CRIMES
&
OFFENSES

CRIMES
&
OFFENSES

J. Lea Koretsky

Regent Press
Berkeley, CA

paperback
ISBN 13: 978-1-58790-281-9
ISBN 10: 1-58790-281-8
Library of Congress Control Number: 2014942516

10 9   8   7   6   5   4   3   2   1

Manufactured in the U.S.A.
REGENT PRESS
www.regentpress.net

SIBERIA
1

EYRE
101

CANAL
221

SANTA BARBARA
239

NO POLO
363

GEORGIA
431

SABA
463

CASINO
551

OAKLAND
615

SIBERIA

GORKIY

Paul said, "Perhaps he poisoned his turkey first."

"He wouldn't have been careless. He would have set his table."

"Assassins are trained, they don't generally take aim at themselves."

Sergiy shrugged thinking it over, sponging the man with light touches. "True, I couldn't have been convinced to sit inside a car on a windy night asking myself where the feathers were if I wasn't instructed to run after it."

"What could he have wanted?"

"He was sent into Sibirskoye all the way down to Mongolian Republic. He would've visited five camps a year that by itself would have kept him busy. But then he would have returned after a year and a half max. They don't permit surgeons to stay. Besides, it takes too much out of you to have to work long hours, be around depressing circumstances. It's dreary, in winter the skies turn grey, in spring there's still the cold and damp, it's not much better than a gulag."

The more Paul thought about it, the more convinced he grew that the man had been followed and his death staged, however meanly. A decent physician or not, his life was not deemed to serve a human interest any longer. It wouldn't be an item that he had seen a plethora of disease or become sympathetic to the infirm. He didn't belong on the perimeter of Kirov in the snow without dozens of agents out there with him. If he had been taking sound imprints in the dead of winter – he had been killed by an aggressive faction who couldn't get rid of him.

Sergiy bandaged in soft dressing the victim's wounds. "These will keep for several weeks, I personally will attend to the recomposition of the head which will be fitted, then positioned without computer use. It's a long procedure."

"Will he then be returned to his assignment?"

"Ah, Paulo, so many questions, so few answers. If my orders were to bleach his hair or change his facial structure, I would say but of course, but I am told he must remain as he is. So, how do I know? If they return him, they are fools, if they remove him, who's to say that is a better decision?"

The trouble was he couldn't download. In the time it would take him to reclassify the material it would be hours if not days. Jacob had identified his fox. He was visible, out from the snow pack, a speedy chump who in surfacing left a trail of prints which while superficial could be easily linked. His problem, if he could call it that, was he had no idea as to which agency in Europe he ought to contact as to the man's identity to find him. He got up, went into Kasayana's bedroom where he found her napping off the winter frost, and nudged her waking her.

"Up for a stroll? I'm getting a haircut."

She eyed him matter-of-factly. "Sideburns maybe, neck shaved, blue black, inch on top, certainly, I'll get ready."

He waited watching as she swung her thin stockinged legs over the bedside, slipping her narrow feet into practical conservative low heels, pulled on a tan jacket and grabbed her purse. The night air was icy, a frost hung in the air. They chatted over a city hum of traffic and blaring horns, discussed the pros and cons of having a meal out and gave no thought as to the need to pick up necessities which they were low on or any other goods to get through the next few days. The barber shop, open even at late hours, was crowded, sitting room only but they removed their gloves and hats and took seats. He had eyed the shop their first week in town, found their customers were average looking pedestrians, many elderly men with already trim hair in for a biweekly cut and shave. The barbers themselves were also old, men who could maintain a conversation despite any commotion entering or leaving, the trade news of the day as informal remembrances of topics forgotten, union hucksters who had opened a shop for their friends.

Finally his turn was up. He described the cut he wanted. The barber, a tall lean man in his sixties with a curlicue moustache and wavy dark brown hair, a white shirt exposing developed muscles, gave a curt nod, proceeded to lather, rinse and dry, choose the color and blend it with a peroxide base. He brushed the texture onto his hair, parting each section with a comb, liberally dosing the black luster until it covered Jacob's head. When he next looked at the seated customers, Kas was on a stool covered with a white vinyl cloth, the youthful barber, a brownish silvery blonde wearing a stylish grey suit and pullover white sweater, a quick study for chipper hair fashion, trimming the ends of her hair. He sat with a timer going, a newspaper shoved into his hands. He had seen the evening hour which hit the highlights, he turned to the sports and read down to soccer wins. The Ruskie teams had a few lasting field plays but the Fins had broken another field. Eventually his barber returned, patted his hair, noting the page and commented on field soccer saying loud enough to signal everyone's attention in the shop that the ice was piling, to which there were chuckles, then to Jacob asked about his preference of soccer huggers. Jacob replied it was in the grip of the cleat, a clipper. The barber rinsed his hair; towel dried it, shaved the back a few inches, pulled out his scissors from a drawer and began clipping leaving a bit on the sides for blunt sideburns. He turned the chair enough for Jacob to see the crew cut get trimmed down to whisker length. The resulting cut with bluish jet black hair kept his focus accenting his gaunt cheekbones, the high bones beneath the eyes, darkening his eye color, his forehead less prominent, and his chin sharper. The hair was cut to his ears, the temples in jocular exposure, his mouth a firm set, his neck accentuated.

He'd have to dress thinner, wear a woolen scarf, and stick with turtlenecks, no dickeys. The barber turned the stool full view. Jacob gave a nod of appreciation. Kas was done, was more evidently the model, and straightened up somewhat, an uncompromising profile for her. His man slapped cologne on him, pulled the mop cloth off him, whisked off his neck. Jacob left a five dollar tip.

They schmoozed down to a deli, walked to the table area and ordered dark rye pastrami sandwiches with Dijon and horseradish. Two tall stouts. The waiter brought their dinner with sides of coleslaw, pickle, and a scoop of cooked diced apples sprinkled with cinnamon. The lager arrived halfway through dinner as a telephone order came into the deli. Kas talked nonstop about the marketplace, rising inflation, tinny production, minimal offsets, next year's Christmas in March, green stamps. She had her list for the children, a new program she had seen on video advertising, a scholarship purchase for the University for Education. She wanted a week in a vacation bed and breakfast preferably in Kirov. Her friend didn't value cruises; she wanted some time in the country. Jacob's only advice was to make it brief. She left the apple uneaten, he did the same. He gave her a thoughtful glance which she ignored and dished out a thirty to pay.

Although muddy ice had piled in the rain gutters the streets were wind swept clean. They strolled to their hotel, she kept the small talk going, making light of the antics of her family's youngsters, despite their recent academic tests which to her mind revealed top scores. She paused taking his elbow to window gaze at a travel Shoppe, calling to his attention a picture of clear blue mountains and rustic accommodations, saying that while the cost was good, the itinerary was better. He pulled her from the window as a sedan slowed to a crawl, the driver raising a gloved finger at them. Jacob held open the hotel door to the narrow lobby, thinking, it had taken too long to verify.

"I look youngish," he said, once inside the elevator. "I shouldn't worry; it'll fill in inside several days, good idea though to have removed the dead weight. We should send up for tea and biscuit."

"Tea biscuit seems about right. Aroma on the light side."

They entered the suite, she to order up, he to check the news. The news station announcer was summarizing the day's events, a storm over Finland, a washout in Estonia, a new construction company approved in Latvia. The tea and complimentary deserts, macadamias and powdered Èclairs, were served in the television room. They dipped biscuits in cups of steeped tea as they reviewed each their summaries. The idea occurred to her that the problem they had had to contend with might have been alleviated by tossing paper at a window with a color wheel posted near the window on a desk. He crunched his cracker looking at the situation from another viewpoint, it wouldn't have said much about an interloper to be situated in the woods far into the trees to listen to a tape without knowing the minute he typed was the instant he was viewed, had he not intended to assess what he may have thought was intrusion all the way from Gulf of Finland. The notion that he was murdered for precisely the reason he appeared not to have responded had obviously been played to his detriment, and thus he decided reluctantly she might be correct to assume that if everything about him from a white sedan with grey upholstery to a man dressed in grey was to combatively suggest a fault in communication her incessant conversation had been to protect him from his usual position. He was aware that were he to have talked for any description he would have been picked up in one place while photographed in another. The photo of him as a younger man suggested by his neat tailoring of response to her could make it seem he was with his wife, once they determined her to be at home they would not be able to view him for at least the night. To the agent's credit, the vehicle backfired first, saying he was killed first, there had to have been a posse waiting for him to drive up, very likely it had been arranged. He said in response, the fox was fired on, but not likely for putting a phrase on his computer, he never answered back. At no time did the agent put that together, the agent, we believe, was concerned for his lover whose brother periodically enters the western defense and then, we think but aren't sure, talks to Fins. The problem for us is that the ships in Bothnian waters are Fin, the Swedes don't as a rule leave their ports and therefore a range as far as the zone is too far. Something has to account for the distance.

He pulled the file on red fox, code name Breaker. German. Idiot. Good riddance. Put the file name on the monitor. The photo was of a weather beaten hard bitten face, possibly from the Khakassia, off the snow and ice without a radio, sight trained for drizzling skies, sub below temperature, see a white deer on an altogether bright glaring landscape. Eliminated, but not by Centralya or they wouldn't have pulled him in so quickly, would have left him to freeze. Kas would have thought he was chatter, silent within a landscape barely without sound. She would be right. Training, a limitation to have to retreat far into a sound proof silent night in order to think. Jacob tried to put him into any other category to place him at a harbor or in a ship, and couldn't. He shot the file to a German prison at Stuttgart for a name and prints; this would determine whether their Kirov was the same man.

He left a message with the front desk to send to Moskva in the morning. Red fox seen at sunrise, snow fell during night, be home mid week. The cipher when received would be broken down and turned over to Command for all its necessary functions. Submitted to telecommunications a first essential task would be to determine the support that accompanied fox in whatever form they comprised, then telephone calls between the parties, fill in the links. A question would be, why Kirov? Because of late winter snows, a slow thaw that could easily be recognizable as background. He considered what other sounds fox wanted to filter from that place. If he had an agent on tap he didn't want to be found. If he had determined she relied on a friend then he could have wanted a collection of identifying sounds. What could he have thought about the situation there? Seasons, no yard, fifty miles from nearest mountain, wolves, no foxes, no telex. He identified sounds only, he didn't appear to analyze, he didn't travel, and he wasn't seen in public squares. That meant fox had been unable to classify unless he wanted to be presumed to be a lone ranger also. Fox was trying to make a generally persuasive identification for someone. Jacob remained skeptical as to if fox knew or was the dead man.

Who would fox know? He was likely to have friends from anywhere he had resided. Home was out. No one from Sibirskoye would ever again return to a life of crime after having to walk across glacially ice sub terrain, have chapped skin toughened by wind, require bandages on their body just to preserve their ability to survive. Three winters was sufficient for any adult. He must have friends from work or an interest. The words scrawled across the screen, Save your breath, prints match, assailant at large, militsya. What a disaster, who in hell placed him there?

GYADINSKIY

Rostrov packed a suitcase. He knew what he was up against. The Soviet technology came and went with their European interests. The photograph of the man was of a treacherous individual whose living was administered by setting standards for testing programs. He devised criterion, admissibility of material, application by industry, staffing, technical support and payment fee schedule. This type of program implementation gave him an immense influence, if for the only reason he had a look at every city to plan for the changing needs year by year. His companies took in two billion a year. His earnings which included establishing periodic overseas expenditures for which his executives reported spending to him alone. In reality, as a major network principal of Gorkiy, he could be a pleasant considerate individual who having purchased accommodations during the summer had not yet staffed his offices. Although he had arranged for new telephone listings he hadn't installed them yet. Everything was quiet, lights never turned on, staff not at other sites, at unknown work stations, moving continuously.

In the air he was studious, contrite, a drink of vodka with a stick through an olive. The novel he sat with, *The Life and Times of Igor Stravinsky* in Russian, was a thought provocative melodrama of a composer who had fled his native Czechoslovakia to first enter France but found it too permissive for his tastes and left after a year for Romania to tend a farm and live beside a creek bed, as it was often dried up and unevenly spilling with mudslides in the driest time of year. Stravinsky did not pick up the pointer until he had taught at the Blevest University for thirty years, wrote a lullaby for his only wife Katriane, and performed it at a tiny rostrum across town in a foreign country, lest he offend the aging officers in charge of a populist movement militsia. "Broken hearted, in abject despondency over the death of his mother, moved to tears by his audience, he burst into agonizing sobs as he explained his composition of one melodic piece, an hour and a half long, written for the most fond moment of his life, running through a field of daffodils, the wind teasing up the grass, catching the only butterfly his daughter would ever have in his volumes of poems. He knew in his heart that whether a man caught her the best, most beautiful flower of a lifetime that was the hand of Life, God's work, not simply a young father enjoying his day off from his long tortuous demandingly complex work, his hours dictated by officers of the Czech court of the long lost, most beloved prince, better referred to as Especial Edward Reminzce Weber originally of Finland, appointed to the throne of Czechoslovakia by then Holy Roman Empress of Russia Domaine." He sipped his drink, pausing to eye the olive that required eating. He took it with a half avocado and rye sandwich and took a nap.

He awoke feeling refreshed as the plane arrived on schedule. He grabbed his travel case eyeing the buildings at the perimeter, four of them, all glass connected by wall ways. He walked in the large rectangle of a waiting area that was nearly empty, blue carpet on a black linoleum floor, past a news stand and a confection counter, through another hall to the taxi lineup. He took his turn slipping into the backseat and gave directions to the site. The driver was entertaining talking about his dog which he said used to ride with him; he also used to like to chase me up the stairs, his hands grabbing at my ankles, barking like a dog about to bite me. Today, he never teases or barks, and he's one of my closest friends. When I was four, he droned on until they reached the elegant four story glass and mezzanine stone walk-up in town. Rostrov paid the man handsomely feeling pity for him.

The mezzanine was alive. Wood paneled walls, shiny green tile floors covered by damask rugs, Egyptian lamps, antiques throughout, a lounge bar off to the side. A crowd stood at the checking counter, people dressed in suits and fashionable dresses, bellhops were carting suitcases up to rooms, a few elderly gents were seated here and there reading newspapers, giant fern flourish in large square gold planters, stunning floral arrangements in light blue green jade on long wood side tables. He waited a half hour to accept his key, and then rode the elevator to the third floor. He counted four doors; he had not meant to place himself in a palatial grand wall street plaza. Opening the door he walked into a gigantic living room with green shiny tile, a Moroccan rug of vibrant yellow, green and red, shelves, two couches, soft lighting emanating from the ceiling, a handsome desk with fully stocked, all steel framed windows overlooking the city and square, a large bathroom tiled in dark tan, three sinks, mirrors, black towels, then the tan carpeted bedroom, overlooking the distant mountains, a large bed, quilted, pillows, an upholstered easy chair of vibrant peach, a shelf and clock. This was the best treatment he could imagine any government official receiving. He unpacked, the closet luxurious with drawers, places for the jackets had he come with any, for the trousers, a tie rack, a full length mirror, the fresh smell of the outside wafting through a slightly open window.

No kitchen, no small refrigerator, no furnace, no bar. Obviously he had never entered a world like this before. He had to add things up pretty damn quick. The contracts man probably lived in suites like this more than he was at home, conducted interviews in his hotel living room, poured himself one too many drinks, and may have a traveling staff of a thousand people in suites. It didn't make any sense if they had resources why they weren't open for business. It would occur to him as he took in these surroundings that the corporation could not go to the building because they were wanted for a terrifying crime. How one proved it whatever it was another question, if there were evidence of a crime having been committed. He thought he knew enough to know agencies investigated the minute a crime was committed, thus he told himself his father sent him to this hotel for a reason, that the suite itself was somehow related to the motivation of the crime, that the man's entire colossal empire was put together for a horrific rationale. He walked into the living room, poured himself vodka, spritzed it, added a sliver of lime, sniffed, and sipped. Excellent. He was given an assignment, to identify a man, until he did that he wouldn't know what it meant that the man could have visited every last city in Russia to plan standards for academic achievement and now not to enter a modern city to begin a new office the government must have encountered an item too serious to be ignored.

When were an individual's rights questioned for public matters, where was the public trust placed? In what ways did the government respond? Why never the agencies themselves?

He was a little surprised at himself, he didn't want to get rocked, the interests of scrutiny was the rationale the social structure made the convictions of life personal and private. They gave the challenge of discernment a promise with livelihoods made possible by security, medicinal, city, sewage. Despite the fact that everything was covered, this luxury of the conference center hotel seemed to represent a realty that was upside down ideologically in some as yet undefined intangible way, a retirement behind words. Just prior to going out to check the registration desk he realized he had copied the wrong phone number for the local office down, he placed in the small safe inside the vanity a rib boned packet of letters to himself before he started the evening with a fifth, outside the clouds were amassing like a caravan of elephants.

When he rode the elevator down to the lobby, he had changed into comfortable tan tweed trousers, a white shirt, and a dark brown over sweater, leather Harrington shoes, a matching neck scarf. The registration booth gave him a badge, packet of brochures, pen, writing tablet, schedule of presentations. He drifted into an exhibition center, began at an education desk, noted the display on language applications, moved past a window of billboards, eyed booths across the floor, eyed a curtained backdrop for scientific medical breakthroughs as a man dressed in a mohair tan sweater and tan trousers spoke to two fellows, his muscular jaw and brown eyes evenly proportioned with blond hair, the view obstructed by the moving angle. He walked glancing at the exhibits, the checklists of standardized testing that would reform education over the sub sequent ten years, passing educational pamphlets, classroom learning, composition and outcome. Rostrov approached the aisle where his target's display sat, the entrepreneurs in discussion, no apprehension discernible. His watch was erectly relaxed, an appearance of facial tension a noted mien from the distance, a brevity of response, a holding pattern contained in his upper body. The floor was masked behind an aisle of poster board, focused scripts about each subject of university education, a hovering of information, alongside which the contained space shrank to an over awareness of their marquis. The curtain backdrops and tables were sparse, light on center, a sense that anything was possible, and a small stack of narrow brochures. He arrived to the table, the ceiling seemed oddly high, a row of orthopedic shoes to one side, a perception overshooting the distance. He had a degree of concern, what made this man need so much latitude, his sense of capability as if governed by confidence alone. A dangerous proposition. A man of reputation.

The file reported to disappearances, this coordinator entered snow packed hilly communities venturing through blizzards, his dominance erased by mist, his form retreated. It was exceptional, a plentitude of information, a clear last known place, no way to track. If there were buildings he passed them without being seen, no way to view him, if there was perception of him there was neither record nor recognition. He came and went unseen leaving no method for anyone to later find. He was the assassin.

Rostrov would have to produce a change in the target making it less possible for him to disappear. He entered a lounge and sat at the bar ordering a whiskey sour. As he thought about the necessary characteristics to change, lazy passersby glanced through the windows at a Christmas tree in red flickering lights. The target wore tan, a mild color that elicited no focused alertness or special consideration. The height of six feet and weight of a hundred and seventy-five lbs. was presumed. His angular frame while admired held no peculiar apprehension as did his mildly bland description. He was at ease, tall enough to be Air. He was used to seeing maps, at his desk or in an airplane, with and without breaks in the focus. Whether he went into an unplanned area with a group or alone, he was given license to be without a cameraman at his back. Now that this problem had been identified the air stations within the sector would be more cautious about when he was in their area to view him utilizing lens perspective. A cursor driven arrangement could subsequently find him on monitor even after but especially when he had already paid someone to lose him. A startle impact would probably be the simplest solution, if not for him to rattle things and make a commotion in the target's presence so as to alter the observer's perception of the randomness of responses.

He returned to his room alert to a necessity to keep his trip brief. Even if he were to enter the other man's suite, ruffle through clothing and order of the room, if he took an object the other man's apprehension would be heightened without his having to do anything else. Climbing up on a stool to replace a light bulb was another option, having to do so involved risk. From his suitcase of tricks he pried loose a responder, dialed the desk and asked to be given the room of Jepson Collier. As soon as he was connected he positioned the device over the headset to record the set of frequency sounds that would record the only tracking sounds and display the number which when unscrambled would give him the front desk three-digit number to the room. He then jotted the number down in a small notepad under the man's surname. He punched it in, the operator replied with a confirmation of the number which rang intermittently until a voice tape answered.

Jepson. You fucking son of a bitch.

He poured himself a vodka rye. The night sky was well in place, in the distance the snow peaked mountain was as he remembered. Lit apartments in tall glass buildings gave the chilly night a charmed effect. Rostrov himself might invite a masseuse in for a towel sweat before he retired. He replaced a refill and tottered into the steam room for a breather. Once he was good and shrunk he would throw cold water onto his face and once dressed, go downstairs for a bite. His vernacular approached sympathy for Jepson, the once forgotten diminutive style of creativity was a lurch to his abdomen. He had almost left the steam when the telephone in the other room rang once, silencing the air with a shocking resonance. The bastard tracked everything. That was probably the only thing he was hired for, was to standardize everything. Like nickels and dimes, a solitary grouping remained hunted.

The morning light shone in. The walls seemed to have moved forward a bit. A thin veil of an aching hangover grew abusive. The fortnight shrugged itself off. Were he an ample man of means himself, the setting might be rewarding but he decided the pristine glow was itself the only reward. He arose and shaved, showered, dressed and ordered up coffee, read the newspaper and took his time filling in a few lines of the crossword. At eight-thirty after he knew the morning session had begun, he dialed the number again. Jepson. Rostrov took a chance. I apologize for my inclination. No need to bother, old man.

He hung up allowing for a certain dry humor to start the hour. He packed his bags putting a fifty dollar tip for the cleaning lady and left for the taxi.

Kirov

Paul looked at his wristwatch. Of his four computers he had brought up a listing of all conclusions of problems which he had worked on since he was assigned the file. This consisted of hundreds of calls, all but one confirmed. In a nutshell when their assassin walked into the snowy silent night he disappeared. Confirmed calls had identified him as the man most ready to receive man of the year award. The confirmations were placed and once placed found people, watches on the Rhine were established, the lead target determined to be inching his way through the mud by cursor assignment through snow, the boroughs it made decided by new curriculum for Sibirisk populations being newly admitted through gates of hell. Oddly enough Neva's brother, while he allegedly worked at a draft in central Moscva, was considered to be on an iceberg demolition crew in the Bering Straits.

If computerized enforcement was the only military job the government paid for and it required a hundred thousand desks, and was easily infiltrated, it had been in trouble for a long time. The desks were made up of banks, investment, and some contracts. These infiltrators called it one thing, landscape, Rostrov called it another, fundamentals, whatever can be made into a program, put into a van and carted to a new location with computers running the show was a danger zone. The reality was telerivalry which wasn't the government, they weren't in centralized sectors, and they were footloose pretending to be enforcers, usurping the government's attention. Code name Breaker was shot in his car and could not respond, was pulled in after having followed the assassin, was revived to go back out there.

Paul had tracked conversations to places and people. The code file assassin was found in towns, in telephone booths, at sidewalk restaurants, and with a situation. The information was presented as follows,

fire department mobilized, which precinct
trunk cable lines, telephone lines offset charges to another
site, system will register what it is
electricity each plug
where is the central cable, how many switches does it govern
how does demolition come down
voltage intensity, crack whip
preparation for demolition
demonstration sites, smaller buildings
underwater clock takes the pressure
requires computers, every other floor, collapse floors
timing device to get there with every time assigned
second hand is necessary
how does crack across floor occur
impulser, wires must talk to each other
what else utilizes the mechanism, watches?, double checks
own accuracy

    The file went on line immediately after the event, the few
shots of the people packing up their equipment were sent by
parcel post to Kallingrad for distribution, the file itself for each
person was broken up into categories and faxed to Moscva for
assignment, and summaries were wired to agencies in every
country. In Moscva the front line read Smith the next line in
BOLD LETTER TELEX, BREAKER. Amadeus Wolfgang
Mozart King of Sweden left European front in van driven by
guards. Paul received his copy of the file when the assassin was
found. Although the target seemed more or less okay, even
though he was a contracting firm with relatively good degrees,
he was the man identified as the most likely to have completed
the act. To put him at the scene was impossible if the watch
could not find him but that had to be yet determined. He had
to decide what sort of watch to arrange, a guilloche would be
fine. Precisely because it would put the file in the zone he was
in by controlling corporation by zip code, the major cities automatically recognized by the inner circle Moscow, Karachi,
Bangkok, Tokyo, Denver, New York, Rio de Janeiro, Azores

with an hour hand that adjusted to the exact time. The Winders hadn't done that, an undetected device that had been created for the Moscva man. If a watch had already been changed for the winders to be ordered in and the assassin was reliant on this change being put in a time zone first, then it stood to reason he had an accomplice who approved these changes.

Paul's file, when he had compiled his summaries, read, what did Moscow know about the assassin, probably not much, just what is in Kall's file, consists of musical measurements, Moscva ran tests to determine breaks for intent of crime.

on night of shooting snow falls as it is raining, question if rain is intensity of snow can watch find man, has someone interfered with what is seen and how would he know, Gorki just listens,

even his computers listen mostly, he only receives confirmation, others receive pictures, and Petersburg receives summaries,

some from brother,

don't know what to listen for, no matter how intently one listens many sounds are not heard,

lab-enhanced color photographs pick up more detail

Paul gave the material careful scrutiny. He would have much preferred to have contacted Neva for her ideas regarding this problem but he would wait for her visit. The telephone rang shrilly its echo like a knell. He was on Gorkiy time. The reference came in at 12:37 pm. He knew this was his personal birth time. He asked Moscva for the pick ups. Almost automatically the color photographs showed up on his computer. There was the assassin at his table. The few photographs showed blurs. He would work on them all day. He began with the most distinct. It seemed to have been taken from a moving van. His good looking man was in Gorkiy having lunch at a cafe with another man. The other man was medium height he would guess. A movie star, also blond, dressed in checkered jacket, greenish tan pants, woolen hat, no leather gloves, Birkenstocks.

Queer. Paul looked at the blond. Just a good time. Nothing ominous. He asked for identification. For this he would have to wait. He walked through the house. It was freezing. No wind outside. No snow falling. Why did the man attend education conferences, the answer was obvious, training, standardization and review of outcome, for which he rented offices. Paul asked himself, what about an office would tell the government he must never move in. That it was too old, there were cracks in walls, not in foundation, it was damp, and lamps didn't work right, use of flash cubes. He walked to his computer. The name was there. WINDER. Friend was a watch man. He had set times. The assassin was his go-between. Go ring your own phone, he thought about him.

It was late winter, normally the season in Petersburg and Moscva to celebrate lighting of the candles. Were he still living there he would see his cousin Rivka who might bring her husband if he was not on assignment. Her husband was lead file for any assignment for which the contract kept liaisons with the western world, he was a thorough, educated FSB who was able to bust apart any nocturnal fox from its lair once the fox was in view. Paul would pack up the youngsters into the sedan to drive to the square for a seven course dinner at Lena's, schlep through the icy snow to the clock where crowds gathered for the lighting of twenty-five four foot high silver and gold glittering candles, one made of beeswax. Once the candles were lit ice skaters took to the frozen pond for an hour long show with music emanating from vestries. Shoppers could watch the stage or mingle through storefronts with lit trees in windows, purchase blanket shawls, pretty watches, wrapped spumoni cake with rum, have ale or toddy at a window side lounge or sidewalk cafe. Photographs all around signed by the Premier in cards to take home, big bears to tease the little ones, teen-run booths along Skivaya Street with handmade art from their classes, surprise gifts in tinsel and carry bags for the tree at home. Then home, a fire in the hearth lit by electricity, storybook with Rivka, everyone in sleepers, bacon, upside eggs, fresh fruit cup for breakfast, about ten adults, always cheery.

He had been stationed at Kirov ten years, viewed the setting as a philosophical life for which the work required six to ten hours a day most weeks. He hadn't seen or spoken to Rivka in at least that length of time and didn't dare. As he acclimated in midlife from a frenzied work pace to a quiet mountain existence with no yard, he found he retreated inward, attuned predominantly to his tasks, wandered little from the house, concerned he could fall through manholes, into streams or creek beds, snow up to his waist. It didn't take but a year before he asked Centralya for a female who could help him.

Neva was herself younger by ten years, an ex-husband who had climbed the ladder to an influential position to oversee assignments for militsya. No children, she lacked attachments that replaced any top official. She was expert, business, keenly modified his summaries to clarify the imagery to find targets including people. His priority with her was to limit her excursions to the Kall. If not for her brother he might not have encountered the corruption for which he was assigned his desk, although he defined her brother as somewhat atypical. It was odd he grew readily dependent upon her entrances which surprised him. The loner was easily seduced. Bitterness was not his style and over years he gave in. When Moscva stopped moving him over the sector, he found himself having never married, social circles far away, the containment of natural wilderness sometimes unbearable, his bed having been made but not slept in. Neva couldn't subtract her contacts and all the while carried the snow through the house.

He was neither a reading man nor a hobbyist. No interest in photography, writing music, neither keeping scrapbooks nor even writing short work. His life was his work. Men better than he was sold out when boredom hit the skids. He knew himself, though. Knew he couldn't compromise a drop of blood. Freedom of thought was the highest value. He poured himself another cup of iced apricot tea and set to work, the heat full blast. Code name Breaker tracked Assassin everywhere. Assassin Jepson Collier still wasn't photographed. He could get many who met with him but not him. Could it be that he held such an important public job with far greater funds than other sorts of autonomous employment that the government satellite system shot around him? What was the key? A Little Mast scholarship was granted every two years to a promising individual of merit and worth, the banks for each city were held in various accounts all over the world, jobs alone with approval were his area of influence. Within twenty years he had increased education by ten thousand people. Too many. He looked again at his problem.

Breaker only cracks, Winder does watches, 20 per floor, 2 floors, 50 watches, 20 a year, each seconds apart, what mechanisms, must others be; he would need a consultant, Paul's guess was this assassin paid a group to grid the interiors of new building acquisitions with flash cubes, paid another watch to set up a second hand preferably who was someone in Moscva sector. He had to try to find him in the snow to put him on spec for murder of Code Name Breaker and who he retained him to keep a clear image on file under the actual name of the assassin. It would be nice if he could find him in rooms of offices he planned staff to move into.

Same old rigmarole had occurred. Education approved another city Gorkiy for an education office, documents were signed, funds transferred, building approved. The State sent in inspectors who cited deficiencies and included a report. Several days later the building was set up for voltage declaration with flash cubes going off all night in each room and cracks noted in other nearby buildings. FSB stationed snag men throughout Gorkiy, all eyes for Jepson Collier, a set of watches that deleted his image off the files.

While he waited for Winder's honest name, he worked on the street cafe meeting between Collier and Winder. Although the restaurant was crowded Paul could locate no one who was a file. He worked on clarifying the section, first sectioning out the two men in a frame and placing the resulting photograph in an emulsifier panel, then using pixels for resolution and enhanced definition. When he was completed Winder stood out in contrast to the scene of the meeting, causing him to wonder whether his image had been placed there to begin with. He filed Winder before he put him into any telephone dialogue possible. Immediately he slipped into his flat. It was his computer contact that turned out to be Collier. Paul put a question mark on the picture. He verified against every telephone contact made by Winder from that location, got a high definition picture of Collier at a convention, and downloaded his picture into its own file. He made a page of copies, each discreet, high resolution, extracted one, punched in date and time of date of any communiqué. The download fit as a shipmate on a fishing vessel in the Gulf of Bothnia outside Finland. He took any person Collier spoke to. Voronad, captain of the floundered vessel that hit ice. Paul laughed. Had Voronad never hauled for Collier, he might not have floundered. Why would it be that Collier required him to offset a planned disruption. It still wouldn't answer the question of the new location he couldn't yet get his staff into.

Paul found the vehicle with Breaker dead, blood trickling from his nose and mouth. He looked for Collier. Still nothing. Took the date and time and posted for Collier. Collier was in a hotel in Moscva. Not him. Paul would have to wait for Neva to obtain those communications.

Sergiy had his own ideas. As he packed his entire medical office into the back of his wagon preparing for a trek to the old fort where the elders lived for a monthly checkup, he reflected on his patient's wounds. There was nothing to explain the massive loss of vital fluids despite the fact the victim wore layers of warm clothing, good solid boots. The snow had been falling all day coming down in a light rain occasionally interceded by hail. For this sort of snow the temperature had to be slightly above freezing, too cold to produce the apparent disruption. His laptop was still on, the cursor still blinking, a message across the top. Sergiy knew there were at least a half dozen stations monitoring the situation, whatever it was. If Breaker had holed up somewhere in order to see who came up the road without them seeing him was one thing. If he had tracked a target into the area and the target was unaware of him until a message was rerouted, that was also a concern. It wasn't Collier, if he was at that very moment in Moscva but he may have redirected the stellar death.

None of the desks would be a double agent, therefore Breaker was correct, someone was already out there. Technically there was no way to do what was done to him in Kirov, too far inland. He'd take the road all the way up the hill to his office and along the way try to give it a guess.

The low lying hills were blanketed white. The road wound through pine forested land frocked with fresh snow. The air was chilly, the sky could be perceived in its grayish lack of dimension. Tall trunks, long branches of spruce pines heavy with fir stood in proximity, dense and shrouded. Ahead where the elevation climbed by a hundred feet, trees knee-deep in starchy snow had almost been obliterated by a rapidly descending wind. The intensity of brightness on the landscape gave the forest a quickly shrinking appearance. He headed up the mountain, a swift incline, sides falling away to lower lying pastures where in spring corrals would pony train young preadolescents. Halfway up he careened onto a dirt access his tires splashing dark mud against the metallic of his wagon. The stone huts filed alongside the road, white smoke rising from stubby chimneys, to the lodge and hospital, a massive terrain of dark green, thin pole trees with white trunks packed in every direction as far as could be seen. He parked in an open door garage for three vehicles and went inside to the nurse station for assistance. The physician on duty greeted him and shoved a chart into his hands explaining that during the night a patient had waited for a nurse to make rounds first, then switched on every computer and reviewed each recovery.

"What did he take?" Sergiy asked.

Sergiy's friend Russ was a male nurse. "Apparently nothing. He wanted information about the critical unit."

"Who is he?"

"Rodney Fane. You know him, the man with headaches."

"Oh right." Sergiy pictured him, a thin blond adept at any system who slept in the recovery ward, had a view of the hills. "How long could he have been at the station?"

"Fifteen minutes most. Don't know why he needed to be there. Nothing much happened."

"Has this occurred ever?"

"The night of Breaker."

That was no coincidence. He'd make rounds, review charts, order renewed prescriptions, and then think this over. He took the items in with Russ' help, set up the medicine supply room, had Russ sterilize.

Rounds took a little over an hour. He chatted amicably with the aging men there, discussing their symptoms, took thermometer readings, pulse, thumped across the chest, abdomen and tested reflex. All were in reasonably well health. Fane was asleep when he entered. He wakened him, took vitals, asked about his night sojourn.

"Just tedious, all this lying about in bed," Fane replied. "Needed stimulation break. The patient listings are incomplete, had to put in to Moscow, they ran an index for me. Room closest to mine has no foreign funds, don't know what that's about. Said hello to my wife, signed off."

"What's wrong with the patient computers?"

"They were shutdown for the night."

"Well, it's a pretty audacious thing you did. The station doesn't talk to the Kall, you know."

"Wouldn't care anyway. It's not my place to do that."

"How's your brother? I hear he's released from Sibirskoye."

"No." Anger flared. "From all the way out there, sub zero degree. He's still there. Freezing I s'pose."

"Possibly he's adjusted, you maybe not so well."

"I'm fine. I only looked, did not print."

Sergiy jotted down Fane's vitals, stood glasses on to study the chart. "Still having difficulty with stiffness?"

"Some. Sleep helps."

"Anyone else here?"

"Sure, lots of shipmates want an SOS."

"Which ones?"

"On the ward. What's his name? Snow shoes."

"Does he go out for walks?"

"No, he watches for his niece. She usually arrives a few hours late, doesn't stay over. He has pictures of her."

Sergiy closed the chart, took it with him. He made his way to each room. When he entered the last room he saw framed photographs on a table against the wall of family, different ages. A young female, thirties, silver blonde, dark eyes, Scandinavian sweater, tightly fitting pants, ski sunglasses.

"Pretty. Your niece?"

"She's older, that's her daughter-in-law. Try the Dracula one."

He looked for a too thin female, darkish bronze reddish hair, woolen cap, dark sweater, black pants, smiling. "Pretty too."

"She's a Leningrad, smart, has her own department."

"Education?"

"Nope, not even close. Medicine."

"Who works for her?"

"Hospitals. You could."

"Not me, I'm Interim. Why would you like me there?"

"So we know who works the train."

He would like to tell him to get lost and to ask where were we going but instead figured Snowshoes was out here as one who prides himself on going after a Code Name individual.

MOSCVA

Neva reworked the file with Paul's additional comments. In the background a party in full swing could be palpated although the doors to the conference room were closed. The cake had been rolled in early in the afternoon after the decorations pinned to the walls, the tables lined up and covered with glitter and party favors. Her associates would bring her a plate with cake, fruit, ambrosia and finger sandwiches, mostly fish paste. The information he had e-faxed her contained a mosaic of files arranged in alphabetical order 'Z' first. Breaker was back on the street, same Volga, laptop, bundled up. Paul's data was outdated with all the accoutrements of a long version come to a close. He had Breaker inside a car, had a backfire on record, a separate photograph sent to Moscva, another sound of a vehicle registered to Collier's fleet. She would work with non subjectivist, wherever the people were found was where they were. The telephone calls for the Institute in Gorky were prefaced by a roundup call that began in Moscva cross indexed in Kallingrad for their shipping to Obirisk through channels. Oddly, education data personnel who worked telephone computers filtered into Bryansk just north of the Ukraine. In Bryansk a convention network formed with over two hundred professionals, as yet no implementation. Telephone rivalry went on line in small cities. Moscva listened. Sibirskaya was contacted for infiltration and none found. Within a year two ships had cracked on unforeseen icebergs. The state approved a conference education grouping for ten cities. Elitists were sent to each city, they established stations for information only. After four cities, convention buildings faced unusual damages for which construction was solicited from both public and private sectors. The contract team was determined by who came to lead booth information. The representatives used telecircuitry to audit the stability of its buildings. The elitists were one by one killed. With this profile put into motion, the Moscva government ordered arrests, detainees who matched the circumstances of their victims were sent to a remote camp. One man had been sent. After a year he was no good to anyone alive or dead, he had refused to name names yet tested for at least one high profile penetration lunatic. Penetration, depending in which foreign government they were trained, were very hard to apprehend primarily because they were absent, never at a crime, or to be found discussing arrangements for a crime, just getting richer by the second.

Tavda didn't know Collier. They had never met. Collier while seemingly on the up and up had new contracts pouring out of his database. Tavda, on the other hand, a lonely non mixer who had a penchant for stunningly elegant Chinese women, stayed to the conservative trends of refurbishing buildings that would rarely be torn down. In ludicrous ways Tavda epitomized the Russian Bolshevik sentiment that resources ought to be minimally spent and banks left alone. Tavda moved in small circles. He had been given a penthouse in Moscva overlooking the river and there he lived formally with the daughter of a Russian diplomat. Her name was Sin Quon. On his arm she was a sinewy female often dressed in deep russet colors, usually a deep dark green that evoked profound sorrow. Her straight hair was long, tied into place at her nape by long translucent needles of matching color. Tavda never let it be said that he wanted children, nor that he wanted monogamy although he rarely traveled without her. In her company he was meditative, satisfied, forgiving of life and its foibles. At the government's expense they traveled on the Arrow to the far remote interior of Russia to stay at a tiny monastery amidst icy mountains, snow packed hills, blue like crystal, the air stingingly clear, no vegetation to be seen. Here he professed to her that even if she renounced him, in his heart he could not separate in essence from her flawless beauty, and they lived tended to by servants an endless spring during which he rose to his zenith in character and wrote her a hundred poems for love. Splendor was his most necessary affection for his spirit, with her he kept to the rigors of virtue, his being surrendered to hers, and were she to one day leave him he promised her he would cease to live. She was seldom recorded. There was some question as to her understanding of his native Ruskie language, she held back it would seem to a life of practiced moderation, an hour every morning before the sun rose to write Chinese characters sensei-style, an hour in the pond scrimping rice, a half hour at night with him in a deep barrel spa. Her thoughtful gestures toward him, ever graceful, ever peaceful, gave him actual subsistence, barley cooked for days and served with rice milk which she also prepared, on occasion fed to him as he stirred from profound sleep.

He slept often in a cellar, body wrapped in warm fleece, slippers on, having stepped once too often onto the meadow, iced over permanently. He allowed his feet to be bandaged, his thin legs to be banded, his eyes to be covered by a dark band, let his tears dry inside himself, until he knew again he had been conquered. After a monsoon he again held her in his arms and subjected himself to her nourishment, salted plum drink, at spoonful, diluted rice milk, a half glass, a few bites of fish stew, long red fish that swam in a glassy section of river, skewered and grilled, mixed with dried seaweed. Renewed again he told her that no matter where she was he would always find her, he would leave when she no longer answered.

Neva supposed Tavda knew little of love having probably already surrendered to some other assured grief. It didn't make sense that he agreed to whatever Collier wanted of him, but the telephone calls indicated only that. Deadly to choose a woman so beautiful that he lost his will to live to her. Worse, to have contemplated leaving, even if she could not be his for as long as he wished.

Neva tracked Sin Quon into the ice on more than one occasion. No person entered an unforgiving zone without reason. It made no sense. There Sin Quon was one of few who lived in bunkers in the ice, tormented winds covering the landscape, bitter cold, where only the truly hated lived in absolute banishment. When she returned she went to Collier always. Always Collier gave her to some other man who disagreed with him. Always she did his bidding. Sin Quon did not make telephone calls, she did not talk to Winder, nor to Kirov. Yet it was Sin

Quon who came into Kirov to set up flash cube light inside the Gorkiy building. She was caught entering the building, seen in the elevator, seen going inside the office, on telescope viewed attaching flash cubes into plugs. It was an outrage. Moscva intercepted swiftly, did not cancel the contract, assigned to every person who had anything to do with that building from contract funds, personnel, inspectors, to Collier himself.

Collier's telephone descriptions were above board. In public he met solely with representatives he selected for each task in his organization. Winder received information from him which he used to build watches. At buildings that had reported cracks inspectors found watches in plugs. Winder had several watchmakers he went to who helped him determine ways to make a watch stop at a certain second. She matched for watchmakers in all Russia, none had telephone contact with either Winder or Collier. When she tried to check outside Russia she was told it was classified.

Classified File

Impulsers on each floor
Thirty floors in all, outlets monitored each office
Clocks for a half day per watch
Obtainable by computer of 2,000 prefix digits per city zone

***

In a small apartment in the center of the government square an elitist worked on a secretive file. All telephone calls were registered by date and time. He worked by zone to determine if any telephone matched any register there. The central sector had already compiled numbers found at random and filed them. His assignment would take approximately four weeks. Once he matched numbers, numbers would be decoded for businesses. This would give Centralya essential information as to who was interested in under employing any of Russia's cities. He worked in the confines of a study. He was diligent, capable of looking at ten numbers scrolled on the computer for hours before he needed to put the parallel processing on a criterion-driven system. He worked into the night, periodically giving a glance to the square where in the center near a statuesque memorial of a fountain of three layers with copper cupids at the top lights of gold shone at the overflowing water the lighting of candles had begun, sparklers which in the night gave an added opulence, even if temporal. He kept a written document with the matching numbers as they registered onto another computer. As the numbers that registered became increasingly familiar he thought the task in Moscva would become simple to position people at addresses of where they were when the contacts were initiated. This was often how resolving complicated matters began, with numbers seeming to originate everywhere simultaneously and then weeks into the job nothing too ordinary to track. His spouse would be cooking dinner, a sandwich of lettuce, tomato and anchovy paste on a slice of dark rye, a glass of iced tea, a macaroon cookie with warm milk taken in front of the television inside the sitting room, the hearth dwindling to coals in the living area, the computer left on for any ideas that might occur to a historian late at night. He and his lover of thirty years had spent half a lifetime inside a four hundred square footpad since he at age forty had asked her father for permission to wed his eighteen year old daughter and the father had refused until he married off the four oldest. Here they were like two old fogies, Avram at seventy and Angelina at forty-eight, compassionately inseparable, her father still alive, and a smarter marriage counselor than one might think. Avram worked through hundreds of numbers as the night chill affected his limbs, the cross matches suddenly in a prefix although he knew the prefix code could be anywhere in the city. Avram was elegant, refined, the ideal elitist, thin and tall, his clothing never seeming to fit snugly or quite right, dark wavy hair, tannish. Angelina was coming into her own at her age, no longer eccentric nor usually teasing of him, a curly blond who wore her hair to her hips, fashionably attired in men's trousers and lace tops, a female young enough to fascinate because he was not an intellectual.

Whereas they had lived through years of discussing whether to have a child, he later learned she had had two abortions. He didn't believe he minded in the least, he knew she wanted close companionship and didn't want to share him. Because he had resolved aging without friends while he was in his twenties, he understood time was met by all sorts of living, but none by the prescription his associates lived by. Angelina's father Hiram had told him years ago quite by accident when Hiram picked him up to go to the smoke room that people who required the same prefix did so in order to become admiringly confused by anyone who knew them provided the recognition of them at a distance filled the person with peace or instant admiration imbuing the person with a confidence of interest. Hiram didn't think Avram had noticed his daughter was more beautiful when seen at a distance than in his arms, but that owed entirely to recognition of her. Avram took in the advice whenever he had to retreat to his study across town. The focused task of catching the numbers, making sure none slipped past without being categorized, causing him to have to lose the world to anyone but himself, kept him at the tedious task in order to check his work. The computer would segment the numbers by any arrangement giving him a way to test his outcomes.

He was himself given over to his government. The aspects of his nature were to produce whatever task that was assigned. Since all assignments were empirical by virtue they combined groupings of numbers, there was no subjective rationale he had to chase away from his thinking. The telephone numbers including those incorrectly coded were verifiable and when he was completed with the compilation he would dial for accuracy. No task was too mysterious, or beyond his scope of capability, merely steadfast alert recognition. He knew at a fundamental basis he was among the most sought-after, second to the man in the street whose uncanny instinct while severely tested was the call for the entire industrialized domain. Hiram's wife was herself a historian, the family made up entirely of historians but none librarians, call codes or any other tangential professions, and therefore not FSB. He would be making history by assignment yet not trapping a single crime to the face. The elitists were not prone to inclinations of personal power and herein lay the fatal flaw of men like Collier who were instant successes to empire relations, neither in favor of helping their country nor of keeping the wolf from the lamb.

When he was done with the task he counted the pathways of telephone numbers called. The same prefix he kept in a file, this likely was the person who convened, and the number that called out over a hundred times was initiated as to other registries. The same with other numbers called many times over a limited duration. The numbers called once also separated by business. Several banks, none contractors to the State. He found one banker on personal time, Collier's cousin Lensk. Prefix went to file name Breaker. Centralya already had the file. Other numbers were Silk, Darren, Ensher. No Winder. It had to be that file Breaker could disappear with telephone numbers. Avram wouldn't sleep while he separated every photo file for numbers called and received. He entered Moscva by mosaic, took copies of all telecommunications. Cities were undefined but he recognized them by landmark. In St. Petersburg along the shore of the inland sea, Collier walked with Lensk discussing problems of educating pupils. Avram opened the voiceprint block for their discussion. Lensk was informing him of various difficulties, infirm age, train wards, snowbound, electricity loss, in-laws. Collier and Lensk met monthly over three years, always at sidewalk cafes, usually inside. Collier usually brought a report, budget line item which Lensk pocketed. Other times Lensk made telephone calls by computer to his old friend Silk in Murmansk. Silk was elderly, dark, brusque, stolid, always wrapped in a dark grey woolen coat with mink fur at the collar and cuffs. Silk had the winders, two of three from Belgium, both had shops in basement tenement buildings, absorbed by their intricately detailed work they put together elaborate small pieces with tiny ruby and granite stones. Picture by picture the men Silk found were found in their benches discussing how watches worked in telephone conversations and as they designed on computers, and were a frail looking group, possibly Greek. One, a merchant seaman named Anaya, developed a timepiece that ticked ten minutes, then reversed, the dial hand moving over half the face, then moved back at same speed, controlled by one smaller wind. The other half of the watch was a harpsichord construction. The third winder had been banished to Sibirisk for his manufacture of operations controlled by pendulums over twelve feet in length sweeping across not onyx for onyx would never permit variation, but across granite. It was the granite, any color but grey that relented to alteration. Avram thought it was tragic these men were involved. Without this work they must starve to death. In walked Death. Although they were only designing a watch, and one without light, they would not be the ones who used it as a breaker would. The two hundred pictures were clear but contained unknowns. In the last frame Silk took his contact to task. Only rubies, a ruby will not crack a wall. It was a beaut of a confession, but the file ended with a reference he could not ever obtain, even in his exalted loftiness.

He spent hours hunting down Silk's disposition. His telephone only hooked up once to the newest office Collier had not yet assumed tenancy in. Otherwise the calls he put through did not find anyone at home. Effan Silk had an envied life as a screen artist of delicate metals, his screens were in houses throughout Severomorsk, ancient looking designs of people and Sibirisk monasteries. To have a screen of bluish copper or one of pale silver washed with stains was considered a height of moderately affordable luxury but to have bronze netting over a copper piece with goldish flecks that seen from a distance were mist over a suggestion of treetops was a rarity. Silk eluded him except for visuals, and thus he had just one number he used for a solitary call. Avram looked for him among streets, in screen shops, and shook him loose in one shot resembling Igor Stravinsky. He had aged pathetically, horribly, undistinguished, as private as his visible would allow. Regardless where Avram looked, there were no other walking canes, he was either a reclusive or a passionate artist who shut the world out.

He tried relations. A pretty young female, age twenty, lemon bleached straw hair came once every half year to stay a little over a week. She bustled about town, purchased food in quantity, everything dried, and beef strips, soup broths in cartons, miso, noodles, rice, matso meal, oats. She took him in his wheelchair to the Mariinsky ballet and to ice hockey and that about did it. Then she was off and he shut himself in for weeks, letting the rubber banded newspapers stack up at the front door.

Danziger strolled daily at noon along the canal passing the cheerful yellow and orange baroque apartments that lined a side. He was typical Lenin, moderately slender, a bit of sag in his late seventies, bony angular face, red cropped hair, blue eyes. He wore a flamboyant Ruskie wool coat, black boots with spurs, a hat and gloves over a typical business suit of silver black threads. Avram found him at synagogue, to be talking with a rabbi, giving bar mitzvah, celebrating high holy days, editing a new version of the holy bible, working a hologram computer under State contract. Abram's computer became too shiny and as he tried to retain these images everything disappeared off his screen causing him to shut his system off. Over a cup of strong chai tea he instantly comprehended Danziger was Collier's sole legitimacy. Holography was the method Collier escaped any detection. The watches might be synchronized for this use to assure protected passage over any landscape. Direction of intensity of light on snow or ice ponds might ensconce an image especially if obscurity could be assured with some idiosyncratic intervention.

In the morning he referenced Ensher. Ensher worked as a telemarketer two hours four days a week in Moscva for an educational product line. His home telephone received calls but was allowed an hour out from eight to nine at night. Thousands of cold calls were directed to educators in major urban cities. Like a gossamer needle in an invisible meadow calls out during his hour were obscured by the background chatter of the calls he made during the year. Ensher was a medium height student prince, wavy grey hair, a dressed up fashionable stepper who was always found wearing grey or black tweed pants, elegant pin-striped shirts with a smart red wool jacket and Strauss watch. Verifying every picture by each call would surely take months to complete. For the first day he would match by computer. At some point he would have to program a means by which to assess if Ensher's assignment for Collier was to handle all arrangements for the network. Ensher was known if only because his father sent him into the unkind world to live as a pauper for thirty years, a paid apartment to his name, his stipend a mere hundred a week, all other living expenses to be earned. The father forbade him to practice medicine in Sibirisk or in the Kazakh or the Plato, desiring him to see the world through the eyes of a beggar. To a degreed intellectual incapable of even leaving his homeland for less than two thousand rubles to enter the European front or fly to U.S. to reside as a resident physician coaching university students, this was his undoing. He traveled on a friend's say so to Pederovska where he slept on a couch in a sitting room until Lensk set him up with a one-room pad, telephone and itinerary.

Avram sent a tentative analysis to Moscva. Anzhero escaped, one building, one airplane, rendezvous to the snow, Tavda? No confirmation was sent. After the incident with Code Breaker, no one would risk it.

KIROV

Early evening snows fell as a rain, too opaque to see through. The candle light in the hall and bedroom flickered for no reason. Paul sat in bed reading Solgenitzen. Neva emerged from the bathroom towel drying her hair wearing a long worn white terry cloth robe tied at the waist. He had been summoned to Moscva. In the next several weeks she would keep the house while he met with the head honchos to decipher a mosaic.

"Tired?" he asked her.

"Not at all. I don't know how you find him a relaxation."

She sat on the bed and tousled his curly white hair. "Would you give me a rub?"

He put the splayed book on the lamp table and pulled her toward him. Slyly he opened her robe and slipped it off her shoulders, kissing her shoulders softly. He could feel Moscva calling him, already he was detaching, viewing his actions from outside himself. He told himself it was the chronic endurance of the work, the fact that Breaker was in the snow again somewhere, this time with many little polar bears. He could not prevent the urging sense that the night no longer fit with this temperance. Somewhere a wolf was hunting tracks silent in a flutter of windy commotion before a storm hit with thunderous force against the hills surrounding the sleepy village. He nudged her onto her front, began his deep tissue massage, working through her tension, managing her body's lean rippling muscles, his hands somehow sensory deprived as though he had been long in captivity. Her back was tight all the way to her rib cage, she was hard thinking anyway although this was more than she generally possessed, despite her workouts at the gymnasium for racquetball once a week followed by tennis. This would not be his file she was reviewing, it would be something else. He asked how her brother was faring out in Finland, only to realize she had fallen asleep. He got up, put her to bed, blew out the candle, grabbed his wool grey robe and walked into the living room and flicked on her computer. He typed in her password, selected a file by date, looked at the photograph of Breaker, nearly invisible, only the color of his clothing identifiable. It wouldn't matter any longer that Neva was reassigned if the FSB Breaker had to sit on the snow to catch a felon, nor that she reviewed his findings only to report them in a new file that became combined in committee over which he had no final authority over his own file. He closed out her data bank and plodded inside the kitchen, distressed over his realization. He guessed no one at Central would tell him because of her newer assignments that he could not remain in his house until Breaker was safely advanced. She wouldn't ask either for her sense of a need to control the file nor think she had lost him, so this enigmatic situation may have been put to a test so that Breaker's contact would not view it as a loss of power.

He looked up his own Breaker file for known contacts and found one, Anaya. The recommendation for typical demolition was not cracks. Where standard demolition occurred other charge breaker boxes consisting of each a diamond, 2 carat, an emerald, no carats, a black smooth stone, non granite, placed within a very small watch were inserted inside all other buildings within a four block radius in order to prevent impact, breakers didn't use electricity, only charge boxes did. The problems that occurred with Collier's groups were the practices prior to assuming occupancy caused cracks, requiring repair or demolition. Russia hadn't had an illegal demolition in a good long time but she had plenty of other problems, ones she couldn't easily fix with money which wasn't there. With her limited tax collection and funding, only certain departments were able to receive new startup and funds couldn't be actual money that paid.

Paul checked into the Astoria. It was a dated, out of fashion art deco building with studios that had a large window overlooking a pedestrian trafficked avenue on which sat few taxis. He left his case open on his bed and went to lather and shave inside the large semi-tiled bathroom with shower, a wall of mirrors, two sinks, vanity and dressing room. Refreshed, up for anything, he read the newspaper he purchased in the lobby, while preparing himself a cup of sanka and cream, until it was time to meet for an early dinner upstairs in the men's dining hall. The interloper hastened to jot along a nonsensical message giving him the instinctive wariness of an agent whose summaries are sent by reference to single letters. At five to six he opted to go up early, his date book and magnifier well in tow. Inside the elevator were other harried looking, somewhat ragged in appearance, educated, thick in the shoulders aging men with female secretaries for whom the frivolities of living were ever spelled. At the entrance into the hall a femme male sitting at a table checked them in, handed out name tags on gold cards and rendered each a volume of poetry by Mandolin and Happledon, and a well briefed indexed notebook with the agenda over the subsequent two weeks. It was early to begin after a half hour breakfast of hard eggs, fruit, fresh biscuits and double strength brewed coffee, a lazy martini and a second order of omelets, all this meant to inspire schmoozing. The Jacob look-alikes had descended the couple with the best chances of promotion into a former KGB post that would control the fair temperate monies of a nation still intent on resisting capital gains and expensive state competitive tours. At the round tables around which there were thirty elegant carved chairs were winders, exposed to their inner mechanistic rotaries like party favors. Six channels, ruby on the largest governing the second hand sweep, diamonds valued at well near a quarter carat, a small emerald, also diamond cut, each with a moving hand, the hour slowly moving around its dial, month, date, day, night, made by an expert.

By eight-thirty the room was packed. Across the room he eyed Code Name Breaker's beautiful wife whose deep emerald green eyes and long brackish hair made one want to surrender within an aimless torrid encounter meant for nothing other than refined sentiment. Command, thin as an arctic Pole, stood the discussion with a handful of province administrators, one who had deciphered the target Collier for new assignment. The winders, he said to get this crash course moving up to speed, posed some notorious difficulties, the watches ran without stopping, joint telex interface was for maneuver,

Rushing water somewhere in the country might do it, or synapses were timed for venture capital releases. Other undesirable events, the timers had set oscillation at twenty thousand with a dial for military time but no automatic, was neither Philippe nor Cotton Club. Without knowledge of an objective course, there was almost no determination possible even for interfering with mechanisms that could offset a timetable of electrifying quakes. Then there were the deep water watches, neither diamond nor ruby, bold sapphire intimidators. Boisterous in intent they calibrated radiance into a myriad of tough quickly unreasonable cracking structures whose foundations would withstand any tough jolt except flashes, those sentiments he had felt would disappear beneath a series of succumbing teletypes punctuated by unpredictable temblors. They discussed the terrain of ice impacted by uneven rolling chronographs. Ice was its own barrier, it could be used to blank out text and pictures, a shiny surface would without a reference on land or water temporarily eliminate something one needed to see, watches would time the duration with elapsed time.

He took Breaker's wife to dinner. She had grown up in the Federated States Bureau, the daughter of a station who had spent the majority of his time studying despite his advanced credentials and time abroad. She had attended a privileged private tutorial for entrants into domestic travel and education, been appointed to a scholastic honors department which she spent years trying to provide grants for honor statisticians who could help create a base of information. She met Breaker after she graduated, he impressed her as a man who was going places and because he already had a group whom he could offer jobs to, she gave his associates services formerly curtailed to them. Breaker was residing in the mountains, trying to come to terms with a monster on the loose that for some reason had to be out there. She felt she had already lost him, not simply because he was gone for years at any one period but when he returned home he was distant, uninvolved, unromantic, a cohabitant with needs she was unable to keep abreast of. Paul suspected she said this to each potential affair, that her actual relationship with her husband, if not a Bureau assignment, was nevertheless protected for each of their assignments. He wondered how many affairs she had had and what duration each was, and whether they calibrated to affection or a sense of necessity or strictly convenience. He asked himself if in her youthful twenties or thirties she would have been so beautiful that she had admirers everywhere and what she could have told herself about that reality, had she thought she would try them all or was she left often to leave some behind with merely a curiosity for who they might be. He knew he would not relent in his wondering of her for he was just that sort of man until he possessed her. Then he would know absolutely if he would like her. He watched her over candlelight, her occasional nervousness, gay laughter, her honesty, the curve of her mouth, her amused glances, his enjoyment. Besides his desire to be consumed he knew Neva had left him also for an impalpable rationale, that she was not his as he had at one time thought she grew an affection for him, she was a weekly excursion, how miserable a blow to his pride. He would never have thought to look over her shoulder, although he could think now had he looked he might have warded off the blow that took the fellow in the snow.

Here they were, two agents in a vast wilderness of unspoken lieges, both knowledgeable to a certain persuasion, presumably minor considerations in common, having had to communicate to other agents whom they had never met. He was past the self questioning as to if he should, or concern for Neva regardless of how superior he had thought she was to him. That she read every last status and selected brief excerpts and sent them who the hell knew where, that she would have tracked the poor fellow by rudimentary telecommunication, she should be tossed into a prison and not in Sibirskoye, if her brother, the asinine man he was, knew an enemy to talk to. The problem with seduction was after the act the forming of a deep friendship took years. He would not leave Kirov, after he had paid nearly two hundred thousand rubles for it, and probably she wouldn't set foot there. Thus, a delicious meal of delicately seasoned polenta soup, very dry white wine, a sliver of fig bread with anchovy, and trifle soaked in rum, they sipped demitasses with lemon, paid each, he tossing a fifty to the chef, he strolled with her through FSB domain. She told him she had come from a living where the pleasure was everything and she told him straight off the pleasure was too expensive. She was reassuring to have on his arm, he told himself a massage couldn't be costly but he wouldn't, especially if it went nowhere. She said she had had a man in a spring year that she probably shouldn't have had, a good friend left him to her, she was foolish to have crossed that line. He took her in his arms and kissed her softly and she put her gloved hands beneath his coat and encircled him, the smell of her faint perfume sweet like lemon. She took him to her, kissing him long to be known. He took her home, her flat a small all glass rentals with balcony on a fourth floor. He permitted her to make love to him, enthralled only to her touch. She was elegant, chiseled in her nudity a soft unobtrusive passion, he fell asleep in her arms, separated by an inner desolation, a sorrow that clung to him, drifting far beyond her alert comprehension. When he awakened he arose to find her in a hot tub on the back porch, a small window pulled open, forty degree cold pressed against the chicken screen. He stepped into the barrel, submerging slowly, the tepid still; water releasing any remaining tension. He was satiated but unsure of how he would decide when morning came as he did not judge himself by the standards of his youth. She handed him a book of poems. They sat immersed, like two older mildly aged friends, the pod light at a distance, the cold unperceived and soaked. He read Jojin, the autumn poem he immediately resonated with. Falling from pitched poles/Feathers scarlet brushes/Why does the wind drift far? Where was this poet standing when he witnessed roosters, ankles tied, heads chopped, getting tossed into a crate for the marketplace. He turned the page, diminutive characters like a column, another vivid image, Points of birch rushing by/Damp dark earth/Cracked coconut milk spilled over. On adoration, rustling crepe like cloth, patter/Stark cries echo/I shiver on coldest floorboards. They would make love again before morning.

He had met a watchmaker once, a narrow darkly silvery tan female who without a sense of direction steadfastly took apart watches in order to determine how they were constructed, tested for timing apparatus and once evaluated removed the stones and reset with granite for resale. She could take the face off and tell by looking if the inner dials were sophisticated to be used for manufacturers. She gave his watch a thorough appraisal and with an eyebrow raised gave him a money's worth. His object was priceless, construed from an older item, four dials, one fairly large flat ruby, a tiny blue tiger's eye, small less than a quarter carat bezel in one, one dial a rotation on another wheel, unlike Rolex, not sturdy to be a Breguet, a classic imitation. He said he had paid eight hundred for it and had never lost a minute. That was his watch training. Command was non compassionate over precise accuracy, the watch assemblage on the table was believed to have cracked numerous buildings causing them to be unfit for occupancy. The Bureau chief only wanted the entire group to assess their use. Because the group was elitists of one analytical type their combined abilities would be needed to come up with times excluding breakers, but relying on use of any composite of watch.

His usual fare was to test. He knew almost nothing about setup. He inquired of the group if they wanted him, they thought not. They planned to start the clock applying ten to twelve watches to assess likelihood of sequence per floor for outcome. The aim was to produce a series of possible sequences capable of creating the extent of deterioration. They figured a day, they had to match against outcomes. He left, the problem while not an unknown nevertheless nothing he would be asked to do, his skills necessary to hone in on sounds that obscured, whatever Central used his analyses for was their business. As with the vehicle backfire he wouldn't include that anyways, it wasn't a regular noise that he would apply to. His data when grouped to other groupings was to assess if other analyzed photographs could become used as interpretation. He stopped for a decaf, took it into the park, sat on a bench and fed the pigeons. He sipped and savored a rare minute of appreciable lack of distractions. The day although blustery was warm, a casual send-off to an unremarkable sedate quality of tension. After he had fed the silly birds he walked across the plaza to Breaker's wife's flat to join her at her hot tub to shoot the breeze about her work. She confided, her husband tracked people who cracked buildings by charge, or whatever the use was of a methodology, they weren't sure, people left buildings slightly damaged, not demolished; she inserted sequences to prevent illegal demolition, always aware her husband had to act against what might be a bomb, he followed a lead, not necessary implementation, what could she do to make sure she acted as a back up – she could stop time but that was not advisable, she couldn't remove a second hand if there was one, she began with the question as to how many rubies were there, now she put forth her terms, she was married, he said he knew, she told him she had developed a breaker system for use by agents who devised for failsafe by groupings of floors and for this reason alone she was sworn to one man. He hadn't realized her expertise, told her he never interfered, he had been hungry for awhile, to which she replied her husband was a way sometimes over a year and at seldom occasions took a friend. He said he found her sweetly delightful; she said she would keep him as long as he liked her. He reached for her in a selfish moment, discovered she was eager, and he pressed his palms over her skin wishing she would hope for him beyond her knowledge leaving him with almost nothing. He finally stood lifting her with him and breathed her into his every sensibility until she trembled.

The next question she told him in a fevered silence was to treble the down motion causing speed to be slower, this was accomplished also by a set of programs she had carefully composed over a period of thirty years. She didn't recommend quick collapse nor swift interruption, sometimes those situations became inevitable, her rule was never interfering with active circuits. But he knew agents who interfered successfully, told himself to remain a slight bit detached as she ran a hand over his neck and back and no less reserved he bent to her caught in a deliberate supplication, supremely marshaled to her, finding his skin came alive beneath her touch, he felt famished, urgently in need, unreserved, succumbed. This was passion, she was yielding, he held only her in his mind, entwined, speech driven to some other part of the brain, cloyed and cloying, he wept as he surrendered. She shushed him, grasped his hair in bunches and cried out and she gave him the refuge he had not known he could need. He demanded her, secured her to himself, and synchronized his need for her, still as yet feeling he did not wholly drain her. Despite the understanding, he knew he was in love, knew he would be at her doorstep many days. His passion was admirable, if because she was an expert, able to give the man who needed her sole provision which under the worst of circumstances would save his life. This itself gave him a feeling of intensified need as he thought in the act of loving her he could also love the strength her husband relied upon to work through the complexities of his work, Paul felt an equality, a concurrence, when he realized he had overnight it seemed developed a shortcoming, knowing he did not wish to restrict himself, wanting her at any cost, telling himself that as noble as he wished he was he had acted only to be fulfilled by her.

He thought to ask what she would do if she had noticed another elitist using reviews for an analyst group any sections of classified notations that they had to correct. She thought what he described happened frequently, some by highly endowed positions, others who needed to dispose of references to non classified groups until the State could make readings and interpret. No single individual usually controlled use of information unless they intended to subject agents to exposure for any uncertain reasons. He then talked to her about his arrangement, the tightly fisted inclination to cede restricted material and the brother who lurked about entering ranks of militsya to endeavor posts that he might someday control. He looked at his own difficulties with fettering out identifying qualifiers especially for groupings of imagery he hoped could prove useful in clear systems detection. He had often encountered faded visor identification, thought it could be due to infringement, knew a trick or two, but really wanted to build in a more responsive three-way detection based upon any condor. This for him meant successful advance glimpses at people for whom holography was the custom, borrowed elapsed sequence, registries of watches, deep water photography as well as speed retroflection, photogamy, series of electrocutions, refracted light syndromes. Her concern was any multiple use as the image was being photographed, the essence of creating a band of holograms lay not in uses of light wands but in preservation. Whereas detection could be compromised, most state departments operated by protocol instead of by meter. The problem for the fox was once he was captured on film, he was known for his identity, and that worked both ways, also for agents.

He put in an appearance at the men's hall the next day to find the group sizing down the buildings that had been affected by each known seismographic detonation. Twenty of the thirty analysts placed numeric hours and minutes for each presumed task and placed it into a computerized databank. The difficulty was that synchronized flash cube use eliminated any ability to classify direction of impact. The watches themselves were then set, attached by rod and measured by the system for resulting sequence of fracturing. Paul took these resulting readings and the darkened photographs of each building interior back to his hotel room to review for detonation center and impact debris quality. He entered each photograph into his database, arranged each series, ran his program and since determinations for each building content by order of recordings had already long ago been assessed, he then lined them up on a map graph, labeled each crack accordingly and applied sequence in order to assess within all cities together whether impact had been generated in solely one building per city or was pieced by numerous devices. Arrows pointed to each identified source of cracking. In most cases it was a five story edifice mostly cement. Within an hour other points had taken, some buildings with insufficient damage to warrant sale to an independent contractor until restoration was completed. Because the original damage report on each building had arrived at the same conclusion, that all affected buildings had been hit individually, the final sequencing determined on what date each building was struck, for how many minutes per strike, and number of occasions. There were twenty computers per serious fault each within a block of the target, corners the most vulnerable for floors, the walls for cracks. He agreed, a group that set up education and took up buildings in order to damage them were interested in construction and that was the objective, to rebuild a country whose authority was situated in Bureau control rather than in consumer management.

GORKIY

Jacob spotted Winder from a distance. Winder was with wavy dark grey hair, a medium height man, distinctive in his fashionable dress. Finally the louts were coming into the marketplace. The man entered the building, in minutes went through the upper suite and could be seen flicking on the lights to each office. The telephone van showed up and men in overalls got out and went inside carting equipment. Jacob stood on the opposite corner cognizant of the men in an office. He left his post, stopped in at the cafe and purchased a cup of espresso, sat near a window and waited for the men to depart. Eventually they left together, Winder folding a piece of paper and pocketing it inside his coat. Winder had a job letting the installers into the building. His question, did the watchmaker work for Collier or did he arrive having learned installers were scheduled. Normally FSB scheduled maintenance after the whereabouts of the critical list was determined, except in this context a piece of information was not known. The fact that Winder was required caused him to consider what he knew of the method by which these files were worked. He walked the two blocks to his flat where he found Kas hard at work on the telephone talking to her exposure contact. She was questioning him as to comparisons. He prepared lunch, took it to his desk, wrote a brief narrative disposition. The telecommunication liaison gave him a series of photographs all of Winder. The subversive target looked adequate, however maintenance was not his job usually, he had a workshop which when he stayed with the man Anaya he spent numerous days fitting dials together and tuning them before he placed the black stone in its usual place. Jacob asked himself under what circumstances Winder met Collier, if they even knew one another. He missed his wife, the warmth of her kitchen, her closeness, despite this he didn't think of going home until he tied up the job. It wouldn't be his construct that gave the job completion or that he could identify by person the group who created their aims or that the executive powers were at least placed within their original cities when they decided to implement. Although he enjoyed the banter of a family and having his enjoyments, there was no replacement for his post. He had long given up on the idea of working on station with another FSB with similar training, as he had also surrendered having to reside with an emotionally available female. The complexity of the nature of a criminal mind had drawn from him a hyper vigilance for which he kept his choices adhering to strict conservative standards. He had been out here at least a year, would be here probably five more years, and while it occurred to him to permit himself to keep a romance, certainly if the agency thought he might require affection, he did not give into it telling himself if he did, he might slack on a judgment call without realizing he had mistaken. If he was criticized for being tough on himself, it was no one's business, the fact that he was given total collateral probably had next to nothing to do with moral decisions. Five years was not a divorce. Only once did he consider writing Rivka to tell her he thought he would be on assignment twenty years and to get herself a divorce, but she wrote him, Never, my heart would break. Her letter was a bit of a jolt because he had assumed that because she would not leave his side even for a few hours filling each moment with conversation and cooking that she would need someone else. He seldom had needs for corruption, not comprehending how he could live to pay such a price, couldn't decide whether to cross that boundary.

He went to join his secretary for teatime. Kas was writing up her notes, adding to them with notations before she would transcribe onto formal dictate.

He asked for her summary on her conversation, for which she readily informed him that Collier had gone to another one of his conferences, arranged for participants to attend orientations to provide support for future positions but as yet had not sent his staff here into Gorkiy and was attempting to post offices at locations in established offices of other departments without getting this office which he had funded staffed. Collier believed his operations were compromised. He had asked FSB for support to deal with difficulties his management was now having, in particular he wanted smaller groups to perform more functions. FSB had refused him. The Bureau asked he go back to Murmansk to conduct outcome objectives telling him his network was as large as it should be and to set up Gorkiy as his managerial zone. The oddity was Collier had spent years trying to gain approval for just such a zone in Kirov. The office location in Gorkiy was intended as a sub zone for independent contracts and had been approved for the maximum one million rubles per lifetime contract to distribute additional funds for the other offices already in operation. It was nearly three months into already distributed funds. In calculating funds FSB came across this discrepancy.

Her idea was Collier wanted an office in Sibirskoye near the medical complex at Kazan. This speculation was given no justification believed to now resemble a crossing. Collier had three sectors each with fifty employees and twelve offices. A hundred was maximum. There were too many problems to warrant further approval. FSB would leave him where he was until they had further verification of why his plans consisted of deteriorating each building his offices were assigned to. When the ship in the Obskaya hit ice the data banks were affected and education was the department that continued to operate. Never in the past had any office been able to be independent of a major problem.

She said, "It's unthought-of of that our worst situation has become typical because we are in a decline between budgets. "

"That's not that unusual, I'm just surprised it keeps going on."

"I've scrounged around for a dossier of some kind on this Jepson Collier to get an idea about his youth. I seem to recollect he did a stint in Saudi Arabia where he chemically analyzed oil for manufacture. While toying with the guesswork I discovered he was a state department contracts man for a few foreign governments, some with very liberal policies. It wouldn't surprise me if what materialized out of that network formed a basis for his contracts in Moscva."

He nodded over his dry biscuit. "That would have been

good fertile ground. I'd certainly like to know what organizational structure he's game for. With so many checks on his realm I can't see where he has any leverage. His potential is limited even if he can enter his own training for prospective upper ranks."

"It has to be tangible. Rundown offices don't get that way by themselves. Who had them previously?"

"District boards for medical science. There's one for most major sectors. They appoint physicians based upon need. Most start in the ephemeral sciences, they are mathematicians applying cures for arthritis, whooping cough, fracture, headaches, whatever afflicts people who live in zero degree climates."

"I'm impressed. Perhaps he wants entrance to new medicine wherever it is isolated. What did he come across with oil?"

"The country uses a quarter ton a year to ward off icebergs. Seamen wind up with more ailments than most. Rheumatoid for starters, deafness, lowered blood pressure, reduced food intake. Education has inroads into experimental treatment. In and of itself," Kas continued, and paused to light an herbal cigarette, "it's a blessing. Jepson was highly regarded when he proposed his fluoridation program. He began with public health nurses at the elementary school, he brought in relay exercises for stimulation of the body, he had research at universities for seaweed and niacin, then he introduced his idea of networking implementation, no one foresaw any of this."

They sipped tea. Kas got up to light a fire in the Norwegian stove. She stood in front smoking her cigarette warming her hands.

"Possibly they get far ahead of themselves after a while," she said.

"I'll turn on the heat," he said, and went into the hall to adjust the thermostat. "You'll warm up. You know, if not for the condition of buildings ---"

"This isn't about buildings alone, Jacob. Whatever is going on goes with numerous entities concurrently because they appear to separate and there's nothing to explain it. "

"I only do what I do."

"That's how I work with the non issue when I'm between correspondences, I attempt to provide suggestion as to the principal. Sometimes I am wrong, other times I have a lead."

"I'm thinking of writing my wife. This is going to be a long job."

"Maybe I could write her, I could think of something you might not."

"That isn't my style."

"Is her mail read?"

"Probably." Without hesitation, he said, more out of discourse than ordinary objection, "I suppose we could give it a try. You could tell her I am in the street all the time."

"I'll think of something."

Rivka's letter sat on the dining room table on pastel blue, green and yellow stationary, unopened.

My dearest Elk, I was overjoyed to receive your gentle warmest guiding words. I also miss you beyond any ability for expression. Filipa sends you all endearments. She is growing tall and happy as only my dearest cousin Clytemnestra will affirm. We took in a tree from the yard, decorated it with home-made crescent silver and pink cookies and made a manger and child for the children's birthday. I long for you in my essence, of all festivity I must confess I am incomplete although the house is joyous. Your father visited and brought me a new coach. Stay for awhile indoors and tend to your heartening friend. May God speed your attentive memory of me. Your darling Rivka.

He smiled amused by her sentimentality. It was a shock to him when her mother after having lost her sixth husband nearly died of loneliness, had to have an attendant come in to prepare a special diet, wash her hair and exercise her limbs, the State having finally ended gruesome nursing homes which little more than warehoused the aged. They added on to their small house over the patio a small apartment of a living room, kitchen and breakfast room and bedroom and handicapped bathroom. Thus for nearly fifteen years all meals were taken on their side of the door, all festivities, cousins down from St. Petersburg and up from Sevastopol for weeks at a time. When Alene's time came at last the entire blended families grouped together, all fifty-five of them into the tiny spaces of the house to hold her hands until she closed her eyes for the final time. He folded the letter and placed it into the envelope which he pocketed into his polo. He would permit himself in the wee hours of late night to reread it knowing this rare intimacy left him not quite himself, but weakened.

If not for the flash in a parlor apartment across the street, he would have thought his watch was asleep.

He went to the flat, cleaned up, sat at his desk, data entered his summary, sent it to Moscva. Within hours the inner central would pack into town. He poured himself a glass of sweet wine sipping it long into the chill night falling asleep on the single couch beside his work desk. He awakened at early light with a slight hangover, the fire still ablaze, thoughts as to the rest of the day. He could hear Kas inside the kitchen typing away as she spoke to someone on the telephone in a hushed voice. As he stood his head ached, a sure reminder he was not as young as when he had this last dance with this liaison. It would be another gripe he added to his list not to involve his family as he was about to submerge. Kas would of course shoot off a communique every so often, Rivka's letters would pile on his desk, maybe Georgann would come again, but the situation was about to go down.

He made soft footsteps in to the kitchen preparing coffee and an ounce of cereal keeping his gazes apart from Kas as she, cornered by a series of instructions, called leap year contacts on a file she didn't need to consult. Once the coffee boiled he poured her a cup, brewed one for himself and squeezed into the booth beside her taking in her status. She had broken the winder case down, proceeded with confirming contacts, put into a watch graph her data and in minutes had successfully concluded the timing mechanism used to intersect telex for the

Volonad disaster.

"They want to know how many women might be involved," she said, after she ended her conversation. "How many shall I say?"

"Possibly one, but red shoes don't complete for a breaker who for some reason is out of circulation a month."

"Not Breaker's wife. She is the goal catcher."

It was not for the custodian who waxed down the wood floors or for the two window washers that he did not stray from his post. The twice folded newspaper beneath his elbow, his long down coat with fake fur lining, woolen hat and gloves, he smoked a pipe with his favorite walnut flavor, sipped a paper cup of strong black coffee, his pager attached to his inside coat pocket, all the while watching the street for signs of an office about to move in. There were no signs of a real life magazine, no furniture vans rolling up to the pad, no actress look-alikes coming down the sidewalk nor moving caravan of sodas and frankfurters or custard baklavas. Just the street. The older style Madrid stucco building with grey gables sat next door to the older ocher tan building of three floors and steel framed windows, for which the work order to stencil bold black and gold lined letters was anticipated. On his side three buildings of six stories apiece, the bronze door for the corner bank, French Left bank interior of marble floors and wooden painted ceiling with lots of antique brass and gilded framed mirrors, the middle building, a retrofit of tan fresco with an elaborate iron gate, and the last edifice to the block, a trim artistic front of elaborate carved wood to resemble ivory over a copper steel door and rows of storefronts for a delicatessen, hair styling salon for men, and a men's wear shop with shoe-shine in the display window. Since this was a lamp-light district in an older section of Gorkiy Square, the effacements of ten county buildings were disguised by a long park of grass and leafy boughs and bronze backed wooden benches around a long necked seven tier fountain into which lovers tossed coins for their wishes of long-lasting love. Jacob had no doubt that lookouts for either

Collier or Winder might be standing at a distance watching for his approach in their direction, but he left the sighting of them to the full exposure group who earned their righteous pay staring out top floor windows looking out at the park. It was a tedious morning without a payoff in sight.

At one in the afternoon the vans arrived. Large mahogany desks with lamps were carried into the elevators, computers and consoles, framed prints were taken in, crates also, large statuary, wooden file cabinets, Berber rugs. Upstairs the lights flicked on, the movers were to be seen laying down carpet, placing furniture, turning on floor and desk lamps. As they worked, the second floor came alive with chandeliers, lamps of every height and color glass, an ebony statue in the end window, stencils on windows for legal and bookkeeping services, hat racks, floor to ceiling bookcases, books onto every shelf, modern racks with manuals, framed credentials on walls. By two-thirty the vans arrived to unload hundreds of boxes of paper files. Four or five men walked box loads into the entrance and left them stacked in view of the top floor windows. Within two hours the men were done, the vans had left and the street was quiet.

Jacob went inside for a coffee and television. A game was on, 1 to 1; the local college had the favorable prospects. A female dressed in a woolen sail cloth white and polished red high heels with white leather gloves stood at the bar, her curved lips an elegant fiery red. She wore her deep dark brown hair tied in a twist without a clip. He immediately recognized the idea. Wounds, but not blood. Winder was on the scene. He was awaiting a turnout. She had ordered a drink which a new mustached bartender poured into a highball on the bar counter. She laid five bills and took a sip, then glanced around, her gaze meeting his in odd recognition. She weaved through the crowded tables to his, sat opposite, peeled off her gloves, placed her drink on the wooden surface and in fluent Russian said Rivka was making out fine, the family from Petersburg down for the winter, and she Georgann was in town to make good on a last mortgage payment. He asked what her ex-husband was up to, and she told him quite frankly he went to work as a bureaucrat in Sibirskaya, not Gulag, farther out past the mountains. He asked her were there findings on Breaker, she removed a compact, eyed herself, powdered her face and coldly answered, Breaker went into a restricted area. In the place he was having dinner off the road he was seen, his concern had to have been when his lead might return. Georgann thought he was still up there getting through winter blizzards. It didn't matter that he might actually know Breaker's identity with FSB. He asked for a point of clarification, who was FSB calling the assassin. She sipped, said that was this fox, Collier. He wanted to understand how the problem came into placement. She nodded out the window as a hat was hung on the visible hat rack. A large industrial complex was shut down permanently when some sort of ship cutting through ice in the north ocean and every last building of a certain flag height was incomprehensively jolted to its foundation. The central government of Moscva found upon audit that these buildings were construed for takeover by an outfit that had monitored another country's output. These buildings were bugged first for light, damp, computerized telephone circuitry. As a result the government had held back the coordinators who they thought were responsible for the bugging. So far they had uncovered three names, Collier, Winder or Tavda, and Breaker, just the last identity was assigned after he was believed to have murdered a handful of Bureau agents.

He finished his coffee, gave her his address and invited her to dinner which she agreed. Leaving her to her drink he walked through happy hour, strode across the street, entered the three-story building and rode the tinted mirror walled elevator to the top floor. When the doors opened he was inside a waiting room with a receptionist, a tall svelte blond man dressed in khaki with glasses, he took a seat, picked up a magazine and took observation of the three offices that let off the lobby with damask sofas, ash blond flooring, a centered off color Berber, a bronze and cement statue of a semi nude male, built-in cabinetry aside the man's decor desk littered with enhanced objects, a opaque green glass pencil sharpener, a note spindle, notepads, telephone console with fifty lines, paper bins, yet a sight of handsome mahogany grain wood. The one office had a broad walnut desk, a flowery red, green, yellow and white couch with teak at the base, a handsome upholstered dark natty green and cane chair; the second office directly in the foreground was long and narrow and contained a long polished ebony table with matching wood white silk upholstery and had two eight foot columns made of marble with lights at the top bases, the final office also smallish wallpapered in a dark rust with white trim, two semi opaque windows, also a flowery yellow, white and green flower leaf motif and small desk of walnut, was thickly carpeted in rust Berber with strands of green. Where the other offices were he could not tell.

These would become the safety contracts for much of the various cities enhanced education departments. At some point he thought the universities might step into take over for their own use. The handsome interior had to reflect someone's judgment for a situation they thought they had to preserve. It ought to give the telescopes seeking definition ideas as to the caliber of personnel, should the clerks or managers be auditors, least known executive head hunters, borrowed from oil technocrats, bellhops, console operators, or professions inherent to balancing average sized county budgets designated to develop rapidly for any rationale the government found desirable. At length the man asked Jacob's business, Jacob said he had come to interview and was informed he was a day early, and became scheduled for the following afternoon at noon. He could hope he met with his next advisor in the other rooms.

On the trip to his flat he stopped in at a bakery for sponge cake, lemon iced, two fingers of ladled fish per person, beet soup and Jamaican coffee. He went to his flat, where the door was ajar, and the pleasant sound of laughter amid intense dialogue from his secretary and government liaison. He discovered Kas in the kitchen mixing drinks, slices of garlic toast on a plate with dabs of blue cheese crumbly dip. He stopped for a bite, handed the food to her for preparation, went to freshen up; upon his return he set the table, lit candelabra of five candles, and went to help get the meal served. They sat down to a lit dinner of politics, discoursed about changes in the militsyaboros, the new opera center plaza in Moscva, various renditions of Nutcracker Suite, Vivaldi and Brahms, Figaro's tragedy, the entire season for a Bureau intent on moving away from contractual era having to focus mostly on oil in order to temperate the cold, into a newly designed fashion based upon city centers such as in Czechoslovakia, a turning down of price indexing, less taxation, a desire for shorter work weeks and family vacations in popular lake resorts. Georgann hummed a rendition of Brahms complete with an imitation of a damsel sighing over her young man's reflection. Just so, Kas replied and tried a few times to switch to the concerns of an entire corridor who could not yet pinpoint the source of several fanatical attempts in Cairo to shake up Russian principals. Jacob held to the opera news and after dinner and before dessert took Georgann for a walk while Kas handled a private call.

Jacob put his arm around Georgann as they headed to the college grove he asked her about the new Bureau palace and she retorted it was mostly for construction for the new wave of two million teens preparing for exams and for a Caspian Sea community about to embark on an agricultural industry. He paused and kissed her and she fell against him rather unexpectedly encircling her arm about his neck, holding onto his waist. He fondly brushed her cheek with his hand almost sadly, everything he knew far away, far beyond any grasp of it. He steered her by the elbow to the bough of trees where well hidden from any public view he ran his hands over her body. She allowed it, he spoke no words and they kissed longingly, she emotionally pouring out to him. He told her his assignment was soon to change and he was to go on the inside. She held him to her pressing against him as tightly as she could, he lifting her skirt until he could pass his hand against her leg. He gazed into her eyes, his stare knowingly hypnotic, and his hand tracing her slender femur. She gently took his hand, letting her woolen skirt fall, and nudged him toward the return direction. They walked silently, her hand in his, his boots crunching leaves, her heels points of red on the pavement.

He met with Collier in his inner sanctum, a pleasing decorum of dark brown wall paper with crème white molding, dark brown Berber, desk, filled bookshelves as anyone meeting a barrister would expect, a floral print of geese flying over reeds and park in vibrant green, dark yellow and white with ebony wood, a fireplace with an insert, magazines on a large mahogany coffee table. The man was tall, blond, brown eyed, intent, a businessman in grey tweeds, long sleeved white collared shirt, over sweater of red, white and dark grey, sleeves rolled up. The areas he required were for materials and records and felt Jacob's expertise would be best suited for records, two days a week midweek. Collier seemed a man for the coordination; there were no indications of corruption or malfeasance or neither of having succumbed to scrutiny nor of wandering into a zone normally closed off to any executive of a department. He was as it suited him, a moderate reminder of an era when education took a forefront and all cities in Russia advised according to her scholars and scholastics.

Collier gave him a tour, showed him to a row of smallish rooms, each in vibrant colors, ceiling moldings, select dark brown Berber, the office Jacob would acquire was ten feet by six feet, resplendent dark rust wallpaper, a large desk, walnut files, a rust upholstered high backed chair, telephones in, laptop computer, window to the street. He took the elevator down, walked the few blocks toward the college, darted inside to a bakery, ordered lunch of wilted salad, a pork chop bone, stewed apples and a tin of hot ale. He deliberated over the scope of the operation, would have considered it negligible to begin with but knew what was in the file, knew Collier was the fox, he was wanted for all sorts of industrial adventures. The tailored sequences were not done without a network of telecommunications in place, the least extensive deriving from mastheads, the more treacherous obvious infiltration, each a recognized combinant of numerous call systems, when one went down so did others, branches of systems responding to frequencies, a government monitored obstacle course removed permanently from silences which this man's agency devoured. He finished the salad, sipped his ale, glanced at passers bustling by, flashy purple and pink shopping bags for the late season, the telephone was the central nervous system, a quick check would tell him the number of locations for which readings were indicated. At some point he thought they would tie in code names for mobile posts.

He took a cab across town to the address he had for Georgeann, it left him in front of a brick walk up, he climbed the stairs to the top floor and went to the near last apartment, removed the key from beneath the mat and let himself inside the overly heated condominium finding it much as he expected. Shining hardwood dark stained birch floors, molded ceilings, a few rooms, and a bedroom with a balcony. He fixed himself a cup of grain drink, sipped it as he looked about for her notes, turned on the radio and television and attached a monitoring device and went in search of her telephone. He didn't see it; she might have it on her person. He checked behind wall hangings and framed pictures ran his hands behind books on a shelf, checked the cabinets. Sat, removed a cigarette, poured a stiff drink, enjoyed the silence, the mist descending. He listened as well after dark Georgann inserted her key, entered with bags and switched on the lights. She was surprised to see him, asked how Kas was, he said he hadn't gone there yet, wanted to stay for supper. She threw some leftovers in the oven, removed her coat, lit the hearth, poured herself a shot of brandy, lit a cigarette and joined him for television news. She went by a bake shop where a grandmother came from behind the curtain with a currant dish for which she was billed twelve dollars. She said they would have it for dessert. Life was going rather smoothly, she was taking someone's place for several days, and asked about his interview. Fox had come down, no telling what that was for, and Jacob thought he was a busy man. He was in the frame now, possibly he knew it, probably was adjusted to it by now. The brandy thoroughly in his blood it didn't make sense to call Kas if he would soon be there, but Georgann put in a message to her which she answered with, fine by her, she'd brought a loaf home and would fix a fish ball to go with a slice. They ate over candlelight in the window, they talked about his interview, she gave her two cents saying the fox ought to know who he was if he ruled out who he wasn't; couldn't be in two places at once. Jacob wasn't in the snow; he could be staffed to Gorkiy during the episode at Kirov. He didn't relay or receive messages; therefore he wasn't available for Kirov.

The currant dessert tasted like mincemeat pie, was warm, crumbly, flavorful. She cut him another portion which he left uneaten. Chai tea with milk chased away the heaviness of beef stew with potatoes and carrots and grated potatoes with cheese. They retired into the living area to see an hour long movie, a militsya flick through well known alleys of Moscva, she sitting across the couch, her legs and feet across his legs. They smoked, sharing a shot glass between them, ate a mint wafer, conversed during paid commercials about her recent assignment. Her van had broken down in Red Square, a handsome militsya devil had taken her to a hotel, within days the place had five or six conventions, she wound up milling about invited by a group of attendees, she poked her head into a day's worth of workshops, went to dinner and saw a wild man run amuck in a garden square pistol firing at people in cars, went straight to a station and gave her report. He thought many females were put in the mindset of public views although it was rare for an FSB to be, she guessed as much when she was transferred and a similar situation occurred which she didn't see much of, but the militsya interviewed everyone in sidewalk cafes. She wasn't put to task nor did the situation follow her when years later she boarded a train into Skoye with half a dozen refugees returning to their families for newer jobs.

He told her he missed his wife and had written her recently, a thoughtless act over which he had a regret. The movie ended and she wrote a note for him about another film by the same director he could see when he needed a bit of relaxation, she wasn't up for much but said her feet were tired and asked him to pinch them, and she coaxed him into a moment of caressing and drifted to sleep. He left her at ten sharp, blanketing her, went down the three flights and exited into bitter cold. Ice had taken the water in the gutters, frost covered windows of cars with sparkling sheets, the cab arrived as the driver departing a stop rushed to him and he slipped inside grateful for the warmth. The city was covered in the first snowfall and heaped onto stairs and streets and fountains. He would be glad when the assignment drew to a close and posted Gorkiy into a distance, but for now he was thinking of ways he would entice Kas to call upon Georgann so as to covenant Collier to public disclosure. By the time Jacob stood inside the fashionable lift, the sting of cold worn off, he asked himself if Georgann's assignment file knew much about any of Collier's non exemplar associates, particularly about Tavda or this fellow Silk, whose name he would've thought attended to some degree of notoriety.

When he got in, he discovered Kas had fallen asleep also in the sitting room on a long chair that was usually pushed up against a far wall, her stockinet legs and ankles protruding from a plaid throw. He left her computer on but took time to clean up her desk, putting her papers inside a in-tray, turning the volume down on her console, fighting every urge to review her scribbled notes at the top of her computer, finally shaving with a brush and lotion, rinsing and patting down with shaving cologne and showering, towel drying, taking to task the day ahead, as he readied for bed with the news section of the Daily Times and a toddy. He was not as some laid-about males he knew, any square advantage a revived appetite for the count of dinners on the town. He himself was monastery oriented although once in France his preference was to stroll the Parisian waterfront, squares, broad avenues, postulate or decorum fancy shoppes, a linnaire and soda water, a bush meal or a wrapped frank on board a sightseeing cruiser. Even as the hour struck a quarter before midnight he was aware a rain had begun to tap amidst a repetitive knocking sound from the floor furnace in the other room, a sincere hope that Rivka was getting the sleep she needed despite swelling wrists from cooking.

Collier's office was sparsely staffed. With the exception of the lobby secretary and an attractive longish black haired medium height woman at the desk adjacent to the lobby he was the only male in the office. He dressed as he had for many years when he walked the Moscva city streets to his expensive workplace directly above a natty tweed smoke shop that also sold men's down jackets, richly woven color scarves, gemstone tie clips, trim toes and backless clogs, and hand-me-down khaki hats. He found the desk in his office stocked for every need, his computer directory, listings of education programs and each liaison. He whipped up a correspondence with an information request, sent it to liaisons and compiled a map by area for each sector by identification, call number and function. Within the hour the liaisons were registered as they checked e-mails and their station automatically came on line by actual location. Once they each reported back, he cross-indexed to employees and each surname and call number appeared. He typed in for numbers ever called by business and independent, lists arrived within a few hours. He organized the files by reference codes, asked for interpretations by conference date and planner, length of time to install systems, education grades by school district and new implementation. He printed the files, placing each organizational chart with respective information into a binder by category, created a separate draft guide on diskette and at noon left the file with the lobby secretary for Collier with instructions.

When he left he stopped in for his lunch of rice, gumbo and sausage with a cup of tea with lemon. Chances were Collier would not respond, at least right away. He left dessert uneaten, walked to his flat without browsing, greeted the concierge and rode the elevator to his floor. A man was having trouble getting his key; Jacob took his groceries while the man opened his door, handed the groceries over and went to his door, letting himself inside an empty flat. It was unusual for Kas not to be there, her table was as he had ordered it, the notes still remained to be convened, and the kitchen cleaned, the bathroom also. He registered on line, reviewed his in-mail, downloaded and pulled up his file on Winder.

Moscva had cleared one hurdle being the breaker identification for watches used for buildings that had to be demolished. Also identified by telegraph was the location for the girlfriend Sin Quon. She knew Skaya because she had a stepfather who resided there, Tavda was a periodic assignment given by Lensk who was thought to recognize Tavda by sight. A photo accompanied her, she was thin and petite as Chinese females from Korea were, had no family to be in photographs and although permitted only for the winder, when she was assigned other men, there was no sex. If she was assigned, then the file was acted on regardless of if it were visible. The fact was Moscva had decoded Collier's implementation for use of a copied breaker system. Zones often were multiplicities governed by decoded crash sites. The analysts were probably done with clock tasks, a new group of building demolition experts would arrive to compare information, and afterwards another group would descend to review minor traction problems.

Sibirskoye
Anzhero

The airplanes out went direct into Moscva International where deplaning took the better part of two days. Arrangements for Tavda had been long in the preparation and when at last a year after his Visa approved the Moscva Commissary undertaking to review his relations he would visit on this trip received clearances and established correspondence points, he was granted a flight with an agreed upon series of stopovers. This being accommodated, and him preferring now to travel at least part of the way by trans Sibirsk train on return, his ticket for the train was fully printed and amount of intended baggage decided, he rode a bus to the airport where he waited for his flight. The day was painfully clear, not a wisp of a cloud anywhere, suggestions of omens dismissed, having served his presumption of self abasement he knew he was prepared for the worst. He had surrendered to his better judgment for which he had become accustomed to servitude, for no rational persuasion could have subjected him to the course he took, not even living in the bare landscape he had gradually come to comprehend. All things were possible, all beckoning, all callings, no more so to flee to a divinity having divested every creative consumption, but having to search deep within for what he knew would devastate him wreaking utter havoc for his mind and soul.

10:45 am
Tavda's Poem to his physician Pechi

I thought I heard a singing lark afar
A wrestled bough a captive heart lament
Descript of muse defied thwarted rebar
Without Piety whimpers scourge repent;
Languished advance borrows not from heaven
Abject miser stored 'against wanderings latent
The heart grows cold over heretic ken
Livid rages at my careless content;
Too late I must obey my Pride's discern
Give tarnished dreams a new waistcoat subscribe
If Ill envisioned preterit nocturne
I was too young of mind to resist chide;
Of all my mortal promises I've wept
Final hours to graves deplored were kept.
Paltry connivance avarice did speak
Dismal progress for sickly old I shunned
The spoon syrup no enchanted vexed cheek
Mean penury its owned contagion;
Likened to invested humility
Distraught complaints were swept into relief
Harsh imploring stayed denied Quixote
Blatant disguise the briefest moment grief;
Had I lived journeys sweet in every port
Were I esteemed of fame or fortune spent
Must I have known that Life renews report?
Steadfast restraint a keen respect had lent;

In earnest Knowledge for that which loves to live?
A vest of worth my merry cap would give.
When early disposed in my youth I came
A male entreated that I ignore the state
Of fetched or nuance made a den to tame
Graceless bold boasts deceived would fee a rate;
A sip of rye complexion finds obscure
A few nights out after being left is viewed
Saddest indigestion hapless endure
Filial destruct becomes misconstrued;
Aging sorrow exacts finer regrets
Intuition snared retracts the distance
Where Reason adhered kindness besets
Defeated folly its own persistence;
For perceived Remorse I waited too long
For fear I remained to whom I belong.
Scarcely a house the buried plains in snows
Driven sleet plaintive awakens sunset
The birds have flown to callings fertile rows
Ice cabbage, blue vines, stalks, lenient wretch;
The tub becalms all agony surmised
Dappled light falls in slats patterns of grace
Wisdom convenes recalcitrance revised
A rush of wings flap leave from dark trees haste;
My Soul repents barest tracked paths o'er hill
Solace fills the cup with tart dislikes again
Pleasures of caribou shadow the sill
Hold to memory the effort disdain;
Lost, dead, the friends I knew ripe plums too sweet
Again, again, the lark resounds skim bleat.

ANZHERO

Pechi had a rare exuberance that delights one to receive translation from a hospital ward. He himself a physician from far eastern Russia traveled west into Siberia once a month to treat arthritis, scurvy, patching, swelling and other physical syndromes, and stopped off on his way to visit an old friend, also a physician, who had frequent contact with isolated Siberians. He as well maintained his own diary when he traveled, submitted per annum with expenses to the FSB.

12-15-07
Chatter on the page, awoke late at 9:40 am cigarette, espresso from the coffee bar
Preparations for the party, added another sonnet, slow creating, month of ideas drawn to a close, talked to handful of friends who can't come, watched another episode of beautiful females, wisdom well in advance of achievement. Picked up 2 pies, two desserts, Mikhail arranged patio, finger food. India walks through the parks as well.

12-16-07
Awoke late, listened to Beethoven, ate, sat on the patio, absorbed the snow peaks, red skin trees like a glen about the base. Read provoking prose, plucked strings on my harpsichord, walked to the trail, picked up my bike, biked about, an afterthought – old man in black coat, flapping, haircut fresh.

Took a lite lunch, egg sandwich with biscuit and paste, the most I've taken at midday, revived the fish in the pond, sat in the garden for quietude from my thoughts. The days are shorter, the dark longer, the ideas spool around another foundation. Another poem from this frail man at the Pass.

Afoot in scarcity brushed by antlers
Adjunct terms stoic acquiescence imparts
Ornamental rosette frost-work branches
Underpinnings nettles, fronds glint flicker greenhearts;
Crisp breath, airy crystalline cobweb lace
Spellbound sterling intricacies snap
Cuneiform alphabet lacquer brace
Up close the snail glistens bark with sap;

Abbreve Braille the chill raises flesh bumps
White loosestrife with abundant spikes climbs stone
Language fails vital mystic strums
I park the bike, retrace the path agone;
The bath prepared I descend the deep well
Before I rise the cleanse lifts not this knell.
Quon sips the clam porridge with cilantro
The wooden bowl repose cheese cream in sum
Sunlight detrims forest's bluest shadow
A cat leans to the sill curtain succumb;
I take leave my unholy state redress
The horse's clip clop o'er cobbles echoes
Winter in retrospect my thoughts arrest
Past darkly stairs and roof garden stickles;
Like one to own delayed delirium
Postscript, the train spools round another pass
Ice cliffs withstand dimorph theorem
The train's whistle penetrates dazed kvass;
Into refract prism rainbows surrend
This one at the end, all holds at the end.

Tavda would know his mistakes, would know a price would
absolutely be extolled, even if he had not yet paid it, he wouldn't
risk his life for what he had already done in his youth. He was
clear, he had to grieve first, empty his well of his own censures,
prepare himself for a long imprisonment, possibly with solitary
confinement, definitively without creature comforts. Only a lunatic having served in Skoye left to go back to a life that would
kill the body, take the mind.

Angelina gave her contemplations to her essays indoctrinated for the Centralya for which, making no elaborations as
to which FSB agent would receive the assignment, she comfortably reviewed the notations of those militsya who kept tabs
with Tavda including document controls. For the purpose of
archives she composed, she would express: "I don't quite have
Tavda's character; he hasn't made the decision yet. He's not one

to give his decisions to circumstance, so if he's inclined to give Collier another go he's also thought it wouldn't be a good idea but we don't yet know why he's reluctant, perhaps it is Sinquon although his rationale is not owing to her. It's possible we don't yet know enough about her either. She is not his, but Collier's. If he bids, she completes, but we don't know anything more of her yet. She must owe some aspect of her life to Collier we think, although it is not clear. Sinquon is in her fifties, she goes where Collier sends her, even Tavda does not know much about her except he needs her. Is it she who visits her father? Or is this someone else? Better I had kept a list as to who is who. At any rate she is the only woman he has known in late life, when choices are scant and the need to preserve the inner circle for Collier is great.

"For himself Collier wants an "in" into Skoye but there is no way in. Education is the least querulous institution he thinks and thus one must suppose he believes he ought to be able to make inroads, Sinquon after all has an uncle who lives there for life. Not without rebels who could want to challenge the fixed system for banishment, Collier while entertaining such a notorious preconception is nevertheless closely watched by the government authorities who now are assured he must be contained and then killed. It was to have been Paul's noose but Paul was subdued possibly by Neva, the militsya haven't proven who takes their code agents. This being the critical complexity to overcome before Collier can be taken; the agent force has seen one after the next loss.

"Sinquon, one must believe, is raised primarily in Skaya in Gulag. When she rejoins social classification as a secretary she works in Berensk where she meets Collier who is reassigned from his task as chemist for oil companies. This is a midlife career change. He adopts Sinquon as a friend, has her in the wilderness to keep his task men quiet and presumably out of sight. Although Chinese origins, which speaks dialects readily and enjoys her occasional luxuries, she maintains a strict fast, rigid disciplines and keeps Tavda's mind alert despite his depression. Fear rests outside her existence. She knows none of the FSB, nor any militsya and lacks any understanding of Tav-da's employment. She knows merely when he must leave that he must have resilience. She asks no questions, does not look to enlighten him by being a sounding board. She represents haiku to Tavda's wrestling with leaving the freedom he has with her, although one feels certain Tavda at occasions revisits the issue of crime. When he arrives he already knows he will be leav-ing; when he arrives he is not at that juncture asking himself the questions he is as he leaves. However it is Collier who has arranged his stay with Sinquon and therefore one would be re-miss not to think Tavda could be traveling to a job Collier has already set up knowing in advance the day the job is to be done. Because Tavda is moving about, Sinquon is also free to take herself from the vast wilderness, although one sees her restive, now more freely engaging with her uncle mentor, she binding her feet as would a ballerina in a method of preparation for an abstraction as yet undefined."

As usual Angelina would acknowledge to herself, espe-cially when her husband Avram was on assignment that her es-says were about real living people with aspirations and families whom they believed in and for whom the subject would not knowingly sacrifice. Tavda had cried in anguish to his supple lover, Sinquon in her solitary quietude had wept. Whatever sat-isfaction she was led to believe was in store for Tavda, she had to know she might not ever see him again. Were she to reflect over their living together she had to derive acknowledge, no less faint, that Tavda planned to enter a decision of great cost to them both, unless she already knew he could never belong to her in any real sense. Angelina was not so naive as to imagine that Tavda was impervious to the State, nor that he was by now watched sufficiently that were he to arrive to Collier's destina-tion it wouldn't spell anything other than instant doom.

Having deleted various document references, because she lacked situations to place them, Angelina kept the referenc-es with an understanding that as they became discussed she would have additional leads and could provide a more compre-hensive analysis. While Avram worked at the task for which he had been summoned, she was without any way to pry his mind, thus her thankless task when disposed of to its proper channel could still require text for tasks other eyes awaited in order to spring to motion. In the interior of her small flat, without Avram, she was left to her own devising, and thus she kept the radio on, her teletext open to the outside world, her notes lined up on the living room table to be checked, a call placed to a friend in Gorkiy to fill her in on any details that might enhance her discernment of the case that already had several hundred FSBs working on it round the clock.

When text came through she was surprised to think she had any response at all. Sinquon had been photographed descending to a platform looking quite the style of a Ruskin in a woolen plaid skirt, white lacy blouse, a red top jacket, tied black boots, grey gloves, her long hair tied in back with a condemnation of tiny pencil curls beneath a woolen grey hat with web resembling in nearly every way Code Breaker's wife. The photograph had to be at least a year old, an abrupt reminder that society females still retained that edge. Angelina copied the photo and e-faxed it in a frame to Breaker's wife herself, saying, "except for the eager sincerity, the train arrived to station."

The idea of freedom with just the few liberties once understood as necessities became apparent as its own philosophical ideology. Kiselyov Mansion would become House of the Press where Yesenin and Blok would recite their works, a badge of acceptance of scholarly achievement for an era felled by cosmopolitan best westerns. Authors Alexei Tolstoy, Maxim Gorky, Anton Chekov for adults and children's stories author Ivan Krylov depicted the advent of industrial individualism as the root of evil, Mikhail Bulgakov wrote about the devil who enters a house for a man's life and poet and playwright Vladimir Mayakovsky, the literary rebel combined language to replace traditional poetic convention, all realized literature as philosophy. The hardships of banishment in Gulag were extolled in Solzhenitsyn to which the microcosm of romance, helplessness and prison life adhered; to study the fiction so as to glean the under floors of modern thought appeared to be the educated route to the solecisms of the century. It would be said without any dislocation of loyalty that fiction authors were given the status of the philosophers of German thought, for in the Russian romantic landscape symbolists rose to captivate a below-middle-class definition of social reform to elevate the domestic health of farm and city collectivism alike.

Out of this historical foundation newer authors Ruben Gallegos and Tatiana Tatskaya hit Europe with unassailable exquisite tales, as promising as Dostoyevsky, philosophy to a backseat. The government would wait for no devolution, no warring upsurge, nor rod in the hearth to make censorious comments for a dissatisfied populace. Although she had poured over their writings struggling in their essences for a sprig of mysticism, her life fortified by steeping herself in the courageous acts of the authors who themselves were bent on denouncements of troubled, dispirited wanderlusts who except for misfortune would have surely traveled continent Russia, Angelina redoubled her knowledge of Avram's world as only one who reads prolifically may. Had it been she instead to whom the FSB assigned the backbone of a horror gone profoundly astray, less besieged by books in reclusive secondary placement to the haste of entering occupied zones to tend to evaluations of hospital-bound, she too would have become enlisted in generations of copious task assignment laid long into nights, often without sleep for days. Yet for the discernment of telescoping into an older female's past, of regrouping files on Red Square anti-bureaucrat posters, she was equipped as thoroughly as an editor who trims for color the selection of under acknowledged film clips. Thus the snapshots in folders were lined up, scrutinized, the cleverness of a female saboteur spied out, a series of photo lens crowds having been worked to advantage, and Angelina cut and pasted a string of handsome assiduously compromised composures. Sinquon was an unknown in those early days of oil rigs and platform stages, a willowy wisp of a crewmate climbing a smokestack, walking across a bearing of thin pipes into a conclave of machinery, a hardhat obscuring her head, an engine room meter reader alongside a foreman whose upper arm strength was utilized by a torque wrench to subvert a misdirection of oil seepage, both found in his small vehicle as he drove her to her station several blocks from the plant. Under close-up Angelina had the wind knocked out as she studied Collier's taut facial muscles, he was anything but brusque, with the arrogant looks of a journeyman who escorted Sinquon to her computers, sat with her and reviewed with her the sequence which caused her to call the plant. Her task was to monitor duct transmigrations, a potentially harrowing risk, where she sat stonily without as much as a lunchbox. Another few shots in a bar, one inside his flat as a masseuse, she was in her youthful twenties naive, earnest, suitably lacking guile, a former spill clerk, in a few more years she would become his wife. A subtle photograph of her on the train through the Skoye, black pants, dark pullover, thick woolen jacket; Angelina downloaded with a text to the lab for the stop she disembarked and a marriage certificate.

BRYNSK

The red fox came into view, the mountain snow was fresh, and the trees were packed in here and there with at least a foot of pile deep. From the nearest window a group of men were trying to decipher a series of complications. As the complications entered their system network, the teletype automatically downloaded to the computers for a cross index to any known code ever used in society skirting through the teletype text for abbreviations, punctuation, or Morse so as to interpret the possible codes for frequency complexities. The group would upon receiving translation enter onto a template for further compilation. Each receipt took four to five hours to code. Only one group followed Tavda since it was he who could interrupt code to regroup it. Infrequently a command station appeared on screen, digitals highly decomposed as though too much fizzle had intervened. The station setting fragmented over minutes but a lasting picture of holiday greenery was kept on screen of a recording. If a series of strident red dashes came on screen, that screen was immediately transferred to an off-line location for identification and the capable entry shut off, at times for almost an hour. The off-line site would try to extrapolate a location for ground level predictability.

At another office Romeo, whose due diligence compensated for his strikingly handsome brown hair and interesting face but who on initial contact seemed prejudiced or overly judgmental, entered his rationale for fizzle onto his computer, writing in shorthand, starting with his usual plunge into his analysis: the only bad complication will be if Tavda enters the Breaker zone at Kirov, if Tavda goes into Moscva to a protective agency he's down completely, he will be detained there, possibly taken to Gorkiy for a rendezvous, if Winder was someone other than Tavda, FSB would try to get Winder to act once they knew what method he used, if it was wire, they would want to know how he intersected a station, if the other winder applied something Tavda needed, all eyes would remain on Collier on his building. The Tavda team now had to conjecture how the thing would work, timers were in place, map was believed to be known, FSB wanted to determine method to interrupt timers. There were still too many unknowns, why was Anya needed if he took no crime jobs; Neva's brother in Fin has dealings with all parties including FSB, he needs to be warned; what does Lensk do for these winders – why did Collier need him if he had a relationship with Sinquon and didn't send her to him, only to Tavda, maybe for this job Tavda had to walk out of a building as it gave sway.

Tavda, like a good Montague, was playing at a game without relief, and Lensk in a presumed truism of a Capulet was thought to be the person who arranged for a cap to cover what would normally be seen to the camera. After days of consultation Romeo decided Tavda could only displace teletype, not in any way alter it. The obvious answer to the central problem had to be that as Collier was arranging all staff, Lensk made sure Collier was not picked up, nor was Lensk picked up either; if Lensk operated alone as he seemed to, if he didn't enter these buildings, he had to have distance to read teletype. Little was known about Lensk except that in younger years he did a high wire act for the circus which kept him fit; because he was tall he was therefore superb, the best in the business because he required no objects with which to balance himself, nor music rendering him very controlled. If it could be found that he used remote, there ought to be the telltale sign that his fingers wouldn't rest easily. Aside from his circus act, with all too few jobs spread out over the years, he kept his verve by studying every word in language dictionaries, this in itself would pose risk of being read if teletype input was transferred to home bases that he intersected to give him knowledge as to stations that might potentially interfere with a target.

In this situation only one thing happened. After buildings were set up for the job then an impact was required that could be put in place by charges, timers were set by computer to go off in a half hour after which various buildings responded for hits. A single nerve was the response team; all others trained their points of reference to the suspects as they were identified, if there were any people working a file that involved them they would eventually be rinsed out. The key as usual was to have enough hands on deck in order to retrieve information while this was going on, the other nerves to the center had the task to determine how it was that although only telex approved documents came out on their computers support for the crime contrived lots of fake orders and someone had to look for those.

The scrutiny of tele-electronics was of course yet to come of age, but for him, a master in religion, whose predominant calling was to fix a path, determine a designee and study music borrowed of ecclesiastical joiners, he had many years of steadfastly pursuing the evil men were made of. Romeo had no false hope that this work was ever anything but extremely tedious, only that to not pursue it surrendered him to grave doubts of having waited too long, allowing for another ruthless killer to get far ahead of the crowd. Teaching seminars hadn't ever answered the passion he felt distracted by, the youth were trained well, capable, driven, knowledgeable, practically applied to forensics, firearm expertise, and computer compatible to detonation arts, behaviorally informed as to abuses, maladaptive addiction, and psychological distress. It was impossible to tell another person when they should have gone into the thicket when he would have acted in some other way had he had the file. He dispensed with teaching after a few years to take a post for which he was required to provide questionnaires upon consultation for the FSB. In developing a routine interview packet for agents he also tested answers for who of those tested had committed serious crimes. The collection data process for witnesses to Collier's crimes included the following queries conducted after each fracture of building complexes.

Questions
Under what set of circumstances were you as a party invited to this country.

Did you make any plans prior to your departure?

Were you advised at any time by your employer as to failure

to return to your workplace?

Could you have made other arrangements to have traveled to another destination ahead of time?

Were you engaged in felonious acts prior to your arrival to the city?

Did you plan to purchase property while you were in the city, could you explain on what grounds a purchase would have been desirable.

Were you accompanied by any person who did not know in advance where you planned to stay on the date in question?

Did you make arrangements to bring any supplies with you on this trip?

Did you at anytime contact your immediate supervisor.

Did you understand if you were required to make arrangements as to next of kin?

Were you ever stationed in our waters or on land as a rank employed by your country and if so, who was associate command.

He began with a few assumptions that Collier was involved with ship plunders that if a ship was hit there could be a submarine involved that if a submarine from another country arrived to any harbor without formal escort of the country; it was an act of war. Never had the air force been assigned to greet a foreign navy, nor could a submarine enter a foreign country as a ship might. Bothnia was established as a pump for submarines and for ships.

The fact was after the first breaker damage when FSB detained Collier for questioning, he had interviewed poorly. He tested for pre knowledge of the use of a breaker system to result in the damage that occurred, the lowering of a partial side of the building in which he conducted evaluations. He had only just returned from Arabia, had accepted a post with the Board of Education to train educators how to decentralize major city zones. He believed he would rent personal habitation until he felt acclimated at least to Bryansk since there was a possibility he might relocate several times in the next ten years. He was interested in building code because he hoped to expand his ideas on decentralization and required the proper structural facilities to have adequate use for the size staff he believed would become necessary. After reviewing Collier's answers and confirming by radio file his day to day whereabouts, Romeo decided Collier had failed to interest the State in storing its own preserves and had selected another route with which to develop a political following for substituting vast uncapped resources which could reduce dependence upon the Middle East. The State did not feel his access to building code was justified because in this lay a trap for an aspired lifestyle it did not permit out of historical jurisprudence such that when individuals became too wealthy they invariably turned to crime, and as a result Collier was situated within any vacant government square.

GYDANSKIY

The snow had piled up again. The heavy branches of damp primeval fir stood in revivification as overhead the purplish sky finally darkened. The hour had been hard won as he could tell by glancing at the teletype coming over his father's telex machine. Tavda was being interviewed.

He hat sat inside a beige four door sedan after two large bodied men hustled him into the plush interior and drove from the train station into the middle of nowhere, far past the Moscva center beyond meadows, apartments and flats, a brick spired church and vineyards and creek beds. He was instructed to catch an early return to Sibirskoye and permanently cancel all plans including his work plan to install telephone wire into surrounding offices in Gorkiy. After this unappreciated lecture, he was tossed into the snow and left. The last thing he saw were the white wall tires of the beige sedan screeching onto the road. He thought he had walked a good five miles before another sedan, a silver bullet government vehicle with stickers, halted abruptly and a man in the backseat ordered him into it.

Tavda slid inside and banged the door. The man was thick beneath his white fur coat and steel toe boots. His face was implacable, governed by thoughts he kept concealed. The sedan shot into the sparse countryside jostling them as it picked up speed.

The man stared out the window, his tense mien the only acknowledgement that there was an unpleasantness up ahead. They passed the brick spired church, a barn, apartments, then careened at the final moment into an alley and came to a stop beside a door to a flat in a weathered tan tile and old cement found. Tavda entered through a hall and to a small room from which he heard typing with staccato rapidity. His suitcase sat on the desk.

"Have a chair, Mr. Tavda," the wizened white haired man at the desk said. "You booked passage to enter Moscva."

"Yes. I am to meet a friend."

"The person's name? Last name first, if you please."

"Kotlas, Nicholai. Militsya."

"Zone?"

"Moscva."

"Wait here. I will be back shortly." The man was medium height, hardened, his boots stamped firmly.

Tavda waited. He wasn't leaving, of that he was certain.

"It would be a shot to the telephone installer?"

"Slightly over a year ago."

"October maybe."

"September, thereabouts, for a man named Lenskovitch."

"First name?"

"Georgi."

"How long have you known him?"

"On and off again."

Nicholai entered his staunch stride even to the last. "Ah, Tavda, we gave up hope you were coming. Has he been any trouble?"

"None. Thank you for your trouble."

Kotlas had reported in, all was well at home. Rostrov suspected his father had had affairs, probably even affairs of the heart. There was his mother, that lace haired compassionate ember of romantic nurturance that he held to fast in memory, and a school teacher he was wont to remember despite her urgings that he adopt a more legible cursive hand. There was the general's secretary, an unusual breathless sort of passionate woman slightly older than he was who worked on a computer intent on knowing when an identifier one didn't know was there, and together when a problem occurred they would spend all night looking for traces of wording that might suggest something they knew, everyone of these young breathless beauties enveloped with his father almost to the need of negating Rostrov's presence. Beauty was fleeting, it was gone before it became truly intrinsically known, low intent voices in the middle of the night like ghosts waking among the dead, laughter reminding him of china tinkling against other china, a remorse emerging from him for no palpable reason, the strings of emotion bursting almost as though he were young in spirit, the eternity wellspring that gave a man his youth, brimmed him to his capacities, but all the same took his father to a greater emotionally distant plateau from which there were few stirrings and all too fewer cognitive restorations. This son, Rostrov felt of himself, was quietly mindful searching for his father's absence among the ancient timbres of forested sunrises, always pinning a soaring hope on the certainty that around his father's habitation lay mysteries that could be answered, could be realized.

Except that he had isolated Collier for disposition and now if Collier was able to step through that invisible net into snow and vanish he had help from an internal source. No one believed Neva was untrustworthy but then no one thought Paul Pechskaya had misread the status. While he surmised the group was sufficient to handle all Russia's criminal activity including in her wilderness, no one had yet determined any reasonable objective to a series of breaker rockers. Whether their families and partners in Siberia wanted into a new country was unknown, for although transfers were obtained periodically people could not enter readily. Georgi Lenskovitch might describe the interests once it was evident who he was. For the moment Tavda was detained. If Neva's aim had been to gather information regarding Tavda, since his shakedown, she could be reassigned although it was unlikely because her brother was playing the part of a double that was given control of Tavda. Until the situation in Kirov was corrected, until Code Name Breaker had identified the red fox in cameo, no one could be certain those militsya were not doing their utmost to walk down the aisle with every possible concern.

Rostrov gave the situation a thorough review asking himself the reasons Sibirskayans might want to enter into a new country at costs. In this provocation Russian philosophers were of no help, neither literature nor capital were suitable to comprehend the dilemmas of the recent historical past of a hundred years for issues that Lenin, Trotsky, Gorki or Plekharov addressed within volumes of writings. Russia's barren ice lands were harshly delineated by her very symbolic Snow Queen ideology of a mistress of no aesthetic or mystical likeness that was frozen emotionally and unable to share her emotions. Certainly a non medical policy of Skoye and a four hour work day in bitter blizzard below zero landscape of Skaya seemed a unremorseful banishment, as well as in some villages for the non Omnis moriar, herbs of euphoria to lessen disease.

It seemed odd to him. Many of Collier's team had formerly lived ten or twenty years in the Sibirsk prior to filtering into less densely populated villages to live and eventually as they grew older went in search of disgruntled inhabitants who professed various anti-government sentiment. After recovering identification about their origins in youth prior to banishment, he allowed for the notion that they were from somewhere else where generally accepted accommodations were more restrictive even than in Sibirskoye. The question arose in his mind often whenever he was sent into find a suspect why any adult who could reside minimally in the Skoye traded in a harsh yet bearable existence in order to become hunted for which the penalty could be death.

The picture was broken into bits of words scattered over the page.

go a w ay go away go away g e t get g et g e t ge tge t g e t g o i n g g et goaway

The man was somewhere out there in the piled up snow with two others walking together but isolated. The two would never separate; one of the two was capable of signaling the man alone. There might be as many as ten separate groups. Simper fidelis. Faithful to their own objectives. Rostrov knew his father wouldn't worry. As he left his father's study and went to the dining hall for dinner, he thought about what he ought to do with the list of Russian authorities that the reader had sent him as subjects of interest, most not dissidents, to the group the FSB was tracking.

Others
Andrei Andreevich Andreev, Russ polit., 1895-1971
Leonid Nikolayevich Andreyev, storywriter and dram., 1871-1919
Leon Nikolayevich Bakst, painter, 1866-1924
Aleksandra Andreevich Baranov, fur trader, 1st gov of Russ America, 1747-1819
Mikhail Aleksandrovich Bakunin, 1814-1876 anarchist
Nicholai Basov, 1922-, physicist
Lavrenti Pavlovich Beriya, 1899-1953 Russ polit.
Catherine Breshkovsky 1844-1934 revolutionist
Leonid Ilyich Brezhnev, polit., pres USSR 1960-64 ;1977-, 1st secy Comm party
Semen Mikhailovich Budenny, general 1883-1973
Nikolai Aleksandrovich Bulganin, Comm leader and editor 1895-1975
Ivan Alekseevich Bunin, poet and novelist 1870-1953
Gavril Romanovich Derzhavin, 1743-1816 poet
Sergei Pavlovich Diaghilev, 1872-1929 ballet producer and art critic

Fedor Mikhailovich Dostoevski 1821-1881 novelist
Ilya Grigorievich Ehrenburg, 1891-1967 author
Sergei Aleksandrovich Esenin, 1795-1824 poet
Aleksandr Glazunov, composer 1865-1936
Mikhail Ivanovich Glinka, composer 1803-1857
Boris Fedorovich Godunov, czar of Russia, 1598-1605
Prince Aleksandr Ivanovich Gorchakov, general and states-
   man, 1764 -1825
Ivan Longinovich Goremykin, 1839-1917 statesman, prime
   min 1906;1914 -1916
Aleksei Maksimovich Peshkov, aka Maksim Gorki, writer
   1868-1936
Andrei Andreevich Gromyko 1909-, economist and diplo-
   mat
Aleksandr Feodrovich Kerenski , 1881-1970 Russ revolu-
   tionist
Sergei Mironovich Kirov, 1886-1934 Russ revolutionist
Mikhail Kheraskov, poet 1733 -1809
Ivan Stepanovich Konev, 1897-1973 Soviet general
Petr Alekseevich Kropotkin, 184 2-1921 geographer and
   revol.
Nadezhda Konstantinova Krupskaya 1869-1939 wife of V. I.
   Lenin, social worker
Sergeevich Khrushchev polit., prime minister Russ 1894-
   1971
Lev Davidovich Landau, Russ physicist 1908-1968
Mikhail Yurievich Lermontov, poet and novelist 1814 -1841
Maksim Maksimovich Litvinov, Soviet diplomat 1876-1951
Nikolai Ivanovich Lobachevski, Russ mathematcian 1793-
   1856
Trofim Denisovich Lysenko, Russ scientist 1898-1976
Anna Pavlova, 1885-1905 ballerina
Georgi Valentinovich Plekharov, 1857-1918 Marxist phi-
   losopher
Sergei Wasilievitch Rachmanioff 1873-1943 composer, pia-
   nist, conductor
Konstantin Rokossovski 1896-1968 marshal

Zinovi Petrovitch Rozhdestvenski, 1848-1909 admiral
Mikhail Aleksandrovich Sholokhov, novelist 1905-
Dimitri Shostakovich, composer 1906-1975
Konstantin Stanislavski, actor 1863-1938
Petr Iich Tchaikovsky, composer 1840-1893
Ivan Sergeevich Turgenev, 1818-1883 novelist
Nikolai Vatutin, 1900 -1944 general
Efremovich Voroshilov, 1881-1969 pres USSR 1953-60
Yevgeny Yevtushenko, 1933 author
Andrei Aleksandrovitch Zhanov, 1896 -1948 polit. and general

His first thoughts when he sat down near the large brown and yellowish brown stone fireplace where a raging fire filled the expansive walnut walled room in which ten tables with tablecloths and a kitchen chef were – how is the subject of philosophy presented through writings to discuss lifestyle, types of commentary as to what should be, if aesthetics and ethics do not discuss crime might they sometimes discuss how a society ought to be, do the various writers believe a just world should guarantee food and adequate shelter to all, have they put forth a social page by which to discuss prose, intellectual pursuits and contemporary art. Or were they each similarly searching for questions about truth, beauty and moral choices, were they each in their constituencies seeking to answer questions of doubt. Under what assertions of democracy did people in their works represent their intended or otherwise stated aims, when did personal seeking enter a realm of enlightenment, when did doubt become a religious questioning, when the person was wrestling with a decision of some sort about their conscience, did they begin in depth discourse with agony or with a less passionate concern, a recognition of having chosen to enter a mortal sphere and how long had they wrestled with this inquiry. Tolerance was a moral concern, it became a social morality when too many people in the society sought damage to the innocent and likewise when social bureaucrats became personally wealthy without remunerating the overall standard of living, and for the unconscionable act that was already in motion tolerance would not be used a decisive blow to destroy an enemy. The drastic situation wasn't merely an employ of a high wire expert capable of replacing already discerned charge boxes but of someone who could in a final moment replace a circuit relay with a sequential implementation which once begun could not be interrupted except for minimal impact.

BRYANSK

The hours were long in the day. The frosted air made a distant sun out of the perceptive bleak overcast. Romeo had run a standard feed on the Gorkiy offices operated by Collier, shutting off computers within the zone that read for support for breaker and then minutes later when machines restored a line of computer text appeared on those telephone addresses each of which was identified to stations. Zone by zone was also read. Within a day telephone addresses were identified by user name which were turned over to databases for actual location addresses, work corporations, and indexed by date of birth, parents, children, certificates of marriage, and other national indexes including vehicle registrations, smog certificates, and letters received. The resulting identities were the same; it was a small group, Collier who arranged the shakers, Tavda who set countdown, Lensk who removed parts of the screen from view of the military, three winders who placed the mechanics in the plugs, and a support staff who diverted impact into other structures using telephone systems. Sinquon was implicated by virtue of the fact that her name came up as an operative for Collier. The tiny group had a huge support that was dependent upon them for jobs and their independent livelihoods. That support wasn't likely to ask the questions it ought to determine if they wanted to be involved with him to begin with.

The second floor had generated no helpful information as to identification. They kept tabs predominantly with the surrounding FSB, they knew when Jacob was on the street, and they knew also where Winder was either in the sector or coming to it and from what direction. By now they confirmed Winder was not Tavda. Winder was as yet unidentified but not Collier either, nor Anya. They suspected he might be Grigori Lensk but because they lacked any means of identification such as fingerprints, driver's license, address, shoe-print by laser, pistol registration or other documentation for him they could not be sure that the man they identified as Winder was in actuality Lensk. He came, he left, and he vanished. Lensk had worked the traveling Moscva Circus for a few years during which he was not permitted to be photographed while performing. He was unusually skilled, dressed in tights, he walked onto the rope, bent and grasped the rope with both hands, twirled with one, put both feet to it and with hands reeled himself back onto the line, walked the rope to the platform, releasing the rope, grabbed the bar, swung through the air, then swung with one hand, brought his feet and legs into it and swung as a partner, a pretty young blonde in glittering pink, swung from the opposite side, she released hanging from him a half minute, her trim modest size perfectly erect, the taut muscles strident, and dropped to the net. He practiced three hours daily balancing on a beam, springing cartwheels across a mat, standing on a prancing horse as it loped around the stage floor, and hauling himself up a rope. This was the Mighty Lensk. If it were too risky to his act to have the audience snap photos, then no one photographed him. Because he had grown up in circus acts he had absolutely no photographs of him to be found. That was the beauty of the beast, he could not be filmed.

Romeo understood one thing, that to identify the person who came through the square, that individual had to be identified in person close enough to see eye color, hair texture, manner. The simplicity of life arrived after long cautiously selected considerations. Thus the method of madness by which to comprehend the vulgarity of human existence would have to stand with the c'est une faute, the incorrigible blunder. Lensk also known as Grigori Lenskovitch could have no reason except an act of incomprehensible gratitude to a man whose existence derived from stymieing a government into an ever unending charisma of duplicity. The ship hitting the ice was essential on the telex to eliminate detection for use of the wire in buildings for the collar. Even if his acts required him to remain undisclosed, the essential concern of motivation as to what Lensk wanted for himself if he remained in Soviet allied areas could not be answered by conventional rationale, if he wanted to serve a country that didn't have a ruler the likely area would be to reside in a remote area like Switzerland, a retreat hidden in a palatial ice canyon far from contact with any population, capable in a moment of springing out of the snow. Since Lensk did not use camera nor did he work security or jail, although it was unknown if he had use of telex, he always had to be under trees, always, even the snow had to have trees, in public he was unable to be captured because the light obscured and then there was nothing to be matched to. Romeo could only imagine these people did a crime first and then thought they would go somewhere and couldn't get there and now were getting a large base of support for the intent that they could get out of the country as a group in order to keep their lives. Once one arrived at this loathsome verdict, the only action to take was to begin a heavy footed campaign to track to detain the people who planned, organized and implemented the crime. Of course one had only the exception, a suspect who could not be proven, to understand it took all types to transgress, smug bureaucrats, historians who felt closed in by restrictive occupations, ambitious bankers who could be comfortable joining foreign countries to a common yen. A breaker box was the size of a floor of a medium hotel of a large city, it was in height over twelve feet high and consisted of twelve to fourteen thousand small objects each of which functioned as potentially separate breakers, usually inside its building in the event any interlocking functions became burnt out. Inside the demolition silk sheeting was plastered over every wall to prevent debris from becoming airborne and from exposed wire neckties attached to walls by a steel stakes alighting with fire. No silk, no fires as some part of demolition occurred. As the floors creviced downward the walls shifted and cracked without doing much structural damage.

When the demolition had finally stopped the breaker box automatically shut off. For state controlled demolition to never give license for use of breaker box data systems, the system was taken over by some other industry that continued to have readable data as a partial was called in. The only thing he knew of that could do this was an electrical shutdown.

He knew what would happen to all of them; he had to ask about Silk who couldn't be a winder because he or she didn't touch boxes if he applied display, silk went on all walls except rosette stone to which silk did not stick. Someone's guess was that Silk was Collier's wife Sinquon. If Collier permitted his wife to make sincere affectionate love to his chief winder Tavda, then it was very possibly to offset a situation Collier was vulnerable to. Tavda therefore must have thought long and intently about Collier and if they never met then there was a reason for that also, could it be that Sinquon after being denied watches from Anya was given Tavda's name and without first meeting him passed his name as a rose on a plate to her husband. He sent a data request to Militsya general, "Silk," another to his chief advisor, "Dancer."

The replies came swiftly. Silk is from China and is used for walls, charges at the floor. Dancer, not a Dain. A melancholia of grievous plots.

He slept poorly waking throughout the night pursued by the demons of a single shot of Portuguese brandy. He could have sworn he heard voices, a movie rolling about outside the window, sounds of madly dashing hoofs, garments rustling, splashes, I ordain you, someone disappearing through the cracks, Danes, red haired men, or Dane sans souci Juliet et tois merci and drew not a straw, a reflection of a man walking on the bank was an upside down man in the ice, golden angels on the Seine upside down gryphons, their bodies rippling in the wake of boats. Romeo startled awake, his forehead throbbing with an aching fever, seeing into the jaws of garish gryphons dangling beneath the water's surface. He downed two aspirin with soda, wrapped himself in a terry cloth white robe and checked his console for messages that had come in during the night. There was one from Angelina as followed:

"Could we but comprehend the mysterious vanishings of space in our torrential wilderness, already a vast enduring description of languid sorrows entrenched with capable fortitude, there would be no small undertakings, nor finite awakenings, laments or other forgotten traces, stairwells beneath the streets encumbered by impervious solitary leanings. Tavda's relationship to the salted pillars of his tragic callings sheds almost no figurative rationale for how we as an educated cultured Intelligence are to obey an instinct that views lacquered scratching as a too remote language and condemns the cranes of brush strokes and misted mountain parlors. Certainly as a desk the miserly reader could induce from this man's outpourings that he suffers yet from leisure to be relieved of his year of solitude, permitted to revisit decorated corridors having not yet chosen not to suppress. Because he has lived a subdued monastic year high in the frozen arches of civilization, verily comforted by tepid baths, trapped indoors by glaciated winds, stripped of diets, we ought to take caution in a repartee that defines a soldierly attitude while neither dismissing return as out of the question nor requesting a more rigid adherence."

He added his initials with commentary. "Ward Subject has maintained observances; my hesitation to release is based strictly on the bias that Collier's activities are unconfirmed." He knew Moscva. The temptation would be to bring Tavda into daylight now that Collier was tracked to a public post.

Gorkiy

Jacob had rewritten a poem substituting words, struggling to get it right and still frustrated; in the last he had sent it, knew she would put it on the mantel with the holiday cards, would call Georgann who would descend again for a coffee at the bakery. It would take weeks before she would remember, the Styrofoam cliffs reflected over Germany. In weeks he would have the entire floor on layout, confirmed the bugging schema, have sent back to floor plan the determined point of origin. The switchboards would be chatty as hundreds of militsya at the behest of call code executives called for information on education management efficacy.

He had had less than a moment of alone time, although during the past few days after work he had returned to the flat to find Kas gone on one of her many walks for a deli meal or to nurse a glass of wine while watching a game of soccer or baseball on the tele. Her agent assigned daughter had taken her winter shopping and the two had departed for an ice rink festivity after leaving behind wrapped parcels one of which the size of a large box had his name in cursive written on it.

He decided after a nerve wracking tedious day peeking into Collier's files the mainstay gib consisted of highlights and hues for all interiors, desks, chalk boards, paper products, whatever it required to subdue glare so as to enhance learning. Collier himself drew vestiges of harmony from design matching fabric to color and strangely these were tested for seasonal endurances of climate by environment. Always there existed a nagging persistence that the man was stressed against a dynamic that was neither light nor dark but of an aspect of remoter life that resided at the perimeters of civilization gnawing at forested vales, drenching down to the culture of dappled shade. Now that the day was over he wore his weariness as implacability diverting his attention from the vivid patterns and signature wallpapers of the office itself to the symmetry that arranged itself in natural situations until he was nearly fatigued. Even quietude wasn't much ease. But he picked himself up and went jingling down the stairs conscious that the waning light from the window on the mid-level became increasingly yellowish as he ran down the last flight. Just as he came to the last steps, the door was pulled open hard and Georgann appeared her hair cascading down her backside. She wore a grey cashmere dress buckled at the waist, a string of red opaque glass oblong beads through which the taut black twine was visible, a red silk scarf and red heels.

"Jacob," it came out as a confession.

He led her by the elbow to the street. The slush thawed slowly, vehicles waited at the curb, shoppers bustled by. "You're a little early. I thought you'd be in Moscva."

"I'm not here for Moscva. When you are completed I will take the first train out. You ought to know I received Kas' note."

"I sent it less than an hour ago. I'm not the one who writes."

"It's the language. Once the codes download off my database I release their documents, I provide myself with a report every morning at which time an article is transmitted. The Collier file for instance says Collier was not in the zone when Breaker was hit. When we indexed for his business contacts outside the government, we found the sources of transactions, two banks, operations, cocoa and associated expenditures. Only one place cocoa is grown."

"To get this far into infiltration they need information banks, that's his rationale for education but all capable uses are for external markets. I have his principals, their support, the databases never vary, and I simply can't find where they are.

"Breaker," he said, "made a run for it into a restricted zone and lost his life. Had he remained where he should have — "

She remarked, "His presence defined, he is named for his target."

"All targets are out."

"Try this; he went where the picture appeared."

"Never has he been known to have used online information, he's information in, that's all."

"Then it must be he's defined solely by his attachment to

actual Breaker, if Code Name said that actual Breaker was Collier, which is who he is. Actual Breaker however while having a brother infirmed will not visit him except by e-mail, therefore it is the track of e-mail Code Name is after. I don't comprehend why at that point he hasn't sent in an unknown. We know Code Name has returned to the workplace although he no longer has to drive into snowstorm beleaguered zones."

"I'm not a man to take you to my flat. I gave you my limit at your flat. Actual has a situation for which his wife takes up the assignment of traveling into wilderness with the only man Collier needs and now that one has turned himself over to a government official we suspect. After I'm completed no further breaker job becomes likely since each has been given a complex lifestyle."

They had walked several blocks past the usual thorough-fares along the ul Minna and entered a restaurant of her choosing. It was softly lit, with tablecloths and male waiters, an expensive menu, almost no decor besides the dark black walls with gold trimmed wall hangings of black and white abstracts. Jacob ordered burgundy wine for each, an hors d'oeuvre of stone bread and natural oil, fresh veal with poached salmon and herbs, a side Caesar, and tart spiced apples. Georgann lit a fag, in the dimmed light her elegance took sleek dominance, he would ask of himself that she was part of the work, as executive class as was Kas who had her martyred affections in Moscva.

He had turned it over a handful of times as they stood waiting an empty table. "Code Name probably has no ability to relist, he goes on his information the same as everyone else, he must have known that his retreat matched the hologram condition for which Actual stymies and so he's where Collier is, however analogous."

Complications of the order of holding tight to assignments was their discussion, posted to theoretical musings if for no other reason than to provide him with a tangible palate of her philosophical saddle. Georgann was at once imbued with the permissive couture of Rousseau, the idea that the individual and government entered into a social contract on which the

methodology of society was based. She did not separate considerably from modernists although in subscribing to symbolists
such as Octavia Paz and Pablo Neruda, she also cut form with
Virginia Wolf, Simone de Beauvoir, Jean Paul Sartre, each
a pessimist to the extreme who felt society had interfered to
an unforgivable degree for amputation over disease, hideous
malformation, closeted secrecy, the typical response was Bar-
bizhon painting, wine parties, excelsior brush art. He practiced
his mode of prevailing concept with her, had she known artists
or interpreters from Skoye, she was familiar mostly with Anzhero, the city, its suburbs, projects, medical wards. He cuffed
a tendency to slight out of hand, yet getting a hand on a belief
of even the sophisticates not having practical enough expertise,
he knew she was assigned him and her job because she was
not conformist. This ought to have assured him to have asked
for her page but he didn't enjoy the mood it enveloped him
because he then often took other recourses. He tried again, did
she read any contemporary Russian works, to which she gave
a sly rebound, saying, of course, all; she stuck to biographies
of presidents, why Androporov resigned, Stalin's dislike of
iron gateways, Yeltsin's monogamy with the west, Khrushen-
tuvo's psychological populace for whom he retreated to the
back country with museo construction communities. He asked
about her own marriage, she delivered the grave logic she told
herself, he was a man of importance, one who would never settle down despite a convened honestly cultivated conflict about
having raised children, a consistent pessimism as her reading
such that he glimpsed in her hidden in dread or surmise that
she felt she could not keep close someone she was incumbent
to love from afar. The job came with the same payoffs for every
last one of them, and while the tendency was once the profiler
left home to seek involvements there were emotional tethers to
avoid, one's own children would find betrayal in the untrue,
they would sip their own ale to oblivion, and he wished for
nothing except their impassioned drama of freedom. He knew
a man who between realizations of toxic ambition comforted
himself with entertaining producers who would drop a coin

into an empty marble, grey stained cold well for a future prose story after souvenir parties extending three days with non-stop festivities in a garden of cold water tile, gravel strips with olive and lemon trees, Italian statues of disc throwers, a vault bearer, a maiden to entice a wife he had returned to after fifty-five years, he was a stolid man, acclaimed, able to see in both directions without impunity, no longer viewing his endeavors critically, who resided as though on a pond with dwarfed pigmy trees, French himself in language. A mesmerizing inability to see past an obvious factor, he nevertheless considered that the assignment gave her a method to combat a realm of conscience, and for that when romance became imminent she walked into the labyrinth.

He conceded saying he too read Paz, Garcia, Gallegos along with apostate writings, as much for the realism of older men on a return journey from the aggravations of dead souls as anything else. His own return from a necessary training at 32 degrees during which he mourned a first romance chided him to whistling ice driven wind although the fallout shelter maintained at seventy degrees kept him three months maximum beneath a treacherous plain in a sixty square foot room with endless bookshelves, a travel van kitchen nook, toilet and bedding with another adult. The roommate was slightly older, in his late seventies, having applied for a Turkish post, a semblance of rough hewn entrenched nomadic, he knew every bunker of eastern Skaya, the illiterate mind vanquished by men who except for their love of freedom would not easily tolerate the mindless existence of twenty-four hour midnight at fifty below Fahrenheit. The bunkers were cramped, barely thirty feet of living, the prisoner five yards away connected by walkie-talkie forty feet into the ice, miles before one might encounter another periscope hood. He knew more than she would ever imagine, knew that having descended into that obliteration there was no remorse, no other finality, no way to make the dead return to life and therefore no experience of pessimism. Whereas once he had read only to remind himself of the discards of human contentment, he now chose his medicine with caution, he told her over a bland dessert of fried banana most which he would forego in order to arrest those less kind considerations of long tried abstinences of indulgence. They bundled up for the return walk to his Hotel Volga Slope condominium, he covered the expense on a credit card, purchased two newspapers and arm in arm they strolled down the ul passing the Nevsky Cathedral in the park, their breath turning to mist, the Volga River in sight, benches parked at intervals.

Psychic isolation has a terrible deafening element to it that unlike other distresses in time wards off the more renewing spiritual comforts of either friendship or living. The ailments of the heart that tore upon poor Tavda kept to a well-maintained indifference which despite his affection for Sin Quon would have to take priority once he was called back to the fore. He must soon return to his beloved Gorkiy to take a man's life, no small task for one who would disappear through streets of apartments until all reality was a mere remembrance. The desertions of service might take their toll but the desertions of the strictly adhered to disciplines of one's maturity would not be easily skimmed over. He could foresee numerous difficulties arising, any of them taking him into visibility which would leave him to become a permanent ward ship, each costly. The malevolence of the circumstance already had escaped detection lay within its own private relationships of ocean bearing vessels to a vast unsurpassed wilderness within which Man was the preyed upon in any instance of sudden treacherous storms. The ability of the capable saw no limit of definition although in a perceptual decline of comprehension limitation such as that which most recognize are fully about wreaking the destruction of tide and ice on men who would seek passage. How unkind of life to assure a bevy of qualifiers to embellish their querulous lives; often he was impressed by this dismal pithy of relief he was expected to rely upon, his sole pronouncement only a strike opportunity at a despised object. If age, gentility and forbearance were his mere staffs he was a seldom appreciated presence for the scourges of civilization were better intended placed into the conniving predisposition of actual killers whose circumference as working agents took them daily to the contact of their targets. So it would be, in an instant he would emerge, choke his opponent and forever vanish, all customary casual elations from that moment precipitously forgotten. He had left Sin Quon a single poem – Only pebbles fall/Scattering in a wind/ Mountains reflect snow down. He trimmed any release to sorrow, made his peace with the featherings of torment, his inner agonies too understated, all clandestine acknowledgements cautiously contained. The year had passed too swiftly, the snow packs permanent. He gave himself over to that momentous state of turning his back on the life of his ultimate possession.

His other poems he sent ahead by train poste to his good friend in Mosckva Centraliya.

WINTER

Pechi

Dormant even in spring
Ideas distill
To the dregs, sweet vinegar.
Ambivalence a tolerance
Regression two steps for one
Knocks once.
All finite, all sparse
Practicality best preserves
Tendencies to drift.
Adhesives shall not impugn
Bald plums like skin
Allow sap to sugar.
Pits dry on a plate
Hard objects, almonds
Objectionable as words.

Dutch hunt hut vessel
Too far north, bidden by shadow,
Moors at peninsulas.
Slabs of icebergs rank
Miles of penguins
Plummet beneath shards of ice,
Translucent blue tinkling
Black capes rise
Sonorous ocean, caw and cry,
Ambiguous pitch
Held briefly or lost
As precious as where to chart.
The shush of tide
Continual rebar
Subdues all who come too close.
Aggression like deceit
Strikes to its chord
Cadence accompanies waltz.

Muted resounds jar
Resonant cacophony
Surrenders taken.
Knowledge keeps to duty
Foresworn solitude
Asks of no cessation.
Go then! Into the snows
Make reason a practice
Logic a devise,
Trotsky must have seen
Thin ray of lighthouse
The Obskaya packed with tides,
A plentitude, white fish
Thick as stones for crossing
Clamoring to live.
Always, always, the silver sun
At night
Nocturne orb on ice white sand.

Chill stillness reduces air
Ice-blind pains
All glass is covered by wood.
Cucumber frames iced
Bean paste in the pot
Impatient days are too long.
We have only ourselves
Weather chapped, aged,
Awakened. Scions of Age.
Old sons, old mothers
Limes, crysanthemums,
Oft' defined intricacies.
Box covered seeds grow
A sip of bitter tea
Love's plaintive wail shrinks.

LOVE SONG

Relentless downpour
Passage through deep woods
Blurred signs to the lake,
Residual demands
Joint abrogations – denials
Tended to.
Less than a year spent
Sleeping in the snow
Love with a mistress.

CAPTURE

By her practiced living
He knows the other
Habits, heresies – proofs,
Acts imply.

As the day waned toward its western most cultivation, as the hour loomed to a darkening awareness of dispirited inclinations, Jonathan sensed his father Rostrov would return from his last journey more introspective than his usual gregarious fashion. Although the forest still stood burdened by a sagging encumbrance of snow, there was a perception of lightness as though a real distraction had finally been lifted. Not all of time would be explained by the rigors of the government's fractions of nomenclature or by the ever demanding tasks wanted of her Centraliya. As seasons eclipsed the aging set in accompanied by no less a periodic distinction of findings, every able and knowledgeable elitist focused to the elements of recovery of information. Jonathan was still in training, his father capable, expertise to a fault, honed in on only predicting with ever sharp clarity those mechanisms that had not been sufficiently protected to begin with. Since he had lived in absolute penury, had determined his own tendencies toward anxious waiting, he was gradually enlisting a repertoire of ways of staving off a perceived desire to relieve or to acquire. The infrequent loneliness calibrated by boredom or anxiety – sometimes it was characterized by a gloaming urgency to replace loss with newness, or a renewal of a once familiar creativity – would become overwhelming, seemingly impossible not to disclose, a fretting, disguised as annoyance, a pejorative slight one gave oneself. The drooping spirit became disengaged, exhausted, yet without giving into sleep relegated mood past its limitation to restore self-examination again. He had experienced this mentally carnivorous reductionism a handful of times such that now as he anticipated the newly accustomed silences with the promise of becoming filled by his father's at home schedule, he was comparing with exactitude both quiet and mind-cluttering sound. Two adults of any intimate duration group their thoughts akin to their long-enforced lifestyle even when the culture of the government calls for separation or acculturated distinction. A preference of the politics of stage by a military presumes that elitists while fitting into any situation also respond without direction. Jonathan's interdependence on his father and his internal need of rebellion replaced by respect of profession, he was seeing his entry into the Armed Forces as readiness, because in the hour the fox was snagged, hung, it would be himself who replaced him. He had only to wait his father.

That same year Tavda's poems were published under the presumed name of Alexander Ovidrimon Pleshrimotaya, poet laureate of Belarus.

FOR AVRAM

Hark! Cold, bitter reward
An abrogation
Of denied fulfillment.
No angels at sunrise
Crimson darkness
Ever spreading entreaties.
A barometer of capitulation
Errant vacancy –
Struck dead.
The body warm to the touch
Cries not, nor knows how many men
Are gone.
Don't anticipate high grass
Nature too recoils
Grows to the roots.
Snow imitates rainfall
Incessant sleet
A door closes, snow drifts.
Destiny restrained
Visions of peace
Seagulls brood aboard a ship deck.
The quilt jacket
Worn wet chills to the bone
Indemnifies against thought.
Yet steadfast, unerring

Russia soldiers undaunted
By the storm.
The Neva by default is dark
Mud slips to sea at whim
Curling fast.
Undertow giving speed
Choppy knife breakers
Sleek catamarans go.
Distance sees mere ocean
Life retrenches
Roiling waves every season.

FOR PECHI

Absence, a grandeur

EYRE

LOST AT SEA

ONE

A female dressed in jeans and a windbreaker fought against the aggressive wind as she made her way slogging through mud to the ankles into a surreal Mars crimson landscape in which an otherwise hexagonal cracked salt flat as large as a thousand miles stretched, terror seizing her normally calm recalcitrance as she shifted the weight of her backpack to leave room to move more freely. Her decision to retrain for special task had taken her into the wilderness outback of Australia with a short out-fit of six trained police. Five weeks camping an infinitesimal red salt lake in a hundred and fifty square miles of the No-oldoona involved many a sleepless night, often in nearly total darkness, in a partially submerged barren uncultivated soft salt landscape in the equivalent footfall of snow-driven sand. She had sought as much emotional distance as possible from her ex-husband's continual outbursts which occurred once she fell into deep sleep, at home in Melbourne these annoyances had been accompanied by his not infrequent blaring horn in the wee morning hours. She had not expected him to materialize at Eyre, but he had produced himself, and she told herself she had reached a point of feeling severely battered, by now a mea-sured certainty, the discomfort was internalized as a psycho-logical torment as much as it was abandonment and alienation of spousal commitment, altogether intentional, well outside the range of impulsivity or thwarted frustrated intolerance. They were once a cozy husband-wife team residing in a house very nearly paid off on an island twenty miles by boat off the Cape with a beachfront and private patio and dock. Their quarter of a million home was two story surrounded by a half acre of lawn and palms, its own long swimming pool, sandstone tiled deck, the shallow clear water aqua blue to the sandy bottom. Mary Finley had planned to become a chef investigator and go out in the dim hours on a fishing trawl to scout missing bodies which for some reason kept turning up in low tide racked out fully clothed on the South beaches. Bryce Finley, her ex, was a cop, a slick investigator, could obscure any loophole and probably had, although his motto for which he was well-known was no technology, all hard evidence, no exception to hot docs, forgeries, fingerprint swaps, bullets, raids, stolen art, kidnappings, and VIN plates. He had trained pro boot camp in Queensland on an attack-charge camp where every breath might prove to be his last. He had trained in at least as many avenues as she had, in forensics dry smears as to shoes, clothing, porcelain, walls, other surfaces for the drug border duty in the British islands; in fingerprints, medical prescriptions, vehicular manslaughter and its corresponding anthropology, but she had rather unintentionally trained for hard-proof photos with the Great Barrier coastal group of International Customs Enforcement agents and was given trauma in skeletal remains beginning with the Brisbane Cemetery Flood of 1993 in which she alone established the post mortem interval to positively identify a serial killing of four victims, all adults. Despite her track record, she was no match for him; he knew every last detail about her, habits, body slumps, ability to get on the go, what she did to fortify her endurance through any restlessness including his infuriatingly precise sense of order; anxiety, disgust or assignment groupings. At the present hour she outdistanced him by some kilometer because she was faster and could travel on foot longer, he'd likely give up in three-quarters of an hour, but he had the jeep. Her sole hope was that his jeep would break down leaving him to return to base camp wherever the hell he had staged himself.

She figured she had the upper rank. She was an expert in homicide, man, rape, indecent infractions, assault, witness interrogations, divorce for incurable mental hostility, no longer defined as insanity although periodically termed hostile brutality, and was every so often asked to train the federal interns at the Cape on physical intrusions and eavesdropping by microphone or wiretap and computer theft by use of interference of remotes. In time she had joined as a member a list of associations as long as her arm including International Association of Visible Doctrine Service Officers, International Association of Bloodstain Pattern Analysts, Australia Association of Private Investigators, and was a recognized missing persons search detective not to mention an asset locator, an insurance fraud and special license joiner attorney, an expert on spouse infidelity, child custody. Then of course he was the assault-rifle pro at marginal skip trace checks, criminal investigative tracking, and the small time, penny ante nuisance stuff that floated across the desks of the privates and retireds.

The sky was clear, not a cloud, striation or whirl anywhere, and below at some invisible intercept where without water it might be clear where the now scorchingly ultra-white salt desert horizon actually lay was the massive inland ocean, plenty salty enough they said to float a pair of shoes, but nevertheless was still, pristine in its reflecting pale blue, not a mar on it, and through this she was frantic, pushing her way through its shallow depth, wishing that wherever the depth dropped from three feet to twenty or thirty feet, it came soon so that he'd be deadlocked in his super-four-wheel-axle man's mean machine, as he called it. Could this have been the first time she had come to the Mel coast, she would have marveled at the stunning clarity of the Jabbul Saltar, for she was exquisitely familiar with the bone and spleen of crimson and crystal salt lakes alike, their seasons, their capable unrelenting treachery and their instantaneous flooding, their special anthropologic interest to science, their glistening mirrored expanse early day and after sunset. Off in the distance a hundred or more high stepping flamingoes like tall, semi African young limber girls strut across the wadi, their pink fluffy petticoats announcing their pronounced flightiness. The dreamy ethereal air reflected in the lake was both paradise and image, sheer pink, phantasms of dried shrimp inelegantly depositing algae in massive quantities; despite this, here and there beneath an antiplano sky were bits of floating salt, cropping grey triangles soon to rise as triangles of salt in depths of water lanes to the horizon like getaway channels for trucks that might be stuck in the absorbing salt, reflecting headlights off in the filmy evaporating abstraction of distance coming in her direction. Like tapas the early morning transcended into a spellbound powder blue, patterns of waves rose along with bits of floating dark gray salt, the lake was utterly quiet, nothing human superimposed upon reality. For an instant without the menacing sound of Bryce's jeep there was no disturbance nor distress, Nature lay like an opossum, space was vast, non-inhibiting, a miraculous bitter sweet aching land of awe and youth, then, swiftly, within minutes the blue turned to searing bright white and the orange sun resurrected itself like the plumed bird of Aztec distinction into the sky.

This was neither heaven nor heaven on earth, as the place was known by local Australians. She ran against the lifeless current, splashing through crystalline translucent water, her mind unable to think of the inspired horror, the certainty that her ex-husband had decided to take her life for the only reason she could seize, that she was the sole witness to an extravagant crime he had committed when he almost choked to death his nephew in a rage while they were on board his uncle's yacht. She had never said anything to him, so she didn't know what he thought he knew, but one thing was absolutely certain. She had talked about the attempted killing to her superior, so there had to be a leak in the state agency.

Two

The wind over the Sealand ocean and its deep space primordial atmosphere chopped the waves at twenty miles an hour. It was the beginning of a cyclone twisting into a funnel that would spew a rainy spout in a dark howling which was to last hours. As the spout rose in a whirlwind of dusty debris and water into the sky, it elaborated like an elephant trunk spinning at a height of a hundred and fifty feet capable of knocking about any outboard, siren motor or small heading trawler. Such a powerful squall it cast its hose thirty feet above the ocean surface, every hundred yards or so nesting before it moved along finally reaching the shoreline taking the opaque sky in its launch. When it descended onto land it ripped house and reef harbor alike, before it sailed off a peninsula into warm shallow water, ascending finally like a dark grey swarm of whirling debris and vegetation.

Forty miles away a secondary current was blowing north in toward the Eyre. On board the Muckraker a party had been getting underway since sunrise. The time approached high noon. The captain James Finley stood at the helm, a seasoned fire fighter who had spent the past two years as a news anchor, winsome blond hair cut crew cut, trim in short shorts after a reclusive retirement year at sixty-six mountain climbing in the Andes with his young wife of forty years, Yvette Finley, she in stockings five foot seven, bronze with tightly bunched up curly hair to her shoulders, always to be found in a sleeveless light blue silk top and stylish white khaki pants and slip-on sandals. Also on deck were their two close friends, Bev Highgard and her cousin Tommy Stael. Bev was a lean gal, same height and weight as Yvette in an all-white bikini that showed off a priceless tan, shoulder-length greenish blond hair due to two hours a day swimming competition sports, a semi-permanent implacable expression acquired training high school students to run the meter. Stael as he preferred to be called was a uniquely tall and thin Scotlander, straw blond hair, gangly arms he'd never put mass on, high waist belt and size ten tennis gear who had walked a ten mile dash in less than an hour and a half. In the ocean he nearly beat his walking time at swimming in fly competitions taking trophy placements for two-mile swim races at dawn. The four had begun drinking straight since breakfast while the ocean was a pristine glistening jewel, not a ripple on her in the cast-off of Australia's eastern shelf below Melbourne, and it was now past three. They were celebrating Stael's and Bev's sale of a house on the desert outskirts and closing escrow on a beachfront dark blue and orange two-story property. Typically house sales with a boat deck ran a few hundred thousand, but in this case it was a short sale, a blessing come at the right time to end an eighteen year marriage and cut free. Tommy's wife, a pricey blonde with a hundred and fifty thousand a year real estate career, a cocktail boozer who occupied her days on the beach, had returned to Sydney and had hired a lawyer to commence the legal disputes which included several condominiums, a yacht, and expensive art. Tommy was advised not to put up a fight; divorce court would split all assets down the middle. He had signed the papers, shoved his copies into a wall safe, and said goodbye to all that.

The air temperature was warming up to a sultry eighty-five. The Muckraker's sails were drawn at half-pole, scarcely a breeze about her, although she ran at half two at four miles an hour, her eighty foot length magnificent for her seven sails. When they backed out of harbor, Yvette started with a score to trim the sails keeping the wind on the windward stow until they advanced to the fifty meter tower on a rock splashing with sea swells; then she rolled down a throw pole as her captain husband put the drive into deep throttle. There were no tugs of resistance with the bow, no arbitrary knife in the water to push the side to sea or fetch a hundred feet of line as the masts rolled down. Yvette reclined on the top deck where her husband could keep an eye on her, Bev and Stael hung out below on the mean deck in director lounge chairs making their way through a steady tankard, periodic seagulls alighting on the bench rail, the start of swells breaking loose as the yacht cruised over the ocean depths.

THREE

Melbourne Cape employed nineteen special task cops to work files in missing persons, homicide, burglary, stolen art, kidnappings and violent acts of intimidation and coercion against a spouse or family member. The spousal harassment division was led by a long time rank and file lieutenant and general practitioner physician Gabby Rebecca who had topped scores for profile analysis fifteen years ago when the divisions were newly breaking into separate departments and wound up in charge of intruder-eavesdropping coercion cases. Many involved spousal injury, but over the years as the military base became the official coast site to train the nation's special task forces for penetration into worldwide assignments, an Internal Affairs sprang into being to oversee domestic violence and wrongful death cases in the special trained police. Forty Sikh families had transplanted from New Zealand having formerly educated and trained in New Delhi into a new suburb on the outskirts of the far reaches of the Saltar Eyre in order to track moonlight and flock seasons across the great iodized red and purple Masseria. Within the first five years of this relocation, setting off a new division for exotic deaths under the category of missing persons, a Hindu was discovered dead, his mouth stuffed full of purplish salt, his mouth running with the distinctive blue that marks the Eyre during the spring after the first drops of rain have been absorbed into the caked layers of chalky salt. He was possibly thirty-eight, a very thin male, wrists possibly four and a half inches, straight dark hair to the nape, his skin the color of burnt sienna, wearing dark trousers and the traditional dark gold and orange wrap across his torso and shoulders. Inside his wallet were two photographs taken in India. The ornate marble columns stacked with marble pagoda entrances made a palace with stairs that showed the dead man and a female, also very attractive wearing orange pants and a yellow blouse, long flowing dark brown wavy hair to her waist, and another of an all gold palace, an ornamental temple with a sky light on the river, the dead man standing behind her, perhaps on a stair, for he rose slightly above her, had his arms wrapped about her shoulders. This looked to be love or damned close to it, there was so much to see, one could travel a year and like the four hundred temples in the grassy flat lands of Burma that gave her a breathless wealth or the carved stone one-bedroom houses that cluttered river banks with stairs to the water, tiny for three adults and a mother-in-law, so the red stone natureza of all buildings spire and lace produced beauty for the Indian seeker like the cliffs of waterfalls in Gujurat or the six story Taj Mahal with white lace stone and dark dried red stone palace, the stone gateway of the river in Mumbai, the Twelve Gates of ancient India-Buddhist architecture including the Bhopal Pillar. Like all spiritual quests during which one gives the self over for penitence, life which began in hardship was cultivated to early death, no explanation seemed evident except this rather infeasible male had arrived to die on a plateau of mining, winter rains not yet rinsed. As the rivers became more the habitat for ornate pier houses, this commonplace one-bedroom house soon took over many a river as a typical eyesore similar to India's Rudall River pouring from Lake Dara, many a winter day resembling dark navy clouds crossing over a crystal bath of whitish opaque salt water as expansive as an ocean, beauty gathering like a pink dust cloud off a radiant silver blue horizon.

Gabby wore a light green uniform daily to work in such a fashion that from a distance no one could tell whether she was female or male. In faded blue shorts and a white tee, she was sturdy, sinewy muscles in the arms and legs, thin in the torso, a scooped-in stomach and almost flat-chested. Hidden by a narrow cap was tight blond curly hair cropped on her head. No military charge who knew her had anything unflattering to say about her; she had been to India, Great Barrier Reef, New Zealand and Figi in fishing boats and with construction diving parties to excavate lost ships at sea and find missing expeditions. Once upon a time in college she had been married, but then got it into her head being single was preferred; there were seldom demands, trade-offs, or responsibilities to fit into an already demanding work schedule. It was often said that the ones who made it up the ladder did so because they never compromised their work; they were available twenty-four-seven even in the middle of the night when a tug boat rang in that a suicide was floating in the bay. Life had not been reasonable – she had been called upon almost weekly to perform a scuttle for a partially sunken fishing boat, once for a Turkish research ship, often for teens who had steered drunk and wound up in the midst of nowhere, just fog and sand, stranded on an island, usually the Whitsundays.

She resided with a sometimes live-in male friend on Hervey Bay overlooking a metal relic ship sunk a hundred and thirty-seven feet in a hundred and twenty-four foot depth. The eastern had proved a subduing sight as much as it had a curious one, and not a summer went by that low tide did not bring hundreds of gulls or moderate tide the frequent occasions to stretch one's legs and jaunt along the sand. In the beginning straight out of internal medical school she and Charles LaMufti, a tan thin, middle-aged Australian with curly bronze hair and the sleek proportions of a long experienced diver from Russell Heads, went diving off Kaikoura for red seaweed. Their find was a boon because it targeted a ready supply of iron. In addition to underwater research for food, they studied waste treatment at Horseshoe Bay on Magnetic Island across from Townsville and prepared iodized waste with salt combinations for burial in the giant Nooldoona and took rock formation in selected quantities to the Great Barrier to Birabean and MacKenzie. Over a thousand trips from Magnetic to the Nooldoona gave Gabby the portfolio advantage over just about any physician traveling by ship through Australia's numerous oceans for the purpose of testing the newly formed soil landscape.

The assignment on her desk came from upstairs. It was an order to interview a hardworking malfeasance officer for signs of domestic deterioration. As with most officers she knew him reasonably well because she hired him. He came as a couple to her division as a husband-wife detective team working graveyard shift on homicide in spousal violent deviation. When the two split up, he transferred to international drugs and forgeries while his wife stayed in domestic harassment. They had moved from their luxurious beachfront home, she to a modest condominium on the sixth floor further down the beach and he, into Sydney to a townhouse hideaway. He was Bryce Finley. Mary had rescinded her married name in favor of her maiden name, Choice.

It was a basic domestic flair-up needing a bit of dusting was Gabby's guess. Choice had her job cut out and for years had taken the dismal, more disgusting deaths found up and down the coastline of Down Under partially buried in mud flats at very low tide. Usually on the coast it was the house owner went down into the basement to set the latch in a storm and was pulled out by an aggressive undertow. On a river the tide kept rising and in a quick six-mile-an-hour torrential downpour inhabitants were dragged along unable to climb out or resist its speed. Some were found tied to initially sturdy crosses trying to float to safety. The Eyre also that sat on the Bight side of the southern tip of the peninsula was yearly retrenched due to the fact that the continental shelf sand bar was rising cropping in the salt flats and pushing them into proximity with the red and purple knife that constituted the iodized low mesas, and from time to time a miner venturing through waist-high water lost his footing in the depth of salt which swallowed him to the waist. Finley, on the other hand, was a herder who had retrained after leaving Cairns on a midway vessel through the Great Reef onto the open ocean. After a year out in sockeye hurricanes Bryce returned an altered man adjusted to the ocean dealings that made sailors near dead on a mast pole incapable of escaping without injury, physical or psychic. This Bryce was a bitter mistrustful man who placed a video camera over the entrances of their home, who hired petty thieves to peer through the window, who stole Mary's mail or tossed it into the trash – the allegations read like a junk movie deleted down to the hostilities. If he was determined to have committed these acts he'd be marched off to Ingorrah prison and held in confinement with a guard to look in upon him once a day. It'd be the end. He'd be taken apart, peg at a time, until he was weeping before any prison panel considered him an acceptable risk for main population.

"So how's the job?"

The man seated before Gabby taped to the lie detector machine was a globetrotter type, large in weight, muscled through the arms and legs, manly, crew-cut, hard mien, chiseled out of intolerance. "So so. I was selected for two shifts a week New Zealand to India, pay's better."

"Four hundred a week?"

"Four twenty-five. I'm interested in making Grade Six."

"That shouldn't be time-consuming." Gabby opened his file. "You've handled Overseas, BOAC, scrapnel for dug-out duty, fence, barrier and projectile, nearly all at open sea including Reef. You were joined by night-duty vessels, square tactics, you're very highly trained, you could go places." She flipped back to the Complaints documents – the file was empty. "Good sign, no offenses, so we have to resolve this latest dispatch report. Did you talk to the penalizing barroom officer?"

"Yes, Lt. Rebecca, I gave him a full report. My wonton and I were overheard blowing the brine, nothing officious, no threat intended."

She flipped to a blue form. "Another party states you have been giving your ex a bad time."

"I'm fine, Doc. It's nothing. Just a spiff on occasion on holiday."

"Not what it says here. Apparently you parked in front of the house and honked the horn longer than a minute at two in the morning."

"Blown way out of context. I went by to collect her signature and I decided to wait until she got home."

Gabby turned now to a light colored purple form which another officer had taken down from the corporal's oldest child by an earlier marriage, now age eighteen. "You periodically took your children out of town to the Territory and refused to notify their legal mother who is your ex."

"What is she alleging? That when I talked to her I was

tipsy or something?"

She read off a green form recorded under oath. "An unidentified person stated on at least an occasion you were grossly out of control, you were shouting, and you threatened to shoot the porch lights out."

"Those are two separate times. I had to drive my oldest to his actual mother's and the other time occurred at Mary's after her boyfriend turned his high lights on me. You can test me. I'm clean."

"Let's return to the allegation. You are charged with a threatening comment allegedly made to a personal friend. The reporting party believes you were drunk."

"Did this personal friend give evidence?"

"Someone else did."

"Some asshole hanging around, I bet. What am I supposed to have said?"

"Quote. She owes me. When I collect my due, I'll take care of her. They'll never find her. End quote. Could you have said something like that?"

He became upset. "Do I look stupid to you? I've got some expertise in lies in insurance fraud. I wouldn't have said that about Mary. I mean, whatever the heck for?"

She hadn't thought he would say much in response. These ex-spouses who bullied their wives rarely were agreeable.

She said, "I've ordered counseling on you twice a month with a priest in coastal down under, one-half hour per occasion, as to how your divorce is going. I expect to hear any problem direct from you prior to an arrest. You will also have to submit a urine weekly."

"Not a worry, Doctor, but you'll see, shoe's on the wrong foot."

The lie detector said he hated his ex so much he might put a fist through her face.

There are incidences when the maddest carnivore outdistances the purest clucking giving way to a steady stream of obsolescence and barbarism. The society as an entirety ignores the obtrusion, the antelope in its haste is driven fleeing to the mouth of a river and forced to swim until it chokes.

Of course, no one who has read one report ever doubts malicious intent when the outcome lies in a wet grave, the sorry individual having supped more than a brandy sniffer worth of death. Claustrophobia itself forewarns, grievous harassment kills.

Even without criminal history or spousal infidelity there are the insidious whims of meanness, unpredictable, impulsive spite which when it intrudes begins as persistent telephone calling. Bryce Finley had once confessed on deck duty that he arranged a signal to transmit whenever his ex-wife failed to return for a night. That information in and of itself, could she get him to admit, was enough to haul Finley in on a charge of domestic brutality.

But she pulled the imprints on him anyway as a precaution. A man who was building up to a fatal blow wasn't soon to come clean. The tapes revealed a bully, a man confident of his position, someone with an axe to bear. In the Tasman Sea or the Bass Strait in the Indian Ocean, he weathered the channels alright, sailed the mainstay mast and beam without any mis-measurement and kept the toddy to the floor in full wind. He was a sight driving his yacht's rippled cloth and bent high dipping one side completely runner tilt to the waves. With each assignment there was less and less presence of his wife until there was none of her, but it was all men, no new female emerged as a singular interest.

From the York peninsula to Fraser Island the bitterly chill Coral Sea ravaged over the Great Barrier Reef locking ships out from Brisbane and Sydney. Below the continent in the Great Australian Bight close to the Tasman Sea sat Melbourne and Adelaide and somewhere west the Eyre Peninsula with thirteen lakes of salt flat mines of pyramid shapes emerging through the crusted salt water which in winter formed mesmerizing lakes, squarely in Southern Australia Lake Eyre North and Lake Eyre South were the more vivid to pronounce bloodshed to a weary misdirected traveler during a monsoon. In spite of the flanks of territorial ranges, Gawler and Flinders emanating like wretched inhospitable stretches of concrete ravines, the newest city Perth lit the horizon far to the west in Western Australia, the smallest civilization off the Indian Ocean. On occasion net darners gathered along the coasts to spread the crimson red salt to bring in schools of red perth. The calmer the waves the greater the catch until at various seasons all that remained were vines of seaweed standing straight up from gloomy sun filtered depths, the undersea world thronged by dense jet blue.

The priest called with his advice. He was a mixed black, tall in stockinged feet, a long time schooner fisherman who from time to time set traps in the great barrier for shrimp, but who otherwise led mass once a week on Friday nights at eight at night and late choir at ten, took monetary donations for volunteers and fed a congregation worth petrale sole and perch twice a week, Saturday and Wednesday evenings.

"Sooo, Gal, I've seen your man twice. Rather nasty bite of jaw he's got."

"Has he admitted to randoogling his ex-wife?"

"Wee bit. He states she hasn't coughed up her share of fife. Claims he has paid more than his share of wage. Says he's been patient, the situation has gone an indecent length far past the separation."

"I have a report that he drives up her driveway at midnight, turns on his lights and tries to pry open the back door. Worse, that he has chased her home."

"Yar, I've tried to talk to him. He says she locked up their cabin at doons and served him papers. He says he paid substantial, ninety thou, if you will compared to her thirty-two."

"Well, you keep in touch."

"I'm thinking you should call in a cake man, someone who knows where these types might die them."

"I assigned a detective."

"Lazy man's appetite. I'd obtain a spooner, who else is going to see a body in a salt lake?"

"Could you recommend someone?"

"Any blood will do."

She thanked him, said she'd talk it over with the detective assigned by her higher-ups and have someone on the case in an hour.

Her detective thought the priest had a good idea. He could work with anyone, whatever Gabby wanted. He had received a tip from an unknown source through the department route system – it was soiled diapers in your baloney. He agreed to fax her the sheet.

Within the hour between deviled egg and a diet tea with a shot of pure cream she received the billing off her e-fax. The attached cover letter read, "Behavior escalated." A string of photo stills showed a rather shorn looking Bryce dressed in jeans and color bone shirt peering through windows at odd hours, wiring up a signal light in the street that flickered on and off, and erasing her computer at work. All this, the report said, was believed to have left her with the idea she had been intruded upon by something she could not easily rid herself of. Eventually Mary Choice put in for a transfer to Cairns and Down Under and once accepted, she joined the special task group that patrolled the barrier reef solid waste crew during graveyard shifts.

"Who wants a dee-tangle in my beau-jangle?" The skinny blonde wore a tight white tee-shirt and white tight tight leggings and sang in a warm melodic wail. "Oooh tell me, when is my boat going to return?"

The ocean rolled in, the harbor had attracted a shift of fishermen with nets and a patrol of mostly female beach patrol alongside the wide tan sand and house pier where the fire department waited in search and rescue boats bobbing in the wave action some three miles off. In the distance rose blue green mountains and the wet tropics, an all-green density of fruit orchards all the way north to Cape Tribulation where the Daintree and its rainforest met the Great Barrier Reef.

The body had been discovered tangled up in a net put to sea off a white fish schooner, each fish in that predawn morning's catch about seventy-five feet by ten to eighteen feet wide, shockingly big line benders. There was not a sea patrol officer who did not spy Mary Choice's poor bloodied face the moment he stepped up to assist. Poor Mary Choice – taken in a Surfer's Paradise, her blondish hair stamped over her scalp, her taut, perfectly proportioned youth mauled by something every diver took caution to avoid – stinging nettles burned on the skin by contact with actual coral, a disease-like pain if an injured party survived, continual contact with coral caused one's joints to become achingly stiff. Someone had remarked that they had seen a light falling and rising on the waves off the misted black rocks that sat in low tide on the beach like pup seals, and as gigantic storm clouds entombed the skies and lowered over Cairns with its chockfull of apartments, there in a glowing surf pool floated the tangled net, stuffs of blond hair showing like lint through the thick embrasure of ropes. Not until they untwisted her body free did they find sticking to her clothing pouring from her pockets telltale java black sand, the only beach in Australia to have black sand at Melbourne, a stunning imperialism of ever-rinsing deep brownish black sand adorned by a crescent peninsula or larger Tahitian-style garden rocks, nothing else, no greenery, the deeply ravened McPherson's shouldering one end of the beach.

The fifty or so jars slopped with paint and varying depths of turpentine in a pine wood floor sunroom with five wall size windows that housed sixteen foot oil paintings of streaks of blue, green and yellow and a dash of cinnamon, peach and white, all small houses on a backdrop of red or orange, the bluish sea in the foreground battling nature. In addition to paint jars he had hundreds of diet coca cola cans in four large burlap bags, some umpteen thirty cans crowding the surface of his only table along with seven dark brown glass drinking mugs of coffee. On a dai up four stairs was the rumpled king size bed on black carpet and bathroom tiled in rose terra with shower and tub and two mirrors where Gabby spent many a morning applying eyeliner and blue mascara and rose blush. Originally a student of law from Bond University, LaMufti switched his field to medicine and went to work the better half of ten years at Royal Adelaide before running New Sydney Yard downtown, miles inland north of the flying buttress symphony hall. Today he was one of the youngest lab coats, in his late fifties, capable of setting up a laboratory on site of a crime scene and dismantling it as soon as he combed the area for trace as to cause of death. Sometimes he'd be stationed on the firm ground of a marsh; at times on the sand above a beach, examining fingerprints and esophagus for drownings, trying to establish feathered fossils, tracts of dark brown mud in oral cavities and scraped thickly beneath toe nails, or looking for any surrendering trail of blood or seepage.

Their original plans to take the carryall to Fraser Island to film pooled glazed ocean water on beige sand was nixed in favor of viewing ensuing evidence. The troublesome finding lay not in the presumption that Mary Choice somehow had time to scout over to Melbourne but in the supposition that her ex-husband had gone to all the trouble to hide the factual whereabouts of her final hours. By sea, assuming her body was dragged from Eyre and thrown inside a van, it was still twenty hours to Mel coast to roll her in java sand and then to tie her up in nets and ditch her to sea in a small yacht. In those twenty hours the presumed assailant had sat through two therapy sessions and been followed by a seawall detective who knew enough to anticipate trouble. The boat that carried her body revealed considerably less. The floorboards had undergone sufficient dousing to eliminate whatever presence of salt might have otherwise stayed, the motor showed utterly none of purple or red crystalline sand and the fragments of vegetation peculiar to the landscape of Eyre was entirely absent advancing the notion that her perpetrator had first removed all her clothing and taken a shower with her before she changed into fresh clothes.

Nevertheless Gabby Rebecca made careful notes. "No final meal."

LaMufti agreed. Thin, elegant braided strands to the shoulders were his sole decoration. An all black satin long sleeved shirt worn loose over light tan jeans and men's sandals gave him the look of incompletion staff left him alone over. "No incision either. If there's an injection there hasn't been time for the blood to develop blood cells at the juncture."

"No foot binding."

"It's not a promise. Her assailant could have stopped her circulation with the weapon."

"But there's sand in her mouth," she said, her voice self-congratulatory. "Orange sand. Under her fingernails also. It's obviously Ayr."

"He could have bagged her with a burlap that had had sand inside it. It only matters we can place the sand. Possibly they went on an excursion first to a cave of water at Ayr."

"You think she would have gone anywhere with him? I don't. She had already filed for intimidation."

"She may have gotten unpredictably stuck. We know from the Bureau of Meteorology that there was a storm chaser predicted on the cyclone tracking map and that NAVMAR had a read for the South Australian Bight to the coordinates of 127 West to coast of Africa starting in the Coral Sea in the Cairns Monsoon Belt."

"Unlikely. She would've steered clear of him."

"Soil, unknown properties, blood, urine. Those are the basic predictors. No other evidence is important. At least one will convict."

The single photograph sheet of first incident of last life-threatening act of violence showed, piles of salt made by salt trucks, tracks of water lanes to horizon, scraped salt, patterns of waves, SUV in flood water up to headlights, the surrounding sand a Mars-like crimson landscape which was the lowest point in Australia described by a sub-file as the worst aching land of indefinite undefined space, rain, reddish murky mud, corrosive salt, and desolate bleak caravan sent by cloud churning winds. In cross-corresponding photo-land placements there were an abundance of flies in swarms at 12 Apostles, miles of lavender fields, the encroaching river-storm rains which expanded the tributary collections of the Desaquadero River and husband sub-categories of a long dry crimson part of ocean originally, centuries of the No-no washing quantities of blood wastes diluted by sewer run-off, and the Uyuni through which men traveling through the rainforest dropped a zip line cable over a thousand foot drop on their way to the coast, with a picture of Mary in a helmet and trouser uniform on a line, to which she had told her friends and associates that waiting for the line made her feel like a chef in the kitchen with about ten people watching TV in the living room waiting for their meds to be passed out. There were photos of them camping on the black sands of Mel beaches; a notation that she must have left with him to go to Adelaide because of dark sand coffee grounds in her clothing. Other photos showed bits of floating salt beneath an anti-plano sky, patterns of reflection by sun in pool rising tapas in powder blue forming arches of risen salt. They were believed to have sailed to New Zealand for a week while the weather was warm, a comfortable eighty-two early in the day this spring, to have gone diving for sea urchins at Georgie Bay in the agua marine water at Perth.

Ayr is in the Uluru Tjuta and both assigned to the Great Barrier Reef has dark blue, aqua water, white beach with lighthouse and 1,200 miles of islands.

Under post-mortem background, the file began with a half page statement that Mary Janelle Choice went to Hobart College to study biochemistry of coral cay formation and waste treatment; she joined an Underwater Research Group at

Townsville as construction diver from Cairns; traveled regularly to Yongala Wreck at Horseshoe Bay on Magnetic Island across channel; and her entire jurisprudence could be accessed through Caroline Islands.

The conversation between Gabby and the poison division was innocuous, matter-of-fact, prior to findings being formally given to each department head as to complicating factors. Gabby was talking to Chief Morgue Administrator in downtown Cairns. He was an ingenious male in his mid seventies whose ten physician licenses, each in use at the five continent hospitals, gave no cognizant evidence he heard anything said.

She asked, "So what appears evident?"

"A play for orange tongue diagnosis. It's open and shut for murder, ultimate death without rigour. See this all over India."

"What finding was made?"

"Tentative for homicide."

"What do you have as time of death?"

"Saturday, Oct. 30, 2011 on the damned side shore. The essential question all along has consistently been, do we know at what point death occurred? I believe all the sand is to mask chemical changes of the body as death set in. There was no rigor. As to any other condition of body, there were damp feet, clammy exterior, orange frothy barf lodged in throat older than seventy-two hours meaning her body lay dead at least that amount of time somewhere. Glucose intolerance setting in due to extreme dehydration."

"What does psychologist say?"

"His query – is the ex-husband a psychopath or severe addict?"

"What are her last known activities?"

"Mary Choice was sent by her agency for five weeks camp at Eyre commencing on September 10, 2011, a Saturday and concluding October 15 th, also a Saturday. For this she drove her jeep and met six other police agents at the lake where they camped in their trucks. They drove out having collected specimens of rain water, salt water, herbs, grass, and salt to the Adelaide lab where they submitted notes and vial trays. Choice had met her parents at Tuck Shop, pie specialties in town, during camp. Her ex-husband joined them. Victim's body was discovered on Saturday October 30, 2011 on a large harpoon boat tangled up in heavy fisherman's net."

Dr. Aarons PhD stated in his report was as follows: Said victim's ex-marital partner was seen in psychotherapy under court order issued by King's bench for purpose of addressing sadistic, morally depraved remarks unbefitting of a custom's clerk. Long ongoing house improper indoctrination including bullying, coercion, acts of unusual intimidation, garden threats, gestures on life endangerment and harm. These involve making intimidating remarks, I will get you; you won't live long enough to tell another soul what you know; not even the basement will find you. Husband is sole marital engagement. Witnesses observed husband drive onto lawn and flood headlights at home; angry words hurled at victim consisting of

You're a deserter. No one could have done more than I. I'll see you soaked in coffee grounds first. During early marriage couple vacationed at Ayr; took a cabin at Cairns overlooking Barrier; celebrated second year on Melbourne beach; took prayer counseling from Roman Catholic friar at Townsville as to getting stationed at Brahma-industrial nations.

He provided a recent transcription of therapy session as follows,

"I'm not a deeply spiritual man, I was bred to believe the sailing man is unexcelled by any force except God. Worst problem along islands is wastes back up in body, bile or gall. Could I s'pose be jaundice, might be heavy diet of apricot and almonds, with over consumption of Adderall to stay alert on those longer voyages."

"Were you ever exposed to an orange tongue death?"

"Just once. Mary, it was her expertise although we did ride into the gold coast to see several exhibits. The subject of trauma has received a good deal of press."

"When did you last go to this exhibit?"

"Let's see, that would've been a year and four months ago.

We saw an exhibit of Josias Bremerton art at the Royal Hall in Sydney called Blood Orange."

"Do you remember your conversation?"

"I said it looked as though the artist had just done smoked his pip."

"What did you mean?"

"Mary was keen on this art. It showed all up and down Down Under. She was given a tract to study to arrive at a rationale as to atypical deaths to elder males. I may have said a better artist should have washed out the rust."

"And by this phraseology you meant ---?"

"To get rid of the impurities, dish out the hops, make a pure paste one can eat without poison."

"Were you each seeing poison cases?"

"Well, she was. There were all those under-toe cases, nearly ten of them. They were all energy fatigue and seemed tied to New Delhi out on the islands."

"Why is it called Blood Orange?"

"Oh, that's straightforward enough. The illness is an upper GI mistaken for bleeding treated by chemotherapy drugs or by hops paste by local witch practitioners for pancreatic cancer of mouth and esophagus."

An attached notation from Townsville Laboratories, Outside Shelton Place, read, "Semi nude body exhibits anaerobic metabolism. Post Mortem shows no traces of drugs, chemical additives, inhalants or other pharmacological. Vomit in throat red rust in color, orange sand presumed Ayr is quite aged. Presence of bile in vomit appears orange. Urine is dark red orange in color. Diagnosis – victim was held under water as is consistent with presence of bile. Dark red orange urine indicates hypoglycemic phalactic shock, untreatable. Gall without blood is severe infection as a result of last meal being longer than sixty-eight hours. Presumed liver ingestion re-constitution at death. There is some indication that Body was in the water in the last seventy-two hours. Moderate specimen referred to Indonesia, fax sent from Darwin to Diu."

From Sydney Bio-Patho-Med Labs, the additional report arrived two days after chief coroner released evaluation. "Blood tests for routine lab studies consist of cell counts, enzyme levels, and electrolytes; HIV testing proves negative; immune response positive; genetic testing consistent. Urine and saliva are abnormal per attached result indicating ingestion of narcotic believed to be taken regularly for stress reduction, suppression of hunger and increased awareness. Skin tests for virus and bacteria were responsive for tetanus, TB, diphtheria and amoxicillin. Skin and lymph node biopsies completed for tissue and DNA. Chest X-ray negative. Breath test is given consistency as to Study Drug."

Mid-week later from Diu Island, Chief Scenic Awareness, as follows – "Food poison causing vomit and stools to appear predominantly black tinged by very dark orange, sufficient arsenic ingested to cause cerebral death."

The first therapy session recorded document typed up by the hospital transcription pool read as follows:

"She came over to my house and insisted I owed her alimony."

"Why do you think she did that?"

"I promised her I would pay her for her half of our rental on the Gold Coast."

"Right then and there?"

"Yes, but she'd have to drive to my house."

"Where were you when you told her that?"

"In my car."

"Were you on her property?"

"I was in the street."

"What brought you there?"

"I had to see my boss. He resides in her immediate neighborhood. When I drove by, she yelled at me so I backed up and told her she should shut her trap. That's when she accused me of bouncing the alimony."

"How much is it for?"

"1800. She was awarded the house and half of any sale from joint properties."

"Did you intend to pass a bad check?"

"No, it's just I get low toward the end of the month. My jobs give me $3000 every two weeks. I pay on my Sydney condo two grand. A thousand boards three kids at Holy Sepulcher per month. It's tight."

"Did she ask for a cashier's check?"

"No, she prefers cash. I told her I'd put it on my card. I said I'd wire it into her checking. She said she'd come get it."

"Did you call for a police assist for when she was coming?"

"Hell no," he drawled with bravado. "I have the restraint order on me; she doesn't have one on her."

Chief Coroner had stayed late to draft up the conclusion on the Ayr victim. Once he closed out the file he'd drive into the mountains until he hit the winding road and head east to the southern shore of the lake to the hotel. The victim was another police officer. It'd be years before the file, once transferred to Whitsundays, could be traced. It meant endless completion orders on phone calls, computer correspondence, any bar conversation, mapping for anywhere the husband traveled, a plethora of minute details that could involve anyone anywhere. In a case like this, they looked for a cheating spouse, illegal use of premises, indicators that the husband was bugging the wife. Technically she had died of dehydration after floating in salt water at Eyre. Red and white salt inside the ears said she had floated underwater. Copse grain course black sand showed almost everywhere else, except inside the mouth where old, aged orange Ayr sand had been stuffed into her mouth probably in the final seconds of life. The addition of sand was to cover the whereabouts of death which he thought was begun at Eyre, then taken east to Melbourne beach for a turn in the tide, and finally far past Down Under on a boat in the sea at night under the unseeing stars. It was a lot of work for one man to eliminate a wife.

The husband was a previous lifeguard at Gold coast who had become a detective for Search & Missing and was always on the go. During long weekends off consisting of three to four days immediately prior to putting to sea for barge duty in foreign shores, he shot up range combined with purple, dropped a few hits of acid a week, smoked high bred marijuana a day and drank coffee blended with spice. She on the other course was well known for her vacation and rotation off-duty. Sydney was the place to eat, every cuisine imaginable. She'd fly in, book an all-glass condo on the top floor, take a dinner of scallops and French fry and a small green salad and order a toddy, and review her month-long activity for any outstanding work. Toward the end on Sunday she put through one telephone fax to him, and flew home. His most recent message from her was brief – "No Tasman or Indian Sea. She has something he wants. He's livid, foaming at the mouth. Too much phallus, bitter in the mouth, bizarre ritual."

And then nothing.

Her death.

Body wrapped up in ropes and thrown onto top deck.

The central question for the death review team was premeditation.

The orange dirt which came from Ayr was aged to a rust grainy consistency, almost as though the assailant had kept it inside a box with filings for years thinking he would use it for some beleaguered idea of finer methodology. Once the orange had been removed from the mouth and the teeth and palate and tongue rinsed, the possibility for diagnosis was much less clear. The tongue was a normal color, not what one might expect were its color in keeping with the bright yellowish orange of orange tongue diagnosis. Unlike the mouth the ears revealed whitish and crimson red bits of salt as did the vagina and labia. Under the fingernails and toenails and in the clothing, her jeans and undershirt and short sleeved cotton plaid trim were clandestine particles of Melbourne dark brown sand, these fairly suggestive of coffee grounds. The entire picture gave Dr. Bialy Ascott a lean persuasion that everything was meant to tie together as though the victim had been given a template of significance as she was being killed. Bialy who was in his early seventies prepared prejudicial analyses of deaths for psycho-vindication spousal hatred cases whether exhibits were displayed in courtroom pre-trial hearings. A Scottish rifle man from South Shields, he was a handsome six feet, unkempt wiry blond hair, brown eyes, dressed usually in cotton shirt with black silk bow-ties and lavender tweed trousers and matching elegant socks and brown suede sandals. Today he was examining each addition of soil that the body had been dressed in after death by pound weight, measurement, description, and color. It would be his estimable conclusion the victim had been drowned by excessive force even though the body carried no bruising, sign of impact or evidence of poison.

However, the perplexing notion lay in the question as to the assailant's idea of death. Obviously there was intent. He wanted her mouth to get stuffed with orange soil presumably to declare her orange tongue. He wanted her to have coffee grounds all over her. He did not want place of death to be recognizable. There were a good many justifications, the typical being she was bulimic and had died of repeated vomiting. Certainly this could account for the presence of black bile in the throat and stools. Or she was asthmatic and had died of respiratory failure; or she was choked to a semi-unconscious state. But she had water in her lungs, so he routed his inquiry to underwater research to the people who knew her best. They had just the one sheet cause of death attached to query who, when they replied with – husband wore ice-based chill pack strapped to leg with vest for ocean disposal. Even had poor Mary a bad case of bronchitis coupled with a righteous infection and fever and aches, standard treatment by Z-pack or Prednisone or Amoxicillin didn't kill despite their strength and side effects. Bialy put his best guess with an ethylic coma caused in fact by profound relaxation initially affecting the toes, ears and eyes, generating a massive hangover accompanied by a retardation of dizziness. More at asphyxiation by choking. Lead suspect was her ex-husband who told his sister-in-law one night when they were drunk that he was going to murder his wife because he suspected her of carrying an informal case on his activities in the Down Under region outside Townsville. Bryce hadn't been too specific but Tommy put in a report which went straight to Psychological after three inquiries were researched. The basic evidence could lead any eleventh grader in tray disorder deaths to accommodate an understanding that Bryce's attitude toward Mary was a resounding Fuck You. It wasn't that Mary had abandoned Bryce, although the very first outburst by Bryce came four years ago when he accused her of becoming a deserter. The next outburst, shortly thereafter, came when they went to Whitsundays Island and he showed her a basement he had built out of bamboo for pipes to carry in water and to remove sewage. They had argued about it all weekend; finally he said it adequately replaced rust from metal pipes even if the depth of metal needed to be at thirty feet, deep enough to cause bends if one had to retrench or replace them. Bechel nut could be eaten and used in chemical manufacture to produce arrow poison as well as orange tongue in the human body after death. Orange tongue was indeed open and shut for murder but it was associated to asphyxia, to upper respiratory failure while in the water, not merely to rising the well, accidental death, cause unknown. Although the poison boys wanted to rest their laurels on a biochemical reaction of almonds from pipes giving sway to a predisposition of substance not unlike Curare which paralyzed, there was no way to know how the deaths actually occurred.

To those who knew him very well Bryce had to have his way. He wasn't one to follow someone else's lead. He had volunteered for expeditions throughout Indonesia and Micronesia, then had been accepted to Borneo, Jakarta and India. He had gone down rivers in a large boat conducting to fallen roof for accidental deaths of Ishmaeli families. If he was well liked, appreciated and invited to celebrations, he was feared also, despised by the one or two who might wind up suffering under the brunt of corruption, but in general adhered to whatever he said had to be. Wherever Mary's file on him was a mystery. If it was in her head, and no one believed her to have been negligent, then the information died with her, all good and fine for Bryce who had not a care in the world. He had hacked through the walls and flooring of her Gold Coast condo and apparently appeared satisfied nothing was stashed either inside a cabinet or beneath one's feet. The dried black sand was meant to match dried blood in her bile which was in less than .03 cm. The telltale crimson red iodine-testing salt which showed inside her mouth was to be found in her ears and in her labia and internally marking Lake Eyre at rainy season the official site of her death. The issue was, had the knocker deaths of Down Under on Mary's investigation been created by bends, which could account for the presence of vomit as well as for orange tongue. Bends was not glucose intolerance. Respiratory paralysis could be the rising of the well, if that's what had been occurring when the ocean tides swept those men out to sea off their rainforest coast and carried them through the lull of tide-churning, bottom-clear, aquamarine warm ocean to the frenzies of deeper ocean wreaking mind-altering under toe. Only the Sea & Rescue could be counted that far north, in rubber decked outboards twice a month except for three months in winter and then once every half season to the islands and bi-weekly out through Cairns to the Great Barrier and beyond. Bryce was a captain steer man so he was already intimately familiar with the exceptions to the coastal tides having already served Ayr terrain and salt seas. Waste was easily disseminated as were blood and carnivore flesh.

Coffee grounds of course remarked on dried black bile and dried bile in stools, but first and foremost it went to Melbourne beaches a tad west. These java color sands stretched endlessly without sign of life, pristine and peculiar in texture, no real estate development permitted anywhere, the borrowed sense of endless time granted by some orchards of bananas, pomegranates and kiwi as though the crating of fruit went with the longevity of unripe productivity. So it was, noteworthy similar to the really gruesome underwater deaths that they left trails of black rust, piles of it, which under the microscope proved to be little better than crustaceans pasted into chalky rock, perhaps the start of or the decimation of fossilized shellfish or protozoan plants that would one day form the reefs. Had Bryce wanted the fish to have found his wife, he might have tossed her in, but he preserved her for death on a boat, her body tangled in about as much net and rope as what the crew hauled black shrimp in. He had had his say. No doubt he profited richly from her silence. But this was conjecture, nothing in the way of evidence to bring in a verdict. One had to figure that even the wall of net and rope seaward-living men hung from their balconies to shut out a raging sea was adequate to prevent dismantling an older wooden house situated on the beach and that this type net for bringing in black cod, prawns, big shrimp or cooee had been utilized with intention to trap Mary Choice.

The number of men whose lived-in houses succumbed to the sea as the tide advanced inward topped an unusually high number of forty-two deaths off Islas Diego Ramirez in destitute Chile, on the other wayward side off Santa Cruz a toll of sixteen; one out of any surviving coastline of dark continent Africa to be found in Zanzibar; two – a married couple – residing in Oman; four alleged fishermen from Perth and seven at South

East Cape of Tasmania; two at Cooktown; ten for the ever-shrinking, crumbling coast from Padang through Banda Lamp, one tragic death in East Timor rumored during a quake, six off Sarmi on Guinea with a heartbreaking high toll breaker of nineteen bad deaths, later stretched out on the beach on wooden window-like racks to prevent rigor in stiffening. In the Solomon Islands in Port Via a man was found washed ashore believed to have been swept away a hundred and eighteen miles north off Banks Island. Solely in the Arctic North in Svalbard above the Barents Ocean seventeen sailors had surrendered while inside wooden houses to the occasional thundering inescapable sea as it roared through the destitute reaches of Veld and Vest at four-teen miles an hour, wind factor not excluded. No where else in the heavens or the stultifying land were the cataclysms of evil as strongly perceived although the number of river deaths any-where for India, Dhaka, and Thailand counted in the dozens with Bangkok at the all-time high.

Very dark navy clouds lined the low skies bustling right above the inland sea of white salt. A lighthouse in the dis-tance issued out a piercing light which during bad weather was a sole comfort to a stranded motorist; likewise on the coast in and around Cooktown half a dozen shipwrecks and galleons watched the undersea for ill will and dishonest conveyances. On their wharves hung long nets tied by ropes. Sand rocks as yet unwinched decorated the shallow bottom and Bramston a mile off the Cairns coast and Russell Heads, about ten miles away, served as off-shore levies to detach motors and repair tugboats. The jetaway at Sydney along the Gold Coast played anchor to the hordes of strange boats up and down its water-ways and prisms of hotels and casinos. The drop line cable through the rainforest which had permitted Mary to suit up to enter off-road wilderness habitats also broke free over the beach that opened onto the barrier reef and it was through this portal Mary learned her job to excavate the mountains, high lakes and florid coasts. If the killing syndrome for dozens of seaward-rooted adult men was an under toe which took life the way the belt of a cable could at an equivalent sixty miles an hour in a sudden rush of unanticipated roar of wind, then she had learned to outwit it so as to produce the closing sund rope to haul hapless victims from out of the sandy plummeting depths of suction experienced in the Deep.

At Darwin where the research society bred big fish in fleets of a hundred for sea bass each a half ton, flounder each a mere eighty thousand pounds, roughy which were not so large and mashali, popular in the islands, but expensive as all get-out, a fryer's worth twice that of one calamari steak. The islanders applied for the seasonal jobs and acquired them, many traveling south with brothers and uncles, an average pay fifty grand per male. Every so often after fishing season was over a family rented a condo in the Sultan's Palace for several years while trying for full-time labor even though in general this practice was discouraged among the younger set. It was training for breeding and capturing that the islander learned to keep his balance on a fast-moving pavement when transporting the tank fish to the seminary along the coast.

As floors with knobs replaced slanted cement flooring two inches thick which was placed into a squared out depression, training was given to predominantly men to grab onto the hand-holds and as the ocean poured in to be capable of withstanding the vigorous ocean waves. Bungie jumping was not just for a rolling road in a flood or eroding street; it also had merit in the pitching ocean.

Of course it worried a man of Bialy's experience that Mary could have been jumped in just such a method as the work she had performed monthly. Clearly she wasn't expecting what had occurred, so used to setting Bryce's intrusions out of her mind, probably more than relieved to have escaped his intolerable behaviors of missing payment of alimony, persistent telephone calling, video-taping her through the window and showing her his tapes when he sent e-mails. Bryce was worse than a bully; Bialy was convinced Bryce had planned to murder his wife all along, possibly from the day they married. But if there were records of spousal corporal injury abounding on Bryce, they weren't to be easily found, and Bialy feeling an urgency about the matter sent for any information from Mariana Islands figuring it would take a few days to a week.

Remaining on his list was to conduct a dilution test on the rope and net covering her to determine where the netting was used – in the Eyre, out on the Mel or only on deck of the boat at sea. Once he had isolated those grains of sand, he could write a summary noting of course intent of design to mask evidence as well as any attempts at purging actual physical circumstance. His concern with aspirated fluid from the lungs being salty water consistent with salt flask water from Eyre, there ought to be a predominance of evidence to state overwhelmingly that despite grains of soil from Ayr and a java beach in the vicinity of Mel, death occurred under water in the dried crimson sands of Eyre. Why Eyre? Was it because his schedule permitted him the availability of free time, or was he waiting for her to be assigned to Eyre, or was there some other peculiar significance? Bialy could only decipher that Bryce had succeeded in creating water in the lungs at a lake depth of twenty-five feet or more which was a rarity in and of itself. Normally the lake rose to ten feet at its deepest. Whereas the circumstances of death mimicked bile, it was impossible to get decompression illness in a lake. She had been choked, strangled or suffocated, pure and straight forward, no less, and it impressed him that it was a keenly deliberate act to require some unnatural reference to someone's investigation.

FOUR

Gabby glanced up from the request for diagnosis for the attached forensic report. Also on her desk was the parent file on the summary and conclusion of the knocker cases at Cairns and in Indochina held by the deceased.

Dr. Bialy Ascott stood in the doorway, his white lab coat dominating dark gray trousers and a light gray sweater over a pale yellow starched cotton shirt, a stethoscope around his neck. It was late, at least seven-thirty. Despite a barely eaten roast beef sandwich from the cafeteria, neither had the lack of inhibition to invite the other downstairs for a late meal of teriyaki chicken and tea. Although Gabby had her usual attitude, the sooner she took care of paperwork, the quicker she could leave, she rarely departed earlier than eight.

"You get to my summary yet?" he asked, fully able to see it lay on her desk.

"Superb, as usual. All the docs in order. I just need a day or two to think it through." She smiled, and he smiled also stepping into the smallish cubicle and seated himself.

"Mary had just met a man, an astrobiologist for Bourke in the eastern range, a specialist who is working on high lakes. Looked to be a cheerful chap. Friends who worked with her thought she'd finally turned her life around."

"Oft' happens that way. What d'you suppose the motive was anyways?"

"It's tied up with her case. Did you get the diagnosis?"

"No, I just sent for it. What do we have?"

She tossed him the summary page which he perused.

"Nothing new, at least not to me."

"You didn't find that all these clam drawer deaths were actually bend?"

"They probably are. It won't alter their cause of death of accidental death, cause unknown."

"They all had barf and purple tongues."

"Presence of arsenic?"

"That's correct."

"Presumes wood was treated with sealant."

"Is Choice purple tongue?"

"No, orange, with barf."

"Eyre water in the lungs?"

"That's the item. These findings to be consistent. We know ears and vagina have Eyre salt, top clothes were rolled in coffee grounds dried sand."

"Does this mean she may have been killed twice?"

"Well, I have a few additional tests to run, but the way it looks she was dropped in the ocean off Mel, subjected to not yet dead struggling to surface, as she tried to kick she lost air and died of bends."

"Does it add up she was killed for her knowledge of an investigation?"

"I wouldn't conclude anything quite so damning yet."

"Bryce looks like lead suspect. He has motive, placement."

"Certainly are some coincidences."

"We impounded his jeep."

"Better get him off a traffic corner stop somewhere just to be sure."

"I did."

"What did Melbourne beach highway show?"

"Same."

"Alright. So we have to show she didn't die of bends in a lake."

"You have to. I have to explain probable motivation. I was thinking he wanted all her money without giving up any of his."

"What's her value at death?"

"Insurance to next of kin not quite a hundred grand IRA, then there's her retirement benefit, plus she has a house. It could add up after a while."

Life must have seemed interminable, undeniably inexorable, each and every down swill another hapless new carnivorous redundancy, always a clavichord of interminable silence, the bastardization of sand moving against pits of marked persuasion of recently lost sand. All too quiet was the breath of enunciations as though every syllable of release carried with it some trace of what had gone before, teems of rill and brine, of baths of sequestered anchovy, the farther the sequel of salt lay a larvae or gelled impregnation as it were, the downs repeatedly spilling forth with slippage underwater, erosion upon erosion, happenstance of mud reviling from its vertical embankment. Of the eels and compressed fish that poked through the soil like a flurry of drills all at once or periodically making a duct for other filmy creatures to pronounce through, there were none bestial to lie at the bottom squid like or with tentacles to vary the cast and dye of ocean as it arose in a distended enormity beneath a boat or like a cloud with petals embracing the fog and chill. The sense of carrying dirt and gravel beyond a series of waves could but be taken up in a feast of crescent as all impurities came to rest in the same displacement of trapped anemones each branch building upon an ever panoramic sea line shelf of strange aggravations, globules and plant-life until at last flora of the underworld expanded in shimmering blue and grey amidst white extravagances of sand.

The cold stung the skin with a bracing immobilization of which consciousness seemed dulled, a minimum percentage use of the limberness as if one was leaden;

In a second the awareness took in the clear clairvoyant blue waters, immobile also, neither drifting nor moving, stagnant, non buoyant;

Next to no sound – the ocean was imperceptible, implacable, without resonance, a massive pooling surface, a nothingness, to wiggle took great compensation and produced a sting of a cramp in the ankle;

The team would jump in repeatedly wearing briefs without wet gear until they could produce the exact spot where the victim had bit her tongue and was dragged in either to a waiting vehicle or onto a boat;

The chill, unusual to this portion of the Australian east, even of Tasmania sea, produced no severity of distress, not the sharp chop to the waist of an under toe nor the suppression of breath as paralysis set in. The glucose intolerant transfixiation could be bends under the right death knell despite contradictory beliefs as to what conditions caused each.

But the vomit squelched it, and she was unable to cough or to swallow. Somewhere in her brutalization she was stultified, unable to fight her oppressor, silenced or immobilized into slow reactions to respond.

It was their job to determine what had occurred and under

exact circumstances.

Almost dead, although she was trained for underwater safety, she had very few responses left to her. It would seem her ex-husband was operating at all costs, she couldn't come out of the water.

The assumption was her ex-husband had never acknowledged what he was doing on Rudall River in India or at the quiet end of the Cooktown coast, but it was sufficient that once discovered he penetrated their base and killed them;

Of all the infamous illegal ocean-monitoring activities, underwater landslides and coastal erosion occurred the most often, one every fifteen to twenty years, during which a perpetrator had to be ready to make certain owners abandoned their houses even if they had already left them disposed of.

Whatever the illegal sham – hurricanes, tornados, spouts, sudden erosion producing sand drifts or fast-moving gravel beds into ravines – the certainty was Mary had come upon it, possibly on a computer, possibly in her investigation of slamming waves into the coasts which produced destruction and debris.

Who might notice while flinging a net and waiting for swells of low waves the precise moment the water reared to a terrifying height of sixty feet and proceeded to advance in, hurtling gigantic amounts of water onto lawns and dirt roads, pulling in retreat depths of feet of mud and cement sidewalks? If blasts eliminated five hundred yards from the coast in every year, and the Search & Rescue resolved these thunderous erosions and sink-wells by rolling in ten foot waves every winter, it made sense people might eventually leave. In time developers could pick up two thousand acre feet for less than ten thousand dollars, no amount of risk able to be offset.

FIVE

Rain was everywhere in the Micronesia twenty, coming down hard, splashing huge puddles with AIS pinwheels in the ocean. The torrential rain made an eerie sound like rust hinges opening and closing, far off long remembering whinny of a harbor motor. The sound persisted, coming closer, fading in the wind again, an improperly working sheller in an industrial yard. Winter had released a glowing silvery light, ample sunlight filtering through all windows despite the downpour. Gabby pulled her raincoat up around her ears and face as she left her car and made a run for the station office nearly evading a turning car which splashed mud behind her. Off shore the boats had come loose. Canoes without outboards were abandoned, drifting on low swells. One couldn't get to them though, they could wind up all the way in the reefs, technically in Australia there were no velocity spouts, cyclones, tornados or hurricanes, almost no rain at all. Except high winds. Plenty of that, and the ocean current never got below sixty degrees. The winds moved sand and empty shells into piles, what was on the ground told weather technologists what type of ocean was moving in before the waves took height. The alerts went out at dawn and at four; especially on the wharves where coffee was grown off major tributaries inland from the gold coast. Guavas and pale flesh melons were also grown on same river. Ten thousand workers were potentially affected in Sydney's pharmaceutical packaging industry that took warehouses off every wharf and harbor.

Through the month of February when the waves surged up like emerging islands that heaved swarms of larvae the peaceful boats were pulled adrift. Powerful tugs carried canoes far past stone-walled harbors onto an open sea frought with entanglements of sogged nets. When the pounding waves thrashed and abutted high tide unfurling an unanticipated drama, boats by the dozens heaved and fell like dozens of crates on endlessly rolling crashers, dark green garlands like chores falling into an hourglass as wave replaced wave. Monsoons churned the seas up; the heat stacked rooms of seaweed in hallways. A mountain of ascending battered smooth-swept sea the shallow blue climbed the grade, ever determining the spellbound glistening film sticking on the sand, ever flowing backward to rivulets of spawning ink-blots, some like murky indentations awaiting the delicate horns of seaweed.

The psychology of living on an island was ever present, an unwelcome homily of containment, consumption and anxiety rolled into one, an untoward anticipation that one could be trapped in an advancing ocean or under the structure of the forest should the currents overcome the soil and leave sinkholes. There were boundaries that brought one in sharp, that exposed non-consensually, suddenly, provocatively, which promised compromised roads stymied by depositions of cruelly crumbling erosion and wind backed branching chemical deposits rained out. You felt surrounded by a finite boundary, the knowledge of it never left, you knew where the beach ended, where depth began, how far out you could walk, where the land fell off like a cliff.

When the news article on Arugam Bay was released about a fishing resort village of twenty-four fishing huts in Sri Lanka burned on the beach due to a petroleum spill and in time after sitting empty for years it became a gigantic resort; this became a hard-felt reality of there being no escape. A journey across the continent took four days; the notion that small peninsula villages were a subdued tropical advantage in some hundred islands was still overlooked, even if many inhabited without consent. This desire that it was possible to live off the land for eight months planting taro and island radish and salting trap-lines in the sand with hooks for eels and clam clusters was sufficient for any size family whose house was paid for. It was something of an inconvenience to travel as far as Perth, an airplane left weekly from Dawson which was slightly less advantageous, and between Townsville and Melbourne three airplanes flew a day simply for passengers. Therefore for reasons of trade prosperity replaced knowing fear that abandonment was possible, large cities sent search teams north of Townsville daily and at least one fishing corporation with a fleet of three ventured as far as Indonesia and farther Micronesia inter-ports bringing fiberglass boats with motors for those months when swamping became life-threatening. It was the mud, always the mud, slippery and slimey and crumbling beneath the foundations that raised many a village on boathouse floors, victims wound up with the look of raised purple shavings on their arms, having operated plantation coolers or turned them into shell shuckers. Sediment trapped like sand mixed clay beneath a slanted flooring, proved a rising well in showering rain, the next worst houses in salty grasses where the tide kept receding, half city blocks, leaving the sand bare, grainy, capable of wreaked erosion, boats far beyond reach, clay uprooting pipes, a marked dominion incapable of offering escape, to traverse the newly formed sand was to break a leg. There was not an analyst who wouldn't say it was the receding soil that took canoes out to sea or caused the soil to run to ruin, beached humps of rust-iron dirt created indentations like footholds that measured the inch to the racing surface, a bluish egg white film covering the sand, glints capturing sunlight, minute starfish and anemone in ocean water brackets, all the food in the shallow, underwater plateaus – urchins, sea cucumbers, seaweed, shrimp – stayed until a new surf, frothy and pounding, sent them crashing.

Gabby stood dressed in black lace vest and girdle, thin shiny black high heels, her fluffy blond hair tied into a short pony tail, Mardi Gras black mask, a constant smile of wine mauve lipstick, showing no disruption of ease, while somewhere nearby metal rattled up and down alleys, tinsel turners clanged loudly to raise the chill on the back of the neck, eerie chimes resounded from doorsteps. Beside her, Chief of Morgue of Darwin Shore Leonard Randolph, also dressed for the Mardi Gras in all yellow lace mask and yellow lace arms and satin jacket with white tight trousers showing off his sturdy debonair physique which was the result of Marine readiness training and yellow and white cowtans, his jet black crewcut complimented by the season that gave his skin a mildly tan color. Together they drowned the effects of a few reefers in high gins and feasted on prawns and pimento and Indochinese pot stickers, a sweet combination of pork, pickle and dumpling sauce. They were joined by everyone in his unit with the exception of Chief Inspector Jean Davenport. All told, some seventeen people peppered by five hours of festivities of reamers, champagne goblets, and allegedly none of the stoned-out behaviors for which tourists traveling into the region claimed shameful, agonizingly stupid acts; having stopped in at Block 18 for Chablis, sausage, beet and cheese bread before making their way into a tavern for linguine, where they met up with four of their airmen and aviation technicians and spent the hour boasting about who could remain underwater the longest and number of general cardiovascular pull-ups and push-ups without going flush, and finally onto one of two big easy bars to evade the local Doppler of low 21, frosted rain and low moving bathing currents.

The night was foggy, drizzling, damp to the bone except inside the bar where heaters kept in a mild warmth and bar glasses chinked. The conversation was raucous, detective and chief sparred in a game of dice while reviling the more recent lab reports, the sensational cause of death listed as embolism while walking not yet in floodwaters, bad enough because of the hoopla it stirred up in the lab.

"Got you on nine," Gabby said, squaring off with a six and three.

He shook the glass and rolled out two fours. "You might have me. What's my score?"

The scorekeeper told them, she had 114 to his 276. He could afford a few losses.

"I found a sharpener wound on Ayr's," as she was coming to be referred to. "Right below the right trapezes, the bullet grazed one of three aortas, but flooded making it a dum-dum rolled or hard lined and not a legitimate steel encasing. The entry was .8 cm and three-quarters inch deep, blood loss approximately a half pint. It's a lot of blood. I'd have to say her assailant knew what he was doing. I asked for a finger and thumb release as to consistency of dummy from Missing & Search."

"They'll take a week because they cross-verify," she said circumspectly with the presumption that he probably knew they gave no estimates.

"Oh, it doesn't worry me if they take eight days, I'm a patient pupil. Let's take a look-see at the presumption. We were thinking she blew the whistle on him on these river-ocean swept to sea cases, that he had gotten the floors on these coastal places to slide into the beach during high wind and was seeing a profit somewhere along the way."

"I'm not altogether certain we have anything on him, at least nothing definite."

"It's open and shut."

"For a rifle death, yes, most likely a small gauge Winchester. Orange tongue convicts. But we don't know it's the husband even though he threatened her multiple times. A court will say that was his style of self-expression. All talk."

"His jeep was dusted. The passenger seat and carpet had Ayr dirt and red crystal salt adhering to it enough to strongly suggest he gave her a ride."

"It's possible he doesn't deny it. He may not be the last person who can say they saw her alive. We don't know. Why a stop to Mel beach? Why when found was she tied up on a boat? These are essential questions."

Gabby shook the die and threw them. She rolled a double one. "Jesus, look at that, will you?"

He played his game pulling a six and a four. He rolled again, this time two fives.

Leonard gave a smart grin. "It'd be easier explained if she was in the ocean, had to be rescued by a vessel hook at five miles out, administered oxygen, IV drip and then died due to blood loss. You would say too much had gone wrong within a forty-eight hour time frame."

"Well, that's just it. I have a revealing statement. He asked a week ago for an available cement-laying reef boat to be on hand between sundown and sunrise for the morning she was found."

"He actually scheduled a last meal fishing boat – you have his voiceprint on that?"

"I do."

"How many times did he schedule this past year? Twenty-five times? It's probably something he often does. Look at where he's going by boat, Indonesia, India, Jakarta, Ceylon, somewhat inevitable I would say."

She conceded quickly. "Well, as it so happens, I have another source."

"It has to prove with finality. To err is to be human, to kill is to covet."

"Where does the burden of the state rest, on the bile or on legal measures?"

He threw a die and came up with two. "How about you just concede the game?"

"Oh, I'm sure I can get you," and tossed hers for a six. "You say Ayr died of orange bile which means the bullet killed her. Coroner says no water."

"That's because they found no water in the lungs. That means she wasn't drowned. It was presumed she was fed Ayr dirt at some point prior to being shot. Mel black sand was put over her clothing to make it look as though she was at a black sand beach which suggests she may have scheduled for Med-Evac as well. Length of estimated time to travel by boat from Mel to Great Barrier was one ten hour day plus eight hours. If he traveled by vehicle the road travel would be shortened by three hours. Once she was dead on deck, her assailant had to have a way off the boat by scuba. That's easily two tanks."

"Travel time from Eyre to Adelaide?"

"Slightly under eight hours with bumper to bumper traffic for the first mile and a half out of Adelaide. All told it was a total of two days to carry out a lethal hit."

"Well, here's a concern. Since there was no way to know in advance when Ayr would be assigned for training, she had maximum a month when she would have known herself. He had scheduled the boat only after she was on site, but he had packaged the orange dirt three to six months earlier. Each medical outcome was designed for deliberate camouflage. Bile was produced by last meal. Knowledge as to when the palms start to turn black occurs after sixteen hours which places the body in Mel at about eighteen hours. That makes the person who assigned her to training an accessory before death."

"Good thinking, I concur. I think there must have been a point at which he decided, this was it; she had to die."

"Maybe before the children reached age twenty-one and when she achieved job permanence and her death would benefit him as lawful next of kin."

She gave another nod. "A man who's so treacherous, there should be something else on him, lots and lots of things people could have gotten wrong over the years. He was after all the one who thought up the use of roped nets as a way for a person to survive the powerful swift recession of waters."

A constable lab couple waved goodbye. Leonard nodded toward them.

She said, "Apparently he complained about her behavior when he made airman. He told his first therapist around the time he sought out Evac that she turned on the hall light before she came upstairs and he couldn't get back to sleep. You can just hear it, she gets home late at night, he's a light sleeper, the littlest thing awakens him, he can't get back to sleep, lies awake half the night being angry."

"That should convict all by itself. Driving onto the grass to set off the sensors."

"Try this. He called someone after that last stalking episode. He told them he had a problem. The man at the other end advised him, 'fire once, move to the van.'"

"How come we didn't send a fire medic to his home?"

"We did. We took a full evaluation including vitals."

"So do we have him locked up?"

"No. He's a cold one, textbook systolic."

"You would think 100/100, a rage bomb walking asleep. Alright, so what do you think you have?"

"Very little name-calling, all innuendo. He told her for example that the children hated her. 'They hate you,' your spine just tingles, he's pure venom. We could use logic for stay-away orders of a hundred to three hundred yards."

"From how many feet was she actually fired upon?"

"That's it, that's the estimated number, one hundred to three hundred yards."

"Domestic violence, court-ordered sanction."

"On the hammer."

"Is that the entire conversation? Go blow her away?"

"No. Quote, 'I have a problem.' 'What nature?' 'Wife.' 'Fire once, move to the van.' End quote."

"The tape tests for all complications?"

"Voiceprint is iron square. Lab said justification was weak because he doesn't ID himself."

"It's one thing to photograph a bad scene, another to not know you have a scene until the photos are developed. It's an expression, airplane from days of the dead. It's just instinct. If it doesn't convict enough, it's a rosary. Churches, las pietas/hear grinding mortar/no one weeps, llorar/but then no one returns, pero entonces ningun se revuelvan/todos piedras/palabras, cruces de tajada, los cielos, hablan el mismo lengua/el razon tiene voces, chico cairoblas, young misunderstandings."

"You're profound, but it breaks my heart, Leon."

"Don't worry. I'll hunt up a sufficiency analyst."

Six

The file was packed with an older case that had bearings of two assassinations. The facts contained therein read as follows:

1960
Death of Chief of Forensic Science and Medicine in Scotland, UK
Coroner for Copenhagen found dead

Body of Dr. Collin Bell found dead of pistol-shot to the head severing the right aorta. His remains were discovered in trenched soil at Lessen Prison in Northern Ireland near Ft. Clevold, Station Island. Surgical intervention to stem flow of blood was attempted by Sir Henry James of Fleetwood.

Three hours after surgery was begun, Dr. Bethany was found dead having suffered either a fatal stroke or suffocation. Despite lack of evidence of homicide, cause was listed as suspicious. Post mortem was performed at Royal Academy College of Medicine, ordered by the chaplain at the college due to number of mortems already scheduled and in progress in Surrey, Essex, England; there the Chief Constable signed a certificate in attendance by two since-revered fellows-in-training, John Mitford and Leith Donegal, 4th and 5th year physician interns.

Request to files —

Any predispositions preceding discovery of Dr. Bethany.
Any prior cases remaining at inquest.

Reply —

1958
Mary Elizabeth Woolsey, post mortem reviewed by Chief
of Forensic Sciences, Dr. Collin Bell. Body found at Cley-on-
sea, England, severe damage presumably caused by speeding
boat, involved parties Teressa Von Mierden, wife of Thomas
Woolsey and relation of Sir Winston Oliver of Cumberland
and two Woolsey sons: Kaith Donegal and Jocklin Abernathy,
both of Southwold.

1956
Police station, Louth, Lincolnshire
Kaith Donegal held on suspicion of attempted murder to a
citizen on the coast of Papua

The file information showed patterns of age. There were
the four crimes to promote an idea that Navy marines who
embarked on the high seas in order to bring medical supplies to
expedition-course islands entered a prima facie sort of embar-
kation authority where they could restore or build any type of
towns as they sought fit. After laying down a sluice, then succumbing a trenched out ditch for the laying of pipes, and eventually having to erect some sort of either prison pantry, hospital
or manufacturer near the sluice, the officers could decide what
other institutions and housing to put down including collecting rental monies and restoring any damaged stair or wall to
house and sea port. It might be viewed as fairly ridiculous that
two great coroner chiefs had been tossed to the well, all for a
luxury tax which only an officer for island infirmaries could
collect, but a season of buttered baking seemed to have clawed
a tithing.

∧∧∧

From the leeward side, the ocean was enormous, engulfing, hurling with disquietude, teeming with sand, sapphire, cold, forbearing, dark and deep, unknowable, clandestine, studied, glimmering and shining, cacophonous, a raging thunder of forceful gales, crashing and assailing and battering, onto beaches these powerful forces became an outpouring of rivulets of sand quickly depleting, rising and advancing uphill, all laboring over rock, flinging seaweed of dark rich green wands wreaking an unfulfilling abandoning demonic canon of booming sound, a wretched greedily devouring barbarous calamity, winds howling through city streets and shores alike leaving in its wake strings of darkly teal garlands where in a bay rooftops like aimless barges float downstream. The ferocity of these gales struck as an ignominious force, denting vehicles, plundering boats, a wrath of turbulence barring passage, clobbering inlets, electricity shorting, towns blacking out, left to endure an after-math of violent solitude, sobering in its redundancies,

The manufacture of flooring was stocked full into cisterns which backed up with bark of trees, and it became an advisable necessity to use survivor bulbs to separate usable bark from twig, having started often during winter as work orders for inmates for prison industrialization signed by John Leicester himself, for which wood was pinned up and placed onto a brick layer assembly for 1' x 4" x 2 1/2" wide, then majored down intended for use inside houses from four prison plants with eaves including New gate in Dublin, Fleet in Clegness, Hoboken in Rumania, and a separate plant at Killeen, Ireland. Built and staffed by the Swedish, their prisons came of use for east Scotland in 1948; although for India England trained her entire physician staff who had to be all physicians, no nurse, no wardens, and applicants had to have done bench law, aside from this Sweden ran Danemora, Dart moor and Ludfenken or Marshal sea, until a man was thrown from a cell to his death at Danemora and it was shut down pending reconstruction and inmates transferred to Ludfen, their leaseholds were under deed-prison plats, the clink, lock-up, hold, penal settlement, chain gang, criminal asylum, one free world to a next.

The listed destruction of Cook town coastal houses included the mysterious drifting of basement foundation and often the mysterious deaths of coast house owners who were expert swimmers capable of running a net and securing against sudden floodgates. A similar list as to the Bell murder was made available for the Cook town forty residents, two who died. All sections were bedded and sifted with a description per pan, rock matter separated from soft and hosing out of all pipes; the lab recommendation was to trench down 4';

The post-mortems for the two Australians were performed by William Oliver, but their bodies could not be received by London due to continuing inquiry of the death of Thomas Woolsey, Coroner, age 81, arch deacon found dead in a churchyard in Arundel, Sussex, England; Arundel sits on the Arun River just up from Little hampton, in the rural lowlands.

Chief of Prisons,

Ft. Clevold
Skagness transfer

Assess Fleet for clogged pipes beneath eaves of plant. Compare to nearby coastal houses. Assign for filings removal.

Office of Utility
Louth

Work orders put out by station asked for demarcation of pipes, Fleet. Investigation finding showed a wall cracked, no outlet, window intact, pipes clogged to plant, no entrance to sewage.

Request for information —

Was material introduced into ground by gauze linen?

Reply —

No. By weed – it absorbs all water.

Request —

What happens when there is no water?

Reply –

When tide goes out water goes down. It is essential in farming bog land that there is substantive water with which to grow fields. Chimneys stand at farthest up to a sixth of a half mile from prisons or bark. Weed in river bottom is deemed the best method to reduce over outage. Per advisement pipes were opened up and bark by-product taken out. Straw bulbs for bark found. No contradictory work order for prison industrialization, all apply; Utility placed all pipes.

Status on 30 prison yard houses —

At Fleet each house is situated on the beach, has 700 square feet oblong, entry into drawing room, dining and small kitchen with pantry, one bedroom, separate small bath, and lower easement level with yard or beach. The addition of a room alongside the kitchen prevented backup from chimney. Kitchen pipes were extended to enhance collection. Where straw bulbs were found in some residences, yards were retrenched.

Brigg became a temporary placement of criminal offenders offset by lack of adequate prison housing or cellblock prior to being sent to Marshal sea, Denmark section. Men only.
No further use of wharf shelf in Darwin, Australia after

1922. Prisoners remanded to Newgate, Ireland for clinical physician observation. Danemora to accept men only. Scottish Borders women's prison opened in 1963 June. Scotland, King's Bench, orders were approved to transport females to Swedish-run prisons in Bangladesh upon receipt by a Swedish military commanding officer. Absolutely no to lighthouse confinement.

All nurse-physicians, male only, were reassigned. This classification was not permitted to travel aboard ships.

Request —

Is there a military prison in Scotland?

Reply —

Yes. Fleet.

Request —

Is there a pre-existing situation as to soil consistency?

Reply –

Land content is predominantly bog, gravel when poured is liquid with low base cement permitting land to escape intact as water re-asserts in unanticipated regions.

Request –

Does soil allow pipe to rise?

Reply –

Soil is consisting of same material, material allows workers trapped in sewage pipes to rise to surface when tide comes in, resistance to moving pipes is assured by trapping.

The Sydney Bureaux d'aide criminel juridique in the Hotel du Parlement sat on the fourth floor overlooking both the
waterway drain and the colorful light blue and sapphire Pacific
Ocean. On occasion the surfer's team paddled out on seven long
flat board scullies, ten rowers apiece, to board a ship docked
a half mile in domestic waters. From his desk Jeffrey Steed,
Constable Inspector of some twenty-four years on the same job
nationwide, a likable seasoned glinty man five feet eight, dark
reddish hair cut in layers, usually found wearing knit compatible navy trousers, braced white shirt and blue sweater with
elbow patches, gave off a confident air that he could find anyone within a twenty-hour leeway. Constable Steed hadn't liked
Bryce Finley at all. The one and only time he interviewed him
in the booth was at upper Perth as the plateau coast at Brooms
was known. Mary Choice was herself a perfectionist, her husband was something of a steelhead fisherman, aggressive to
a tune, a male who had to be on the go at all times. Choice
proved she could be dedicated. For Finley everything was super
fast, he gave no reflective time to the job, whatever was on his
mind was a mystery. He described himself as a tackle coach,
a tumbler who was capable of jumping the road as it turned
over, a usual panoramic field task for new Med-Evac marines.
He also took pride in the fact that he could run across a rope
bridge in a minute flat and sit-fly on a zip cable down a mountain through forest or jungle in implacable silence. He was the
man who by his own description was all ears and all eyes to the
job, a job which gave him ultimate latitude over entry and departure, both over land and under water. He placed a bumper-
trailer on his wife's jeep to determine where she went, and then
was stymied by the fact her jeep wound up parked at airports
and he had no further access to information without arousing
higher-up suspicion. That was around the time he purchased
a high powered telescope to take pictures of her at her house
from a nearby friend.

Jeffrey Steed had one solid reference. He had the ram-
charger being accused by his wife of having murdered a half

dozen men out on New Guinea coast. It was one of those hold-your-breath responses in which it was obvious the man knew exactly what his wife was intimating and then in a cold blood-ed, casual telephone call to a hit man, he asked for a rifle draw. Steed had pursued the line-up certain he had the case. The inquest examiner, an unduly cautious individual, didn't think it would sell the case in court. Ideally Homicide had to nab Fin-ley at the scene – obtain a photo of him obtaining keys to a van with high powered sight rifle or drunk sitting inside his jeep in traffic with a body wrapped up in the trunk, or best of all captured in a photo taken by street Intel laying a string of clam shells on the beach draft-scale-level into a home or attaching it to a fence of a dead man's property. Indonesia or Twenty would do. He sent for a status file through Fingerprints.

The desk sheet showed five photos across and down for a total of twenty-five per sheet. The storage had grouped the positive fingerprints by incident of domestic violence but had not looked for on-site incidents nor for non-spousal related in-teractions which meant someone had begun an inquiry. The photographs corresponded to twelve separate harassment in-cidents including eavesdropping of her answering machine, video target surveillance of her driveway, intimidation with use of her house sensor lights, tagging her vehicle with a bumper-beeper, and obnoxious content telephone calls to the home. Two photographs gave his home on the Gold Coast below Sydney, level drive, three story condo facing the harbor, amply furnished, one photo placing his telescope and corresponding E-fax. When the call was made to the rifle silencer man, the telephone from which the call was made was photographed through glass of a second story study, a red couch, recliner chair, light stand with swirling colors and glitter and a long desk with a stereophonic computer system on it.

Macklin William had pulled the deaths of which there were ten men in Indonesia and nineteen in Solomon Islands whose bodies had been swept to sea, at least six Micronesians who were tangled up in rope nets saving them from having sunk far below. He always considered that the fifty-eight dead in Chile and the seventeen from Veld had been submerged in partially frozen water. The British Isles had a few files for any of these deaths. The cross computer pages gave some ironic facts which Macklin thought might impress any investigator. The dead had all been expert swimmers varying in age from sixty-six to eighty-five who had at one time demonstrated proficiency at around age thirty-five years old for avoiding rapids, tumbling inside a net while underwater, and riding surf inside a canoe at forty miles an hour wave action. At least half had semi-frequent experience sailing along a forest cable zip-line and could do the same in the ocean between small islands. Thus it made no sense that when the ocean hurled up the beach incline and seeped into the basements that even with walls giving way the well-trained, agile men should have been able to grab their rope net which was attached to a cable line and prevent being ditched into the scandalous sea. It made even less sense that when the waters receded chunks of previously pristine smooth beach had been gouged down to half a foot up through the yards of long-secure houses, many surrounded by wire fences.

Macklin was himself in his late fifties. He had ocean-rinsed blond hair, a fit physique, tanned, with all the attributes of a handsome man, small nose and ears, square chin, dreamy blue eyes, a shy smile, who the women loved to tease. In his youth he ran a diver's bureau hiring out fifteen divers to retrieve submerged boats in the water ground cover, repair cable, find flooring that had washed away, siphon off water by hose after ocean water flooded yards, any task the military marine already did for the counties but not for residents. He himself had gone with the Missing & Search into Indonesia after report of the initial death to discover the yard gouged with string-ups some-times mistaken for clam bedding or land mines which they were neither, and not really detonators which could destroy a place. String-ups were used for tough lime walls after multi-ple seasons of seriously eroded embankments. It was his good judgment that what had occurred may as easily have been acci-dental, something on the order of slightly arthritic men whose first sign of age was that as they climbed the few stairs that led from their cellars to their kitchens they weakened in hip or leg and fell as inside those four walls the water rose suddenly and swiftly threatening to eradicate the walls, floor, stairs and pull the crumbling debris past the yard and down the beach and into the churning waves topsy-turvey. But the photographs were misleading. The backyards looked trenched, the interiors of many a basement had withstood the pressure of collapse, only where there was still four feet of water sitting in a room was there any sense of what other houses had withstood, and in few places the wood walls and stucco had caved in and resembled smashed exteriors, trees blown away, roads having been truncated and washed away.

In one lone photo in moonlight where the Randall River in India had uncharacteristically risen to sixteen feet, for the rivers were maintained at low levels under seven or eight feet during howling monsoon warm weather to secure against drownings, the photographer had ambitiously captured three men all similar height and stature as Finley casting wide nets onto the stairs emanating from the river and darting the entry doors from sting guns, very thin rifles manufactured by a Sri Lanka store. Macklin removed the darkish photo and placed it beneath a magnifier and the men sprang to life – unfortunately for life Finley was not one of them although his unit joined that other unit on occasion. These three were feared throughout the deltas of India rivers, if for no other reason than because they were from the Mekong jungle where rope nets captured a soldier on foot and placed him high among the trees with snakes and the ground covered with dense vegetation nevertheless contained rut mines which were capable of blowing a foot deep hole. The entire situation was checked against Bibliotheque et Archives nationals at the Centre d'archives de Universite Dundee, Scotland as to suspected causes of injury. The Ministere de l'Immigration contained a file without photographs of infirmed citizens from Malaysia who had shipped out to the islands after suffering an outbreak of cholera. The incidents were reported at about 0230 when high tide whipped in with stiffening at the joints, inability to move easily, homes being assaulted by running water, the noteworthy sound of fizzing coming from all directions, water pouring through vents, calls for help and no one coming, survivors trying to get away from a flooding swamp and unable to out swim it they drowned. The bodies pretty much had the same look to them – rigor at ten hours with greenish skin, at twenty hours purplish tone, and at over thirty hours pale black tinge having taken hold of the surface skin color and rigor passed. Choice had gone well over thirty hours from initial time of death and her grayish skin showed it, so unlike river deaths in the Bengali where the ceramic heating had exploded and hit the victim leaving an odd brick layer look to the skin when in fact corpuscles had broken at once just prior to drowning. The hundred and fifty bodies worldwide that washed out to sea had very little of any injury about them; occasionally an orange or purple tongue revealed gunshot or poison by arsenic, but usually by the time the lifeboats caught up to them their deaths were deemed accidental to the monsoon wreaked weakness of the land of islands. Many elderly fell asleep sitting up having watched television; the moment a wave crasher hit, telephone lines went down in an instant, lights doused, if a levy or containment wall busted, the wave action that had occurred four miles away rose like a shock, crashing every which way, bursting with hurricane force, jetting down every street producing a city under water in minutes. Fishing traps laid into the sand with snares rose with a rising tide and could snag a person in the neck or in the gut. If the sea threw a wall down, floated cars, it was a very powerful tidal force that could not be escaped as one might during a wildly raging fire in an underground shelter. In hurricane strength of a pitching sonorous high wind, new mud washed away fast, cars upended, houses caved in, everyone had to leave for county shelters. Where bodies were recovered and found to have clear orange tongue, then they were shot. Even if with vigorous action of turbulent flooding a bullet was shimmied free of its wound, the tongue would still be orange.

Macklin studied weather for Eyre and decided that during

the weekend of her death the sun was shining and the temperature was a hot ninety-six degrees. It was the equator that ran through Lake Victoria, Indonesia, Micronesia, Kiribati and Ecuador and kept these waters warm seventies all year long. Even Tasmania had lost seven to the sea below it. Choice was anaerobic strong, she had tested in the top two percent of training camp marines, could stay underwater three minutes, cable-dived to fifty feet below and could pole vault through low river and marsh. In addition she had an ability to suppress bend response in surfacing for any aquatic environment. But fear was a mind-bender, a minute-by-minute reduction of endurance. One individual's long range telescope had produced the appearance of an act of madness, a dashing, arms held in rigid posture at chest height, Mary Choice, the salty sea in its tranquil blue beginning to wear down her flight. It was an odd photo because it caused him to be uncomfortably aware of a knife in the water shot. It reminded him also of a wrenching photo of a youthful Micronesian man, dark curly hair, deep tan skin, lithe weight, five feet seven, his tension worn over his face like a tight hollow grin, which he pulled out of his desk drawer for comparison. He too had wound up on the constable-inspector's table, dead. He too was tripped up around the ankles by two feet of shallow water; God only knew who or what was stalking him. At some assailable point his calves would have become too pained to keep up an advantage and when the rifle cracked, down he must have gone also, flung to his death like a fleeing doe. Macklin couldn't comprehend the image, as though the assailant could have been standing in a jeep he was also driving as he leveled Mary to her watery grave best western style, but there it was, a recognizable image, of a woman being ridden to her last moment.

He hummed Lover's Quarrel by Louie Sable as he examined the suspected scenes evident in forensic photos. 'You've got my number, I've got your face, I'll see you around that bend before you leave me.' There was Mary driving her own jeep through the Eyre during the warmest January of any year by Meteorology charts, then there was her running in wild madness, her body found on board a fishing boat, her face stuffed with orange Ayer dirt and a notebook worth of training camps at Ayer Rock on the table and inside the cave in the water. Dozens of marines carefully measured out an ounce of orange dirt, labeled it with a ruler, placed the evidence inside a folder. 'You won't leave me, Girl, oh Girl, you won't do me that way.' Macklin segregated Finley and his constable troopers and decided anything was possible, he could have realized he had a problem little sooner than he'd put a ring on Mary's finger. Maybe Finley married her to figure out just how much she knew; maybe he hadn't crossed the line yet; maybe he was operating a goon raid through Indochina's houses when the first victim showed up floating off the spillway on the north shore of Jakarta's back country; maybe Ayer was where they had their first fight. The subsequent dead showed up in the Tasman Sea after an exceptionally wet monsoon season which occurred during March and swept up through the Indian Ocean in forty knots westerly sweeping up into Shark Bay to Broome and across the ocean over Indonesia's large islands; two in the Gold Coast apparently having been blown over deck of small vessels; five at Timor were discovered clutching at vines; the very hot and wet season normally between December through March at eighty six degrees easterly high winds moving steadily taking up trees, bridge lights and harbor masts before rushing a downpour of three knots an hour into the clay and sand orchards; and everything vulnerable to the pernicious oceanic currents which increased in speed as they tore over land through ravines and dumped particles onto mountains. The course of climates altering none during a dry season April to August until the chill stepped in during July lowering the spell to a chilling penetrating receding ocean.

He finally shot off a query to Evidence asking, how much weather is capable of producing swamp and quicksand in the New South Wales?

The sand on her clothing and body was definitely from the Twelve Apostles along the far southern Mel coastline. It was spared that terse quality of being too dry like volcanic debris and instead was as fine as the deep rust muddy sand peculiar to the Ayer's desert from which it originated before being mixed with slate rock. Because the distinction of sand permitted no other location, it was exceedingly odd to find out the last occasion Mary was in Twelve Apostles was two years ago for a deep-sea cable descent to a hundred below in cold ocean. Even with a demanding reorientation schedule she was consistently assigned to the Timor Sea and to Great Barrier and thus saw almost nothing of the major cities bordered by the Tasman. Any combination of marine tidal and shallow water and fishing ocean travel had been routinely coveted by the marine themselves.

While inside his studio Chase LaMufti had run his dark colors through a sieve until he acquired the darkish brown he was after and threw it with force onto a wall-size canvas, flitting dark blue which ran in rivulets through the brown paint. It wasn't possible that the dead woman had acquired the dried blood off a long dead haul but that's what it was, a mixture of squid and dried blood that stuck to her clothes as though once placed in the net she had been turned onto her front side. There had to be a reason for it besides a possibility she had been stabbed with poison that the black blood of squid camouflaged.

Now at the lab he placed the small jar with the paint filtered mixture into a tube and the tube into a centrifuge and spun it down to a brown color and dipped a test tab in it. By degrees he had managed to come close to deriving a close match to the flecks of color stained off her clothing, causing him to determine that she had to have been saturated at some collection place where an entire haul was docked. Could be Melbourne, Canberra, even Sydney or Gold Coast, any that took in early morning catch to distribute to the restaurants. The wharf the boat began at was essential in order to determine estimated number of hours dead, but more so to rightly assess who might be the boat owner and taken her body into Great Barrier some ten hours away.

Or the black sand also was another diversion as the Ayer's dirt was. Any spoonful of dried blood identified itself by smell and color as squid. Squid came in early morning once a day for eighteen days from below Tasmania and sold at twenty dollars a serving. It was trail meat as white fish was called that was netted off any reef formation of at least ten years or more. Homicide freezer had already cleaned her off and with a microscope picked over her skin in as meticulous a scrutiny as any coroner routinely assessed, and that's when the bullet wound was found and orange tongue diagnosed which was insufficient to have killed her immediately in the instant of impact that the bullet struck her body. For it to have fallen out within minutes or hours of being shot, it was reasonable to consider it was made of a dummy material. At least that much wouldn't be known until the wound was scraped and the abrasion examined. The destructive properties of this particular black sand when combined with the effects of bloody squid parts seemed to have been deemed useful. He himself was neither a ballistics expert nor a coroner, but the reality of the situation pointed at the necessity of producing fatality. If after being shot, the sputum was orange barf, then she was dead, unable to be revived. Black bile said dried blood internally. In the absence of bile dried blood of squid had to serve a purpose. Maybe it was the prescription these killers fed all victims they killed.

He had typecast every palate of dried blood over the years. Few were the result of gored fish. His best guess here was their victims were snared intentionally or otherwise. In the past he had matched to dead dog and dead bird. Bird was black blood. All color determinants of relative value to orange were removed, this included yellows, flesh tones as well as variations such as peach, salmon or tangerine.

The victims suffered no smashed skull negating they were toppled after a rope bridge unraveled and pulled apart despite the finding made in Poisons in Hobart that one male was hung in a tree after having stepped onto a target net and another male dead after involuntarily falling face and shoulders into underwater grabbing clay mud contaminated by a brine-like substance and was unable to climb out. In Indonesia it could be the cement beneath a house was inferior or that there was no foundation to begin with. LaMufti wrote his diagnosis as followed, Hematocrit 38, death not due to blood loss, presence of dried blood presumed two days from many gored fish. He added a notation, if severe weather can be determined, for coastal wind warning or turbulent wind and mud-gouge-capable rainfall to which victim may have been subject, please define probable latitude.

Thus, there was no need to assess for prior weight of the body, since blood in the victim was not dramatically reduced nor was swelling evident. Constable Steed evaluated severity of range of motion. Victim had one pickle, not two, wound above the waist, not in the limb. Pickle was gone, removed by a surgeon with a steady hand or designated somehow to fall out or was accidentally gone. Bullets were that way – unpredictable. But despite no recovery of a bullet, the body lacked ease on the right side of the spine. Had the victim been propped, there might be some lack of motion permanently, but because she was assessed over three days dead, it was assumed the sting of squid and its blood anesthetized her wound causing partial temporary paralysis.

Of all results including lab, ballistics, poisons and soil composition of environment at death scene, Evidence still came in with a problem finding. It focused on legitimacy as to next of kin, shooting the determination of domestic violence back to Psychology.

The first authority under the Barbaric Act was to eliminate seizure of properties through any act of intentional homicide if death was imminent in the eyes of the law following any threat made to the person by a recognized individual of acquaintance to the victim. An inquiry found sufficient cause for homicide. The buoy lights at the harbor entrance of Townsville and after, at the one-half mile, showed the deck view with Bryce Finley at the wheel, rope net on deck. He was given a lie detector test which he failed. Normally he would be kicked out of service, but there was no direct proof that he gave her a goodbye. Psychology reported that the widow had described a felony to a psychotherapist as follows –

Her husband told her over dinner that a group of owners of small houses built on a western beach of Indonesia were already losing cement siding to their yards and as a result he stripped them down and tied them to their bedding. She reported that she told him his act was unjustifiable and immoral and told him she had put in a report to India authorities.

In addition it was revealed under redirect that he set off the sensor lights in the driveway and copied her messages off her home telephone and sent them to her work telephone and her cell phone. The Department reported that Finley traveled for work sixteen out of twenty-two work days in his capacity as a coastal marine for which he increased his regular salary of three thousand one hundred take-home pay by twelve hundred and fifty dollars. His therapist sent an investigator out to see his home which was described in a written narrative as in the affluent condominium high rise estates on the Gold Coast. It was a five bedroom, three bath flat located on the third floor overlooking the ocean and waterway, all dark blue carpet in the hall and bedrooms and wood floors in the living room and flagstone tile throughout a kitchen with modern appliances, immaculate to a fault, the entire floor plan taking up one half floor, costing Finley twenty-five hundred dollars. The therapist went on to say further that Finley was quite forthright about the problems in Indonesia and India that all victims bodies that were swept out to sea were saturated in black sand, many did have Ayers-looking sand in their mouths and many were found strung up by rope-net traps in trees and some discovered underwater in similar nets. A few who survived their ordeals described that they were pulled by their legs by unusual force into the current. Almost all suffered floods to their houses that took walls and basement floors and windows. The therapist asked Finley for his opinion, to which he replied the circumstances were unknown, some men were strung up over rafters, several were shot, a large number drowned in the middle of nowhere with no one to see, their aging, very small houses on coasts with pretty white beaches. He said most houses once they were destroyed were never rebuilt. He said in rivers in India where he was sent to patrol, it was a common sight to see flotilla type floaters at night with full sensors on bright with a man steering, one to two who set shells and one who manned with a rifle. He had never done that sort of patrol himself; he was sent in with the Red Cross after a flood to secure people and look for bodies.

On another occasion Finley was asked about a man who had suffered a rifle shot and was given a diagnostic medical examiner evaluation of yellow tongue. Finley said it had happened just once in his entire career, a garbage runner who dumped quantities of refuse on an island in the Mekong delta had soaked the black blood of a cuttlefish into a wound already prepped with an IV congealing agent which after two small dark hours of loss of sight killed the man. Finley was given the man's job for the better part of a year before being transferred back to the rivers of India. Even with the necessary point by point plotting course, along with infrared to locate the men who were swept to sea, it was a tough line of duty to get to the sites in time and perform any number of enlistment protocols. Usually the current was swift moving, the boat task force although adequately staffed called for numerous rescues handled by stepping out into mined waters to grab a victim and haul him in. On tape for all eternity was the adviso, "That's my girl, good, take the towel, there, there, now we have you." Finley denied saying those words or hearing them spoken.

After careful scrutiny the Constable Inspector turned up evidence that a sea marine hook intern had suppressed a man's life by smothering his face with a cloth, for which all cameras were shaded, and rumor of this started an investigation for the man's body.

Gabby slammed a return serve that sent the ball at a direct delivery into charming bleached blond Constable Inspector Steed's opposite court and got it back in equal time with equal force of delivery; twenty back and forth swings before Steed hit the ball hard but low into the net. Gabby had been reassigned to the Gold Coast to a luxurious pad on the third floor facing into Finley's flat, the kids were fine despite the regiment tasks they performed at sunrise which included making their beds, polishing their boots, making closet and drawers neat, and cleansing shower stall and toilet and homework laid out with corrections, a set of four who spent their afternoons after school let out running about the beach. On Tuesdays and Thursdays she played tennis and Wednesdays through Saturdays she returned off a boat from the Great Barrier Reef often late after sunset at ten-thirty or eleven in summer months, these being January, February and March, and in winter cold months July and August putting in dark nights at the office or jostling over terrain in her jeep on lakeshore roads doing surveillance stints on drug patrol of warehouses. The Constable Inspector had opened an evidence warehouse on the Dry dock wharf on the Gold Coast with the skipper's boat that had contained Mary Choice's body and live photo scenes five feet by seven feet of Mary at Eyre along with placement of the rifle-shot dummy into the right shoulder, photos of Mary's two-story house and street, joint excursions with her husband while living to training camps at Melbourne, Sydney and Whitsunday Island, and a confrontation of Bryce at his home. Psychology had it on advisement that Bryce had taken her to a refugee base in the South Pacific and showed her detention and bayonet fence perimeters miles off a tar road that led through choice oil refuse container basements;

and that she requested separation from him after leaving the base; launching off the tirade of hostile actions that led to the investigation of Mary's charge of severe domestic violence.

The tennis match drew to a conclusion, nine to two. Gabby was soaked through with sweat. Steed tossed her a wet cloth and slipped into an over shirt for the drive home to Sydney.

"There were some additional complications," he told her, as they left the tennis court and walked past an Olympic pool to a grass plaza and pavilion where bands played during the summer to an outdoor concierge for two sodas. "The suffocation cloth was ID'd to a male nurse aide who punched a marine on a ward in a base camp hospital. Apparently there was discussion that same weekend between Bryce and his brother of intent to stage a demolition on the coastal fronts on Fraser Island, and Bryce's brother sent a telephone inquiry to Mary during demolition."

"It could just be an unfortunate coincidence."

"Or it could be Bryce set a few things into motion just to make sure nothing could be tracked back to him."

"Was the telephone call received?" Gabby asked, not having heard this bit of information despite the considerable amount she had accumulated in the file.

"We know it had to be because Mary left the following Sunday from Townsville on a fishing vessel headed for another camp Bryce described."

Gabby said, "That's where she took the photo of the man in the water."

"Brave act," he replied. "Did anyone overhear what she told him?"

"She went straight to his home on Gold Coast Waterfront Drive. The neighbor heard him. She screamed at him, 'It's not your place to make that decision.' He said something like, 'He was drowning; he was already good as done.' He demanded to know what she was going to do. She said she had already taken care of the matter with the appropriate command. My guess is she thought he would be reassigned, but no decision like that has been made."

"What is the unofficial diagnosis on him?"

"The Darwin Yard thinks he expected her to agree with him. It's entirely possible he hoped to introduce a spouse legitimacy into their rescue unit. The belief has not been submitted yet, that he killed her in order to acquire her house and death benefit which is at least fifty thousand."

"There's always a financial motivation in these domestics. The money is the motivation for the job."

"They also agreed with your guy."

"Chase."

"Yes, Mary was injected with epinephrine into the wound and smeared with cuttle blood to confuse any black bile she might spit up even though it's pretty certain she was very dead by then."

"I'm so impressed, Steed. You're always much better than I already think you are."

He bent forward, dreamy eyes, his light silver blond hair ruffled by the wind, and pecked her on the cheek. "You're better at everything yourself, Gab."

They walked to the parking lot.

"What's Chase's idea?" He asked her.

"Well, I honestly think he's going for the Finley yacht. It's my guess that's how he got off his cod boat. It's clear the man has gone everywhere with his brother on that thing including flying sails in the annual Rolex Sydney Hobart race. Probably early in their marriage Mary went everywhere with them as well."

"How're we doing overall?"

Even if she was not yet reasonably content, they were beginning to acquire a clear case. All the ten typical pointers had been identified. The skin color and temperature of the body, wounds and ankle and joint swelling, scars and marks and fingerprints, presence of poison, everything but a weapon, probable environment of death, vomit placed into a jar and smell of death. The real issues had to be addressed: where did his brother dock his yacht, where was it right this minute, did he have a house somewhere, and when he took it out, where did he go?

She drove home to the beachfront property she shared with Chase. The living room was overflowing as usual with taped prints, sample voice prints noted by crimson and green charting designating matching telephone calls, assorted other evidence from the lab brought home for her perusal, dusted surfaces for prints, spool to spool documents including running scatter, shouts – far off and near, battery shoves, slaps and raised voices, his most useful document was of Finley's voice on board the yacht with filtration sound bars of other vessels on the ocean and dates of collection when Mary's voice was picked up by his yacht. At this stage the inquiry was focused on the telephone and computer contacts picked up by micro-technology, also charted on a separate diagonal band. Chase worked in the dining room at a table fronting a wall of windows, some cracked open midway down a series of slats, on the other side of which was a wooden deck that ran the length of the five room house along the beach. Fifty yards separated them from the water which never advanced all the way to the house. It was a complacent living suitable for detectives who were almost never home.

She parked her notebook and camera on the kitchen grey and black Formica counter and made herself a plate of yabbies on toast and poured herself a cup of brewing coffee. Sipping it, she added a bit of cream.

"Were you to the surveillance?" she asked.

"Several hours. That Finley is a sly snoot. He denied following Mary to Whitsundays and out to Fraser and hooking several lines in through the reeds, but we've got spools and camper beepers both."

"What about feed off roof tops, antennae and the sort?"

"One radio scoop, but that was months ago. He's been extremely careful since then. We sat out with a long speaking wire on the beach where the boats dock and he hasn't been back since."

"Are there many strips of photos without landmark identifiers?"

"Hundreds. The crackling chirping wires are the best bet. The problem aside from the shell firings by sniper fire is the drownings that occurred due to weather, and I accept that. Winds are thirty miles an hour. Everything flies, shuttered windows, fences, satellite dishes. It's a real gale."

Gabby sat at the head of the dining room table, the door open, waves moving slowly up the incline, the beach an abalone shell patina on the damp beige sand. She ate three bites of yabbie crabmeat and set the plate aside.

Chase was rinsing out a solution of sewage to eliminate impurities most of which showed as greenish gunk in a tall jar. "Before we can make a determination as to where her unwashed clothing in her wash says she was, we have to obtain as close a match to the contamination pattern evident on her jeans. To my way of thinking this should not become a major disagreement in the lab."

"Inspector was impressed with your idea."

"Yeah, her blood tested for epinephrine, so she was slaughtered with octopi."

"I thought it was squirt-fish."

"Cuttlefish have almost no blood; octopi are infused with profuse amounts of blood. Bryce must've had some reason to string her up the way he did."

"All the bullet deaths were similar. They landed face down on orange dirt, were unable to move, were bathed in eel blood, and left on a boat out in the reef bobbing up and down inside a net. According to the morgue docs, it's positive proof for gunshot orange tongue, ashen black-tinged skin, evidence of over thirty hours dead by fatal injection. The java coffee grounds don't lie, but there you have it, she could as easily have died hanging aboriginal style in a forest jungle tree, pomegranate to the flies."

"Did he teach her to sit zip cable through the forest?"

She replied. "They were still a couple when she was doing a chair drive. The morgue reconstruct on her puts her in the water ankle deep at Eyre with Bryce standing in his jeep driving two miles an hour rifle aimed safari style. She may have had a head start but I think he gained on her. She was a mile from nowhere when he shot her. I think he took her down pretty fast at that distance. The impact of the dummy probably tenured an aorta easily."

He poured another rinse into the jar turning the gunk at the bottom to a light brown which he held up. "There's nothing like this in the Great Barrier. What's your guess?"

"I think he picked that up on the boat," she surmised. "Tasmania Lotus stem possibly; it's definitely not parsnip, that root is yellow, not ginger brown. We have to learn what he did after she confronted him with actual murders, not as much to know why he shot her in salt or made her grovel in Ayer's red dirt, but why he hauled her in his jeep to his boat, wrapped her in a rope net and cast her adrift."

"I think he'd done that already to half a dozen drowned victims. Maybe they couldn't be convinced or they barricaded their houses against the threat of winds and flying electricity, but it looks like he killed six by spatula, each with different color tongue, blue, yellow, orange, plum, whitish, black. If you ask me, all thirty-four in the womb of Indonesia died of unusual exposure to cold."

"Definitely we've seen a variety of death due to different unusual circumstances." Gabby sipped her coffee. Consulting the clock on the kitchen wall, she saw it was barely eight, the sun a bright orb dipping toward the horizon, rays of orange like a varnish on the placid waves. "Bryce was also flood relief. If your house wound up floating downstream he'd rescue you in a boat and take you to a shelter."

He added, "Or rescue boaters who got lost and wound up in the reef."

"Where is their billet when they're out there doing rescue?"

"Their boats, I would imagine."

"Well, that's what I thought. I didn't think they were dining at the Marriott."

"This black bile stuff – what do you think got it started?"

"Yeah, it's pretty weird. Practicality maybe, if many deaths resulted in day's old dried blood from the intestines. I've been focusing on definitions – bad tempered, maladjusted, malodor-ous. "

"How would you note the phenomena of his apparent obsession with overkill?"

Gabby closed the door and the window slats and switched on the overhead light. "It's not simply that he was defacing her trying to leave no clear traces as to where she died, because I don't see that he succeeded with that, but it's obviously a criticism he wants to impart in disguising the outcome of her death. She died of orange tongue in orange Ayer's mud. The wound sealed over quickly because she was covered in black gooey repulsive blood waste. He trapped her in the net, and she was captured. He gained possession of her life in death."

"He must have been pretty furious at her for what she told his captain's physician. He refused to bury the hatchet. He never forgets the injury she has inflicted, so he executed her."

"That could explain his vindictive action. His type always looks over their shoulder to check if anyone else is after them. We are looking for any previous crime spree, possibly blackmail or battery, any unlawful personal injury."

"You weren't at the inquiry to hear his defense," she said. "The inquiry came at him very directly. Had he ever arranged Indo-Chinese to be isolated in life-threatening circumstances? He answered, Never. He was aware cards in a box traveled between the smaller islands, but these were well-made boats with AIS systems. He doubted there were any Jakarta's to be counted among the ravaged dead. He said no one would ever be as responsible as he; he had gone out to every advanced training and overseas assignment offered any seaman; he went in for boat rescue during the floods, rescued people off floating houses, secured towns against voluminous momentous waves of land advancing into the ocean. There was no one who could contradict his loyalty and industriousness. There was a day when he had arrived onto a foreign shore of Pushkar to assist with sandbags to the riverbanks and had to remove strings of Christmas lights from the sand beneath the layer of loam. He trenched down looking for more erosion but found none, only the orchards behind the banks filled with ocean water. He thought any device that made rivulets for the ocean to pour into was a destructive thing and therefore a bad thing? The strings of lights caused shoals of sand to continuously wash out to sea eventually taking dozens of houses, rutting their yards, causing basements to slide off beaches and adhere like barnacles in shallow coastal bays. Monsoon after monsoon, waters rose beleaguering swamps of entire cities, the devastation of roads later to be found gutted, wastrel for any populated area, requiring the transposing of a hundred people into mountain towns.

"The duty suited him because he was single and eager to become established in the down under world. He quickly climbed the military ladder and was eventually assigned to night patrol working levies diving to find tears beneath the fifteen foot murky water and sheeting cracks and laying slurry seal asphalt. He met his wife in a bar on the Island. Frasier was where the Great Barrier Reef Patrol brought ships to be restored. He was in his late twenties, Mary was barely twenty-one. He had given her his standards that evening over baked salmon and chilled white wine – never be late to a date, never be out of uniform including at home, and no special favors, everything per its listing. When the children were born, the rules became tailored to fit home management – there was morning inspection of chores, dress in a fresh uniform, and breakfast at seven. Over the years the four children adopted all rules to perfection, when the oldest turned twelve, Bryce installed the night sensor lights and answering machine and the children were taught to take telephone messages and send important calls by e-fax. They notified their dad when mom had to work late, when she had to ship out unexpectedly or when she was required to handle rifle patrol or fire repellent house to house inspections or sit down prisoner discomfort frisking. If she had covered another person absent for sickness or family death, then she had to stay over to transfer for graveyard shift duty.

"This was Bryce's only marriage, first or otherwise. In college at Adelaide at Dundee Police Academy, his roommate sliced his fiancée on the hand during an argument and was ordered to serve seven years labor camp. Other than that, his father made gunnery sergeant and his mother stayed at home and ran meals, laundry, shopping, petty cash and errands, and when he was eighteen she took her life with a pistol to the jaw as she walked into the ocean at the base. It was his hope to someday command his own night raid flat vessel for river rescue anywhere.

"The inquiry board had solicited four signed documents that gave permission for the deceased woman's statements to her off-base therapist to be read in court. The therapist stated that her patient feared for her life. She advised her patient to leave her husband and file for custody of her dependent children of whom there were two."

"Mr. Messiah he's not."

"Well, I'm certain he knows he lied in the witness box. My impression of the case as it existed prior to my receipt of the referral was that this was a My-lai boy who'd decided to come to Sydney for its proximity to Hobart. I think he did his nine month stint, got the hell out and made like a seaman half way across the Indonesian Ocean for any environment similar to Vietnam. They have those picturesque rocks, a bit of coral, they're a stone's throw to beaches with huts that wash to sea every year. He came to us, he knows out type of sea, he's worked reefs, he's fished off fishing trawls and my guess is when we find a record on him, we'll have his training."

"Digging for clams, planting roots, tying up orchard gardens ten feet above the top of the tide line," he said.

"It's a possibility," she replied. "I wouldn't deny him that, but you have to ask if he told Mary he did these crimes solo or with one or two others. Maybe he wasn't one to steal from the commissary because of the risk of being caught; maybe he does his crimes at a desk where an insurance check comes to. If he has a forefinger that gets numb often, possibly he injured his hand using a device that is placed where the clams are dug out. This could turn out to be a regular bridge over river Kwai, it's difficult to know what this guy has lived through on his own."

"I wouldn't have thought it likely he'd want a family with

this sort of military exposure. Many special forces steer clear of children. They regard young ones as an inhibition against the heavy-duty missions where they'll have to go in armed with Kiowa and dagger and slit a few ears. They aren't able to be photographed in public or lined up with their pretty Filipino bride."

"That's what I would've thought as well. According to surveillance he's got them fairly well commissioned, they awaken at six, brush their teeth, make their beds, scrub the bathroom, fix breakfast of boiled eggs and toast, then do fifty sit ups and push ups and dress in uniforms. It's a simple way to raise a family and prepare them for a lifelong career. There's no need to pack them off to college, or to trade school for career orientation."

"I'd like to know if he's taught them to fire a weapon, light a campfire, or build a latrine," Chase added, giving the rinse a final dunking. "The determinant is very straightforward, I'd imagine. Can a case be developed for an easy-to-define event he participated in with his wife? Have we found it? I don't think he was a spy but she might have been. It's even conceivable she wanted an entrée into Internal Affairs with us."

"Right." She agreed giving a finite nod. "This was her case – death due to orange tongue. So she knew what to look for. Where are her case records?"

"There aren't any. She seems to have worked it coroner-morgue style."

Gabby guessed the photo lab showed some sort of oddity of laminate commonly found in river settees along the fishing rivers of India's main artery which led to her older abandoned palaces. It was a trick of light that gave off a queer incandescence like glitter emanating from beneath the green linoleum fixed to the walls. The lab presumably was a base of a kind having an ability to offset camera takes causing each indiscriminate photo to resemble a brownish green malleable material. Since two of the three men holed up inside for long hours with rudimentary henna face paint on, she would surmise there was room enough just for two, the third somewhere in the brush or on deck. In fact she went further, the oligarchy of the serpent came and went with the dead of night with a bare light bulb that swung overhead from some boat perched above a door to the ground.

Ampo-lite was shipped in wooden boxed crates from India for use as a wonder drug in surgery if a patient had to be conscious for example reset a dislocation. The effect of the tranquilizer remained active for two hours, sufficient for any complication with a twenty minute surgery involving in the water injury. For the operation the arms at the wrists were wrapped in muscle looking plastic which while usually used to bandage colts could asphyxiate a male between the ages fifteen and forty-two. The drug was administered by needle in syringe without tubing attached to the right temple just above the eye before the skull bone which numbed the face in a relaxed smile. Death followed when two toes became hard, a grocery flesh colored plastic bag was slipped over the head tied in place by ductile tape, all murders believed to have been committed by Philippine bodyguards out of island rock Laos. Golden netting was placed on the hands of victims and from the air resembled gold. The guns were used in surgery to affix skin to close the wound.

The soiree squandered its creative celebration in style, a gusher of champagne poured into a tray of long stem glasses, a blade of grass on each, wine mixed with brandy filling goblets with a sizzle of whipped cream, in a lounge bathroom on swirling golden and beige carpet girls prepped pistol whip IVs made of methadone, speed and heroin; out on the terrace couples dressed in orange and silver and transparent blue high heels beneath chorus girl satin dresses, men in trousers with white bow-tie over ruffled bib discoursed the comings and goings of milking ones tits, Lord Mencken set the newest trade agreement between Sydney and Indonesia into flame where in a summer breeze it burned like a piece of chintz. With well over a hundred of the parliament house, the trade winds secretary was dancing the lala atop the polished long dining room table, while trumpets blared and strings defied. A staunch address and peppery mint defined the ballroom stage, two hours into a round the more chatty celebrants kept their ties wilted or repressed, gradually taking a palate off a dark gray tongue. The draught had taken hold of lies and ingenious little darlings which freed their noses to upgrade their whiskers, the avenue that took all midlands from their shores. Brevity of promises couldn't contradict a season's barometers, the realism one wrestled with had to include the compromises of cut law bills on the parliament floor, so much of a tunnel to a gate could fill a path to the door, a token of filings to an underground of computers, a barbershop razor open on the pavement like a calculator, the door through the warehouse with stone pavers on a wall displaying a snaking column, drew nine flasks of kerosene which even a match could ignite serving five instead of eighteen. The botch must have occurred when a poor dim little light filtering through a taped pane shrouded. A tunnel light caught on film loose shards on linoleum as good as an umbrella computer as a lunch on pier beneath a wall with a glass plank resplendently reflected as an extension over water; this tunnel passed a wall with red I-ching letters on a red opaque window of a restaurant grease lounge, where inside the dishwasher was broke and a spider lay behind a thick prison cell door. The night celebration was lively as a speak easy where rumor was thick that a male Joseph Santer, a Czech pistol out of Hungary, who made a descent of destruction when a soil avalanche descended under calving ice, who was known to the parlor wine house to have held a spigonometry welding device up to a four foot steel door. He left by a ride-down to the work tunnel through a bank three-story elevator into a chamber of darkness, incandescent green light spilling from a warehouse along a joint wall of numbered posts, on the other side which was the fast-speeding train, when he came upon the room where bank notes were stored. His instructions were go to America, buy a pentagonal turning cylinder, set it up in a room across from the storage warehouse of textbooks and break into any row of three shelves for greenbacks. On a first round of quick pix by Intel 270 the analyst found a sheet of clear scene photos, rice paper over a window in a subway basement and a rifle stored in a closet, Santer and his wife came on scholarship to Julliard to play cello at Fortieth Street Academy; he fled to his death in a subway yard during a transfer of tools between compartment boxcar and home, his body was sent home.

Lord Stevon Mencken spent a pithy duster on a yacht tracker for the Rolex 2000 in order to sail his one hundred and forty foot yawl between Storm Bay and the Tasman Harbor at Hobart. Life had smiled upon his tall elegant frame and ruffled top hairs in the nick of time just as the Carlo Borlenghi team went before parliament on bended knee to request another portside wharf at Hamilton for a yacht berth worth two hundred and eighty boats. Mencken himself lived in an apartment situated in ornate pink tile in Mandalay in the Golden City while he raised a daughter born to a Pushkar India nightclub singer. Once she reached age eighteen and entered the internal medicine practicum at Royal Hospital in Sydney, he left aboard his yacht, the wind flying his sails, the taste of salty air on his lips, the fresh catch endeavoring enough to make his heart sing. A mariner for a father he wasn't far from the waters, a testing pistol and rifle driving range expert he utilized a welder's lamp to examine pieces of the firing trajectory from each and all barrels. It disturbed him there was no abrasion ring nor clear muzzle imprint because the retained shrapnel was particle-assaulted, even less was the amount of retained shot, but upstairs had rated it a man-stopper of sufficient velocity to produce an ultimately fatal wound. Gunshot residue proved provocative as a forensic study anyways – always there was debate on any similar wound pattern if it were usually produced by another weapon. In this case Mencken wrote that the victim died of hydrostatic shock from a .38 dud carbine, a very high class rifle with partial sandbag producing a massive slug impact to the trapezius muscle causing cervical cord dysfunction. It was only five years ago that the victim brought in a man believed to have drowned in a fishing boat accident. After careful scrutiny Mencken deduced a pressure time record of a shock wave resulting from impact of water of a 4/21 inch steel sphere moving 2700 speed per second on a thirty degree angle path. He formulated that Mary had come close to discovery since her death so similarly approximated the shooting orange tongue victims of her Internal Affairs case. Hers at peak pressure was nine hundred yards per pound square inch. No one would say there wasn't definite stopping power. There were eight causes of death per body, each identified as defibrillation. The assailant possessed uncanny classified expertise.

In addition to processing some thirty-five thousand lab tests a year, Inspector Steed reviewed a checklist of the toxicologist team forming a resolute but recidivist perusal of the procedures. The bureau had produced its general status evaluation, positive toxicology, a crime scene reconstruction was still proceeding, a fingerprint analysis was completed, blood splatter presumed, ballistics assessed and pathology of the still body processed. In his report he summarized it was cold blooded murder consisting of serious bodily harm, assault and battery with a deadly weapon, including a longtime history of breaking and entering. The history included assault by a marital spouse breaking plates over the wife victim's head and monitoring his wife in the dead of night with cell phones with built-in Samsung cameras; Internal Affairs regarded the case as a cheating wife case despite the fact that it was Mary who complained about Bryce's harassment. This was one of those enigmatic conflicts, most probably over the family business, Tasman Investigations, a mutual husband-wife detective agency that began with their first year of marriage and included personal and business authenticity, insurance, surveillance, dating scams, missing person, fraud, record search and assets profiling. Their more recent cases took in business background, on site inspections and scene photos for actual business verifications.

The troubling bailiwick consisted of the extensive firing distance as to Mary's mort pathology. If it were far back enough the helmet would lose firing speed. Her husband had to have carefully researched haulage or made his falling stake with it, this was the distance of producing death as a result of one cracking high speed barrel. If he were a pro-visor at distance target fire, then he easily stag-horn stalked her, while knowingly conveying petty rankling callous behaviors. At the top of one report Charles LaMufti scribbled a continuous line-up of adjectives which the inspector found he gave some thought to – dominer, dogmatic, obstinate, servant, distress, guarded, resentment, ingratitude, retaliatory, remorseless, bears malice, never forgets an injury, vindictive; and then hyper vigilantism?? Steed had sailed one year with Carlo, it was sailing speed at the whips as well as flat sails for miles on the blue ocean, cruising at ten knots to an even cadence, all hands on the lean, conversation physically impossible. Into and home again out of the stone gate of Tasmania, dozens of challenger boats briskly confronted the horn. Even there, Search & Rescue conducted a rigorous duty, in time all their sailors voyaged to the opulent Pushkar Palace, the mind spiritual peace of the Bahrain Temple, the petulant Ganges, and the devastatingly stunning gold and rust colored palaces of Pink City before they set course for the stone ceremonial heads and Buddha's of the jungled terrain, flying over the meandering rivers low hung with an abundance of wooded trees, garlands of vines and screens of mats hanging over abandoned clandestine porches sitting in tall grasses amidst gone-to-seed vegetable plats as though the garden area were still regenerative. Steed never regretted his decision to separately categorize hair and fiber for these elusive vignettes, because while blood stained light or dark was conclusive, too often it was a combination of factors that gave no conclusion – blood was blood, there were no markers to determine racial properties, nor definitive skin color or characteristics to give origin of whereabouts be it Queensland, Western Australia, Melbourne, or islander. Over decades Parliament separated Australia into three regions – Sydney Canberra for health, royal hospital, and trade of pharmacology with Africa, Brisbane and Perth. The one political crime they treaded through in the late Eighties was a Watergate-type burglary during which a suspect ransacked photos in a warehouse and set fire to "calling you" tapes. These tapes showed streets with high walls on Tasmania, all at street level with no run-off possible. The river rose too high; it was three months to drain once the levy was rebuilt. In Australia ten rivers flooded in the Australian winter during June, July and August when the weather was very dry, the Eyre was maroon soil which blew over the entire desert consisting of some two hundred miles. Of all archives the photos which marked the "calling you" files contained the Harari River in dark sand in Melbourne, fish tadpoles in shallow water with primitive white outlines on rock, and a fish skeleton in water in a Wadi, someone looking for their ancestors from another continent, a mythology that sprung up overnight as far back to marsh salt growers who carried large bags of dredged salt on their shoulders to train cars on the plain that supported the raised railroad track.

The Chili Rooms in Sydney featured Wayne Ashton's Interior Subway of a metal of centrifugal lines in all directions posted onto metal display of a clock with a thin red second hand at 11:35:07 of a presumed vehicle zooming into a future crash. Mike Sawas Full of Love had an attractive slender brunette inside a room with an infinite number of predominantly blue and white globules, both reported in at Sotheby's Australia. New South Wales Museum cavorted Perry Sandhill's modern ink blue on a beach; a series of realist artists including Vicki McInnis painting of corn, Glenn Hoyle's plaza, Rob Fulani's Water, of color. In Tasmania at Wineglass Bay's Francine National Park were the Color field Paintings of a corner at night, New Orleans and a green highway, each as remarkable as a plate river in the rain or time lapsed painting of autumn trees, each line going onto the canvas as trees were drawn and sky and seagulls etched. A blur of King's Canyon and Ayer's Rock basin with swimmers plummeting under water in a cave by Ptarmigan, colors positioned in long horizontal columns across a canvas representing ocean and sand, and then the works of Ken Done in light blue, white tan, wine, black and blue.

Gabby walked, arms folded, deep in thought contemplating the problem of proof while ahead Inspector Steed and Charles scribbled notes in their mutual pads comparing notes to one another. They had just left the Sherman Galleries prior to brunch after viewing a photo of an I-Ching of sunlight and in a brick effaced room the youthful face of Craig Walsh entering through an open door, artist painting his model by Ken Done, painting of an austere blonde. Canberra from outer space seen in crimson, purple and blue sky and Lewis Moorcroft earth in space above a river juxtaposed by a territory blur of sand, yellow, red, salt flat with a grey sky track with Olga's in North Territory titled, Gone. Her favorite was Vanpool Pop Art for its redwood texture painting of stick trees in snow and horse racing of three disc jockeys in red on horses. Inside Australia featured Peter Kovacsy, Dianne Gall, Kristine Zelve, all at the University of Leeds, artist collective, international art exhibits in Turin, Italy; Tallinn, Estonia, and Orneau Baths, Belfast, North Ireland. Of eight hundred and thirty-five paintings, it was two shiny airplanes standing on their tails that stayed with her.

Proof of Mary's cases came at long last with the doors being delivered to a warehouse established for the sole purpose of evaluation. In it were the eight restorations with dummies who were penetrated by man stopper bullets at a presumed range of nine hundred yards positioning their assailants in jeeps or on the ocean on boats. All other victims lost their lives when the beaches where their houses stood formed cut- always and washed out to sea along with tidal crash breakers carrying a tenth mile of debris of housing and street lights. On a narrative summary she had written, The physical state in which the initial victim came to be tangled up on a moor craft on the ocean estranged from a modest abode inside which during a full frenzy storm the door to the basement banged closed permanently forcing said victim to leave by an open window and take his small boat out into the ditch well-rising streets but getting instead washed out to sea at four knots per kilometer. Also determined to be shot was a Two Island male resident with a man stopping bullet that pushed the victim onto his back as a fast moving curling wave seized a rope wrapped around his leg pulled him out to sea over formerly a yard of weed ground cover. The photos shot by moonlight with a canon show five to nine assailants wearing Search & Rescue jackets and marine dark trousers. These men were also to be found in stock photos M-612, M-628, M-713 and M-891, referenced in Great Barrier. The carbine gunshot victims advanced to inquiry before the general magistrate of the king's bench in Townsville one week prior to her death. The presumption was she was killed because she had new evidence. Her ex-husband had threatened her life verbally telling her one day she would disappear and no one would find her in time; had harassed her for over ten to thirty years snapping pictures of her inside her house, sending her videos of dinner dates, camp and undressing; and there were no eyewitnesses to these threats. Mutual friends said they didn't want to get dragged further into their stormy divorce; his friends stated he was ambitious opening a detective agency in Sydney, Melbourne and Perth; wife Mary Choice ended her relationship as a detective with the agency when the divorce was finalized; and cases the agency handled did not consist of her case although the detectives worked missing persons after storms involving floods and researched personal and business credentials in the islands.

Gabby conducted the first series of interviews herself, they were brief, merely routine question and answers, five queries in all – Have you taken trips on your own to patrolled areas; have you dated a female you encountered while on assignment; have you met with any families during monsoon seasons; have you on your own investigated or taken under warrant any drugs, weapons or devices of equipment; and have you purchased any of the following: jewelry, expensive food packages of golden curry; cane teak; mass market supplies of sneakers, rain-wear, insulated pajamas, or other product? She had already reviewed their reports and looked up who was sent to New Guinea islands during flood season, respective rifle permits including permit to carry rope, net and scope; been placed temporarily in charge of a station for a unit; took vehicles into custody and locked up evidence; and ferry rides from any port to assignment bays.

On the other hand Bryce Choice spent a season farming pink lakes releasing truck crates of flamingos on Lac Rose and scraping salt into pyramids on Eyre. In summer the Choice family sailed the Western Australia Rolex Sydney Hobart Yacht Race on December 26th of every year they were together, all fourteen years; this was the age kids missed their mom, so the oldest ones, now at the end of the pubescence, were applying for entry to the marines to be close to their mom. Once accepted to the new marines, they would erect simple villages, two hundred occupational buildings surrounded by salt slats, a river filled with cranes, and rows of houses each able to reflect the setting sun. Flamingoes walked on tip-toes, their fluffy feathers buoyant on their backs, necks tall, proud and astute. The pink lake was just that, a saltine pinkish blue that changed color as though opalescent, the sand as white as the blue tint it became toward nightfall. Through encryption files a semblance of Arabic characters and symbols described a picturesque past of engravings in stone in underground passages in India. Mary's case on deaths in islands throughout New Guinea and Indonesia not to mention Tasmania's six, all described nets in the water or underwater above the horn, one shot by barrel gauge, almost all drowned, black bile, grey skin, found in low lying orchards, swamp conditions; the majority of investigations that the Choice agency took on was concerned with address checks, marital status and lifestyle; Bryce was both Australian marine and Military police of India – he was deemed dirty, a man on the kill, who had joined an out-there force in order to qualify for entry into Iraqi Forces. Everyone knew it was the Iraqis who were sent by their overseas government into the jungles of the wild to knock over heads of stone statuary, build rope bridges above gullies, farm mangoes and salt dried plums for market, and establish a hundred houses made of stucco and wood along coastal beaches in the jungle, all this for island governments whose governor had separated from the parliament houses of authority.

The reef analyst, a Whitsunday man who wore snug runner's wear and a striped cuffed shirt who in stockings had a slim cut yellow jacket and parted his dark hair on the left side, from Sydney in wharf harbor borrowed on good over time to formulate his opinion as to where the Choice yacht was docked. A perfectionist of thirty years standing, John Coffin could identify any sound as to town and vicinity. At the moment he was tuning out a choir of Christmas choral music to hone in on the Darling harbor. Gold coast scatter had been picked up all way to the actual sail and boat pier, it was unmistakable, no one who had ever detected the dock hotdog hawker missed the identification once it entered the masthead. Even the bell at the one half mile buoy was pitch clear despite a slog of ocean water lapping against the peninsula sound.

The final blur took him well over a half hour, initially it resembled laughter of school-age children except there were no schools close by, there was a park beneath a steel-arced bridge that on any afternoon carried store traffic, but in general his feed adjustor gave little indication as to what it could be. The shush grew louder but not more promising in distinction, just a slurping of water moving over a plank of some sort. When John distilled the item he realized it was the sand factory laying a stack of sandbags onto the platform off an enclosed ram-tray onto a palette crane. Now he tuned in for a sure draw. The sound was unmistakable, the boats on the starry plow dockside were mainly large sailboats, an occasional ring indicated a telephone call but once the sails went up nothing was heard over a din of flapping sailcloth. No matter, he'd switch to a harbor universe of call forwarded telephone numbers and try to prod out a cell based upon pictures of the swilling ocean in sail. The faces showed aboard the Hobart Run, a mad wind dashing sweatpants and nylon parkas, hair blowing every which way, the sun shining in living glory over the deck and ocean. The Choices knew their way on a leaning yacht, they dressed and stripped down to bathing suits and trunk shorts for the men and sipped drinks and tried a bit of marinated fruit and steak. After all of a few minutes, the number read in clearly, 683-1145-01. John crossed it to any listing available, numbers swept onto the cell operator station in hundreds of line item running through indexes for the better part of two hours, listing each found telephone number for origin of call to the cell. Every few minutes he sipped brewed coffee; after the first hour he lit a mentholated Cool.

His schedule was very straightforward – he awakened at five, took tea in the greenhouse large room on the garden, at six was served omelet, hash fries and bacon by the maid, at seven drove his black Macerate to the office; it was all he lived for, his car, job, and condo on the gold coast waterfront, right on the beach. He was always dressed in striped silk shirts and black trousers – purple-black, blue-gray, tan-red, and white-black. His specialty enlistment was filtering cell phone calls from all types of environments from an interior walled room where he had a desk and studio-worth of headsets and channel dupes to dilute out abstract city scatter until he produced a single discernible element. Off hours he was a chef, took his young Zealand wife Imelda on weekends during Australian summer beginning in January to Hobart, regularly prepared a vegan parlor for pearl onion, clam and yellow bell pepper on pizza; vegetarian crab on dill toast, seared pan fry artichoke and cilantro in pear-mint laced eggplant, and a side salad of diced dates, spicy curry, and a condiment of chopped strawberries mixed with bite-size chunks of honeydew melon.

It was nightfall, the lights of the city's high rises twinkling up and down the bare beach corridor reflected on the pitch black ocean. On the television in the family room Hunt for Red October had played billing after billing. He had left a long stem filled champagne carafe after two champagne drinks left him dizzy, barely unable to think clearly. Through the glass his picturesque graph measured speech, telephone and computer fields, every so often hour to hour, the tape spooled with a whir alternating graph for synchronized measurement response. He had been taping for days since the court order was signed.

For this sting he set up twenty computers, two to receive additional info from anywhere, twelve broad band to coordinate restorative scenes and accept feed simulation from 22 agents, and five to review news clippings, feedback, archives all day, etc. from city stations reporting in, and one slim-line record, no play computer to district to a central government relay. His real question was how much scatter was capable of being heard from a yacht and planned to sail as soon as there was clear weather.

During these intensive episodes of car-tunnel taping, he would tell himself that it was far beyond anyone's ability to grasp the violence people seemed capable of, the analyst who could accept that fact didn't pause too long over the inscrutable inhumanity that cropped up every so often, but to discover in the midst of a homicide that a spouse had caused grievous bloodshed consisting of knifing the victim in the neck or stabbing through an aorta took years to get over; when obviously it was done for the money, lots of it, the spouse pension, individual tax annuities, their mutually owned house, her timeshare, her savings, all total over nine hundred thousand pounds. No matter how comfortable the lifestyle – drinks on the terrace every evening after work, a driver to pick up the children, a maid to clean once a week, a five-mile stroll on the gold coast past the column of hearse-like line-up of glass nails, built pier houses or sailing the yacht one weekend a month down to Tasman, purchase of a Ken Done city-abstract and seeing the stars across the ocean from one's bed – the cruelty that people were capable of was so foreign to life that it took one's emotional resources past one's comprehension to absorb it. In fact it was about as imposing upon one's emotional defenses as it was to walk in to see two people killing someone in their bed. There was a big idea this was boat he took after he killed Mary from the great barrier because it was easy to motor.

Once he had possession of the docket of listings to the particular cells, he then spooled for photographs for each telephone. Almost immediate to several days the spool-catch gave him India's Pink City, Bryce dialing in to speak to Marine Corporal Dennison; India, The Golden City, number to number from a pretty mansion on the river to speak to first wife and daughter of corporal Choice, which ranked him as a cheating husband; then to Indonesia on the ivory coast, to talk to another marine – Coffin would have remarked rather unkindly that there was no one who didn't comprehend what these men were after, they lived in Jainjupur for over twelve years, married, had children, and left one day to work the corp. and strike it rich by building inadequate caked cement sidewalks, yards and basements. His guess was they were good sailors who were probably offered to take more assignments than many and quickly became relied upon. Not many of those stay married, the rise to the top was complicated and most females had a hard time anyways putting up with living on the edge of life, the last photo showed a small town in Solomon, a tiny town on the second to last island and an airstrip on significantly lower island above South Pole, if he could match the cell for the conversation between Bryce and Mary with any other photo he had a bin he could introduce to a Dundee court of law.

There were so many variations this could go, he ate two for the price of one, beautiful sweet strawberries, fresh out of the box; with a bit of poured cream and sprinkled brown sugar he was in seventh heaven; he sat in the dark with only a fan whirring, cigarette burning, a jigger of tequila watching the salvation of the abstract Italian artist Modigliani with his wife after a defeating blow of reputation by the gluttonous Pablo Picasso; following this movie over panfry noodles and broccoli, a wild espionage adventure in Ronan and drunk now to the spirit of a quart of tequila, a melodrama attachment to a heartbreaker rendition of a musician cellist in the Soloist on a freeway in Manhattan; every so often when he consulted the computers and noted the gradual list of governing prefixes and numbers he also realized with shuddering appraisal that they were mostly at the end of the world, Perth, an odd assortment of berths and docking saloons, not quite as he had expected the berth slip to be solidly Melbourne harbor slips or barracuda boats which telephone numbers rang into the harbor station house where the desk paid out on the size catch, forty thousand per man for abalone, two hundred thousand for rock clam, or fifty thousand per stack for cucumber eel and rough tuna. The proof-worthy variation placed both Bryce and Mary at an old lighthouse in Chairns and again in Darwin labs, several parasail red balloon jet ski on board a boat, lunch on a tour through Standley Chasm, inside a canoe wallowing up the Alligator River through a forested remote marshland, joined by a Royal Flying Hospital physician into Katherine Gorge to its flat clinker like, grey greenish chimney rock squeezing through low willows and a toss of slate rocks, then finally as a full moon rose on The Ghan, the Great Southern Railway through the Kakadu National Park through the Outback. In a Marraiku cottage beside a pool and restaurant young husband and wife lounged on the Mary River, in a jeep they followed the Mary to a waterfall where they notch-belted down seventy-five feet over red canyon walls into a wet glade of ghost gum trees and a husbandry of farms. To Mary who began as a newcomer to Australia, the scenic rivers must have carried her past realization that time began in these aviary wilderness narrows, that the Saint Charles suite at the Crowne Plaza offered her a season of epiphany, red long plumed feathers interspersed by long pink tassels in a showy headdress, accompanied drum beats and Mardi Gras regalia were eyes in disguise for a Jazz Nawlins, black and white small squares covering a mask, silver tinsel turners and pink, green, gold and black beads and light green plumes gave any street-goer an impression that mystery and fetish were plentifully abound.

John Coffin slept through the night. Round about seven he came to, his bed sheet kicked off in the night, his bottom green pajama still starched. He got up, labored into the kitchen, opened the sliding glass door to the balcony, and steeped a cup of French roast taking it with him onto the balcony to wait the new morning where the sun as shadowy as the moon rose from the barrier reef. He had slept uneasily, tossed as yet another heat wave churned through the dispelling chill, a call from the lab at Darwin to say they had isolated the couple's honeymoon and he'd have it by seven. The blissful shots gave a false impression of surrender, hardly the déjà vu of a man intent on murdering his wife once their children entered pre-maturity. In the distance of a glistening sandbar where fifty or so flamingoes gathered and strut about, their plumage of white feathers lifting. They walked the sandbar, tufts of flounce afloat in salty waters, pink bodies like flowers stretching in a breeze. Hilarious delights squawked up a lively chatter. Endless forever chores kept running feet splashing through the aquamarine waters. From the highest mountain in Papa on snowfall, the government brought farm-grown flamingoes in crates and upon release fed them tiny eyelets in wet sand. Above razor-striated skies kept to an everlasting scrutiny of an opaque sea, salt dunes, and strip of land crusted with orange. Two swimmers clad scantily, the male in barely briefs, the female in briefs and a string top, dashed for the waters, droplets splashing around their feet and hands. Out of nowhere the mustard, brown slightly blurred photos revealed Bryce with rifle drawn, sight lens blinking green, masked males robbing a wall unit of a bank or government custodial safe, shelves fell and floor released to an underground, all dark bars, almost no light, technically there were doors leading out. A next photo series of some twenty pages showed the ultra-bright sun, a glaring orb with a summer halo of grey and blue as though the all damp sky might suddenly obliterate the day with a good soaking. In part of the same series the low, modern life of Darwin's sultry nightlife on Mitchell Street caught a photo of snow so thoroughly blanketed it resembled a white curtain with no abatement, no visibility, nor recognition of a town, no buildings, plaza squares, trees, parks, houses, docks, or vessels. Whatever the gold coast produced, it was the same nightmare vision that every artist who painted her had, a detachment deployment of slaves to sand, skin and eyesight ruined by the forces of nature, skin rough, a dismal departure from any reality of a beige skyway of sand to the Stuart Highway on which Tanami livestock trucks beat a path to the crimson dirt and vast orange plateau. John removed two photographs out of sequence and clipped them, one for a feature, and the other for an extra.

Inspector Steed removed the three documents from the clip marked Combo and spread them across his neat desk. The top docu-proof photograph showed a narrow opening into a predominantly glass walled bedroom of a red cloth bedspread, a chest of drawers and trousseau, both made of blue oak, and a swivel chair at a desk. Accompanying the photo was a description of a sector of the great reef by coordinates with a new small island for real estate sale, someone's idea of a nasty wee joke which had been sent to Coffin and lastly the actual graphing for AIS and chart race from Mel to Hobart for the recent blue cup trophy sporting the Voodoo at the Showdown from Derwent Bay with two hundred and fifty deck homes enveloped by a forested stand high on far bluffs to the iron pipe stone cliffs of Van Demon land. Justin Clouger had just bagged the Illingworth trophy at Perth sponsored by Sydney Heads for the 12-20 north-easterly. In the International Dragon Race there was braggart Tony Lyall for a grand prix in the Sydney Hobart sails, and at Maria Island off the Tasman East coast, Greg Prescott sailed his strident blood orange yacht into first place. The indent photo in the corner of the Showdown showed a keelboat at Sandy Bay featuring the new Audi IRC sailing under the Tasbridge in the direction of Lindisfarne. Newspaper clippings for the race and for a subsequent February tennis open in Hobart show placing Sugar Hill Serena Williams accounted for the Herald Sun from Mel and Victoria and the Telegraph out of Sydney as well as the Cutline whose front page ran Cricket winner Michael Clarke. All the way from Head Beach in the Bahamas came upstart Lleyton Hewitt who began training young at age two and was so known he had to fly in from a private resort for the Australia Open. Steed worked backwards. He had already compiled vacation photos for the Choices. His first in the set was a tense photo of the Victoria Lady in a board bent sail chase at fourteen knots whipping through high spells. Everyone who worked Southern Canberra was straining against the top sail including Bryce, his brother, sister-in-law and her personal friend from Ormiston Gorge parasail boat company. A string of savvy shots eventually brought Mary aboard the Ghan train, four family friends having departed the yacht harbor at Darwin were now playing cards and sipping cocktails, each couple in a separate barroom, enough luggage to keep a train porter in silk suits. There were photo wink shots of Bryce in bikini briefs, Mary in bedroom long gown ice blue lace and a teal lace mask over her eyes. Another grouping of lazy safari-style photos for yet another, much older trip across the continent through Katherine Gorge in a canoe on the lake with dozens of other boaters; a resort on the sand at the end of the world, Perth; in quaint Sydney and modern city mile Mel. They had topped the charts at Fox Glacier on New Zealand rope and pick climbing the gorge; staying at the Marrakai cottage and pool and they drifted downriver in balloons through the remote outback of wetlands and hundred feet high stone to a waterfall over red canyon walls. It was these remotest areas that drew Steed, the crocodile farms, national park orchards and four-day preseason sailing training camps, radio operator training on series sailboats, zip cable lessons down mountains terrestrial forests, through underwater zip cable from ocean depths. Had he to have met the couple for a first time, he well might have awed their ambitious lifestyle, but he went further back, to their late teen dating years, searching for any shred of ludicrous naiveté while his abdomen strained against hope that there was nothing at all to surface. He had a brief list of employment as much as could be discerned from Mary's notes. Bryce had a shady past – years in training were spent at age 16, when he entered foreign forces for Philippines; age 19, he transferred to the Mekong Military for India; age 22, left the Mekong, bought a house, and met his wife in a poker game; age 27, for some reason he began plotting her demise, and at age 29, having just closed escrow on a condo on the gold coast beach, he became identified through both Office and India Interpol as prime identified domestic killer, all identifiers tagged despite not being in a killing finish photo – his rifle is, his jeep is, but he is not on board boat where her body is found. The Chief Inspector wrote two queries on a summary – (1) Who else knew of the existence of these gunshot victims? (2) Did Mary confer with anyone?

The mist rose off the billabong. Early morning fog had settled along a settee of low hanging branches resting slightly above the dark flowing snaking river. Except for an occasional dappling ripple, the forest river gave no notice to anyone or anything on its banks. There was a permanent sense, like a stain of death, awaiting a traveler, always at the rear of one's short viewed perspective an enemy stood on firm ground, boots supported by layers of matted grasses which subdued sound. A wet season photographer known to the state for salacious expeditiously pertinent sex scandals crept over the salt banks, his Canon 205 trained to the crumbly ground like a blood hound. The domestic violence case had been forwarded to the desk of Gregory Valentine. Valentine was in his forties, a youngster all things considered to have landed a job in the Intimate Apparel department which staged surveillance sets usually through car or bedroom windows to snag evidence. The Choice case sat in Valentine's office unattended to for days before he closed a month-long case and reviewed the hits. Stevon Mencken was still working on details of man stoppers for the gunshot victims in Indonesia's and India's jungles. Steed was testing extravagant distance. Gabriella had pulled summaries on man stoppers and conducted second stage interviews of assigned marines who worked gunshot case territory. John Coffin, reef analyst, had made a determination as to the harbor the other Choice docked at, Melbourne City Wharf. The real evidence hinged on a series of hanging clips brought to life by honing in on any water surface including splashes to meter up any image of a person. Done all the time, it usually took upward of several weeks to sufficiently abstract out an entire governable setting, but for an entire lake the time needed to restore shadows and assess time of day and month could easily take a few months. At one time, not yet a half year into his new career Valentine traveled to every scenic stage to produce his own baselines. Twenty-five years into this work he was known as the cheating lover's tag.

Valentine ran along the salt beds. Every foot run was a slogging dense footpath slowed by the torturous pull of sand. He shot photo after photo of bright glaring salt, some gray with age, piles and rivulets and creeping and statuary daily for seven weeks. He estimated this single weather changing from mist to shaded sunshine photo shoot would take a good hour; updated to his already justifiably judicious capers he could then produce from charts on rainfall, evaporation and traveling dust storms where the victim entered the lake, speed per hour she drove, when she left her vehicle and where her assailant was when he physically fired upon her. The lack of vegetation at the water's edge made a clear finding all the more assailable. Once he locked in on the direction of her assailant he could speedily produce the one road out of four he had traveled in on producing him by facial draw in the event there had been reductions in military-industrial sectored taping.

Back at his lab surrounded by light blue surface drywall Valentine carefully sifted through his own restoration until he matched any draw to a light flash caravan that raised Mary's borrowed jeep. Prior to leaving to the lake, the four-door, light blue vehicle with white wall tires stood in a five-stall lot at the Eyre National Park Station. The jeep was almost impossible to discern once it had entered the lake, but outlined on the computer, the three hundred and sixty degree pin was a cinch to research. He could alter the color of salt and did so for each two hours of daylight utilizing the colors of the spectrum, dark pink being the latest between three-thirty and dusk. Because it took him nearly an hour to map through a county verified terrain all that stood out were odd concentrically formed circles, no cars, houses or buildings able to be seen. But as soon as he correctly estimated distance and direction he produced the other vehicle, a dark brown travel-all flat on the terrain surface from county to city zone. From a speedometer distance the driver did not resemble Bryce to make a reasonable guess, although Valentine assumed it would be proved in due course he wore a wig.

The effort to find splashes of Mary running through the saltine water came quickly. Greg distilled to the hour. Almost intuitively he assessed for high noon. No matter – this was not the first time he'd come across a clock-clever inducement. The droplets, once he isolated them, would read as clearly as news print. He selected the angle at which the bullet flew, and he pulled out the entire panorama in which the splashes could be encased. He chose three hundred multiplication to begin. Despite the fact that the droplets showed a dimly perceived photo not distinct enough to work with due to brightness, he teased out the dimension adding color to the shine of metal and creating a tint to the glass of the windshield and passenger windows until a very large jeep vehicle could be seen in the daylight. He barely shaded the interior reducing both glare and reflection and traded an exterior pixel profile for an interior as close to the driver as he could manage without distorting shadow. He moved the multiplier to three hundred and seventy, then to three ninety and up as high as he could without losing the clarity of picture stopping cold at five hundred magnified image. When he had the driver in clear shot he placed each separate surround as a separate photo, measured hairline, fore-head, neck to shoulders, and length of arm to hand. The bird sailed into view – the bureau of registered motorists listed him as a Renault Chesboro Roice, age 42, born in Achan, Western Samar Island, Philippines. Address listings gave three different photographs which Greg decided after running them through an alias compilation were three different people, none of which was Choice. Valentine spliced for known observable identities, for military induction and assignment – one for Philippine army red beanie and green sport shirt with tan dark brown uniform, motor vehicle, boat registration and mortgage which was the same as his military record. After some verification for all current listed photographs Valentine returned to his assailant and looked for him at Ayer's, Melbourne and Great Barrier particularly roosting a net out on a fishing vessel at sunset.

In fact the buoyant sea of the light blue lake carried a some-what indescribable effervescent appearance as did the airy light blue sky to which the water was matched. On a clear day the salt dunes were visible, on a hazy day nothing was distinguish-able; in the rain the lake seemed as shallow as a pond, and on a windy day the sky lost its horizon. In order to determine level of water in the lake or to decipher time of year for purposes of reading in a crime, there had to exist noteworthy descrip-tion as to climate, probable likelihood of month or year, moon-ing of moor-craft, presence of flamingoes, isolated herbaceous growth and new amoeba. Season to season one unruly cloud created enough doubt that the High Court wanted an expert study of the ecosystem. A side division gave some durable idea as to what should have been in the sky; yet a fortnight to com-prehend where the sea was unfurling to, but in the form that LaMufti was expert in his definition of fish blood, so the de-sired pan had to clarify its stir-fry.

SEVEN

Half submerged, black sand Piha Beach at Melbourne resembled a cove filled with barely visible bloated squid to the one-third mile buoy. On an otherwise clear day the water receded several feet displaying an ashen black shore originated from the all black rock found at intervals. The rope line crew had stayed an hour or so past low tide waiting for the dark sand to again become engorged with ocean run-off. Since they had to provide a guideline as to when a boat might have entered the cove and anchored, a court order required them to document by the hour for two weeks taking into account any twelve hour sequence for the start of high tide or two wind days. Over the course of a week the tide sprawled in covering the entire shoreline on a Tuesday reaching high tide an hour later lasting a complete forty-seven hours. Within the span of a day and a half approximately between 10:03 am and 06:00 am of the next day a vessel could have arrived by pulling alongside a dock curb to remove Mary's body. It wouldn't be the craziest thing anyone had ever heard.

For Valentine, the difficulty with honing in on already adapted photo-file print sheets was that a few were missing, likely to have been pulled by Chief Inspector Division for reasons defined only as problematic. Non-sequential camera shots showed up on a media file consisting of public program photographs with undeniable references to the Intelligence file. It was in these that adult males aged twenty-one to thirty-four wore navy shirts of starched cotton and bluish gray trousers, regulation boots used by many swamp government itineraries and sailor-profile fence-perimeter caps. Probably none other identifier existed and thus a commercial enterprise series had been created for public television and radio. Thus, as he formulated consequence panels for the surveillance unit to receive automatic prompts, he nudged in from top right and assigned automatically to template for Piha Beach for the church tower glass panels of the campanile; row of beach line storefronts, houses and medical library. Because he had to catch the right time of day to obtain any reflection of a boat, failing this since the assailant's fishing boat had to be found on any reflection and none was, he went back to his basic premise worksheet – did assailant's boat leave barrier at Townsville before it was found on the ocean. Knowing the orange sand was used to doctor the body to mask the color of mouth and barf, if it was a different color then it would have suggested to Morgue the hour in which she was killed. He presumed it had been twenty-five hours since; and black sand to mask when body turns black, that was around thirty to thirty-seven hours after death. Then scrapings beneath toe nails took on morbid significance; there wasn't any coroner who wouldn't take anything but those; certainly wouldn't look at fingers which could be misleading. Passing rigor around thirty hours might be noticed if morgue had received body, but if assailant still had her, he'd want her on the boat long after, probably at earliest thirty-five to forty-two hours around time black discoloration could begin to recede. If it took seventeen hours from Eyre to Adelaide, then his jeep had to have her stretched out inside, could have her curled up, rigor normally set in at about five hours after complete death. If she still were breathing but was semi conscious she might have become unable to resist fleeing. From Adelaide to Pihu Beach was around seven hours placing her at morbidity for severe dehydration when orange mouth might ordinarily become slightly green. From Pihu Beach stopping at his new condo in Sydney could put the jeep roughly at thirty-two hours, give or take a few hours, and north to Townsville about forty hours, earliest launch to sea through the nearest portion of reef should be estimated at around forty-four hours. There was nothing to say that the length of time exceeded past forty-four hours that she lay defeated on boat but by this time she had to be dead; fact that she was smeared with almost black octopi blood might have aided in keeping her alive. Just to say she was found covered in black, clot filled, coagulated blood that was still a bit gooey despite her lying under a bright ocean sky was enough to convince any respectable constable that this was a nasty death, vulgar in its inception, utterly derogatory in every respect that his wife had appeared to have hemorrhaged; otherwise she was clean as a whistle.

Perhaps Bryce originated the underwater net in anticipation of a futuristic idea he expected to kill her underwater, except her assignment was abruptly changed by Internal Affairs to lake bio-sphere plant life origination. His inherent message seemed to be – you'll just have to wait; the rifle is used in the event residents actually saw something; the net because it reverses on the cable flinging them minutes after being submerged onto the beach; the tide was swift, no one survived it, if they reached the surface there were boats to escape in. There was no rigor that wouldn't cause an investigator to question facts of death. Maybe there had been no blunt trauma. When a person passed on during sleep there was often no stiffening. There was a facetious saying for inspectors that there were many ways around extinction – a threatened species was always reborn and it was a matter of time before they were seen again. Possibly in Mary Choice's situation she was removed off her case which held him bound, perhaps he had waited for the Internal Affairs to make a finding on him. They kept a case closure code BUNDLED that signified the agent was killed for the rationale of their summary. Bryce therefore had all sorts of reasons to dispose of her but if he were educated by military complication codes he wouldn't want to miss any action the agency might be required to take. Then again it was possible the sole reason he married her was because she worked all jungle zip-cable death cases. It was entirely do-able that he was tracking down an actual witness to an illegal commando raid in one of the islands.

What did it take to make a case? Valentine had seen numerous cases get shoved into the files, never to be reauthorized. There was more than enough medical evidence on Mary; there couldn't be more had the victim slashed her wrists.

Were it not indecent, anyone could have said he struck them as much older but that was par for the work, it was the work that aged these boys so rapidly, caused them to look as if they had aged far beyond tender years. But rarely was anyone rude. Lieutenants wanted their green horns to succeed, at least to get through the horrors of many deaths with deep appreciation that because someone had to do the job, it might as well be them. His own work pushed him past his comfort level to challenge his thinking. The octopi with one eye, sixteen to twenty tentacles, there was nothing in that; it was just bloody.

"To whom do you plan to assign?" He telephoned and asked Gabby.

"Someone's already on it. They don't tell me who it is."

"Better tell him to be cautious. He'll probably get himself killed."

"There's nothing to be ready for. It's not mine to oversee."

Greg put down the phone, disappointed. It wasn't the end of the world not to learn who had Mary's case. It was possible her case was thought to be mostly completed anyways which would mean another analyst department was handling final valedictorians. Probably it was a desk job discreetly approached by an advanced description code. Were the case still required to use the standard IAD rigmarole, some poor slob had to sit on the street with their parking lights on waiting for the family to come and go and recording time and name, while another had to watch the garage screened gate. Two retired constables were the limit.

Valentine dropped in on the surveillance crew. Charles was in a small office with Steed. They had two sight lens with listening track speed cameras aimed at the Choice condo. A spool clicked on whenever anyone spoke. The blinds were down making the rooms seem discreetly covered. Only the bedroom had a visible interior.

"You got a beer?" Greg asked Charles.

"Yeah, sure, refrigerator is stocked. Help yourself. Steed brought in some smoked eel and apricot jam fogged hot dogs on buns."

"Don't mind if I do." Valentine disappeared into the kitchen and prepared himself a dish. He removed a Red Dag from the refrigerator which was filled entirely with cases of about eight types of local pub beers. When he returned to the unlit room, Steed had begun smoking, his eye plastered to the peephole.

Steed said, "Choice has a log that charts every journey over to India. Everything else in the way of work is entered on the computer."

"What's your read on him?"

"Oh, he did it alright. Guilt's written all over him."

"How much do you think he learned about her case during the course of marriage?"

"Probably everything," Charles said. "You've got to hand it to him that he knows how much blood fish produce. I'd say knowing which ones are the gushers are something right there."

Steed advised. "Well, he started off Mekong. That's all they did, the trained rifle militia black hats, they walked through river after river pulling bodies from floods. He probably learned all sorts of things in infantry."

Greg quipped, "Which bamboo makes the best snorkel; yeah, it wouldn't surprise me."

"Look at all their outdoor sports," Steed remarked.

"Well, you have about as much under your belt." Charles remarked to the photo-journalist lover boy.

"That's the work. It takes me everywhere."

"So does Choice's job," Steed interjected. "He's going to be a tough nut to crack. How're the reflections?"

"I have a filter on every water hole they went to as a couple."

Steed said wryly. "Lots of Whitsundays I should think. Anywhere where the cable moves a barge of autos."

"Well, if they went there I'll receive it, I'm sure." Valentine drank his beer, sampled the eel. "Excellent, that's the way to live. What's he pay for his apartment?"

Charles answered. "Twelve hundred plus services. It's not outrageous. He's hired counsel for their house."

Steed was matter-of-fact. "He'll probably get it seeing how none of the children have turned a majority yet."

"Yeah, you think he boshed her for the property?" Charles asked.

"It doesn't read that way, but you never know," Greg replied. "I'd really like to know if there are any restrictions placed on his job by now."

Steed said, looking away for several minutes while Choice went to the bathroom, "Oh right, do you mean like how much information can he send for?"

Greg Valentine said, "He should be off Special Ops at least for six months until a verdict of clearance is pronounced."

Steed shook his head and turned to them. "Never happen. We never tip our hand."

Charles LaMufti, lab coat, added, "That's got to be a mess. I mean, look here, the guy's a bloody family bloke, helps with their homework every night, packs their books, stuffs lunch, the eldest son is on lunch allowance. I wouldn't have gone so far, bound to be problems in a year what with their mum newly deceased. But he's got them overloaded on video games, every few months it's a new computer game or a television package, or clothes, these kids don't lack for much."

"It'll hurt his capability if he can't earn that extra two to three grand a month," Steed said. Then:

"Can you place him at the shooting?" Steed went back to his monitoring.

Greg said, "I have him in the shadows. The joker's wearing a nylon."

"Man, that's fucked," Steed replied.

"That's the whole problem, I have to find him on anyone's camera." Greg finished his drink.

"Maybe he's cautious, drives at night," said Charles. "Maybe he's so inconsistent he's difficult to get."

"Intolerant, I would've said," Steed put in. "So intolerant he doesn't give a damn if he's made a mistake."

Greg: "He lives by a death code. He kills everyone the same. Ayer's dirt in the facial orifices, black sand on the limbs and torso like the victim rolled around in it first."

"Maybe killing gets easier if it's repetitive," Steed offered.

"Good answer," Greg said in return.

Suboxene was generally administered under the brand name Prednisone or in a three-pack mass marketed as Zithromax. The drug was prescribed for aches, fever and chills often to the marine crew who worked the reefs after they experienced ocean fever requiring an ice based chiller unit strapped to the leg. In the Mariana Islands just due west of New Guinea the presence of lead in toxic quantities in the soil had more suspicious barf cases than run-of-the-mill booze, grapes and rice cheese for a positive lab on glucose intolerance. In the loop where the squall line was its most wind-bent fury, where sand was regularly pulled to sea by high ranging ocean waves and cement and sand were daily spent by blue dyed asphalt and grime, the crescent shaped newer island formations changed color from aquamarine to deep blue within weeks and sent toiling back through the currents large debris that came to be liberally sprinkled about the very white sand beaches until a high wind scurried the dirt into high tide. It was during the late autumn weather that the substance of this debris washed anew through the drenching monsoon tirades through the islands of great Papa holding firm to any recalcitrant bone in the yards of modest beach houses.

The Underwater Research Group at Hobart College which studied coral cay formation for waste treatment disposal sent two construction divers to Horseshoe Bay to Magnetic Island across from Townsville to appraise ocean photographs so as to recommend subsequent disposal procedure. Since there had been a research committee formed to identify deaths due to barrier reef circumstances at Birabeen, MacKenzie and Russell Heads, ten miles from Bramston, recommendations for fish extinction included black cod, shrimp and red shining eel but saved prawns, big shrimp, and both the popular mashali and couee without which the common northern Cairns coastal Australian would lack precise enjoyment of French cuisine. By the next year of the new research study the sapphire inlets of the cement crescent rising off the ocean surface had extended a half kilometer. Thus, despite the obvious attraction for potential photographers, the trade reduced its pertinent layovers to the Perth coast and to the national forests inland.

Valentine stayed at the surveillance over the weekend through the first two week days; checked in mid-week Wednesday, got to sleep at two, and returned to office; left description for the final photo for the ministere de la Culture des communications, sent photo of artifact to Muse de la civilization, and a copy to Muse national des beaux-arts naake along with a card index to the ministere de l'immigration, programme d'civiques et intercultures to track foreign whereabouts of the suspect.

The final photo was produced by an attorney who specialized in Ethics and Professional Responsibility and Financial Investigations and Money Laundering. Into his sixties, refined and an honorable speaker on forensics during budget season, brown curly haired Nathan Carley had just finished a courtroom case on the flight characteristics of blood that spring when he was thrown the bone to dig up any photograph bearing incriminating evidence to the suspect from any government or military gauze bandage profiles in performa. The photo showed three males inside a room off an underground tunnel on Papua inside a sewage treatment operations performing grinding at the core of a lock located inside a drain in the floor filing the side to make the acoustical barrier smaller to slip into the turn key to open a wall. When the final grinding began, the mirror at the side cracked a bright whip streak of electrical light. The telegraph receipt read March 22nd at 0116 am in Room 322 on January 16th, 1952, a work order signed by one Saco Amarillo. Two telephone calls located the specific tunnel; a third telephone call placed by the Armory cable crew who were trying to track down the receiver found the use of the drill; but it was the fourth telegraph call that produced a contractor who climbed down to talk to the three men and get a good look at them. One was half concealed as he stood between floors allegedly fixing a pipe from the above floor.

The question as Valentine perceived it was, what made the work of the three men inside the operations room illegal?

Despite the query, evidence was stacking up in the file for case completion. Matching site forensics revealed hard-proof photos of a man wearing a hood taking aim with a rifle barrel shotgun, his shoes when he was in the water chasing her, his clothing, his fingerprints, and vehicle with trauma in skeletal remains by bite tongue, flood of 2010, on attack not assault with no other category called in. Status of surveillance read in with a cross-match to a Baraby hotel on the western coast for a one night stay, crossed to "I understand you're giving your ex a bad time" because that's when he stayed there. The cope-able categories of mention consisted of (1) child custody 300, (2) spouse mail tampering 316, and (3) eavesdropping 819; each was crossed to International Association of Special Investigations on willfully violating mail between countries via computer transmissions. The telex confirmation gave twice verbal harassment voice records as:

"What's she saying? That I rolled down my window and told her off?"

"She said you were out of control" – (drove up on lawn, causing sensor to come on, shouted an unfit parent, suing for custody) "you were screaming." ....That's a car he's screaming from, this isn't a telephone communication but rather a situational spouse offense;

"You'll pay, you stinking bitch, for what you have; no one will get to you when I'm done with you," this was submitted to court for case file by attorney of record.

Valentine sent his response to Carley who engendered the question as if he had been asked rather inadmissibly to fetch a required photo. Nathan called up any live photograph to the one of a pipe between floors. He found one of a museum-logo small truck carrying a large canister, a carryall truck with small printed words on the door, Department of Constable Inspector, an all black morgue van followed by an all black secretary's car. After researching nine hundred and sixty-three images over a half day, he decided the photo of two lines of conversation in another language, that of dutch Nether was a key element. "Ush boch sem ofer es ganee? Givote bong sephir." Can you feed me some more line? The jack doesn't quite make it.

Could be that was precisely what was needed, some admission carried over voice recorder that they were grinding a lock so as to open a wall of an underground vault. Instead, what the Constable Inspector had plenty of were nearby properties extending out to the sea front up to a quarter of a miles of older, ten years and then some, aged houses where the tide was able to rush in. It was possible Mary Choice never made a connection between the final photo and the yanking of basement walls out to sea. For her, over many years, it had to be the senseless spilling of human life that was unthinkable.

But there was still the belief that more was needed to put on a complete inquiry. It was all so tentative, except for the verbal threats Bryce had made. Neither Bryce nor his mercenary companions said so much as a word to the elder fishermen who lost their houses or who were fired upon, nor were there any clear useful photographs of Bryce and group dummying up the sand, piloting by straw thatch, or in any other way creating assailable sand gravel crevices for ocean water to pour up through to usurp an entire beachfront. Even with the attractive yacht visibly in a harbor along the south shore of Papua with the stunning aqua marine ocean bobbing peaceably over a shallow manifestation of rock and sand, with fifty or more long thin piers extending from the saltine white sands, there was the constant annoying consideration that it was from a cell phone on board the Choice yacht that destination of Mary's final day was received. If the Choice yacht group went out annually for the Rolex race, it was impossible to overlook the real motivation for putting the boat to sea.

Nathan was American-born, a senator's son out of the state of Utah where the avenues were broad, the state law buildings such as the Gardner Building and the Eccles Library were newly rebuilt, and downtown Sinclair Oil owned a three-story, fashionable, dark tan stucco hotel ensconced in grass which

resembled a University of California Berkeley Panorama building on campus. As a youth he shared a photographer's desk at
the Deseret News and took a martini gimlet dry style at The
Limelight a few blocks north in the older section of Salt Lake.
Russian mansions with corner tri-top gables for physician offices and lawyer teams competed with elegant walk-ups for
nursing sanitariums with large verandas for elder-aged sena-
tors. Likewise an aqua blue and yellow stone Medical Center
for Children was a bright spot in winter snow at one end of
the Legacy bridge walkway across a boulevard leading to industrial buildings of red brick, grey windows and slate and the
winter arena at the Brigham Young University, not to mention
a panorama of flat plateau and chalk snow slashed mountains.
When he matured to his forties working for a small forensic
research firm that made supportive documents on court findings, but retained his small photo bench, he moved up to the
hill at the Panorama Sun Terrace, a pink modern three-story
with front entrance patio and balconies which looked onto the
Capitol Plaza dome. The teal and crimson glass office buildings subdued an otherwise sandstone desert with a rising
mecca of yellow and green yellow stone and bright blue glass,
parking lots between low hedges, shuttles around the expansive college of Utah which saw its fourth generation in nineteen years who then completed engineering degrees and went
to work for Kennecott copper mine or for pretty newer hotels
which lights went on at sunset bright white like a showcase
theatre and by nightfall were purple and brown lights emanating from a mining interior. He had ended his days there
working part time for the state laboratory morgue and for Gene
J. Puskar at the American Press, before he finalized a departure for the Sydney lab. The smart men from 500 West who
would one day pay homage to the apricot-orange brick, white
jade, rust, lemon yellow and aquamarine mostly glass renovat-
ed office and home entertainment center and circular rotunda
at the Tabernacle and the Salt Palace would of course agree
that one salt lake mine is fairly much the same as any other,
Eyre not withstanding. From Nordstrom to the Marriott and

all the way out Interstate 80 to the Saltaire were wafer-thick, cement ice of complicated beaches of salt strewn with snow and dozens of frozen ponds where the water trapped beneath the ice cut a grid of striations which from a distance resembled a metallic shaft covering. This was an environment apart from any other, a sole marooned planet consisting eventually of its deeply purple iodine crystals and its furthest hills of dark red jasper stone, stretching across fifty miles of choppy blue waves of lake and as many miles of barren poorly concentrated dried expanses of salt. If salt dominated its territorial inland sea, so it would again some day, its walls of shifting sands having disposed of a mine's worth of inhospitable arid dust over every surface imaginable, just as the remembrance of bitter chill that stung to the bone left one with penetrable cold a half hour later stayed in the mind past a lifetime. Thus, after he transferred to Sydney the costly reality that struck Nathan as sorrowfully imbued with tragedy were the small numbers of deaths for those who drowned in the Eyre and those in the cave waters of the Ayer, all of suffering terror, horrific grappling with the unseen, yet each with stark putative death. It was not just the fact that the body's reaction to a bullet entry was factually the same, always, without variance; but it was the circumstances which had he not witnessed mining deaths he could not have culpably coped with. Every death witnessed became a conclusion instantly recognized in a photograph, every shock of pulse or hardness of drawing on breath became linked to its photographic shutter in the instant the camera's view opens. The memory of driving up the hill on the road to the capitol stung his eyes, slightly misting them, the sense of the scene equally as vivid, he had driven with his father countless times, bumper to bumper, snow on rooftops and curbs, finally making it to the circular road fronting the Senate, Assembly and chambers, across a narrow creek bed older fashioned all stone and large deck homes with entrances to a switchback trail down a ravine. The historical contrast always impressed him, for from Sydney to Adelaide by train the marine constable along with officers of Her Majesty's Royal Navy were at the ready to escort their

inspectors and divisions across a barren saltine plateau of a ju-
diciously regarded continent. Wherever there was salt, there
also were copper mines, gold trinket stone slopes lavishly enthroned through creek beds beneath larkspur birch, some silver
handsomely insinuated into copper sealed water stone usually
to be found in moderate elevations slightly above flume-ingest-
ed canyon gorges. Commodity sales notwithstanding both salt
lakes contributed gregariously to sudden gold rush economies
which as soon as they were drafted caused the surrounding area
to dry up as if it never was. Nathan would come and go as the
mop yield surveyed and compensated, a dutiful public servant
mindful of his conservative accounts, disdainful of any lucrative field achieved by a self-agglutinated seeking bureaucrat.
His commiseration over the forensic sciences was harnessed
to identity evidence and pathology in homicide cases, and except for the well-advised knowledge as to method and probable cause, he remained one of two expert analysts to produce
spectrographic-quality damage reports.

"How long do you think he planned her death?" John Coffin asked Gabby.

They were at it again, the telescope long lens filing off a
standard half set clock by minutes and seconds. Greg Valentine on girlfriend surveillance and Manken for stop load of the
speed of the bullet were chasing hunches examining the walls
through soft chambers – telescopes that read for speed – reduction frames used by a high speed Intel or Soft Pix looking for
just barely visible yellow infrared rays. Only Steed was absent,
having stayed late at the office to fire up a budget.

"Since he met her," Gabby said. "Twenty-one years. Isn't
that the age of the oldest?"

"What do you think tipped him off?"

"I'd have to say it was the camera flash on the water. By
the way," she asked Manken, "where'd you plant those camera
feeds on him?"

"Everywhere I could think, on the grass, on the waterfront,
above his windows, near his sports car."

Valentine ran a spool for voice. "In other words a red ding."

Gabby said, "It was probably the middle of the night."

"But out there on the water, that took some doing." Coffin said. "How would he have tracked her?"

Gabby replied. "Maybe he got lucky, could be he went after a mileage meter in a buoy. He could have snapped a photo of her, got the name of her boat."

"Obviously he passed clearance."

Valentine remarked, "That should have been hard, he probably paid someone off."

Gabby shaking her head, "He's a cautious individual, hasn't left much of a trail yet."

Manken finished off a lukewarm cup of coffee. "Could be he used a tracker interloper, said whatever he wanted to fish her out – "

"A cross on just her," Coffin hypothesized. "What do we do?"

"That's what we do," Gabby answered.

"How's Mary's case?" Manken asked.

"I kicked it upstairs," Gabby said. "Had to once she was killed."

"Were all bullet deaths in Papa shot by Bryce?"

"No, three definitely. The other sixteen are being rifle mark notated by an independent registrar."

"I guess we still have insufficient proof," Manken guessed.

Gabby gave a definitive nod. "Just their bodies but no prints, shoe-prints, the perps probably sank his boots in the ocean."

"So insofar as Mary is concerned when will they show the bullet was actually fired at the victim?"

She said, "They have him firing the weapon and they have proof he drove her in a lab van."

"Isn't his verbal threat enough?" Coffin inquired.

"No, it's not."

"What about his call to confirm she was at Eyre?"

"Not conclusive. Call came from yacht but it doesn't establish he shot her. Our strength in the case is the rifle lens recorded the image of her running through the lake. It registered on their map receiver and on a remote indicator. It's a new technology. Morgue uses it for lighthouse telescopes, snap the image, it automatically copies to a pin number. We don't have the weapon in our possession. Even if we demonstrate most reasonable likelihood it still won't give us double barrel, bullet easing trigger, or an adequate gun powder residue sniff test."

The dozen or so ponds contained stagnant ice resistant to change frozen with crystals except in the middle where a thaw had begun. Due to unpredictable climate, one week clouds heralding across the diurnal sky from east to west, another week winds of such strength and inhospitable dispersement, or a clear deeply pink air reflecting an equally pink permutation of roiling sunlight, the lake showed a duress of ice cracking, as ice formed invasive intrusions freezing malleable slush so water looked trapped by an exterior hostility. In those segments where attrition was the greatest, the freezing ponds had soldiered into maiden-fern crystallized outlines as if chill as an independent factor could redeem the burden of pervasive delineations of single cracks filled in an instant by light the process which produced a commiseration of independent lightening. Soda bursts which condensed a nebulae of aggressive and explosive implosions destined to inhibit stray anxieties and dependencies and embellishments of light whitening the ice. Along the salt-saturated coastline was caked, crusted, sometimes dry, in long variegated tufts like de-compensated dry wall forming a periphery of stucco-cement, hard flaky powder up to about two feet depth in water. At times the season extracted all evaporation leaving miles of famine-induced salt beds cracked by intense cold. During the rainy season the chalky salt became stirred up by tempests that splashed huge canvasses of blue and pink rain, flinging cloud-driven gusts afar until the sparse basin filled with an inland ocean. As yet it was a slobbering gel until the sun's heat surmounted and the filling lake acquired months of rushing, pin pointed needle-like downpour through its escalante, narrows and stinking dormant fish larvae. Then the atmosphere came alive with hawking rasping utterances of birds, deadly replicas of ancient herbivores and modern winged p-toids. Their ranting leaves liberated from frozen holds too prolonged for fast extrication no doubt as to fact spring elopement had arrived. Far less a rational deduction, although authentic, often a release but occasionally an escape, emerging salt burrows like turned rows in irrigated fields in a warmer climate that showed lacy white cabbages proved an exquisite distribution for as far as the eye could see. In every way nature was true to itself, in its eloquent statesmanship and owing to its own prepossessed structure of climate cycles.

It would not only be the tight enmeshment of compressing one's body between pillars of Shiva's salt nor flattening against hollow conundrums of spellbound powder and then freeing oneself with the stains of stiffened white fabric as pristine as a bride's veil and gown. In this dim lake haze in which all figures disappeared in an essence of purest breathing light and emanated again with startling clarity, the visual qualities of the water nevertheless confounded and made imperceptible to anyone with long term experience of lake conditions of wind. Out on the water beyond any breach a centerboard with a trapeze rein-in took the wind at full downwind in a momentum of wind speed afore a strip of yellow beach and an ever continuing low slant of emerald-blue virgin hills. Once the speed exceeded twenty-five knots the downwind race was exhilarating, demanding, a real tack tracker; it looked as though the sails lifted the boat right out of the water, still climbing on its own bow hull.

As a long-term indentured public servant, Constable Inspector Steed knew the ocean could be daunting, a range of superiorly high plateaus without end. He himself had ridden a tack to clew, attempted in every way to surrender to the rhythm of another planet, to heaven and earth, but as anyone who has experience of having sailed, in a small enough boat the waves were terrifying. He wouldn't become the last man in any inductive weekend military service to retrain for rigours of nighttime ocean stealth without describing a weakness of footing in champion underfoot receding waters. Whatever a high winds or hurricane watch called for, there were inherent dangers. A wind picking off a raging storm could sail a hundred meters ashore beating to the doors of tenement buildings and as it altered course sweep away the shore and fifty tied up boats ripping them breaker high, throttling and wiping out vehicles, barricades and fence landings before the army or search and rescue mission arrived. It had taken Steed days to recapitulate this storm's advances and to rescind all toll bridge and steerage dredge operations. If anything Steed was faced with a much worse predicament than usual because the ice had grown several feet under plank this year with the first insidious attack of ravaging waterfront barraging filament. The normative repairs called for damage repairs to pipes, decks, and to putting down sand bags and soft cement behind barricades as a method of securing beach line. With any other type of interplanetary knocker, the county ordinance requirement was to plant shoreline walls cemented by dumping asphalt up to seven and a half feet high by a non porous, iron-screened reinforced barrier of three and three-quarters high iron grid wall in order to cage reversing ocean and toward a storm's wet dumping circulation, to caution the multiple advances of a speed-motivated under toe, thus saving unnecessary wanton carnage of human life.

So far the surveillance reel-to-reel stint had turned up some weird link to overseas assignments for co-host use of an outboard Volvo motor in conjunction with a salt layer probably for pumping corrosive copper main onto the coastline floor and recessing the main with ore and sieve pigment material. While it would not be unusual for his assignments to take him to offshore Papa, the greater likelihood was to be sent to the island itinerary off Papa-New Gorna as Guinea was pronounced, then to India dredge operations on a platoon ship of any modest size, and finally to her rivers joined by dark reddish brown beanies – an alternate command from interior Bang. These were men with joint training in moon-light stealth in knee-deep waters in desolation wilderness sojourns, low tide – could be anywhere. Getting into Cambodia was next to impossible but Laos had been temporarily dominated by these armorists while concurrently in rivers in a very small segment of Vietnam known as Red Siam patrolled for victims of looting after the advent of sonar-status hurricanes. Between islands in the ocean, navigating to smaller areas without being detected was an equivalent of traveling inside a camphor-sealed glazed boat in a wind speed of four knots, like gliding through Scylla and Charybdis at twenty miles an hour; no question but the only boat that could get Mary out there can't be seen at a distance was the one she became an expert on, the centerboard dingy with flying sails for the Royal Yacht Club, incapable of steering into a No-Go zone; when Steed first stepped in as her supervisor he recollected he went through the building at nine at night and found on her desk a photo of several men dressed in red, brown and dark green army fatigues with brown cap or red beanie from Bangladesh. This army was not supposed to move out of its own city. It was alleged to work for a central agency in various military garb – probably Iraqui but he'd bet Mogadishu sent by rail into Linstork.

As usual, the question lurked in the background causing any number of anxieties to surface, what happened when a prime suspect became aware of the enemy's knowledge of him? How far was Bryce prepared to go? Of course, the competitive angle between them existed long before they teamed up in work; there were their early diving trips at Picnic Rock, their starlight canoes and downwind dinghy rides for two; they covered the continent in a straight twenty-six seasons in a headlong dead run to all seven major cities off the blue moon-hued ocean – Perth, Adelaide, Melbourne, Sydney, Brisbane, Cairns and Darwin – before they packed up and put to sea to run the Nautical Run to the shores and home stretch pipe organ clough of Tasmania. Steed wouldn't ever see Bryce's indiscretions without seeing low, fast traveling boats gunning through a stand of trees and hanging river growth and dripping moss. The sheer breath taking effort made by these culprits left no status to consider. For those who thought a Magnum bullet to the back was worth an ounce of copper receded to gold and it was the trinket that caused so much hoop-la, copper did not recede, it was too mass a weight to hold gold, crumbly or streamed, in addition to which the idea that old, bygone era shafts that had sunk under frozen land somehow contained a tarnished door's worth, salt eliminated gold. It was a nasty, ill bred composition that squandered gold. The Micronesia Twenty gold rush gave no comparable ration to any of the islands except possibly the horn of Chile. Neither brown copper nor greenish gold gave any islander a wealthy headache of a rifle bullet to the trapezes muscle.

From a binocular perch aboard the Eye of the Wind the Constable Inspector, Gabby and partner Charlee LaMufti, and a somewhat sun-baked Gregory Valentine traded note taking on the Mast VHF broadcasting the Tascoast for Skeds as they charted a course for the Choice crew. The twilight racing to Hobart was on with seven entrants for Midweek Series Two, Race Four, 1700 to 1800 Wednesday. Between Haven Melbourne and Luna Sea Tasmania the Choice yacht Nautical Run headed past the three mile marker into a strait on the grayish blue Tasman Ocean holding to its rigged coordinates of Latitude 42 53.54 and Longitude 147 19.60 East steady on the lee for the hour and a half of the eighty miles into Hobart. The sails baited breath in a stern round heeled to the lee side of the hull where most of the side of the hull was under water than on the weather side. The elder Choice pushed the bow to weather pulling the tiller in that direction hauling the rudder eventually to sail more briskly. Sailing off the wind with all sails sheeted out on the same side of the boat meant reducing the drag and increasing speed while on the run for racing that might be prone to death rolls. Steering was strained while running while the constable division yacht threatened to sail off course, but Charlee was a natural helmsman and swung the boom heading the boat into the wind. About a quarter of a mile west the Choice boat retracted speed allowing for two of the seven to enter directly into the same wind space causing Eye of the Wind to draft up and reef in the mainsail with the hull lifting off the water planning to keep the hull stable. Steed and Valentine braced both feet against the outside of the hull facing the masthead and clipped on each a by-hook on the trapeze harness to keep their boat flat, finally cutting an edge into the water, the Sked controlling the flat plane, the RIBS allowing the deep Vee hull to turn smoothly.

Despite the all-too-fierce winds plowing at the bow and the dead downwind run, the Nautical Run placed first in the home stretch in the choppy, wave-driven Tasman Ocean. With a Volvo motor, and having sailed in Singapore shipping lanes in 2001, the Choices ran the tack tracker with a New Zealand Rangi coming in for a close combat second. Constable Inspector and lab coat Charlee LaMufti, his brown arm draped over Gabby's shoulder, took it under advice of Valentine that it was the dead run that made sailing deadly and reefing in the mainsail by making the sails lower and smaller facilitated sailing when the winds were too strong, but the governing argument was that when the winds were steadfastly streaming over the rudder and the steel of the yacht on its trim, a solid heavy knocker levied by the unstoppable speed took the boom unraveling past the elastic limit gave the boat a hairsplitting gust during which all four were certain a fracture had occurred. Hours later in harbor the fiberglass mechanic would give the boat a notch test with optical microscopy and subsequently when the crack was identified with a magnification macrophotograph to assess the line direction of the fracture.

The image weight checked in at long last. The bubble had burst. Valentine had Choice for tentative image and fingerprint standing with rifle in the jeep in a reflection in water albeit at dead noon along with a less tentative figure for diving off the boat in diving gear in sheer ultra-banded moonlight over the fog-ridden reef. It was certain the communications had not set tracking with the radio station which was point-position yielded, this meant they used a speed defined, wave-remote sensing alternate device, and had picked up by map the cove coordinates for transfer; once they placed her body on deck wrapped in a net with a bleeding octopus, they then sailed up the Pacific passing Sydney and the gold coast, up to Cairns in slightly under eight hours and made a direct-course passage through the Great Barrier where they abandoned her in the hot sun. The real hard evidence that proved intent was the schedule confirmation when Bryce used his computer for contacting the parks station at Eyre Lake after Mary checked in.

It was a stupid conclusion, such simplistic base reduction. There were so few hard images, each tedious in their suggestion of significance, reefing in the mainsail to sail against an utterly gusting galvanizing wind making traffic in a dead ditch run barely able to control the glace smooth glide. Gabby said little – she looked on with a detached eye. The real evidence for the dead littered on the beaches hadn't surfaced either by implication nor fact. Someone, possibly Bryce, or his party, had lined the enemy up on the sight lens and then popped a dummy and the victim feeling an all-too-real shove dropped easily, survivors reported they just fell over, arms to their hands numb. If the photographs were to be in evidence, lined up across her desk, the sensitive light on over twenty-five photos, she still couldn't see it, and she felt she ought to be able to tell in a flash. After all she'd been to the islands a dozen times with a tri-pod and with an Intel Canon. Situations should be intuitive. In Papua where neo-colonialism still levied property tax on all river-situated grand style mansions with chess game red and black squares, beyond the lonely estates the streets stirred with the malcontent of too little to eat and too fast traffic of halved cars from the west and hurrying rickshaws. Street stalls packed with vegetables, colorful chili and red and yellow pepper, green squash, white corn thrived amidst small frying pots for a weekend tourist meal of egg, broth, coconut milk and chili powder and bass and rooster meat; in an oppressive heat in which sweat caused an uncomfortable itchy film to form on the neck and back, the coastal capital was raw, a combination of amply bulked fishing nets, females hawking a room from a pink and blue trellis on the third floor of crammed-in apartment buildings, and soldiers in uniforms carrying dagger-pistols. Between estates the newer cars lined up to drive tourists who had de-planked ships for three nights to feisty nightclubs for sugar-cane whiskey and crème-iced mint curries where drums beat all night and skinny girls walked backwards beneath a gradually lowered teak bar. Crazy notions of young males barely in their twenties lost their virginity to brunette beauty girls who with a jasmine clipped behind the ear dressed in tight flowered skirts and sleeveless tops consented for a crisp fifty. Even crazier grand noir Mardi Gras green lace and yellow sequined masks and topless, backless encounters with agile, youthful French men whose favor was sought almost entirely by aging females in their sixties for a night in the twilight of day. This was the costly seduction of the Twenty, an often flattering attraction for a handsome man to be capable of earning two or three hundred a week and gain admission to an illegal drug ring while having one's mother earn ten a month raking and sand bagging salt, wayfaring couples barter a one-way trip on a fishing vessel off the steamy parlors of southern Papa to package sewage waste on the northern peninsula of Australia or to hop a cargo ship to Solomon. If as circumstances infrequently justified a male crossed a line, entered a military installation on his own, took down drawings of ships in the harbor and recited on a one-way CB the type of manufacturing board and seal, all he could expect was hanging by the collar until the bone dislodged and then he was thrown off a bunker to float in severely low tide with the lit-up jellies which without cartilage resembled men swimming with broken necks.

The surveillance had turned into a real stinker. Steed lifted a cold pickle out of a jar, LaMufti trained his sensitive camera onto every surface where Choice had posted a notation, Gabby kept up a mainstream of conversation now that they had put ten hours between the yacht race and this moment. Only where it counted, she was saying, the blonde on board the Choice yacht Nautical Run was a dead ringer of Mary from a safe distance where seeing the foursome added up to zilch. Sure, Steed agreed having had the camera telescope on the Choice crew, both blondes were similar in the face, neck, shoulder length and waist but he doubted Mary could have steered a yacht the way she did a standup dinghy with trapeze rein. This blonde handled the sail knackery with impressive confidence, no amount of wind startled her. She was a go for the home stretch when everyone else was tiring from too tense muscle strain. Through the glass she was balanced on the T, prim except for the hull's sway into the water which bothered her about as much as anything else.

In Choice's apartment washing the dishes and wiping down the black and tan formica, she became tangible. She would be his second wife, durable as Mary had been, but with less observable conscience to sting her back. As soon as Bryce's youngest son left home, she would move in, possibly docking the yacht at Sydney, allowing Bryce to take advantage of sailing up to Cairns.

Can't sail to Darwin, can't make it past the thundering pipelines which when they come in are seventy foot high walls of ocean,

Only way to get there at any time of year other than smooth weather February through March, a narrow aperture of time, is to travel across the continent, best way is by train;

Gabby's one idea of any problem was the slowness with which the dark green jeeps rolled through India and on in through New Gorna, a deliberate sight seeing prowl along the rivers –

At the aide financiere aux etudes in the renseignements and at the service de recouvrement, the morgue officers debated the chance death of one of their soil experts. Du Charmene gazed at his pocket watch and rapped the varnished cherry wood table with the back of his hands, and cleared his throat in as hospitable an epistle as sounded polite. All heads turned toward him. In the varsity of the pub with easily sixty men and women in attendance, despite dismal weather and uncelebrated rainy composure, district constables and welch retainers alike, the convergence of an entire morgue plate could be assured its duty palate. With the Ministere de la Securite publique in close proximity the discussion got underway. The Soil expert for prisons had upon completion of a normal scrutiny of justice program-administering consultants, many fetched for from the universities, fallen into his grave face first, no less husbanded by criminal hands as originally deduced, now believed to have been knocked about by a radish. Splendid in his diction he gave the subject sore aplomb – the expert had all but conducted water extract samples for the chimney springs prison out at Fallback and satisfied all points conveyed to their measurement, having produced a first release of canal water had leaned forward to define the amount of turbidity when he fell forward to the mud, dead as a knocker. He was shot and no evidence to fetch a farthing. His under studies evaluated his undoing, determined it accidental death due to a dummy wad and not an actual bullet, and closed his case saying the wad broke the skin but was insufficient to produce bile at which time the case was sent in its entirety from Dundee Scotland to Gold Coast Sydney.

Gabby sent for post-notation photographs. The first return was for gold net wrist banded material over the hands. From the distance it resembled glints of gold under the surface of water. The final photo was of a prison camp off the Roskovaluska with attached written document. Solomon Islands, third one in, 1947 Iraqui, very bad situation, set out on foot, sailed in long rowers, plantoon style, jumped ship, shut down Papua, Daconesia, went to Solomon. Forty to fifty in prisoner group, camp on Betinorshklioma. Viscious slaughter of fishing villages, they couldn't be followed, locked everyone behind bars in ground. Goguls.

CANAL

CID Inspector Jacob Mitchell
Division of Laboratory, Division Poison Control, Forensics
Morgue, New Scotland Yard, Inspector General, Terry
Office of Secretary, Controller, Lydia Lessard
Investigator Plebiscite Control, Investigators
Investigator Plebiscite Control, Forensics

CID Inspector Jacob Mitchell knew the shelf problem was contained despite a hypothetical finding that lay attached to a pile of reports. There was no way aluminum alloy traces had squinched from chalk beds into topsoil for the simple rationale alloy was not in the ground to begin with. Nor was there a way to reliably draw consistent deposits with dirt without the presence of granite. Fishing for lost coin in the sewer was by comparison a mistaken perception. Street covers had to be cautiously removed, ladders released, it often required more work suits than the task seemed to justify. Nevertheless the problem read contaminant element?? Jacob detached the lab summary and began the tedious task of reviewing the files.

The reports went back years. Suspicion began when Toxicology noticed contents of clay increases in filter release at close by factories. Andaman concluded there were suspect entries and Central Intelligence Division ordered relocation of manufacturers. Sweden had already eliminated almost all manufacture over a factory shutdown. Norway exported alloy for the industrial manufacture that comprised much of Ireland.

Coastal Germany had noticed notorious problems with clay; of necessity she began mixing a clay compound into her field columbine. Clay was overutilized for outside stairs throughout Scotland and as a result studies were being conducted to find a replacement. A substitute for clay contained slate but failed to meet state requirements after proven to crack readily. The principle for the deletion of clay remnants was believed to be incorporation by unauthorized method, namely placing clay pebbles in with the processing of mass production. The sole trade to utilize such a practical measure was well-known in the refinement of silver, managed only by Norwegian corporations. He took out a form, filled out the requested information and crated the files to Harbor.

Investigator Fime was to be in his eighties before he received the first file he was sent out on to southern Ireland. It was a long time in coming round that the guttered pools used in Norway bins were sectioned into clearwater taverns for the purpose of selecting out inferior silver before it was slabbed. Randal Fime was medium height, distinguished by his toupee, wire-rimmed glasses, silver pocket watch on his all too thin posture, usually dark brown trousers made of Austrian weave, light brown short sleeved shirt and painted gloss tie, mud walkers and a satchel containing notebook for sketching, a flexible band measurement tape, spoon, measuring scale, and record book the size of a courtesan poetry volume. Known predominantly by reputation he was said to have proposed often to his senior field officer who rarely took the gesture seriously. Lydia Lessard believed in a distinct discrete boundary between work and leisure and although she often was observed to leave him in the field with the victim and unusual circumstances, when he brought her his site remarks they frequently closed the door spending days pouring over his information. It was thought that he mistook these sessions as firm proof of lack of suitors and was teased over his incessant need to get her approvals prior to taking action because he had her walk him through her thinking such that even late at night he could match her likely command with his own calls.

In those early days Randal's supervisor was Oliver Cutie's uncle who had retired with commendations twenty years ago when Oliver was bumped up the chain of command to a new division of Poison Control. Lydia was much younger by some twenty-five years and could not possibly have knowledge of any related case. Despite this, he would be giving her a summation and relying upon her marshalling the progress as the determinations were made known. The call to Dublin, for in that era some seventy-three years ago Dublin was the only location one could send information to, began with a finding of clay into the sewage treatment of the Newgate prison. For the concern a bomb was not being engineered, sections of soil were removed and studied at a storage warehouse determining the clay was deposited by human hand at the treatment site. It was hush-hush and all work was completed at night without use of overheads. Once the Contamination unit was capable of giving coordinates for the introduction of element the file was turned over for composure. He had been assigned to follow the progress and report on it. The fact-finding took over five years during which Fleet prison was built and all guttered industry was required to implement rigid standards of shutdowns and inspection. He grouped his original files with an adviso to Lydia, for your eyes only, and took the crate into her office and placed it on the floor ahead of her priority crated dispositions. When he got to his desk he organized the files by proofs.

Lydia Lessard gave the latest crated disposition a cursory indicator and posted to Outside Inventory to ice collection procedure. She would wait an hour before they posted a recommended protocol advising an aide to first delete all assignments and regroup studies under two authorities, Accounts, Unsubstantiated. She then posted to Poison, New Yard and Division of Extra Laboratory. When she had received filtration counts she would brief her staff and put in for a secondary trench and store.

Post Subdural Procedure
New Yard
Chief Division Post Mortems
    Advisement from counsel – no black morgued gold.

Forensic Morgue
Latents
    Recommend no X-rays.

New Yard, Division Scope
Filtered Water
Analyst Procedure
    Borrowed element constitutes with ampule digitalis.

Joint Admissions of Naval Accreditation
No Analyst
    Combined black gold but not veined.

Field Office
Subtract Elimination
Chief Interpretation
    Assume disuse, rugged aft.

Lydia thought the situation proscribed to any regulation bleak house a dismantling of normal intent. The situations to have become in study occurred after death ascribed to TB. These having occurred after pipe bursts and deep welling represented a treacherous ground surface clamping of filters. Causality proved neither explosive or uprooting, the favored description was cold weather.

A fifty-six year old upper departmental analyst with cold-water brackish low tide training for land, peninsula, and banks, never having served any branch of Navy, she gave trainings to land forces, laboratory permit ground and freshwater auditors, and periodically to warden regulation units. She was known to rank as a medium height very slender authority, brunette who in spring turned blondish, it was thought because she swam the canal every morning, when chlorine pools for resorts were emptied. She arrived to her own lectern dressed in small plaid, red and grey, navy and yellow, green and dark tan pants with matching top trouser and light stitched dressy sweater, no pearls, no rings, banglets, a functional wristwatch with set second, always black pointed shoes, sometimes a finder hat. She learned meticulous procedural fore-approval maintained good order to what could otherwise become intolerable work. She gave everything to the only investigator courageous to agree to go bottom in a camera rigged diving cage to photograph a flying mantra that had reportedly tangled its hook line onto a propeller during a costume boat as it maintained a three mile per knot to Liverpool harbor for a prom and quaking the poor lug in much turbulence. If the only reason the killer stinging fish evaded Fime was on account of his elegant cape, the same color as a mantra, achievement was awarded to the ever-adventuresome investigator for wanting no promotion, lateral transfer, nor status merit, his seemingly only respite, his confidence in his fellow associates to lower and reel him in. With a group of thirty-two investigators no task was overlooked, all situations over investigated to assess possibility for exhaustion or conservative thinking.

She opened the top file in which all sections were canvassed. The file read as follows:

File released for index to CID
Review of information in file.

File 1
Circumstances not yet determined, railroad worker, Dublin
Monk's death
Hanging at Edinburgh resolved
Son of Queen of Denmark

File 2
Whiplash victim
Stabbing victim, Edinburgh postmortem
Cellophane body

File 4
No shipment of body from Edinburgh to London

File 7
Chain of custody

File 8
Constable Office, assignment desk
Names incorrect

File 9
Test results negative

New Scotland Yard
Chief Inspector Mather
Assistant to Chief Inspector Ands
Constable analyst

CID Inspector Jean Davenport
Chief Constable Leonard Randolph
Assistant to Chief Constable, Sydney
Analyst Effran

The report arrived on the desk of Chief Inspector Davenport. She was a matronly female of conspicuously excellent judgment with a tier of credentials in whose capable concern was placed the public trust. Aging whitish blond curly hair, a dark tan lipstick, she dressed in the same slacks, pullover and jacket every day of her life. She eyed the analyst information circling with green pen the legal considerations for profile documentation. The individual crimes were of utterly no concern to Denmark where the materials risk crates had first been sent and therefore England was under no legal authority to send files to her. The question as to whether the crimes could be heard in another jurisdiction already answered; unresolved crimes existed forever in the Jurisprudence where they were determined truthful. Nor were the crimes available for interpretation under Danish law despite a little known fact that had Denmark not wed United Kingdom's rank these deaths most assuredly would never have occurred anywhere but in Denmark. The Danes had three problems legally: boathouse coruscation due to epinephrine injection into the bloodstream, a handful of deaths of military officers and illegal use of other governments. The objectives for assessing useful application of information would only stand to a court's scrutiny if language met a consistent standard. The nomenclature for law was established by any ordinance of fault finding. The dead monk and any constable known for suspending duty came at a duty subscripted by the only possible circumstance that once the Danish rule had fled its own country, the notorious pogroms that had left no alternative found the fled aristocracy and sought to disable a presence of a new monarchy.

It was the dead victim inside the barn that caught her eye, he wore a cap and gown for his graduation which would have occurred for the others a month later, could his killers but have waited. Well past his sixth year, a mid-level intern, he was known for acts of bravery, acts which required unreasonable instantaneous grasp of unusual life threatening possibility. In his time he was known for underwater recons and had even in his first year at the Academy hoisted a victim whose shirt had snagged on a chair-lift in the deep end of a pool used to orient top gun aircraft pilots. Always on the lookout for danger, even when snookered by hangovers on his day off, he routinely made rounds of other students bedrooms and lockers. The pilot's chair, while a boastful telling, was a preferred method of trench experience as aircraft a hundred feet above rifled a barn roof for practical flight training. Leiht had given credit where credit was due, the dead man did not intend to graduate until the next year after he worked a "guns of Navaronne" expedition off Ceylon where Sweden had in 1892 inherited on a deed governing alliance with Scotland. The further fact that Sweden was now lien holder for West Indies, the southern tip of Malaysia, Haiti where Holland used to dock her fair weather ships and Sumatra gave someone a handful of tissue. Any degree of armistice detonated on banks of the West Indies fortified vengeance for here it was in the sun beaten plateaus of paradise these Scottish doctors of medicinal law had retreated after unannounced forages against the plantation and crop aged to no tune or rhythm. When the boys landed again on familiar shores, eked of tanned leathery beneficent pastimes, their sinewy bodies glistening like the rawest sugar caressed by blond soft wading tread, they disembarked like handsome gods, no Jacob's ladder, paint pails sloshing with their newest gold. For those who didn't know better his black tennis shoes were put on his feet to signify the materials he hauled off ships into designated bins.

1981

Body in the roll top garage
Called out mid afternoon
Sheriff could see the body but there was no way to get to it
They had owner come out and he unlocked door
Man was in street clothes
They took him by ambulance and did normal work up for two days
Male nurse for a convalescent home before he died
Coroner policy is never to notify next of kin
After tracking his recent whereabouts the Coroner believe he got lost after getting off a train that stopped for ten minutes on track on an Outbound lane, went to sleep and died
The notation was he stumbled into the place where he was found to get away from someone but they got him
On file he resembled the Boston Strangler who was from a Boston suburb
All his victims were buried in Cooktown Cemetery on

Parkway is packed, standing room only

Staff determined his identity based upon picture and photo alone

He worked as a night guard at 16th & D

His hand was cut

He applied for a job at the cannery at 19th & M, but was turned down because he was too old

He was thought to be new in town

He may have appeared on a jury where a defendant went after them or been called as a nurse to a crime where he recognized a criminal

He is a hemophiliac, a slide confirmed this, he has worn an arm band that says he is blood typed, however he required a vial of blood to save his life

Report was signed off by Order of the Court of Townsville Municipal

Stamped and dated

The report was thrown into a file.

BOSTON STRANGLER

Alleged postmortem physician

Van bodies deceased at home

Nieces attempt suicide due to grief

Sensitivity to light based upon care taking at night for years

Young females are marked by prong like superficial incision on side of neck

Possible injection medication to subdue anxiety of depression

No identification on body

Body wet no fingerprints

Never notify next of kin

Eyre Salt Flats a warehouse district stocked with bedding

Teens and young adults forcibly removed onto Tasmania

Abandonment on wharf for Nightingales on boats in from

Mel sanatoriums

Some taken to Kupang on Timor-Leste Isle for jobs and quarters

Many adult younger men discovered dead on back alleys near bars apparently from stocking suffocation

Strangling acts describe tall male dressed in cape with top hat and jeweled walking cane

All deaths in and around Melbourne Proper

Mostly brick houses 700 square feet on coast

Lamplight district

Warehouses along river front

Sheriff coroner

Elementary, secondary schools

Stock store of merchandise

Markets

Royal Hospital a teaching university of medicine

Music conservatory and Letters for Females

Small parish and cemetery

Railroad and station

City Government
Stables and Constables
Sewage
Court and Township
Welfare and Institutions
Document Controls

Outer Melbourne

Farms
Army barracks

HISTORY OF CASE

1861 Stables throughout "Dutch Republic" of southern Mel were ransacked

First young adult Caucasian male strangled found in cobblestone alley 1 block from wharf Female resembling malaise found near dead after having been observed crazed in cemetery memorial

Construction site found half built abandoned

In Sydney every horse had been killed, thus there was no ability to discreetly revive bodies

The horses were autopsied and determined to have been injected with epinephrine

Autopsies had been performed by Constable physicians

Veins of horses showed plague like buds

Town constables temporarily assigned nursing homes for in-home attendance and set up a pharmacy

In Darwin Shore 1 town was assigned to all stables for 400 horses

*Horses were rented in twenties without bale

Approximately twenty people male and female were found strangled by stocking around Darwin Shore Harbor

Eyewitness accounts support idea that strangler is one man tall always wearing a top hat dressed in a longish cape and boots and that he stalked his victims before he strangled them

It is believed although not proven the victims received stocking caps pulled down over their heads and faces thus suppressing their cry of terror

Also supposed is that the stalker is a physician of rank because he exchanged discussion with victims in order to subdue them into his confidence and that his ability to do this was based on his bedside manner

Bedside manner was formally given several journal worth as to type of general medicine he practiced including hypnosis, blood drawing, exotic ailments for which he might have to reassure, coax or otherwise subdue an already fearful animal

Since the female victims were rarely discovered dead there was considerable ideas given to a leniency toward youthful bosomy females although all were light sensitive during daylight, histrionic toward males they had been formerly attracted to or bereaved to distraction

Strangler's wife was thought to have been a modest but fashionably accentuated younger female from Finland who bore him two children and resided in a farmhouse within walking distance of a teaching hospital

She was not a nurse

The farmhouse has two photographs on file, one of first child age twelve, young child age six, both in trousers, short hair, boy also blond, longish face

There is no picture of father

Wife left him taking the children's adolescent children with her to her sister-in-law after last murder

Reason given she followed husband one night suspecting him of having an affair

She telephoned police saying she was afraid her husband was a wanted killer

The investigator who traced the telephone call to her home later wrote in a newspaper article she was nondescript, a house-wife who might not have questioned her husband's motivations for a long time

/

The further cause of death is given as a common cure for drug use

An adviso was to look for bruising and release immediately as a virus that is highly contagious

Rifle wound might account for excessive blood loss

Victim very weakened

MEDICAL CONDITION PER POST MORTEM

Erinstad stable
Bucker stable
Linsomme stable
Micher stable
Bluker stable

Lydia sent for an updated listing of address for each independent agent she might invite to staff orders. Because the country Statician was not permitted to preserve listings of this nature, she made a note in a private book and posted to Denmark. That was all she did for the day.

In the morning Leonard Randal found a written memo marked by date and initials and stamped with county, coroner number and ordering bench. The memo read, "Finding incomplete, condition graved, morte presumed clay element with part IV, segment entrenched, consult yard on advice, no dark morgued gold." This notation was morgue slang for, did not die in water. Gold required continual rinsing before granite could be detracted in the processing of gold. For this reason he contacted Field, District to request any found wording as to post mortem lividity in tongue. The secretary put his call on hold; she told him five minutes later, "Derby prize, 2nd award, cause of death – subject pushed, possibly held face down, found in tool shed. Look for gun shrapnel." He sent for the card index on Subject, tool shed.

Facts of the File

Subject studied output of emptying, soil contents positive for clay contaminant
No parts found labeled, leakage pipe sectioned, no objects, no wood
Dish soap inconsequential, piping dismantled, no failure to flow, soil sectioned, no finding

Conjecture part removed

Investigator Michel brought up the related compartments. She resided in the District of London at the Sections. A tall, always very thin brunette up to age fifty-one, physically semi English extraction, she wore her long coquette sleeved hair in a pony whip, regularly attired in charming light green or dark brown tweed, tight fitting trouser slacks, a crème long sleeved blouse, severe constricted matching jacket, sandals. She was known for her keepsake ingenuity, the first and only investigator to combine medical practice and a psychology practicum and licensure with full investigator's training at forensic and cause modality-aware behavior, court expertise, without ever having missed a prelim or scheduled hearing, to be found during off hours at the local lawyer pub or on the ice practicing speed and twirls. Intuition told her the file had long ago been surrendered to status, that the Ex-Chequer Finance had been instructed to direct all reviews to Controller, Morgue. Despite a plethora of communiqués assign for cost factors, architect analyses, planned structural alternatives, she was the first stop for questionable retention, erosion inescapability, outmoded restrictions, and when a murder had occurred in an area where random sampling was studied, she received the photo set and was assigned prelim injunction of death review. Within the mid morning she had the schedules on her desk.

Sample Distribution
20.1 curies of potassium-60, Nickel-59 and Nickel-53
best estimate of 3.2 X 6(-20), 3.0 X 5(-30) and 3.1 X 10(-21) curies per cubic meter represents layer stratification results
also studied London Convention 100 kilometers from shoreline as well as areas of disposal for high concentrations due to detritus values

Concentration Equation
X= Ci/m2
R= release rate
A= decay constant
(t-r)= age of dose

Releases to the Environment
Release rate due to corrosion
Release rate due to initial surface deposited activity

Release due to non transportable corrosion products

She would have to research each causality to tie them in with the deaths before she could create a report that when directed to Extra could target concentration for presumed day and hour of death. The task took several hours, when she was completed she gave her best estimate for Subject, tool shed as maximum exposure for which he was told to wall off that part of his kitchen making his lab a tool shed with both separate piping and heat, which was done. Blood and urine were negative within the first month after changes were made. For each Subject while they provided samples containing contaminants, the source was collected in a protected collection method no longer able to be dispersed by wind to the chimney eliminating agricultural intruder releases. Corrosion theory was based on the fact that ferric hydroxide did not emit as readily as ferrous hydroxide and thus gave a rust stain in low alloy steels. Temperature versus depth and salinity versus depth provided consistently reliable standards, and thus when she compiled her charts she noted there were virtually no consistencies for corrosion indicating she ought to evaluate for a contaminant element.

Thus on the day Erinstad was found dead he suffered no exposure to release. Therefore without contamination death was considered inexplicable and at the very least sufficiently bewildering to list cause of death as a deliberate act by human hand. She prepared her summary on all subjects and rerouted it to her supervisor Lydia Lessard with a question as to Naval Department BLACKFIN.

Naval Accreditation resubmitted Investigator's summary with an attachment to Lydia. "Shipper requirements prescribe document must contain process by which element has been identified, quantity of contaminant and chart of where it was found in the soil."

Inspector General Terry was at his best while enjoying a scoop of Scotch in the company of his CID chiefs. He had dined with two from Telecommunications and Finance to chew on a particularly overly heinous peculiarity as to the significance of a spirited bubble traced to the new sewage installation in Dublin and after a thoroughly entertaining meal consisting of a dressed down descript salad with croutons, shrimp and escargot and an after chaser of tonic rye, they sat to the task of scripting a request for combat troops to Ceylon. A surge of bravado had broken loose from an adjoining lounge causing them to change seating into a nearby bar. Terry wore a plaid pinafore of brown and placid orange over trim naval officer stripes with neat bow-tie ankle shoes. His calling expert wore all white trimmings, his finance control man sat stiffly in a bow ensemble as he crunched a pound note in exasperation. Usually they drive bowled on a terraced hotel lawn with their wives at the light speed crack of dawn the first weekend day of the month before groups of elderly men came to quibble about political state matters. Terry ran down the formal problem of this joint boulder attached to a surround of hard clay not unlike the stuff that adorned roofs. The notion that some Norwegian lost on high pounding roller waves had once he stepped onto a Coast Guard boat was that something ought to be done to inhibit roller waves in the extreme unlikelihood that officers could become missing. Finance Burroughs was having a muck of it as they tossed the queer thing like a two pence. He was looking forward to a new alloy for concrete, one that would save any size building from weatherization, but hoped the bubble was only for pipes on the ground; on the other end of the spectrum liked the idea he was a pioneer able to steer this outrageous smoking cannon out of Dublin somewhere to any country that predominated in the worry that mud chalked oil would be relieved of infrequent blockage. Terry disagreed. Except for his status as a ship captain he ran his departments free of newfangled uses and preferred anything outdated if only because it was reliably proven. A nasty bubble that could anoint a solderer as he packed drills into a trench was scarcely his idea of a find. All those rust shavings, the thing was as impractical as a knife on iron and no matter how pertinent it was in industrial manufacture, it could not relieve adequate stress. But, there was a troubling item on the horizon to spill the stature of men who worked towlines. Longshoremen ought to be able to lift heavy crates without all that rummy sewage lifting also. If the bubble kept the sewage from clapping the aft, it might be worth a look-see. Finance suggested shooting it into committee, Burroughs said, can't fancy that, surveyors wouldn't welcome the sort of competition if it made them hose down the decks with a bloody pool.

Terry toyed with a rather odd idea, that if the only thing that kept sewage in the can was the very thing that rushed oil from its cisterns, then what the heck did it do inside house pipes to knock bricks from mortared chimneys? He couldn't help the skepticism he had, a device to lay out a line for property was also a device to eliminate pebbles from copper alloy. He threw a two pence onto the table for the servant and said good night.

SANTA BARBARA

PROLOGUE

The well-known British voice of Tel Aviv radio announcer Dutcher Lang delivered with sincere menace as he read: Ten minutes ago at noon Monday, October 20th, a masked gunman entered the U.S. Embassy in Haifa on Herendon Square a block from the flowered gardens of the Buddhist Temple and proceeded to fatally shoot the security guard in the office on the first floor severely wounding two information specialists in the office on the second floor. Shortly after the body was bagged and the ambulance had departed, a small bomb blew out the window of the vault room which stored a hundred thousand in American dollars. Israeli authorities have responded to the scene. We will keep you informed as further developments arise.

His cue man signalled him to take a breather and turned on a segment of jazz. Dutcher felt in his vest pocket for his cigarette case and removing it took out a cigarette and lit it.

"Good work, Dutch," his secretary Lynn said as he exited into the sound room. Her short dark hair was waved. As usual she wore a loose blouse to hide her weight and tight dark pants meant to rivet the eye to what was once a great figure.

He got on the phone and called his contact. Sheridan was a real sly cat at times like this, getting past police tape, able to get to the front line with camera and cassette.

"His room doesn't answer, Sir. Would you like to leave a message?"

"No, thanks. I'll ring back later." He placed the receiver in the cradle hoping to hell Sheridan was able to get himself to the scene before the evidence got up and walked away.

In another world a man was staring out his window overlooking at the mouth to the bay the strident magnificence of the Golden Gate Bridge, its slightly curving span abridged only by its color and thin steel chords. He had lived on this hillside at the outside perimeter of Sea Cliff tucked behind the Presidio

Park and army quarters for nearly thirty years. The ocean today was a bluish grey, choppy, with a wind of ten knots, a swiftly moving current few boats on the bay could impede.

He was one of six men whose signature could alter the course of any commerce, be it shipping, air express, rail or truck. At various intersections throughout the city he had installed his five younger brothers in homes which looked upon a major commerce route. His father while he was alive had instructed him that to be the primary if not sole proprietor to assure safe passage of assets it ensured it necessarily had to know every last ship that came in beneath the seven hundred and sixty foot style and put to port. The least expensive view was to see everything.

His grandfather was in his mind the single most important man ever to come to San Francisco. He was an immigrant from Naples and was twenty-one when he stood on the Marin headlands to appraise the worthiness of building a bridge with a high enough clearance for naval ships to pass beneath. The mountains were the problem – smooth but high backed, descending like a fortress to the ocean with almost no beach nor harbor that would be free from the roiling waves. When the bridge was finally built it was positioned between two flanks such that with fog rolling in, it could not be seen making it an imperative to steer or fly not by landmark but by navigational notation. His grandfather was Almo and he was Deo.

When he was in his pre-adolescence and his grandfather was still living, his grandfather's solicitor said kindly, for one day it was presumed Deo should step into his shoes, he would have to purchase the entire coastline surrounding San Francisco, if he were to adequately insure commerce. Only the piers could be separately purchased as berths for the great maritime industries of the world; but the decisions concerning coastal development should necessarily lie at his father's and in time at his feet. Oakland across the bay ought to remain a lesser commerce zone by virtue of the fact it was distantly placed further inland, sufficiently far from ports and airways.

The bank, Deo was told, BancNaples was one of those

great institutions remaining from the Old World. In its day prior to the twentieth century it was a world bank kept anchored by a board of trustees comprised solely of physicians whose contemplations consisted of a palate of surgeries, research and pharmaceuticals. Deo too like his father before him would attend medical school, be sent to Rome and to Tivoli to study the compassionate arts, and then sent to New York or to Singapore to perform medical care for the better part of three years before he could hope to assume a position as trustee. The belief was that life in its essence was greater tender than the money whose rate one would forever exchange and the thinking man, or woman – for the Italians were not adverse to donas – must take into account and into perception this appreciation.

The bank functioned at all because it funded and underwrote all commerce. If needed, it extended a line of credit to branches of the government and military. If the bank had no real control over its assets, it would eventually lose everything. Control of the continuous coastline would give the bank control over all development up to the three mile marker on water.

The fight was waged with every successive county government for the county destined it should be out from under with regard to rate of interest and penalty and so inch by inch it sought to wrestle from the dominion of this very powerful institution control of its lands. Across the bay in Alameda county the University of California, having learned the most unscrupulous lesson since the catastrophic fire of 1923 when the bank – then BancItaly to be replaced by Crocker Banc – took back officers' housing and those of trustees, had since purchased holdings piece by piece and converted them to historic landmarks.

In thirty years the fight continued with the county, who withheld consent for the bank to purchase segments of the coastline now annexed as South San Francisco. Thus to own these previously unincorporated lands his father Almo would have had to purchase them illegally thereby risking loss of major if not all assets. Also in the last thirty years BancItaly and its earlier incorporation BancNaples had reapportioned itself into a handful of distinct separate entities, BancWorld, better known as American Bank; Mercantile Associates Bank; and Bank of New Jersey. Into the foray came the Landhold banks representing Britain and employee-based banks, among them Charter Bank headquartered in Oakland.

The single largest threat to the remaining BancNaples were a complex set of maneuverings by the county to award leases to Mediterranean-based shipping frigates which in turn because of contractual wording shared twenty percent earnings with the county, thus permitting the county to write off a percentage of city costs. These preferences had nearly wiped out BancNaples holdings. Seizing a new marketplace was becoming ever more difficult as counties established their own lending corporations made viable by lower interest rates and higher buyout leverage. Twice in one quarter his father had come back to the trustees to request a change in negotiations with the county, only to be told the bank had to approach the State, because the county could not redirect its charter.

Deo cooly appraised the span. He had lived his life in view of the accomplishments of his family, had set his future by the unrivalled excellence of design and tensile durability. Now forty-six, he was fully inured to perform any transaction above two million dollars in the realm of foreign investments and ventures. The problems of maintaining a bank were further enhanced by a long bitter history with a county who despite the line of credit proffered by the bank were permitted to retain holdings as landmarks, once the line of credit was repaid. The issue of landmarks was long ago set aside in favor of redeeming value by entering into new commodity markets. He stood before all time, with all its immortal equations, trying mentally to balance the impossible. How would they survive yet another wave of competition? How would they supersede themselves?

The telephone rang, and he turned from the view he knew so well. Even before he picked up on the fourth ring, he intuited that this call could indelibly shatter all hope. By the time he hung up, immobilized by incredulity, he knew his greatest hour was upon him. The financial backbone of one of Prince

Edward Island Bank's mainstay ports had been pummelled with artillery fire, one of three staff dead on arrival to a hospital. In spite of all precautions, all knee bending and sacrifices, all overtures to accommodate smaller interest rates and to expand offshore ventures, Oakland would supersede San Francisco, Oakland by a transaction she had entered into half a century ago when she agreed to accept all cargo flights out of the Middle East.

1.

From his room on the third floor of the Dan Hotel, Robert Sheridan packed his suitcase hurriedly as he listened with one ear to a radio broadcast and with the other to a live telecast from Haifa.

The situation which a week ago had begun as an embargo against Turkey had suffered retaliation. It was the only logical deduction to explain a counter to the U.S. Army's entry into Cyprus and sending her Marines to occupy the beach from Mersin to Antakya. As soon as the troops had seized control of the three ports, Syria had taken responsibility for launching an attack aimed at U.S. ships in the Tripoli sea. Syria's offensive was joined by Iraq and in turn by Jordan. Allies stationed in Saudi Arabia withdrew leaving behind mined waters to the three mile markers. In his mind he considered the vast wind blown sandy desert, an implacable face to the smaller, humble sections of habitations that dotted the coastline and whose politics, often as barren as their rulers' desire to turn a wasteland of poverty into governable suburbs, left a pallor of fatigue to an economy given almost entirely to the production of energy. He had spent a week in Nabulus, another in Gaza and broken up a third week between Beirut and Hamah. Little of interest popped off the squalor and disintegration of cobblestone streets amass with livestock, both dead and alive, and with yelling vendors and outdoor shanties. Except for the periodic glimmers one obtained of opaque glass walls and

244   J. LEA KORETSKY

chalk apartments along wide avenues and a growing populous of affluent businesses along the Lebanese coast, life was sordid, a mixture of declining port activity and dogged restaurant and soda fountain storefronts. An American had gotten shot at during the noon to three fiesta time while he was travelling by bus through Sidon. The only other event he recounted was of seeing bundles being set on fire and of police issuing out of shops as a result.

The embassy killing was a shock. Foreigners as a rule were acquiescent to Americans. With an oil shortage reported in Al Kuwayt and ocean bearing ships unable to accommodate passage to Europe or to China as a result, tensions were felt as banks closed an hour early and rationing on staples began. Not only did rationing contribute to a revisited resentment toward Americans and Britishers, there was a perception that if American troops cut off commerce with Turkey and Israel maintained a lion's share of trade, the Arabic world was isolated, relegated to waiting out a crisis over which they had little or no leverage.

This was Thursday. The embassy attack had occurred on Monday shortly past noon. By end week violence in the forms of overturned cars set afire, road blockages leading into the mountains and shelling was certain to break out along the Israeli borders. He wanted to be on a plane safely dispatched across the Mediterranean by then. Although it made more sense to fly south to Egypt or to Nairobe, he reasoned that once soldiers saw his passport, they might detain him in the event they wanted to make a political statement of solidarity to Arab nations.

He started as the telephone rang. He picked it up jerkily. The voice on the end of the line was a stranger. A guttural report of French slang and Arabic verbosity stung his ear.

"Hold on," he said, in broken Arabic. "Start over. What about the airport?"

The speaker paused with the implied silence of being affronted. Then in English he said slowly so as not to be misunderstood, "The airport at Tel Aviv is closed due to a bomb. The strip outside Nazereth too is closed."

"There must be some way out!" He yelled.

"Maybe by jeep."

"Can you send someone? I'll pay American."

"No American dollars. Israeli shekel."

"I'll get it converted. How much?"

"Three hundred to Beirut."

He'd never make it across the sea to Nicosia, let alone safely out of Beirut on shekel alone. But he agreed thinking it was better than sitting on his ass in the middle of a crisis. "Okay, give me an hour."

"Yes, good, an hour in front."

"In front." And rang off.

By the time he exchanged dollars, the borders would probably be closed as well, especially in the north. Egypt was the most sympathetic neighbor but even with a freeze on the dollar and sundry shops shutting down early for the weekend, a trip into Cairo meant a lonely advance through the Gaza with no telling of the hostilities that could erupt there. If the best thing was to hole up inside an American hotel for the next week, then he was slitting his wrists to attempt to wing it to Cyprus.

He found the small storefront next to the tobacco shop facing the lobby helpful. The Customs agent assured him that in Arab countries the officer system would be in effect in the major cities, regardless of the political climate. Robert took a hundred and fifty American in lira and for good measure exchanged another hundred for Arabic lira. If he made Acre or Tyre, he'd make Beirut without incident.

The driver was a guide he'd stumbled across in Afula, a small town inhabited predominantly by physicians whose medicine was the equivalent to the dark ages. A man by the name of Abu Raqqah, the guide was tall, dark sienna complected with a dark grey beard which Robert thought he should shave because the beard was bushy and unattractive. Abu helped him with his luggage and then counted the bills Robert handed him. Satisfied he could take Robert the distance, Abu ushered him into the backseat of the yellow car, offered him a pack of cigarettes and soda, and proceeded to exit the hotel and the city of Jerusalem in the direction of the highways and back-roads so that as they travelled up the coast they steered free of Haifa and of the crossroads which linked the seaport to the single road to Acre.

Robert smoked incessantly as Abu postulated as to the identity of the gunman. Someone with good English, who had cased both interior and exterior, who knew the layout, where the vault was, number of security, was able to gain access to the reception – was not this terrorist someone who either trained with Americans or who had special knowledge of the suites because he had constructed the building or laid the marble?

Robert did not care to speculate. The whole inquiry made him nervous. By degrees as he dodged questions, redirected the dialogue toward shipping and the embargo against Turkey, feeling perhaps with too much discretion for threads of information that could cast clarity over the terrorist's objective. Wasn't an ambush on an embassy a grab for positioning by a special interest group such as the Al Fatah?

No, Abu retorted. Turkey was not the object. Radical Arab groups were not interested in floating barges to Adana or Mersin because there was no strategic advantage. Cyprus was closely watched, as the American occupation proved. As long as Kuwait had oil to release, no Arabic nation would jeopardize her holdings.

"Well, I'll tell you," Robert mused, concerned they would cross the mountainous border by nightfall without provoking the attention of the Lebanese military; "the embassies by and large don't impact the economy to the extent this gunman may have thought. In Tel Aviv the function is simply for Americans to wire home either for communication or for banking access."

"That may be, but this gunman killed people rather than extort money. His mission was to close the embassy."

"Any precursor to the event that you know about?"

Abu gave a nod. "Talk of eliminating the neutral zone."

"We wouldn't be able to fly in."

"Well, be comforted. That will never happen."

But neither man was assured. In the banter was the reckoning that in this corner of the world life was lived in segments. Peace came at a tenuous price and often not at all. Concessions were granted to appease mighty nations into cease-fire, and some concessions worked because no one lived in the zone whereas other concessions were caveats to land grabs or political preeminence.

The terrain became creased with ravines and waterfalls spilling over rocky faces of hard red stone. Past a forest of aspens and into the far reaches of rocky wilderness, the road sprinted toward Mt. Herman and the inland Sea of Galilee. The sun waned behind a bluish, snow capped range. Here and there stood tanks abandoned and rusted, beside open trenches and foxholes, seeming indicators of a war zone that could produce return fire if Syria walked the mile to pummel the vestiges of resorts and kibbutzim with air raids as it had done in the early Seventies.

The sound of jets flying overhead caused Abu to pull off the road. They put in at the Galilee resort on the lake. Once it had been a monastery for the initiated, its stone walls and wooden doors and balconies offered the semblance of relaxation. Robert paid for the room and Abu erected a tent which surrendered him to a makeshift bed.

2.

The same way the money was generated it was lost.

Michel Gandt bent into the wind hurrying to an appointment with his solicitor in Santa Barbara as the rain lashed against the street in slanting sheets. He had decided hours ago when he heard about the Herendon shootings that he needed a trustworthy authority who could, without much checking, divine what the hell had gone wrong on the square.

The gunman had been prepared, or had had help from someone on the inside. Of the four doors off the lobby, he had known which to proceed through, presumably the number of people who were working, where the vault was located and when it would be open. The Agency was heads up over any international scandal but this, with an estimated five hundred million in liquid assets worldwide, would bring in Milano and Zagreb, not to mention chase the Americans out of the Dutch regions and forward them to Haifa.

Michel avoided getting sprayed with muddied water by a passing truck in a haste to turn a corner. He stepped up to the bank door and letting himself inside absorbed the sudden quiet the windowless room provided. At the far end of the establishment across a polished sheen marble floor and past a row of frosted glass teller windows the manager, a bald man with a tied bow at his neck and formal suit with handkerchief tucked into his breast pocket lifted his hand in acknowledgement. Michel made his way to the manager's desk and sat.

"Quite a morning," he said, relieved Mr. Colton had the contracts waiting for his signature.

"Yes, quite," echoed a sonorous manager. A gold fountain pen lay at the ready. He picked it up and held it to Michel.

Michel was aware his signature was illegible. Like most transactions he had engaged in both during the war and subsequently as an agent he had had to decipher as well as to consent to numerous agreements. These were mere letters stating to an auditor that the papers maintained by a firm he had audited were correct and in proper holding accounts. This done, he remarked that he was relieved at last to have these notarized.

"Well, you know, we no longer hire the service," Mr. Colton. "Once a week she sits at a desk," and nodded to the empty cherry wood table and upholstered high-backed armchair.

"Thank you all the same." He rolled his thumb onto the inkpad provided by Mr. Colton, then placed his print onto the notary ledger beside his signature. He wiped the ink with a wet cloth and wadding it tossed it in the trash. "Think the rain will lift sometime today?"

"Certainly before nightfall," the manager ordained. "I can't imagine who will drive home in this wet cold."

Michel left. He hurried to his white sedan parked in an alley. Once inside the car he turned on the air condition and a classical music station listening for a moment to a Vivaldi concerto to decide whether he recognized it before he started into traffic. The rain was to a drizzle but a mist had settled in making it hard to see. He rode to the freeway where he expected rush hour traffic. Instead he found the congestion surprisingly light. Vines crept over a fence in the divider zone and interlaced with honeysuckle and peony for an other world appearance.

He thought about the embassy attack. It was unlikely the terrorist was a newcomer to such attacks because he had cinched the time to under five minutes. He had advance knowledge of who was armed and probably with the type of weapon and the security and third eye. He wasn't concerned about the camera trained over the entrance that recorded his movements and had known where to stand when he murdered the guard. When he departed he was seen walking, his weapon no longer in evidence. It was a pro job, hired in by pros, captioned and delivered.

He exited. His car became a reflective object that shimmied in the salmon colored marble of storefronts above and below the sedan's level of movement. The speedometer made a sweep across the mileage markers as he accelerated and turned onto Roble Drive in the direction of the ocean. Passing gnarled oak trees, opinioned by a bevy of palms, ferns and Aspen, he discovered the road quickly became windy with hairpin curves offset by dappled and shaded light that suddenly spilled like a blinding glint on his windshield. He had no time to look for street numbers nor for landmarks. As he swung wide to avoid a curb he came upon suddenly, he swerved into the path of a fast moving sports car, the couple inside it a little too gay, or drunk. Between estates of paved circular driveways and Tudor mansions with impressive slate facades came barely perceived glimpses of a squall line and yachts bobbing on the water.

The storm weather was recreating itself. Large raindrops fell with ever increasing morbidity until the rate and velocity of rain characterized a thunderstorm. Branches shook letting loose yet more sprays of water. The wipers swept from left to right and right to left reminding him in one instant of radar antenna in the cockpit of an airplane. He heard a screech and then felt with shock as the passenger side of his car folded inward, compacting metal in a surrender of sound and impact. The steering wheel swung free, rendered useless. He tried to downshift to prevent further movement but the steering column was locked, braced by whatever mechanism fell into place when the car was in park. Screw it, he thought as he realized he didn't stand a chance of reducing the damage; the assaulting vehicle had succeeded in making a small intestine entry.

3.

Across town in the Hilton hotel Joe Daughter was again preparing for a one shot entrance into the headquarters of the Prince Edward Bank in Caracas Venezuela. A paratrooper from the Korean War he was trained to move in very quickly, look at the situation and get out. With the broadcast of the Haifa situation he had realized there could be half a dozen crises worldwide with at least one in Caracas. His rule of thumb was to situate himself as soon as could be arranged at a strategic base and observe who showed up.

The Prince Edward Bank had long backed the forested mountains of northern Columbia and fishing and military ports along the Venezuelan coast. In addition it handled trading for isolated settlements through its neighboring coastal cities, from Port of Spain on Trinidad Island, Mon Repo on St. Lucia, Salibia on Dominica and at various cities dotting Nevis, St. Kitts and Martinique. Whatever domain the embassy at Haifa controlled, most likely Israel's shipping industry, the collateral bonds to back her losses were assured by the Prince Edward Bank in Venezuela in the Antilles, the secondary bank holdings located in Campeche in the Yucatan and by a collection plate of trapping and forest settlements scattered across the District of Mackenzie and its upper regions consisting of two dozen islands and districts. The real resource for the bank was of course oil and there were a dozen shafts dropped through ice caps which were in various stages of being mined and actively utilized despite treacherous roads, eroding ravines and shifting bergs. The bank had authorized only two platforms in the past year but its ability to deliver on schedule ocean liners carrying lumber and precious metals into the Mediterranean and return with textiles, freight and passenger vehicles, and German plastic. This commerce enjoyed a long residence beginning in the 1950s with a treaty called the Six, as the Common Market was called. The Six had as a twelve, twenty and forty year goal to remove all obstacles to inexpensive trade and to create a trade base with the rest of the world. Tariffs were cut, chains for gasoline distribution spread overnight and warehouses sprouted throughout Europe and then to five other continents in hopes of creating a unified worldwide base to sell to.

The attack on the embassy in Haifa signalled any number of difficulties in the Common Market, the first being the use of a single currency. With the run on the Carte Bancaire in France in 1987, ironic after France finally and reluctantly joined the common marketplace, and subsequent releases of banking authorities in Hong Kong and Macao following the end of the hundred years of domination by the British, the rush to capture new markets suddenly leapt to the fore. Even Joe Daughter whose now infrequent business trips to Middle East countries had brought in behind him the CIA, RAF and a string of pearls changes in postage stamps and airplanes to transport mail, formation of iron ore deposits, relaxed borders to open new slopes for wine grapes, creation of lakes and bounties of fish, even he recognized that once an embassy was perpetrated yet another currency note had to be swiftly adopted to prevent a run on banks and the insurgence of counterfeit notes. Additionally, if the integrity of the embassy system were to continue to have authority in far-away countries, the dollar had to be changed immediately.

The substitution of a new currency was regarded by many bankers and outlying posts as a troublesome venture if only for the reason it usually produced a devalued economy in the countries dependent upon the former dollar. With bombings of airways, trains and the holdup of transportation and checkpoint delays, the urgency for additional currency could strain cities to collapse. Banks awaiting dollars and coin could wait weeks finally resorting to the sale of territories to acquire necessary notes.

He reached for the knife he had carried in a pocket holster on his right calf when he last dropped from a hundred feet by helicopter into the forested terrain of Columbia. Two days in, two days out. He almost hadn't made it out. Latin American terrorists pelted the mountains night after night with ear deafening mortar blasts and the yellow light as the bombs fell created a shadow effect for any group trying to escape with businessmen. This drop would be different. He'd be landing on the coast in waist-high water, making contact at first light on land and then joining an outfit of a dozen men to the principal site. He wouldn't need to gain entrance or capture or interrogate suspects. If the observation proved uneventful in the first forty hours of continuous daylight, he'd be swimming back to destination.

4.

The stillness of the land at daybreak was an uninterrupted measure of silence. Only the silvery light gently diffusing the glacial bay brought change. Kiev sat on the bench, her mittened hands holding a tin of breakfast tea. Tea like shards of filaments kept the dark liquid from freezing. As sunlight blew into the sky, indistinct shapes of the small weather station took form. There were three cement block structures, the farthest, some two kilometers within sled distance, a dark rectangle inside which the central computer and teletype communicated with a further remote station.

The outpost was situated at the eastern end of Lake Athabasca in the wilderness glacial plain of a corner of Saskatchewan. She had originally put in for a post in Manitoba thinking during her time off between shifts she would be able to fly into Ontario, but her skill at being able to correctly decipher shifts in ice formations from other erratic erosion had landed her as a first mate in the heart of the Northwest territory. Initially the isolation had been disconcerting. Byrd's tale resonated and she kept his book on her lamp-table for weeks, until she surrendered night reading to a semi permanent condition of eyestrain due to the cold and the brightness of snow.

Five weeks later having interpreted cracking ice and calving snow as it became too thin to remain a mantel above water, she was the expert in a two hundred mile circumference. She had assisted in Alberta, in the District of Mackenzie to the north and as far south as Manitoba at Norway House on Lake Winnipeg flying in storm conditions to remote and barren areas to identify solidity of ice, measure infiltration of water, hunt down fallen radio receptors and fish out of semi-frozen lakes and rivers overconfident staff who had misread weather or had assumed that the ice, twenty to a hundred feet thick, would not or could not crack beneath them.

Distant trees rooted in ice cropped up as the sun became ever-present in the sky. The sky had been overcast for a week and subject to snowfall and windy rainfall. During this most recent advent of wet display, she had chopped off her formerly shoulder length dark hair and taken to wearing a bandana over the lower section of her face to minimize chapped lips and leathery skin. When possible she wore a face mask made of velour but the lamb-like cloth irritated her skin and so gradually she had discarded the apparel and aids she had been given when she arrived, among them goggles and caps. Layers of flannel worked best beneath sweaters and windbreakers and gloves and several inches of socks and protected boots.

She heard the sound of the motor of the ski plane minutes before she saw it enter the dense cloud-cover like little red riding hood. She saw the skis first, then the body of the cabin as her ride back to the States descended. She ran toward the plane, jumping onto the step and pulling open the passenger door, thrusting herself inside the cockpit. Jack's face was a ruddy red. He wore a thick lambskin cap and warm jacket over blue jeans and a yellow flannel shirt. They exchanged a few pleasantries and then because she knew he couldn't carry a conversation and simultaneously chart a course through a no-visibility wind, she removed a bound notepad and began scribbling notes in pencil as to the events of the previous few nights.

She had been the last to leave. Jack had evacuated three others of the crew, trusting her as most did who worked the weather line to stay in for the final recordings before the ice finally gave way and took the floor and sides of the walls. Everything was expedient – the maps, the measurement of rising water, the shifting ice, the formation of new bergs. If the mother station accurately received daily teletypes that was the most anyone could expect in these conditions.

The shaft which was lowered into a hundred and fifty feet of ice had been expected to remain for several years, at least until other fingers of sludge had backed into the primary feed. But there had been problems. What was thought to be marsh land along the Taltson had been undermined by fluctuating tides as far north as Fabom Lake. When it was determined that the oil had thawed, the problem to retrieve it became severe. Emerging sites appeared at a hundred yards and conversely at a quarter of a mile away. After the platform was put in, although the oil recessed into a specially created recess or ravine, it could not be quickly extricated and formed pockets of shale at seventy feet.

Because secondary sites had proven productive, another drill was lowered at Selwyn Lake. For a year the site yielded rich healthy oil. When the river feeding the small lake flooded, the oil froze and the pack could not be excavated. Only the Yukon rendered happy returns. The pipeline captured a steady flow to fuel industries to San Francisco. In the last month Prince Edward Bank had sought to relocate most of its wells, flooding and cracking fields as close to the Trans-Canadian Highway as the laws of Nature and gravity would allow. She had been offered a post in New York and she had taken it.

5.

Robert awoke to the smell of bitter, putrid smoke. His heart raced as he grabbed his possessions and in a night robe and slippers hurtled himself into the chill night to arouse Abu from sleep. In a week's time when he was on board a ship bound for Cyprus, Robert would remember fleeing from the resort to the road where a gasoline station and row of shops had been decimated and the ashes were fiery hot, water pipes welded to the asphalt, gaping holes in the road were joined by stone fragments of stores which days earlier had comprised a town and postal stop. Now he pulled at Abu, shaking him from a deep slumber, and terrified they would be struck by spewing mortar or burning asphalt, Robert began shrieking, aware of his mortality and of the fact they were still far from their destination. Unable to calm him, Abu pushed Robert to a fallout shelter and there they spent the remaining hours of night wrapped in an odd embrace as though life could end in an instant.

Morning brought the horror of the maimed. As Abu and Robert ascended their underground chamber to face the realities of war, they found much more than one row of stores had been hit. The road to Zefat had taken a severe beating. The asphalt was impossibly gutted. The dirt that showed through steamed and a woman lay bloodied and brutalized, her body having taken shrapnel throughout.

They returned by the road they had come. Haifa was to be unavoidable. They gassed up twice getting back to the valley. Despite a hundred miles between Mt. Herman and the rolling hills littered with communal settlements, Abu drove with all too real terror. He refused to stop for food or for information and would not allow Robert to listen to the radio. He had an irrational fear that if the sound of his radio was picked up, they could become the target for unfriendly fire. Abu drove with the recklessness of a madman and Robert held on to the upholstery, concerned only for his eventual safety at any city that would be beyond the reach of machine guns, tanks or air raids.

At one point, as they flew down a steep incline and passed blocks of abandoned small houses, as burning debris fell to the embankment from some unnamed source and the land opened up and spit up dirt, Robert thought the tires of their vehicle could burn also. Yelling he pounded Abu to drive on the opposite side of the road. The air became lit up with falling embers and Robert thought they would die.

6.

"The Air Force wants you to take a month in St. Lucia," her physician supervisor Seth Yelland informed her.

Dr. Mary Right gave an appreciative nod. "Does this have anything to do with the Haifa matter?"

"They think Caracas is going to blow."

"Really?"

They were seated in Seth's small office situated at the closed Mare Island in Vallejo, California. It was a windowless room made attractive by oil painting pattern designs created by a San Rafael artist. Seth was a good looking blond who had relocated from Berlin in the late Seventies and married a mousy looking scholar whose compliment to the marriage was she was a nurse.

Seth answered. "Well, it's the next best target once the Paki's realize the Saudis don't ship to anyone but the Europeans. We aren't looking at simply penetrating secrets any longer. The difficulty is we're seeing a greater number of acidosis in the Caribbean."

Acidosis was her specialty. She could read the symptoms long before the breath smelled of fermentation. "Who's it hitting? Not just itinerant farmers, I gather."

"Agents, some of our very best. We suspect we're going to see more tangibles as we increase shipments for oil to the States."

The process of acidosis was frightening and perplexing to the medical community who twenty years ago considered it primarily the result of drug ingestion, largely methamphetamine. The breath stank of a chemical malodor, the skin was hot to the touch, and despite traces of cocaine in the bloodstream, there were also traces of iron. By the time the victim reported to a hospital, any serum was useless and the body reeked like gasoline.

"When will I leave?"

"Tomorrow. I apologize, but it was me or you. I told them since you work emergency, I could find a replacement for you fairly easily."

"It's fine. I'm free. Will I have access to a lab there?"

"I have no idea what the setup is. It could be state of the art or a rudimentary clinic. Your contact will be a woman named Jean. She has no idea of the assignment. She's arriving with a friend of hers."

"Okay." Mary stood, and pocketed her stethoscope.

She'd made plans to spend the weekend up the coast at Sonoma and would have to cancel. It'd be one more cancelation in a long list of agitations between herself and her man friend, a resident physician for Vandenberg Air. As she slipped into her Datsun and inserted a tape, she thought with regret about the researchers coming from Norway at the end of the week. She'd long awaited their arrival. Their knowledge of laser to replace surgery was world renown and would someday become the hallmark of American medicine.

As she sped onto the freeway, she thought about the modernization the direction of medicine especially of data acquisition had already taken. Digital imagery, orthophotographic studies, heat tests, dye infiltrations. It was a wonder anyone died before age ninety with the degree of specialization and responsiveness.

7.

Ann Smith had accepted the post at the request of a friend. Her employer was Richard Askew, formerly a pilot but now retired who consulted for the air force and marines on both domestic and international trade problems. Her duties consisted primarily of correspondence – of taking dictation, transcribing notes, translating letters into various languages and then making certain that once sent they arrived on time to their destinations.

One of five children born and raised in northern Russia bordering the Gulf of Finland, she had spent six years abroad in the year 1942 as a young house manager and tutor for a family whose estate was located two hours outside of Rome. While there, she learned fishing, mending nets, boating and scuba diving and although these pleasures were primarily to assist the young cousins who resided at the estate upon their entry into the Royal Navy, she viewed her time spent on the lake as enhancements which hopefully would be used in the future on a more challenging assignment.

Her oldest brother was ill with tuberculosis that first year she left and as a result could not enter the United States with the other siblings. Motil, Aleutia, Nossin with his daughter Evie and Harry were the Noamens, into whose family she also was raised. Her mother was in fact her aunt, who abandoned the family at age twenty-one to travel to Moskva to join the army. When her assignment ended in 1951 Ann was denied return stewardship to Russia and went instead to reside in Britain for the next ten years, meeting her second husband, raising two children and joining her family in Maryland.

Motil was in his seventies and had adopted a child. Aleutia had married a Slavic woman from Danzig and had a daughter named Elizabeth and a son named Nossin. Nossin was living with a woman without being married to her and the youngest of the family Harry had put marriage on hold to study law and was a corporate attorney.

The years had retreated into kind abdication. The two story cottages of the last war had faded to the glistened edges the photographs taken of them. Ann had gone to work for a finding agency to research the whereabouts of her mother and friends. Because they had lived on the sea in an area neither the Germans nor the Soviets possessed access to, it was her hope the community that had schooled her had fled across the water either to Denmark or to Sweden and Norway. Documents stored in synagogues were destroyed; the information she had catalogued while living in Italy had been forwarded to unknown archives. Even the family whose affairs she had managed was allegedly dead with no viable way to track the children. By degrees she settled into a sort of quietude which had as its release the weekly perusal of newspapers written in Italian, Russian and Swedish.

Her friend from the newspaper service had told her the post for Richard Askew would be a good call for obtaining information about Europeans who had migrated to lesser known regions. Barrister Askew was in his eighties also and like her had lost a family to the Germans when his only child, a son Cowper, joined the Air Force to fight the Nazis and was gunned down in battle in 1943 and reported dead. The barrister was a very private man who isolated himself in his study, sometimes for days on end, and then emerged grief stricken, aged, unable to be consoled.

She kept to her duties, careful not to impose. She made for herself her own peace with the well-to-do, attending mass in order to surround herself with elderly Italians and their generations and taking a taxi once a week with a young woman from the Jewish Services agency to read periodicals at the library and then go for lunch at Ledbetter Beach.

On her employer's desk lay a copy of the notarized page of a transaction signed by a Michel Gandt and witnessed by Samuel Colton. Beside it rested a contract for the Prince Edward Bank. Of particular interest to her was the pouch of photographs of young men presumably in their twenties. Most were clearly of Russian descent, some looked to be Finnish or German; one was Slavic, from Yugoslavia or Lithuania. To whom were these faces worthwhile information? As the slanting sun fell across the carpet and desk, Ann considered ringing up her nephew and then thought better of it. His professional training in law would be helpful up to that certain point when he understood the scope of the problem facing Barrister Askew and then in all probability he would view the wisdom of his acts with jurisprudence.

It was best to observe who came to visit and who left with advice. She glanced at his calendar written in ink and decided that since it was Gansk Boethling she ought to wait inside her office on the first floor close to the room in which they would meet.

8.

In 1940 after years of cataloguing numbers for museum artifacts, Evelyn Noamens married the man of her dreams, Abba Bracha, a Belgium scholar who taught language at Yeshiva. Their first apartment was a furnished studio on Washington Square. They applied to an apartment complex on 72nd in Manhattan and lived there for two years before relocating to Mississippi where they lived until Abba received his notice 1A for the draft and entered the Navy. His mother moved in for the four years he was sent to France. When he was discharged in 1946, they moved to Berkeley, California because Asilomar had no available housing.

Through a professor at U.C. Berkeley, the Brachas were introduced to Ezra Congress, a surveyor who worked for East Bay Municipal Utilities District. He hired Abba and secured a secretarial position in the Engineering Department at Berkeley for Evie. During their first year on campus Abba and Evie lived at 1715 Hearst Avenue (today a park) with Ezra and his wife Winnie who booked artists and musicians at the Trumpetvine. The Brachas lost two pregnancies to miscarriage before they had a son whom they named Nossin after Evie's father. As the Congresses prospered and rose out of the university squalor, so did the Brachas. When Ezra Congress died in 1982, then living in an affluent community in Oakland on Chelsea Drive, the Brachas had moved to Santa Barbara Road and after putting their son Nossin through four years of high school they relocated to a condominium at the entrance to the Tennis Club in North Oakland behind the College of Arts and Crafts.

Nossin Bracha followed in his father's career becoming a scholar, but of dead languages. Once he opined a job as a teaching assistant at Yale, he spent summers traveling to Europe and the USSR visiting professors whose careers were made by publishing journals and family bloodlines in now non-spoken languages.

An Officer System is a naval assignment in which the man at the post – the post being the geographic locale where the position exists – may neither travel far from the area unless a commanding officer designates it so or can relocate a residence outside the city limits. This is how the CIA understands national safety. The state of California for example is a chessboard on which the players manifest their lives and all schemes including international foibles are wrestled with on these squares.

Into this panorama Nossin at age thirty married Sonia Farzeheis, a tall elegant Jewish woman whose parents had fled Nazi occupation of Vienna. Sonia had two older brothers and a third eldest who at the time of migration was sent to live with his uncle in Los Angeles whom she never heard from again. Nossin served in Korea where he witnessed a degradation he found deplorable. He came across a detention camp where massive numbers of people existed in sickbays, where underaged children ran through the halls in the middle of the night, the smell of death like a sick pallor reaching beneath doors in an off yellow light, people huddled in their presumed dying, given up for dead. In trucks people lay stacked on top of one another, IVs still in their arms, dehydrated, some shoeless, some shapeless entities, as if on the seam ready for being sown, scattered throughout the fields of wherever planes would fly over.

Back home his new wife had filed for divorce, returned home to Ocean Boulevard in Long Beach where her parents now owned a sleek two story block building with opaque corner windows, a veranda overlooking the wide street and grass. Later Nossin would recall her tall, reserved parents' large bay windows with drapes and the exterior of the building done in Art deco. Across the water forever glinting on the skyline like a throw of a million tiny diamonds on the bar sat the Queen Mary, a hotel anchored permanently on sapphire blue water. The point of Sonia's family situated on an avenue which a mile away sharply narrowed like a too thin alley went a long way to the dead end where for the price of two million an apartment beach houses crunched together behind tall partitions while on the beach a bevy of patrol cars and helicopters patrolled the beaches.

By the time he wrote his own orders to get the hell out of Korea and head home three and a half months early, he could honestly say he was sick to death of the war and of the exacting way he was given over to learning the technology that was to save their lives. He was transferred from the detention camp to a ship. Divers shot photographs of mines and where possible, dislocated the device from its stem. Nossin's job was to break down each mine on film, shining blue light through the metal head to measure how much space there was between floating rods which resembled pennies. They brought in a specialist who threw up as a result of drinking too much vodka and died on the job. If not for his death, the entire operation might have been bombed.

A trick knee kept him in Alabama after the war. He met and married a southern princess whose family was originally from Boston and purchased a gracious antebellum home with flower beds in front of the home, tea cups and crystal plates containing dry sweets and ghosts in the unused wing whom one saw at a distance. But the aftermath of the war relegated Nossin to the submarine quarters where he sat for hours taking apart Spanish-made mines and French ones and numerous others placed in someone else's waters. At age forty they had twins and at age fifty, now retired from active duty, a levy on property made them turn over their antebellum and downsize to a former firehouse on the water.

The year was 1966. The Navy sent Nossin home to California to Monterey to man a post. It would become his post for the next thirty years, following him into retirement. He would shuttle from the FBI training station to Camp Roberts for long walks on the beach with his mother, sessions with salvage divers, and fireside dinners with his sons, Aleutia and Gedalea. Of the two Aleutia was the more materialistic while Gedalea insisted on staying close at hand, informally an officer at a roving post, and learned to operate a teletype. As Nossin buried friends from the war Aleutia became critical, and rebellious. At age twenty, clearly not the favorite, he moved in with the Congresses with whom he played golf, kibbitzed with aspiring musicians and eased into the lifestyle of the happily satiated, working for a synthesizer studio.

Internationally focus was on the eye of the hand. The country was pulling out of one war while preparing for a second, shifting from the country below Russia to the far reaches of the Malaysian peninsulas, hoping by degrees to retread into the depths of the colonies of Great Britain. The most logical route for penetration was to take an air circuit into the mountain climates and when crossfire ceased as it periodically would to permit ships to bring rations and incidentals, not to mention motor cars and goosedown jackets and woolen coats, larger aircraft would fly in fog conditions for surveillance reconnoiters. The colonies most suspect for having mined Malaysian waters to India were the Asians themselves. After all they had access at night and knew their own bays and inlets from having grown up on them. Not only that, the more ambitious youth had farmed their own adventures, skillfully towing ski planes for repair to small outboard stations when weather or enemy fire dented a wing motor. Because the aircraft was old fashioned, the American Navy could not pack in behind with modern day revues to enhance expeditions. Whatever course they selected – sending hikers into desolate snow blankets or divers to plummet for downed aircraft or sunken treasures or spiritualists or cartographers – the Asians delivered the same meal ticket, a downsized Bossa Nova style six seater whose engine was able to cleft mountain heights but only able to handle short distances before the knocking engine would empty its fuel.

By the time the British had talked the Asians into a share of the marketplace, the Americans had staged more than half a dozen coups of its political Left seizing not so much the vote but strident ambition to outfox the fox. There were real gains to be had, the first being to establish a boundary south of its own borders without actually taking jurisdiction of any part of Mexico or Central America. The second was to establish through a series of links a marketplace for the sale of European items. This was done by expanding the Right, by strong-arming churches and insurance lenders as providers of health plans and a network of hospitals. After came the concept of the consumer with consumer price indexes as the new language. People were no longer individuals who belonged to a family and were loyal or disloyal to their country. The bullies were brought in to castrate the average driver to force millions of consumers to purchase new vehicles after being rear ended or to buy caskets after their car exploded on impact. If a college education did not net a higher paid job, if the government eliminated controls as to who would earn more, the cost of living zoomed like an out of control elevator. And all the while in every defense attorney's office the guilty, charged with abducting safety or with years imprisonment sought vengeance by impounding further stresses on a beleaguered country and importing families from foreign countries where corporations had become the cities and their streets and maps were borrowed in total from cities dotting the western seaboard from Bellingham to San Diego.

The eye was retreating. In its place cities and countries sought funding of large scale revenue producers such as movies or buildings. In Great Britain who supplied most of the free world with loans, in order to raise funds for these projects which were defined by ratings, a group of business people had either to approach the military or the royalty, if there was a royal family. In America, Hollywood or conversely a construction company gave its own permits. In Scotland for example the military would arrange for use of a castle for a charity ball to raise two hundred million. The manager would send out a guest list to British, French and Scandinavian royalty, known actors and attaches, have lunches and art showing or concerts for a week. That's the Riviera. There might be fox hunts, a masquerade ball, tennis open, a Red Death rock concert. This would sell at ten grand per couple to a guest list of four hundred people.

9.

Michel Gandt tucked in the large white cloth napkin into his collar and looked with satisfaction at his borscht. He added a dollop of plain yogurt into the center, then took a sip of white wine remarking to his evening companion, an elderly gentleman with whom he took dinner one night a week usually on Thursdays, that if two or more embassies had been held up, one could without doubt attribute a problem to currency.

"It's the Swiss," his estimable companion Harold Bixby stated, as he dipped the goatsherd bread into his soup dish filled to the quarter mark with icy cucumber soup. "She's refused to trade on the open market and she was the sole supplier of ore," he explained. "It's been a perpetual problem for the French of the last century. She owns other ports for her coffee and lumber and chances are those'll be seized."

"But Israel."

"Yes, I know." Harold was fair complected, with a broad forehead and flat, proportionate, somewhat British features to add to his height which was well over six feet. "Her succession from the Common Market takes her franc out of circulation, notwithstanding what is in other countries. Imagine," he said, pausing to await Michel's consideration, "it takes two weeks to get a new franc distributed to all bank locations, yet within the first thirty hours of banking everyone freaks out and withdraws money forcing a run on the banks wherever the franc enjoyed a sizeable venue."

Michel gave a decisive nod. "This will push the French into a crisis causing them to declare bankruptcy."

"Indeed. Worse than that. Let's say she obtains a loan of two billion Italian lira to tie its contractual arrangements over for two to four weeks. What are the practical considerations?"

"This puts all airplanes in the air, its ground transport does not move, international holdings are sold."

Harold answered, "Problem is when they get their new money they cannot pay off the loan. To pay off the loan, France must allow the lending country to take any resource up to the amount of feasible payback."

"But this could permanently close its mines and mining operations." Michel responded with uncharacteristic feeling. "What in tarnation caused the French to drop out of the world marketplace to begin with?"

"No one knows, except that we have to take into account there was a run on South Africa's mines first."

"What're we looking at here, Bixby?"

Harold shrugged, and pushed his bowl away from him, his meal largely uneaten. "The minute the French government leaves its country, the location of the country is for all practical purposes somewhere else. Once the new location is determined, and proven, she is subject to attack. If attacked, she will seek refuge. When she runs out of refuges, she will have to withdraw."

"This is severe."

"Terrifying. South Africa is oversold on her diamonds and gold rendering her banks undermined to the last particularly in the face of a potential heist. If she attempts to retrieve any degree of balance she is left with satellite development which in many ways damns her to hell because her titanium levels are rapidly depleting. Switzerland, on the other hand, has an entirely different set of circumstances. She holds the largest world bank in her borders and to lose this could jeopardize her ability to maintain any industry at all."

"I'll call Joe Daughter. He'll know what to do."

"Yes," Harold said, remembering Daughter as an effective margin hunter who could without much effort enter a small nation and size up a potential disaster within a matter of days; "better get on it straightaway. Don't want to lose him to the train station at Delhi or to the rain in Bangladesh."

"You're a pessimist," Michel said and drew a thin wooden carton of Havana cigars toward them. "Care for one?"

"With a sniffer, if you don't mind."

Michel rose and walked to the liquor cart and poured two brandies in sniffers. "Israel was heavily reliant on the franc," he said, and handed Harold a sniffer. He watched as his companion removed the cigar, cut it and lit it, puffing to get it started.

"Oh the Israelis will recover," Harold assured him. "Their dependence on the Italian lira is worse. That would have been fatal."

"Any possibility Switzerland was the target?"

"Not likely, not after Bloody Sunday in 1987 when France lost her cartels."

"Sixteen years later and the French have not recuperated. They still cannot return to ventures with the Germans."

"Why should they want to? It's not as though the Germans have much to offer."

"My good man," Michel was exuberant, "the Germans farm steam. What else ought they to offer?"

"Well, I meant simply regarding the issue of ore. It's ore the French have lost. Car manufacture without ore will be extremely expensive."

"They have steel and tin."

"Not for long, not without ore. They're going to wind up in hell."

Not that the French hadn't walked the mile for years. Since the two major wars, having learned her lessons well, she had recompensed her advantages by trading with Norway and her hydroelectric functions closer to the cradle. In addition she had laced underground cities with the economy of steel bearings and bright lights to produce electricity and heat. Small but adequate with enough snowmelt to supply a multitude of nations with drinking water.

As he sipped hot milk at his bedside table with calcium to make himself drowsy, he wrote in longhand the letter he would wire the next day to Joe Daughter. In it he urged Daughter to fly into the Middle East and to bring with him any journals he might possess written in Hebrew which realistically appraised the embassy front.

10.

At that moment Joe Daughter was crossing Sante Fe, Columbia on foot having secured a flight out at dawn with a private service. The planes were still notoriously ancient, relics that had been dug out of a shutdown military base and carried by ship into Venezuela and driven rather than flown off the tarmac. It would take two hours into the Port of Spain where he would be shown maps of those channels the British had mined. Until then he had less than a fortnight to conduct the reconn mission and get himself back to the small airfield in time for his flight.

The city was a busy marketplace, a large bustling zone into which a half million people poured daily, rode metro trains and buses to work. It was also one of the oldest cities in South America and had seen its share of earthquakes and rashes of fires. Joe knocked against a man's shoulder glimpsing his scrawny face for an impossible second. Almost immediately, before danger had registered with any real posture of memory, he fled, hurtling himself forward, advancing himself by extending his long arms and walking on the balls of his feet. He checked the button on his lapel to be certain the microphone device had not become dislodged. He remembered the man's thin bony face from a sea of faces in the Yucatan during a mining operation. The state had invited the gold mining agency in and then as the trucks burrowed into the forest and chain saws ravaged a thousand acres of virgin forest, carloads of men arrived with guns. The standoff had been bloody, a short-lived war in which the interests of the entire Peninsula froze as military men from South America poured in to squelch the rebellion. Many years later he would contemplate as to the folly of these men chasing off real jobs and continued prospects but in those hours he had fought off the sinking dread of kill or be killed.

The British embassy stood in a square, a timepiece to the mechanistic growth of the city around it. It had been built out of glass and steel, with five floors, balconies on each floor, and a high wall around it. Beside it rose the Prince Edward Bank, a handsome and stately dark beige colored building with cream trimmings and an intricately carved door. The object of concern lay across the street – it was a two story building inappropriately identified as the Department of Education inside which at the back of the second floor permits and contracts were archived. Joe scouted the street, then made his way inside the two story building through a rotunda containing eight foot high marble figures in partial dress. He moved up the carpeted stairwell, strode down a long hall with portraits of heads of state, flashing a badge to the security at a desk and disappearing through a series of hallways which were tiled black and white. At the end of the last hallway was the repository. He climbed through a small sash window onto the fire escape, stepped onto a narrow catwalk and when he reached the repository office, he threw open the window and then stepped aside, his back pressed against the stucco.

A woman's voice was heard cursing as a wind scattered materials over the floor. She came to the windows and glared to the terraced garden below. He took in her profile, a tight chin, small forehead, short red hair stylishly worn. She turned in his direction as she reached for the hook on the window and he saw she was an infrequent tourist at Santa Barbara's waterfront. He waited as she closed the tall windows and locked them.

He withdrew equipment placing an ear on the window. Made like a stethoscope, the ear was connected to a wire that operated a digital pad. She made two calls, the first to a number he didn't recognize and the second to the embassy across the street.

He waited until five o'clock, then made his way to the series of hallways, colliding with her as she jaunted from the women's bathroom. He pretended to drop a notepad and as he mumbled an apology he reached into her carrying case and lifted a badge attached by a clip to a handful of cards. While she took the elevator, he ran down the stairs, two at a time, leafing through her identification and the cards of people she must have done business with, depositing these on a desk inside the door and exiting onto the street in rush hour.

He was confident he had lost her. He moved in long strides through the gate and into the Prince Edward Bank. He withdrew a checkbook from a pocket inside his jacket, tore off a deposit slip and asked to transfer forty million to a private account in Zurich. The check was drawn on an alias he used when he travelled to the Middle East and on occasion to Belarus. The cashier arranged for the transfer by wire.

He booked an overnight into a cheap motel. He placed a call to the British embassy to the Passport Office and left a message for someone named Magra that the rate of exchange for the franc to the dollar was expected to fall by afternoon of the next day.

The Bay of Pigs had been a near disaster. Fidel Castro was a brassy politician whose belief was he could unload destitutes, drug dealers, criminals and domestic violence abusers into Florida to stop the drain on his economy. The U.S. had had its boat rocked enough in a dozen years by thieves, arsonists, prostitutes, drunks and any other underprivileged and undereducated deviant now stacking up on welfare. The government had ventured its drug enforcers into international waters only to discover the Cubans were mining their waters with stingrays developed by the Russians.

Joe Daughter was thirty when he sat down to examine a live mine. They'd brought in a rookie named Barack who had an eye for triggers. Together they had dissected the pin from the detonator a fraction at a time until Barack was able to identify the one wire and truncate it from the sadistic piece of metal which would upon contact explode the firecracker. He could use the other man's expertise, he thought as he dwelled on the design of what was possibly a Guyanese mine. It looked to be of Dutch design but he wouldn't bet on it. Any little difference no matter how slight could blow his arm off.

He sat for hours and toyed with the configuration on the computer. The wires were not precisely linear which meant that to crack this coconut could mean pulling at each one. In the blue light the cross section gave little additional information. From one angle they lined up as thin reeds, not much larger than the standard width of a chain.

He produced a series of Xrays from which to study the orbs. He ordered in dinner from the mess hall and then did not feel like eating when the straggly spaghetti arrived. A central wire ran the width of the head. Where the central nervous system of wires met, a pin when dislodged would hit the hammer which would produce the explosion. Because the mines were submarine mines with acoustic metal attached to them, any sound like a submarine motor could detonate the nervous system. The problem was to render the head useless as an explosive to a sub or conversely to a large ship. Judging from basics, if any of the wires were cut, the individual mine would release away from the string.

He e-mailed Barack with a cross section and his thoughts as to weight and sensitivity of each device. Then he went for a walk around the base and for a beer at the canteen.

^^^

Nossim was on the wireless to his mother when the transmission clicked onto the central processing unit. He uttered his assurances hoping his father's health would improve as he refocused his attention on the long document instantly recognizing the pattern.

"Gotta go," he said rather briskly and then aware he might have hurt her feelings he said, "Don't fret. I'll be home in a week."

He ripped the paper off the computer and dialed the number for the naval base at Port of Spain. "You're dealing with a magnetic device," he yelled, when the voice at the other end answered.

"Hold on, I'll transfer you," and the line clicked into a recorded radio message.

He waited for what felt like an interminable time. Then, "Barack?"

"Is that you, Daughter?"

Joe chuckled. "I've got a string of these in the trench and harbor."

"The head is responsive to sound. Each wire is hooked into place by a magnetic function that can be triggered by sound. You with me?"

"Yes."

"This can be any consistent pattern of sound, most of the time by a sub motor. You can't scalp the mine or lance it like a coconut. To cut the explosive wire you have to go in through the central nervous system. When your stem is de-armed, then you can cut the wire to the head."

"I'm in Trinidad. Can you take a plane in?"

"Not with a hurricane brewing. If you give me your configurations I'll chart the pressure scheme for your diving technicians."

"Will do. How long will it take?"

"Few hours. How many do you have?"

"A hundred."

"You've been cluster fucked. What's your average depth?"

"A hundred to two hundred and fifty feet."

That's relatively deep water. You said this's a harbor?"

"With channels for five oil frigates a day. Not only that, we have a basin of subs sitting on bottom."

"It'll take a half day, up to ten hours."

"Okay. I'll relay the heads."

By the time he had transmitted the string of globes, he knew they had the first in what was probably a real windstorm which if they were unlucky might sweep halfway around the ports. If the devices could not be easily intercepted, frogmen could be days or weeks at each operation. On instinct he wired Canada to the troubleshooters at the weather station with the hope they might have run into a similar wire stem device used in cracking ice. He left his computer line to the Navy on and switched to a system at another console on which he proceeded to the next step of measuring depth of water and wind current above and below the ocean's surface.

The site was located directly on Trinidad on the leeward

side. The shallow water was a good hundred feet deep. This meant that the shipping traffic was in and of itself the intended mark, as was cutting off submarine passage.

The Lesser Antilles had for long been the subject of sore debate. After all it was the smaller islands from Aruba to Bonaire, held in possession by the Dutch, that gave rise to grumblings that Venezuela with the lion's share of military strength should control the entire sea passage. And although Guyana to her south and Columbia to her immediate West shared in the profits of oil exploitation, the more sinister implications for embargoes were ever present. Settled in the minds of the Europeans were the cast of northerly islands, among them Barbados, St. Lucia, Martinique and Guadeloupe, from which the African French tended farms and windmills and dug trenches for fishing and planted rice on mile acre stamps in knee deep tides. Without the threat of embargo the islands provided respite and prison relief for the malnourished cities of Venezuela where crime was rampant and the function of the middle class was to be an ever sinking burden to royal families who had elected to fund plantations there. But with an embargo, ships would be grounded and no commerce would enter or leave, possibly for up to six months.

The lineup for the trade winds enjoyed a calm along the shorelines of the islands and the Venezuelan coast. But farther out beyond the two hundred foot drop of ocean underwater pyramids, the winds crashed into one another making for hundred foot waves, impassable channels and static communications. Flying over this stretch also was treacherous because the squalor at the water's surface rose like a wind tunnel grabbing onto and twisting off course any small plane including those with superior instrumentation.

When he went back to check the other computer to see whether he had messages, he found the computer line cut, the static having asserted itself over the chart of the Dragon's Mouths. He flipped onto the frequencies that would give him eyes into the half dozen submarines parked below Bonasse and wondered how in hell they would put to sea if it was discovered the trench off Venezuela was also mined. He decided after checking several dozen windows that no sub was answering back. It was a dead man at sea alert.

11.

"You have too many friends," Ann's employer told her.

The correspondence from Great Britain had found her barely able to contain her horror at the idea that a registrar of surviving nurses from the war had been forwarded to Barbuda.

"One less should do the trick," Richard Askew told her, winking as he closed the massive oak door behind his guest Gdansk Boethling. "Any possibility you'll require time off?"

She debated. Barbuda, St. John's and Montserrat at Plymouth made up the British loop. While safe enough to travel in by ski plane, winds would make it nearly impossible to leave the huts and could keep her housebound for months, until a plane could land.

"I think not," she replied definitively. "Not that I wouldn't mind the time off and I know you could do without me for a spell, but if I go I'd want to be certain of the passage."

"Yes, well," he said, still partially engrossed in his guest's visit, "you'd want to leave at your leisure. I can appreciate that, Ann. Certainly if the weather turned, I might have to see to my own needs for a while."

Hearing her thoughts echoed back to her, she reconsidered, and said, "I might if time permitted track some of those faces on your desk."

"You have reason to believe they are survivors from the war?"

She met his gaze head on. He would permit this bit of confrontation, if only because of her age.

"One is a spy, Ann."

"Which one?"

"Yes, which indeed?" And laughed. "One of these days that small matter that occurred in Haifa will find the assassin with a bullet to his brain and that gun will be one of these men here," he said, inferring the subjects of the photographs.

She gave an assent thinking it would be her boss who flew into Tel Aviv and drove by car to Haifa, not one of those faces.

"You must have an opinion," he said, taking her by the arm into the large sitting room which looked onto a forest of twisted and gnarled ashen grey trees, "as to my invitation to General Boethling. Do you know what he told me?"

She waited as he poured two glasses of bubbling water and took the one he offered. Normally he would expect her to guess at the subject matter and the two would banter it out, a stubborn teacher rehearsing a slightly younger student at something they each knew intricately and disagreed upon.

"No?" He asked when she didn't answer. "The general told me it is far better to store the past in photographs than to discourse over it. This, I suspect, because he has invested in movies."

She knew it was not the subject he wanted to discuss. He seldom went to the show or rented a video. He was closed on the subject of actors. He was instead fishing for an elusive thread which when he attached to it would explain something about his guest that had worried him.

"The movies are not his passion," he continued, pausing to take a sip as he surveyed the garden of twisted trunks and clinging ivy. "His passion is for steel. He has decided to open an ore farm."

She thought his friend the general had fallen into a rather foolish quarry but did not say so, or that her employer was joking.

"In addition he expects he will tamp out in a number of foreign markets other companies who process metal. I told him I thought it was a waste of his time. He looked at me through his monocle, quite humorously in fact, and informed me that leisure is the number one industry worldwide and why not join with him to commit to investment capital."

"What will this cost you?"

"Two million." He said, and laughed.

"Will you see a return on it soon?"

"Probably not." He chuckled. "What do you think he really wanted?"

"No idea, but I think I will take a week to go to Dominica."

"But not for coke."

She stood as he approached. "For my health," she answered enigmatically.

Both she and Richard understood General Boethling's query. Underwater film processing gave the submarine expert a handle as to how much pressure the collective rods could withstand inside the mine head. The general was suggesting that the French or Chinese or whichever group of radiographic technicians who had set the mines were looking for mine heads which could not be penetrated by normal methods thus delaying the Navy's response time to potential problems that arose with the bombing of Israel's port. Sir Askew had served in the Royal Navy in his time and was no spring chicken. If he were concerned about the safety of subs in shallow water as divers attempted to safely disengage mines, then the queries he had put to her were to be understood as child's play. If or when he received telex communications regarding the spy in question, she would have to be quick to appraise the faces and determine which in the group might also be endangered.

Gdansk Boethling was British and Polish and somewhere in his eighties. Unfortunately he was easily recognized because of his broad physique and his balding, shorn presentation. The glasses did little to change him, nor did his vehicle, a Buick which resembled the Lexus line, also forwarded him. Ten years ago Sir Askew would have delivered his concerns into his home as a procession of dignitaries and would invite each successive guest to comment on opinions proffered by the former visitor, but the duration of a decade had convinced him that neighbors are their own grievances, sometimes more dangerous than the events that have spurned the need for information.

Today Sir Askew was more deliberate in his stirrings. He probably knew the general could be asked to appraise the damage rendered by the bombing by studying photographic material, or he was one of hundreds of contacts the embassy had on hand to pull in. She decided after plotting the steps through her head that he had asked the general over in order to spark the curiosity of the neighbor whose new country house overlooked the ocean. Her small office looked onto the patio and garden of this neighbor. It occurred to her additionally that it may have been the neighbor who had begun the search for the identity of a spy.

History like most important things was small when situated on the large intricately complex map of millennia. In her late seventies, Ann had survived the strong call for spirituality in her forties, the equally compelling latitudes of an end to her mothering years in her fifties and by her mid sixties had recomposed her life and livelihood to make peace with the unanswered questions of the early years. How little old age was compared to the impulsivity of youth and the breathless beauty of not knowing age could embitter one! Ann had assumed as most women who have had to work the better part of their adult years do that all needs would greatly lessen after her first retirement and her desire for change would diminish. But she discovered after planting a garden of vegetables, citrus trees and flowers and moving her patio twice that being made tired by physical activity does not in fact still the mind. Learning quiet came in spurts because she resisted it. By the time she understood patience as the young at fifty view it, she knew enough to know it was a state one took in at forty if one could but did not succumb to it in one's seventies because to do so felt too much like resigning from life.

She paused to glance below into the neighbor's garden. It was oddly lit for so late in the afternoon. She puzzled over the strangeness and when she realized the estate was alight with bright bulbs from a theatre of light, she pulled back into the shadows to avoid being seen for a person glimpsing the Askew home would no doubt catch sight of her.

A woman had come onto the patio. She was tall, dark,

dressed in expensive white raw silk pants, her wavy hair tied behind her head in a french braid. She lit a cigarette and jammed it into a cigarette holder and held it as one might a pencil. She sat on the brick ledge that surrounded the garden, picked up a newspaper and read it, discarding it after she had read the front and back page.

A man came out to join her. He was tall with tan features compared to her swarthy blue. "It can't be as bad as you let on," he said, and swirled a brandy in his hand.

"Well, of course it's bad. It's worse than bad if I've been chopped out of the will."

"Saying you won't inherit the house is not chopping you out of the will, Gertie. You still stand to see the beach house, not to mention the cabin at Inverness."

"I think we should ditch him at once."

"How much are you in debt for?"

"A quarter of a million."

"Good heavens, Gert. What in hell did you spend it on?"

"I made a mistake is all, a stupid senseless error. I didn't realize I'd live to pay for it the rest of my life."

"You're just being melodramatic. I can extend you a hundred grand if you need."

Ann retreated from earshot. They were silly children probably used to overspending who had been caught up short by the realization that too large a debt can become grounds for sudden impoverishment if only for the reason that eventually it cannot be repaid.

But their conversation reminded her of another conversation she had had with an American she had encountered during the war. He had ridden by bicycle into the countryside and presented as a forger. He was there to produce passports which could pass the scrutiny of the Germans, allowing her teen charges to escape through Rome into the mountains because the sea was watched night and day. He had showed her the small changes the guards had sought over a single year. Unconvinced, she had turned him down, saying they would risk escape by going to France.

It proved an insanity. Crossings at night were dangerous and mixed by those trying to defect to any nation that would not turn them over. At the last she dressed them as herself, put them on a train bound for Spain and hoped to God they did not return in winter.

The woman in the courtyard below would come around to her unabashed impulsivity and wish she could recall her words. Life and death had been two sides to the same coin for the nine years she lived in Italy and after, she compared the rest of her life to those days. Nothing was ever again inconsequential nor dismissed. She felt a sorrow well up within her for this young woman's vacuousness, and for her vanity. At a young thirty she had attained what few could attain at any age – young or old – and possessed it for the simple fact that it was part of her parents' estate and would someday belong to her.

Ann felt remorse and a pang of envy. How much easier her life would have been if she could have inherited an estate in a place where there were no Europeans nor miseries of war. She picked up her calendar and proceeded to her suite to pack her belongings. In a day she would fly into Miami and from there to the Caribbean.

12.

Harold Bixby told Michel Gandt, "I took the letters to mail them and threw them in the chute. In another chute I deposited my laundry."

Michel was busy with half a dozen deciphers which had come in on the teletype from Afula, an inland town with a handful of Arabic physicians and a local pharmacy which as he recalled sold liquid opium over the counter.

"And this has some bearing on our conversation of the other night?" Michel asked.

"Only in the sense that if two submarines pull up to the same salvage yard, the first being towed to a floating shop, then one should wonder if there are submarine cables and acoustic hydrographic survey equipment in the vicinity."

"Who handles that sort of thing apart from the Maritime?"

"Maritime is still deployed in the Indian Ocean. Strategic Sealift provides whatever is needed in the Atlantic to deliver materials and take petroleum to the States." And then as though to jar his friend to the key matter, he said, "It was the Israelis built the drones that both the Italians and the Spaniards use to sweep for underwater mines."

"So you made some inquiries, I gather."

"Yes. The only way to obtain any information as to mine detection in the Mediterranean was to consult Haifa. It's my belief, although it's not documented anywhere, that the Pakistanis attempted to go after Haifa's database first by electronic methods and failing that, tried to establish an agent-in-place."

"A mole, you say?"

"Yes. Perhaps they obtained some information; what with all the British scandals in Tel Aviv in the early Seventies, certainly we would have seen the same number of airport bombings as we did at the European Olympics. But these targets expanded once you Americans took your corporations into Asia and Malaysia."

"Any idea what Military Intelligence thinks?"

"MI-6? No idea."

"Someone should really ask them before we ruminate further."

"I did learn the event preceding the dissolution of the French cartels was the closure of Port Said in 1984. As early as 1976 you had the bombings of the airport at Tel Aviv by, it is speculated, the Berliners."

Static disrupted the connection. "Berliners? You mean, by the Arab quarter," Michel asked, and then strained to hear the answer.

"Well, it's the nature of the beast, isn't it? Competition, that is. We no longer can assure New England she will receive a hundred tons of crude without a percentage winding up at bottom. Who do you suppose wants the fleet oilers, anyhow?"

"Must be rebels in Venezuela."

Harold spoke. "Oh, Venezuela doesn't give a hoot. Try the outstations. Try The Alfatah."

"The Palestinians by themselves don't make up enough numbers. The British have some access to the Saudis," he said and paused, adding, "through the Arab Commonwealth, I suppose."

"Well, the countries which follow similar counterintelligence measures are Israel, France and Italy and their protectorates."

"If you mean the Caribbean, the islands there are merely ports. A handful – Tobago, Bonaire, and Curacao have farms and the Dutch influence. Oh, by the way, I've received a correspondence from Bob."

"Yes, Bob," Michel joined his friend's enthusiasm. "How is old Bob?"

"Doing spritely, I should say. He writes from Jericho. The post says, This is some swell place. We've traveled from border to border by four wheel drive, small plane, boat, school bus and shanks. Seen sights and had perfect crepes at an outdoor cafe listening to Mozart."

"Who's he with?"

"It's signed Bob and Stevie."

"Must be a woman friend. Any idea when he'll be back?"

"Doesn't say," Harold said. "This is dated almost five weeks ago."

"He probably didn't get out in time before the Haifa incident."

"Well, you know what the Australians say."

"Is this Stevie Australian?"

"Or New Zealand. I seem to recall his mentioning he'd met a woman when he was in Aukland."

"Oh I thought he'd never left Macao or some such place." Michel adjusted his bifocals.

"Could be. Could be I have it incorrectly. So the Australians say that the woman's husband wanted to be left. The husband apparently had asked his wife to keep his bed while he went off to India for a year. He had wanderlust. Of course we all have something incurable. The woman in this story says she had left this man a year too late. He could have been a rich man."

"It's like the penney story, don't you think?"

Harold was quiet a moment. "Oh, the one about sticking the penney in the automobile lighter? Yes, a bit. Of course those pennies count for quite a bit. They open with the Dow up, the NASDAQ also up and the Du Maurier at a low."

They chuckled over that one. Always the Brits took it in the shins.

"Are you still expecting me Thursday?" Harold inquired.

"Yes, indeed and it's your turn to cook."

"Lamb be alright?"

"Fine. I haven't eaten a good stew in months. I'll supply the house red."

Michel remembered the defector who had joined the parade in 1938. The Americans had withdrawn their troops from France and unbeknownst to the Germans had regrouped in Russia along with the British, the Danish and Norwegians. In underground silos they readied squadrons of aircraft fighters, some of the best planes the world would ever see. Factories of adult laborers volunteered for the list. They trained first as divers to handle underwater reconns and then flew into the Netherlands and from there to France and Germany to scour the harbors to assess military strength. As their numbers increased, as they secreted men into the German military, they bombed harbors, cut off communications, misdirected radios, and established their own checkpoints.

Vidal was French. He'd been raised in the Alps when war broke out. A robust youth with dark hair and a reddish tan complexion, he could outwit anyone with his knowledge of tangibles. He operated all farm equipment, could replace generators, interrupt and if need be monitor transmissions, and he was a superb diver.

The defectors were among the best and the worst. Those who retained their political loyalty to the Party while outwardly operating as a double spy took many lives before they were finally apprehended. Vidal went in on a handful of underwater reconns before he joined the first squadron of fighters. Not until 1943 did they understand he had been sending cables by underwater transmission to the French.

The Haifa incident reminded Michel of Vidal, of his ability to enter a place heretofore unseen, move in and within minutes have pulled the plug. Just as Vidal had been interviewed by the Mossead for deftness and willingness to kill, he thought this assassin had also been prepared. The training was standard – focus on one object and blur the background for all others.

He had not contacted Tel Aviv since the war. He placed a person to person call to Liam Coyne.

13.

Vidal swam to shore. The row of colorful pensiones stood midway on the only road, somewhat camouflaged by verdant greenery, steep gardens and terraced fields. As he bent to retrieve his towel and sandals, he caught a glance at a motorcycle edging onto the path along the sand. It was driven by a woman he knew from the university. That she wore a wetsuit struck him by surprise. If he had suspected he had been followed into the water, he would have postponed the dive.

He found his way to the flat and checking to see he wasn't observed, opened onto the small studio and loft. From the foyer he could see he had a message waiting. He switched the recorder on and listened as he changed into slacks and a shirt. It was already four and he had a good hour ahead of him before he made it into Rome to meet his contact at the church on Via Venuto.

The road winded from the rocky shoreline past a tree with its roots exposed and grassy hills to the main avenue. He looked instinctively over his shoulder seeking the woman on motorcyle but she had long gone. As he drove into town, he mused over the recent radio broadcast. The French were changing from their reliance on the Swiss franc to the British pound note in hopes of salvaging half a dozen industries which had been affected with the market decline due to the Middle East Crisis. A refocussing on the Norwegian coast also might move dependence upon oil closer to newer ore deposits. In the meantime the world markets would seize the port and in so doing ward most commerce to a neighboring city. To keep shipping free of Arab-dominated coastal communities would be difficult.

As he neared the center of town and switched lanes, approaching the cafe opposite the church, he saw the man the Agency had sent in was Zagreb. He was a Yugoslav born in France, with the typical outsider look the Yugoslavs have of modest height and curly brown hair, and had made a narrow escape to Holland where he hung out for half a dozen years until the war was over.

Vidal parked, and slapping the other man on the arm, he pulled him into the cafe with him to a booth. "Nostalgia bring you back?"

"Oh you mean here? No, I'm staying across the street in the church basement," Zagreb said, and bent to light a cigarette.

A waiter took their orders. Vidal said, "What's the Agency planning on?"

"Swift offensive. Someone else is bringing in the artillery."

"Great." It meant a bomb, probably to Arafat since he was doing the talking these days for the three Arab nations. "Any possibility we'll track these gunslingers into their rat hole?"

"No way to track them without blowing half the countryside. Once we know who responds, what their connection is to these sluggers, then absolutely we'll drop the floor. But you better believe, they've gone into hiding where they'll be for the next decade until someone sets up a new job."

"Where do you intend to strike?"

"Haven't decided yet. Maybe outside the net. It will take me sometime to work up a strategy. My guess is I'll bring in four men, five tops."

"I've been asked to put out feelers for who brought the gunner in. I'd like to be a string along."

"Sorry, Vi, I can't. This is going to resemble a quick throw. I haven't decided – maybe a car bomb, but you know the baggage will cost me a hundred grand. I thought a swimming pool or a vent."

He could see already they were moving along separate lines of inquiry. "Where's Milano?"

"He's detained."

"Literally? Arrested?"

Zagreb smiled. Because his chortles often resembled snide barbs, the smile struck Vidal as amusing.

"He's in the States unable to leave."

"New York?"

"California."

"Unbelievable. Leisure?"

"It's a job."

"Someone I know?"

The waiter brought coffee and Italian custard. They performed the rituals of pouring cream, adding sugar and tasting the dessert.

"Kiljoy," came Zagreb's wry reply.

"Oh no one calls him that anymore. Time table stuff, wasn't it?"

"Right. How many minutes until the Express pulls into the next station. Tiring. Everything timed to the minute, rehearsed until the rail yards pulled their newer lines off track and just ran with the clunkers. Oh, and by the day."

"So, who is he today?"

"Points South, who knows? He's got a list of code names. None of them adequately put any perspective on his brand of insanity."

"He should've stayed behind in Britain."

"Well, the British like the countryside."

"So I'm told."

They sipped coffee. Zagreb changed subjects and rambled on about his desire to return home for a summer.

By the time they had paid the tab, it was eight o'clock and the sun had dropped ushering in a mauve darkness and a string of lights in the chain of vehicles streaming past them.

Looking at the fare sheet to the Peninsula via the Golden Gate Bridge the mileage from San Francisco to Alameda County was thirteen miles and by air was twenty eight miles. From San Francisco the mileage to Sonoma was forty-five miles and by air was thirty-eight miles. Jean Wilson reviewed the chart for the radio cabs until she was assured what the round-trip to and from Belvedere was. A trip to see her grandson was a must if she were to prepare herself for all the young people she would encounter once she arrived in the Antilles.

Not only that but her son had married a Jewish woman convincing her that the British actually do have superior brains and she wanted to bring the family a picnic basket of Andoulle sausage, lamb cubes, locally made strudel, dried apricots and an assortment of goodies that a mother who rarely was able to leave the house might enjoy. Besides enjoying a few hours of conversation without her son, Jean was hopeful she could learn what her son thought about the Caribbean situation without having to ask him herself. He had held a job as a core map reader for the Navy for twenty years and it had taken him to the Caribbean three, four times a year. It was he who had told her tongue-in-cheek one night that oil was the only commodity the government couldn't supply enough of without exhausting reserves overnight. Venezuela was where America went; the United States was in charge of oil there. Europe, on the other hand, went to the Saudis. Although China oil had been optioned, it had to travel across Pacific Ocean where the waters were still mined, predominantly by the United States.

She was going to meet with her good friend Ann Smith who had raised hairs when she alluded to a handful of neighbors whom she considered might be in the business of blowing up sensitive targets in Egypt and Oman. She stated in her usually dry wit, she did not think the gunner at the Haifa embassy had been concerned about oil.

But they both knew that Palestinians who bombed did so because the price of oil was not high enough and that they were frequently from Pakistan, Afghanistan or Kashmir. Inherent in Ann's tone was bewilderment, which for Ann whose experience of skirmishes was so extensive was a rarity. Could be, Jean thought, the Haifa tragedy had been created out of a religious rather than an economic problem. But then that meant the four powers of Syria, Lebanon, Jordan and Saudi Arabia were reasserting the veil, and possibly the steam.

The steam was an enactment of the worst type of oppression. Prisoners were held in tiny cubicles which were overheated by steam vents. From tiny outlets rose torrid steam which in time burned the skin of the captured. Political prisoners suffered worst of all because they were essentially kidnapped and held unknown to guards who might be sympathetic.

She packed her suitcase with several conservative tailored suits – grey, navy blue and black – and a half dozen white, collared blouses. For Antilles she laid two pairs of slacks and one pair of shorts and sneakers. Through the window she saw the Yellow Cab had arrived early. Zipping the case and grabbing it and her purse, she went to answer the front door.

14.

As she window shopped in the underground bubble in Toronto, Kiev thought she saw her father who had been dead twenty-two years ahead of her in the marketplace. She ran to catch up but he walked quickly, losing himself in the crowd. His profile was as she last remembered. White wavy hair cascading comfortably to his shoulders, high cheekbones and narrowing jawline, a bit of a tremoring to the hand left from the medication she remembered he once took and the too slender frame over which his clothing draped. Gone was that death stare and gaping expression. He could have been twenty-eight years younger, or perhaps her father's natural-born son, had he had one.

Out in the snowy wilderness, she had had years to reflect upon family resemblances. She and her brother while looking somewhat similar with their hair cut to the quick did not share the bone structure of their youngest brother who when he sucked in his cheeks had two layers of ridges making him like a New Zealander. She couldn't make the equation come out right however, and after toying with the idea that the hospital mislaid two out of three infants, she abandoned her ruminations as signs of restlessness, or desires for a new and substantially different life. It was the mid-life question after having spent years isolated from the world inside a tin shack at an oil station to imagine that when she reconnected with life, she would somehow be shaped into a changed person.

Her family was painful to be around. Her older brother was energetic and talented but iconoclastic and as a result limited contact, and her younger sibling was domineering, used to bending others to his will. Their parents were considered by all of them to have been lost in a world to themselves, their father's death causing their mother to retreat far from the world of social engagements, entertainment and art. If she had been entranced by her husband, having spent every hour of their retired years in each other's company except for the hour he went for a four mile walk every day, she was now locked into his memory, consumed by his research and by the books he wrote and the ones which he never agreed to give his publisher. Wherever this was, when she was with her children, she was far away, her ability to want to be with them depleted by her inability to soothe herself adequately.

It gave Kiev little relief to escort her mother to a matinee movie or to the museum, although when her father was alive, these enjoyments filled them with the purpose of being connected not only by presumed genetics but by common interests. They spent hours laughing, comparing notes of the days when the three were young, and holding hands as though nothing but their sharedness made them whole. It was this rapport that had carried Kiev through college and grounded her, making it possible to span lonely hours in scientific research. The wholeness she had identified in her mother as humor was now so diminished she felt herself to have been wounded as well. Attempts to rejuvenate her mother failed, leading her to purchase items for the home she thought her mother might require and instead creating a void because her mother did not want to replace her furniture nor her automobile nor any other possession, no matter how small.

15.

They took a boat to Acre at midnight. The half moon shone strangely through amassing clouds skimming the water. The walled city from a distance stood on the peninsula, its turrets like slanted windows at angles. Their motor sputtered in the night. Here and there lights appeared or were extinguished in windows of chalk buildings where the residents of the city lived. Robert spied out the entrance to the catacombs on the far side of the shoreline, pillars of ancient brick or sandstone rising above the flatness of the precipice and at their height slats through which the moonlight shone.

During the war the British had captured and tortured members of the Jewish Underground. After, the castle was converted from a prison to a mental institution where shift change occurred between three-thirty and four in the morning.

They docked and tied up the boat. A vehicle had been left at the roadside. Abu found the key under the carpet beneath the driving wheel.

By the time they made it into town and booked a motel and had ordered in toast and eggs, it was five o'clock and the first light of day cracked the horizon.

"Where's the number for your contact?" Abu Raddaq asked.

Robert gave him his passport with the number written inside the flap. "Once we hook up, you can drop me and go your way."

"Not such a good idea. You will need an interpreter, no?"

"Doubtful. I'm fairly certain this man speaks English."

"But you'll be meeting out here in the country?"

"Possibly."

"Then I will wait."

Even after Abu had arranged the meet, Robert was uncomfortable. He was clear Milano would not come into the open, making it necessary for him to enter the knoll. Abu would have to be told he could not join them and would have to wait in the car. Since 1971 when two young Jewish women were nearly gunned down after dark, the strip along the waterfront was heavily patrolled by Muslim and Jewish police alike.

Robert catnapped for most of the morning, rising at noon to shave. He went to the lobby for a newspaper and sat in the front room listening to the water fountain as he sipped tea and read for news of the mortar shell raid a night ago. There was no mention. He scanned the news for local tips and found to his dismay that boats bound for Acre were actually being rerouted north to Sidon.

He showered again around two to stay cool and took another rest until five. At six they went to dinner and strolled along the waterfront. When it was dark they drove to the Catacombs. Abu let Robert out in the square near the stairs and retreated to the road to wait.

Robert climbed the flights of stairs that rose above the knoll to the turreted walls through which it was possible to see glimpses of the city below. A figure stepped out from a turret and approached as Robert crossed the roofless castle floor.

"Milano," Robert said, and clasped the other man by the shoulders. "What's happened? You've lost weight."

"I've been through a dozen wars since we last met," said the thin Italian with close cropped hair and a beard. "I've been busy."

"How's Zagreb?"

"The Israelis have hired him. That's about all I know at the moment. If he learns Acre or Sur had anything to do with the violence in Haifa, there'll be hell to pay, but I don't think they did, so it's a matter of waiting."

"Will you join him?"

"No, I'm too old to keep building pipe bombs for mosque shuttles."

"Ouch."

"Yes," Milano said, stepping into the moonlight now.

Robert saw he had lost his tan and had a swarthy look typical of Indians whose faces at night seemed bone white although by day they had a good deal of color. His leanness was noticeable, and Robert refrained from commenting a second time.

"I was in Haifa when they struck," he said. "I went by Herendon Square as soon as the news broadcasted and shot a few rolls but I haven't had time to develop them. I was hoping we could go to your mother's so I can develop them."

Milano considered. "We can do this, but tell me, what makes you think no one saw you, especially since you're known as a face with a camera?"

"I'm not sure. I just need a place to hole up to figure out what I've got."

"Maybe you ought to return to Jerusalem first. Get yourself some cover."

"I'm not sure I can get that far. There's bound to be detours by now."

"Okay. You remember how to get there?"

"Draw me a map."

Milano did, then said, "Tell your man to return to the motel and you'll meet up with him in two hours."

They split up at the stairs. Robert returned the way he had come. Catching up to Abu, he told him of the plan.

Abu laid a reassuring hand on Robert's. "If you're detained for any reason, call."

"Don't worry. I won't be," and jaunted off to the gates to the inner city and to the maze of cobblestone alleys which would take him to Milano's mother's home.

Thirty years ago when Robert covered the early airport bombings at Tel Aviv, he had met Milano at an outdoor cafe. Milano had just met the woman who would become his second wife. She was a tall robust Muslim woman from Beirut who had relocated with her family. He had been living then in the country with a handful of Arabic youths who ran fishing shops and small markets in the Acre harbor. His mother was a stout woman with large breasts which sagged to her belly. She kept a log of his calls and set up appointments in the inner city for her son and businessmen who would later help Milano link resources for the CIA.

The cobblestones glinted with steely light. Robert entered the gates and followed the series of streets that led to his mother's condominium. He climbed the fifteen or so steps to the chalk canopy and knocked on the door. A man opened it and ushered him inside past a living room of talkative, loud women, one whom Robert recognized as Milano's first wife's sister, into a hall and past a handful of small bedrooms to a bathroom at the end. He opened the door, then locked it behind them.

Immediately the man raised his shirt to show him a scar across his back. "Last job I took I got sliced." He let down his shirt. "It was over something far less significant than producing photographs," he said, and climbed onto a stool to remove the light bulb and replace it with a red light. "Just don't take too long," and slid open the shower to reveal a board laid over the tub and tin tubs with chemical in each. "I use this half a dozen times a week but after tonight I'll have to relocate because someone is bound to connect your face with my condo."

Robert understood. He locked the door behind his departure. Then he removed the film from the plastic containers and slipped the negatives into the chemical tray. After ten minutes he clipped them on a rope string that ran the length of the tub and waited five minutes for the film to dry. He removed a magnifying lens from his belongings and inspected each frame. They showed the open door to the embassy, a man smoking a cigarette in the street, a baker hawking pastries, the Buddhist church and the block of flower beds around the church. He then cut the frames he wanted for pictures, slipped glossy paper into the chemical and placed his own magnifier with the negative over the tray. In minutes he had verifiable prints of the open door, the man smoking and the baker along with a multitude of tourists mulling about.

He bagged his things leaving nothing behind. When he let himself out, the chatter had stopped and the party had left. Even the man was nowhere to be found.

Someone had gone through the room with a fine tooth comb. Abu lay sprawled against the furniture, his head tucked into his neck as though in deep slumber due to an alcoholic rendering. Their items lay scattered across the floor, their backpacks and duffel bags shredded, the furniture gutted with stuffing showing through. Robert brought Abu to, passing an inhalant beneath his nose, then left. He strode down the street to the bus depot, got aboard the first bus that arrived and rode it to Afula, where he figured he'd be safer than in Haifa. From there he flagged down a cab and rode it to Tel Aviv. He figured he'd sit at the airport until they resumed scheduled flights, but when he arrived at the check in counter, the officer checking his belongings told him a oil-bearing ship in the port at Haifa had been bombed and said everyone was being detained and led him to an office where airport security worked.

An hour later the airport police transported him to FBI offices in downtown Tel Aviv. Tel Aviv was modern, a hub of outdoor malls and digital neon billboards amidst glass studded office buildings and four and five story sandstone condominiums built for professors and physicians who constituted the State's upper class. The office he was brought to was the only fully furnished suite in what resembled an empty airport hangar. He was shown into a room with a desk, book shelves, computers and a blue upholstered couch.

Night fell over the city. Lights focussed on a walkway made of sandstone and the light yellow colored concrete of the Technitron Institute of the university. Around the city billboards lit up with a product commercial and retreated.

When still no one came after another hour, he curled up on the couch and draping his jacket over his body fell asleep.

16.

The ship docked at Castries in the coral reefs of St. Lucia. After a day in a hotel overlooking glistening white sand on Montserrat where the ocean liner replenished its fuel, Ann was relieved to have arrived in the countryside of St. Lucia. The farmhouse from which she would use as a base, faced the desolate expanse of ocean. The breath of beauty was the un-cluttered coast, a sight she wanted to take in for a good two days before she went in search of Sir Askew's problem.

She walked across the knoll to the small stone cabin where a gift shop and cafe thrived and purchased a newspaper and a cup of coffee. The winds had died down making it possible to enjoy the sight through the opened window. She eyed a row of cottage houses and past them a well and trough. Although she could find no animals nor cattle, the landscape possessed a surreal reality as though all time was arrested somewhere between the finite and the scarcely forgotten. The mostly African population was no-where to be seen, although here and there a farmer, usually Dutch, appeared and disappeared through the arrangement of cottages.

She had meant to stop at the base in Guantanamo, at the southern tip of Cuba, and then to traverse by yacht to Jamaica, Haiti and to Puerto Rico but the ship's captain was hurried and needed to reach the Venezuelan coast within three days. The newspaper boasted of a new government project off Tobago and reported an unusual response from islanders. Over a hundred men had volunteered to work fishing boats to scour the waters for itinerant mine heads, along with navy men who would go in. It would be two days on, forty-eight hours, then a day dry with accommodations in Canaan and in Trinidad at Toco. The call for labor would destitute the availability of boats, causing her to take the first crawler that promised to leave.

There was no sense traveling as far south as Guyana, un-less she couldn't get back. The sensible thing to do was to stay put until her friend Jean Wilson arrived and then take a flight to Kingstown and from there to Grenada.

Joe Daughter packed his belongings. By two o'clock, weather permitting, he'd be on an island flight to St. Lucia and from there to Puerto Rico and the Keys. In a week he'd fly to Tel Aviv with an assistant Kiev Houtely to take a look at the embassy situation in Haifa. By then it ought to have cooled, unless the shootings were tied to a bigger picture, and then heaven help them all.

He had stayed the night on the telephone to Gandt, his contact in Santa Barbara trying to discern how much money the Prince Edward Bank had left to draw upon. Houtely allegedly had the latest info on capped wells, but Gandt was the one who would approve substitute currency to Israel's principal cities. The lira was going strong and after that, the American dollar with a quarter million tourists visiting the Holy Land and the Wailing Wall. Gandt hoped there wouldn't be many delays. Daughter told him Venezuela oil was on schedule and from his point of view, despite a run on the branches in Sante Fe and Cumana, there'd be enough cash flow in the next twenty-four hours to boost the coastal cities back onto the map.

The minute he hung up the telephone and switched on the television, he saw a gang of terrorists had shut down the ports on Sicily. He watched with stuporous fascination as the broadcaster elucidated on the as yet little known facts. A handful of bandits had overtaken the two southern ports, shut down the monitors and barricaded entries to the radio stations. The telecaster speculated that since these were the next most frequently utilized ports after Haifa, ships in the Mediterranean would be forced to put into Arab ports in order to travel from Egypt and Israel to Italy. If ships ignored the entire Syrian coastline, without either Haifa or Sicily, they might not have enough fuel to reach the boot.

Chances were, even if the airport at Tel Aviv remained open, he'd have trouble getting to Haifa by any method of transportation. By now the Israelis had to realize their shipping industry was not safe to dock and had to secure alternate de-fueling stations.

Robert Sheridan was aroused out of sleep by a dark complected man with dark curly hair wearing trousers and a blue shirt with abstract blue and white tie.

"What took you into Acre?" He asked, in a thick accent that characterized him as Spanish Jew. "Did you have business there?"

"I was trying to find a fishing boat which could take me

and my driver to Sicily or to Greece."

"Why not fly from here?"

"Because I have photographs taken of the Haifa incident and did not think I would make it safely this far south."

"May I see these photographs?"

Robert fished them out of his backpack and turned them over. "My driver took me to a photographer and then he wound up assaulted."

"Who's this? The photographer was hurt?"

"No, my driver. I must have panicked."

"Yes, well, I will show these to our director. You wait here."

He'd wait all day. He stood, went into the hall and bought a cup of coffee from a vending machine. Sipping it, he glanced at the front page of an Israeli newspaper which showed a ship bombing. He scanned the section, and absorbing that it was an oil freighter, he took it and the coffee to the office with the sofa. It wouldn't be daybreak before Tel Aviv asserted martial law and the streets and shops were patrolled for known anti-Israeli agitators.

The officer returned with a senior officer, a small stocky French man with wire rim glasses and a suit of white polished cotton. "We have to ask you to come with us."

"Right now?" Robert asked.

"Yes, immediately."

They led him to an elevator and rode it to the street, then marched him to a waiting automobile and drove across town past a myriad of closed restaurants, stores and apartment buildings. They followed the road as it wound above the city out of the financial district to a parking lot beside a long yellow brick two story office building. They ushered him inside to a stylish office of neon signs and archeological diggings and deposited him inside someone's office.

The man whose office it was sat behind a large desk with a yellow ceramic light. He was light skinned, with wavy reddish brown hair, typically Israeli, probably from a kibbutz rather than city raised.

"You're a professional," he said, and then introduced himself as Jordan Betrabi.

"Yes, I was staying in Haifa when the shootings occurred."

"Well, these are very satisfactory. You've captured a man's face here."

"Yes."

"Any possibility you will ride with me to the G&E plant at Gomorra? It's about a two hour drive."

"I can do that. Would you mind telling me why?"

"I'd like you to identify a man there."

"Not this man?" Said with the revulsion Jews have for bombers who live within Jewish boundaries.

"No."

But Robert suspected the agent meant it could be him.

As they drove inland, the sun rose high over the flat land. Although there were a healthy number of tilled fields arranged like a checkerboard, the distance looked to be uninhabitable, mountainous hills on which nothing had grown, or could grow. The water canal filled to capacity did not reassure that the needed water to feed the population would indeed reach the population centers. Alongside the road, ash was piled from a source Robert could only guess at.

When they reached the salty flats that constituted Gomorra, the man Betrabi had meant for Robert to identify was in the lot engaged in engrossing discussion with another engineer. Robert readily pointed him out to the Israeli officer who escorted him inside the plant without appearing to take note. Once inside the concrete enclosed hall, though, Lt. Betrabi showed Robert to a series of meters.

"Any knowledge of these?" he asked the journalist.

"None."

"They're standard meters to record output."

"What are they meant to show?"

"Performance of steam vents."

"Not electricity?"

"Well, allegedly the man in your photograph monitors output."

"What brought him to Haifa?"

"No way to know. Any possibility you could release all film taken in the country to us?" Lt. Betrabi returned to the parking lot and to his jeep. As Robert buckled his seatbelt, he asked him, "How well do you know the radio broadcast crew at Tel Aviv?"

17.

Claudia ran the piece on the Israelis launching an Mx in Gaza, then spliced in a segment on Jordan's King Abdullah II. She wove in the usual commentary saying it was up to Arafat to deliver this time by clarifying what the political end game was. She concluded the half hour with a delivery on the American spy Robert Hanson whose sale of secrets had destroyed a culture of trust.

The Cold War was still here. Spies were breaking safes and stealing secrets. We screwed the Russians, the Saudis were locked into a juggernaut with us and not even a hundred miles to the southeast off Florida Cuba had her weapons locked in on our southern most ports.

"Joe's flying in on the red eye," her sound man said, as she exited the box. "I said you'd pick him up."

"Great. How long's he here for this time?"

"Probably a few hours. Then on to Manhattan to meet a contact, some woman flying in from Canada."

"Sure, I don't mind. I thought I'd run a piece this afternoon on the 1956 Suez crisis and feature John Foster Dulles work with allies in Berlin. I did the research."

"Yeah, I can excerpt previous tapes as well. You think we're headed in that direction again with this latest intrusion?"

The attack on the embassy had proven a security embarrassment, not to mention the difficulties it could pose for transfers. As a base for economic espionage activities, without the numbers to issue advances for operations, the theft of the registers for issuing release of money could temporarily harm stability in the geography. Not only that, but the ability of the

Mossead to launch an investigation was also hindered.

Claudia dampened her short reddish hair and combed it back from her forehead in a feathered tapered look. She'd last been to New York four years ago but it felt like a hundred. She'd gone to look in on Roger after his prostate surgery and found him in the throes of lust with a junior lawyer in his firm. Never one for discretion, he promised to put her up at a motel where he took unconventional lunches, offering to drive her there until she put her foot down, took a taxi to their daughter's private school at Stoneybrook, yanked Cheney out of the semester and took her back to Boston with her. His affairs had been painful during the twelve year marriage, but it wasn't until she sat down with Cheney and learned he had indulged a handful of women at the expense of cancelled dinners, missed recitals, forgotten shows and a handful of other broken engagements that she let him take her to Divorce Court to win back whatever it was he thought he was capable of delivering. It hadn't been much – a dinner once a week, having Cheney up to the cabin in upstate New York once a month, and two weeks every summer between quarter breaks.

The long and short of it was that as soon as she landed her job, she managed to fall out of step with Roger to the extent she could honestly tell him she was overlooking holidays and in-between times. If he needed her to pick up slack for him, she was not around nor available to be consulted with. In four years Cheney survived his emotional distance, stepping up to bat with clarinet lessons, tennis once a week, swimming twice a week and high school concert and eventually local symphony performances.

She exited the studio to the parking lot, stashed her duffel bag with jumpsuit in the backseat and made a beeline for the Logan airport. It was a half hour through semi rush lunch hour and she found Joe standing in front of the art deco entrance by the taxi stop.

She parked and went around for a hug.

"Jesus, you look terrific, Claude."

"So much for couches for you." They kissed, and she

pinched his ribs. "I mean it, you're in terrific shape." She opened the trunk and threw his suitcase inside. "Up for dinner?"

"It'll have to be at your place because I can't afford to be seen in public."

"We can do my pad."

He grimaced. "It comes across poorly but this is very covert stuff."

They got inside the car and she headed for the beach.

"Where're you returning from?" she asked.

"Sante Fe, near Caracas. I was sent into defray a crisis."

"What does Intelligence honestly think could happen?"

Joe had settled into the seat of her old Dodge with a look of complacency that worried her in men she was on the verge of falling for. "They're afraid this could be a sizeable ring with a far-reaching grab at the international dollar."

She lit a cigarette. They were travelling now on the speed-way with departing planes flying above them, as she took the road to her beach home. "Do they have any idea who pulled the job?"

"They weren't known. My key contact last I heard was holed up in the Golan Heights."

"Oh Jesus. You going to fly to Israel?"

"You know me, only if they ask."

She had an idea they wouldn't have to. Within a forty-eight hour period, Israel would bring in sensitive agents who could calculate penetration and set up a round of counter of-fensives designed to shake any rat free of the ventilation. Their agents would want Joe to maintain a vigil outside the suspect's quarters.

They unloaded his stuff into the guest bedroom. She made Margaritas and guacamole with chips while he talked to her about lancing mine heads in a naval building in the Port of Spain.

"Who's your contact in Manhattan, Joe?"

"Her name's Kiev Houtely. She's returning after two years stuck on an iceberg in a lonely ice wilderness."

"What do you need her for?"

"The usual. She's a pro at pulling up sediment and evaluating core material to determine whether the exploratory is capable of producing oil."

Claudia sipped her drink. "Have they run out of oil?"

"We're in good shape. Venezuela will never run dry; we have four hundred ships in a week which arrive at destinations inside of a week for every dock on the East coast and in the Gulf."

"So what's the problem?"

"No problem. The British are forever seeking new wells. If a two year run can increase production, the bank views it as a worthwhile investment."

"Did this embassy attack have any bearing on Prince Edward Bank?"

"There's the potential. Israel has a refinery as you know as do a hundred other ports dotting the Mediterranean. With the embassy at Haifa down for let's say several days, international banking will necessarily turn to Tel Aviv and she's in no position to handle anything beyond the scope of the region."

"I didn't realize that."

"In addition the attack puts a crimp in her ability to put diesel on the road."

"Any expectation there will be a problem with the airport?"

"That's where these attacks hit us the worst. If I go in on this which it sounds as if I probably will, I'll be looking for the tourniquet action."

She fixed a dinner of lamb chops, salad, carrots and rice and watched him eat. He was ravenous and cleaned his plate twice. They talked about the Navy's watch over the harbor in the Caribbean, its vigilance on nuisances and on more serious disruptions, and about the people he worked with whose task was to assure secure national boundaries. She described the last fifty hours on local radio as tense, tiring and simultaneously provocative. Around the city, dot-commers were initiating contact points for family members in and around Haifa and seeking to draw upon information sources as to access to airports, roads and outlying areas.

When he was done, she was on a third cigarette. He helped with dishes and damp cloth cleaned the table and counters.

She slept with him because it was the thing to do and she had not had a man in over three years. She was insistent and impatient and kept him to her rhythm until she felt he could run on empty.

In the morning she found him gone. It was a curious feeling, to be alone when she expected to rise with him. She wasn't certain she liked the emptiness she felt.

His note to her said, Claudia, you won't remember this but the last time I stayed the night you wanted me to leave before morning so I took the liberty of calling a cab. I could've stayed through mid morning.

She'd never been clear as to what men wanted, let alone what she wanted from a man. If she liked the intimacy, she was afraid she'd become dependent; if there wasn't enough attraction, she ended the budding relationship before it got started.

As she stood in a silk negligee in front of the window overlooking the ocean, she was aware of feeling the time with him hadn't been long enough.

18.

The advance car was Zagreb.

A Yugoslav, he had all the advantages of the British without the ties to the German-born Irish. The money was in the account. Now he had to act quickly before his presence was detected and then retreat to Belarus equally as quickly. There, he'd be confused for half the population.

He rented an A6 27T model Saab outside Rome. When he went to pick up his new passport, the weather had changed to a dull grey. By eight he was on his way to the Trade Zone complex and once his business was completed, by nine he'd be on El Al to Tel Aviv. At eleven his man in Toronto would retrieve the A6 from the airport stall, bring it to a chop shop for a complete breakdown and by four have it back to the rental in one piece.

A fire truck sat at the curb in front of the trade center. Inside, the various firms were bustling with businessmen. Zagreb rode the elevator to the second floor and passed a sign that said, Expect delays. He passed the shiny tinsel diner for Fog City and entered the next establishment, a shoe shine mart with twenty stands occupied by what looked to be a predominantly Swiss traveler.

His chair became available. He climbed onto the platform and placed his steel pointed shoes on the iron bar. The shoe shine man whom he suspected was CIA or MI-6 was an elderly gentleman with wavy white hair and a moustache expertly toweled the left shoe.

"Encounter rain on your way in?" he asked Zagreb.

"Some drizzle."

"You know what they say. Better to change your route than to wait a day."

"Any idea as to venue? I'm headed for the Via Venuto." If he was sharp, he already knew Zagreb's itinerary.

He appeared thoughtful. "Good place to find statues. A bit heavy though on the mental fare." He proceeded to the right shoe. Dabbing polish on the side above the top lace, he took the

306   J. Lea Koretsky

towel as though it were a leather strip and expertly moved the shine over the shoe. "My own preference is for a museum and a respite of lunch."

He hadn't considered a museum cafe. Too noisy, too congested. But it gave rise to some ideas, as his shine man said, without expression, "Stay off the pavement." Which translated to, take a bus.

He tipped double. He sprinted downstairs to the travel office to book a return to Greece. The shipping agent asked the usual tiresome questions and asked him to complete an address statement. After collecting fees and assigning a berth, he was given a ticket for the QE2 which would depart Haifa in two days hence and arrive in Kekiras just beneath Albania. With that arrival the mission would be complete.

Then it'd be a waiting game. They'd wait for hours or years. Transmissions to and from banks and cartels would be scrutinized, as would redirects for container ships and air cargo. The money was often sent in half a dozen different directions with spies assigned to monitor as much of the officer system as possible until the conflict was perceived to be stable. Then they'd act, whoever they were. They'd hit another embassy or the Games, or take out a handful of banks and the event would become dubbed another bloody Sunday.

He dumped the rental at a stall in short term parking depositing a sack in a locker in the airport terminal and mailing the key by express mail. He checked his bag and went in search of a bar nearest the assigned gate. On his way he spotted his number two man coming out of the men's room. They acknowledged one another with a glance and kept walking.

He'd done this dance a hundred times. He was the best in the Western world and his tactics although costly to the jurisdictions they affected produced a suspect within days of the final act. His second man would fly to Logan in Boston for a night before flying to San Francisco and picking up a vehicle at Bauers. The 800 vehicles confirmed what was already suspected, and Zagreb, his style varied and unpretentious, allowed for any number of alternatives. If he received a confirming telephone call in any of the cities where the explosives were to be wired, he sent in a second team to tail suspects. If he then received a confirming memo, he'd bring in Vidal. If Vidal had somehow picked up a lead and joined him by entry from another route, they'd switch teams and bring in another group, probably out of Sweden. The idea was to keep the revolving doors moving, too fast for a small ring to identify who was stepping into the entry. As time wore on and new aspects were determined and catalogued, they'd slow down the revolutions per minute to see who was watching who and where there were leaks, if any.

He had his suspicions that the attack on Herendon Square was one of many similar acts, part of a string of consequences spread out over a vast trade zone beginning in 1969 with the bombing of Israeli airports and the Berlin Games intended in the end game with the seizure of a major American port to become the next installation for the termination of a death-star, most probably of Hong Kong and all her powerful financial hubs. Just as the USSR had gone under ice and her cities relocated throughout an immense territory, so now China too and all her civilization would merge and reformat itself on newer continents planned for by the Spanish whose colonies were now a receding sea, too fragmented and usurped to remain powerful.

He deposited himself in a quiet bar not unlike the numerous airport lounges scattered throughout Britain and Canada where he had spent countless hours awaiting replacements for cancelled flights. He ordered a beer with an egg and tobasco and retreated with a newspaper to a spot by the window.

At midnight Italian time, the men's rooms at airports in Rome, Athens, Istanbul, Constantinople and Aleppo blew out causing irreparable damage to plumbing. Onlookers would be rushed to hospitals for shrapnel and would later describe the sound as a large whoosh. At three in the morning Turkish time, pipes fell in causing major avenues to cave in effectively shutting down one entrance into Istanbul from the northwest.

At five, an unidentified frigate moving at five knots an hour across the calm waters of the Aegean Ocean exploded in smoke and fire and falling debris was instantly scattered as far away as Paros and Nikonos.

One man was reported injured in Syria. All others except for the frigate crew who were presumed dead were released with minor bruises within hours of the bombs.

Around the globe teletypes rattled printers on land and at sea carrying the news to a chain of command of wire services, media centers, newspapers and broadcast systems.

Dutcher Lang was roused from sleep by a voice he did not recognize. It was muffled by a sound box and further masked by the fact the caller was reading from a script. You are to postpone your morning show to eleven. At eleven you will begin by playing Beethoven's Fifth for precisely three minutes. You will read five minutes from the Bible any passage a Talmudic Jew might consider relevant and you will follow with any news item you desire for a maximum of twelve minutes. Failure to comply shall result in an explosion at the home of a member of your staff.

The neon clock sent pulses of aqua green light. It was six minutes after five. He checked his alarm as to why it had not sounded at the usual time and found he had set it late.

He called Lt. Betrabi. "I've received a ransom demand. It didn't record."

"Write it down as close as you can recollect. I'll meet you at my office in a half hour."

"I can't go to you."

"Okay. We'll meet at Channel 2. You know where that is?"

"I do."

"Call no one, not even a girlfriend if you have one."

Dutch knew better. He could feel the erratic pulse of the sadistic assholes who were intent on wiping out the Middle East financial zone with one maddening elation. This end of the world created time, lived off it in magnificent castles on the sea, military encampments inside its major cities, and paid homage in the west to the best movie and cinema produced. The Arabs weren't sitting in the lap of luxury as was frequently portrayed in satirical displays on British airways, and the Israelis weren't having any fun with the concept either. Their lives had been recreated in terror and they had made do with terror every year the Berliners or some new fanatic or right wing crazies produced yet another airport bomb or took down a plane.

He'd been hoping to hear from his contact since the embassy attack and the fact that he hadn't heard anything yet concerned him. It meant his contact was detained or worse, stranded, and he had no way to contact him. It was a fact of war that as the police scoured the roads for recognizable terrorists they frequently became more vulnerable because they were seen by people they would never come to view as terrorists. It was an irony he sometimes sarcastically polled by saying, when someone gives you keys to the city, the trick is not to open the gate. He would often say after a ten hour marathon reporting a straight course of news that it was the Chinese who built a bank on electricity and had in years to come gone bankrupt the moment the British returned to turn off the lights in 1997, thereby rendering Hong Kong to its Mainland.

By the time he reached the commercial sector the sky had lightened. Dawn was still a medieval concept. If not for billboard sized neon screens, Coca Cola signs straddling buildings like long bibs, spoon shaped complexes and rounded obelisk towers, all Tel Aviv, her avenues of outdoor cafes and old style Russian Jewish bakeries, her swanky clubs and stylish Swedish apartment buildings would be diminished in their essence, mere comfort for a growing upper middle professional class compared with the sophisticated collegiate scientific boundaries set by the itinerant international dollar. Lt. Betrabi stood by the elevator in the lobby with two officers. Together they grouped on the second floor of the corporate offices.

Dutcher showed them the note. "I don't want to alarm my staff."

"We can't afford not to bring them in," the lieutenant said. "They have to be rehearsed especially in answering the phones.

One perceived slip up and we could all become yesterday's excavation. We'll go to work as your staff and mill about. We'll change all posters, bring in our own electricians, check your sound systems – "

He was shaking his head. "No interventions, please. For all you know one of them is already on my staff. I don't want to broadcast with my lunch in my mouth."

Daniel Betrabi became impatient. "This is not just your life. We have our own officer system to think about here. Even if you were to have such a person on board, chances are they are not hooked up with this same group of current terrorists. In all likelihood they are brought in by a person who at their level knows other networkers."

Dutcher glimpsed the reality too late. "I have a contact who is God knows where."

"A photo journalist?"

"No. He's not media, although he has a badge to get inside the door."

"Does he have a set occupation?"

"In the States he used to do percolation testing and soil analysis. He was the one they'd bring in to determine how much heat a foundation could withstand without cracking. When he travels he stays usually over six months and works on a visa."

"What does he do here?"

"He bolts girders into slab."

"How did you meet him?"

"I've known him forever." Then: "Since I've been at the station. Twenty years."

"Twenty twenty. Either of you have surveillance technology that feeds a line to take pictures off the other's computer as you are entering it?"

"We'd both be dead."

"But you're not here to read media?"

"No, and neither is he. He's not with the State Department; he's a freelancer."

"Is he brought in as a specialist for a job?"

"You mean to build the box and then to pour the cement? Well, he's able to perform lot line adjustments before they dig stakings. He can leach field testing; back home he researched the underground aquifer beneath Montana and Wyoming. He does both topographic as well as orthophotographic surveys to determine how deep the slab has to be."

"Gotcha," was all Betrabi said. "I'd like to talk to your man when you find him."

"Yeah, no kidding. So how do you want me to handle this?"

"Exactly as you were instructed. To the letter."

19.

He was antsy as he watched the tube. From his room in Elat, he had spent the morning arming himself with quietude. He had turned off the squawk box because the station was game playing to the tune of the blown frigate. Sentinel hours made him nervous and he could afford no irritation nor interruption. In all probability this was a CIA bid along with the broadcast spacing for music, prayer and feature.

The program was a replay of C-Span of the Investor Summit Securities and Exchange Committee in America featuring Corporate Finance Director Alan Beller and SEC Chair Harvey Pitt. Discussion centered upon disclosures to investors about insiders and about the formation of a new Public Accountability Board which would oversee auditors.

He had until dark before he went in. He'd be wearing a black seal suit that covered his face and black gloves and shoes with flexible soles. He wasn't worried about what he'd find. The Liftmor crew always brought in the material during the work day and left it on the top floor where it was presumed no one could get to it anyway.

He was careful. He didn't eat until the job was completed. He took ten sips of Gatorade throughout the day until three and then stopped. Once he climbed the rope he couldn't afford to pay attention to anything other than the timing of the task at hand.

He'd been up on this building twice, once at the twenty-sixth floor and again a week ago after they had poured cement and hung the picture on the forty-fourth floor. Despite a modest wind, the building was wide enough to accommodate an hour stay without feeling heady. He'd trained himself in twenty-four years not to get gripped by the inclination to look up as he operated the crane or as he climbed a rope. He'd known men who retired early after discovering that the continued motion of looking up caused their neck vertebra to calcify. He climbed the rope by floor, utilizing grasp with feet and toes and hands. Each rise was accomplished by direct level glance and as a result nothing could take him.

In addition he was a diver. The weightlessness underwater prepared him for the tenacity he needed to maintain during the hour it took to ascend to the top floor and connect the charges and to descend. Only once he had taken the crane seat to ground level to create the illusion that he relied upon equipment to handle this type of work. In fact he could climb any face, no matter how tenuous and could scale a building by side railings if he had to. Upbringing had placed him on steel walks at the age of three and thereafter had set him down from an airplane on top of the mid range Alps to claw his way with a steel pick and rope to civilization.

20.

"What do you think?"

The manager for the Speyside port on Tobago winced at the photograph. It had obviously been shot through wide angle lens at night and showed his skyscraper cat hitching himself up the Securities building in the southernmost part of the Israeli desert. As usual his form was tight, close to the rail. But it was the tiny lights positioned on surrounding skyscrapers that worried him.

"Can the assignment, if possible. Pay him an extra two million for his troubles."

Michael Gandt pursed his lips as he regarded the telegram. Another commitment was required, this time to appoint a team of Olympic mountain climbers to San Francisco's financial district.

He called the Overseas operator to place a person-to-person telephone call to his brother in England. "How's the weather?" he asked, shouting into the mouthpiece.

"Dreary, as usual. They've sent one of yours to Cyprus."

"Really. To chart a crawler to Beirut?"

"No interest. They've sent in a team to squeeze the gelato."

"And?"

"They think they've got a tentative match on a catwalker. This is a German, thin, undernourished type, balding, no fuzz. Been walking a high wire since age ten. Does it all with a rope. Grew up in the French Alps."

"The Americans are bringing in scientists who specialize in breath."

"Well, you like them, I guess. Here they're calling into the field every agent who's been stationed at sea level operations and anyone who's hoisted a crane. I told them they should bring in hand gliders as well."

They laughed.

Michael said, "Anything you can do for me for an advance?"

"Sure. What're we talking about?"

"The job calls for forty but my guess is you'll have to put up a hundred and forty before all is said and done."

"We'll stage it in increments."

Michael gave him the account number and the translation subsidiary name. By daybreak of the following day, the agent Vidal could bring in the best catwalkers anywhere in the world.

You couldn't pulverize a tall building, but you could dent a corner or blow out a floor. Or as occurred in the September 11th disaster, someone could throw a big rock.

Building one was relatively straight forward. First the

foundation slab, then balancing the beams, setting the floors, then the face for color blind windows, elevators, amphitheater, density of the grave. The architects were known, so were the construction companies, the pile drivers and for the quiet buildings the lattice boom, the hydraulic crane, the tonnage capability. What the hell wasn't known? There weren't so many buildings that the architect planners were hidden.

So why did anyone think a handful of airport bombs were related to skyscraper architects?

Of a multitude of air jobs, at least one employee had to have gotten wind of something.

Solla Data eyed the list. They had positions for major airlines, for commuter air, cargo, mail carriers, agri operators, corporate aviation, the government and aerospace not to mention for the pilots, air traffic, safety inspectors, techs, engineers, flight attendants and management. In her role as investigator, she had a handful of months to direct fifteen hundred interviews of all ground personnel, run central indexes on temporary personnel, and forward a list of employees who worked the areas where the bomb had taken out the bathroom to the Americans who were coordinating search and seizure for terrorists connected to any American airline.

21.

In a tall high-rise in Herendon Square in Haifa situated on the waterfront above the pier, Philip Van Dorn studied the photograph under the magnifying glass for several minutes puzzled by the inconsistency in depth for the objects he was looking at. His associate sat across from him in the red leather chair one leg urbanely crossed over the other, and waited. Between them on the massive walnut desk lay the photographs surrendered by the Tel Aviv precinct for the photojournalist who had captured the moments of a gunman entering the embassy on Herendon Square seconds before the shooting began.

"There's a man hiding behind the driver's door," Scotland

Yard Detective Van Dorn remarked.

"And look now to the photographs of the stairs," his associate Detective Bertrand Hopeley said. "Don't you suppose that too is a person rather than a blur?"

Philip leafed through the body of black and white photographs until Bertrand leaned forward and tapped a succession of them. Lowering the hand held lens to the first photo in the grouping, he studied the shadows.

"Yes, I agree. This here," and pointed to the wall immediately behind the door. "This man's quite good. Very thorough."

"We told him half the prints did not turn out."

"Better for him security-wise not to understand what he captured on film."

"How did he explain to himself what he saw?"

Bertrand answered. He was thin and stately unlike Philip who with his American looks, medium height, dark grey hair covering the start of a bald spot, and constant companionship after hours with two friends also in their early sixties – one a curly blonde who wore a painter's smock as a style of dress and the other a Filipino man who owned a speakeasy on the corner – had most of London and the crown's protectorates dogging at his heels.

"Lt. Betrabi said there was a problem with the mail delivery and shortly thereafter one man posted himself out front for a cigarette and the other sat in his sedan until the gunman arrived. He speculated the job was meant to resemble a youth bumping into and making off with a parcel as the gunman entered the embassy."

"Which explains the dispersion of the crowd here," pointing to the lower right corner of the photo, and adding, "not to mention the appearance of a scuttle."

"Yes," Bertrand said, satisfied he had not wasted his time in the dark room enlarging the yield. "Of course, Sheridan was followed to the Ha Golan."

"As well as to Acre."

"Betrabi feels the technician at the PG&E plant knows or can identify the gunman. He dragged Sheridan there."

Philip said, "To Gomorra? It's a hellish place. Parking lot, industrial plant, not much else out there." He studied another three or four photographs before he said, "We have the looks of another war here."

"I'm surprised they didn't seize the airport this time, or bomb half a dozen roads between here and the mountains."

"They may in fact get around to it. What do we know about the situation as it stands at this hour?"

"The Parliament has hired in a double agent who's proceeded to blow half a dozen toilets between here and Turkey and we've countered with one of ours, a quiet man who never uses violence to unearth a spider."

"We have names?"

"These are codes. Zagreb, he's from Yugoslavia. Real name is Guy Sender. If you want to get on his good side, you send him a dozen yellow, long stem roses which he hangs upside down in his closet until they are dried and withered and then sends you the dried arrangement in a glass vase, usually opaque cream colored yellow, light green or light blue when the job's completed. Real style, good eye for glass.

"Vidal is French, at least ten, possibly fifteen years on Sender. His real name is Carl Fox. His forehead is lined, all that worry, and he's dark, as you would expect a Frenchman with a lean, oblong jaw, reddish deep tan, dark eyes, soulful guy.

"There's Milano, but it doesn't look as though either our military intelligence nor the Israelis have thought to bring him in. He's a placid looking man, tall, brown hair, pasty complexion, travels with his secretary who for all anyone knows may well be his daughter, and is known for his postcards especially from China."

"No one thinks this has anything to do with the Chinese, do they?"

"Who the heck knows? There was some talk of evidence of Macao money floating around the Middle East. Then again, I think the Cold War's brandishment of Red China is overly cautious."

"Better safe than sorry. So, you planning to pull together a team of operatives?"

"Gibson said he's good for a few months."Philip said.

"Oh? The Queen wants to send him to Egypt again?"

"He just returned from Johannesburg. I doubt they'll rotate him back so soon. He can identify these guys. Not only that, when the opposition retaliates with similar looking players, he knows the board so well, he can call the shot for what it is and then determine what the end game is and where it is being delivered. Like take this thing in Port of Spain with naval games being tampered with. Clearly a target is onto our launch pins --"

"That's very dangerous."

"Worse than dangerous, because we have so much at stake in the area. There's shipping, refineries, farms, a string of penal colonies. One blow at us and the whole area could be sealed off for weeks. Imagine not getting oil frigates out of the staging area."

"What's this I heard about ice caps in the Canadian wilderness?" Bertrand let his attention drift to lighting a cigarette.

Philip waited until the match caught. "Prince Edward Bank has continual explorations on many ice capped regions. It's nothing new. They sink shafts all the time. My guess is on the international picture their call led to this attack on Herendon Square. Not that it matters to our investigation, but if it isn't the Arabs we may need to re-evaluate where the driver came from."

Bertrand was quiet. After a long moment, he said, "Is this attack about oil?"

"It seems to be. Prince Edward's leading export is oil."

"Who do we have who can get identities on these men?"

"I've been thinking who this could be," he said about the man whom the surveillance camera had caught a glimpse of as he glanced up into the seeing eye. "This is Carroub."

"Oh right, Carub. He sinks canes," Philip said euphemistically of the equipment the Turkish man used in initial oil exploration, "and rotates them until he can feel the groove slice into the rock to tamp the sediment bed. In fact if you come across him actually in employment, he'll show you a candy cane and illustrate the point by spinning it between his fingers as to how the screw is lowered. That's how he got his name. It's a joke."

When Bertrand did not get the joke, Philip explained, "It's the small mound of dark sand that gets produced as the blade is sunk."

"It's exploration drilling."

"Yes."

"How many drills do they sink in any given area?"

"I have no idea."

"I think it's several rows of nine cores apiece," Bertrand said. "But don't quote me on this. I'm as much in the dark as you."

"Look," and pushed the photo across the desk. The man behind the door wore no mask nor shawl to obscure his face. A direct-on had captured a man in the hall with an oblong rounded face, with round eyes. "Isn't this the man behind the door?"

"Could be." He checked, then: "Sure enough, I think you've got him."

"What about this fellow who took the outside photos? I think we should assign him a tail. Someone competent."

"Oh at least one. I thought maybe four or five."

"You're talking about a large team. Five for Sheridan, another five for each of these jerks, a team to pick through who had access to the airport bathrooms that blew --"

"Those cameras are lost. They blew along with the plumbing."

"Oh that can't be. They must have another set on spools."

"Find me an operative willing to illegal access airport security and we'll see if he can prove you right."

"Just call London and tell them you need a new budget."

Detective Van Dorn smiled. "Headquarters will tell me to take a jaunt."

"Yes, well, no one's going to take this assignment for free."

22.

Across the ocean on board the U.S. Naval Ship Mercury, Gedalea Bracha was burying his father Nossin at sea. The old man had made it to a spritely hundred and four and had managed to outlive his wives, including a third whom he had married ten years ago. The time for seasons had come and gone. Now, with six weeks to go before Labor Day the day was quiet, reflective, and the ocean in the gulf was without waves. Beside him stood his son Nossin and his son's wife of two months Andrea. Nossin would continue where his grandfather left off, in the Navy's employment, secreted to the tiny cubicles of an officer's quarters on board a submarine or alternately on an SL-7 tanker.

Gedalea had a sense of time fleeting to an extreme degree. The lower East side of New York where his parents had been admitted to after they fled Russia was far from being the protective haven it had been in 1912. His father's entry to the Navy, the loss of an uncle Milton who had enlisted to fight the Germans, his mother's recalcitrant stand to shut out her sons up to her death – all had taken a toll so that by degrees with the estrangements that come about due to separations over political ideologies and over taking one parent's side over the other, Gedalea felt his life and community were with the military. His own son and a daughter who was tracking planes over Antarctica were all that connected him to the vast numbers who had preceded him and who linked him to the czar. As his father's body was shot off the board into the ocean, he knew he had lost that to which one becomes most endeared. He had lost his identity, and the feeling of safety that a parent provides as long as they are living by being the older surviving generation. He was seized momentarily with an urge to wail, and then was drawn by recent memory to his father's wail when in an instant of terror he knew death was upon him. Gedalea would not wail, would not cry out, would not beseech Elochim or God Almighty for the clutches one reaches for in that hour of surrender. He knew simply as tears sprung to his eyes he had at last become emptied, dragged down as it were by an undefinable weight to the desperate depths to which the soul is finally laid to rest.

An officer fired off a round of booms from the canon as the body sank. The air seemed to lift and a spray of ocean caught them on the face. Forever he was seeing his father bending in prayer, the shawl raised to his lips, the gilded bible written in the one language of Jews the world over in one hand as they prayed for deliverance from an unseen threat a thousand miles away. From the corner of his eye he saw his son break into tears and embrace his wife. Someday young Nossin would stand at the bow as they did today and it would be Gedalea who would be cast out.

One would never reconcile with death as one attempted by piecemeal efforts to do with the mistakes one made in living. Death was final; not even memory adequately consoled. As the service ended, Gedalea smiled at those in the party and feeling oddly disconnected felt he would never live long enough.

∧∧∧

Aleutia sensed the time was upon him.

Even within the confines of the Cuban camp at Boqueron, some forty miles south of Guantanamo where the Navy had its naval base, he was unable to obtain a two day pass. He had not foreseen his father's passing nor was he in any real position to have put in for sudden leave.

Only a short week earlier he had brought a contingency of prisoners in from Marsh Harbor. Since then the southern end of Cuba was fastened down and no ships nor airplanes were permitted in or out. In his capacity as management for Customs for the transport of raw cane, tobacco and coffee into the West Indies, he was on shore duty and would have to maintain the radio for a good two months. During this time the six prisoners would walk the plank half a dozen times, build latrines, soup out oxen manure and make cowpies in fields where eventually there would be a small plot of green leaf tobacco or a blue patch of cane sugar. Because each season for bringing prisoners to this section of the islands lasted four months, the rotation for transporting them back to the penal colony worked around the monsoons. Periodically the Navy would bring in officials from India, Burma, or Indonesia and they would come with the bamboo furniture or the pound bags of coffee.

The only reason an officer wound up in these far reaches of apocalypse or hell was because he had been selected to exact justice. The wheels of justice were far flung from the marble pillars and chalk colored concrete stairs of courtrooms across the country. A man learned he was never again a free man the moment he pulled the trigger to take another man or woman's life, or the moment he committed the heinous and felonious act of arson or bombing, which was common in areas in Mexico and South America where a person could live an entire year on several thousand dollars.

Aleutia had permitted his father to draft him from the world of materialism in which he had found immense satisfaction as a ship captain for companies exporting household goods around the world. For twenty-five years he had shipped goods, tea, tobacco and coffee made in factories in India, Ceylon, Mainland China, Bali, Borneo, Java and Irian to the Americas up to his mid-fifties when his father, then in his nineties, told him he had not seen enough of life to understand why trade needed to span oceans. Reluctantly, because he felt his brother Gedalea although favored had followed a modest living by staying with the navy when he could have gone to work for corporate giants at Sandia or Livermore or Lawrence Hall at Berkeley, he came to Cuba and travelled, although sporadically, to the various penal colonies in the Antilles and in the Java Sea.

By nature he was not a man who sought or felt he needed forgiveness. Thus as he entered domain he considered his brother's, he found in himself emotions he rarely had felt, among them anger at having to regard Gedalea for his having followed orders. Aleutia was a man of the sea, he could come and go as he liked from any enterprise, and he was in a business in which if one merchant did not treat him with courtesy, because there was a limited number of shippers, Aleutia could cut a man off and think nothing of it.

Unlike him, Gedalea was soft, even keeled and patient. Aleutia needed the ocean to temper him and was most at home steering across any vast sea that required more than several days passage. As he resisted his brother's influence and sought a peripheral field beyond him, he discovered unkindly that he was relegated to posts which gave him no overview. When he realized he would have to accommodate his brother, during the years he felt himself subjugated to a colonial type of mediocrity, he was abrasive to Gedalea and the men and women he worked with.

It was during these years he felt most censured by their father Nossin. Nossin himself had not strayed from the embrace of the navy and the father/son bond was firmly attached because Gedalea had sought outwardly to be his father's son. Aleutia believed he knew more than the sum of his family and in knowing felt himself to be the one who should have been admired and pursued emotionally. Instead he had been forgotten at best; at worst, somewhat despised.

His response to his father's death was mixed. Nossin had lived long and had been hugely valued during the war and after. The navy had kept him on as an adviser and he was known for his influence. But he had been to Aleutia's way of thinking a hard father, hard to please, hard to get close to, hard to appreciate and to love. It did not matter he had no one to look up to; he had not enjoyed that privilege since he and Gedalea were children. If he had no one to turn to again in his life, whatever was left of it, it would not matter as much as he imagined it would to Gedalea who he sensed would be decimated. He was his own man, the maker of destinies, the finder of solutions. Nothing was impossible, except how to repave the road to the one person who should have been kinder and less withholding.

He walked through the long, somewhat darkened hall over the green linoleum floor to the glass door, and stepped outside onto the freshly cut lawn. His gaze took in the row of cabin quarters and beyond them, the mess hall and the infirmary, each separate buildings that had been rebuilt after the Korean War when the islands were temporarily abandoned. The equivalent of several blocks away was the beach and firehouse. It had been a year since the incident when a group of prisoners numbering fifteen had broken out of their barracks and set the firehouse on fire. This had necessitated warplanes hunting down the group with firepower, eventually killing three and seriously maiming the others. Because the infirmary was originally built for two men in sickbay, ten were transported to Grand Island Bahama and the tourist trade was cancelled for one Spring. Aleutia had had his first real taste of war. With no one to talk to who was willing to fill him in on any real detail, he called his nephew who directed him to Gedalea.

Their conversation took him from Cuba to New Orleans. Gedalea told him about justice, about the CIA's telepathy and how without it, there was no hope for society to track down greedy and sometimes powerful wealthy criminals and their pawns. He showed Aleutia the missile room, the launch codes, and how navy games worked to punish people who would otherwise use insurance or loopholes in government code to their own advantage. In one brief glimpse Aleutia knew the men he had traded with, some who owned corporations, were guilty of hundreds of felonies, the least being arson.

That dialogue had occurred a year ago. Although it filled in the distance between them, today, in this hour, as he knew his father had been laid to rest undersea, the stirrings of resentment swelled up and he felt as though in dying his father was diminishing him. The fight should be over, he told himself, as he hurried across the expanse of lawn, feeling the willfulness of a hurricane wind begin. He darted into a cabin where he knew Miranda, a young forty brunette who typically wore mechanics coveralls, would be oiling down an engine which when finished would be placed inside a skiplane.

She turned toward him as he came behind her, his hands already on her hips. She smiled and dropping her greasy rag and pliers encircled his neck and pressed herself against him. He was hungry for her, hungry for the passion that sprung to life between them, hungry for that part of his youth that had no comprehension that death could split a man into fragments. She helped him with the snaps and struggled to free herself out of the tight fitting monkey suit. He held her with his legs and breathed in her essence. She was so fresh, her skin was so smooth. She unzipped him and took him and they kneeled and slipped to the floor and he mounted her. As he came, he saw a scene he had not remembered for years. It was of his father studying an aerial shot of a communication grid beneath a blue light.

23.

Joe Daughter stepped into the banquet room of the Inn, a pricey Victorian hotel that sat on the beachfront road on Mile Marker 87 on Plantation Key. The air was salty, the road a worn dirt path beneath leafy palms and colorful ground cover, and the view of the ocean was as a placid stretch of glittering blue water. Seated at a large oblong table enjoying a lunch of oriental stir-fry and coffee were a group of women and men, some of whom he had fought with in Korea. They were engaged in intense discussion over a mole who was believed locked in a suspected apartment in Afula near the bus station. Airports into Arab or Turkish sections had been closed as a result of a series of bombings.

"Daughter," said an Egyptian man he remembered named Moudi who had traded citizenship when he left Canada in the late sixties and came to DC. Randy Moudi was a specialist in tracking British-born moles, many who relocated to Middle Eastern cities where the lifestyle traditionally included a nap midday and evening work hours from four to nine.

Joe took a seat and dished out a portion of stir-fry onto his plate. He made a mental note of who was present. At the head of the table was a man from the State Department, nondescript in his grey suit named Williams; to his right a retired intelligence agent named Hansom who handled distance surveillance; the next agent was a woman, in her fifties with silver-blond hair to her shoulders, named Cord who was raised from her twenties in the Air Force as a paratrooper; beside her was the newcomer named Kiev Houtely whom Joe had expected to hook up with; beside her was Moudi; to Joe's immediate right, a Britisher named Fielding who had spent half his career in the African savannah; to his right a South African minister named Miles whose primary function in addition to resembling a blond man with pinkish skin weighing forty pounds over a preferred one seventy who might stoop to molesting choir boys in a bad year was to watch airports; and the woman at the end was named Ersatz, a Muslim who after losing a son to a well-to-do ex-husband who kidnapped their child and departed for parts unknown had joined the growing host of American agents as a walk-in who worked almost exclusively on kidnap terrorists.

Absent from the gathering was a man named Hand, a black man of Puerto Rican descent who spent the second half of his career stationed at Puerto Lopez, Columbia tracking information made available by foreign newspaper and radio broadcast.

Vladimir Williams was speaking. He was tall, thin with dark grey hair which he wore short. His life in the State Department had changed when the Department became the Bureau and ceased tracing forgeries and began planting agents inside government systems in an effort to track leaks. "We have our agents-in-place both in the Antilles and in Egypt and Israel. Also our information systems are reliable as to the problem we are facing.

"The British it seems drilled a hole somewhere in a Canadian ice cap," he continued to a round of chuckles. "They didn't disturb anyone to do this. They didn't produce another Exxon Valdez nor cannibalize half the territory to exploration drill, yet as a result of producing two years of oil, a gunman robbed a convenience store called an embassy and made away with a check that was intended to cover costs of fueling naval ships to leave Haifa. The check was a hundred million marker. In addition he stole plates for currency effectively eliminating use of the lira note until a new dollar note could be made and circulated.

"Because of this theft, the Israeli government has to rely

upon francs. These are Swiss francs. So we now must use francs until the new money is ready which at the earliest is two months. For two months we are to rely on francs. This in effect drives up the value of the Swiss economy and her products. She knows that as a new lira note becomes utilized, her franc will again be lessened in use in this part of the world. But she is smart – she does not produce new bills.

"This gunman is located in one area, we think near the Afula bus terminal. The Israelis have hired in a Bolshevik who bombs the toilets of a string of airports thus eliminating this man's ability to leave the area discreetly. In addition it destroys its own roads such that this monster cannot flee through the mountains into Jordan.

"There are ideas as to who he is. The Israeli police have tentatively identified the gunman as a known terrorist named Fashee." He turned on the overhead projector and placed the man's head shot beneath the light source. "Fashee was believed to have bombed airports in Tel Aviv and Beirut in the 1970s to prohibit United States agents, once they arrived in Israel and had spent two or so weeks there, from leaving. Fashee's friends have traditionally come from the walled city Acre and from the desert between Jerusalem and Jericho. They reside predominantly with Bedouin and are veiled. In the past he has used two men named Abdul and another named Haminahfarq, but the men who have now been identified manning exterior posts are unknowns."

He sipped a glass of water and continued. "The intelligence agent Vidal, known to us as Karl Fox, was brought in because he grew up in the Alps. The Israelis are positing that the people who brought in the terrorist team did so to eliminate ships returning to the Antilles. This would increase reliance on oil from Saudi Arabia. With greater oil production, in order to meet supply and demand more Arabs from Jordan would be taken from the workforce and given jobs on line, thus cutting down the number of bus terminal robberies that have been occurring for ten years at inland city bus terminals in Jordan, Israel and Egypt. The people most interested in this plan are thought to be a group of physicians who have medical practices nearby the various bus depots.

"We are going in behind Vidal. Zagreb who the Israelis paid to eliminate access out of the country will be watching all exits with a team of highly expertised professionals. The primary difficulty for us is once we arrive we cannot afford in any way to undermine position reporting, which means we will have to fly by the clock, not be indications which may stem from local events."

"In other words we will need to assume some type of radar contact," Randall Moudi said.

"Yes. We have target hotels out of which we will conduct games but we will have to assume their electronic surveillance is equally as sophisticated as ours and they will be watching us."

Antonya Ersatz glanced up from her note-taking. "Will we be going in under the aliases of couples?"

"To some degree. We want to keep intact as much as possible our ability to respond to crisis or to flight and thus the paratroopers will reside at one unit, the information processors at another unit, one within radio distance to the suspect's apartment, and so on. Since you are intimately familiar with kidnaps, we will use you to entice these men."

"But will it do any good?" She persisted. "If as you suspect the second man is a mole, then he is someone who was recruited by foreign intelligence. Surely his loyalty will remain with them."

"If we have to, we have assured both the British and the Israelis we are prepared to penetrate the terrorist group once we identify it. The crucial piece for us is to be able to determine in advance the intended location and identity of victims and if needed secret sources of weapons. Any questions?"

Of course, Joe thought as he rode into town with a silent Kiev Houtely, no one had any questions in the first briefing. It was only with repetition, going over the target area with use of maps, rehearsing scripts, studying communication and radio detection and ranging that questions would arise. As members of the team understood documents they were expected to photograph and people they could recruit as defectors, their roles and the amount of supervision they would need would become clearer.

"Any questions?" He asked her somewhat humorously over dinner.

Kiev smiled. They'd make small talk, perhaps chit chat about weather contours and echo transmissions, and then set aside the meal and move on to the enchantment of the evening which floated on gardenias and a slight breeze.

She knew Daughter by reputation. He was the man who jumped out of planes at a thousand feet, hitched himself by rope up the sides of buildings of sheer glass, infiltrated safes and walked off with verifiable high-priority information. He was the one who over time honed in on the key players, broke their codes, rewired their transmissions in order to out maneuver them and then set them up for arrests or for closures. While she had been stationed in zero visibility, monitoring the success of oil production, she had listened to higher ups talk about his ability to keep the oil companies honest by putting trouble spots on the map the moment a crisis broke out.

Here he was in person. He was the system itself, the basics applied to proficiency, the corrections and adjustments that made for smooth operations. He was one of Prince Edward Island Bank's key contacts when it came to handling sensitive operations. She could sip tea with him, order a Port Sherry, share an eclair and through all of it he was accessible, real, a person with thoughts and feelings, and a sense of purpose.

After dinner he took her to her cottage and pausing on the stoop he asked her to brunch the next day. Then he jaunted off, apparently connected to whatever reality she would later find him in when they sat down to conduct some real work.

Inside, the rooms looked onto a vast ocean and sky. The blond hardwood floors, wainscotting, ceiling fans, and french doors separating the sitting room from the bedroom and porch made up for hours spent escaping snow-blind and blizzard

SANTA BARBARA 329

sub zero conditions. Here she would relax, take walks on the beach, swim at the pool-house, sip hot milk at night. As she prepared for bed, she organized how she would conduct her activities while abroad. She would rise at six, walk or play tennis, eat breakfast, read the newspaper, begin her workday at the station she was assigned to, break for lunch, leave at five, stop at a library, take a meal, then return to home base to discuss the day. Even if it was she who was meant to reside alone, she would make a point of bicycling the distance to one of the others. But she sensed this was not to be the case.

Over semi-boiled eggs in porcelain cups and toast, Joe told her they would be going in as husband and wife. They would be situated at a small house on the Israeli coast, several kilometers south of an artist colony, and would remain there for up to a month, if need be. Daily he'd drive to Afula where he would see a physician for a medical condition and he would leave her to herself. She could do as she liked: become acquainted with artists and sculptors, take tours, or take a studio above the greyhound station in town if she were so inclined. Together they would be an American couple from the Keys who travelled yearly to a spot on the Mediterranean.

This said, he turned to the subject of her recent experience. Why had the Prince Edward Island Bank hired her and what did she learn after two years of monitoring sludge? She settled back in the high backed chair and sipped a glass mug of coffee. First off, she had worked in Toronto for the trading post affiliated with Prince Edward. While there she read film clips, appraised land values and monitored ice conditions for fissures, cleavages, calving, depressions and avalanches. Over time she became able to identify by sight how one surface of ice would fare over others. The geologists were brought to find shelf water within the ice and to assess fracture once the drill was lowered; and then meteorologists determined the presence of strong updrafts and down drafts. For each section, they worked in tandem, identifying weaknesses in rock ice and looking for cores of strong winds or precipitation that could indicate areas to avoid. As they targeted what they believed were low risk, maximum yield fields, she came in to begin the meticulous process of logging movement surrounding the core.

"Believe in dreams?" She asked.

"Sometimes."

"At age fifteen I dreamt once a year I was fleeing down the cobblestone frontage road surrounding the city of Acre and the prison turned hospital with a hoodlum in pursuit in a pickup truck. In my dreams – I had one a year for six years – I am fleeing with another man several years younger."

She was enigmatic. "What year?"

"The first dream began in 1966."

"Might that not be the Six Year War?"

He had managed to pull her out of that odd place in which time infrequently arrested her thought. "Yes," she replied. Curious, she had not wondered that very thing herself. In the icy landscape one did not dream, or perhaps could not dream.

"What does one dream about after a year up north?" He asked.

"It depends what you've been looking at all day. Generally I was seeing actual conditions, whereas the five or six scientists who rotated to the substation every six months monitored weather-radar screens."

"What instrumentation would these have been?" He asked.

"We used passive storm detectors."

"The same that are used in commercial flights?"

"Yes. That's all that's out there besides you and the ice and the atmospheric conditions. You can't operate equipment, let alone shovel the snow from the drill site. Depending upon what the engineers see coming in, whether its drift correction or a severe amount of rainfall over a short distance on the horizon, if your radar closes its eyes to that area or a storm has so much rain that all of radar energy is reflected on screen as a bright echo, they keep you indoors because chances are they can't see the storm on other side of the mountain."

He nodded appreciatively. He laid out a diagonal course in smoke. "Ever seen something like this produced on the night sky?"

"Sure. On the night sky the plane is moving at same airspeed for distance but at an angle to you; on the weather display it's your visual glide slope for descents; and on an aerial reconn it's the first line that defines the grid by which all objects above and below on your screen will be referenced."

"Good. Ever seen the difference between a photograph and an aerial?"

"Numerous times." She spoke with confidence. "Initially before the first drill bit was submerged and the crew became covered in mud, a ski plane took photos of the surface. Sometimes all the photos showed were white on white, making it nearly impossible to delineate people from ice or to appreciate hilly areas or depressions so that we could later find the area on foot, so we brought in aerial devices. At a distance of a hundred feet which is your typical runway plus fifty feet, more or less, on a flat surface if you are directly overhead it's difficult to tell the size or distinction of the person, whereas at the forty-five degree angle you can adequately see people in motion."

"Any notion as to why someone might produce a burn using paraffin?"

She considered. She felt he was no longer made self conscious by the twenty year difference in their ages but was now honing in on the problem he would be undertaking the moment they arrived in Israel. "Paraffin smoke burns black, correct?"

He gave a decisive nod in the affirmative. "It produces soot and masks any source of light in bloodshot red."

"Then it would have to be the dark smoke would mask whatever helicopter pilots expected to see on the surface."

"A diagonal smoke line would define wind factor and could help investigators later pinpoint the original source or area of smoke."

"Is this an actual event?"

"One of the men in the crowd outside the embassy was tentatively identified as an arsonist. This is his modus operandi, to always try to chalk in the line by obscuring prints with black or blue smoke. If you came across this type of fire in or around reflective objects, even if your radar screen was blank, you could toss out a bouquet."

"Except a blank screen would mean there were no reflective objects on the horizon."

"This man has been identified at airports, both large and small, and near buildings with minimum visibility upon approach, and once below a forty-seven hundred foot mountain during a thunderstorm."

"He brings down airplanes."

"Very possibly. So for you, the information a passive storm detector gives you is what hours are a good time to get out on the ice to drill –"

"Or what installations need to be set up in order to pipe oil to a pier and to a lineup of frigates –"

"Right, but for me weather advisories are about what route should I fly, am I cleared to destination, have I recorded takeoff time, can I find out from Center how high I am allowed to fly given weather conditions, am I on course or will I have to fly on a heading before approaching the inbound course, if I've missed an approach where do I begin my forty second turn, how much wind, and so on."

"And in the absence of assigned enroutes its 4700 feet from hazard to STACY intersection."

"I see. That's what tells you he's interested in airplanes and airports."

"It's probably the reason the Israelis have not built an airport landing in their mountains."

He was seeing the picture more clearly. "A photojournalist in Haifa just happened to wander onto the scene as this gunman entered the embassy and shot the first guard and wounded another two. There were three men inside; he and his two lookouts made three. My belief is he was ready to assume their positions and shoot anyone who walked through the door."

"Based on what he stole, I'd say he had many more men than two posted at the door. Did he knock out the cameras?"

"He wasn't even concerned about them."

"Where have the Israelis posted state police?"

"Two at the airport in high-rise complexes. Of course a high-rise for them is twelve stories. The British sent in one of their codes to a home nearest the suspect's apartment and the Italians are rumored to have sent in Milano."

"I met Milano when he was in the provinces. He's medium height, sandy wavy hair, spectacles, somewhat near sighted, nice man."

Joe laughed. "If he's there, we'll have plenty of lunches with him. He's known to both Fox and Vidal." And then, seeing the disguises she had accepted as the world were slipping, he said, "Milano makes subjects nervous to such a degree they give themselves away."

"That must take years."

"It does."

She sipped her coffee finding it had cooled to a warmth she enjoyed. "Joe, Vladimir brought you in because of your expertise at infiltrating a building, correct?"

He gave a nod.

"And they called me in because I have been around geologists and meteorologists and engineers enough to know when a visual landmark has too many reflective bodies around it, because face it, there's no ice in Israel so no one's going to be banking on my expertise to assess fractures."

"Probably."

"And most of the members of this team are either astute at scoping out distances or able to call a kidnap in advance of it occurring. In many respects we're a boot camp that will be filling in for intelligence."

"Who will be there, trust me. We're the moving targets, the avenue of troublemakers this man will be watching. He won't be aware anyone else is actually there."

"Even though logic should tell him we are not the answer he's seeking."

"The practical spend-down for this exercise is that after a month he is not going to be able to tell who is coming for him and he's going to in all probability take swipes at the wrong people, thereby further exposing himself to risk."

"But you expect him to be in close proximity to the people who may have paid him to rob the embassy to begin with?"

"We think that's who they are. So far nothing connects him to them."

She was quiet as she made sense of the plan. Joe would be seeking medical treatment from at least one of these physicians based upon his complaints. She herself would be farmed out, able to get about predominantly by bus or cab, from the coast to any site that could be reached in a day but she was not to venture to Afula or come into contact with him while on her excursions.

Depending upon physical findings would tell them the sort of man he was. Marks and tattoos notwithstanding, he was going to attempt to pass himself off as someone who might enter into contact with a gunman or some such terrorist. If he had glass shrapnel or he had tested chemical devices, his body would bear witness to such tests almost as certainly as did Milano whom she had inadvertently encountered half naked in the latrine. It had not occurred to her that the two inch diameter marks all over his back were growths resulting from contact with shrapnel or burning debris.

Finally, she said, "Your purpose is to test their medical knowledge."

"That's very thorough," and smiled.

It was clear he considered her ready. For herself she wanted to know more, be made clearer as to the risks as well as the desired outcomes. For an instant she wondered if he were chauvinistic, then doubting this was so, she recalled no one in the group of nine had been fed on much information.

He said, "I'm divorced."

"Yes, me too."

Hesitating, he said, "You're too young."

She laughed. "Well, if that's all you wanted to know, we can take separate rooms."

He had decided long ago in his early forties that he bored women. He was a straight shot, made for the jobs he handled, but rugged in personality, without the kind texturing the women he found himself attracted to seemed to want. He decided after four years with a woman who was a thinker that the best relationship was one in which he could forget or put aside these recalcitrant leanings. After an on again, off again twenty year relationship he grew convinced the type of woman he fared best with was one who daily was a good companion.

Kiev had no ability to take him. She struck him as a child and while not needy nor particularly emotional, he felt himself wanting as though for her he had to become either mentor or lover. Life was not to be discovered through love-making, although he had no doubt that for this attractive blonde with slight features her inclination would be to seize the first buckaroo that came her way and sip him as she did her coffee, tasting it as though she were not wholly drawn to it, ambivalent to the last. But for this separately perceived anxiety, he looked forward to the trip. It was on this piece he floundered, for in a state like Israel where he had travelled in his mid thirties when Eugene Burdick had just sold The Ugly American a couple was frequently viewed as a political entity. Little did it matter how they dressed or whether they travelled by motor car, or even whether they ate out a good deal, they were looked upon by Israelis and Arabs alike as a sort of peculiarity, capable of embarrassments and then too off diplomatic contributions, or mistakes.

Had he been told he was joining the female paratrooper he would have begun outlining trips to the Masada and to the Golan in preparation of descents they might be expected to make at point of capture, and together they would have been seen as a military couple, at once serious minded and complimentary – a negotiator and his wife, either a translator or a transcriber. Or if they were separated by incidences of street violence or bombings, someone would think to send for her.

Not so with Kiev who judging by her cottony dress and white gloves and hat with lace would be regarded in any quarter as a somewhat spoiled debutante, clearly separated from her element. To be associated with a social class he had sought to avoid since Korea, he felt he would have to make explanations or apologies. If she caught him at it, she would become offended as he was certain she had been at brunch. All this would require time and would drain his attention and thought process from events at hand.

He had reached his car, a plain colored blue Pontiac. He reversed his steps to her cottage and stood feeling foolish on the stoop. When she opened the door he was relieved to see she was surprised.

"Well, Joe Daughter. So soon?"

He followed her into the cottage. She had changed from her dress into shorts and a tee. She was tall, tan, narrow shouldered and oddly, because he hadn't paid much attention to her proportions, slender through the body and in the bones. Then, as she stepped to his side, he found himself looking at the magnificent vista of sky and ocean, of the blueness, the calm, the slightly slanted beach, its chalk white color.

"Did you come to seduce me?" She asked.

"No, I came to bridge the generation gap."

"I think the best thing for me is to purchase half a dozen suits before we depart and leave the expensive gowns in the closet."

"We're not enough alike." He said.

"No one will be. We're varying cultures, different temperaments, different ways of thinking. Have you considered asking for a replacement?"

He had, but he wouldn't. He intuitively trusted groupings assigned by higher ups. If he had a hard time of it, then he needed the distraction she created to study the environment these men surrounded themselves with.

"We have until 0800 hours," he pointed out.

"Yes, indeedy. I don't drink."

"Perhaps we could sit on the beach on those wooden chairs."

She tossed him a hat with a visor and took one for herself and a beach bag and they strolled to the sand. As soon as they were seated, he knew he had been right to return. But it was she who deserved the commendation, he realized as she removed knitting needles and a swath of wool for the project she had begun. It was the fashion he supposed that men would come to the beach and their companions would sit and knit pillow cases or jumpers or baby garments for their grandchildren.

She opened with, "This will be the first real trip I've taken in five years."

For no reason he could think of his eyes watered. "I'm sixty-six. I've seen more than I care to see or know of other people's lives and it hasn't humbled me."

"I don't think I want to know much about what people are made of."

"I should've had great grandchildren by now. I'm old enough."

"When you live at a sub station and the weather is below zero, you're bundled up in special thermal with masks and mittens. It's survival at its worst. The thought that you have a family somewhere rarely occurs. It's hour to hour. You worry most about saving your eyes from the glare. Chapped lips is one thing but eye strain can put you to bed for a month."

He was about to argue with her about who between them had more to worry about, and caught himself. He didn't need to say it and thereby produce for himself a morass of self pity to compensate for the latitude or longitudinal differences in their life experiences.

She said, "It's okay if you want to fuss," to which he burst out laughing. "I don't have to be comfortable on this trip or become envious that you will be having all the fun," she continued. "If it doesn't look right from here, it probably won't look any better when we pull up for the close up."

"A month is a long time."

"For all you know, we may get stuck there. Let's see," she mused, and counted the stitches in the row she was working on, "I'll buy silk pajamas also like a suit; I'll leave the house before you shower so I don't run into you and knock you off course; what else? We can dine with another couple at least once a week and I'll listen. Obviously it's not going to cut it if I tell you I've known about your intelligence work for years and I admire you tremendously."

"I didn't know that."

She continued knitting, picking up speed. "When you thought you were flying in for an overnight, what did you hope to speak to me about?"

If he worried she could not keep pace with him mentally, she implied she understood him. He lit an infrequent cigarette and focussed on the water, thinking how to answer. "I wanted to know the degree of turbulence you kept encountering."

"You felt the fog zones were being manipulated by enemies of the British."

"It's a possibility."

"Any likelihood there's a connection to the Haifa incident?"

"Yes, especially if these people had insiders working the drills."

She sobered. "Is that why Milano came?"

"It could be. I wouldn't know."

"This could be brutal," she said, about their trip.

"It most probably is."

"What do you think these folks want?"

"Possibly to stop ground transport, to bank airplanes, to alter road signs – "

"When are you going to tell me what it is we are really going there for?"

24.

"The mother pool that was tapped was shallow, a mere seventy-five feet, although the petroleum was a paraffin that was easy to process," Philip Van Dorn said to a room of agents and Israeli state police.

"Did the Israelis ask the Saudis for assistance? Is that the problem?" Someone asked.

"The problem," his Scotland Yard associate Bertrand Hopely answered, "is that with a multitude of embargoes the Israelis turned to Italy to receive shipments. The French in Algiers upon discovering this arrangement determined to place sanctions against any sympathetic nation. We stepped in with assurances that we would ship Venezuelan crude to Israel. With this, a handful of nations inquired as to how they might trade and thus began a fight to the dogs. Into this fray Israel discovered a gusher north of Acre producing an expected yield of some quarter million barrels of crude. The embassy at Haifa was attacked. What was not released was there were a series of targets where devices were placed but not hit, and we have since eliminated them."

"What were these targets?" The same person asked.

"The hospitals, the Dan hotel, and a handful of public service routes. A threat was also received by Dutch Lang, a local radio announcer, whom we suspect brought in this photographer Sheridan from whom we confiscated his film."

"In addition," Van Dorn added to the growing excitement in the room as agents realized that once again oil was at the top of the fore, "Joe Daughter has received tentative identification from Leavenworth as to Bandarprahi's lead."

Joe stood and walked to the chalkboard in the center of the room. He had dressed for the briefing in standard army gear and as he pulled down the map of the Middle East he looked to most like a fighting man who had scaled out the enemy's fortress and was prepared to advance. "Bandarprahi is not from Saudi Arabia but from Syria. The Israeli Mossad tells us his post on the coast is only meant to give him advantage if war ever becomes imminent. He has been sighted periodically as far north as Istanbul and as far west as Libya. Although he is not welcome in Algiers he draws upon Syria's purse strings and thus financiers come to him on occasion.

"I am told that when he leaves, he does so at night travelling often in a covered van with a curtain so that for the most part he is always behind a veil. When the Israelis closed gasoline stations at four in the afternoon he was believed to be stranded. Because Egypt also shut down her gasoline marts early afternoon, it was perceived that as a nation she had joined sympathies."

He tapped the Aegean Sea with his knuckles. "A small outfit of international agents sit on these islands. They maintain live posts in fishing boats and coast guard ships. They have mined the waters. For Bandarprahi to pass through unharmed he requires passports and numerous permits. It is therefore believed the Aegean waters are a successful net."

"Have the Libyans been known to provide egress?" Another person wanted to know.

"The French dock ships in most ports of call along the northern coastline of Africa and up until Port Said was bombed in 1984 she brought her cargo ships there as well. But in recent years with the British introducing sharks into the Mediterranean, the French have adopted a more conservative stand and she docks usually at ports which carry her customs houses."

"Ibn Saudi was replaced."

"Over ten years ago," Van Dorn replied to smiles. "The Saudis have become more aggressive in response to the global climate. Remember, it is the French who enjoy title over transportation. Thus for her to assure neighboring nations that in building fifty thousand automobiles, thirty thousand which will be exported to the Americas, there will be oil, she has had to join with the Saudis to a large degree. France, mind you, is sympathetic to Jews; after all, she had underground tunnels for escape. Also she prevails in a national policy which permits no anti-semitism and her courts punish violators severely.

"Thus the measure of violence perpetrated against the state

of Israel does not start in France nor in those countries that have sought to remain affiliated with her by capital. It is perhaps coincidence that because groups of terrorists have penetrated competition, it was the French cartels that were penalized and this, to put the vehicle motor on notice."

"Which was responded to by waves of violence, most typically road upsets that were purloined as earthquakes. In Russia, China, Romania and America there were reported large quakes, up stemming freeways and highrises."

"So is it surprising that after such colossal damage China promised to become a new market for the Saudis?"

A glance across the room at Lt. Betrabi and his handful of state police told him that the best offensive was for the moment no offensive. Better to let sleeping dogs lie until more information as to the lair and possible points of penetration were uncovered.

In principal Joe Daughter agreed. But he was a paratrooper, better able than most to capture support networks and disarm them, and that's where his strategy would rest. "We know based upon activity in the region that this insurgent group cannot be far because they have returned approximately once a year to stage a major hit. If they set arson to Ben Gurion a year ago and this last month struck the embassy in Haifa, they came from somewhere close by," he said, to those who nodded in strong agreement.

"Not only that," he continued. "Reports to various corporate administrations show various personnel were stalked by women thought to be associated with these insurgents. Because there were scheduled shutdowns of platforms in Canada as well as in Columbia just prior to the embassy incident, the support for aggressive action has fanned out most likely into the US where any number of spies are looking at what impact these shutdowns will have on worldwide production."

He had the group now. They were joining as one mind. Assignments, when it came time to divvy up the workload, would be seen as complimentary to whatever officer system the Israelis had in place.

"We will stage as our first act paratrooping onto all communications bureaus in the surrounding Arab countries. We will break up tasks by skill and allow two days. Code agents will be in place. We will retreat to assigned vantage points for a pulse. If there is no attempt at violence, we will move in on Bandarprahi's last known address and dismantle all access to it. Within forty-eight hours we should know what, when, where and who is seeking redress."

It was a plan, Randy Moudi thought as he hurried across Tel Aviv to join his mother for an early dinner. He was expected on board John Fielding's yacht later this evening for a by night surveillance of what they hoped were members of the group that had taken the embassy.

On the surface, the man aiding Bandarprahi was a fisherman who lived usually off Cypress but, not to be outdone by coastal merchants on the mainland he maintained a shop on Syrian waters and another further south on Jordan's coast. Nor was he favorably prejudiced toward the Arabic; he was a realistic man who knew that with the Mediterranean ports closed or restricted and the air access limited especially for the Israelis, this would drive the cost for gasoline way up and both the tourist and the airline agency would suffer, not to mention the shipping industry.

The car was a monster; a man got behind the wheel of a car and by the by he did not even know who he was. Or so it seemed as a multitude of reckless drivers swerved across his path.

The Arab world was cognizant of what it asked for, as were its representatives flung far abroad. OPEC was not merely a bird with wide wings; she was a home away from home, far beyond the known waters of an ocean it had long feasted on for its revenues. If the Saudis who came to operate the farming of oil were known to say, Venezuelan oil was had at a steep price because although the oil sat in depths of ten to fifteen feet, each pit vastly dark blue in the enormity of each field, the oil was had at a hard price. It stuck to the mud the way varnish might to a table, inured of its disposition, unable to be coaxed at a steady fueling. So, although Saudi oil in Saudi Arabia poured through pipes, in the South American environment it was another matter, a steeper price, an annexed territory awaiting a claim, a turf on the verge of war, a murky and inky desolation, at once made beautiful from a height but succumbed to in the last as the pit in which the field was submersed dried from pressure and became hardened with clay, thus shrinking the reserve.

If Venezuela or Columbia or heaven forbid, Ecuador on the other side, the Pacific side, produced shareholds of oil, then her masters, in their jet liners and ocean vessels, were concerned merely for their own transport. The fact they were unwilling to sell for any less than forfeiture and demanded this in a seizure of small cities and governments in order to fatten its own treasure chest gave rise to the American sentiment that we were forever perched on turf, ready to surrender the dollar rather than go to war. The dollar being what it was to the small man, the middle class who swore loyalty to the mighty industrialists of the era, was shrinking in this vast globe, easily conquered by men on whose testimonials of national defense solvency rested.

Thus we were at war with an unknown villain, one we would not successfully touch or insinuate despite our need for information and the need for caution. Greatness might rest with leaders who were willing to chase after civil reform and help acquire for the majority the most savings in all arenas, both at the gas pump and at the national polls, and but for the wanton lust for mightiness and simultaneously for vengeance that the public could be made to suffer for showing sympathy for unpopular political platforms, these powerful leaders could render followers incompetent of thinking on their own, or wanting to. Individuation came at a cost, for it only was doggedly pursued when freedoms were most curtailed. This ebb and flow provided earnest men with sustenance for an honest dollar and tried to restrain the men and women who controlled such dangerous fortunes.

He hurried beneath lit street lamps whose auras cast an obscure yet silvery glow until he reached the wharf. He could make out Fielding's yacht sitting alongside the pier surrounded by a surreal fog. Fielding had gone in on foot after Daughter, contesting to the habits of the physicians whose practices engendered privacy by virtue of the patients who sought treatment. Although Randi anticipated their discussion, he felt certain that Fielding, if he were unable to persuade his evening guests to the proposition that following various subjects back to their vested tax dollars was ill-timed, he would at least attempt to discuss the profiles of these clients, and who among them worked for the Saudis and who for the Israelis.

The yacht rocked on the incoming tide with the inadvisability of the damned. Drugs, contraband alcohol and watches, and ivory chess board pieces might share the den beneath the deck, but the real sale, or real opportunity, was to be had in the certainty that only the men on board knew who the targets were and where they might be likely to drift toward once they motored through the straits, rounded Africa and came up through the Red Sea. Nothing was certain, even the booties to be garnished by men who counted on piracy for their steady income was subject to unseen levies not to be admitted to by men in customs. If money capsized, if men were lost at sea, if damnation visited the young and left the seasoned sailor for the high sea; all were estimable losses which spelled gravity in the face of utilizing the Red Sea.

Except the men who had bombed the embassy and blown a handful of routes knew the consequences of their acts. They knew for example that within two hours the economic currency could be replaced, substituting the lira for the shekel; they knew worldwide stocks could plunge leaving countries with little to hang onto but a plug; and they certainly had to foresee that jobs in addition to transport could become strained, hampered, costly, or eliminated, too costly to keep going in the face of Wall Street rollbacks.

Fielding was working his way through a bottle of Brut from Reims, France at thirty a bottle. It was good stuff, sweetened with honey from a wine cellar in Saxony, all but melted in his mouth along with a double edged sword of fine chocolate, also velvety in texture, both made for a middle class who wanted to sample the sweet life. Ah, it was indeed a sweet life that allowed for the best of everything, set on the counter awaiting special preparation first for a rum souffle, then for fruit laced with champagne and finally scones, buttery and light, finished off by Bengal spice tea, that balance between having overeaten and having tasted the succulent, a dialogue for the rich who wanted the flavor of the sweet without also becoming poisoned by having too much.

"They've run for the beach," Fielding said, as Randi stepped through the small gate and climbed on deck. "Just as I suspected because, dear fellow, where else can these men have come? They are used to napping until noon and equally as used to chasing women and driving in Masseratis through the dessert. Spoiled, rotten men," as if he had said tsk, tsk and it was appreciated or understood he was establishing a mood of ironic whimsy, one that would carry them through the night, at least until Joe Daughter and that youthful affair of his showed up to wallow in the late hour.

The lights along the pier came on; in the suffused ethereal pallor of mist, the water seemed at once a blanket of a dream and a wandering into hell. Randi muttered that he had chased Daughter into Afula and by degrees captured these young men on film, their hairless chests, darkly tanned smooth skin, their needs as transparent as their habits. They came to town often on a bus to sip liquid heroin or belladonna or to seek advice reserved for the damned, alleging they had been tortured or abused and left for destroyed. Through doors kept slightly ajar, Moudi had wandered down their hallways to spy on these men and had only discovered by profane curiosity that one or two received bathing and massage or as in one instance, a locked embrace of breathless passion, such was his doctor an outlet for needs that would never survive on the street.

"You won't make the grade," Fielding responded at once, and then tipsy on the Brut he reached for Moudi's hand and held it a shade too long. "You will have to reduce your observations to the commonplace, something even the tilted aristocracy can join with, you know," and bent to kiss Randi on the mouth.

Randi took both John Fielding's hands between his and made room for John to step up to the plate and then because he wanted to and saw no reason not to, he caught John around the thighs and drew him ever so closely, raising his chest to catch the other man's taut desire.

"My dear," Fielding swooned; "oh, my dear," and brought Randi's face toward his, thinking as he did so that if Daughter failed to show or any of the others stayed too long at their own carnivals, he could endure these thrills without any notion of guilt.

Randi Moudi permitted himself to be seduced. He knew he had walked in on more than one tryst; he had considered following any of these young men back to town for endurances, even setting one up in a room in order to gain his confidence and so by degrees get him to open up.

Fielding had sunk to his knees, pushed against Randi's legs and with the entreaties of a man who knows he needs to be undone, let Randi unbutton his shirt and unzip his pants. "Jesus," Fielding said, the minute Randi reached for him. "Don't stop, oh, just this once," and Randi moved a hand on his stem, pulling hard, flattening his chest to the other man's face, thinking it was as easy to go to hell as to give the government whatever the hell they wanted.

Kiev's breasts strained against her blouse as Joe Daughter pulled her into the moonlight. "What is it?" She asked him.

Joe watched the young man enter the phone booth where an older man waited. It was an old gambit, living by the money a few blow jobs a night would provide.

"It's the man you followed, right?"

He had meant to follow Moudi onto the old man's boat but wouldn't. Respect for privacy prevented him, and so he had pulled at her hand hoping she had not seen what he thought was plainly there to be seen, and then because he was embarrassed and alternately somewhat humiliated at the idea of having seen more than he wanted to about anyone's life he didn't care to know all that much about, he had put his hand up Kiev's blouse, surprised to find she anticipated him.

The man in the telephone booth was plainly seen in the light and his contact, or lover, or prostitute, it was hard to know which, had his eye on Fielding. Wouldn't it be interesting if it were Fielding who was getting made? Joe Daughter cast a hard glance at the two posts, certain Fielding had no awareness of the man in the distance.

The moment Kiev tensed, he knew he had hesitated too long. Now she followed his gaze, sensed his tension, appreciated his task. Her body resisted him and he had to refocus, feel her sensuality beneath his hand and then feel her give in to whatever was required of the moment. His groin ached. He fumbled with her bra, and then because he would not jeopardize whatever was in store he drew her to him, kissed her and pressed her to him, giving himself the ability to observe unnoticed the man in the booth.

He was getting jacked off, the young man's head visible above the glass. They'd go all night until Fielding or Moudi tired, and then depending upon whether Moudi left or stayed on the boat he'd keep the man in sight.

Kiev rocked him until he himself felt the insanity of the moment. If Randi Moudi had been prepared for this ambush, he was better than good, a man who could hold his breath under water, as it were. But if this was simply part of the job, this ability to leave one's senses and venture for whatever gain, then he'd beat the other man, no matter what he was prepared to risk.

It seemed their collective strength of infiltration lay with Moudi's ability to surrender without being affected, and Joe found himself watching as if for signs of knowledge that he was being watched. As Kiev went through mindless rhythms of caressing him and he of allowing her to work him over without becoming drawn in, he found himself wondering what sort of training Moudi had and if he wasn't on some level prepped for the life of a penetration agent.

"Bit of a voyeur, aren't you, old chap?" Moudi asked as he

stumbled across the threshold into their room.

Joe hastened out of bed, careful not to awaken Kiev who slept soundly in the other bed. He caught Moudi as Randi fell on weak knees and grasped his nightshirt. "Caught you, old boy." Moudi said, stinking to holy hell of cheap liquor and belladonna. "Can't catch a bird without a chore, can we?"

And Joe thinking Moudi would not make it to his quarters a few apartment buildings away across a courtyard of lawns and paths situated him on a bed in a guest room, opened a window and closed the door ignoring Moudi hoping Moudi interpreted the denial as fact. Why on earth had Fielding tossed him out? As he stumbled back to bed, he thought it was possible Moudi had in a state of drunkenness left the boat, zigzagged up the wooden planks and drove to the complex where a few of them would mark time over the next two weeks.

25.

The series of bombs ripped through the coastline from Adama in Turkey through Beirut in Lebanon, Tel Aviv, Port Said in upper Egypt and the Suez, and in Shahhar, Libya. In addition the rail was detonated, eliminating passage from the Red Sea to any southeastern country in the Mediterranean Sea. Arrivals would enter by Bagdad and pass over land, hopefully without getting shot down.

The extent of damage, while it did not destroy aircraft or shipping vessels, closed the four airport strips and the routes for ocean bearing frigates and ships. If no ship could arrive at destination for at least a week, and no courier could get on the rail except by car, it stood to reason the roads would become inordinately congested and the cost of gasoline would skyrocket.

It was not simply the countries with coasts who faced risk. Half of Africa relied upon commerce and trade by sea as did Iraq, Iran and a significant piece of the Soviet Union. For as long as it took to repair the avenues for transportation would be the price of silence.

The Free World turned toward the West represented by Europe. To the Aegean, Italy and France, not to mention Great Britain and Holland, the Middle East implored her need for a swarm of agents equipped with surveillance and infrared to stun this terrorist wave and put every last community on hold. To Joe Daughter as he rode the bus into Afula, and cast aspersion on every swarthy complected male who refused to make eye contact, the bombings were meant to draw out spies whose normal silence was misunderstood as a lack of presence. The West would be hard pressed not to draw upon these operatives and to attempt to conduct business with the small numbers already in the areas hit. Even if the Saudis sent in a hundred agents, which the government would do in order to affirm its revulsion to violence, they would be unable to do more than provide security to the six areas.

Across the world Michael Gandt had received another telephone call. Although the connection was poor, he still appreciated the agent's thoughtfulness.

"The chessboard has been hit," Zagreb told him. "There is literally no way out except through Iraq unless you are an ally."

"Were they insane?" Not meant to be answered of course, except he was unprepared.

"My belief is because these governments were backed in the purse by Britain's hundred year bank, they believe their dollar to be worthless."

"But my good man, this is 2004. Shouldn't we have expected labor and delivery prior to 1997 when Hong Kong financial institutions reverted to the Mainland?"

"You had that with a series of events drawn on various high yield securities lenders. Try the World Trade Center fiascoes 1991 and 2001."

"Yes, yes." Impatiently. "But Syria. These hoodlums are from Syria." And then the loading dose of reason kicked in, because he thought that Zagreb in all probability was correct, and he said, "At whom were these launches aimed?"

"Not the Emigrate."

"No, I suspect not. Perhaps at Daughter?"

"No one realizes he's there."

"I see. At Intelligence?"

"My hunch is they did it to prevent airlifting evidence."

"We're still looking at the arson attack in Tel Aviv?"

"That's my guess. Somehow they captured Bandarprahi on film."

Joe Daughter had been smart not to tip his hand with the aerial reconns taken at night. "Anyone on the team going in after him?"

"There's some underground talk he's gone from Cypress to Sicily. They'll put a boat for him."

"Doubtful the Sicilians would allow that."

"They'll allow damn near anything if it means successful capture."

"Did you receive the money?"

"Yes, but I suspect we have a leak."

"From the bank?"

"Try the wire service. I've made other arrangements for deposit."

"With whom?"

"Gotta run. I'll catch up to you in a few days."

But Michael was worried as he hung up. The situation was escalating fast. Not only that, the CIA would begin disappearing its pieces throughout the Middle East to make room for British Military Intelligence players so that this band of terrorists, however large they were, would think the scoreboard was smaller than it was. Once the CIA vanished off the map, these agents could wind up anywhere, inside or outside the boundaries of trouble.

He knew Daughter was a cautious man; hell, he admired the man for that. He was also a man who lived tight to the waist. He wouldn't discuss strategy until he was certain what he was dealing with. The team could go weeks without a word in or out and another six targets could be hit and disposed of. He considered calling Vidal and then thought better of it. He'd wait twenty-four hours. If in twenty-four hours there was even a single incident, he'd arrange for another team into the territory.

The Prince Edward Island operation at Selwyn was now a thing of the past. The company would begin dismantling the platform and they'd depart, leaving not a trace of even penetration. It was money well spent if it predominantly figured in this chain reaction around the globe. Then they knew that the areas most severely affected by the redistribution of oil were the countries from Turkey to Libya. If Sudan, Ethiopia, Somalia, Kenya on down suffered no losses, then overall these countries remained dependent upon the British and the throes of China had not dented them.

They should have known, he thought as he turned his thoughts to the utterly fantastic notion that it was the international telegraph service that had sparked these acts. But for wire services there was no way to communicate with the Middle East. A leak had to have stultifying reverberations.

He wouldn't wait. He picked up the telephone and dialed his contact. He instructed the secretary to get word to Ann Smith that her family had been located and he was sending someone in to bring them out, if at all possible. And then Michael Gandt did the inconceivable. He placed a call to Gdansk Botherling and left word to release the prisoner.

Ann Smith picked up the message. It read, identification positive; subject purchased inexpensive vehicle; parked it and left it for tenant; left his own vehicle running at the convenience store while he went inside; he redirected mail to former wife; he stole tenant's tools; created a public scene for which the police were called. Question: was there another man?

And the last sentence – The United Nations is our federal government.

As opposed to what? The Pentagon? She thought with mild annoyance. This was a message that Michael should have sent to Gdansk, not to her.

He would not make a careless error. He had meant her to receive this.

Rereading the text, she wondered why it read like a World

War II extraction. She had handled numerous such correspondences in Italy, especially when the Germans were trying to eliminate people from public and known addresses. Identification positive. For whom? Her Italian charges? Or for one of the photos on Michael's desk?

The memory of the neighbors sprang to mind. Of the petulant woman who had spent a quarter of a million dollars and of her brother who would bail her out.

She sought her friend Jean in the farm feeding the animals. "I've received word from my employer. He's found one of my charges from the war."

"Amazing." Jean approached her and set down the pail of feed. "Did he say what has happened to him all this time?"

"Tell me what this means," and thrust the handwritten note into her hands.

Jean studied the note on the lined page. "The person in question left a vehicle for another individual at that person's address and then identified him in certain acts. The tenant must be wanted for a crime. Not only that, it's someone who has dealings with the police. Your employer is asking if you think there was another man."

"He's not posing any of this to me. This must be a mistake. He sent it to me by mistake."

"But it was posted to you. That could indicate you are not the target or you are expected at some later date to offer this information to the target."

"But why did he go to these manipulations?"

Jean stooped to pick up the pail. "He trusts you with the intent of the letter. Plus, he says the situation whatever it is rests on a center of the United Nations, not the White House per se or local government."

"Why is he unable to tell me exactly what he expects from me?"

"Because he is concerned about who has had access to this information in sending it to you."

The point hit home. "I had this very thing occur when I took my charges by train through France and Spain during the war to escape the SS."

"Yes, you see? It is easy. I would suspect a tap on his phone before I worried about the wire service or worse, about an infiltrator."

Ann returned to their cabin. Yes, it was increasingly clear. Michael had some sort of difficulty and she was the method by which he could adequately test it. She composed her return giving thought to the wording so that as her employer read it, he would not have to puzzle over her intent. It took her until lunch to rework it. When she was ready, she transferred it to a postal letter and sent the draft with its revision and then took it to the market to drop it in the mail slot.

When Ann's reply came two days later, Michael was working his way through a crossword puzzle, his mind sufficiently at ease. There had been no further development. The ball was in their court awaiting a response from any number of agents, operatives, secret service or correspondent. A blunder would be understood as a reply, so the agencies had tightened their belts and probably sent everyone indoors for curfew.

Her draft tumbled out. Seeing the errors and rewording, he set it aside in favor of the letter. "We have two weeks here to feed animals and tend to the one prisoner. He is an American in his fifties with a damaged leg he says he received during the last war. He sympathizes with my neighbors, the young set who has spent the family's retirement. He is inconsolable because he did not realize until we heard the news that the Lebanese now wish to extend their border north. This would mean his friends in Syria would flee to Turkey. Perhaps Greece is under the same despot. It's been sinking sails for a long time."

This was a partial transcript of an interview conducted in 1991 prior to the discovery of an attempt on a building in New York.

Where did you fly a mission in 1941?
A: I flew Japan.
Did you authorize missile target?
A: No, that was handled by your command.
Have you ever authorized missile database.
A: Never, that is not my authority.
Who does it belong to?
A: Scottie Alexander Walpole.
Do you know the number and site authorities he has authorized?
A: I think he authorizes target data for Canadian rivers under a contract seen to by South Africa millitary.
Who is his command?
A: I am.
Must he answer to you by document summarization?
A: No. He provides all docs to Special Home Office command.
Does this change?
A: Yes, depending upon missions flown.
When was the last mission flown?
A: I flew it over Egypt in May 1977.
What was the purpose?
A: We were receiving incoming transmissions to the effect that information was being subject to older authority code.
What specifically did you receive?
A: We were given obelisk readings. These were in the form of meccas.
How would you describe a mecca pictorally?
A: It is a pyramid made of ebony which has a minimum of seven tiers.
How many appeared on a sheet?

A: Twelve. We considered at first it was a bit of humor until we tracked it to Palace Nekira. We contacted the palace and were told they were under attack.

What procedure did you follow?

A: We called Lineage Bank, Zurich and satellite. Receiving no confirmation we contacted Moscow. They told us they had received a different sort of communique and wired us theirs. It was a rudimentary pyramid unlike Egypts. We gave this to an Egypt doc expert who told us an inner chamber had been breached. We anchored all images and shut down the palace with a black out code. This prevented further invasion. I then summoned Air command and told him I required an aircraft that was swift and silent. Command sent me in a Blackbird with ten target data flight experts. The mission itself took two hours.

Did you attempt to learn who invaded her drawer?

A: Yes. This was done by an affiliate of MGM movies which was making a movie produced by George Lucas. When I cleared him I discovered he owns fourteen miles in California.

How did you use the black out code after this finding?

A: I learned that the family for one of our royal families stationed in California was an employee of Lucas Films Ltd and I ordered a black out on every member.

In what year would you have done this?

A: First in that year 1977 and then again in 1984, 1985 and in 1990.

Why so often?

A: This particular family had many people in the liberal arts. Two are writers and one works for Hollywood.

Did you attempt to open sub files on any?

A: Yes, on all including their spouses.

What were your findings?

A: The employee working for Lucas Ltd was brought in by an Irish movie producer. The writer who appeared in a popular rag was married to a man with connections to the underworld and the last writer tested for intent to commit a crime.

Has this crime occurred?

A: No, it is scheduled we think for summer 1992. It is referred to as the summer plan.

We have checked your answers and are concerned about your stated findings. Do you wish to amend any of your answers? (We gave him a copy of the transcript.)

A: Yes. I may have exercised too much of a rush when I attached a black out to all parties.

Have you recalled the code?

A: No. I have continued to make a finding for a spouse.

Have you also made a finding for the wife?

A: No, not for her. She is a Scott.

Wouldn't it be prudent then to at least remove her since she has never worked for the movies?

A: I consulted with my cousin who did not think that was a wise course.

Do you know why your cousin made the recommendation?

A: Yes. She has extended family in the air force.

I've now taken the opportunity to check this latest information. Before you on the table is your statement about the wife's extended family. Could you sign it?

A: Yes. (He signs.)

Let it be recorded that you have signed the statement willing. Do you agree you signed this willingly.

A: Yes. (He consulted with his attorney who confirmed it was willing.)

Did you at any time try to ascertain who the wife thinks she is related to?

A: No, I didn't believe I needed to do that.

Would you like to check this now?

A: (From attorney) Are you advising us to do this?

Yes, I am. Which clearance staff would you like?

A: British French.

I will arrange this first before we continue.

What are your findings?

A: The wife does not know that she is related to two of the parties. She has not had any contact with the third party who is her aunt since 1972.

Do you wish to contact your cousin?

A: (Consults with attorney) No, I don 't feel I would need to. I am the one with the authority.

Then will you remove the black out at least for her?

A: I don't feel I should.

Will you state for the record today's date.

A: (Consults attorney) Yes, today's date is April 21, 1991.

Thank you. Let's now talk a bout your 1977 flight mission?

A: Alright.

Will you state again the reason you made the flight?

A: We had received a document that provided us with the whereabouts of Prince Andrew, left inland Scandanavia. Because Moscow also received a transmission, I felt a flight plan was in order. The Russians do not do business with the outside world and thus someone seems to be trying to allege that there is a connection.

Could you elaborate on this.

A: Certainly. Moscow received a similar transmission.

Why is that unusual? Moscow built the Nile. Egypt is her satellite defense program.

A: I was not aware Egypt was put in place by anyone other than us, UK.

It is based upon an air force system. It is based on the A-10 and not the Porsche.

A: We have an eclectic system for Rolls, Porsche, your Martin and our Falcon.

In 1941 the Falcon was outmoded. In what form do you use it and for what purpose?

A: (His attorney requests a minimum two days.)

(This is granted.)

(They ask for an extension for a week and we grant it.)

I'd like to repeat the question. In what form and for what purpose do you use a Falcon drive satellite?

A: We use it for satellite image enhancement.

What do you mean by enhancement?

A: We convey images and representations of scenes to Vest, Berlin and to Cairo for documentation.

Do you have any site control laboratories in this country?

A: Yes. We have funded contracts with approximately twenty seven of your publishers.

Do you have funded contracts with Canadian publishers?

A: Yes. With about six including Exxon which just purchased a hotel in Florida.

I see. How do you use these scenes?

A: To protect our shipping fleet worldwide.

Do you use your satellites with air force?

A: No, never have.

Do you use your satellites for your submarine fleet?

A: Not directly, unless we are required to deploy.

(We take a break for three days.)

Who has access to your satellites?

A: Air.

Who has command positions for Air.

A: Myself, Sir Edwin O., and Lord Alexander.

In what capacity are positions employed?

A: They are minimum third class in rank all the way up to eighth class and they are overseen by lieutendant authorities.

How many authorities do you employ?

A: Twenty-two.

Of the twenty-two, how many work with rank from other countries?

A: Only three. They are Scottie A.W., John Douglass W., and John Alexander, son of Lord John A.

Have any ever taken missions to Egypt?

A: Only one, Scottie W.

In what year did he fly a mission?

A: 1974.

Have any ever taken missions to China?

A: Not to my knowledge.

Have any ever taken missions to Canada?

A: Many have.

Would this have included the Great Slave Lake fiasco?

A: Yes, but that was headed by Senior John Van Damme of Johannesburg.

Under whose advice would that have been?

A: D. Bayer, Secretary, Legal representative to His Royal Legion, and her former husband Thomas A. Betterton, Esquire.

Do you know what the purpose of that particular mission was intended for?

A: Yes. Canada's banks were becoming rapidly silted.

What do you mean by silted?

A: Mud was building up at an alarming rate impeding our ability to get vessels to our river ports.

What techniques did you use to get rid of silt?

A: A #4 missile, a #1 dart and a #12 dart which looks somewhat like a mining cannister. These are colored orange, gold and rainbow, that is white with navy blue sails.

In what years did you sail these darts?

A: I'd have to check but I think they were used in 1979, 1982, 1983, 1984 and in 1988.

We will allow you to check by any method you desire. Were these years all for Canada?

A: All except 1984 when we used a similar dart for Cairo's port Said.

Did you ever attempt to track these darts by forest or land reconnaissance?

A: No, we've never viewed a missile or dart because they are used in rivers.

Do you know whether you have ever caused accidents to boaters.

A: No, I would not know.

Would you please check? We will aid you by giving you a

copy of this last transcript and providing you with a reporter.

A: No need for a reporter. I read transcription fluently in most European languages.

One will be made available if you change your mind.

(We took a break for approximately four days during which we verified the whereabouts of every military class and rank worldwide and verified each person's intent for use of military operation.)

(We sat down on the fourth day when he brought his cousin and we chose not to interview cousin after we saw who she was.)

Today is April 24, 1991. We have checked for the current whereabouts of your classes and their rank and we would like you to look at our photo pictorals. Can you tell me who is in this submarine?

A: Yes. (He identifies them. There are four.)

Can you tell me based upon the digital information on the panel where the submarine is in this photo?

A: Yes. (He puts on eye glasses and reads the digital information.)

Can you tell me where this location is?

A: Not without the aid of a nautical map.

(We have a map unopened in packaging brought in and ask him to open it, which he does.) Please note the map is unopened. You will have to remove the packaging. Can you locate the coordinates on the map?

A: Yes. This submarine appears to be sitting underwater in the Gulf of St. Lawrence off New Brunswick.

(We give him another photograph.) Please identify the people in this photograph.

NO POLO

1.

The return to the No Polo base in Patagonia took the teams working under Lewis all of eighteen hours in the dead of night to fly west on a red-eye charter. After the high court signed and stamped a mandate ordering the Miami South Field Office to report to duty ready for indoctrination of lab perfunctory detailed analyses, the twelve field officers arrived at five in the morning by the time they descended onto the tiny runway of the No Polo Institute situated in the arid, inhospitable temperature and craggy rock affectionately referred to as the first U.K. overseas weather air base. Winds as usual bent tall swaying palm trees and caused smaller shrubs and forsythia plants to get scurried about down a long aisle of lush green course entirely surrounded by dark beige rock strata at the bottom which lay the shallow sparkling aquamarine Sea of Cortez bay. The admiral who greeted them who would oversee the essential question as to the amount of underwater damage was evident in the photographs of non-accidental incidents, wore standard regulation attire matching their tan and dark green uniforms with jacket and stiff leather, hard wear desert boots who was familiar as a Churchill man from the good old days in east London's air industrial corp. He operated the Daily Truffle on equestrian dash having long ago purchased into the Prague Post after winning the spring event fifty thousand dollar silver cup. Resembling a del Nero, Daniel Maggie looked like a French premier who was older, balding off the forehead, elegantly shown in an addition of a brown tie strap style. The group entered through the main gate, followed Daniel inside to the registration desk where they were assigned quarters, Lewis and Rhonda to occupy a couples suite, Jones next door, the others on both of two floors, five suites to a floor.

The air was at once stifling and consumptive. Lewis parked his folded trouser luggage inside a closet and took his routine luggage bag into the commode, unzipping it for shampoo and bath soap, each a light cucumber mint wash which under the warm jet stream removed hours of stress and exhaustion, tying on a bath robe, helping himself to a tall glass of chilled water before he settled into a purple and black upholstered easy chair. Rhonda had been up all night tracking the whereabouts of a whiskey train out of southern California's Imperial Sea bound for St. Louis guessed to have stopped anywhere on the port plagued red bean Missouri line through West Virginia. She lay curled up fully dressed in Union Pacific garb, yellow skirt, blue top with a thick red diagonal across the front, asleep as though she was now impervious to the demands of several harrowing days. He felt little desire, more a tightening in his chest as he gave his gaze to the packet of photographs the chief engineer had sent with him. The red bean crop was the leading producer coming from five states each having about two hundred farms apiece. Wyoming, Nebraska, Kansas, Arkansas and Missouri shared the fame for carving up their states with chili, stew and spice that the red bean claimed title to in seven hundred tonnage weight per seasonal train. For as far as the eye could see from May to September when the harvest columbines threshed the crop in the turbulence of red dust thick as smoke the red bean crop gave an appearance of light red abundance, an ever prominent dust rich in nutrients, a significant as the barley wheat that crossed the Imperial that was transported to the Appalachian mountains of dark stratified ore where fifty-three mills churned butterscotch wheat barley into a drinking man's whiskey and dark ale. The photos conveyed a shocking horror as six bandits boarded the Imperial Kansas Birmingham Mid-

night Special in June 1978, took over the train steerage at gun-
point, dislodged and tossed the time recorder box out a window
into a barren city wilderness along with two conductors, and set
course for one of the greatest collisions of the century, achiev-
ing a run-in at a hundred and forty miles in rural Kentucky
with five passenger trains each destined for Chicago. Without
warning the bandits jumped train as it circled the high yard
rendering it defenseless to any of thirteen switch lines. The
mess was severe, the damage so utterly consequential that the
wreckage could not be hauled off the track, box cars welded to
rail, parts of rail, some over a block long, uprooted as though in
a whirlwind of charcoaled debris. Its relay by systems that took
over as the recorder box severed station to station communication sent a half ring to Florida, another to Chicago, and in the
moment Morse code read into Florida's coastal line, the high
rail reverse snapped and catapulted a southern bound train to
its demise some hundred and fifty feet below just west of Pensacola, destroying her in a rocky, dried up shallow creek bed.

The crash in Kentucky occurred at 5:04 am and involved
the silver Lincoln Nebraska, the blue Huron Memphis, the
green Boston Kansas, the black Chicago St. Louis and the tan
and red Florida Everglades. These conductors described a me-
thodical progress into central Kentucky when they experienced
a sudden gravitational thrust not altogether unlike a dynamic
storm-gathering pull which wrenched each train onto one of
two rail systems moving far greater than their applied braking
flanks could reciprocate. From the tower station warning lights
flashed issuing an unmistakable warning to approaching trains,
but as the center silver train slowed, the other four were unable to break free of the path of the runaway whiskey train flying above the rail narrowly escaping track, its blue-gray-black
compartments combatively erroneous, charging like a bronco
in the throes of a burning branding iron. Even a parked orange
tan sitting the night out from El Paso was hurled into the air
in a sizzling burst of sparks as the steel mesh of destruction
whipped past it. The station dispatched a helicopter from an
airport a half mile away and a pilot descended a swaying rope

ladder onto the runaway in the hopes of rescuing the train. Despite this the two forward compartments separated and force of air spewed the pilot into the air lifting him in a non-directional wind that flew him into a river. Rhonda herself had stayed with dispatch in Pensacola until the south bound train there barreled over the embankment in clear view to the incredulous dismay of ten train engineers and course-chart coordinators.

He'd never know what they should have done. No way to predict the unpredictable. Despite two tragic train crashes in previous history, each a plundering so god-awful the routes were permanently shut down and redirected, both took red bean Carne lines into Texas and the gospel South. It was hard to discern cause where coincidence played out; Carne was the red bean distributor that transported to Campbell Inc., Progresso and Boston Baked Beans, but there was no man alive who was willing to declare on Carne. In the blurring dust wind that covered the state all six trains were lost, not even infrared situated the yard within any discernible quadrant, this then was the only reason engineering could photograph by Kodak cam recorder, and nine camera men shot six packages apiece not available except to live studio action film. The 971 out of Alabama ran four years straight before it collapsed unable to proceed past a second station. Even the 532 from Baltimore was eventually affected giving way to an unprecedented sale of car leases.

First down was station systems along with camera on-track ghosting, out for six weeks, All video burned out, except in Warden, Tennessee which experienced a pile-up a week later, telephone went out, shortages along the line affected three states, an ensuing green out resulted in no gas or electric hiking costs well past manageable rates. Viable hammer sockets in transient locations which shut down after dark could not be revived once station imprints booted up, nor tertiary routes stabilized. Clandestine mills took the heat finalizing brief portrayals between days-long charts of ocean released satellite. In the Carolinas where satellite sponged up monsoon and tornado calls the sole relay came from a small company called ACME, known as American Consolidated Metro Engineers with forty-seven transmittal receivers to read for hail, weather and damage and flying debris. After a joint congressional hearing during which all carriers were reviewed, ACME was mandated to insure all red bean trains. While it wouldn't dock passenger lines, it was ordered to down-read all material connecting lines. Ninety congressional hearings later, all casino draws would be required to carry eastern coastal storm warnings. Despite voltage frequency changes, storm negatives were conducted to Philadelphia matching her short train carrying safes which derailed in 1974 falling some two hundred feet onto an interior valley plain. Fleetwood 9 would in due time transport all Miami products through Florida and Alabama to West Virginia from where distribution to the Great Lakes would get routed, thus steering crisis off the flurries of the eastern seaboard during high wind weather systems. If anything was to go wrong, the light foot lines would be spared accumulative tidal dust winds and whirlwind debris knockabouts common to Kansas and southern Nebraska.

All things considering, the best photos were taken in the dark at pre-dawn, not even enough rail light to produce speed. Normally an underline function described broken track split by a motor powerful enough to cut rail and a tone-out of a yard showing non-moving trains meant camera maneuverability was postponed. When toward nine o'clock in the morning the brown and yellow ten compartment white bean registered in, Missouri being the point of origin, Birmingham destination from West Virginia moving at twenty miles per hour through South Carolina, it was the start of a hellacious four days requiring the double staffing of agents from as far as Trans Am Hookston in the Rockies to Houston Flight Center. After all, white bean was the replacement bean for red bean, although its use as a marinated pickling in bottled salads removed any need for use of the can.

Gabriel Roscoe was the man who invented canning of the bean. Descendants of God-fearing sinners of the state of New

York would swear his eldest son Steven was the devil having stolen food certificates in a heist to operate a cannery contract to strike it rich. However, Gabriel's invention was used in Turkey during the famine of 1943 and because of him, lamb and vegetables were put on any table day or night. He was a man of his word, rarely quarrelsome, a devout parishioner whose deeds went to assure that Nature could not take a toll with winds, sand or dust. In the Midwest he manufactured two million cans three times a year from his square buildings in Germantown, Iowa. Tall, sturdy, tired red brown hair, he was seen oiling his machines for a straight run of five weeks in seasons when electrically charged dusters wore down engines. All hundred families lived at his table and followed him into the mill each work day. When he was nearly to his mid-years, he married a winsome blond from Tairn with whom he conceived two sons, Kevin Steve, one a strident buckling lad with gray black wavy curls, and Sticky, the young one a deaf mute whom he packed off to a board and care institute for boys in upstate Wisconsin who would at age nine be pronounced almost dead of fractured bones and contusion after a boxing match and sent home for hospitalization on the all black Langston Express out of Green Bay. Gabriel sold his company to a righteously indignant man and took his boy to the windy cliffs of the old Jesuit monastery where he surrendered to drink and reefer. Not until fitful years abandoned by wife and family he returned to work to drive the Sunlit Prairie over the mountains of Ohio into the ill-fated denizens of blue grass Appalachia.

The lean plains could drive an undecided man to toss away his comforts. These soft shouldered ranges were steeped in drifting sand, white as bleached soap, the underlying swept mound of hard sage and tufted brush, at once hearsay and conversely points of reference for the land was never the same twice. Before the sun had risen, the sparse landscape stood out as though powder, deep ravine-prone snow or sandy bits of pebble like a driven expulsion carried by elements a foot above the ground, governed all plants, obsessions and possibilities. During winter the land fell beneath snow and crawled out from under. Avalanches did no less, their glacier-like remnants of gravel, sand, clot and carry pushed the soil into small hills good for retaining water for growing so that over years the plains extended in slight depressions, funnels, craters and filled with icy ponds and lakes. The sharp sting of frost kept the flat spaces and roads free of travelers although by spring with thawed creek beds, raging canyon narrows, an occasional butte split by an aspiring tree, gnarled and tempered, the pump men were exchanging pipes and resealing ground water wells. From summer to summer a feisty gust sprang a spout of quickly evaporating rain which threw half dollar sized drops onto the sage and otherwise bounced a brave set of mud to stain any windshield with tan chalk. Gabriel envisioned the prairies as a calling. He bundled his near-crippled child in the observation car and saddled him with oats and strap. The lone afternoon light, shrill as a bone, kept a more than thin vigil such that by early evening the bluish shine of cold northern wind wreaked havoc with an ability to keep alert, gaze fully comprehending hundred foot high lemon yellow and chocolate and salmon orange and pink stone spire hoodoos, magical splash sounds on the river, the oddly tightened crab grass borrowing off river banks or just ending short of any realizable water source. All the world was a hunkering down of stiff, combative flanks, in those long pitch black nights when the only green or red light could be seen for tens of miles was the train switch stop on the tracks, the warehouse depots alongside the tracks turned on their lights until platforms looked to be bright yellow, misted and stinging with trim halos, from a distance a light overflowing from the kitchen.

The finality of wilderness, an unrelenting perpetration of endless miles of slowly spinning dust as though spirit and shadow might be making figures in the wind, until the daylight was spent as sickly steeped as a glowing orb offered no consolation, it became a burden to pass through it, a gauntlet of macabre flying wind, of errant soldier-abandoned peaks of snow rilled with gamboling vixen, paraded sails of sands spinning into a universe of a receding sun. In his mind lodged in his conscience was a dim realism that it was possible that somewhere in another country a train waited as stampeding suns blasted furnace-hot onto a pavement of sand. Throbbing sunlight, mercenary heat, contrasting freezing nights, a hundred moons seen in water over a bridge charged through his senses, at once leaving him parched, heaved, fatigued. Despite his eldest son learning to drill a well, Gabriel was into settling down in his job, finding solace in the stretches of sun storm weary uninvolved prairie, learning to tolerate the brick line as mortar was called that strew milky limestone in every direction, keeping pace with the dark tunnel of prairie misbegotten wind, adjusting his fairly habituated eye sight to rolling light, waiting out both night and gathering sand dust as the roar of machines howled into the gray visage of morning. He had hunted pheasant with better hold-outs, sitting in the brush silent as can be, holding the birdie until the very moment the bird swooped onto the windy loughs. He'd have to sit equally as patient, cautious of the spilling rain, of non visibility, quiet thunder, ultra whitish opaqueish silvery sky with a golden orb at its momentous center, until a duster flew across the sky there was no convincing method by which to appreciate the fact of a slow-to-start hurricane rainy eye. As soon as the sun lifted the wind to it, the sun-pervaded smog cooled to the ground summoning sand and dust in alarming veils of drifting turbulence spreading west and southerly as thick as a sepulveda of night, a frightening stampede without hoofs, the air staggered by coyote and turkey eagle, gagging cries like someone being murdered. It had taken nearly ten years to understand that a factory churning glass back to usable industry created a high pitch noise that gave a pig's squeal a rather unsympathetic whine. Always a small bag containing a half sandwich – rye and corned beef or pickled onion or beets and gravy smothered turkey – gave the shotgun seat the best view during the nights of flying shoe sparks, the calculator was within an arm's reach.

After Sticky turned majority and went off to work camp to study cog-wheel stern, Gabriel set his well-engineer son Kevin into the caboose to feed the coal manger. Together, his twenty year old, now a foraging dusty elbow, and he churned the bed-ore coal, fresh fixed the connector clamps, shortened the chain, and otherwise de-accelerated the altimeter, waiting for it to fall three feet below thermostat. Stevie and Pa stood watch on the side row their shirts flying, dark yellow dust choking the night sky, waiting for each passing sign to record the train's journey into Kansas, and then over the bean pass through wash basins of lower Nebraska as the putrid gasoline air became thin and the stars shone through. Once over the elevated rail deep red volcanic rock and side-arms of waterfalls gladed through forested canyons prominently showing through sometimes glaced frosted holy wings of frozen escaping floes. The even bar that kept a train stable despite fast-alternating downhill speeds traveled through abutments of solid knife points, treacherous look-outs, winding eroded open space. The practiced skill for de-climbing made for the sense that the train was locked into the great wilderness, the pillaring towers of trees across the night sky given seldom to anything but countenances of awe. Just ahead, tuned to the capricious envelope of an aerosol shot off to prevent a speeding avalanche, the Nebraska to New York train was climbing the high pillar, the small airplane pilots grounded due to the plunge the storm took, Stevie's good friend out of Missouri, William Nash, manually timing the southerly entry to the station at Fork. At that precise moment the Nebraska line pitched off the rail hitch and five compartments fell dangling mid-air as rescue trucks with screamers on zoomed over the intersection. The incoming west-bound line put on its brakes and stopped and kept passengers on the train for three and a half days.

The first photograph in the eighteen page series showed a brownish sky with a field of grass alit by a slow-moving uncontrolled fire, typical for mid-west telegraph station areas when train holder agents switched onto silent mode on walkie-talkies during storm electric outages. Crickets as big as crabs emerged like a disgusting evil festoon all over a stationary repair train crawling out of grain sacks, a certain visitation of plague. Four photographs were all that deservedly remained of insects that had to be covered in dung and gasoline and burned upward of seven hours almost to the pink of sunrise. The burning had gathered wind of howling proportions sizeable enough to conduct windmills unless the air was thick with hordes of gnats, as evidenced by the photographed yellow mark in the upper left corner, it'd be at least a day once he requested a logo tape of it assuming the numbers correctly corresponded to the labeled photo; but it was a shock to come across a picture of William Nash, nephew to Kevin Roscoe, his flaming red hair flying wildly as his shirttails, green and white diagonal striped tie waving past his shoulder like some characteristic independence declaration, his slightly arthritic lithe body looking as if he rarely ate, the hallmark thumb pinned to his forefinger known for the injury he acquired when he ran moonshine out of a cabin in the Everglades and sold molasses sugar-turned whiskey diluted by crystal pane and inadvertently jabbed his entire arm through a electronic wired door. Lewis Lewis enlarged the picture before he sent it to photo lab but he was absolutely positive there was a match for at least one earlier derailment, possibly that contained the deaf and dumb nephew, heir to his father's payout.

The confirming photos arrived on dateline at the end of the transmission day. Sticky had been punched so hard in the mouth he lost speech owing to his upper jaw taking a bit of climate. As a result he was perceived as taciturn, although enabling to adult males who knew him, an affable autistic capable of basic word pronunciation, some mild stern locomotion, action drive in situations where there were essential obstacles such as too much dirt or brake oil leakages. Despite a content worthy brakeman's pay, he was a joiner, caring only to assist his wage-ready uncle with the chores of a train castaway run rider, an extremely complicated task of disassembling box carriers and reloading a hitch. With about as many photos of them hitching a lay-back compartment, there were also an unusual number of holdups, suspected audacious piracies, each accompanied by step ladder or shakedown step, some tough to imagine earning them a reputation for pony express, bandana covering the boniness of their faces.

The real dismay was captured by Maggie whose consultant John Mixey had trained from Ft. Laramie in Wyoming. Mixey started his career of investigating derailments over water for which drowning occurred, already he added Costa del Sol, Spain, Naples, Italy and Nice, France to a lengthy resume of credits. His Bellevue statistics on Nash were itemized – he had never been seen except as a shadowy figure in a dense storm, he was a known soldier of fortune, he had been employed by the Greeks of Minnesota as a train yard completion mechanic, reversing throttle and leaking fires off the engines, he knew every transcontinental pigsty where old money was burned, and he worked the slow dollar trains that carried other monetary exchanges such as diamond truck, gold copper, mixed nickel, and a regular shortage of damaged food. Tobacco out of Mississippi was regarded as cash damage shortages when it grew with mildew and frostbite. Prior to the Wyoming stand-off where a short train had gone over an embankment into a lake, Mixey was last seen at Cambridge Square, Massachusetts. He had taken miners into Patagonia by bus and left them there in huts in mine interiors where they recuperated from extreme snow blind. His areas of investigation included sub-rosa for documents filed by subject, counter industrial treason, abductions, boating season and tracking by Intel X. At age seventy he had never taken lunch, he didn't own his means of transportation, he walked or took the metro and he lived in hotels, saw movies at home, hung out in bars, did not enter museums, talked to one senior field agent Hoyt, and only worked in places where there was a metro, such as District of Columbia, San Francisco, Seattle, New York, Rome, Paris, Berlin and Amsterdam, a good place to be, changing sites every four to five years. He typically looked at markets, trench work for resorts, high trams in the mountains and Paris counters – hub news stands, magazine racks and liquor bins. Never certain where he would be, he might spend on credit predominantly and show no predictable cash outlay. As an agent who called every city Berlin, he got sloshed all weekends, never entertained and gave over most of his efforts to studying how victims became imprinted. He was not interested in art or ships, was not into fashion or night-clubs but had been to every city in twenty countries, knew all television and every city desk producer, had never laid out a contract, and with the chemical vapor cloud over the default line above York, was gone, vanished, not a receipt to find him having wired to Hoyt that once in the jungle there was nothing to get one out of it.

Thus the picture Mixey produced was of a chalky snow cloud at three hundred feet elevation to zero showing negative proofs of seventeen men on presumably white stallions, buckle around the head that shone like tiny errant train lights per-plexedly stranded.

2.

There was no theft of money for the 1978 Nebraska derailment or the 1998 Kentucky Derby pike as the Warden Tennessee crash later came to be called. It was assumed that the rationale for creating a non capable exposure lay in either a necessity for stealing train compartments to build an illegal train or in hiding compartments used previously in a crime such as the New York heist getaway or any of the following, the destruction of the Akron Bridge pass into Chicago, the box car theft of fifty safes outside Boston or the runaway train carrying lost postal declarations out of Biloxi, Mississippi and then blowing up each stolen compartment individually so as to obscure evidence once the compartment was tracked and found. There was also some idea that refrigerator cars removed off track in order to replenish empty coolers had gone to storage housed by transfer companies whose staff turnover resulted in negligence in hiring adequate security guards. To Lewis' way of thinking, research had been exhausted on the subject of motivation as to who had control of schedules at the time of the disasters, leaving him with the belief that the crash incidents were not accidental. The day of the 1998 crash was a blustery windy morning during which neither shipping container nor truck carrier had arrived off schedule. Abroad, in 1961 the Quanchar train on the silk road through Tibet fell dangling over a thousand feet of white stone, in 1983 there was a collision of two trains in Bagdad station which caused the yellow and green box cars to scatter onto their sides across rail; and in 1990 in India a dark purple and blue train descended over a stone bridge when an oxen stampeded a compartment sending the short train over the easement into the river under water. Within the U.S. in 1981 the Birmingham train to Texas shot off its track at seventy miles an hour under a full moon amidst gusts of high wind and torrential rain drenching an otherwise arid soil; in 1987 the Florida-Delaware charged full lantern gear into coastal swamps despite admonishments by kitchen manufacturers – the soup plants of Virginia, the bean industries of Wyoming, the chili handlers of Missouri and the all white bean stews of Dunsforth, Ohio which produced sixty million cans a year – to proceed at safe speeds during rainy hurricane weather.

But for the Tennessee 1998 crash into the West Akron River which flowed north to south through small college towns periodically cresting above four feet for unsuspecting downriver winders, the blue smoke hilly Appalachia train submerging baggage car first pulling twelve cars into a greenish intensely murky water with such poor visibility afternoon warm sunlight barely penetrated underwater eleven feet maximum would not have required twenty retired well-expertised divers swift with bait and riptide knife to free drowning bodies of vestibule or vine entanglements. It was a summer day, the law schools were still out, bicyclists everywhere, dusty roads on back country pastures, campus church white brick plazas quiet and un-intruded-upon, the only intersection active with shoppers and vehicles a few blocks west of the train rail station platform. The divers dove off the bridge simultaneously, Mixey showing up miraculously out of nowhere in a clear arc off the embankment, into billowing steam and bubbling water, amidst a broth of bobbing bodies with obvious rigid limbs, insufficient survival, undeniable castrations, any victim might have felt the tumultuous boom, males descending, their bodies weighted by a heavy slackening of the scrotum like a shoe leather affixed , toiling about in fast-rolling, churning over adequate rock heaps in white water rapids, few hands having clutched at weeds as though to pull themselves to safety, gathering crowds as though to a tramcable accident, men stripping off shirts, shoes, relinquishing jackets, wallets, backpacks, the shore drawing attention, by the end of day dead bodies lined up on the bank wrapped in tarps awaiting the coroner morgue undertaker. It was the sighting of Mixey that suggested the case, whatever began the derailment-crash incidents of which, thankfully there were less than twenty worldwide, for the Midwestern deck of U.S. traveling trains. Mixey's actual appearance said maybe not an utter disaster , a derailing crash that definitely depended upon skills to take a high narrow plunge without incident.

"Just look at the fall," Lewis said to Jones as they took a path behind an observatory through purple wildflowers of crabgrass on their way to one of four restaurants. "Obviously train snapped, it toppled, hit the water hard, submerged. For a person, falling or jumping, even if he'd hit the water hard, he would come right back up. "

"What did Maggie have to say?" Jones asked.

The interior was instantly relieving. Booths, shiny and sat-in light blue, looked as if one might surrender, lose one's dizziness of altitude and return to the extremely wearisome commonplace rocky strata of tan stone and seductive aquamarine ocean considered a paradise to kayaker and distant-satellite analyst both. They were seated beside a window, a box shelf of ferns placed behind Jones on a dash mount.

Lewis lit a cigarette, ordered a vodka straight, the usual whiskey gimlet for Jones. "He put it like this, two trains smashed, one train was outgoing, one was incoming, the trains crashed and spiked cantilevering. No one knows why, either the track relays are wrong or communication was cut off, but there wasn't much room on the bridge for a western roller to unhitch, two box cars went into the water, it was Maggie who ordered signals to be redesigned for a hundred miles."

A waitress with enviable thin torso served their drinks, took their orders for breaded sole. Jones sipped his drink, it was tight the way he liked a working martini, always up to the rim.

Lewis continued, sitting back with the ease of a man who has delegated the rough assignments to staff he expects serious answers from. "You know, the doer is waiting for something, he's got it figured out, either a plane has to land in the river and fly the bodies to the morgues, or our doer is hoping he'll find the morgue labs. There have only been three derailments in U.S. in South Carolina, Nebraska and Washington state and only four crashes there. Mixey is the agent we'll look for because he is a Maggie-trained cadaver specialist, the splashes automatically involve drowning, we don't know what we're looking at yet, it could be something very very straight forward."

"Why do we think these are actually crimes and not

weather trauma? Fifteen derailers not due to human error went over in blizzard conditions. Mixey is water entry, not necessarily crime intent."

"Well, how many crops are involved? There's only beans, not even wheat is an objection which is thought to be the only item through the dust bowl, but Kansas has never had so much as a stoppage. Arkansas had the slow down just prior to the Kentucky pile up."

"Time of year suggests tornado. High winds, night time visibility, blizzard dust, unpredictable gusts, unfavorable reverses."

"All true, but the Texas train to Kansas never left its track. The train stayed put for as long as it took the weather to die down. If these were underwater escarpments, if there was no other compelling item, then we would expect to see just that in the photos first row of the sheet removed."

"I think there's a possibility Nebraska was a downhill escalator," Jones put in. "Look at the fix, one train smashed into another train carried by sailing high winds setting it on fire for three days that a passenger train in the opposite direction had to wait and then buckled off the overhead, it took mechanics ten hours to get it back onto the track."

Lewis remarked, "At this point we have to start making guesses as to why these human error crimes occurred when they did. We strongly believe there's a can involved because these train problems have all occurred on can routes. Since the result was to use another route for four years and red bean had to relocate its night passage, it's assumed the derails were done for alternate transportation such as to increase tractor trailers, the thought being to give each person their own route."

"Well, the documents reveal single line row, that right there says a heist of money but no advantage, so it can't be spent; five plus one was a bad row unhitching one or more box cars, but there's also double digit numbered photos suggesting different intent and on Washington state there's one double and the rest each a four number, that's a derail even if blamed on a bear."

"These are tiny files that cut off at 1437. Tiny files are human error, always."

Over the bar on the television Detroit played against San Francisco. One play was down made by Lacey and Crabtree was darting between a squirm-ish all the way to the yard line.

Jones had gone through the pictures cautiously. An avalanche cloud opened and the dust clouds evaporated leaving a big opening through which stars could be seen; in seconds wisps covered over distortions of wind carrying hallucinations of images of bears, tigers, blinding lights. "Looks to me like someone out there thought he had a fight with old rooster carne."

"Looks like old news to me, maybe the man who put up the money for Melrose Place."

"Bee sting nurse?"

"Right, the oil can for the train. Italian chef, Hawaiian, out of Landers. I heard he was an astronomer, had a system for charting the big dipper in night skies, rightly projected large images off steel basins."

The temperate part of the day was winding itself into something of a bastion. The winds had picked up a duster on the prairie, embodied in the fury that normally pelts all abbreviated living leaving no one unaffected or unbothered, nor nondiscerned in weather drizzling with abated wind churned wheat dust, smoked from the sun's very abundant copper hell storms, in the winter Maggie needed to know where the snow was, as well as from which direction was the wind coming, so he could anticipate difficulties for stuck-ies, the men who worked the reverse rails. Maggie was a tobacco-salt man who had grown up in the chalk-white icy range of Patagonia and come of age in dense icy cloud turbulence, endurance trained under the strong searchlight of the glowing sun, the ever bleached white nocturnal blue landscape of moon luster bathing the foothills of the Muertos Mountains, bellowing calls of the evening train as it sped through the unlimited divination of monuments, desert, eerie cold, barren wind backlashes, where days droned on amidst imaginary statuary of mountain formations, tresses, sheaths, languid shapes among errant shadows, possibly of vanquished men, their wives and children. Life might come and go, or reshape itself from houseboats, rocking jetties, abandoned piers, to dust saturated cliffs, desert narrows of straight-down sandstone walls, buried crevices, an entrenchment of forgotten scorge blasted nights, hooded figures fighting through the thick presuming rugged force of a twenty-mile-an-hour wind shaped as a funnel wreaking a gritty, pumice-integrating debris full throttle, castigating and vengeful, deadly, carnivorous, recalcitrant, combative, monstrous. On camera stills the weather just hours prior to the crash was oddly speckel-flying, contentious, bound to become an ash spurning, contentious bondage of subjugation, a penitentiary of closeted odious screeching phantoms. An artifact recovery of a pistol had been discovered at five in the late afternoon above Mississippi state hatcheries in a pond flowing with a waterfall filled with red bellied trout, the twinkling water spelled by dozens of coot ducks bobbing in the twilight of a gradually plummeting orb of bright white sunshine as it fell like an October moon behind a succession of dark blue mountains like waves. In this eerie pencil haze dusk a morning water dive by an underwater photographer produced the 27 millimeter gun suspected of jolting a month-earlier train through Bellchester, Arkansas with its sudden blast. The team studying the phenomena of derailed steel underwater usually convened at car race tracks at the last weekend of each month to test durability, steel shocks, front end absorption for dents and smashes. They filmed impact and took the wrecks to the lab for evaluation and concluded even with powerfully enforced struts impact succumbed under a bullet firing speed of thirty thousand frames per second. For Maggie who worked the entire line sitting removed from other passengers, he could recollect most passengers after being shown photos, after fifty years of evaluating a repair work expedite, he possessed an unerring instinct for idiosyncratic behavior, hair styles, shoes, facial structure, indifference, muscular exaggeration, he had no trouble recollecting them, there was no question, battery of downright illegal or questionable access to the train engines, clock and altimeter as to when the train was losing speed, use of baggage car for overflow, all were subject to mortification protocols of examining where someone not permitted examination might come to have it. The days could line up accordion rack file, in order to determine which photos gave a suspect, he had to look at billings, leases, loans, supplies, borrowing, other rail lines which brought in needed goods, chili powder, red peppers, rice, onions, barley, tomatoes. On the Kansas line into the whiskey towns, both Kentucky and Tennessee, barley was king, more so than wheat which produced the Turkish and Israeli philo dough for baklava, strudels, fruit-filled rolls, more so than the soups, more than the bean. The bible belt and the U.S. Army shared their demons of moonshine, molasses butter, quick spun scotch and a horde of any number of liveries where booze was amply sampled with mutton eggs. Thus, when the question was put to Maggie, it began with – how did the arrival of an off-schedule train occur? For him whose job it was to see every last photo of anyone who stepped into a train, who had tangible knowledge as to who boarded the trains, the queries soon became a multitude. What condition got met by a runaway train whose pilots at each end, forward and thrust reverse, had been gunned down? If these trains all rolled downhill, was this the necessary element for causality for a derail? Which engine cab responded to the bullet implosion? Who benefited by a crash on the barley train? Who won for a skid-over on the red bean line? Why did white bean never receive a crash? Were these series of explosives the staging of a white bean plot? If red bean followed every whiskey into station, was that the reason one crash knocked barley into the river and burned the red bean to bloody hell? For barley mash ale to be the ingredient that softened the red bean, it seemed to illustrate to Maggie a hell of a point to increase the value of the bean by eliminating a transportation cost. He pulled up bulk capacity per compartment, it was exactly 4,666 tons each, and then looked up the thumbnails on both loads. Freight handling for operations for containers by port, canal and dry dock including load shifting transfers for food, excluding coal and iron ore, showed the five plus one row, the first photo #41 was of the Idaho derailment, a projection around midnight of a drunk bear that hurled into the side of the train at such speed, the train lost its rear engines; the second photo #47 of the yucca cactus plant which was used as a dye for non gins; and next #59 the silver shoe into which the heist money had been tossed on the Birmingham postal mailbag; but no Roscoe or Nash as might be expected; instead another Nash was caught in a hitch and roll in a glimpse in #70 of rain and snow falling onto winded birch pine leaning tall like pitchforks into the forests along the Columbia River of western Washington state which was freezing over with ice trapping small egrets and trout alike; #80 of the same dust churning, locust burdened, sand driven wind that gave no true indicator as to whether the hooded apparitions in long robes were real people, lights somewhere barely penetrating the density of opaque-ish howling dust; and the final photo #95 of a male hidden by shadows of the wooden gray-dark brown bridge legs several feet immersed in the river shooting a roll of film of a train coming clickety-clack into station. Someone, an analyst, who had made an initial foray into the matter, had jotted down a notation on the steel-methods page that read, lantern man shooting photos with 130X Intel of second and third box containers, which told Maggie in no uncertainty the staff for the derail into maybe twelve feet of river already knew which part of the train they wanted to start the derailer, for under usual circumstances it took thousands of pictures to decide to go for the third cab, did they think by this time they had locked the schedule in place. Maggie assigned each photo with an idea or two to each agent who would prove barrel shipment designated route choice to look for photos of entry to that station, as well as time of week, and any suggestion as to situations when train compartment steel would break under high tensile strength and dents and wear in toughness.

3.

Using the Intel 130X Maggie searched the river for Mixey among hotel traffic. Mixey lived a basic life – he stayed put once his target walked into the public eye. Chances were since the plunge into the Akron, he had studied the trams for a likely subject who had access to the train locomotive engineering and could predict adequate damage for a rollover. Maggie guessed that John Mixey had found the money man who was attempting to find a fence for conversion to modern year dollars. Mixey left Cambridge Square without a forwarding address, but always the same stratagem so he'd turn up on a wharf in a large city or stretched out on a hotel balcony overlooking the waterfront and train yard. Maggie checked long wooden avenues in harbors, ship crane yards, ships in dock, no docks closed in by land, busy thoroughfares, taxi curbs, strutting hookers and young models, buses rushing along the wharf front, Intel found him in a non-descript light yellow with railing balcony apartment nine-story highrise across from the all white sand beach and aquamarine water between a YMCA and a newish light purple renovation for fixed income, semi retired garden suites. Within the hour he had Mixey's origination calls.

Is there a patio deck?

Grass, ramp down.

Boat access?

No avenue dock, no yacht club, sometimes a tug.

Storm service?

Unlikely, small quay, pebble bottom, houseboat on occasion.

Another call gave a status find.

Has a girlfriend at Gables by the Sea. Hot crab, toasters, rum mostly, tie-ups, outboards, wave runners, spotlight cruisers, off Highway 5 to the Keys.

Children?

Not a one, no federal aid either.

Can you tell me who else is watching?
You'll want to call back in a week.

Mixey had not acted yet. His small data box with weather reports and projected storm warnings that permitted five lines of text each day had been opened once since he resituated. His first message after reading hospital charts of the injured for the derailment into the river was, who got off in Warden, Tennessee regularly; just prior to the departing month, he asked, who is moving the money? On the day he left, he wrote – train law states all trains must be in the open and underground trains cannot pass beneath buildings, only beneath streets; inquiry as to possibilities that can be eliminated.

A city desk editor put on the wire about the Kentucky crash.

Charge panel gave off significant impulses seconds before derail.

Parts of train – sabotage or human miscalculation, as to:

Track especially on high rail,

Engines, front and end of train, were irregular sounds heard,

Transmission, was it flooding or overheating?

Coils, for interior light system, did these short-circuit,

Heat and air,

Call box

Jones had the removed photos on his desk of hands swimming through doors in murky green water, legs pushing up looking like dozens of feet vigorously pushing to the surface, the passenger train that was always on schedule having been busted by the incoming Boston-Arkansas-Nebraska line causing Mixey to wonder on the morning after, who was on the street looking for a missing getaway container. This was after all the going idea that a group of smugglers heisted an entire vault of a treasury certificate deposit inside an empty horizontal tunnel after crawling through sewage grime and headed to 7th where they boarded a late hour express to Yonkers, switched to a ferry and headed for the Boston fellowship wing. Too much rain and hurricanes aided in their escape, they slept at an inn before heading inland in canoes down an intricate river drainage system toward the Mississippi Valley.

Lewis Lewis was surveying a plethora of identifying photos for the single lane high up rail that wound through the evergreen and pine of the mountains. Concentrating on winter and summer, on desert sagebrush, prairie wheat and corn, forest maple for sugar, marsh for legumes and wild river fowl, and river straits along the inland deltas and angling steep ravines fit only for burro teams of miners come to snag a few plots of mountain ash, there were nine passenger trains and eight main points of residence travel, Seattle, Chicago, New York, South Carolina, West Virginia, Alabama, Louisiana, and El Paso. No crop train went to all destinations nor every passenger railroad to every major city. The Nogales entrance at the border was watched closely by Border Patrol SWAT and Disrupt Teams with dogs and their surveillance and raids was picked out weekly by Lewis; Omaha helicopters patrolled inland seventy miles in either direction. There was no proof that the train was crammed with a shitload of money, the money was somewhere, maybe not where anyone thought, and was carefully hidden. Possibly at Puget Sound. The state had taken just one measure and that was to spray passenger and crop transportation with illegal fertilizer in hopes of illuminating the stolen bills; something had worked because the federated boys had retrieved fingerprints, although no one knew who they identified, they weren't born or employed in the U.S.

In a week Mixey had made contact.

Birmingham-Tuscaloosa is a definite, Naples no photos, Everglades looking for a bathosphere.

Thanks. Can you get me a boat?

It was two in the afternoon. A squall was forming a winding spout out at sea. It was the first sign of storm weather during the entire season, small craft advisory warnings were on the radio, sea kayaks were boarded up, Loreto Bay teemed with choppy water, a crack of lightning hit the horizon. Lewis had left for the poolside with Rhonda to catch what remained of the hundred degree heat. Jones remained at his desk getting hazed on rum and barbiturates to nurse a sprain while he hunted down a few references on his assigned stack of photos. He had a hundred rolls on the Arkansas-Kentucky fiasco with more than forty of track by itself. Straight off he saw the photos were out of order. Money packages had been tossed into crates booked already for train passage, a repair train had picked up a crate, that container wound up on a Washington train along the cliffs of the Columbia River where the train derailed, the crane responsible for raising the container out of the river was subsequently put in Miami port and the container was removed to a train yard in Spokane, but the money was missing.

Jones returned to wharfs and ships on the eastern seaboard. Perhaps the money had traveled west, or to an off shore site until the hoopla died down.

Hoyt invited Jones for lunch and a stroll.

"Was the problem the Kansas dust or the Arkansas locust?" Hoyt asked, as they rounded the point overlooking the bay.

Jones said, "No idea, could be the Kentucky crash was done to affect supply."

"By farmers? You think they want more value on their beans? We're already two cents a bean."

"Could be someone wanted a more direct route to kitchen manufacturers. You probably didn't realize but the government already had contracts to can red bean prior to any of these crimes, either that or it is refrigeration taking too big a bite out of the bean and rice markets."

Hoyt was thoughtful, a celibate already on bended knee to the Dateline reporting of criminal headwaters. "Where have you searched for who travels into the mountains who doesn't reside there?"

"Everywhere," Jones replied with a laugh, four marriages by the wayside, dark brown hair brushed back, sticky brim hat lending his rare conservatism of oceanography training at

Obispo a more servile demeanor. "Restaurants, grills, sidewalk cafes, fish and coconut chili, stuffed grape leaves, hotels with ivy, speeding taxis, verdant waterfalls amid icy trees and snow capped peaks, fly fishing, casinos, wheel of fortune and black-jack, pool halls, hamburger joints, skiers on slopes, lodges, gift shops, breakfast eateries overlooking a ski lift – my lead claims he is African German, probably in his thirties, done with col-lege, an astronomer or bucket photo colordesk, if only because he deliberately evades detection, he may even have gone down with each derail."

"Guarantees his outcome, you think?"

"Strong possibility, I'd say."

"Well booked?"

"No way to know, probably trousers, men's shirt, tie, light coat, nothing to call attention to himself."

"Monuments or national parks?" Hoyt queried.

"Didn't come across any repeaters."

"Occupation?"

"Might be a stucky if in fact he has a job on the trains." Jones replied. "Here's the summary, they think either oil man or lantern because the switches were open."

"I would've said impossible without administrative help from the junk yard. It's the computers that have to open in order for another train to go onto the other track. The comput-ers check a standing train before they release, so it's got to be sabotage."

"What makes a train keep rolling?" Jones was on a differ-ent line of thought.

"Well, aside from the Florida train where the tracks were chopped out, I'd say it's hard to do, the incoming has to call ahead, the station tells them when the train can proceed, so a crash into an outgoing train has to have help because both trains would've been on the monitors."

"Then the monitors went down or didn't show for extend-ed homebound standing. Who would've had an independent computer with farther than immediate preceding range?"

"It could've been the reverse or the thrust once the train

was allowed onto the platform incoming rail track." The concern was apparent. "Obviously the crash was rolled in, the only track answering a wait-for-release instruction was another incoming train and she never got on the platform track, she was told to backup into a hold until the engine car could be changed for the reverse direction. They should have done that with the crash. As it was the crew had to take it apart with a crane."

They eventually sat to lunch at a small Chinese café overlooking the golf course and swaying palm trees and ordered crab, egg, scallions and fried rice and a plate of Szechuan shrimp and tea. Hoyt was talking about retirement but the brass wanted his appraisals on a handful of investigations in Florida and the Keys past the mile markers. There was the Birmingham Route 66 devastation of the Sable Island peninsula where two boys had taken their uncle's Thunderbird car, driven it into a large pond, ransacked a few cabins, and mistaking the embankment for sturdier soil slipped and fell prey to ocean quicksand. The fact that these boys were seen hours before at a deepwater bar with a young man named King who worked constructing sky ways in Appaloosa, Birmingham, Spellchrist, Ford and Omaha, sometimes with young Davenport, the two on occasion in Kansas to walk the top of trains in order to verify the camera mechanism, was itself a coup.

"Are there any names on the dead?" Jones asked, having left half his plate untouched, tea now lukewarm enough to sip.

"One was Torch, he was a hood out of Texas, nickel plate covering the face to prevent contact with flying debris from the thrust reversers beneath the compartments, much as on ice trucks into blizzard wind in Wisconsin up to Green Bay; and the other was a relation to a troublemaker named Braines, possibly a cousin to Torch, although I heard Torch is Braines and he works both reverse and thrust. We've sent for the full photo table, four rows if a judge will approve, if not we'll have to try for long haul footage, police bookings, especially bar skirmishes, snow mobile bangers, what have you."

"Any witnesses?"

"Half a dozen; three were on the Tennessee roll. It's so

perplexing because the Nashville train runs at an optimum."

"My own guess is that because a train can be recorded to what part of the train has a problem, it can also record unusual sounds that shouldn't be present at all, this pistol finding for example."

Hoyt was ravenous and dished out a second helping of both plates and poured tea. "The tape that examines where the train was when there was pistol fire out off the ice that gave off that whipping sound, was it in the mountains or on the ground, said on the ground near the fisheries, but the Florida crime wasn't on a tape."

"Is this Mixey's case?"

"Just the drowning. I'd say since he didn't need to excavate the train and all bodies, drowned and survived, were account-ed for, he's only going with a do-er; this old elm, elephantine roots in the swamp might tag along with a refrigeration closet on a compartment, but I honestly think these crash derails are all the same crime. The Florida situation is probably a double cross."

"Sure. I'd buy that."

"Then there's ACME's 45-playing records, the ones sent to Nashville to the sound studios. While we encountered all the correct photos on the train interior – the mail was in the chair, no obstacles to get to the furnace, all phones are work-ing, connectors aren't loose, recorder box is working fine, et cetera – the fact is that the label wind-ups recorded the Ohio-Illinois flood with downstream charging bronco-bucking logs, track that sank with timber, not to mention some sort of pitch vowel resonance. "

"Of what?" Jones asked, making utterly no assumptions.

"Sirens. There was an ambulance at the intersection." They sipped tea, paid the tab, left a fiver as a tip. After some con-sideration, Hoyt said, "There's always a possibility that no one could get to work and the station was down to the two who sleep there, one to staff the bridge and an outside tinkerer to run signals."

They strolled back the way they had walked, on a path

with flowering fuchsia plants, star flowers, overcoat plastic looking, red antheriums amidst a fairly well-watered golfing green of eighteen holes.

Hoyt said, "Lewis will probably say he does all his own underwater; I certainly wouldn't nor would you, but the river raised track has its own barometer read, if what you think is that just before this crash was a fall of altimeter, on a train this indicates a slow down, over a crossing it may not amount to much but as the train climbs a high rail, the train may lurch forward as it prepares to pull into the wake, when in reality it is already off track somewhere falling."

Jones gave an instinctive nod. "How many reverse gears had to be replaced on that one train?"

"Prior to the crash? Once a year, standard service. To ditch a train, you need to know what pitch-roll recording is for off schedule ascents. You'd want to be able to see with your own eyes the extent of wilderness, while Amtrak passenger allows for a hundred fifty miles terrain between towns the crop trains are notorious for playing cards at a longer stop. With the hour to four hour waiting you eventually get known for the amount of fog on the mountain as the sun comes up. Had one to know height of rumble road, paving, become very familiar with where the river bend starts and when the lakes churn, one might be able to predict high rain as well as cracking land over a levy-like surface. And then fairly commonplace releases, a train crash will get filed between two all black fade-outs which prevent any theft of those photos. "

"Actually I came across a black as night passage through north Virginia that has seen some dark mirror activity, I suppose somewhat like Washington state, but it's the ocean being right there that tricks the tape that defines altitude and makes the tape record a much higher geography."

"We've looked for these roughnecks in the woods with no luck. Since the mirror gives chase to the wrong direction, many a horse and cub have wound up stumbling onto the highway in the face of oncoming headlights."

Hoyt would sleep off lunch and then go all night waiting for John Mixey's five line message off the tele-reporter and then attempt to snag all outside jurisdictions for matching description. That's all he would ever need – he was from the school that gave its investigators little actual information, like a shot in the dark, a still candle inside a boat cabin, an overhead lamp in a storm cellar, signs of tampering or an actual conversation with voice identification imprint and fingerprint matched to photos of the crime-in-progress, not necessarily stage 4 interviews or public proximity or even money in the mail.

Jones thought he was on the verge of the worst boredom of his career. He'd checked out the singles at the pool, Marva a seductive dreamy blond who daily dressed in stretch jeans and a long white stiff shirt was nevertheless too young, a mere forty-five; Nila, an unenthusiastic bronze, shoulder length haired, over-the-hill seventy who sat in the bar until closing time who knew everything there was to know about saw-fish that chewed on bodies underwater who had lived with Mixey for years in Constantinople, that by itself was invitational itself, who had discovered stinging nettles and a strange symptom of bleeding underwater; and of course Quince whom Jones had known forever and took to dinner a few evenings a year when he needed sympathy, a few bottles of wine, and no hassles, a brunette almost to her waist, fair skin, dark tan shift and sandals. Quince was on her way into counter industrial treason abductions on a shockingly terrorist case that had been open for not yet twenty years of a highly mobile group of tree trimmers who dug out the basements of houses leaving the house without a foundation in a flood zone of raging waters. He had said no to himself for Rhonda, spoke infrequently to Lewis, told Rhonda it was over, that his first wife wanted him back which wasn't true, she was still nursing in Cincinnati at a rural hospital but it created a sought-after distance and despite this, he felt guilty, even thought he ought to apologize, hear her out; but she and Lewis arrived to the lounge daily at eleven, ordered martinis and split an olive, cheese and salsa omelet, she wore a tight black halter top and long white stretch pants and black backless heels and

Lewis, dark grey tweed trousers, a striped black and dark green short sleeved shirt and light jacket, they piled into the booth and sat side by side talking, oblivious to life.

In the end it was Mixey's female he chose. A first night out Nila took him on a boat onto Loreto Bay and brought fresh catch snapper which she grilled with coconut curry, a twist of lime, spicy red breaded corn broilers, Tangeray gin and tonics and her notepad cluttered with notations, remarks and sketches. She had thrown on black stretch tights, a light blue sequined blouse over a sheer white sharkskin sleeved top, hair twisted up and white throng sandals. Jones had slipped into black corduroy pants and a long white sleeveless men's top. In the distance were No polo hotels with golf courses, the moonlike subdued Giganta Mountains, a week tournament at Cabo winding down and tourists going home.

They sat on the bay, the two of them. Without awkward silences Nila kept up a steady stream of dialogue, Mixey had taken her to the French Riviera to see the drowning of a parliament figure, it was a notorious case, the man was in his eighties, had played football polo in Peru, was a name in lounge polo; he had just been to Australia where he came in second in the Rolex yacht races, always someone who was better at a loved sport. She and Mixey played the casinos on a cruise ship where a man leaped to his death into a pool, lots of tourists on the upper deck snapping pictures, he usually didn't handle ocean liner drowning but this had been the exception because the victim owned a condo penthouse in Bariloche, Argentina and an all white Arabian horse had won him the fifty thousand dollar cup. Every so often as the night wore on, they paused to listen to the wind, plug in another few martinis. She had seen it all, deaths on beaches, in rivers, on sand, in lake trees, she could explain when the body had been fed on, fish larvae and that sort of horror, yellow bellied exposed torn flesh, desiccated and stringy, it wasn't a sight for just anyone, the morgue cronies waited weeks for the bodies to toughen when the skin took on a rubbery appearance, such were water tombs, most detectives said no thanks. Mixey hadn't thought to give a damn, every summer there were half a dozen drowning, it was somewhat inevitable with drugs such as paint and vial, life eventually became inhospitable, whatever the underworld was made of was his bite, there were no complaints, rarely he got drunk; then last year he turned her out, said he was done with sex, the job needed all his energies, it was better he wouldn't involve her another month or day, she'd get over him, men were a dime a dozen, other dimes out there.

Are you a dime? She asked.

She disrobed. Her body was striated like her mood, firm, rock hard, swelling breasts, somewhat caved-in abdomen, tapered legs, very tough. "Should we?"

"We can."

The sense of her reality caused him to throw away all instinct. He took her in his arms, felt her pulse in her neck. When she pressed against him, he thought he could ache with emotion. He was ready, seized by desire, unquestioning of his surrender; had she suffered years and now without flaw opened up to him, undeniable in a need to be possessed, he took her. He saw she held nothing back – in the moment he felt himself transcend, molded her to him, all the while he held her arm against him. She was all he could ask for – unequivocal, unselfish. The fact that she seemed to accept him, went easily with him, no discernible contradiction or reluctance relieved him of feeling left out.

"What does the Agency have you doing?"

"Identifying adventurists by category, money invested, marriages."

"Would your Mixey be doing this type of work?"

"Not usually. He is figuring out why his show relocated, what's there for him, who wants him."

"What convinced him about this man?"

"Photos. He had first five plus accomplice, track was put onto existing track false plated which lowered track permitting a bungle. Without a manual override, it's an outside system, the train can't enter the bridge but this did occur, track buckled, and four people on board died and many drowned, John lived in the blue mountains of Akron Tennessee and traveled to the western Virginia mines where the train system is based upon a turn gare, although John said the sail created a drag in such a way the train is cavorted along, a blind alley."

"Is there a history on him, what's his code?"

"Braines, and yes, extensive. First job in Virginia he replaces steel pike rods that control brakes, this caused train stoppage. His second job was Great Lakes Chicago runaway of 1958, it took a crop train to crash and stop it. In 1956 he hid a train in a building and painted it black and red. He worked signals on an old line not in use, sent the Bantam train south to Florida and derailed it in 1961, that being the Boston-Antioch-Amarillo-Montana line and then numerous pony mail express theft of document bonds across Missouri. Mixey has him on fingerprints but with aliases and different looks, the target allegedly has flaming dark red hair, brown eyes and is tall, handsome and secure."

So they would hang out, kibbittz, take coffee, sit on the balcony, edit their bylines. Jones would cook tortillas with spicy fish and rice and serve full blooded burgundy wine and top off the meal with an herbal French fag beastie. After a fashion he'd have to acknowledge even to himself that Rhonda had proven an expensive second youth, a quietly coveted crazy spill, a release of wicked hunger, so foreign yet so instantaneously satisfying as though all arousal led to self knowledge. In retrospect he'd probably ask of himself, what became of motivation or rather of despair, he must have been depressed, burrowed under reports, dead to emotion, certainly he had put his sentimentality on a shelf. He would never contain Rhonda as Hoyt had, she wouldn't agree to leave Lewis, he would bring himself to that realization and cast all cares away, awaken himself if he was able to another female, despite her relationship to the famous, much demanded-of underwater excavation-ist. If he had never been inclined to fall into someone's world, he would comfortably tell himself he was hiding, trying to rid himself of numbness, hoping the pull of a woman could release him from a joint tenancy with shutting out being needy. He would lie awake in the night trying to piece together stray possibly desperate realities such as a photo of the falling boxcar, bluish white until it hit the water, cracking of joints and a sting to the inner thigh, stiffening limbs, smashed digitals, freezing rubbery skin that lasted momentarily as the compartment sank rapidly shorting circuits as oxygen bubbles rose, the amount of boom was the sole predictor that amyl had been used to roll the car off its rail hitch; Jones mentally walked the walk. Who knew trains who had been around forever? Hickle and Spark? Chain and Zoo? Klamath and Fitch? There were a good ten stuckies who had hauled mileage who worked mate-shift during the brightest side of day until the mountains fell into a color of bluest blue, each more true in blue than the range preceding it. The uphill steeping of an agonizing engine of thoroughbred capability, a Schermer or Rothschild engine, removed the distinct burden of winded thrust after climbing a mountain of over three thousand miles. Any Godiva who convened a thrust-conveyor- landslide usually started with a mortared headstone situated on its side on an outside track with switch. If the train hit with enough force it could lose the train uphill velocity. His problem once he determined incoming speed was to decide how much overdrive to shut down in order to force the train to proceed at a speed necessary to crash and then to unhitch and fall. The fact that the chief station engineer wanted the crash summarized as a quick fix said the outgoing had to back up onto an outside rail line just as the incoming slipped forward to the hark. Who cared if two danglers needed an icy ski if the felling motion was the eventual release of speed of the Plymouth part of the trickster, the middle of the train's crank, that caused it to zoom right up there? Eventually he got out of bed and slipped into his gray-blue flannel robe and slippers and walked into the kitchen, poured a cup of coffee and went about reading his book on monsoons in the bay. The fallacy of the boxcar that it could easily dislodge in water and float to the surface was for a crop train; for the passenger train, it was a nightmare one hoped never to live through. Jagged ledges, stillborn cliff lines, bottomless canyons, spill-easy ponds, glacial mud, carry-all ice quenchers, spit-ale caverns, filmy quakeless anchor-ruts, all could pitch a train for any greenhorn conductor who was unfamiliar with his track. Sleep notwithstanding, nothing came between the engineer and his load. For an average of five days that the steel-horn rover forewent sleep, the rail was his filial oath, his terrain crossing, an only call, no other Clementine heard or wandered near to.

4.

Lewis turned onto his side placing his arm across Rhonda's hip as she lay napping. She was having a hard time catching up on much needed sleep. Station completion narratives kept being retrieved and she had to evaluate them and send them back by next day mail. She stayed up nights when there was nothing hectic to interrupt her concentration until she became so exhausted she lay down and fell into a deep sleep.

The report for Lewis on the Nebraska wilds had come in a few hours ago, the bogle had slipped off the track and wedged on the inner wheel causing a derailment but the bad damage rested on a raised portion of platform with a snap wedge where both wheels had come to sit off the rail after a boiler explosion. Obviously it was a bomb, probably beneath the track, very possibly a disruption caused by a shoelace that separated track from ground. It could take months going through photos to determine why an assault occurred. Nebraska lacked the stunning blue ridges of Tennessee, moving north from Oklahoma through Kansas City up the long prairie and desert through Omaha, she sprang from grass roots, bent under a whip-storm breeze of herds of bean heralded by the shining yellow light of a lonesome train wail, which when it thundered whistling into a station for an hour stop five men de-planked to check fix plugs, cable attachments, noise ducts, line installations and a host of other mundane, seldom went-wrong connectors which on this one journey unlatched in a blizzard while waiting for the station go-ahead and moving unsecured through Fork split a trough and spun a latch pulling the runway into the air without sufficient force to slide. The train crashes took up residency throughout red bean country for no reason he could think of except that the heir to canned chili and soups owned those weather-beaten plateaus.

The photo straight off the station computer showed a man, quite tall, stringing a shoelace some seven to ten feet long into track during a blizzard, on the day the track buckled the telephone-to-station photo went entirely black on the monitor seeming to remove all monitor viewing. As a result the signal apparatus closed at 04:22 am. It was a little known fact that despite plank loosening or wood softening, the rail itself stayed firm to the land even during fierce blizzards. When the night crew came across the missing tape hours later, they found two blue Chevrolets under a telephone pole stuck in the snow, five very thin figures in black tights, masked, gloved, hooded running over the tracks. By the day Lewis received the photo strip, his questions were simple – from where was the photo taken, and for what subsequent train disaster did they need a derailment.

As best he could assess the telling photos were shot on the ambling prairie where the plateaus were uneventful, dubious shallow waterways, quagmires of no importance, seasonal transcendent green to rust and gold, yellow and pastel blue shading, grazing meadows for horses and moving herds, indexed blue-silver pinecones rich with sap falling onto pine matted soil, a dominant presence of a red-orange moon inhabiting the sky. There was the typical program difficulties following the loss of visual – down radio, station couldn't pick up, same crazy photo sampling of blue mountain ranges forever – that indicated a crash was imminent, and then people who might be witnesses to something produced in all sorts of mundane pictures, it'd take weeks, possibly longer, to frame any suggestive and actual knowledge as to who could be involved. Would field interviews be needed? He wouldn't know until he had picked through the samples – and then came the first photo as damning as the individual who shot a photo of a very tall hooded man slapping an independent air condition unit to glass from inside the Alfred F. Murrah building; this was a pipe placed the suppressed month and year 1998 of the derailment approximately six and a half feet long attached to a lead stick intended to make obsequious the actual explosive tagging that gave investigators their data. It would provide a plastics-identifier worthy hitch blow, but after tagging it to a shop he'd have both the builder and the man who put it on the track. Although it might take upward of a few months to profile the entire group, if the man who laid the explosive was the same man who Mixey was onto, the photo might be the only essential summary that was needed.

Up close on the film gastrometer, the dust in the air was wheat coming down like rain over water, so faint it was barely noticeable, but evident for six seconds approximately, no actual rain. That's all he needed, that by itself told him the derailed compartment was removed off a wheat train that had not yet been cleaned and thus could be classified as to probable handlers; a wheat, not a barley, train was one of three routes but not the Tennessee line – wheat came in on Montana-Montreal, on Nevada-Dakota, and it's most revered of lines Minneapolis-Chicago-Akron where wheat became bread, pasta, and dessert. But why a wheat train? Were there trains that moved out of New York which were the same color as Chicago black trains carrying wheat? Train products varied but in general the high volume included corn out of Louisiana, bean into canneries throughout Missouri, rice from California, oil from the state of Washington, lettuce from Idaho, molasses and beets also grown in California, lumber out of Oregon, dirt from Tennessee, and beef from Texas. Administrators of the trucks which were considered part of the complex train industry would concur that no bomb was capable of blowing up a truck on or off a railroad, the containers were made of perforated U.S. Steel, most often drivers weren't aware a bomb had released; and then they were built of wood interiors such that the space conducted air calibrations. The sole photo of a bomber without any hood or loose clothing wrapped about him came of presumably an employee, red hair somewhat lacy, brown eyes, Munich face, who worked aging repair, usually bolt down, a switch changer who had to open track available routes in order for one train to leave and another to enter the platform viability. Their chief analyst said it was impossible he was a descendant of James Hesse known as Jessie James, the man didn't match any corridor; if anyone, he might be a Silver but not one of the knife-haul-down for a lynch hanging. Again, the motivating question for the Nebraska lane switch was, where had the train spent the night, in a striptease whiskey parlor or in the cold wrapped in thermal listening to the chill wind and whining coyotes? Lewis sent for fingerprints and once identity prints were determined, any other bagged evidence no matter how long saved.

The pertinence of a creed came with seeking to renegotiate the pathological enormity of stigma. There was seldom contradiction to method despite a florid gratification that if one lived outside the law that one eventually became bound to a distribution of tide, tide being the moon; and what appeared as formidable was renounced. Thus, pony mail came to be seen as logging, an industry of opportunism of conjuring, money itself as a coveted steed. Wanderings throughout the night over rugged terrain was not the least these prairie rooms became known for; the men had no income, no address, they were criminals in a caste system, moving with cattle on vast thunderous desert, Bedouins in veils, every so often riding the rail cars, living in abandoned vans, covenant living for the dozens without insurance, fires only to insured churches that rented. The prior weekend was a harbinger of low to the ground cloud cover, varied darkening, violent snowfall, pounding rain, driven sleet defined by thumbnail; thrashing trees, a howling twister, a sudden storm over an early morning without anything much going for it, awake at seven, coffee on the patio, chilled grapefruit and pork bow at eight, collating notes on chronologies of the crime and reviewing interviews, and the big "do" brought in by dinner over the Dateline summary – the target's fingerprint obtained off the counter in Spanish Cay at a 27/11. Knowing Maggie's affectionate description of Mixey, Mixey must have changed his mind six times as to whether he should fax the fingerprint to island police, these were after all drug bordello cops, Mafia-men, hiding the money as fast as it was being made, who knew who was safe to tell, a much better idea to find a city desk and send the info to their felony-docu-proof correspondents, but finally he sent it. The sketch Maggie received he distributed as a tear sheet to every agent. The box went over in Tennessee and it was a Perskoo with the alliga-

tor staring out the ship portal window. The target worked repair track, he had taken a boat to the Everglades to Old Man's
Cabin, No. 42, hidden behind a boathouse dock, on his most
recent job he had placed a weather balloon on that mountain
train. The photos matched along the lines for employee engine
release and valve check for the Boston to Nebraska line as well
as the Kansas to West Virginia line; but there was none to explain what had occurred in the state of Washington and none
as to the Philadelphia to Marathon, nor were there Roscoes
or Pinters to be found. The night watchman stepped onto the
track. Voices could be heard as far as the yard.

"Hey, Shawn, what are you doing?"

"Don't worry none, the cowel's got to catch a rift of moonlight.

"You don't say. Isn't that a right damn counting of carts be
sold?"

"Don't know. Who's going to the lock-up?"

"Bit of blurry. It'll be a show all night, run right stray of
the hedge."

Their talk faded into the sounds of winter – dripping ice,
rushing falls, trout jumping out of the lake, wheezing thaws,
hawk shrieks, a barely frozen car motor trying to start up, then
not another disturbance.

The blue ridges of Nebraska became dusted in shades of
blue – gray wisteria, smoky sapphire, grieving cornflower, shadow chalky summit and gas-cracked whale blue. The mountains
finalized breath with slaked ore in its ponds. From five shafts
buried deep beneath her hills and ghosted tunnels, fog emitted
in early dawn, traverses of mist down to the flanks of foothills,
the train's call penetrating the air, air compression increasing
to mask teal light, obscure mouthbreeder trout that carried its
eggs in its mouth, a recovered pistol with part of a man's palm
print laid along its barrel in dust enamel, a signature of a sort of
a derail stucky expert, apparently a tag gun authorized by the
City of Philadelphia, several shots on the telemeter dated and
captured in Breathless, Arkansas.

The photo-advance that was routed by Maggie's stunningly bewitching huntress of a detail analyst read, "Apartment without any clear resonance, no photo, all evidence rendered in brown," to which Margi had in her own small handwriting asked, "Are they still in Spanish Cay?"

The periodic rain ran in rivulets drenching an ascorbic landscape colorless in the way deserts become after snow leaves the ground tired and sorry. Each of the trains had departed after an hour-long stay having served dinner around midnight, gassed up and made a final boarding call. The little known incident had produced almost no attention despite the nearness of passengers waking at the late hour and descending into the chill air for a breather. If anyone heard the pistol fire, it had registered to none that is what it was. In fact although many would later contend that the conversation had a menacing quality to it, most had simply ignored the likelihood of a conflict and went to purchase a cup of coffee. Between the thirty passengers and stewards, a handful had crossed the tracks to see the garbage put out alongside each compartment on an adjacent walkway. The man Gerard in the last compartment had written his last conclusions on the efficiency of the passage and was preparing to walk to the dining car for a sandwich. Inside the entrance stairwells teenagers playing at Gun-smoke on the video players were wide awake and looking forward to the steep twisting ride through the reservoirs of ice to the Colorado Rockies prepared to be mesmerized by staggering ice falls, forests of pine, swamps and ravines as tall as striated skies. Life was wondrous for those who saw it, bone aspen and ash trees crowding out gray skies and moss cascading banks to the low river which evaded icy rapids and governed many a silver ore deposit. On the terrace dust winder along the railroad track a Stebbins blue collar with long steel, pack and chain hiked beneath the moonlight all the while trying to eye the track for breakage. He was from a miner background in Jerome and had stayed far past any charitable season. Now, paid good pay to hike track he pitched a photo periodically and recorded the chug-a-lug of any passing train. With any luck the chill ice packed onto slopes and left the soil firm. Even approaching nightfall the bench lay high in the range, the stabbing darkness looked to be climate governed, all around lay evidence of nests and reeds. Boots placed on trees gave an eerie accommodation while elsewhere jackets hung like hides. Familiar caves were sheeted with ice, long ago trenches sodden with carried earth, discarded boxes still retained their shapes. Where the river diverted course, human hand was still avowed to creating livable ponds. The high walk peered out from on top, soakers, roots and pestilent ivy hankering for even ground. At one time he had laid cinnabar over lead, measured distances for cleavage and corrected with pure soda nebulae which over time became strewn with bark, leached saplings, moss, bulbs, wild strawberry, and lobelia forming a tough recalcitrant ground cover. Although he took for granted land nests and the ease at which a man might break his neck, he gathered instinct and experience to shallow landfall, symmetrical hills, joined paths, and wind exploited ridges along with the muffled or piercing hollowing thuds the area might convey. In another day he'd hike the segment and meter the sonorous tribulations on his return, then he'd be days attempting to match stray vowels and longer flights of prey until he could accurately produce the irregular dissonances. The train proceeded through towering ranges agonizing through forest, piled snow, dimensions of ice, stopping once at a school yard where he disembarked at one in the morning.

He picked up a taxi between here and there, retrieved the one-night room key at the unattended desk and took the stairs to his room on the second floor. The window facing the mountains had been left open. He unpacked, placed a long distance call to Mixey in Houseboat Key and left a message – turnabout. It meant, stay only where you can be seen. For Mixey it would mean only one reality, walking the train which invariably was anywhere between Colorado peaks and Wisconsin drawer. On such short notice, Mixey would have to infer that his target routinely was captured from above or showing him leaving. He then looked up Maggie and assessing for passage sent him, bail out, no return, and hung up. Sleep was eventual, the drowning deaths of a train compartment would cause comparisons around the globe and be released to any city newspaper with any reference heading. He was the man they read on dateline, Mixey was their under surface problem finder. Whether Maggie spent any time retracing his travel was doubtful, he'd be looking only for Mixey.

The chill was soon replaced by the bathroom heater. As he grew tired, he put the phone next to him, turned on call waiting, and fell asleep thinking only of the ten days of walking that lay ahead.

The phone jangled. Without any real alertness he handled the receiver. An automated voice relayed to him, the restaurant sits at the station on Forge Pass. Forge lay unremarked on any map inculcated by weather, its cable open to the crowds. Around it sat iced lakes with moving trout, mating delayed by frost conditions. It was an adequate place to place an ad, but the scenery had never won him over. Any season it was barren black plucked of most appreciation, the photographers avoided the area, ranchers moved on, trees canopied and grew too many branches to be milled, fishermen had to rely on poles, and jacks were replaced with each blizzard. Gerard put his socks and thermal blanket into his pack, everything else he wore, windbreaker leggings, flannel shirt over thermals, lightweight risk jacket, gloves, shore man's boots, woolen cap. Downstairs he purchased the usual – water flask, 8 oz., dried salmon strips, nuts, chap stick.

The cold stung his face raw. The wind was obliterating in its whipped glacial carnivorous fury, a turgid stalking for anyone in the dense wilderness, he felt his fingers stiffen, his skin burned, he bowed and headed past the school yard in the direction the Boston-Nebraska train had traveled, running for a fair twenty minutes to become heated. Ahead the awe-inspiring magnificent snow ensconced Rockies stood in unequivocal undefeated stature, shadows of clouds moving across them. The angle at which he strode kept his gaze turned upward causing uncomfortable stiffening pain at the back of his neck, there they sat, miles of impenetrable igneous rock, glaciers once, slanted steep caravans of indomitable inhospitable eagle's nest. For several hours until the range altered direction, he would be eclipsed by soreness no matter how often he climbed the route along the river past the lakes. He would operate his recorder at ten minute intervals for seconds, the whitish cast to the air was a threat he had long trained himself to endure, and his sight adjusted in spite of the spotlight glare the falling snow gave. When at last he slowed to a brisk walk, he had entered a plateau of sorts, shaggy trees appeared impoverished, a flock of crows stood in a pond of ice and frosted grass. Perhaps he had made this journey fifty times, he gave it about as much atten-tion as any report he recognized he had written in a year. The sounds came to him from the nearby flanks of peaks, circling prey, many turkey buzzards, the gunshot of servicing ice cliffs, a dramatic gust of downhill wind, a tower at the lake crack-ling, the faint sound of an aircraft. For years the silence hung in impending doom, an astounding quiet, the oncoming train blast a relief to hear. Every so often he heard a vehicle and then because it seemed intrusive, fortunately the wind overtook it. After years spent measuring location of noise, he could find anyone presumed lost. Errant birds brought an awareness of distance; thawing ice and rushing water overcame the dulled senses as nothing else did. By dark he had walked forty-one miles, the night pass would be made uphill for another two miles before he would rest sitting, the safest thing to do.

He sat rigid his sense of the intolerable attuned to the dark. He slept when he heard the train's wail, the recapitulating re-sounding capture of the mountain range by the train's blast and light. It traveled his subconscious along the remembered continuity of land, if the lake froze as the train blared past or the skies moved in proximity, the presence was assured for an echo of hours. His body absorbed the blanket's warmth and his numbness became finite. The clarity of the mountain disaster had to have occurred around five, just an hour before any soft-ening of light, it had to have come with a jolt as the train was jagging to a stop, its wheel freed from track, its furnace gone dry. The lack of furnace meant the engines would stop, once that happened the interior rim caused maximum overload. The sole sound he found to place the train by coordinates was a sound he had heard every winter, the splitting of ice on gravel.

Cases came and went, the least dangerous usually the more thoroughly worked. Industrialization lent a complaint to scientific enhancement, the Washington-Nevada craggy plateaus and ghostly staggering forests, were trees darting onto false landings. Errant rays – what ought mining corporations think that photographed visual sightings of tumultuous light soaring behind trees and conglomerating as shining orbs reaching for tree tops or conversely toward rivers? Who was there to worry that light spiraled along a bluish wind in the direction of a speeding train? Or during the last of day catapulted beneath oak, pine and ash like a charging ram in a wake of an impending storm billowing below tree tops in fitful speeds? Thus, as the dark penetrated and the train moved into the forest it wasn't until early morning that the same train was discovered unhitched from its engine standing stationary on a track. Both colliding trains of the Nebraska derail had stood robbed of engines in the Colorado Rockies for hours before being hauled into town for repair. The mechanics asked but one question, where did the conductor go? The Tennessee engineer had been found under a tract of leaves shot in the back but still with a pulse. Therefore the chilling reality lay in the few confrontations between bandit stopping a train and conductor. Many a windy night took a man's life, many an engine was seen drifting cabin visible in thunderous Columbia River crashing water sprints, in the Rockies there were more than a hundred flowing meadows with glacial ice to turn havoc into, the least winding up through the open vistas of the spiraled staircases of sunset glowing golden pink brimming snow avalanched tomahawk peaks.

Mixey had other thoughts. For this target every act of train robbery ended with an underwater entrapment. The nature of living was far more complicated. There were acts that greatly hinted at train regrouping of various compartments, the train scoured the foothills looking for them, finding none but rain-stained shipping crates left like discarded dumpsters on mountain passes, officials ran operatives to motels, Rancherias, any spoon-feed in search of hideaways, tram-style garages. Where it came to looking for discards the choices for ocean depth tended to be few. He had found the last engine in the ocean at the mouth of the Potomac River attached by a barge crane surrendered to an isle in the San Juan Islands already getting broken down, the encasement separated from its chassis. His sense of his target was there had to be another banked somewhere below the Galveston current awaiting removal onto a nearby track although the man had made no effort to sail a hitch there. In his submarine pilot car he studied the shoreline for any caboose, the more likely a Birmingham masque marauder dumped off the Alabama coast into the Battle Creek River and then barge pushed downstream into the gulf, Mixey cavorted through tide breakers and tide crashers seeking any elevating platform capable of lowering such a machine, he decided the risk had gone farther to sea possibly as far as the island off Alabama on the ocean side. At length after a steady hour at the Trevelyan sinkage depth he came across a cave which showed through the bubble shaft lights into a surface tunnel. It shone like a dead giveaway of intent. He disembarked without flippers or cable, attached his oxygen apparatus, and swam free rising to a barely lighted ocean tide into the scare way. The tunnel sloped downwind making any removal out of the ocean entirely realistic. The curving cave was solid, without fracture, and made its descent to a mine shaft elevator at approximately a third of a half mile in; the shaft rise emitted up to a floor where presumably a train of six or seven compartments could travel north despite a shallow rail railway. He shot a roll of film and dropped it into a cellophane, then he placed a counter meter onto the base of a dirt wall clamped to the rail, and set the timer. At the ear deafening blast he had leapt into the water and floated far underwater playing dead as above, earth showered into the water plundering into the depth. Mixey waited a minute as the sphere of light blue ocean returned to visible rays and plankton again became apparent before he swam back to his pilot-maneuvered capsule. The water as he rose thirty feet still showed dirt debris, the water was predictably choppy, the tide drifted in with chunks of wood. Only the strata of ore rock bed protruding above the misted current seemed unobtrusively applied. Within hours after he returned to Creek Harbor, he'd take his boat and sail close enough to the blast site to see who came in for a look. His recommendation was to cancel the light weight train traveling through the forested woods of the South Georgia Passage to El Paso North to prevent a sabotage of the whiskey barley train, not to overlook the Nebraska line into Flagstaff to the La Plata silver mine. The original conductors who took silver out by shaft metal antagonist oxygen shakers loaded up the dark reddish brown open topped cars ran the trains from Texas into Kansas east through Appalachian blue ridge mountains into West Virginia and north to Nebraska and Colorado through the lonesome peaks of Idaho and eastern Spokane. The sole breath of the entire line gave its dying declarations to a signal changer by the nickname Dusty Silver whose single minded pronouncement was to stage train stoppages for mine shutdowns of dark rum ore, bushel-load tonnage steel or mix-wheat silver, all which led to the embarkment of trucks onto roads.

Mixey had all their instructions given by his target to seven hitch anglers, men who detached engine from single standing compartments, three from Utah who worked the mine. The target had allegedly obtained his nickname from having been the man to sit silver flake inside a dusting tunnel which permitted short change of cool mist to wash over the product which compacted it prior to it being utilized.

Could I have a bit more of that? Asked of a line man's soup lunch.

Will get hard cold if you leave it all night.

Can't get much more sorper without a toast.

Should get baked first a'fore one has to eat it.

How many days up the climb?

Four, I'd suspect, might be a ransom o'er the Lift Away of the Colorado Rockies.

Stand her in a clean barb in lake – could go for that.

Best burr past Sunday, off year.

Looks like a beak on a snowman, jumps right out at the flour.

Good to sleep, first off the line, don't keep him waiting.

Every man who heard the tapes considered the notion of running a bad train down the Tennessee absolutely out of the question. The Tennessee was the final threshold before the train entered the blue ridge sea of mountains where the country's mining origins lay. Beneath the soil of wheat and coal lay the formation mines of ore where every train runner gained experience with the trains. It would be a generation before a small set of outlaw bean keepers would leave the fifty door entrances of the Appalachia to produce stagecoach robberies in the dark corridor of Virginia hammering off line short cars of coke deposit for an eventual dynamite caravan through the territory of slaughterhouses along the incoming tide shoreline of the San Pablo Bay.

5.

The last ray of visibility lost its sky as the train slipped behind the hills of the Virginian wagon plains through a purplish quiet of rambling valleys known for their russet fields of mares hold grass. Soon within hours the purple color would recede to an eerie unsettling darkness that was neither shadow nor dark. Here despite numerous rivers, some as shallow as swamps and others lucrative as bench havens for late thaws, the area was without a well supplied watershed having to share its infrequent effluence with a rather proliferated movement of hills, erosion never quite seeming to rest. The elastic turmoil queered by white clay combined with elements of mercury and cheater's clay made an unusually strident porcelain beneath a capable potter's wheel shine, a cannibalistic emollient that could be molded to any shape as it dried with no use of sharpener. For most train engineers this twenty-five miles of ensuing dark brown tint to shades of grayish night was palpated like a gauntlet and were it not for eleven bean factories the usefulness of the area could be described as scarcely worth its finest plate ware. Into dank darkness the train bellowed taking to it an itinerant meager homesteader who as soon as a government agent pasted a lien on the property headed out on foot looking to replace a column of disparity with a new riverside ambience. A measure of stern wheel of potters who made use of the land inhabited trench available room houses between sunsets. Out of an umber landscape Dusty Silver Simmer torched his weal burning off sparks long into the day stilling iron out of caustic clay pretending that the stupor he periodically borrowed from would in time decrease. He was a backstreet husband herder unknown to these hills who nevertheless would one day weld the best steel into shifting plates that could catch and hold a rail with steadfast speed. The Virginian No. 28 careened through dales and hillsides without so much as a care shrieking in its pursuit of destination, a steel dark horse bound for the outer bastions of the earnest Iowans and from there to Cincinnati where after a four hour dispatch stop it ran a tankard to Wyoming and Washington state. Nearly all of its seventy-four hours took it into summary quiet where eagles perched high above watched it soar into tiny seldom visited platforms. If as men camped west they envisioned merely a demise to the screaming sparking locomotive responsible for their penury they one day conjured up a terror of burning carnage by the time they came upon the Rockies. Unlike its predecessor of the Fifties, the Balboa which ran from Texas to New Jersey through the russet hills arrived to its final resting place along the Idaho River well within view of the emerald forests of the Tuskegee River, all metal stripped off both engines. It also carried wheat chafed from those dark lilac hills. This was the environment of farms that entitled train renderings, in the height of sweet smelling lobelia adrift in charcoal earth to otherwise stillborn mountains, amply staffed by mottled Manzanita as rich in petrified bark as any on the Salinas Plain. A finding of gorge suffered only the unworthy who plummeted off its lowest foothills two hundred feet to captivity along with grazing cattle and sod hoofed goats. Proportioned for a willingness to nevertheless beckon a livelihood of agrarian interest the new desert saw in its rank an unyielding attribute of bankment holders who clamored for tin and upholstery and heralded to baggage and silos equipping themselves against dirt holdings for cinch jobs. The manufacture of booths gave them a survival amidst tenancies and travel to assure duration over thousands of miles until they came to a pass through lit daylight. Whether endurance stood at the felling of old trees aged by lightning or across leg deep fields, the test of rein took the harness of plows to comprehend when animals became weary; at that stake the boom was held for hours until oxen were fed and then the group bore forward transferring load for the travel into the wind. All except ten surrendered to the chill, the men who succeeded as far as the west coast capitulated to nothing, not even to hunger.

It was the fashion to hunt trains. Well intentioned bronco riders seeking a carry-all lifestyle who one day would work oil can in the furnace junk room would start on a prairie job turning beets for beet sugar canneries and both five coal barley and buck corn richer than wheat in nutrients in ale. For Mathew Jordan who rode as oil can extra up the steep eight thousand foot escalade to Fork, an abundance of wheat lay in every direction green as healthy stalks could make the landscape its wealth. Mathew was a sparing lad, an earnest rodeo Buchanan with red brown hair and green eyes, a sympathetic expression which won him friends, a driving hand that could pry anything off a stuck oil-slopped release, and plenty of stamina. His favorite route was the Wheat King, an all charcoal black and beige train leaving the west out of Chicago all the way downhill to Kansas and Wyoming and then uphill on return. Often when Matt rode the Kentucky Cannonball he wore a winch on his apron and kept a cinch lever for the hookups for the last three cars; once every few weeks he went assigned to the Birmingham Four to the prison coast, an all nighter that ran eight hours and paid a lift fee. Give me a train without a hitch was his jovial expression for the winter runs long after the high rails were partly closed to accommodate spell blinds and storm warnings. If the belt was not attached to the pad, the train could roll in from an off-track location and it was not all that unusual for stackers to stand on the platform or sidebar, from time to time truck compartments designated for train transportation were found in rivers with an interior file drawer or leaking fluid running out drying a creek bed. He was one of seven oil men to come across a dismantled compartment in South Carolina inside a shaft cable line underground with packaged red vine money in packs of fives, tens, twenties and fifties, and sent the train car dock on its speedy way to Birmingham to the tin pan refuse fire block cinders to be banded, labeled and re-jacked and sent by ferry to Long Cay to the armory. Periodically, now that he knew what to look for, climbing down sixty feet into underground tunnel adjoining rig and fueling tugs, he sought interiors for suspect cargo. It was all the rage to follow ski patrol over the wine ridge to cove layaways. He ran shower with four brothers named Wrangell who took turns carrying the barrel, a device that measured length of travel, how long a detained train had to go; but the Wrangellsteens intended to leave Vergne, Tennessee and stop working apricot and peach season inside the dozens of square backed umbrellas round the clock, also leaving the Chicago west denizens of candy bars, chocolate bean, hard work on the runner anchor-steam carrot-bed mills, it was typical for hands to get cuts, for the body to await irreversible strains during the can month – and they intended to travel far west through the grain farm hat to the California fruit orchards on river basins and start their own marshmallow factories manufacturing boysenberry, cinnamon apple, peach and pear wine liquor cordials. Ten cents a barrel was a knuckle-joist finger complaint for fruit men who lifted crates all day, a rugged tedium of labor with little relief unless you worked raisins.

That winter Mathew shoveled snow off the track in the Wasatch peaks of Colorado for the rescue patrol on avalanches. Clean sweep whisks took hour after hour to keep school sidewalks chaste, road shovel to free roads, bean hammer to prevent snow piles in the tracks, branches were blown loose to get piles to relapse, and roads washed down until gutters saturated. Wine, stout, vodka and tonics like rum, brandy, chocolate cordial, rum cider, were stored in knock-overs in brick facilities being turned nightly, but whiskey made in great stills containing white bean mash took a cannon musket before it poured into the stew pot was shipped by special train to storage in the bins of Nebraska to be casked in sterns like cold rum liquid caramel glaze. It was around the year the wine casks purchased a train to run a dozen harker-operated rear axle rod bearing train along the six rivers of Florida to reach the St. John's Gulf. Many rod-harkers were born in Northern Ireland and went to tithe Harker's Mill in lots of two thousand journeymen, the chief employer run by the Bishop's Charitable Council commiserated under Cal Sperry the track masters John Kerry, Smitty Sams and Duggin Lieky. These four men trained able bodied crews to operate engine-dominated cotton mills, wherever was a mill there was also a hospital with ambulance. In America, where there were prison rum cantilevers there was the Midnight train which stopped outside the high wall, transported the tail Inside and took the rum to Alabama's coast wharves. On occasion the prisons manufactured a house bin coke like a WD-40 used in oiling vents, machines and cranks and this was taken to Kentucky, Oklahoma and Kansas to aid with mechanical improvements slashed out of twenty-one ore mines where a hundred and fifty men worked each mine, among these the clinker mines of Pennsylvania the strata ore blown by canister off shelf into open Union Pacific cars and transported to Colorado to freeze-combine plants to freeze loads into more easily managed turbine baths.

The bather as the oldest prison line was referred to took a car of paint mixed with pieces of wood and coal bin filled up a fifth down the speediest part of the Vergne run to Post Office City along with freeze ore and once dispatched made the rail in thunder speed to pick up the whiskey slew. The bather resembled in color an older man with blond hair dressed in blue pants and a striped red and white shirt was said to march the post mail and the barley rum plantation oil check from the Nine Yard to Post Office City with funds to construct towns for two hundred to reside and work. This was real money, tendered by the cattle mart, driven across the plains by saddle bag, the one and only pony mail money for people from other countries with little or no means. As luck would have it, upon completing the harker run and sweeping the trenches, Mathew returned via the Galveston Wind which sounded like a rail tinkerer clanking through the desert tornado dustbins through El Paso, Armadillo and Galveston along the coast to Florida's panhandle where wood from port battered long boats were burned. Moving through the spawn pools in dead of winter he stopped off in the countryside for a month's worth of stout and beet bread to visit his longtime friend John Wrangell whom he figured had to be in the thick of it whether or not he was aware of it. His older brother William had served the Flying Huntsman off the coast of Virginia boating about looking for broken boats and steering them to harbor into covered berths for examination and repair. Obviously a train getaway gone awry had other steerage, in order to obtain warehouses in the west, one had to have a way to get there during all seasons. Backed into a passage by hurricanes, they must have underground railroads, Mathew reasoned, and all beneficial expertise eventually became drawn upon like a dormant account. He knew it was a matter of time before the eldest sons took the Appalachia railways apart, they were a fierce set of narrow framed, self absorbed, cantankerous ditchwater blonds who but for their impulsive ruthless ideas may have been capable oil, bag, or steam shutter. For Mathew who perceived an unusually accepting and non judgmental nature in his friend the weekends spent at the Wrangell Ranch were looked forward to along with a cloying degree of persuasion he could learn a thing or two. There was nothing quite so relieving as good whiskey ale, meat stew pie and sugar crème custard to forget the sailing avalanche blizzards and stinging chapped skin. He had his heart set on John's cousin, a long legged sassy dark honey blonde who was studying milk canteen at the whiskey run college in New Angst ell. It would be a fall invitation to ask her to ride with him to low tide in Matamoras to stay the weekend in the tepid Laredo heat. When she agreed, they boarded the Sundowner; silver thistle barley blowing every which way, fields looking crimson dusted, they took a coach on the gulf side, ocean rippling like a bright oar dipping in gleaming pale blue. Mathew brimmed at the idea of having no thought except that his bonny lass Eloni in hiker jeans, a black red flannel shirt, and boots would by nightfall be his and he could pull her away from a morass of impending violence and degradation.

Mixey swam against the powerful current. Utilizing a long continuous crawl he swam miles, infra-blue goggles spying any shallow cove upon which a grounder might rest, her usage unpredictably scuttled. Despite prevailing winds and scoop full waves he took the weather with fortitude fractioning against exhaustion and heaves. At length some five miles from shore, small towns in evidence east and west, he spotted the railing of a submerged schooner, high berth, three decks, two lifts, and long platform on which sat a dark black and silver train compartment presumably capsized by big waves, speed or grounding. A glimpse through the hold told him the ship carried pulverized stone and gravel and was probably bound for southern Louisiana. The waves ran roughshod over the bulwark, the contents would have done better on a barge tow, oddly weather to course must have matched in order to plot course. When he returned to his cabin on Spanish Cay he'd check the number of ships anywhere in the gulf which he expected was twenty to thirty per month for all carriers despite the fact he didn't think loss had been declared. This idea of giving a small ship a send-off far from the assessment of port station command was the sole rationale he could think of for hiding money, stuffing scuba diving protected sealed packages into the boom of the throttle bench secure from prying indictments. Always the desk task for any strip assessor was first to determine whether systems were accurately recording and then to look for loss; must be the oldest trick in the book to vamp goods at sea. Mixey was convinced this group of bank thieves turned to his target for many needed capabilities, the most desired methods to move money, let alone to move advance cars in a fast running herd. He unveiled his Coolpix and shot twelve underwater photos of the ship swimming onto the deck, unhindered by flippers he walked the stage, climbed through a portal into the carrying trevass beside the radio room, removed a package good as gold, slipped it inside his wetsuit and shot another dozen of the remaining marked bills; his next job would be to move the schooner south ideally to an inlet with tracks and replace the compartment with a burned engine from the Nebraska red bean fiasco. Once this was achieved, there would be hell to pay, the target would surface. Newspapers on the subject would report the find, the waters annihilated by sportsmen having only the aim of getting the payload west would run the trains seeking what sped along the coast which was the Sundowner.

The finalizing methodology for this group had been to scare down the containers removed onto other rail lines and grease them with shoveled breakages. There had been the notorious South Carolina derail followed by the Birmingham stoppages and the Tennessee plunge into the river and then the Nebraska derail and fire, and the crashing Washington state derail by an awakened bear that ran headlong into the train while escaping alleged lights of a gigantic storm. None of the states fared well, the Carolina track demolition closed the line into interior Florida, the Tennessee derail shut down its line, the Nebraska lost its coveted contract with white bean and never regained corn. Whiskey Ridge went home to California for six long years. The gospel South went dry, strata ore workers boasted the least tonics in bars throughout the spendthrift. The lines through the west shut down their transportation through Detroit and car manufacturing grinded to a halt. In time California instituted car manufacturers to take the slack while new unemployment rampaged the older columns of the once well established world of finance bringing seas of men seeking work to a coast formerly known for its wheat and barley.

After two days spent in the gulf waters he and three penalty hard drivers had all but eliminated cove track replacing the New York railways into the Deep South, they left wheat king compartments standing dry in Houston, Yuma, Parker, and north in the Rockies, Boise, Spokane, and Portland to be encountered, the money vanished, the roar and squeal of train lines running throughout the night – in rode the fruit sugar gin makers of the east coast inventing new ways to discover money carrying torches invading small farm towns, government city hubs, docking bays, marsh canyons steering delta water from dams through rice and corn fields sinking prosperity at every turn bringing a gauntlet to corral the orchards and burn the beef. These men sought the persuasion of control, as a group of self willed despots they opened a slaughterhouse in Richmond's clover fields, they supplied every butcher and restaurant, taking over the growth of fields of acorn, poor till of Aragon wheat, oats, apples and sprout to feed cows, until they had sufficient call once more to obtain a rail line monthly, enough to compete with the Carne beef out of Mexico and the fruit and herb wines used to marinate beef. Until they shepherded cattle which grazed freely in the wilds of Colorado, it was veal, poultry, pig and carne for regularly consumed staples of diet, and fish brought in in crab trawlers, bass for Petrale sole, tuna albacore canned by Albertsons and Nifty, scallops and prawn, another Carne weed feeder from the gulf. The original bandits came from twenty-two families from Naomi Place above Sturgeon Cove flooded the Appalachia for apple and wheat gins earning their production on nets at sea and filtering stouts made off fruits, canning jams, syrups, wines and ladle. Mixey's last recommendation was to scourge them away from sugar production which was to presumably drive them off the coasts leaving them without benefit of irrigation, cove track, dock bench or sail.

6.

The night ripened beneath plains of red chili, sweet and fulfilling. Mathew stood on the porch of the El Centro Rose, thousands of stars commanding a warm breeze, in the distance high tower tiny yellow effervescent street lights aglow over the barren basin of desert, tumbleweed careening about blowing against herbaceous sagebrush on the pink and beige sand. The clock read ten-thirty, a wayward man's time to consider destiny and the responsibilities of raising a family on an agrarian or mining pay. The train had reached its end destination and awaited the delivery of the week's saddle bag which when hailed into Amarillo would begin construction of a wharf and town of a hundred and sixty homes, two elementary and one secondary schools, a law library, a sheriff office and clothing shop and breakfast diner. He had grown accustomed to fetching saddle bag disburser government funds having obtained finding checks for a city in Washington state to be known as western allied Sea Cattle Stowage, a township in Minnesota called Green Bay to manufacture cans for fruits, another township on the Great Lakes known under the little used penmanship title Barge Run, and a host of train towns in western Missouri and eastern Nebraska. The saddle bag itself was insured by Safeco at an previous unheard of restriction of a thousand dollars. The job offer from ACME had come as a surprise although offered to all bag handlers, but to accept meant travelling on ship to Mexico and to leave his close friend John he felt like a traitor. The risk work meant less available time, the only real way around the dilemma was to pack Eloni and their daughter Lou home to John despite a knawing concern that the older brothers had conducted to a train crash with Sinner. He had thought about it for the entire day what it signified for John to wind up without close friendship, to have no one to take long walks through the wheat, to be alone in a fishing boat on the winter snow fallen lakes. Because John had imparted a good length of discussions having at their locus trips into the forged mountains of the Wasatch and further, to the canvassed peaks of the white plains, it did not strike Mathew as far-fetched to believe the burning collision of red bean with wheat was planned to remove the eight thousand foot high rail in favor of an easterly route descending into Fork from on high through the rugged river basin of Iowa as had been considered if Missouri took over chafed wheat. Many a lonesome awakening was chased away by John when together as they socked away a quart of whiskey they wept tears of laughter at the finer items of life they had each foregone in favor of work. He would be nowhere without this tall skinny man, he'd still be driving the coal without a house to sleep in.

The tangy peppery spicy scent of chili collected around him much the way fireflies did when he was a boy living in his aunt's home in north Charleston. He came from a boy's institution after his mother, a young fifteen, eloped with a married corn harvester and his father left home to take a job in the strata ore mines sending half his check for the boy to his sister. Mathew came of age with ninety other homeless teenagers learning to read and write and study a trade which for him was furnace shop. If he erred on the side of conservatism, it was because he watched many a foolish notion of older, headstrong boys' intent to have their way over short term ambition get roughed up and become recalcitrant annoyances to their priests. When after repetitions of coaxing failed to engender tradesmen of the lot of five or six of them, he forgot them also, joining the church choir, preparing lunches for the college students and going off to work at sixteen with his uncle to the Braxton mills to pour ore for steel and at twenty with the help of his father took his first job on the New York to Georgia railways hauling lumber. Such as life for an inwardly shy young man, he kept to himself, a good natured wave to the Wichita linemen, speaking when spoken to, recording in his passbook and otherwise fetching pail and shifting up-gear. John was like him in character, a conventional bicep, on occasion a repair train stuckey, a saddened expression which became him like a mask, talkative in private opening up with scrutinized observances and rare humor. Together they made a family, knowing every little detail about each other; John had not married because he wanted always to work the line, a mild flirtation gave John no hope, girls liked to tease, he didn't believe they saw into him. He'd raise the matter to him and John would reply it didn't matter and Mathew would intuit he was crushed neither to have been asked and to feel abandoned, but Mathew would go adhering like an adhesive to John's inward denials that things would change much like the sting of betrayal.

"If you considered it from my point of view you wouldn't go so far," his young wife replied, pregnant with their second child in her nineteenth year.

"John said he would help raise the children," Mathew put out, to convince her. "It won't be forever, it's a half year in Guadeloupe to learn top to bottom astronomy, five months to run the repair line on the Boston line and then a year in the Virginia peaks before I am eligible to take my first four and a half months vacation. Then it'll be like you won't be able to get rid of me."

"William won't know you," she answered pleading with him to reconsider, already determined to mend any rift that might exist between Mathew and her eldest brother.

"He'll take to me if you tell him I'm working and I'll be

returning home."

"But he'll be walking, you won't have held him in your arms, awakened for feedings, I'll be alone."

"My dad worked in the mines."

"Yes, there's that, having to live outside the home."

"I lived with my aunt until I was nine."

"William said it is tantamount to desertion."

"I can't persuade him to any reason, he's not a thinking man. Please don't fuss, Sweetie, I will be home soon."

"It's just such a long time."

She was right, it was a long time to be absent. He resolved as soon as this run out of Centro was over that the first moment he was home, he'd talk to William, see if they could tussle through their differences, but Mathew grew uneasy at that idea. William was jacket width, bull-headed, a bit of the tantrum when he had to explain himself. He was also steeped in bourbon pitch frequently sauced to his eyebrows, a ladies' man at the speak-easy, a bouncer in the parking lot. Life for him consisted of proving his iron fist and the older he got, the more chiding he became. There were numerous times he had attempted to mildly coax William, but his argument was always the same, the red bean used only the carne meat out of Mexico, that by itself brought in the illegal aliens even if the beef itself was Texas marm. He and a bunch of the boys rustled cattle through the loop driving steer as far north as Colorado corn and one day they were going to run the cows into the Pacific as far as anyone was concerned. The Appalachia was designated for ore by the post office, thus no one could stampede so much as a steer and the Missouri plain, flat as slaked lake water, was meant to farm beef, not simply to put it into a can with chili and bean.

The eye witness ducked out of the blue ridge Tennessee sunlight fast before someone recognized him throwing himself into the pig car and releasing the brake immediately speeding out of control down the rail track. Anyone who rode stackers knew there were two brakemen and two oil cans per eighteen hours. William stood out like a sore thumb, so did Silver who joined up for furnace pot on single engines causing a red bean man handler, who did the chore of taking excess fluid from the radon room, to call him Simmer. Shouting as though to invoke thunder William said no to traitors; Simmer sprang to life with unguarded menace yelling no to carne men. Their argument with John took the bucolic absolutism of rim exchangers, steel crate shaft buckles, an unholy charge of assault and battery wielded at a well meaning substitute dad who in recent months put in pool spill work in the weather mines. The penetrating climate killed a brother, young John, putting a mere twenty-six year old into a grave causing the insurance corporation to send Mathew home.

The body, the pistol clean center wound near the left ear restitched, lay inside the nine foot long box outfitted in blue woolen leggings, a ruffled white bib starched color, confederate gray with red weave at the cuffs, dark brown boots, a bolero to winch a hat. Eyes closed, John appeared given to God, his taciturn manner a pledge into death. Mathew was astounded at the sorrow the sight of his very good friend aroused, tears smarted and he wept openly, his wife pressed against him, her lithe petite figure a reminder that they had been cut adrift. As the minister intoned the memorial, Mathew swore he would one day find a way to take William for his meanness. He lovingly wrapped an arm about Eloni's shoulders, her calf-length lilac silk dress blowing in the slight breeze, a handful of rich Tennessee Bulgur wheat dirt tossed onto the coffin. She lay her face against his shoulder in contrition; beside her the two children, a girl aged three and a boy age one, stood in confirmed obedience, their uncle's presence reassured by a half dozen oil can and tinkerer.

It wasn't just an ordinary argument. John lost to his brother because he also went to work at Consolidated Engineers at their train ties. The understanding would always be an uncomfortable suspicion that William who worked there first before John did had learned a method to flood the poop and submerge a train engine. The witness drafted a disposition to the insurance carrier that read, Simmer drove the barrage to the hearth.

Lewis Lewis had the letter with the engineering report on his desk. Hoyt had given an analysis of the condition of the poop. There in old town Galveston, along three city blocks that ran north by four county blocks that ran east, the unhinged poop had laid waste permitting an unheard of depletion of coastline to become submerged beneath tonnage weight of ocean until it put unauthorized banks, western telegraph and separate track twenty-eight feet underwater. Inlaid tile rooms the size of a train station sat immersed, hallways, stairwells, janitor closets, ticket counters, all gave lost fare into the devouring tide. It was anyone's guess whether the furnace cans on the Galveston Wind had unwittingly stumbled onto this truth, whether William or Simmer was sent by other killers to straighten up the mess. Lewis compiled his own conclusions that the poop was blown intentionally – the objective being to eliminate the whiskey train, the Dueno Norte, a fire engine red banger-knocker sounding locomotive dubbed the El Centro Rose which tore down the coast one day a week to meet fate at the exchange to the Kentucky-Tennessee bound Gal Wind Express. A much coveted photo had been taken of her as she charged cattle-run style skipping all stations hell bent on arriving to a Tennessee crash that cantilevered an incoming train to plow right into the outgoing one shoving the outgoing into the river. The fact that it was William at the stern and not the assigned engineer made the crash a hostage saddle.

He had a dirge of photos showing William, his brothers Ed and Darrell, and Simmer along with a Roscoe lookalike wearing chin masks on white and brown appaloosa horses galloping alongside the rushing train as it gained momentum traveling at a hundred and ten miles an hour having left Arkansas and entered Kentucky, staging a jump in unison, killing a train conductor and oil can and tossing the other engineer overboard to befall great injury. Each photo required lists of documentation, and he sat at his computer pulling up last known addresses, work registration permits and thumbprint, proof of mail delivery under the correct name, copies of cancelled pay checks, physical whereabouts at work yards, and any toxicology lab slips or pharmacy documentation. It was going to prove hundreds of hours to reconstruct each known crime scene, to institute some sort of ballistics, blood spatter and pathology, proving who held the killing weapon and who attacked solely by their hands. In these train takeovers, murder was proved by serious bodily harm, assault and battery, assault with a deadly weapon, or armed robbery or any combination of forcible entry. In one photo each act he had Simmer beating the injured conductor with a billy club such as what police at the ore mines used to break up a skirmish and breaking his dinner plate over his head. Each photo would convict. He had come across all types of bad violence in his career, but these were slut acts most probably paid in advance by someone who worked a business that these trains supplied. It was entirely possible no one who could reasonably be expected to have seen these robberies would come forward in person, less likely they would always deny. They had gotten lucky. The lineman who mailed the letter was the best they could wish for. Thus, he wrote on the file cover, all witnesses eliminated.

The fact was after he received Mixey's underwater photo he had a clear enough file of the target and could cross correlate the man to the Tennessee derail. The target was selected out by his legs swimming through the open train doors; he pushed upward without observable arm movement, his leg length being remarkable, like strong tentacles practiced at swimming in weeded murky waters, his length was one of those circled, he rose up through the twenty plus feet with few thrusts going for the circle of light that coalesced above the river, no stranger to the water. Had he to guess they had him point position fixed in Washington State in the Potomac River angling himself to the surface in minutes, swimming in an expert crawl making his way from the frenetic disaster relatively unseen to the shore. Mixey had gone the dive with this culprit who was proving to be support for hidden money, a Muni fix operator beneath the ocean who possibly arranged the east coast, South Carolina-

Georgia derail, who made overtures to ghost riders, who was as familiar with dustbowl and corn train lines as the ten to twenty mud pile track plows who held seasonal jobs in springtime. In Mixey's P9000 underwater carryall shots the target emerged a mile off the cay at midnight, a sharpened figure in a rising wave who made the beach in an hour, a spritely running man in moonlight without a shadow losing his ability to be seen several minutes after he was on land. A match to a fully hooded canister man wearing retardant wear on the Nebraska rail he had flung himself off a tunnel onto the speeding train, and in seconds was a sprint runner, a tangled web with the wear and tear of an inside-shelf safe builder knowledgeable of plank flood, sewage compartment fire and moving terrain. Within seconds he had disposed of the clutter sieve, poured a fluid into the car and tossed in a flame, moving stealth capable to each latch and issuing the same fury until the cars raged like demons in the night.

Lewis searched days before he found his man again. The target was filmed underwater somewhere south of the Galveston plunder in a safe made from a two-hole detonation into ore for which the interior was the sixteen foot height of a train engine with two top feet to spare and a block of track too wide for small case bins. There was no corresponding photo of an idle engine said to be sent to a repair yard in Mississippi after it cremated during the Nebraska crash with the victim red bean crop train. An all out concerted effort tracked Simmer and Wrangell but without success. The self styled wine makers evaded encroaching dragnets managing to retract their fleeting footsteps into small towns along partly flooded coast tracts. He decided there was a war at large, Rhonda described it as the populace fetching their honey walked the line from the silver ridge foothills into the charcoal brimmed boysenberry footloose journeys of moonshine bottle makers to secure their version of rum vodka.

Causality was a problem to determine. Jones left a vegetable beet, leek and tomato salad and afternoon tea barely consumed. It was not in his nature to look for a rationale, his task was to take apart crimes and provide convicting photos, conversations, and hard evidence, he did not invent news opinion, a crime was whatever occurred, wherever it had happened. Voice match was brand new although Tennessee State had recently installed a voice-recognition system to match against established documents, Department Motor Vehicles, prints, birth registration, mail trace, aliases but it was controversial getting kicked about in the courts by defense attorneys, advocates rights and illiterate rights. Because the system borrowed after an Australian indoctrination also required a repetition of documents over a span of four years on boat, train and resorts to be operable, the use of it although limited to confirmation of address was a big bang throwing onto the computer additions of employer status, vital statistics and credit bureaus, and then came the stuff of which martyrs were made, the actual physique, facial bone structure, color of eyes, shape of nose, mouth, chin, ears, location of scars and tattoos, and speech deficits, accents, idiosyncrasies. This made the identification field wide open, trimmed criminal associations, determined any trespass, break-ins, vehicle theft, run-of-the-mill robbery, shoot-outs, with a half sentence containing name.

The trademark surfaced with one question heard above a dog barking and snow falling. Auto recovery automatically filed in numerous indexes, the entry being, "Hey, Shawn, come take a look, no more bark line, the creek is gushing water," William said to John, as the two brothers de-planked the Missouri kitchen in the snow and while the gas truck fueled the train engine they wandered along far the path to the pond filled by the fisheries. In two days the mark had collected other voice imprint matches. It came as a stunner that although John Wrangell never met Bob Roscoe, because Darrell Wrangell reviewed train yard photos for a living and recorded the original threat made by Bob to William about John working an overnight train that captured John's plea of terror – don't do that, don't hurt me, please.

Jones kept the tape locked into place as he searched for any archived photo zoom lens shot. Even the Pan Am 747 from Tokyo to Honolulu was collected in less than ten minutes showing the sixteen year old boy blown out of his seat. Despite the fact that forty agents had been assigned to investigate the Wrangell murder once it was known that John's chief assignment aboard the whiskey train had taken a bomb, Jones couldn't recuperate the data as quickly as he might have liked. The computer listed queries one after the next primarily for work schedules of years ago as it considered whether a device or chemical had been used and who besides William could've obtained it. His fingers did the typing and he flew through notepads for any item any on-track camera might have taken while the trains were unloading. The train world was less complicated than the airplane scene, with no loss of image as a result of damage and debris, but the main frame ran slowly, accumulated even more deliberately and cabled by phone through other countries at the rate of a snail. Intel was the winner, the amazing wand of calibration, zeroing in on utterly minute seemingly insignificant bullish detail, having been trained by Hoyt's first expert trainer to stampede the field while separating congruent sounds; over time one eventually did everything and built a repertoire as to how to look at new requests for information. Underwater was highly specialized, Intel Block 5 recorded splashes, drops, wind ripples, Westerly's, light blizzards shedding snow in water, then tracked the environment to an individual when possible; often a domestic argument had fought its way to the sort of sounds which were produced, often the bale net contained a dead dog or some other ridiculous blind and this had to be researched for weeks to make certain a weapon had not been utilized. The Intel radio band station operators were always on standby listening for the presence of Iron Curtain, Czech, and anarchists on the loose. In addition underwater often recorded using an overlay of a dark shade measured band so as to produce instantaneity of watery depths. Just because the operative Mixey had not yet produced a verifiable name or a frequently traveled vehicle – car, German, French, Dutch, Citroen, Volvo, Bug, jeep, van or sedan – or often traveled luggage, American or Italian to Lake Como villas, Santa Croce, or unmarked pistol which had a signature bullet-cork-stopper for a European, Greek, Spanish or Israeli leverage, it didn't make sense that John Mixey nevertheless knew where he was likely to be found.

They agreed after the target was photographed by a clear underwater visual that the flowing red hair was indeed the man everyone was after. No matter who followed, waited across the street from cafes, traveled with him on the train, chased him to the acropolis, to Avignon from Paris on board the TGV, on a coach for days to the museums of Buenos Aires for wine tasting a good porto or dry vermouth martini and tour guided sightseeing, the comments remained the same, "looses you on a train or boat, no good under the canopy, not a newspaper or snappy drinker." The four three course shipboard dinners and buffet breakfasts placed the target agents who used similar techniques to John Mixey or Steven Might best tracked bringing target into view occurred in the islands and in the South America cape. He was at each no more than a day, taking photos through a view finder, needed to dive a train off a coastal shore. No one knew whether it was the Parthenon or the nine days on the ocean running off the ship plank every afternoon to see a new ruin that became the source of his clandestine functioning. But for service charges, baggage handling and taxi fares, he didn't exist except on the brackish water rivers of the prairies and low ridges where he impressed those he came across that he was a mere hick.

One had to get used to living with disaster. Tension was unending, stress burned, deadlines pushed, determinations while a relief relied only on tested reliability and proven hypotheses delivered by conferencing weak proofs. He left word with Mixey's wife Nila that he was taking a break to walk down to the kayak deck, strolled to the bay, the sky a severe metallic grey indicative of rain. He found himself thinking over the years with Rhonda, he resented her presence here, felt in having found her newly closed off emotion stifling, a long lens burden lay in retrospect, he was finally beyond her, again by himself willing to give himself over to Mixey's wife. From his point of view although she wouldn't be typing up his research as she had done for Mixey, for Jones allowed no one into his inner sanctum, they were a two person team, support active but nowhere visible, retreats taken abroad or in the woods. Tomorrow they would return, lounge on the beach with sugar rum martinis, compare notes, probably inside of a week rent two sturdy jeeps to Quantico to review the sum of photos on overheads. Mixey would fly the red eye to Italy, Might to Cairo. Once the target was tracked worldwide and was recognized, the job was over, information denied, team coordination would dry up and become elusive.

Nila waved from the restive kayak completely in control of the rocking waves. Jones waved back, waited for her to pull alongside the porch, stepped in and took an oar.

"Ready to depart?" she asked.

"Ready as I'll ever be. I found several good likenesses of our bed knocker."

DATELINE, Kansas City. Received over communication train conductor screaming, "Oh, my God, there are four Falcon airplanes swooping at moving train threatening to crash us. They came out of nowhere."

GEORGIA

ONE

His tires screeched to a stop before he started up again.

Jones chased the blue 1985 Maserati in his Carolina Chevrolet coupe, half black, half white roll-top special at sixty miles an hour through the dockside asphalt yard of brick warehouses that constituted the southern Quantico packaging station. The Cape Fear inlet of beige, yellow and silver glass high rises six to twenty stories at most with trim wood balconies stood stark against a clear blue sky. On the canal a row of cabin cruisers teemed with morning sun bathers washing down decks, fueling up, preparing for a weekend on the ocean in the jet stream tradewinds. Out to sea where the bluest of curling waves collided surfers paddled on fiber glass boards. Jones gunned after the Maserati intending to fence him into a dead end. He circled past a restricted demolition sandlot where an excavation crew had brought in three tractors and a scorpion shovel and clipped him on the right roadway that led to a forsythia hedge lined frontage road and clamored yards behind him, steering wheel spinning, up the curved driveway to the second floor of the car lot and kept pursuing. On the third top floor the Maserati slid to a stop in front of stairs, the driver jumped out into the open, a brownish face, black tight fitting garb, pulled open the metal door leading to the stairs and disappeared. Jones considered driving down back onto the street but thought he would miss him and parked grabbing his key, leapt from his vehicle and ran after him. He could see him escaping through the half raised car lot, he charged for him gaining on him until the man careened through the air over the railing.

They ran through the warehouse alleys. The other man dodged Jones around corners, beneath a newly built steel floor of what was to become an elevator lift for large equipment, and darted out onto one of five docks, up a narrow plank onto the Queen Elizabeth entering the velvet and gold ensconced ballroom and pine wood lounge where when the ship was three miles on the ocean dance entertainment, nightclub singers and fashion shows paraded down a runway. The man climbed the center stairs, exited onto the outside deck, gave chase to an observation deck and flew overboard. Jones cursed, he should have seen it coming: the target was obviously extremely fit, agile, a mean bullet logjam. Seeing no sign of security, he called into dispatch again to notify them that they had a floater.

The file had been bumped up to Field from Domestic Division. It was a routine splash of color glossy photographs primarily of the college town Bremerton on the coast, of windows, nothing too exotic, except that the exposed graveyard galleys of basements in surrendered high rise office buildings constituted every single last file Quantico Recovery ever looked at. There were dozens of bare pits, cement block and foundation dirt that a group of a hundred men had removed by chain saws, digger picks, turn shovels and water hoses. Despite the fact that the Federal Bureau had formed solely for this reason, and had over the years added floods that submerged entire suburbs, the dismal reality came in a swift comprehension that although a high rise had been gutted no one knew until a discovery was made, usually by children playing underground in a tottering building. Attached to the folder was the deciding question, where does the target live. The terminology target actually originated with investigations for which architectural design developers staged high rise buildings far enough away from a major freeway but for one reason or another wound up producing vibration to adversely affect the amount of time buildings would stand. Target became moving target when impact zones were evaluated for potential debris as a result usually of hazards.

Jones had thumbed through an eleven year-long hazard inspection conducted by the U.S. Attorney General Office listed as AGO so as to find a probable site the targets wanted to attack next. Although the assigned agents made every building contusion angle to Ground Zero, no links had been proven. Of the beliefs the team had kicked about, two stood out as probable – first an illegal demolition meant sellers and advance men were more readily induced to be fences and second, once the property was laid clean real estate was cheaply sold. There were other ideologies involving foreign renegades and beefing up police regimens, it was convenient storage for weapons, it relieved instant pressure of water mains indicating reduced blockage, toilets didn't overflow, the list was usually misconstrued. He had been with Field so long, almost forty-four years that he had viewed virtually every ground beneath government buildings. Few began as grassy knolls or were laid bare that he had not stood on, fewer contained any ruptures or fractures indicating potential slippage. Despite the fact that skyline property did the worst – the waterfront was either too chilly, not dense enough, at the surface of the water, or had been erected without proper foundation – these frontage roads extending a few hundred yards remained choice land often fetching fifty, sixty thousands before buildings went up. He had often thought there was a group that gained access to landside turf no matter who bought or who built, unless houses were put down, then all was well, suburbs fared the best.

He had encountered the Maserati man emerging quite unself-consciously around eight at night from an older, thirties tenement brick and stone Harry Belafonte style building along the lower east side below Sixth. After dark the moon shone like dark fluid in an inkwell shimmering on the coast of Cape Fear like a rogue making a debut butting against mortar and steering himself home staggering and bumbling. A near-miss caught Jones' attention and he decided to have a look-see. He was anticipating a drunken party well underway, but as he turned into the stairwell fascinated by four or five descending levels of wood crafted pigeon-cage stairways with bric-a-brac floors, as he stepped down he became aware of a dank chill that burned the body with its cold. He gazed up at an equally impressive series of ascending stair levels, small white and black hexagon shaped tile floors barely perceived. At the last as he landed on the bottom landing instinct caused him to open the door. He stared into a boarded up room of sorts, he thought the damp was a leaking pipe because with the draft derived a sense there was an ice vein rising through the soil. Jones punched at the boards on the other side and wrenching one loose discovered that three basement walls were mostly eliminated and the tarantula wood, most of it virgin new, that held up the building enclosed dirt-like cement that had been removed to form a tunneled shaft with several vehicles lined bumper to bumper. An hour later when he returned with a building inspector for the Norfolk County they consulted the aegis for what ought to exist to discover more than eighty percent of foundation had been reduced. He would have placed a leasehold on the useable part of the building prior to renovation, but the county listed the property as condemned, tacked up a sign to that effect on the sidewalk, sent a work order to the industrial cost repair department, and that was that.

Under the street light of the Intel, the Maserati man came up like a sweet-smelling daisy, clean behind the ears, slicked down wavy black hair, a cheap cologne three piece tweed suit and rose colored man's shirt, and equally as casual gentlemen's leather mock-toe wingtip shoes, looking all the sport for a day at the races or a stroll-about the fairgrounds carnival. Fingerprints brought up another man, older, more jounced, sags pulling beneath the eyes, not so relaxed or mindful. Jones went for the credit card for the business suit tailor. The credit card read Jim Mills, and the fingerpints agreed, but the expensive white wheels said Nicky Coventry. Some alias, if they were the same leech.

Neither name resided in Dutch town; neither was a boozer or Greek tavern regular which is where the angle-work placed him three out of four days. Jones tagged Coventry for months visiting office buildings until he had a list of eight rim-shield buildings each good as bust. It looked as if the man were inspecting his own fleet of ships for readiness until they bust or fell, Jones couldn't decide which even after the obvious sign of disaster when they swayed or cracked.

The four inspectors for Bremerton Department of Agriculture itself made a half day tour of one of the eight condemned. The brick, metal guttered, once handsome city center on F Street and Steeple crossing avenue stood between the sagging Harry Belafonte and Mildred Mortenstern building where the once famous German actress from Bork on the Rhine lived. These inspectors had been trained as morticians but due to the incidence of building land erection declarations after the fact they worked for the state evaluating both garden and roof. As had occurred with its neighbor, the ten story city center which was over fifty years old had noticed condensation under the floor space. The inspectors went through in merit bag suits, large puffy white or light red suits that covered them ankle to neck, recording on a clip-pad for drainage, attics, vent and air condition systems, exterior wall insulation, storage, halls, crawl space and interior cement room, kitchen, bathrooms, surface and slope of site away from outside window or stairs. There were other sorts of problems as well that indicated real trouble including buried oil tanks already leaked into the soil previous to an addition, crumbling stucco, rust, a hundred and fifty feet of foundation walls below the basement room, piers, wood columns, joists, and thick all wood beams. These problems produced sags in old plaster often inside closet extensions, flickering lights, but the severe items gave these men a stir. Even the Inspector Chief Thomas Pynchon, a understated slender accountant-looking blond haired man in his eighties, whose expertise came with college overhangs and heating and wind draughts was horrified over the condition of neglect. They wrote on the citation report – life was a garbage heap, a damp paper smell emanating from below the basement, cement plaster falling, electric live-wire lines poking out of ground, path like tunnels through the dirt to interior stairs, a floor hole looking into big wall-framed damp depression the size of a series of rooms stacked with a debris of sticks, rocks and glass and no stairs and door to the outside.

Five points said the problem was technically under the basement; the entire building of eighty offices or residential apartments were intact but couldn't be used for a damn thing. The county had twenty-five days before the building had to be torn down after the warning signs were noticed. The first problem was lights wouldn't go on inside the building although they might be glaring under the stairwells. Both the Belafonte and Mortenstern buildings possessed the identical look except for the underground lights. The rooftops gave in, water spouts on an exterior wall shut off, lights and outlet appliances in use crackled like crinoline paper, and hoses caught on fire. The Chief said it was the worst nightmare he'd come across in all his years of diagnosing sick buildings. Nothing was to be done to renovate this site short of wiping the slate clean. The trouble was demonic, the pipes were turned off but the gas was left on. Before submitting a case to Field Division, Chief Pynchon always looked for who was inside the building who could have entered the ground either from the street or by elevator down. Field had come up with other descriptions on past cases, the most common was a trench through a unused yard and the next most typical was a set of demolition wires connected to at least one vehicle draped into rods and were held concubine in metal rod like posts to every floor, when the vehicle ignition was started up, the building quivered indefinitely. They checked the original blueprints for where lots and garages should be found, but none had been built that far down. Exit egress, driveway slope, rain run-off, and stone non-porous and non-slippery pavement would in a final analysis contribute to the rapid decomposition with which a center wall shifted gravity essentially booting a building to its knees as occurred on campus at A Street and Steeple on the traffic row of the Princeton College Plaza when the men's college dorm slipped and fell into a hole.

Two

Princeton was the male ivy league school located in Bremerton for anyone of principles aiming to become a physician of physical medicine. The college town was separated by five bridges and packed in between A Street, F Street, H, I, J, L and N Streets and in the direction westerly to east coast there were the busy three straight thoroughfares Honoree, Steeple and Governor, each northwestern corner along I Street had an industrial hospital rising seven floors and ambulance dock with three ambulances ready. Approved buildings were constructed on non wharf avenues, streets and alleys that despite being situated at one end on a coast or interior boating canal and bay nevertheless did not share ramps leading onto the wharves. Where problems arose, especially for soil sedition and loss of determined road ends due to encroaching water, the roads on rising sloping hills did far better than their boutique and ski rental with boat turn-outs off dock. In interior state situated Cape Fear the small town of eight hundred Bremerton homes, nine hundred square feet with ample living room overlooking red and dark salmon bulbs, kitchen off a deck and three bedrooms screened for the oppressive heat and jagged lightning and sixty, eight story stucco office buildings lay on the coast some two miles from the high high bridge into District of Columbia, in an utterly muggy complaint given summer season and in through autumn lifting clouds over oily squalls jetting on the Atlantic muddy choppy gray. As a result of the dorm corruption, the streets nearest the college were redone every year to year and a half, new dark salmon color stone stairs, annual changing of extravagant flower beds on the central campus, hibiscus, dragon fly and thorn-less yellow, white, dark crimson and blue rose bushes, cafes, restaurants, smoke and magazine shops, camera stores, paper supply, bookstores, dress shops, hotel lobbies, bakeries, and medical clinics were torn down on a regular basis, but without observable entry into the ground, the closest place which any hard hat entered was at the waterfront into tunnels that extended from the bay long past

Governor Street to the edge of the industrial financial hub. Crews came and left within a day to clean up the mess left by the college corner dorm. Inspector-chat alleged floor detritions were done by people living in the building at night while washing their clothes, joined by six foot two stolid shouldered men drank coffee until all hours when they departed into a parking lot and walked into the street covered ground of a baseball stadium.

Upstairs on the fourth floor of Quantico the seasonal Field agents arrived by the dozens pouring into tiny cubicles each of which contained a desk, phone and endless manuals labeled by year for changes in law and policy.

Three tips had ever come in by call-in's, each stated a location and implied demand.

"It's in the basement – no ground," possibly a reference to the World Trade Commodities Headquarters; but more likely was a quotation off an interview given a group of twenty campus students after another building lost its capability to turn on lights, or the call was made out of sheer horror as a result of having been there.

The second call, same voice tentatively identified by Voice Intel, was made during a spring semester break. "It's a axe pick."

The final call was transferred mysteriously to Jones' telephone. "Balancing act is inside; it is no Rome, Tennessee," referring to the bridge derailment.

Digital-direct dial by Intel Federal response by nearest camera and automatic capture for identity spit out a photograph of a tall wavy red haired male, who was no one known to any local agency. A walk-in claimed to have dual circuit housing authority experience for which he was questioned in a cell block room, as follows:

How did you get there?
Who brought you?
Were others there?
What was length of time you worked per night?
What did others do?
Were you paid?

How did you apply?

His answers gave nine men who turned out to be mathematics students who worked as bus boys at non cooking restaurants that served prepared baked goods and coffee on campus; three had to close out the register, one set the lights, one left a door open to a gate closing alley at predawn for the garbage truck. The chart map for campus security placed each man on the campus town at any somewhat frequently attended address, all went two days a week to and from Stilton Hall to one of eight math courses taught by three professors from Harvard's engineering department, all ate dinner nightly at the Addison-Montgomery Hall a block off the plaza on Grosvenor; seven rented and two lived at dorm buildings. Intel gave photos at eleven at night to three in the morning for unauthorized underground shelf demolition at which they shoveled a three foot wide path into the foundation of dirt. The man who opened the door for them to enter was Nicholas Coventry.

There was little to do but sit and wait on the waterfront for any sign of Coventry to show. The waterfront was like a maze of alleys and docking berths, there was nowhere a man in the water could go. Even with an outboard motor there was no out way from the bay which had been built like an aquatic park. Jones' guess was he would attempt to return at night. The situation was frustrating if only because he could not afford to put his attention on anything else and risk losing sight of him. Quantico prided its agents on their assiduous concentration of never losing grasp of a chase. The inspections could be re-evaluated again, but an agent on the prowl had only his wits. There was no time for exhaustion either; age was never expected to become a thwarted measure, if anything because he was Field Customs Jones was regarded in a classification by itself. Inspectors did not approve cooking, kitchen permits were granted by the state which oversaw licensed electrical and construction abeyance operatives. Life ran a short wire line to install an elevator. Inspections promoted up to date safety, did a building have safe stairs, sturdy floors, adequate lights, useable faucet supplies, flushable toilets, outdoor parking lots, safe furnace, non slippage of sidewalks.

The stack of photo files at his lab showed men pulling ropes hitched by cables with a good heave-ho as though they were ship deck hands working an Argus to steady it onto the ocean for sail. Dozens of photos taken from different angles, shot overhead from the sky onto a map of streets, interior of men slicing up the thickness of walls, cement-solidified soil, installing drainage pipes, hosing by use of a hydrant until the path became durable, a sick profession which depended on no good returns.

It occurred to him after two hours his target had chosen another avenue and was waiting it out in a boatyard. He didn't get out of his car, the target might steal his car, but it meant he had to be on the road when the target was. Jones turned on his computer, fixed coordinates on the beachfront park, checked seeking where Nick had entered, where he had gone. The agent group found his tracks in less than a minute, the B Street Bridge evidently too far to swim to for the stone stairs, he had climbed the G Street Bridge much the way parachutists climbed the Eiffel, looping a rope by claw and lifting above the perch line to stairs. His anger was momentary, a shooting star fleeting realization – he felt he had missed his mark, he had all but charged into Coventry, for which he could imagine paid time off, an embarrassment no agent was supposed to live down, but the more he thought it through he believed he had erred not to have exercised more aggression – during which in an instant he sized up the picture, the target was an underwater destructionist, probably turned everything to fathom-deep right there on the sidewalk grass lot. If he relied upon bomb diving, releasing magnetic nets as he descended by torch alone, they were in real trouble, because a man substantially agile to underpin in turbulence might be able to survive a planned descent to Zero. False addresses were a dime a dozen, although stolen usually from the obits, just as easily co-opted from old building addresses, claiming children they never had, trading off streets like they were names of immigrants engraved on a wall. There were many ways a person might disappear through seemingly legal identification.

Jones produced the analysis that these were adjuncts to stadium halls like the reception halls of concert or museum buildings, but perhaps the inspectors were correct, these were actually garden holdouts through which campus staff housed small tractors or made their way across campus emerging into gardens with statuary and ponds.

The computer gave him seven pictures on the target simultaneously for the past twelve hours. Coventry was at the courthouse on Governor and G Street off the bridge lift waiting on the steps for some old man, wavy curls like a patrician judge minus robes, at two o'clock he tanned on the beach in stretch stripes and went for a swim, at three-thirty he dropped off a brown parcel wrapped shoebox at a sunshine garden roof terrace on G Street near Steeple, and ten minutes later he sped from the Belafonte building having entered east off Spring Street and come out on the Haven Court western end of the stone plaza, drove his flashy collector's sedan barreling onto the street at a rocking horse speed of forty miles an hour. The parcel by itself would kill, a nice juicy split of Nick's underground activities were all he lock-framed onto his search designator.

Acts of deception organized themselves into target cornice and image-agreed searches as the man lived day to day, same with the nine winch handlers and rope conveyors. Jones had completed a mountain of image rockets on the art trash bin assignment just to find a breaking loose shattering piece of airplane window. After what seemed an eternity, the chase temporarily ended, each quarter hour the pillars accumulated until dozens of abutments, staircases, lawns and city signs created open drafts and cars parked on the street were tracked to determine if the target ever rode inside. For the six who got accepted to clerking jobs they enjoyed, had lots of friends, took photos of wonderful scenic vacations, the good life was over. The compiled photos doctored in four targets with no common sense who had a draw in their pocket, the Spears-Arnold paper shredding plant that rolled in easily fifty trucks in four hours, and their unscrupulous manager-waitman stored a half load for a stuffer job scheduled for burn, and out of the blue, here stood shaggy dog building owner Bartmueller and pretty blond grovel-at-your-feet Sameas, they drew a contract with Nick for new parking.

But a drive to the bridge took what remained of his mental calm. A lookalike Bridgeman-Adolf Gurion state mansion with leaded glass windows, four stories, beaming chandeliers in every room facing onto the street, chalk brick exterior, and marble-glass insert window panes showed the roof had sliced open. It meant there was utterly no ground beneath the basement.

The city had less than fourteen days to get the building down.

Typically there was a witness in the kill group. Jones betted on it especially since someone on the inside was talking to him. Difficult to know how bad it had to get before someone would tell, in the office they all took turns at guessing what act led to the turnabout but they knew they'd have to wait years for a kill to turn themselves in; when they talked, the whole city turned itself upside down, paranoia was at its worst, no one came out, they did all their work at their desks. He dialed Nila's number. He hated himself for calling to ask for help, but he told himself that Nila was a strong minded female, a skilled trench-dive broad-channel operator herself who would gladly come to his aid. Jones parked his coupe under a tree and walked across the grass to the docking bay.

In No Polo cove she had heard him out, listened intently as though with a taken by surprise understanding, long time away from intellectual input, and he hadn't missed the point, nor had he forgotten that one small act. Years ago, a seasoned operative who had more than one fall, Rhonda excluded, he still hung to the idea that all information was knowable and known, was manageable, despite much information to the contrary. Jones waited on the side dock in front of the fenced repair yard, a yacht propped onto a saw horse, boats steering out to sea at three knots an hour. Until Nila arrived an hour late steering a large canoe, he had time to decompress under the bright hot sun, nothing was ever forgiven, the dorm tragedy had housed forty to a floor, thankfully most were out to dinner; land zero was an entirely different idea than zero-frame landing which was a dead on the clock stop on a runway. He needed some crystal ball gazing right about now, in standard demolitions the ground was eliminated directly beneath the lowest kitchen, all gas mains opened, a balloon placed inside and tied to one main filling with air and once the balloon was filled with two tubing attachments to secondary mains and these were filled so air could escape, then building itself was detonated by wrecking ball.

Already he had wasted too much time waiting for her, he could have swum the yard to the undertow by now, she didn't seem to appreciate his schedule demands, who had energy for this, in his mind it was love them and leave them, who needed them anyways, the priority remained, Don't get involved. He turned to the jetty, began to walk to the stone wall on the ocean side and hit a wall, the pain to his foot so great he could barely walk or put pressure on it, he wasn't a beach bum the way Lewis Lewis was, it could be he was at last a resigned bachelor the way Hoyt had become, unused to the rigors of outside surveillance, almost an entire cadre retired at forty due to stupid, hair brained oversights. There was the element of surprise as an outboard with telephone ringing pulled into the harbor with a short change box attached by wires to the motor situated high on the deck cabinet at the rear. He ran like hell to avoid the blast as the switch was pulled, the man fell backward overboard and the boat exploded in plumes of gasoline fire that gushed into the sky. It was over in less than a second, but he knew he could have been killed in a second.

The crowd formed within minutes. Acid rain debris fell through the air. The black smoke with red flames spread across the sky singing the onlookers. Only the burst lost its detonation appeal except for wooden shards which floated on a surge of wave action. Somewhere a small child wailed, his mother's soothing voice attempted to reassure. A coast guard chopper and flag ship hailed onto the water from across the bay, siren captivating, as a wind whipped up. By now Nila had to have seen the goner and sailed to another wharf landing, but he'd let her find him, knowing that would be easier. He returned to his car, ears ringing. The blast occurring at the moment he arrived onto the dock couldn't have been a coincidence. He had to have been sighted, or one of the targets was waiting for him to step into the open. It made him wonder if the target couldn't do a job because he was being chased.

Jones had tracked a train murderer to his roots and it troubled him to know he could have let the man slip through his hands after he went assigned to a course of duty not even Lewis particularly welcomed, he returned to his car feeling a whirlwind of emotion, his nerves tingling with bracing rawness, his mood dejected. The crimes were piling up, two train bridge crashes, a murder of a train conductor, detonating three blocks of Galveston, all paid penalties of heavy metal, no one who killed would live. The target seemed to think he had God on his side, for a college such as Princeton with dozens of stairs everywhere including onto the beaches so no one could get stranded during high watermarks there were few inaccessible egress. This was a morgue town. Political appointments were granted to graduate practicing physicians with specialty in ear disorientation illnesses. There was a convincingly held belief that the disorientation was the result of having attacked a train. This was the presenting case of the surgeon brother of the famous author Lewis Carroll and these were his malcontent students.

Since the day the agency flew him to see the hole which was under a house and dorm he possessed no illusions that he was dealing with physicians whose practical expertise accompanied childhood, being reared and swam on the river with fifty boys from a boy's lower grades institution in the spray of a hydrant, who lived to see a child strangled underwater in the river and laid out on a sidewalk slab. Youths retained unmis-takable resins of despair and horror, and these crimes reeked of abasement and futile rangy futures. Even the fog that rose into the hills of the bicycle walking trail and drenched stillborn oaks and entangled wild sickly pungent gardenia covered so much as to sufficiently cloak the bay until the tide came in.

He had no reason to believe Quantico which dealt with basement floods for Homeland Security could handle such an eventuality of no land or zero windfall, let alone detonation-prone behavior. Here he sat waiting a competent below zero land scuba diver who might be late or merely an advertiser whom he wanted a relationship with. He glanced up at his rear view mirror to see Nila lying on top of his trunk and rear win-dow. She looked stridently youthful, her short black hair pasted against her chiseled face, trim in a wetsuit, promising.

THREE

They swam into the chill current.

She tapped her watch at him to signify eight minutes for the one tank and kicked into the murky depths. He followed closely behind. Here and about lay rusted pipes, some big enough for eleven year old boys to climb through. She adapted well to the tugging current staying adeptly on course. They passed below Washington Street Bridge looking for any underwater hatch. The water was warmer because it was in direct sunlight. Oddly enough the photo that hung in Sebastian Hall where the medical reference law library was of a centrifugal drainage seemed to have been photographed where the sunlight turned the river mud and vines bright catching green. He checked the air tank gauge. There were less than a minute.

When they came to the foot of the Charles Bridge monument they weaned their way to a platform. In minutes they were lifted into an out of water cave of dry paved dark grey and brown slate rock where an old rail line and corroded metal compartment stood. It was plain to see that the college at one time sneaked drowned victims into its warehouse garment district. A hiking trail led from the musty enclosure upstairs about forty feet into a clearing with two large older pink and beige, four story dormitories with sash windows and a door that led to a garden with blooming hyacinth. Several stone benches around cupid girl and boy statues served as respite for the weary who had climbed above the oceanfront boardwalk three blocks over from A Street past the sandstone medical college, law library and past the glass paneled cafeteria that was situated high on a hill.

They laughed when they reached open air, relieved, their eyes smarting with the intensity of cold.

"Jesus, I thought my lungs would about burn."

"I know what you mean," she said, but the experience had done her good because she radiated with the brisk cold.

Students congregated in an adjacent plaza, some with

take-out food, some with bikes mulling around a hot dog cart.

"My treat," he said, and purchased two wieners with mustard and beans.

They walked in the direction of his car.

"How did the dock look?" he asked.

"Like hell. I knew it was where we were going to meet."

"It was sudden; I all but glimpsed the detonator."

"I bet it was all shells and micro-radio-scopic flash."

"Seen much action of this sort?"

She gave a shrug. "More than I'd like to think."

"You know we've got an underwater downhill racer dirt derailer."

"I thought so."

"Yes, as the train moves the hitches release. It's referred to as heavy metal."

She kissed him lightly.

Worth the kiss, he decided.

She told him less than an hour later when they had boarded up inside his vehicle that she berated herself at mid-life for putting on a few pounds.

They made love in the sun room between sips of whiskey and samplers of vanilla frosted gingerbread cake. She was easy, matter of fact. He kissed her sweetly, passion stirred gradually, he was still asking himself how long a season she intended to stay. The wind shutters knocked about in the slightly open window like a clock slightly off tap. He wouldn't leave if he could help it, but four divorces were expensive putting an entirely different twist on love. From time to time whenever he felt not quite himself, a bit off track or queer as the British would have it, he convinced himself the long distance was better sprinted without a live-in romantic notion. He wasn't the type who could often win over a female; they looked him over and usually moved on. The idea of having another pro in the house seemed a good consideration, although he knew himself, he didn't enjoy the continual attention it took to start over. Half way through steak and eggs, she threw on her tan high waist jacket and a touch of purple lipstick looking decent in brown suede pants, a crème silk collar, tan raw silk scarf, and said goodnight. She was a bit too detached; he realized that Mixey must have been away usually.

She had left a note placed on the outside mat. In dark letters written with a charcoal brush, she wrote, "Next time let me know when you want your alone time."

He stuffed it into his breast shirt pocket and walked a block beneath the spring cherry blossom trees to his car.

At the office the floor buzzed with telephone conversations like opening hour on Wall Street. Agents with loosened ties and bedraggled looks, jackets hung, leaned back in swivel chairs tensing for new information, as the office mail clerk distributed bundles of mail. Jones had scarcely leafed through his small stack when the itinerary analyst called him to bring his notepad. He jumped to, walked through a center aisle passing the smell of burnt toast to the wire tap room.

Stoller ran all bugging. He was a shockingly handsome man in his mid seventies, icy blond hair bouffant like a female's evening style on the town. His office was immaculate to preserve his seventeen recording computers which meant never coffee, no donuts, no crumbs, a clean slate.

"I've got your foot sliced under the in-step," he said.

Jones opened his pad to a fresh page while Stoller switched on band receiver playbacks as though he were in the cockpit with his rubber finger.

"It's not there, I left it on the boat."

"How will I find it?"

"We'll send someone."

"How old will they be?"

Stoller shut off the playback, saying, "That's what I consider a good wireless conversation."

"No kidding. How deep do you want to go?"

"Let's get ourselves an actual obliteration chat." He flicked on another six switches on the calibrated monitor. "Here's the outer limit," he added, and plugged into the switchboard.

"How fast should it go?" said a voice from the previous tape.

"Ride the Wind, shoot for the wheat, calibrate without a recorder."

"Who will be the chase?"

"He is a dozer."

Stoller removed the plug. "Obvious connection between the Mexicali Rose and a boom box. We could convict the murder now that we found the pistol. Only wine draws a pistol. Voice brought in senior Wrangel. The dirt racer is another crime. That one is a projection off the Idaho Range."

"It must be that wading through snow compares to underwater dives."

"Actually we've never failed to find him. He does the lantern downhill run in late season. I have one more." He changed a dial setting. The voice was instantly familiar as John Mixey's target.

"We're in the home park. It looks like safes. The other is red beans."

"Who did you arrange?"

"Joint transfer. He did the House of Usher in Daly City."

"Oh right, the red brick tank house that fell onto a San Francisco bound line."

"I thought it went swell. We might try a little further up."

"Can we shoot the Carne on the route?"

"Depends."

"How many grids are there?"

"One, but it's not a good notion."

"What do you say if the high car gets kicked off?"

Stoller interjected, "That's the Nebraska crash. That's the ground car that flew off."

"Is anything else needed here to link these crimes?"

"There's no real point until the outbound through Emeryville, California, but that recorder stays with the engine."

"What would you call their outside gain?"

"It's probably to store ore coal coke."

"In Martinez?" Jones asked.

"All the way up. Vallejo."

"Ridiculous, there's no use for coke there."

"Not so, they did it for the eventual industry of producing car keys."

"Can't have car keys without purchase of a car. Doesn't make sense."

"That's nevertheless where coal ore coke has been since spent."

Stoller let the tape continue.

"How many times, powder on the track?"

"Three big piles, a dynamite charge stick per pile. Give it to the Wind, the long range, and Whiskey Mountain."

"All to wheat?"

"Don't ever touch a white bean."

Stoller turned off the machine. "Silver went into the air as a plane. That's all coal coke manufactures these days. Silver emasculate."

As far as Jones was concerned these vagrants worked coal for fifteen dollars a day, six days a week for four or five years before their bodies crapped out, two bucks a day went to pay the rent, two dollars for a week's groceries, fifty cents for the raisin mashed rum. They weren't satisfied with marriages, they either were domestic complications or more argumentative than living allowed.

Nila had left a message for him. "When I first met Mixey we went to a bar and got smashed. Every night thereafter we threw ourselves a big party. I hope your day's going okay."

He returned the call, but her line was busy. He thought he shouldn't say he did not need alone time or that he didn't know what caused her to say that. Perhaps she had given Mixey every consideration, or maybe she needed emotional distance. He thought she had lots of nervous energy, that she could pick up a cigarette and never put it down. He didn't think she ever relaxed. She impressed him as an 'eat and run' gal, it was probably the reason she was late. He couldn't read her yet.

"I love you," he said. He felt satisfied he had kept it brief. There were moments when he knew he talked himself blue past the tolerance of being listened to.

He was immersed in a plethora of building photos, corner gutters, uprooted parking garages, nails protruding below stair level stucco, peeling paint, unaligned bricks, pipes poking through soil, when Rhonda walked in, nice tan, blond curls swept off her neck, wearing a sequined black halter top, tight white pants and peeking sandals, toe nails polished pink. He glanced at her indiscriminately watching her arrive to his desk and place a report on his desk with a note to sign. He signed and handed it back to her.

"How's Nila?" she asked.

"Good. Thanks for inquiring."

"She was a diver on Galveston."

"I didn't know. Want to grab a drink in the courtyard?"

"Sure, I'm not expected for another four hours."

Three hours later he pulled into the drive. If not for the attitude that winner should take all, he felt certain he could have brought in a billow of anti-constitutional leniencies priced at the handsome penalty of an endowment. Rhonda was exactly herself, seductive, relating, a cornerstone of highly classified information. He listened to her for hours unaware how quickly the afternoon passed. For one item to be in the forefront and not be identified, in absentia, not realized at a token worth, that trains which ran nowhere near any corporate office was still an overriding design drew the entire matter into question.

Four

The rowing association building located in a pink wood and white stucco building on the Millstone River gave canoe and kayak instruction to students every spring and summer despite demands on their time for advanced research and intern law library sessions. Through archways under the scrutiny of silently querying gargoyles engineers from Frick Hall and Whitman passed their admittances to Penn Central and New Jersey Transit while invading the warehouse ponds and tropical rainforest wetlands utilized by the cotton mills for sport. Fishing for yellow perch, catfish and pike commenced in Kingston where the Millstone flowed into the Delaware at Griggstown at Suydan Road bridge. Of all the counties including Bergen, Essex, Hudson and Union all the way to Trenton Mills, it was Bergen which overflowed its banks and flooded roads off highway 83 on a yearly basis increasing marsh by an average of six inches per month beneath the Conrail Bridge at the west end. Rising above the historic civility of stone landmarks stood the gold dome of the Trenton courthouses, the eventual aim for local Princeton law graduates from the Whig and Clio campus honor roll sanctums of cathedral interiors. End summers were spent far from the scenic ballrooms on Passaic and Delaware River basins and in Atlantic City on the beige sand expanse of beach that made up the seductive monies of east coast gambling and racketeering of clothing and trade moguls. In all of this learned capability amidst Lenz Tennis Courts and Brown College of mathematics lay the perplexing identity of the blueblood family origins for Nicholas Patton Coventry III, the man for whom fingerprints registered to a Penn Central and Rome Tennessee crashes. His father ran a spoiler room at Princeton Station and his mother won tennis tournaments. To his father with whom he spent adult years devising chemical bins so as to filter sludge he owed his knowledge of ground depletive storage for strewn cloth waste, accommodating essential barge floats upriver while taking material wastes into vast landfill reservoirs. Although storage was viewed as a temporary measure of docking floats, its purpose became an entrapment for re-trievable minimum sediment used in controlling the flow of sluggish water from manufacturing plants. Many a warehouse succumbed to the course of interior devastation of floors and ground until the firmly packed dirt gave way to its mulch.

His uncle Oz Roscae while attempting to perfect a flex-ible wood window pane purchased thousands at any one time of stills worth of strewn waste; remnants were sent by railway car north to be combined with oil for pounder to be used as roof slate edge emollient for ice, the unused portion stored in basements, contaminated by wood for furnace burned a trough, massive use accumulated at Lavender Hill with stupidity, deep gate troughs burrowed at ten feet down in grass switch-backed like narrow canals through meadows, they did this to the Illi-nois wheat and grain fields making them too tough on elevated dirt hoofs in order to irrigate when the ground had too much clay in it. They moved to where they could live, packaged the dirt for drainage to build land, a service offered to the projects along waterways to enhance newer planned buildings.

In 1979 David Orion Kameroff, a dramatic tall fiery dark wavy redhead, left his wife of 22 years, tried to get into the draft board on an August weekend and when he failed to get the guard to open the door and talk to him to give him a re-ferral to a psychiatric hospital, he removed a pistol and shot himself in the left foot causing the police to call an ambulance to admit him to Highland county hospital in north Oakland. During an admissions interview he said he was concerned that his father-in-law Nick Coventry III had told him he intended to bomb the Richmond Oakland Corridor by cannon fire if he Nick was not paid for his still.

The interviewing officer, Michael Ketter, another bay area native from Dutch harbor off Pt. Richmond through the tun-nel near the five yearlong docked Exxon ship, asked politely, his Spanish accent clipped, "What type of winery is his still?"

"It's not wine; it's a seethe waste production plant off Trent."

"What is seethe waste?" never having heard the term.

"Goes with the train, it's an engine with five locomotive motors."

"Where is it today?"

"Off track in northern Colorado being tested for speed. We thought he had a purchaser in west Benicia but at the last minute his well ran dry."

Kameroff had an unusual idiom. Possibly he was eastern European or Mediterranean. "What has Nick threatened?"

"He said he's going to fire with both guns fully loaded."

"Do you have an address on him?"

The address proved bogus. With Kameroff's fingerprints and vehicle file, the Oakland police began an urgent pipeline for the suspect Coventry running Department of Justice inquiries in New Jersey to Delaware and from Pennsylvania to Colorado on a missing persons automated dragnet. The Interstate system posted a bulletin through their crime bureau on regional broadcasts.

Meanwhile, Kameroff was comfortably sedated inside the Permanente Kaiser Hospital on MacArthur, ten stories in the Dangerous ward having undergone surgery for his self inflicted wound. He told the male ward doctor who contacted the family that he had come from a place in the mountains high above the snow line where he had a small two story house that he recharged engines for the Kansas Line and once the engine was again functioning to par he returned it to the track that connected to southern Oregon coast and northernmost Delaware through a contingency of college stations. Nick was his wife's relation; his use of emollient gave him a status of riling hills for which he was considered quite mad. The brother visited each evening for a week bringing pastries, bottled tea and dried fruit and together they conversed about old times fishing off the pier and riding the empty train cars through the meat warehousing district of Richmond below the wells along the park land on the waterfront into Emeryville. The brother Kevin was a contrasting lookalike with much lighter wavy red hair, willowy through the torso, a convincing sign changer on freeways who rode the hilltop vans from the merchandize warehouses to the

San Pablo stores. Scarcely two years apart Kevin was old man wisdom to his older brother David's flung-one's-whims-to-the-wind attitude, probably a sane measure of restrictive behavior.

The dialogue registered in. Lewis Lewis regarded it with a thin scrutiny.

"It's a turf bind," Kameroff said to his young brother.

"What's the point? Station sits on a canal."

"Lights shut down during high flood season. You watch, they'll move the station off Coventry and onto Kingston."

"Meaning what? Who'll know you shot yourself in the foot?"

A draft dodger to the end, David required cautious attention, a sobriety all his own. To have so much as confessed to forming underground caverns of air would prove a fallen saddle to bring him down on his own bended knee; so much for his notion of reducing a genuflected aristocracy, no more jury rigged julienne interludes, these reckless, improvident, wasteful columns of geography, his sardonic value of the trains as absolute and autonomous never quietly dispatched, the only legroom in the soldier cloakroom was a bleak house of cards, joker's wild playing to the ace of diamonds in quintessential blunders on floating draft ships on a veiled mildly opalescent blue ocean seeping in by sleight of hand, a prima facie fulfillment of theft, a nocturnal false elation of pride, possibly confused as nirvana or extinction of intellectual individuation. For to participate in a heinous act, of which every parcel of land was combat, laid ready for siege, men such as Kameroff and Coventry whose intentions reached no greater than marginal parity of stooped relief, there was no checks and balance on reality. The cement under low weight buildings were found to have been conjectured by a silvery gray damp slope in through which air calibrated, various flashlights wedged into the ground so that they shone out like a stopped train on a track meter, each a lone light penetrating the dark gray of pre dawn, each candescence recording swirling dust in the contaminated crude expressions of their dull miens, Coventry's eyes glinting with instinctual ferocious greed, a man of few words, for whom any attempt on the Verne pony express required a suitable passage not far below the surface to derail and demolish descent through water.

Lewis reviewed the notations of the thick file. Jones had run all the various types of clearances. On camera Coventry was obvious, an evil man with a sly mission, posing twice a year as audit evaluator, a property manager with interested buyers, whose stable was invented out of pay-outs to the state to take a money guzzler off an honest man's end balloon loans. He had produced a name list of aka's, a federal number despite no convictions, fingerprints to match vehicle and boat but as quickly unloaded them so that he appeared in less than fifty photos which was hard to do; he had never married; even Mixey said of Kameroff he did not sustain identification and didn't expect diver bomb suspect Coventry to come in either; Lewis Lewis had a cumulative file of wrong person occupational licensing queries up until now. Neither showed proof of work. Now Kameroff would forever read in as a Mental Health Firearm. Despite this, evidence tracking was still not enough; his analyst said there had to be better proof of linkage to pull in Kameroff for tidying up and Coventry for road-right-of-way designations. So Lewis gave the Coventry case to all his ten agents with a first-find status call. Inside of four months he should have his lead.

Lewis could have been dying his death at age seventy-seven. File divination gave little proof. Hindsight was passé, hunches mere discussion, food the single most incentive for creativity put him to fitful sleep; he could cook for hours if Rhonda supplied enough wine at least until they agreed on the elusive matter of an assessment. He pulled up all information the computer contained, Coventry was seen climbing out of the hole when the dorm fell in and he was seen leaving at least three other Princeton undergrounds, his voiceprint surfaced on all stings, he had signed the county contract on the Passaic Canal for Princeton Station, he was seen diving with a boat handle package, and he had called his nephew for an automated firearm expunger, a device which caused the sewage to release and then to pool on top of the ground making it lay waste and have to be dug out and replaced, none of this a crime yet because once lights stopped working the sites were posted for demolition. Oddly it was not enough to convict.

He wrote the problem. Neither man took the Rome Tennessee by rifle or pistol. They weren't seen tying a bomb to a rail line either; they weren't on camera for shoveling dirt, or placing a device on or in the ground. This was to be slow evolutionary work to investigate.

It was a few hours before telescope would identify an underground match. The dock Coventry had been seen at off shore was finally in with the capture of shadows. The boat jetty and canal he had spent time at were read at night. His cell phone signal booster read in as soon as he stepped onto dry land. Receipts led nowhere, a full tank was just that, fingerprints although partially viable did not exist. The fact that he was to be found in cavernous undergrounds didn't mean a damn thing.

Since he had lost twenty pounds in the abdomen, Lewis could fit easily into the elegance of dress without stress in undershirt, dark socks, garter for a 22 mm pistol, beneath off green silk and linen trousers, white stiff collar shirt, and jacket; he no longer wore Mock Toes, he wore brown saddlebacks; non-existent nape fuzz and smart crew cut. In matters of precision having to do with final outcomes he awoke at five, swam until six, took coffee and the daily standard newspaper, rode to the office on the beach, and left by seven when the building closed. With trim distinction he found he could stay put for days and hours, reviewing chart quarters, dozens of submitted reports, notations, calendar assignments, mileage analyses, pathological studies, evidence loss, tip edge sheets of who was on camera, missing person list or dead, chases and falling rooftop bites, highway fatalities, break-ins of any type, water and salt evaluative inspector general field reports tracked by revolving video camera on roofs, locator charts for mapping accidents, matching debris pastures, and so on and mountains of photo reviews. Everything that could be obtained was. Thus, direct evidence of all sorts was turned over until controversial issues and soil infractions were able to be guessed at and probable conclusions indirectly established for circumstantial evidence.

He looked for use of lobster manufactured by a New Jersey firm on the Basin called Mer-curie which could be tested in its sweet pea pervasive scent, dark bluish trace right off the ground up to three years after initialization to hoist land for future population in advance soil enhancement. If lobster trace was able to be established, its presence could tie Coventry to the Nebraska derail and costly mountain hideaway under Colorado snow of a missing smashed engine from the Chicago-New York wheat train. On the other hand if there were no ties to the Nebraska smash, at least there was ample sweet pea scraped from box cars that burned for an entire day.

He checked. He had no positive toxicology test results. Only one mention of a previous tenant name which Jones had come across that led him to a telephone number of business manager Coventry. Together with a wide angle one-stop Nikon, Jones was able to come up with tentative fingerprints which gave him a car in a restricted zone of a warehouse.

Of thirty locations worldwide, which was preferred minimum target dial-ins, Coventry tested for eight. Not all were isolated places, several were as crowded as Syria's bazaars. They had no profile on him, didn't know where he was born, whether as a teen he robbed stores, was a runaway, Indian welfare, applied to the youth corp and was denied, wanted on lewds, tested for paternity, or acted in porn videos; he had no known stats, wasn't on a trust fund, had no credit recognition, didn't own a house, wasn't in an ESL school.

The boat debris had been taken to an undisclosed warehouse, dried and tamper-proof resin tested for any capable evidence consisting of fingerprint on an explosive. The waterway was being combed for shoes, gloves and trace. A half print had been found on the underside of the boat motor box. The explosive itself matched a short wire circuit deducer of three hundred and fifty yards, a typical device for boats producing a wind up to twenty miles per hour with hailstones about a fraction of an inch in diameter. The half print cross matched to a man named Series.

An analyst sent over a query – how many deaths were intended. One bad injury and any number up to three seated on the back railing.

Another analyst called in. He thought Series should be looked up in forgery, hot doc's, raids, peering through a window. Did the analyst know the number of suspects who appeared on camera for staring out a window; but Lewis fed it to his photo contamination section for Mobile Spy and Real Spy databases.

So, while any good file ought to have criminal history, vehicle registration, academic and work, history on addresses, small claims, marriage, Coventry aka Series had none. With the partial print and alias Lewis classified him under Fugitive.

Port of entry, out after dark, if he was a foreigner, had to be extrapolated in complete scrutiny particularly if he had ever washed in with gas tanks, illegal fertilization or detached control bands, uniforms not to be ruled out.

Hoyt raised his right hand as he stood inside the witness box and was sworn in.

"Do you swear to tell the truth and nothing but the truth, so help you God?"

"I do."

"Please state your full name for the record."

"Edward Hoyt."

"Please be seated."

The counsel for the Office stepped up to the witness. "Where were you on September 4th, 2008?"

"I was on a leisure yacht in the bay at Cape Fear."

"Who was with you?"

"My wife, Mrs. Hoyt."

"Were you married legally at the time?"

"We were separated."

"Was anyone else with you?"

"No."

"Can you state what you saw?"

"I observed a cabin cruiser leaking fuel. It was slowly overturning."

"What was the name of the boat?"

"It had no name."

"Did you attempt communication of any sort?"

"Yes, I approached it up to nine feet and asked on my loudspeaker if they required assistance."

"Did they respond?"

"No. I realized when I channel changed, they had no antennae."

"Did you do anything?"

"Two things, I radioed to the Narragansett Coast Guard and I steered my boat to the distress boat and boarded."

"Did you find anyone on deck?"

"A male and female scantily clad in G-string swimwear were asleep and the boat was in cruise control."

"Could you awaken them?"

"No. I tried for about fifteen seconds. I determined each husband and wife were under the influence of a powerful narcotic due to hypnotic stare and weak pulse."

"When did the Coast Guard arrive?"

"Three minutes later."

"Thank you, Agent of International Customs Enforcement Detective Hoyt." Counsel turned to opposing counsel. "Your cross."

"Were you under the impression the couple was drugged?"

"Yes."

Hoyt was excused. It was the sole time he was asked to testify. A senior Field Office agent was seldom invited to testify; a unit chief never was.

The male on the boat was John Nash out of Rome Tennessee and the female was his auto mechanic. Nash was responsible for all recordings along the Kansas Trail train line. It was he who identified and placed the pistol shots that killed an oil can train employee on the return trip.

SABA

SABA 1

The chase was on. Up ahead the Turkish cabin deck three-tiered ship, the Fog Horn, slid ominously into the misted waters moving at nine knots an hour, its metal reconnoiter rotating at medium speed, every so often the rotating denzil of green light could be detected through the fog. The ship had departed Bermuda carrying twenty-five illegal aliens against advisory having missed the three mile buoys and the island call stations. Despite the fact that Bermuda had a healthy fleet to detain boats, all helicopters had been temporarily called off due to rough swells expected to last several hours. The weather at sea gave a storm warning of showers moving up the coast of flat Georgia with a highlight of severe thunderstorms. The fog would persist all night, tricks of light played havoc with the least incidental object, driftwood became a partially submerged plank, portholes in ghostly light resembled bobbing bodies, this stretch of murky ocean contained a hundred or more illegals in the worst pitching weather anyways. When the shroud of air lifted there would be the canteen ship looking as though it took a crash with a smaller vessel; such were the plights of ocean battered hulls stolen before they could be rebuilt. Lewis reviewed the storm path looking for any oncoming signs of distress likely to create an immediate retreat. A hurricane spout gathered speed starting in the Pacific on Middle Island 31S by 27N. As it picked up velocity over the northern tip of Nassau – there were an estimated ten per year over this very spot – it became capable of rendering an aircraft invisible in the lashing, whip-bending rain. A downed aircraft hadn't far to go – Bermuda, if she were lucky. He estimated the elusive cabin deck would sneak past their scrutiny, possibly sailing into a secluded beach, mystifying even to their remote lens. It would be hide and seek through morning, nerves lacerated with blunted edginess, illegals castigating overboard, hiding out underwater, giving up and dying, or yet more sinister floating as far as to a farm island. These entrenched migrants were like porpoises, to be found usually in fifty degree water or warmer including up to ninety degree making a dash for an exclusive abandoned house with plumbing having identified it by conversation alone on a tour boat. Under winter circumstances they were anticipating a more conservative held battery of immigrants who hoped to make it to anywhere the crackdown hadn't yet penetrated.

The weather was a devastation, the deck awash with swirling ocean, fog on every swill, the ship a cruise signatory spelled high on far climbing waves. It was for every regret imaginable that the slave ship had sped through a deep water blue light buoy into real ocean; even a lament her crew knew barely passable English and were all men in their thirties who had already gotten busted once for swimming a barricade of ten boats. Lewis Lewis understood their one law, nunca direccion olvidarse, never forget direction, which of course was a plague of conquest and who could fail to understand there was no comparison in lifestyle, despite the irrevocable sins of stabbings, suffocation, wrist slitting, gunshot in the ear, and countless speech recognition wards for untold years. Lewis attended to the scope as three captains stayed with the ship through cabin-light dousing winds, shouted orders lost in a flooding gale, wind wailing above the breath of life. Where deepwater left the primitive sea and misting sunlight shifted in the water like shafts to a cave, they dragged a chain, snagged the Turkish anchor by trowel line and pulling it tight took it round the crest of St. Barts long peninsula some twenty-one miles to warm-milling water at one point two miles off coast where depth began.

The starboard was shooting gas, its painted waterline sinking by inches to the blue line. Ten pilot cutter officers in studs boarded with pistols drawn and once on board ran down the decks opening all doors – to the cabins, mess, engine, starlight, radio and bridge, while on the first deck tanned males wearing striped teal green and orange high neck shirts and apache pants jumped ship and began swimming, no fear to the eventual waves. Based on the reality their garb was prison plantation off Barbados, Lewis who knew ships like the back of his hand looked for any obvious deployment. When he encountered a bleeding man with injury to the hand split in the grain elevator, Saba pineapple bright red, yellow lettered crates asunder, he thought mutiny, no doubt for a drug market and proceeded cautiously, lifting with a crowbar tucks in walls, floors, ceilings.

An aircraft jettisoning fuel from a dangling engine tube crashed after catching on fire in the cabin. Although he would receive a written docu-file in two days with photographs, he had few answers. For starters the vessel had occupied a dry dock lift for the better part of a month before being lowered to ocean side view. The border patrol and fleet rigging and crane through International Customs combed every panel where drugs were often stashed. The Fog Horn was as clean as a whistle. Despite tests she had attracted a ton of Mexican marijuana clipped and bagged for ready street sale in half ounce trim cellophane hidden inside the wheel box all the way down the turn hoist shaft to the engine propulsion. Back-taxing work, whereas drug smuggling occurred by the hundreds every season, weather no obstacle, enough marijuana cut with cocaine was found to outfit a standard size bulkhead's available floor space. Sixteen hours later inside an on-shore gymnasium size warehouse, the contraband lay labeled on tables awaiting the chemist.

Saba lay a hundred and twenty miles to the west. She was calm, almost no high winds. She was a relaxing, comfortable life where islanders worked seven mornings to nine nights.

Houses faced east, they were pink, salmon or green, and were sheltered against the disparate winds by an enclosure of trees, windows covered by thick wood slats, small lawns close to the main structure each, and nestled near a hill with wide veranda a half mile from the beach. There were an infirmary and market at each of twelve docks. At nine every morning was an air raid and on Saturday also at seven at night. There was no tourism, no one was allowed on the island. For the fifty-eight islanders whose trade it was to build boats and staff the docks, there were fifteen coffee shops open all hours; one radio station, no airport, nor ocean port. The closest station lay through deepwater at Puerto Rico off sand island on the southern coastal plain. There were no cars, the island had never experienced a crime; the mere hoopla of having a ship enter the trespass zone at ten knots placed it on the AIS scope for capture.

Saba was the home of the SABA pineapple advertised as "the one that satisfies." The SABA was the same color as the red orange papaya and took the entire island – all 644 kilometers, some three miles by seven miles – for growth for the chief export. The plantation operated around the clock, seven days a week. One half billion SABA pineapples every two years shipped only to Egypt left the small balmy island in crates on fifty steel platform boats destined for the two mile limit to be transported by single hung declass-ier crane onto two ocean bearing ships. Of Saba's three exports which included mica, slate and providing test gauge mechanisms on boats, its pineapple took all twelve docks, four boats apiece packing thirty crates loaded each with ten boxes of pineapples on swift currents that traveled away from the coast. In Egypt luxuries were hotels, pineapples, papaya, British cognac and specialty ice cream rolls decorated with multi-colored pansies, blue, yellow, aqua and rose.

The gauges used in boat manufacture produced forty boats a year for delivery to the nearest of two islands, St. Maarten and Antigula. From the Antilles, the dependent imported cotton, beans and corn from Nevis, pharmaceutical products from

Puerto Rico, albacore from St. Maarten, spinach and papaya grown in Dominique, and mate tea from Mexico.

Lewis consigned for the blue test used typically in cocaine powder evaluation despite the fact that the best, most reliable test was to smoke it. But for the purple stain indicative that the product contained dye; if testing produced a yellow stain the product contained penicillin. It stayed blue if it was soaked in crystal, but then the trick was the crystal hairs on the weed could not be found to have been produced by a food. The chemical strip on first go-around revealed methamphetamine blended cocaine – the presence of a faint violet used to perfume-card greenbacks tested on a second flashlight read for drug storage contamination. Product dyed back to sapphire blue inside of a minute and then it had to be air-dried and sifted before it could be approved for release as a medicine otherwise left untreated in a toss-away bin it eventually resembled a tranquilizer for animals.

The Saba ship labs were a throwback to an older era when all that was needed to provide expertise on tests were culture and sensitivity stains and Q-tips, gas spectrometry, solid waste and a few centrifuges. The marijuana was scored, half was set aside for the slaughter house to be shipped bulk to Hawaii now that the mainland United States had perfected a simpler methodology of feeding large quantities of feed-nullifier to cattle which helped the meat bleed less. It was after the dope was tested for juice substance on the marijuana crystal under a microscope that a match called a fingerprint was declared. A non-match was a dye. Standard dilutions consisted of 1 part to 25 yielded a match which read proof there was food in grown tobacco – which was illegal.

His small house sat at the northern edge of a bay from where on a wrap-around deck he could identify both boats racing out to the long black lab ships that would single-crane lift crates of boxed red-orange flesh pineapples and sail non-stop to Egypt. The day was blustery, made silkier by a cloudy breeze breaking low over an aquamarine jet stream current. The bourbon stayed in his throat like a half digested irritation of things to come. His investigation had wound up costing him a relief nursing chemical-medico staff to draw dilutions of food syrup used as rum; distilled two parts or greater it could blow a hole through a wall for a slender child to crawl into. The wounded man in the grain elevator tested for lithium fiber in his wounds. He was arrested, put into padlock on a leeward masted stow accompanied by five detention guards. A wind which blew stern for a good hour bending oak trees in a flap made for an interesting sight as often pre-hurricane stormers that gradually subsided did lose their fierce throttle. Lewis awaited Jones' vehicle, his having flown midday from Houseboat Keys where a Field unit sat bleary-eyed over dozens of baking units for a new entry of crystal. Lewis himself was skeptical as to whether he might be called back to the station to repackage and bill a new saddle worth of green. His energy wore thin, ribcage showing becoming more pronounced, he was losing weight at long last, sleep was occurring more readily most nights.

By the hour Jones arrived, a slightly jocular figure all in white with gold eagle sunglass clip-ons, Lewis was on his fifth drink. They exchanged a warm handshake and embraced briefly and moved onto the deck on lounge chaises overlooking the airy, placid warm blue sea.

Jones said, his beige blond hair giving a bit of sport, "The blue test read two parts to a quarter."

"For trade cocaine?" Lewis ventured; now that the problem was explicit he wasn't as concerned.

"Hairline juice to make marmelaide meth."

"That's really thick. Is it fish trank for the slop trough?"

"I gave it a red circle crayon for prawns to enhance them but I s'pose it could be albacore."

"Put it to sleep."

"Queer sort of situation," Jones said.

"Can't imagine smoking it."

"How many were affected?"

"No idea," Lewis replied, but thought it through anyways.

"Complicated occurrence, still have three other islands to go out to inspect. There's a plant allegedly somewhere near anchor."

"Voodoo fire sticks detoxify only a witch doctor."

They chuckled.

"Any base rhubarb on it?" asked Jones.

"Test didn't prove for it, just the plantation. Patrol called the ship – they'll hold out the crate batch number, send it back with paperwork including testing for drug and spoon."

"Wouldn't care to have to mark it. Voodoo fire stick surrenders the chemist aide himself semi-drugged with intoxicant, smoking it could induce a fever."

Lewis removed his sunshades and carefully folded them and slipped them into his shirt breast pocket. "I asked myself why the unusual contraband. I asked the chemical analysts to scrutinize which awarded us blood, a match to the same filtration as on the wounded man in the grain elevator."

"What did you make of it?" Jones inquired, not the least concerned a wounded sailor might in fact be guilty of deckhands misconduct, possibly of a small fire inside the brink or engineering a collision accident by incorrectly speed information.

"Well, after verifying the AIS course I discovered one explanation, that our man handles radio room and he was intercepted on deck as he was about to come across an on-board money stash worth hundreds of thousands."

"That I 'spect would explain it although the batch test confirms the ship was illegal. Who knows what else is being trafficked?"

"It should be easy enough to determine what with the ship being delayed at four miles on account of fog."

At Lewis' insistence they took the stairs to the ground and walked the grassy path to the beach from where the waves charged in pounding steadily up the ten degree incline. They removed their socks and shoes, left them on the sand, and hands in pockets strolled through inches of frothy water discussing the pros and cons of storing medical supplies in dockside lockup along with medicinal rum. No telling what concoction some of these seasonal coke sugar-rum-plantation dock ship loading recruits might devise; on what planet were these youths stationed? Lewis said it was occurring these days with greater frequency: quench-thirsty perpetual island tourists looking for a niche. He was convinced that in a warehouse in the middle of nowhere, tiny Nevis Island to be exact, approximately some thousand yards from the shipping wharf, a compound had tested with a chemical similar to Litium which was devised of incubation of testing dry for morphine. The resultant chemical which had been utilized routinely for batching was excessive in its particular strain. Sooner or later the lab would be found where the combination of crushing the reddish SABA pulp, compressing it for liquid, combining with some strain of sugar, preferably brown, had obviously produced a milk sugar cocaine stained on marijuana. The satellite photo in evidence was an appropriate, evidentiary yellow blur against dark dark brown or near black; teal and red were mapped also at the same facility by an inland channel where alleged cocaine shipments were teal. The additional appearance of lint on the crop-cutting formica tables revealed the use of linen fabric for absorption of scavenger powder. Penicillin in water made a base for cocaine milk, pineapple juice was the fixer for speeding up the processed density of cocaine crystalline meth. As far as Lewis was concerned, Lewis told Jones, the crescent shaped beach taking in clusters of coconut palms, frothy ocean spraying over barely emerging rock surface, the entire occurrence smacked of computer enhanced off-shore product reorientation designed to at some point transport a real product during real time. The thing with getting illegals across the invisible ocean boundary had gone far enough and before long there would be a necessity to pump the fat bankroll into seemingly less attention-glaring markets. He didn't know which was worse – the desire to run for the crank or a perpetual need to be admitted into the Keys for purposes of crime.

By the hour Lewis and Jones boarded the cruiser at Miami beach it was well after seven and almost dusk. Lewis and Jones joined a unit of six patrol paraffin agents who used torch weed blowers to rub out any clandestine operations, once found. The hide-aways were usually a worn down house with an unpaid judgment or an unsecured debt in dire need of paint, stairs and new flooring and drywall, often a large room inside which a capitano observed all labor as refried beans were poured into a boot and batches of cigarette weed were left to air dry over two days. The cruiser sped like a flying porpoise over ocean scintillating in bright lights onto aquamarine ocean and through the night without so much as stars to steer by. The errands top deck cabin boat ran a gauntlet between smaller islands from Sable beach past the lowest Keys out to Nassau where it was common for satellite computer posted to any site to read yellow blurred on black, figures moving about, possible teal or red blocks of color indicating illegal manufacture. Once deployed, in the end the border patrol would take the walls to the lab, board them onto trucks and test them for blood, splatter, food and chemical sub-infuse lighters.

By day these waters were pristine, warm. A yacht tour group could bathe in eighty-nine degree heat, masts giving full tether to the West Indies trade winds. Evening they might deplank on a pink sand beach for grilled abalone steak and a late game of volleyball before finally retiring on deck inside their cabins. The pernicious scent of penicillin waxed like a violable substance of disease ever present. Certainly the black nurses from Viejes across the channel from San Juan's high water wall checked the purifying soaked branches as they hung high over an electric heat for hours in some unnamed room situated in a remote village, buds stiffening, crystalline hairs lining the stems with tenacity. All illegal activity came with censured inducements. The soft warm waters gave off no hint except of sandy beaches and luscious green plants and grass. But as the cruiser slowed to a minimum speed slowly approaching inlets and coves, when the satellite computer yellowed over in a row of pretty peach colored houses, the captain pulled onto sand and doused all lights. Donning head masks, gloves, all black wetsuit garb, the eight men tucked in pistols, clipped on walkie

talkies, and sprinted up the beach to the first two houses, shouting at the top of their lungs, slamming through doors, firing at
anyone who attempted to flee. In a main kitchen shelved with
a wall-length grill and fruit crushers on four tables, marijuana
crop steeped in light blue stained rhubarb, residues of powder,
baking soda, digestive antacid, coke, rust colored heroin each
in a different strong box tray wearing the night hours away.
Already packaged cellophane banded rolls capable of bringing
in a million in street value lay tossed in gigantic drawers meant
for transporting money obtained from deepwater raids.

Had he but thought it through – the water purification system for drinking water subverted by top barrel somewhat floating opaque orange wrapped bricks of marijuana or heroin hash
– he would have sent in advance for the illegals homicide expert stationed at the repeater station on the resort side of sunny,
lusciously verdant Nevis. The island expert went out for every
ship steerage on the ocean for which there might be sixty in a
month. Trained as well as beneficent expertise at a look-ahead
distance system which could read backward calling systems,
satellite inducement to read behind islands and land masses
as long as the speed over ground was less than two knots gave
this man his proficiency. But the positioning of ships, course
and speed, call to port, navigation system, and a host of over
fifty other symbols and references made tracking and monitoring ships commonplace, scarcely out of bounds nor mystifying.
Thus Lewis called forth Fixed Access Time as it applied to
collision avoidance especially of reckless unidentified schooner
vessels and proceeded to chart by night-vision deep water scope
the dismal hunt for the Fog Horn. Boats might fill with water,
flood into the cabins, drown the sleepers.
But he hadn't so much as given a guess. It was the tension
of the raid that removed an ability to reason why it had come
about at all. Whereas it was a regular tour to inspect quarantined wharfs, the statute said where voodoo carousels were
determined to be likely medicinal, all lockers, shelf and dock,
had to be looked at. Typically voodoo was wrapped in bright

red cellophane with yellow letters often mistaken for garden nutrient to soil.

They sat in the dark listening to the stillness amidst lapping waves. At some point a crow cawed raising hairs on each man's neck. The satellite photo continued to show yellow on blackish brown, teal and crimson mapped by an inland channel where coke shipments were revealed as teal, as their boat floated down the causeway to the dock in question. The patrol proceeded across a lawn littered with smallish concrete pebbles to a patio and hammered the door with a pistol and staggeringly bright lights. As the front door swung open the patrol team ran inside, eyes straining through night vision gear at all sorts of objects, sinks, centrifuge, bum sticks for making loco dust, milk tray for crystal leche, bags and bags of empty capsules, liquid hydrogen. The room was large, maybe four hundred square feet, without a window or access door to the yard. There was a stove but no oven use, chemical trays for mixing, a crusher; a deep fryer the length of the wall presumably for scoring marijuana with hash; this batch couldn't be sold to humans, only to animals because of the small amount of mold from the milk powder. Off the fryer kitchen was a medium size room, maybe a hundred and fifty square feet also without access, defined by a good layer of ash-barium soot covering the walls exposing fingerprints. The border men trammeled through a hall and series of twelve bedrooms, each of them tiny, barely adequate for a duffel bag, shower off the center of the hall, through a pantry packed with packages of material supplies of all sizes, into another hall of an attached house into a large room inside which six bodies zipped into white plastic bags the size of a ten or twelve year old prepubescent adolescent lay scattered about along with fifty or so bath towels, the sickly sweet morphine smell of urine overpowering and dank. The bags lay partially in water, size-worthy cracks in the walls having been without security as stacked sand bags like heavy weights seemed to suggest or the presence of the towels to abate an ever stemming seepage. In this type of setting all things could happen; despite this certain acceptance on the part of each man, they were aghast at the sight, their sensibilities forever compromised. Fear stared over their shoulders, as they fanned out now to conduct an indepth search and cart the bodies into the central hold of the radio room onboard the vessel, although the closets betrayed the semblance of camera rinse on ceiling, walls and floor to obscure packaged drugs, there were no television monitors to display quantities; all stored goods were on a looksee basis of discovery.

In ten days there would be a post mortem once the facts of the case were researched. There had been some tell-tale signs of a bad wind blowing through, the first observable sign that crime liked to swim with crime was a man from Nevis was admitted to the clinic at St. Kitts for extreme mental confusion, distorted reality, out of body experiences, he couldn't add or divide to save his soul, and eventually he fell unconscious. Because of the hair crystal evident on his skin and clothing, it was established he had handled methamphetamine, known as a fragment substance formed from an alcohol derivative. Once the bodies were dispatched to St. Kitts, after a thorough batchchem process to investigate both houses taking into account the similar manufacturing to cheese of the milk crystal and long stem tubular lab droppers, a makeshift ice stem of a heater for control of heat for ampules, during which there would need to be lots of release, one man removed the latents and unsecured evidence off the soot wall; thousands of cigarette butts and beer bottles taken from the bedrooms were bagged and labeled for eventual lab process; multiple swabs were taken from the urinals which were filthy with a putrid stench like sewer flowing through city streets; there was rancid sand, bulbs were wet emitting spectromagnetic emission like mist; the grill of the oven was removed to determine what source caused the electricity to blow out; and electrical outlets in the bedrooms were singed as though by use of pressure. Closest to the houses trenches with bared pipes had been sectioned and pipes cut through and through to find whatever obstacle prevented flow of water due to theft of smuggling. The question had to be asked – were the deaths the result of an event or of an illness that shut the house operations down. It seemed infeasible there was no stifled resentment in rooms that reeked of absentee supervision and all too brief departures from poverty.

The air in the sitting room reeked of fried donuts, there was curdled hardened milk in a pot, it was possible to walk over the ground, narrow spaces of dirt showed through where floor boards had been removed, over these like worn placements tape binding rugs ran the length of the room. The victims were scrawny like unfed horses, worked too long and unattended to. These men probably began as joiners, teens with nowhere to go, whose mothers would one day weep a thousand tears. In the next ten hours when morgue ran Interpol clearances on all to identify fingerprints and name, whereas none turned out to be boys in the hood, their bodies were nevertheless void of personal regalia, no marital rings, registration cards, blood bank donor cards, company employee permits. Neither had any male tattoos, scars, neck wounds, injection sites, bruising, or earrings; certainly no wallets, no checks, nothing anywhere under a mattress nor inside a drawer to say who they had been in life. Men fleeced of their identities in exchange for a month's labor at a drug camp. They were suicides zipped in bags for the permanent dead.

Favorable in all white captain's suit with gold trim including on his solid cap, Lewis Lewis took a bowl of teriyaki steak for lunch along with his usual Mai Tai chartreuse rum on the patio nearest the lush green lawn that fronted the pools and lounge. Across the square wooden polished table Jones in blue jeans and a polo shirt with Geiko sipped his rum for the moment awaiting grilled prawn and savory New York filet with due diligence granting the coroner a keepsakes of secrets each tied to its own stake of savage brutality. The other man Coroner Davey Randolph who dressed in khaki colored jeans and thick sandals, a sailor bib and red scarf was a hard study of drowned jowls and even worse, pityingly scarce accommodations of polite entreaty or willing acceptance of complicating circumstance of stooped slouch and thick blond dutch hair, rambled on about hurricane gale winds segregating the islands and house lights fizzling out just as the hour after sunset went mauve.

"Been to the inquiry on the young turnip found in the gallery?" Jones asked his returned superior.

Lewis weighed his strip of meat down with a good dousing of Worcestershire sauce, bit a shortchange and washed it down with his spoon-fed sip. "All dead of the same. Turnip took in excess governor's fifth meal, as well as the six washboard. All smoke inhalation."

"Impossible, don't you think? Couldn't they push through a barricade outside?"

"Possibly not. No windows, therefore no way out, that's a real stinker."

The coroner spoke up. "We dusted exits, doors were nailed, no equipment to saw through. My hunch is they were walled off for some time."

Lewis responded, saying, "In span of a day and a half they were asphyxiated, incoherent, unable to act."

The coroner asked, "And you're asking what occurrence produces that affect? Could be damn near anything when it's drugs or inhalants."

Jones said, "Well, I'd like to know where else this body bag syndrome of death has occurred besides Nassau, would you know?"

The coroner checked a tiny spiral notepad. "All told twenty for five crimes, all stacked in the water, the first incident in 1774 there was a plague death at Spanish Harbor on Houseboat Key, adolescents placed in shacks behind barbed wire. There was no electricity, plumbing or livable habitation. Absolutely it was a disgrace. Two bays were abandoned on a fairly extensive island due to the plague syndrome."

"What was the cause?" Jones wanted to know.

Randolph replied. "Blood cocaine, dark red powder tinged black, it contains amino ethyl phosphate. The black tar makes it sell a thousand dollars American per half ounce – it's known also as black flower, probably because it derives from the blood red poppy, opium. Downsides are life-threatening cardiac arrhythmia and damage to blood cells in the brain like after-affects of the anesthesia-like drug Special K; after a meth binge, it's all sleep lasting days. These boys have done it to themselves. They fly below radar, so dead stone blitzed they're pursued to the last with nausea and vomit and loss of consciousness. About as bad as LSD or mescaline from spotted lizard looking Mexican cactus, or PCP damn head trauma. This voodoo stick is like dark grayish black incense, with an absorption rate as rapid as THC but with such slow elimination it can still be detected in the urine forty days after initial use."

Jones asked, "You saying it's like PCP sprinkled on marijuana and then smoked?"

"Aye, and burned in the barrel first."

Burned in the barrel meant it was quota-generated for a fingerprint match which meant there were a host of sins that accompanied this voodoo scratch, forgery, deed theft, drive-bys, rotating in and out of jail; syringe drug crimes of possession and sale, aliases, narcotic dependency, and drug manufacture. Only the camera of choice, a Canon EOS 300, knew for sure.

Lewis gave Jones a nod, and said, "They say if you enjoy your miseries you can have considered yourself to have done well in life."

"Almost as well as a café black with a peppermint stick and an ocean view."

Lewis Lewis played nine holes in four hours. Toward noon he sat on his deck with his telescope waiting for Jones to finish forty laps. He had already sent a caption to dateline in the Azores as follows – the daily routine depends upon beach patrol at dawn and espresso and blackboard news at Eddy's. Exchange sleep for surveillance, fix steamer cup to lift fingerprints off soot in death room; who's been stalking the orchard? Within a day Azores replied, fingerprint match. Known to FBI, Island Customs and Interpol. Aliases, forgery, human slavery, smuggling. Dead first jailed in St. Maarten, thereafter periodic ports guard patrol at ten miles to sea, St. Martin, Santa Lucia, Martinique.

The day spilled over with humid licentious heat. By ten when shops opened and the first abalone rock had been pried apart and admitted to the grill, mostly females had decided to avoid the beach and parkside and fan inside their parlors over a cool steamed frosted glass of café and biscuit. Lewis had opted out of an indescribable precognitive sense to spend the early hours in his study instead of playing tennis, given over to a need to know who was hiding in the Antilles wet dish of newspaper runs. As was often typical right before monsoon cyclone season, the mid islands filled with mean light lipped mustached acid blotter and sniff drinkers from interior Florida and their head crowned fluff women of purple tan skin dressed in draped beige and tan silks over their absolutely flat bone ribbed bodies. Every night was Mardi Gras; jazz trumpets and bongo drums to celebrate rum crystal, males adorned with head flowing feathers of green plume, serpent daggers of orange, sickly purplish hibiscus falling stars to complement tiny strings of butt-naked bikinis. When the floats paraded through town, beautiful girls had not a sliver of cloth.

A fan whirred incessantly, the long walnut oared blades stirring up a palpable breeze. Jones had left at four in the morning to return to his hotel for a shave and change of clothes after laying a legend and walking through the evidence proven by the first two hearings that made up a preliminary injunction of the postmortem. At some point around midnight despite three hours very carefully laying out information and backing up each act of circumstance by section of international law, they broke into an argument as to estrangement to answer a common skull drudgery matter of who should have been held responsible for loss of crated crops which later turned up to be used for preparing seed for illegal trade.

The notification documents arrived banded together with

passport issuances and several time sensitive insurance docu-proofed certificates. Inside the notification were textural cop-ies of the latents per each man killed that had been removed from the death room, evidence found elsewhere, and testing results which consisted of oral swabs for various drugs, sensi-tivity cultures for ejaculate, anal smear for stomach contents, and confirmation as to hair and fingernails and clothing. In a separate manila folder were copies of medical exams, nursing home stays on Martinique in the winter, and fourteen dollars each for a full year medical coverage for ankle alert bracelets, all worn at time of death. Even as Jones returned spruced up in freshened linen weave dark yellow tan trousers, a dark tan shirt and crème colored jacket with men's brown stretch socks and mocktoes, slapped on spice lime cologne together with the newest in fashionable ties, a Parisian street scene below the Eiffel done in yellow, white, brown and black remarks of paint, he was dubious as to the amount of trafficking for slavery they had uncovered. The crime was treacherous enough to warrant full attention to ship orders, time-entered recordings of bell ringings as well as hoisting up of mastheads in foul weather, closest station entries and an assortment of other ballyhoo's not to mention dock sightings, weather spools, under-ship status warnings, tipped bergs, physician evaluations including clair-voyant hallucinations brought on by heaving waves and con-tinual nausea.

Jones began the moment coffee was poured and French toast buttered with apple spread. "How were these men previ-ously associated?"

"What makes you think they were?"

"Medical was performed by one physician."

"Could've occurred prior to cabin assignment and blanket and vouchers given."

"Wasn't. They weren't all stationed in the Keys. Only one was."

"We received a fingerprint history on them. They trav-eled a fair amount. We have photos not just of these bedrooms mixed with mold, series of twenty-five sells for two hundred and fifty dollars in conjunction with live voice seriestat."

"These males were wet bloods." Jones said, and opened a fresh pack of Winstons.

"Shore labor," Lewis corrected him and helped himself to a cigarette. "They arrived by float from who the hell knows where, the assumption was Lower Keys."

"It's definitely not straight out of Nassau which is patrolled like it's going out of style; can't go anywhere including renting a car unless it's a tour by an approved state-registered escort. Could be this blood cocaine gets them there for seasonal work."

"Not a chance. Five rolls worth of photos shot out of the trees show planking and assignment by twos to the top forward with a deck working the bin prior to being found in the crate elevator. They ate amply, slept in swing hammocks; on Nevis they constructed four pools, built a restaurant with grill and clubhouse; on Barbados the poured five pools, nice trim patios, laid turf and on Lucia erected a handful of supermarkets, police station and a stock warehouse of a block long. What does all the activity say to you?"

"They wanted youthful teens but settled for undersize males. The fact is if they didn't arrive together then they weren't friends."

"They were obviously migrants. Fingerprint division matches them to tobacco, hurricane sugar, orchards in lower ant. They applied for ships."

"What about church vagrants?" Jones hypothesized.

"Oh, certainly, good one."

"Or stomping cotton out on Maarten's. It must pay alright for what it is, no experience or diploma, no US residents."

"Okay, let's look for day of week for labor camps through hospitalities, see what corresponds."

It was an indecisive argument. One could hardly examine hardship of the seasonal wayward without seeing random settings – a perpetual endurance of dank ominous slavery. In a black wind folding over the ocean with lightning cracking its streaks of bright light, thunderous howling wind driven in sheets of rain and flailing snapped telephone lines that left the asphalt of streets glinting, the downpour chased after gusts. A shout permeated from the dock. Another softer roll of thunder spit forth a crescendo of rain and a spike of fissuring lightning, hailing rocks across the pavement with the speed of headless chickens run amuck.

Into this sightless storm the patrol crew returned. The crime scene retained its chalk outlines of the dead. The rooms absent of bodies and drug paraphernalia were vacant as though they awaited life, no matter how cheapened, to invest their atmosphere and negate an all pervasive scent of purgatory. In the cloudless night the rooms took on a shroud of lifeless chill which burrowed deep like a penetrable damp cold to the marrow of bone. All victories to the absentee landlord – whoever that was under such an onus of borrowed time.

The agent in charge of migrant trafficking who had to be called in for his unusual capability of information was a man of notorious reputation, a handsome Hispanic from southern Florida around the Miami South area, tall, in his early forties, dark wavy hair shaved trim to the neck showing premature white streaks, conservatively dressed in tan uniform of polished cotton of short sleeved shirt and trousers, a clipboard of half a dozen forms for drugs, no prescription, drugs, forged prescriptions. A wicked smile left the indelible impression of an officer who had no other work experience in charge of everything about ocean and land and air transportation. Nicholas Santiago Cordones Randolph was such an officer. Assertive with an air of finality not to be contradicted, although he had rescued many indigents and from time to time displayed leniency, he was old school; and in this regard a ratchet of a team player. He had begun twenty-two years ago in failure to obey, climbed easily to driving reckless, exhibition of speed, addict on highway and drunk driving with open container, and after ten years flawless performance was promoted to possession of narcotics for sale and transportation of dangerous drugs, intent to manufacture drugs and cultivation of marijuana together with bookmaking, forgery and fraudulent document, and counterfeit and forged bills. Night raids were his baby, he nursed them back to health with swift arrests and operations shut down. Tonight he studied Lewis' and Jones' tracks, his six patrol officers having blockaded all entrances to the two houses by water and dock, beach and road and for twelve hours closed the wharf in town and redirected the one anticipated container ship to unload at Dutch harbor.

Lewis admired the man for his sentencing policy on code of marine patrol. In the U.S. where code was rigidly employed, the codes were defined by the Customs that maintained cautious scrutiny of the islands. These included drowning, marine accident, accident with injury, fatal accident, operating a vessel under intoxication, moving and non-moving citations usually involved with ramming a wharf, search and rescue, boat theft, fraud, reckless operating a vessel, and petty theft. Of course the bone of contention would eventually consist of whose jurisdiction and whereas he was fine to toss Marine Patrol a crumb, Lewis knew that even they came under the eye of his courts.

Nick was explaining his in-depth investigation. The bright lights scared the rabbits from the yard, while inside the two establishments a handful of Island agents still poured over the walls and floorboards looking for objects that might have been used to obscure light, hide cameras, dent resonance or any other simulated environment.

"These were outcasts. One had a malicious mischief non-felony from way back when, another pimped when he lived in San Juan Castro Fidel at the jail in which he spent three years; one discharged a firearm while joy riding, one peeked in windows of teen females residing in a pleasure park, and the other two had drunk in public on misdemeanor records. None of these devastating, but someone must've advertised for these types."

"Uncontrollable juveniles," Jones replied. "Unless they qualify as inebriate detention."

"It's a bad scene to have been raised to prowl on a wild side," Nick stated; "but it's what we haul into our judge classrooms. If they don't reform by fourteen then they're headed straight for lock-down."

Lewis asked, "Any recent loitering charges?"

"No. They were seeking restitution, three looking to support young families."

"Someone damned them," Lewis gave an honest opinion. "That blood opium – treacherous stuff. It wouldn't surprise me if that by itself stopped them from breathing."

"You wouldn't like what's peppered inside our foreign fugitive files or our boat files."

Jones agreed. "Between Lewis and I and twenty other Field operatives, we could count thousands of gun files, missing person, unidentified, not to mention securities and violent felon."

"Yes, sure, violent and unidentified. Those categories will knock anyone's socks off."

"So," Jones injected, "how do you figure these males were disposed of in morgue bags?"

"Tell the truth, my homicide release unit is stymied. It looks entirely plausible to find each man OD'ed, but it's a hard truth to assume he zipped himself inside a masked grave. There has to be one or a few who made a grab and run for it once they ditched the six. But here's the problem, we examined the street and there's no sign of other relief. If they're there, they are getting in and out by tunnel."

"Might be stupider than you'd imagine," Lewis said, lighting up a Canadian rolled cigaret. "Could be they pulled up a trap door in a field nearby and were killed, or someone called a beach coroner after the men were found asphyxiated."

"None this far in," Nick answered, and lit a Dos Fuma looking like a brief vacationer. "We scour the meadows and the ocean jetties regularly," in defense of the police he worked alongside of. Then as if recovering rarely lost posture, he said, "We're as thorough as our computers permit us to be."

"Hear, hear," Jones gave an affirmative. "We're shown the goods on an even basis through port defiance at least once a season."

Lewis scoffed. "Yeah, newer and more clever ways to carry

contraband. Did you arrive at a determination on the kitchen batch?"

Nick said, more to Lewis, "Definitely scarlet poppy infused into a milk crystal which the marijuana is strained in."

"That was our belief."

"We tested for the cocaine milk and found they purified for over three days."

"Our chemist concurred but said negligible amounts on a separate grate-drip for angel's dust."

"We haven't actually found much use of PCP going to sea. Each captain is expected to declare health of crew or let them off at nearest port."

Jones inhaled deeply, and remarked, "We ran exotic that produce lack of consciousness and found near matches for eighteen substances."

Nick grew more comfortable. "The more extravagant the production, the more likely the particular drug can create unacceptable risk. Voodoo and tar run neck to neck with similar symptoms, the more bizarre being floating out of body, seeing water everywhere, choking and distorted thinking. Who's to say they weren't sampling the weed as they processed ingredients? Ethyl fumes are pretty damaging to breathe."

"They must have experienced numbness in the foot," Lewis said.

"It's what the bromides cause."

"That's what I'm told, although there's no one to waken to ask. Seems we already checked on the inquiries of neighbors conducted by canvas as to what they heard or witnessed."

"They heard nothing," Nick Santiago said, as his man Renaldo handed out cups of Guatamalan coffee from a thermos, and he took a sip, then waited politely until Lewis and Jones had theirs, "it was dark, bit of rain toward daylight. Houses here are built to shut out even loud sound."

They bantered about the complexity of busting trappers, of tracking the right fox to the chicken coup as they sipped their drinks and smoked.

"Too hard a fish to grill," Jones said about going after cargo in tunnels. "Where did the intoxicating venom come from?"

"It was it brought in, I thought we dealt with that, it was blended right here," said Lewis, rather snappishly.

"My guess is there are small rooms off these tunnels, houses are rat mazes really," Nick remarked, adding, "We are notorious for sniff dogs on a chain, I'm surprised no one heard that."

"Oh, well, it's sufficient. Life's a lime in a jar," Jones said,

To which Nick said, "The coffee's worth twice the wait, it's the rum trifle one can learn to live without."

They chuckled.

Nick said, "A man on the inside placed these workers hands in juice extract and cleaned off their prints on a man's shirt and sent it to the lab. We gave it the EDX line read, that did the trick."

Lewis remarked, "Clothing is the least predictably known. Almost nothing requires us to test it for changing hands."

"So you sent the prints through to Interpol," Jones joined in.

"Process for testing for pineapple liquid was standard, .01 product per liter to rinse, run on centrifuge for a half minute, sampled in ten test tubes each designated by proven method as the substances most probably selected," Nick continued.

"What'd you wind up with? Opium, dark stain?" Lewis speculated, thinking the status of laboratory generated completion through.

Nick nodded. "Exactly what you'd expect, opium purple stain, no blood, matching prints on beer bottles and roughly a few hundred cigarettes, marijuana."

Jones finished his coffee first. "Rubber soles, fabric shoe imported from Columbia, socks provided on board along with blanket."

Nick said, "We have our eye on northern Mexico Verde area for the entire drug ring export to the Keys but not in the pineapple."

"You cut them open?" Jones inquired.

"An entire shipment worth, but not a single fruit."

"Were all goods moved to border U.S.?" Lewis asked.

"To magazine spiller, kept the yellow print applicators from becoming too claustrophobic."

The slight non-affixed remark was the merit they worked to; once smoothly going like trim to a sail, they were at ease, competitive cheer had flown at mist. They were each of them non-complaining despite a dampened enthusiasm over the cynical nature of the clean-up that remained. If the lab found blood of these dead men smeared all over the floorboards, that was one thing, unless the blood corresponded to unknowns, fingerprints on remaining cigarette butts belonged to other unmatched traffic.

The incident was over and done with before the Customs Office sent its evaluative team in. The only thing that allowed a vessel in illegal waters to gain entry to a wharf was the discovery of a dead deck mate in the elevator for transporting materials from deck to deck. It was the problem of extreme drug inhalation and ingestion and the fact that someone had been sent for to bag the bodies that gave the death scene its complicated sinister twist of fate. Each death when post mortem was filed was adjudicated as accidental death. Within a year of typical crimes – an inspector aide had gutted his own chest to transport over the boundary packaged pure heroin when he was detained for having too fresh a wound without corresponding medicine; a boat was held up at San Juan harbor when a savvy shipping metropolis border inspections clerk thought to zero in on the gas tank with a camera and could see two hundred thinly wrapped topper syringes with injection tube of dark crimson fluid; a couple was frisked and arrested at San Juan on a pleasure day cruise boat and discovered to be wearing jackets of tubing, lighter fluid gauges, wire and stoppers connected to watches with open back mechanisms; and a host of other highly explosive devices, among them detonator switches placed inside cans. There were numbers men found dead inside small shacks shot in the forehead or through the chest in the midst of lonely garden terraces of darkly thick green soakers; younger aboriginal looking young male adults presumed to have wandered through the sugar cane flooded fields in seasonal labor houses having processed raw cane bamboo who were found dead by a tourniquet tied around both arms and a needle jammed into the arm; one male in his eighties found stuffed into an attic, the telltale sign of death the overpowering sickly sweet smell like urine penetrating beneath the doors to the outside. After a while of seemingly endless harassment cases, fatal boozers on board ships and yachts, and more than one homicide per early summer somewhere along blowzy jet stream ports, the crime scenes took on resemblances of one another, art valises were often predictable, distillery joints opened and closed by the dozens leaving sorry trails of unpaid loans and promised taxes, and knifings, overdoses, torch scares that charred only a wall, pillow case jewel thefts, abductions of boats and vessels all began to look oddly familiar as though the drug and criminal rings that monitored living conditions ran random death killings to improve upon theft, embezzlement and downright product tampering in areas where housing often went vacant year round. Even while sedatives could go on any type of duster crop, and Custom officials had to determine once product was grown, sprayed, picked, dusted off, tested and crated – how much was toxic – and for that estimation much of the rough stuff got cut and sifted with the finer seedling. The questions of how did they get marijuana in bulk out of the safe house onto the dock into a vessel was still unanswered despite a twenty-four hour camera posted over both front and back doors. What caused the dead men to be bagged in morgue bags? Who was in charge? Why were there no signs of struggle? How many ships were implicated – were these cargo or passenger ships? Had the men as deck hands become covered with kerosene perhaps as a result of a cleaning chore, the ship had it discovered a fire in the cabin at sea would have been quarantined, precisely as was done for the reason of a man being buried inside the granary. Container ships came to dock at stone quay pilings and deck mates filed into captain's houses that sat at the end of a wharf where warehouses ready to load stock by shipping crane would begin the burdensome task of transporting crates into the ship hold.

By the time Lewis and Jones de-planked onto solid ground in southern-most Florida, exhausted from their three-day duty, their condominiums off eight story high rise were a thoroughly welcome re-entrance. They slept like men who had forgone sleep and comfort for months. Midday Jones stopped in having picked up coffees and a newspaper at Starbucks on the circle. Lewis' place wasn't greatly changed, he kept the two chairs and small table in the immense glass walled-in living room, the sliders open, ocean breeze blowing about, his own penthouse two addresses down the beach, a fabric flowered sofa, green, red, purple and midnight blue, both long kitchens exactly identical. In the dining hall Jones came across a canvas in progress of man in boat on glinting ocean, barely begun.

"Well, I just don't know where I want to go with this. It's not like there's some great mysticism lurking about there."

"Why go anywhere with it? Just paint it in, it's quite good," Jones said appreciatively. "What's happening with the bookmark?"

"Oh, yes, number of ships ahoy floating an illegal grocery. I'm sending in half a quince worth for standing notation, should be most of three years, catch wind of every damn sail in industry."

"That's sound advice. What do you think will sail into port?"

"More rubbish, if you get merely a syringe. I can't predict it thoroughly."

"At last we'll know which fleet down south of Puerto Rico it is that's pulling in stray shore up."

"That's for certain."

They took their coffee out to the balcony to two deck chairs and newly purchased square opaque glass table. Overlooking the golf course on one side and the causeway and strand of pure beige beach and bluest ocean on the other side, they relaxed and took in the leisure of beach living.

SABA 2

The weather was a drowsy neurotic September. Lewis took his morning coffee and fruit cup out on the balcony where the view of the warm aquamarine and sapphire blue ocean at the mile point lay like a vast expansive non-intruded upon field. He wondered about Agent Nick Randolph's remaining tasks and knew that despite the back-up testing Lewis asked from Nassau, it was nearly impossible to predict what evidence would match and which could contradict. Every job required four days to walk the scene, dust for laser print photography, bag the fiber, fluid and other evidence, look in on morgue, and analyze reports. In a case like this the list was routine, despite the exotic findings of burned mouth and tongue and the bodies sealed inside morgue bags. Dusting for prints and laser red enhanced photos allowed the lab analyst to detect whatever was invisible to the naked eye; charting and labeling the whereabouts of prints and shoe patterns in the houses and outside, to match with vehicle tread marks, and match to prints in and around the islands to include warehouses, spectator booths and storage attics and compile and send findings took about twenty hours. A bookmark file consisted of sending for all subject-matching reports, analyzing circumstances in view of the total parent file to date; ongoing and new investigations, and pertinent information. The first task was to examine all reports for problems on wharfs and suspicious trade between islands and mainland. In due time Lewis Lewis would send two agents with expertise in rotary to eye activity at ports, check out incoming shipments, and obtain destinations as to where cargo picks up deck hands, location of ports and type of week-long employment. Common exports were textiles, special dock crate men for overage, and verification that the route was from islands to Mexico to vessels into Florida. Their clearest photo showed about ten nondescript men pushing off from the Martinique coast in three greenish gray large boats. The second task would be to rent a cabin cruiser and put to sea to take photographs and channel radio talk. In the Caribbean it was the gas tank that had to be evaluated for transport of drugs and for explosives. Within hours the radio room would warn control units and broad band units as to locations of suspected illegal border crossings, Swat teams, border patrol disrupt teams, evidence of smuggling, and assign Blackhawk and Commanche and dictate on an Omaha 423 radio, monitor for weapons, and corral suspects in for inspections, usually through Nogales or Cambria Verde, check for human cargo and ports of entry.

As command lieutenant Lewis was given a bulk weight list with instructions to check for any uncommon information. He had already sized up the lower Antilles as the place to be for ship repairs and lay-outs between ships. On Martinique there might be as few as fifty officers stationed there year round assigned to docked cruise ships or mingling at the diner clubs, but on Barbados the primary objective would be to randomly test sacked flour, corn and potatoes; the physician from town lived on Nevis for two decades tending primarily to the addicted and wounded. Short silvery blond hair cut severely to the ears, green eyed, thin through the collar bone and torso, always in navy uniform, Michaela was of London extraction and had served aboard ships most of her youth. She had ridden by island taxi from the King's dock, a stone harbor on the leeward side of Barbados with a beige long two story building with Ciudad di Mexico embassy windows and a dockside walkway bordered by grass on the estuary, to the crime scene while there was still a sliver of moon in the dusky glow of evening. Beside the jetty ambulance boats awaited departure with bodies; they bobbed motors on in the periodic wake of a ferry with siren cresting to shore. In the yellowish pink distance the two towers at the entrance to the cove blinked red lights on and off as below through a narrow station boats of every medical and legal effort pushed forward against rippling waves at four knots an hour. She was shown into the yard from the rear street and through a gate and covered entry way up a few shellacked pine wooden stairs past a laundry room to the death scene. She felt the bodies, gave each a cursory assessment, examined pupils, throat, wrists, chests, armpits. After a brief examination of trauma in mouth, she stood.

She dictated to the aging African-Puerto Rican border agent at her side who took dictation in a scribble standard to courtroom stenographers. "Why was there no odorless substance that might have dissipated in a half hour? Shoot that query to Pathologist Aaron Stubb. Cause of death is intoxication due to opium, open and shut as evidenced from constricted throat, soft nail pads, solely excellent fingerprints, no smudges, pupils not dilated, burnt tongue."

"Are there any attempts to revive?" he asked her for his notes.

"There may be, no way to tell. I'll know later after I look under a lens, but I doubt it, there's usually no indication; if so, there will be two long hypodermics to the lower gum and one injection under the tongue."

"What do you advise?" he asked, flipping to a fresh page.

"Crime scene mock-up, do both earlier crimes and this one on site with package of marijuana, one half ton, opium in vials, cider in ten-gallon jugs, crystal cocaine, tubing and no burners. It'll probably prove they were gone in an instant, minute amount of blood, as I've always said, the fact that the oil for fingerprints was gone at Baja says those men were dead at least a year, but the fact the walls were light green meant discovery was not possible and that they were probably dead years. Just remember my boss said because of the color of the walls, there had to be a pay-out even though they were illegals; so the wives collected without there being prints.

"Here," she pointed to a myriad of clear ten-prints, "these are unmistakable. Now if we find any matching relatives we can look for extortion and who owns these death scene occurrences. Maybe these deaths were meant to occur somewhere else; possibly these boys went for a walk on the beach and surfed, then returned freezing, crawled into bags and were suffocated. Let's look for a photo, inquire whether salary arrived weekly to the door; above all, you should ask when does the owner do this sort of scene."

By nine the next day island constables had a quick list and

Puerto Rico Customs had dispatched a first row of photos to Daytona Beach dateline.

Lewis had snagged a wine taster from Pensacola where sixteen wharves from Bayou Tex to Bayou Chico shaped her ambitions while working the far side of the moon for Puerto Rico barrel for aged ruby and brandy ports and expensive wine. Basic rules were no drugs, aspirin taken to clean the mouth before the first sip, almost no coffee, okay to tea and sweets.

"No mileage without consideration," she touted once the beach cabana lights came on. She was a pretty blond, long dangling curls to her pronounced collar, green-brown eyes with a hint of gold, comfortable in the torso, the suggestion of long established reserve become complacent. Black stretch pants, beige strapless shoulder with large chocolate pearls and backless heels, fifty-four to his seventy-six, she represented all the sins of the flesh without the canceling stigma of too much wealth. "It's the thumb demarcation for a rating on opium molasses – I suppose it might well be hash oil – the rush is like hiking a small mountain."

"All six deck hands responded identically. May as well have supplied a casket for a hearse."

"Could explain the duplicate identification tags you found in drawers."

"I thought the tags raised the cost of shipments."

"Well, that's crass; if you care, don't say you don't care," she said.

"There haven't been many cases where a free newspaper has already bagged the bodies. You yourself must have files."

"Sure we do," he said, ready for anything having arisen at five, gone for his walk on the beachfront green, stopped in at seven for coffee, newspaper and poached egg, easy up, on dark rye with a dollop of Tabasco to clear his sinus. "Commonplace; but tell me, how much tasting would be considered adequate?"

"In the business of wine, it's twenty minutes between sniffers with five maximum per week-long evaluative period. For the opium booster, it's probably less. They do have to be able to sleep it off; might be what the cocaine is for, stimulate them back to reality."

"Can one taste after they've been starved? Our book says not likely; good health is a pre-requisite."

"I know they have to know their own limits just like anyone else. The six were on a goodwill crew hoping to gain a little experience in order to get hired on the boom."

"Well," she toyed with a cube of sugar, "wine will require restitution, absolutely no crabmeat, could be petrale sole, but no oyster on the half shell at all. The palate has to be rinsed, because opium, unlike soccer practice bum Mary-Jane, is extravagant. Poppy requires the one short finger of chocolate but it's no to mint for the timing of the high. Then the final sleep is delirious in sublimation, and rating requires that as well."

"But how long until the smoke was too high?"

"Less than an hour. The male stuck in the elevator was inebriated to a toxic level. No telling what he thought had occurred. Do you have a suspect yet?"

"They have one, an Ant who works the car rental at the airport, occasional drug dealer. I put in for a tale document and a report with my signature came back with a target in Cannes for the Riviera."

"What do the runners say?"

"His fingerprints surfaced for container freight by ship to port. He's handled logistics, ocean freight, freight forwarding, warehousing and pallet freight, shipment orders on a rugged mobile Logic 125K predominantly for packaging for marine. Cargo sheds, water pipes, thin pipes, he's been dock at Long Wharf up in Boston, sand at Shipley Wharf, knows dock hands at the Port Arthur Expansion, at 4837 Jacksonville and at Dundee for office buildings, warehousing, hotels, berths and resorts. Real man about town."

"Where did he get his jump-start?" she inquired, and removed a small bound notepad and pen and flipped to her notations under a heading noted as Tideway tankers, Baystreet River Warehouse and Wharf.

"Oh, who the hell knows? Counterfeit maybe." He replied.

"Soften up, maybe."

"I'm sure there's plenty of unhealthy money in that."

"Well, if when he surfaces all he sees are docks and warehouses and forklifts and semis, then at some point he's going to throw out bait to learn what he's up against." She had found the searched-for reference. "Listen," she said rather breathlessly, "here's the amber. Amber gives the bridge or high shelf sway. He has cove access probably on cement under shallow water; it's going to be a refrigeration-generated mechanism, but definitely a casket."

He removed a French cigarette fag and handing her one, he lit them despite a strong breeze. "Any idea what he's into besides round toes, black socks and ankle trousers?"

She blew out a steady stream of smoke, her face pricked with alert observation as if just now made aware she had caught his attention. "I'd say he meant them to die."

"I'd say so too. Might as well tell you. The dead had no scars on their bodies at all, literally nothing except tightness of the vascular over the neck due to the burned tongue, and they each had it, so it's a known reaction caused by a drug which even I'm not well acquainted with."

"What has the lab said?"

"About hire to unlicensed entrants? Just what I said, a practical way to get in the door to better paying wharf work." Then catching himself, he said, "The drug hash in mixture tends to be neither inhalant nor ecstatic. It's a weed. Not quite spice tea; it has a bit of odor that lashes if one isn't careful."

"Could be just the excuse he wants, with a quick death there's bound to be a fast retardant applied to exteriors in an effort to hold off any other chemical contaminant reaction."

"How many men are you intending to send into scour the area?"

"Two. It's the most I can cover."

He took her to a tiny restaurant with tablecloths and lit candles for lamb, sautéed potatoes and cubed squash, and sorbet with biscuit and frothy café. Over dinner he held her hand, small talked her to pearls of laughter, anecdotes about his early days in the field when just prior to the extension of the Panama Canal he had to send wireless halfway around the world out of kitchens, always on the move, another deck under cover of moonless ghostly lit skies, at lunch when family men went about to conduct errands. He gave her the spoon, watched her swallow softly, kissed her ear, drew her willingly to him, an old man on the prowl.

Precisely at eleven after three hours dining they stepped into the cobbled plaza where he hailed a horse and buggy to his doorstep and they rode the elevator to his penthouse, her arm about his waist. He kissed her in the hall, gave her time once he admitted her to his glass shrine to admire the flat, to wander through the living room, walk onto the balcony and momentarily glimpse the stars and come back inside and linger in the kitchen, then put on soulful jazz, removed her blouse and placed her on the blue marble counter of the kitchen and kissing her skin began to make love.

Prior to his trip to Saba, he had spent an appreciable month locked in a deadly embrace with a port manager to assess what had happened to the billing for ships carrying tile from Montenegro. German spy glass had lost over a bidding war to the Finnish starlighter. The news reported longer delays than usual citing tide irregularities, the Westerlies had met with climbing waves out of the tradewind loop causing oceanic ships to be delayed indefinitely. The Grin herself had been boarded for South American ivory, all ships thereafter sailing the horn recalled to Nigeria to face an inquiry. The Ivy Glade report rang late – at the end of the third quarter after gale winds swept across the swaying fields of the Antilles.

Lewis Lewis scanned the flying jibs for the taciturn Belle Fleur, wherever she was, her rust can hull speeding into a fortnight. Was it a wind down, he asked himself picturing her half till swallowing bale tonnage of ocean. The fancy mariner had met fierce resistance over the southern cap, emerged into Magellan Strait, aft lowered, scouting for a protected inlet. If she relied upon faulty cracked instruments, flying by boom, she could be anywhere. He must have contacted the Australian manufacturer a half dozen transmissions before he turned it over to a choir wind tuner who could perceive sea storms in a lashing viper. Probably she had docked, the easiest strait was Tasmania, currents easterly, from that direction the wind could but fill the blowing sail full till.

During these uncertain hours which stretched seemingly without end he kept to a rigorous schedule; although worry was scarcely alleviated, only the line at the bottom of the glass of whiskey loosened the tie. He had finally succumbed to a realization Abby had left and with her the chapter on Baja Canal closed without so much as a steady blow. The Kellestra case of a year ago was piled in boxes around his desk. Its sorry wharf for warehouse sections four to fifty saw the shut down of rubber and a swift change to rail as the new replacement certificate. Steel ligatures sat on three docks awaiting shipment, disbursement long paid. Even with crane cargo it waited for the Kellestra to complete its journey to port. The team of physicians had six months ago departed also, logistics made for equipment provisions and boarding.

Inside the rebuilt wharf warehouse, walls outfitted with actual wood walls, the twenty chosen agents, all men and one female sat in a large room facing two offices that overlooked the other desks from behind glass, one in which the Nassau chief came to oversee deaths two days a month, and the other given over to Lewis to oversee his units. Jones was up the hill at the new Fairmont with its elegant portico building, gigantic rolling green golf courses all the way to the windy sea, upper estate penthouse offices occupying the top eighth floor, two rooms apiece, black carpet pile, mahogany cabinets, desks and phones with television Intel monitors, desks, computers, two upholstered pale blue George Smith chairs and chartreuse Armani Casa stage show sloped couch, a frameless in the bedroom which opened to a balcony. For Jones, this was the step up; but at the brick building with boats lined up alongside the docks and products coming in all hours of the day, the office with sizable table for a desk outfitted with seven computers, each a dire necessity, for dateline wireless, AIS charting, notes on cases with instant agent assignment, a console to look for any physical address for name constituted the ease for command. Since his promotion he had forgotten women, turned his back on socializing at the office and at the green, and put his energies into catching the target the chief had finally cornered through receipts for events established by X-Interpol. The year reports from his own agents had finally come in from Jones, Luster, Gannet, Wasoe and Gornne who between them provided an arrowhead tablet of billing for photos predominantly of collections of fingerprint post-mortems of color, art painted on building exteriors along and near the port, curtains, outside lights, walk-ups, any demarcation there was new activity to be considered. Any photo of an overcast day was a headache; blue sky were good days to find people schmoozing at outdoor markets. There had been some five years earlier a strikingly similar crime in which seven bodies were discovered beneath a dock house in white plastic firemen's body bags. The only narrative permitted to be released was the description of these youth as shelf stocking clerks out of South Carolina's exit to Lauderdale. Across the interior plaza wedged between the museum on reconstitutes and a newspaper press was the teen porn magazine produced by Benjamin Ween, a disclaimed physician whose nurse at the Philadelphia office center choked her husband after a scandalous infidelity with a sleeping patient. As a result the Whimper editions contained disgusting photographs of females predominantly who had been murdered, a veritable photo catalog of smashed heads, stabbings to the back, wrists and legs chained to kennels, young teens locked up without food or bathrooms, bed scenes, child porn, legs spread, chestless and boyish, anyone's whimpering dog, blood dribbling out of the mouth, rare occurrences of murders of mind-twisted indelible images, knifings, sodomies, dried vomit, it was hard to believe anyone chose to defile the young.

His quarterly crime journal listing The Islander had arrived and lay splayed front and center over books to be reviewed. Sometime between issuing a finder for the Belle Fleur and the arrival of his list, he had received a photo junket of a much older crime that originated in Saint John's. His desk reflected the very cosmopolitan way in which the bodies were disposed of – behind wrought iron fences, celebrated pastel pink and terra rosa mansions smothered by leafy fronds and overgrowth of hedges and trees as though the owner in departing for whereabouts unknown had let the high tiled martyred roofs vanish in the very growth that probably gave it beauty. His desk held stacks of dateline tabs, old tattered files, ticker indexes, narratives, day old coffee, a half eaten tomato, bacon and cucumber sandwich, an appraiser glass to detect forgery, rows of newly developed photos on the adjacent table waiting for the crime to be laid out. Four old cases lay deposited like glinting gold in pure warm aquamarine water, all easily identifiable. A car full of seven French-looking tall tight-chested sailors, an overnight in the Florida second key among the storefronts of mumu's and knit blankets for rainy, humid, sometimes torpid summer weather, at a resort owned by a contraband mover, his vanquished garden isle two story properties raided at least every few years by border, the recent raid which produced evidence of human cargo, torched curtains leaving charred green walls, photos of homosexual rapes lying about, food left on plates untouched, the carpeted floors a mess with evidence of blood, drinks everywhere, tins with mediocre marijuana on bureaus, counter tops, bathroom drawers, bedroom headboard, kitchen; an old boat in the slip, the crime scenes borrowed upon for the dank interiors of the abandoned houses as though the business he were in was to recreate the same scene every few islands. All he saw were the oldest suburbs in the warehouse district of Miami port, slow to be replaced, tiny studios, an illegal barrio surfaced from an underground through basements and damp beaches running along a series of cement escarpments, boarded up storage halls, closed train stations, rundown sections along unused train track, evidence of abandoned train compartments converted to form a quick bed for escapees or drug addicts.

Lewis ran a dish for prints on the Nassau fiasco but found no verifiable prints. Someone high up in Port Authority or

Border had either squelched release or there just weren't any. The charred bedrooms had the look of professional jobs – stick homeless, drug dependent families in an out-of-the-way place and then periodically send in a do-er to crash the place. This was old tired police work, the haggling end of new-age living out of a dumpster. Lewis did the next best thing; he looked for entries. Most had their backs to the camera, most teen girls resembled boys. In a line-up they'd look the same; from a distance they'd be a tribe. He took faces never-the-less, square-cut them, clipped them with letter-number queries, and sent them to hostage tank. Although the first dribblings on the Nassau crime described summer labor who worked mansions with basement coolers, because files were denied, the mystery became imbued with the same ghastly revulsion as lit torches used to see into the feverish darkness were cancelled by gusts of wind blowing from the sea. Not even an hour later the men were trapped when the river sludge backed up drowning them. The seven men could have been asked to cook hash oil or guard storage for that matter, or await delivery of raw materials for drug manufacture, or they were renting a house, or they were hitch-hiking on the highway and wandered in, who knew what circumstance gave them access?

Jones found a haggard Lewis inside his dockside office below a whirring fan, a green desk lamp light on, felt pen writing on the white board the essential questions as to how the bodies came to be bagged on Barbados, where any illegal tunnel that emerged at the wharf might start, and who was interested in hiring human trade who were left for death. Lewis looked finely attired, wearing rolled up starched light yellow stiff collar shirt with all black tie, pin-striped black and pale yellow Dago trousers, and round toe black tied shoes. The effect of nine coffee cups amidst a file-stacked desk, all seven computers on, three notepads on the calendar blotter was that he was intense at work. Jones himself wore brown tweed trousers despite the heat with short sleeved white shirt and grey chappy sweater with open toed heavy sandals.

"These people are extremely vindictive," Jones said, uncapping a paper cup with espresso. "Just for turning over that Florida couple."

"We don't know why six men were killed. This sort of kill-or-be-killed has been going on since the war. That seismic tidal plateau in 1938 that wiped out the coast of North Carolina is just the tip of the crisis. The war was on. We had our boys up and down the east coast watching for any shadow that moved out of the shrubbery."

"It's just such an unpredictor. Then, those seven men were found floating inside morgue bags in a basement."

"Nothing is what it seems. That was a real shock; this only looks as if there is a connection. There may not be."

"What's come down from the recorder, anything?"

Lewis said, rather unremarkably, "We have their names, matched to the overabundance of evidence, prints, matching clothing, vomit, beer bottles, handprints on walls, clear shoe impressions in mud, spatter marks on all sorts of surfaces, walls, doors, bathroom tile, refrigerators, fuse box, tables and product strainers almost as if they thought they ought not to wear surgical gloves."

"Are they cross-indicated in the earlier crime?"

Lewis gave a laugh. "No way to know, all information was denied."

"If prints were denied, doesn't that say we have come across a previously unknown Doe from an Eastern European Bloc country?"

"It says to me that someone wanted to gain entrance to see various remote islands. In the war we thought we had an Internal National Service leak because some group was stealing the postal letter service off the street."

"Was that in Germany?"

"Three miles south of the Hungarian boundary, yes. We were losing by air stamped mail mostly. Our letter bags turned up inside a train station right outside Dusseldorf without any apparent overseer except it probably was delivered by transom auto-coach because that was the automobile of the era used by station guards. It caused quite an inconvenience when as a result medical papers did not reach the lower islands of New Guernica or the new ship base outside Panama. My honest estimate is these men may have started their long origins on board these vessels."

"Are we seeking a German-based operative?"

"Probably a remark column reviewer who came through those islands to the Caribbean on board a ship passing as deck or kitchen. I've requested info on dock handlers able to target-identify any such individual. By now it's entirely possible the one or more subterfuge operators have remade their identities."

Jones set aside the lukewarm coffee and removed a cigarette and lit it while Lewis poured himself another line of whiskey and added a cube of brown sucar. "Didn't we have a case involving bounty in the wilderness of the Indian River marsh reserve?"

"The boats that were rifled with bullet holes? Awfully recent."

"It might be something, a fast and dirty way to put off a chase for wanted men, could be dinghy docks in the Florida everglades, marina store, small motor boats along the river."

"You could scour the photos," Lewis said, agreeable. "These men are from somewhere. The scenes where death has occurred are similar. All baseline sewage, two beds per room, bathroom large enough for six, lots of drugs, access between houses, low frequency radio on boats, little lighting at night. We should know for starters what brought them there – just to manufacture opium ---"

"Seems the most straight forward," Jones replied, writing it down on his lap size calendar. "I s'pose it could be to await delivery of cash for the drug."

"Most likely, but assign it anyway," Lewis instructed. Fingers interlaced, he thought it through. "Who is our man? Does he ask them to guard storage, rent a house; could be they worked for the mark, or they wandered in although less likely that it's accidental chance; our mark has to have owned any number of properties, even without evidence of bombs, he might not be interested in converting to ready-made cash."

In his cubicle Jones perused the listing of seven photo-file tabs. All focused on angles of the death scene of bagged bodies, one showed the sooted room with five clear sets of prints. He square cut each negative and Xerox-faxed them to Fingerprint division whereupon he received five identifications, each from Nicaragua, coffee hills, seasonal workers from June through October for six years, boss-man also Nicaraguan landowner and segment plantation hombre of four four hundred acre foundations. Boss was named Stiegler Maartens, aged 65, seven houses from Blanca coast to Verde on the other side of Mexico to Homidad to Guadaloupe to Florida Mean Town some sixty miles north of Miami South Beach, all seven dilapidated salmon colored ochre mansions with dark blue tile roofs, newish brick patios front and back, wrought iron gates surrounding each smallish estate, two-foot deep India-Taj-style pools, grass overgrown with palm leaf fronds and packed in with gladiolus and large white perfume-smelling flowering bushes. Inside was a plantation tile-laid foyer, orange wood stairs that led past a living room with open hearth to three bedrooms, each a hundred and twenty square feet with windows peering above the growth to the ocean, and a blue tiled bathroom with cabinets for every use. The houses had sunk into disrepair years ago as either tenant or owner had remarried or relocated until with merely the damp monsoon howling winds and gales of rain, the interiors slipped into abused and untended corridors.

Rather abruptly he turned a corner, having cross-indexed each of the scenes for who if anyone had ever stayed at any of the scenes, he came across Abby's picture, her lanky beguiling body in a posture of languid endurance. He found himself chilled as if someone much higher up than Lewis may have dropped the photo into a bin, now could be in search of the agents who laid track for wives of unsecured gemstone analysts. Lewis had been discovered by black thieves during a bombing of Haiti. He didn't think it could ever amount to an irrational fear for him. Although Lewis's experience was commonplace – they saw him, he probably memorized the people he saw –

Jones considered him an exception, untouchable if not incontrovertible. No reason for the sensation, there was someone who looked out for this and who classified it, but he was nevertheless unnerved.

"You were both on film with Abby," Rhonda said to reassure. Despite a penthouse on the other side of the island, her voice was distant on the phone. "That's how we all get there."

When Jones conveyed his conversation with Rhonda, Lewis was on his way to becoming sauced, but he had put the coffee on and propped open a window and laid out a folded blanket on the couch to spend his overnight in his office if the case wore through to morning. "That's life in the fast lane," Lewis quipped. "Get yourself a lifestyle, get yourself a Rhonda."

"It's not for me, too haphazard a way of life. She didn't want the divorce, I don't think."

"She sued for the divorce to hurt me. At least I wasn't cookie-cutter love."

Jones reconstructed the rooms of both houses and placed the various sets of ten prints by color laser – red, blue, green, yellow, and orange – in each room to chart foot traffic. In the room with the bodies the skin color had retained its normal skin color, the injection into the gum inhibited reviving despite a faint pulse, the subcutaneous cut to one man's upper thigh was dark orange which indicated forty-five hours dead. The others had succumbed at different hours, and probably all fatigued at the same time. The heat had blown out in a storm outage two days earlier leaving the houses cold below forty degrees. The men had been seen five and a half miles down the coast at the wharf helping a ship dock by pulling it in with rope. Someone had gone down on their knees and never recovered. Based upon where sets of prints were and shoe prints, he expected to determine what the men were doing, who was cooking, who packed, who ate by the demanding task of deductive reasoning. Wharf photos showed the men departed wharf crew at four and began the walk back; they did not freeze despite walking in wet clothing after standing to the waist in ocean because the presence of a quarter inch of water leaked in during the night prevented it, but there were blanket fibers inside their mouths wedged onto their teeth that said they were suffocated. Green had run from the second house at fast clip judging by the imprint on the carpet to the front yard. There were cast prints leading to a creek and pooled tarn still with muddy water that reflected trees and palms. He could feel it in his torso that this was a big find. If the best photos possible, then they had to make guesses.

"The closet obscured the early stages of the crime," Lewis remarked as he entered Jones' office with two cups of coffee for the late night they were putting in. "No way to say where the place is; it gives the criminal a safe yield."

"Nail pads were soft, meaning the vaso-vagal nerve went numb as a result of being pricked by some sharp prick causing numbness to the sides up to forty minutes."

"Maximum two days dead."

"I agree," Jones said.

"Where did green finger and shoe turn up?"

"No proof as yet."

"What do we know? Was this a wife?"

"Could be, one set of linens tested for semen and foam. Lab is hopeful she is one of the wives who inherited in the Baja scene. They think whoever is behind these assaults is eliminating witnesses."

"Possibly someone died in prison is on a tear."

"Maybe it's expediency. They can't afford exposure."

"No kidding, they have worried about coming to a new country since they were brought in around the time fifty thousand other people come. They're a group that has lived in houses underwater. They know how to cause a panic to escape – just flood a suburb and drown the police."

"So where is green and when did she arrive?" Jones asked, tapping his monitor having mapped her actions by the evidence computer.

"Well, what do the prints say about the boyfriend or husband, whatever he is?"

Jones looked up the blue set of prints. "Chief packer. It's his prints all over the cellophane packaged closet. He's in his fertile years judging by the sperm count. He had a thousand bucks French on his dresser which he entrusted presumably to this female."

"Let's get wireless in on this. Maybe they received a report. Did anyone hear cries; how many seconds before they lapsed; was anyone seen; where did the doer reside; how long before a body was recovered?"

Jones determined that a female by the name of Dollar had come in with a cruise ship a few hours after the Turkish meager vessel was boarded; her ship was ten decks and sat in the customs harbor for a half day as officers gathered everyone sailing in a big room and processed passports and baggage; and she was originally destined for the J.N. France General Hospital to work four days which she did under an alias, Denny Bradshaw. Border Patrol had prints on her for Frigate Bay for standing ship at a rum distillery;

she stayed at a nice trellis apartment pink and green with a balcony overlooking the bay for five months and played tennis at the adjoining red tennis courts while her boyfriend worked Sydney Tower for the Caribbean Hurricane Network for a half year in hurricane weather driving the crew out in gales;

her boyfriend was a jovial sort by the name Niguel Meeker but his prints didn't put him in the soot room;

whereas Life put her on Roseau, Dominica working for a canteen truck service which she drove to the dockyard weekly when the ships unloaded their containers near the wide road across from rain-streaked warehouses, silos, modern high school, all brand plaza and bar set against misted dark green hills off the ocean; for a few years she owned a flat in a boxy stucco painted yellow cramped in with a hundred other stuccos with balconies dotted on a verdant green forest at the coast; compressed by a small college, stadium, four window balcony with an upstairs, dock, cruisers, a string of lights at Dalta dock; for a year of well-to-do living she had a studio on the third

floor overlooking the ocean, a tree-lined drive to the campanile tower, comfortable, some modern glass front, plantation
apartments, fenced-in pier, stone harbor wall, A-line and flat
roof tops, van transportation instead of taxi cabs, below mountains of dark green trees like a sea of verdant green; around the
coastline over hillsides was an agricultural reserve with a creek;
    at the ocean was beige sand, light blue and clear water,
seaweed lazily drifting in, a rainforest of moss green trees. She
was in demand having taken her truck to all cities on all islands, recognized by her pretty mauve curled hair and known
to travel all the way to Florida if the money was right; she married a sugar cane field hand in Basseterre at Mt. Misery whose
cousin in Miami applied and received permission to work for
SABA Packaging Plant as had four of the five ten-prints found
at the scene came through church-hill where Sobba was murdered; most days found them working for church lodging and
meals, evenings in a bar with teal green lights, small glasses
serving greek rum, eating a plate of cold steamed crawdads of
sitting outdoors on the sidewalks smoking French cigarettes
or inside beneath Greco and Rivera listening to flamenco; one
was all the way from Saint Angelina back roads of all wood
forty houses sitting in Appalachia high grass potting plants
over the crumbling ceilings of cold storage rooms built right
inside the ground; one was from Vasteras where boats and
dock houses floated down river into a wide river plain in rainy
weather; she had dropped off a female at 1:59 pm who crossed
the parking lot to a set of buildings to Still House; she knew
people at the Christian reading room in brick Tudor roof with
open front room leaded glass; ivy covered separate red and
brown brick churches with towers, stone walls leading to stairs
with gate, greenhouses several blocks south; eye witnesses said
– they heard female cry for help – help me, please help me; ten
minutes of screaming. A person called police to report where
they heard this, a young girl curly hair accepted cigarette from
a policeman in patrol car she got into to say what she observed,
said coffee fought with person who knifed her in leg, she ran
but he caught up at still and pushed her into water and climbed

on top of her to suppress her and cut off her letter box finger; people parked in cars at the still fled, one entered gate of cemetery greenhouse for a rescue jacket; lunch that had been delivered was in back of truck. It was said the man who murdered her married his mom who was a blessed virgin, this man was described as having left his flat in a tenement two story house a half mile away on the main strip, walked to the parking lot and stabbed her and dragged her body, subsequently he delivered the finger to a park where she first rented a room to the man; it was conjectured that he murdered a guard at a crossing for identifying him as a bomber of Dresden and then hid in a submerged house on a river in Holland; he was suspected of having a job as a taxi driver, he had been seen on Antigua boarding a ship for destination Miami; a dockhand reported seeing him at Champagne reef waterfront; another person who made an anonymous call did so at 2:20 am and said they thought coffee was killed in a still three blocks from Our Holy Worship cemetery.

SABA 3

An all night sheriff posse and border patrol police dog working to turn over the soil of the grassy knoll came upon the mangled body of a woman buried inside a kennel beneath the ground several yards from the Barbados still. Her body was mostly buried, part of an arm and hand could be identified beneath leaves and soil. She was slender, dark brunette bouffant hair, her soft face badly scratched; a missing severed finger proved she was the object of felonious assault. The still itself was less than a mile from the house where five men lay dead in morgue bags. It was evident the woman went for help, yelling for someone to attend to her; the fact of where her body was found said she also was murdered.

The state coroner ordered a full workup on this latest victim. She had three superficial marks on her face on her chin from a blunt weapon. Otherwise there were no other signs of perpetration including torn garments or sexual rape. Her body was covered in dry damp mud, much of which clung to her facial skin. Twenty tests were administered – seven for scrapings to determine whether she had scratched at her assailant's skin, three for the presence of unknown substances inside her mouth, and ten for hair, fiber, and prints. The fingerprint computer gave her name as "Dollar" Coffey, age 41, understudy, married to an island warrants constable, and born of a Sable police officer Benjamin Mason and actress Rissa Worth, star of a remake of Black Velvet who after the death of an infant entered a sainthood order. An information sheet on her provided information as to how to interview a candidate for bondable employment – what is your name; have you ever committed a crime; how many DUI's have you had; and have you ever operated a wireless.

Lewis wondered whatever happened to Robby Mempis, a slender college boy on a bicycle who gave the impression that beneath a patchwork cap the wavy sandy hair and high buttoned stiff collar shirt was the rudimentary makings of a choir boy at the organ cans. He would be a lean seventy to-day, tooting at the bridge of an ocean vessel making its way stateside through the Ant. If not for his most accurate wireless four damned would not have been caught after they robbed a farmhouse in the German woods and slaughtered the house animals.

The belief in quarters was that the five men and man in the third deck elevator were justifiably slain if because some person at lab knew these men had had a first digital of one hand sliced off. These were traitors, who had all committed treasonable acts, sins far past reasonable indictments of dishonesty or per-jury. The movies that Dollar and her chemist physician super-star had made consisted of Spartacus filmed on location at Old Mill motel for the fire scene, Leviticus II at the Hell set, Little Women at Legion Park and two films of minor distinction. These production shots were fore-noticed as no coffee on the studio set, houses only, no lawn shots.

He had one witness-heard statement – "come back after dark," remarked to the man who had walked four blocks to the scene who wanted to shoot keel in the next movie by one Jim Haserman. In an attached file, obtained some weeks later, a screaming match that led to the brutal murder of Dollar's business associate who was also discovered stuffed inside a stile in Legion Park, Brutus Country, the heard shout was, "You're crazy too." Both bodies, when found, were removed to county morgue for identification. Consideration had been given by Island Border as to where each body could be shipped to – UCLA at Pendleton Camp on the beach or Presidio at San Francisco, both California, United States; Martindale, Iowa; Twin Peaks, Wisconsin; Heather, Idaho, run by the second disposed female; Medford, Oregon; Ranch, Wyoming; or Bel-fast, New York. Lewis found the belief impossible to accept once he obtained the first lab evaluation from Belfast, New York that stated fingers off one man, Dollar and Dollar's co-associate were illegal.

The ocean at Miami South, Florida stretched to an infinite

horizon, the sand an impure tan. Lewis walked along the sand, the skein caught tight like a seal's skin fur, darkish tan color of a moth. The morning was bright with a mere suggestion of restrained wind, the surf coming in cocoon-like amidst cresting shallow froth up the slight incline, the early sun charted by mist rising off the sand in plumes as if driven cattle. It was low tide, the grainy brown beach a thin slick of water creased on sand, further out teal waves rolled in, apartment condominiums on a brown soil cliff made of wood, erect steel and glass of three and four stories overlooked the ceaseless blue. Insanity seemed to walk the planet among a thin cloaked pine forest through which a mid-afternoon train wound its way through steep terrain, green light filtering down, a blur rushing by, dirt ground spelled with herbaceous lush creepers, whiskered trees, utter quiet, the last compartment taking in only a well-made, slightly raised track over reddish, rock anointed dirt, golden brown lichen, the barest glimmering course of the river below, slicked, murky, in the sunlight it appeared as a clear reflection of mustard and bay leaf in tint slime mud, in other places dankly teal. The fingerprints placed the second female on the tragic scene, perhaps it was she who bagged them to prepare the men's bodies for transportation to the tiny morgue on Antigua. Her name was Gemma Bauterrie, born in Hague, Amsterdam, resident of southern Florida, formerly a polygraph agent for a Hollywood movie service. Because Florida had no morgue, her body would be shipped to the Heather morgue in Idaho state where the coroner knew her. Lewis himself had been called to Heather on numerous occasions to identify islanders, it lay north of a small freshwater lake, snow peaks blue in the distance, forest showing in bald patches, the train on the ridge moving slowly, lake waves were grey dark brown mud, mountain towns with lake resorts and piers awaited.

The fingerprints on her tested to a residence on the Norwegian coast at Armar and a summer sport of a hundred mile run from her town west along the coast. She led sprint races for eighty trained long distance runners, each section run approximately a half hour at four miles per hour with forty minute rest for a total of fourteen hours. Bauterrie herself placed first over a half dozen summers. She also placed in southwestern Hungary at the Vesper Memorial Institute of Psychoanalysis for studies in test taking, psycho-diminutive shallow personality, unusual occurrence of presumed aberration to solicit drugs from suspected volcano bombers, as well as microchip sunlight tracking. She was living in the city Vesper when three super fast robot-piloted jets crashed into Rock Mountain thirty-nine thousand feet above the highest road there. The report sent Lewis for the referral on her came from San Joaquin Delta as follows: "10:22 pm, Thursday, 1960, nurse from city medical legal library, corner Baker Street, across from park through stile heard to scream blood chilling cries for help; a young man rescued her and dragged her into stile; no breath, 'she is dead.' Sheriff dispatched, body admitted to Joseph's." Further information from police closed files read, scene was location for filming The Little Women and for Pride and Prejudice, originally starring Gracie Knapp who resigned after discovery of Gemma Bauterrie's body and by understudy Janice Coffey, who was filmed for four scenes for distance. Sets were built two houses with seven acres including small lake by Matt Hennesy, Dustin Maitland and Philip Carter for foreman John R. Westly, Licensed. They designed a park square bordered by three blocks of average size houses between Baker Streets and Main Road, and by two blocks stately manors at far end of park. The full account staked that Gem Louisa Bauterrie went to the lake at four-thirty-one in the late afternoon while the sky was still daylight to enjoy duck feeding and a cup of milk custard drink when she was startled by a rather large broad shouldered male cutting a section of fence and slamming it into the water. She walked twenty meters and told him, you can't do that, whereupon he said his friend would do her if she did not get going. A twenty-four year old handsome male, dark hair and tan Italian complexion entered the park where he struck her across the back of her head causing her to fall and left her for dead. They then sauntered across the park green, crossed the street, knocked loudly for a carry-lamp from Michael Baten, the resident obtained the item, they set off to the nurse when both men struck the resident, battering him extensively, shoved him into the lake, positioned the fence over him and proceeded to deck him. Upon arrival to the said same hospital, the victim was pronounced dead of a broken collar. Estimated time of death was given as between five and seven that evening.

As far as Lewis could make out the dead man found crushed inside the ship elevator on the third deck had been killed because he possessed the turn key for the ship radio, this same key could be used to operate a letter box typewriter equipment. Not a ship clerk agent of which there were three adult men over age fifty-three, nor either two docking captains, one who worked mess, or any of the twelve necessary deck hands knew anything, in addition to which this radio ship to land officer was newly assigned from Twelfth Dock High Bridge which contrary to public belief did not lay asphalt but instead carried vehicles by ship from one side of Miami-Delray to the other side. The crushed man had been snuffed out by a rag soaked with baby urine and the drug for manic-depression lithium. Lithium was known as full life for reviving where there was a slight pulse, however erratic, taking up to well over forty years.

Upon discovering five dead men previously ship deck work hands for three days work duty out on Nevis, Janice Coffey ran into the night shouting for help. No one at any of the nearby houses responded. She ran as far east as the closest Nevis wharf where ten stone warehouses crated a thousand Saba pineapples bound for Egypt every few months. Someone there took her life, a substantial slash to the back of her left thigh and a ring finger off the wrong hand, thus it was a murder. While she was gone, someone went into the house of the dead bagging the bodies with cellophane to the left hand each, and then bagging their bodies, two in blue opaque body bags, one in a off grayish white body bag, one inside a brown body bag and one inside a black body bag, all bags except two legal disposal for morgue. The exact reason Coffey's body was to turn up in Florida at a hotel on Miami South Market Gardens was unknown. Lewis sent a complete correspondence to each church in Florida to request whereabouts for any of the seven except Gemma.

The dictums were returned within a month through a central district administrator office. Attached to a short letter which read, Thank you for writing the Monsignor with your interest in seeking information on the five medical mates. It is with regret our office can only attest to the facts that all five were in Angiteren in the late 1950's. The accompanying information listed a massacre of predominantly children who fell into soft soil extending approximately a quarter mile. No one could get to it. Many survived. Survivors report the shifting soil was very watery and thus hard to move in; however was not sewage. This information follows a query as to when are married actors kicked off the set? Our military parole agent wrote: drug use, alias or lied on resume; and an in-home murder of unexplained causes.

Man in ship elevator originally lived in an area of forest and mist – extensive mist that rose off no water, seemed only to seep from mountain roads, spill over orchards, through crop hectares, over miles of farms. The office added that he could have lived in Norway but not Baptise, Poland, nor Wakken, Germany. Oddly he had arrived with Gemma after her brother wrote her to dispense a stuck ship case in the ice in eastern Norway. It was his sister who married the man who would one day murder a young physician on location in a lake setting at Legion Park in a Hollywood suburb some four hundred miles north. The dead man crushed inside the ship elevator owned a house in the Legion district on the set; the other five homes and medical clinic were owned by Dollar Coffey.

When a group disrupted a country they resided in, what did they want? The case had become a pestering headache. Lewis was still left with an essential concern that something alarming must have become revealed on several of the polygraph tests. Someone who worked a set on location must have discovered incriminating information on someone. The Austria-Prussian war had sent many a worthwhile agent into Hungary as a result of radical anti-government madness committed in Hungary after the government withdrew its populace from five towns on a summit at a caldera. If hundreds of people fled across boundaries to clinics that stayed open all night to receive them by train, the surrounding government also made arrangements for displaced people. The night wore on. Somewhere in the balmy dark a howling dog sent shivers down his spine causing him to be poignantly alert to the human sins of mortality. The brief interaction on Saba and Nevis left him with a judicious season for death, out in the Caribbean Sea drifting on a yacht or vessel were the culprits, their task un-prevented or already over, their sail bent for lantern-steered waters. Had they emerged from across the pacific having fled an utmost corruption or taken non deceitful flight, the terrors of escape weighed upon their minds. They were presumably the first to have fled a conquered homeland, to have gazed at life with prevailing remorse, to have possibly even placed themselves at risk by fleeing with the actual culprits. Who knew, let alone suspected, where these cannibals might eventually come to and the risk of recognition? There was every reason to believe that Austria upon seeing dark smoke rising into the sky charted the source, sent trained forest arson investigators in, and having discerned who the spill guards were and their last suspected addresses prepared for war. Certainly the aims had to involve toxification of drinking water, ground disposal for non sewage waste, as well as instantaneous elimination of forest stands, the life of that nation discarded with her ditches, commemorative landmarks, her towns falling to the last like rubble under the pressure of gas emissions. No one who awaited ships from Europe in Miami's port, the only deepwater channel along the eastern seaboard for any vessel to enter, would imagine who the newcomers might be. Whether ships crowded in by day or lights sparkled from afar reflecting on glittering waves mattered not, the lit wharfs could take fifty ships a day, feed and house people, and create jobs for five thousand arriving from the leg-embattled inhospitable trenches of devastation. It was not a simple matter to view the sudden influx of homeless without looking for those original inhabitants. The world of

Bauterrie already enhanced by running marathons would not seem quite as placid as the celebrated authors and entertainers whose twenty-nine years were spent seeking the wretched of their own underworld.

SABA 4

Lewis Lewis went for his usual morning walk on the beach. The tide rolled in slowly, a continual cadence, reassuring and familiar. Already the sun had burned off the night's steady downpour of overcast skies. Beach Patrol was on the water in boats to check for tired swimmers. Their vehicles parked on the sand near sunbathers lying beneath blue parasols. He strolled to a few chairs where Jones sat, lounge and polo shirt wear, sunglasses, blond sandy hair ruffled by wind, the morning Dade Source folded across his bare legs.

"My inquiry came in," Lewis said, settling onto an available chair. "Elevator man injected with lithium, can't revive. Presumably he was killed for his rope key for his ability to start up an engine."

"What do you suppose for?"

"We know the vessel was seen over closed circuit."

"Is there anything that ties the Bauterrie gal to the five men?"

"We know she had to be on site because it was she who ran for help and was killed at the harbor stile."

"Yes," Jones agreed, waving down a beach vendor for two cups of café latte in striped vertical light blue and white shirt, blue trousers and white navy wear cap. "A ridiculously bad scene."

"Very bad. It had to have been premeditated, Bauterrie's name means low bridge walk-through."

"The very idea Coffey's body was discovered in South Beach Garden Condominiums strikes me as odd to say the least, why in Florida? Fingerprints put both her and rope key in a husband-wife relationship." Lewis sipped his drink. "Given any thought about that promotion?"

"I've considered it, but it'll put me in Bermuda. I was hoping to get a flight deck one-way to San Juan."

"You think you would like a desk on paint restoration for ships? Awfully tedious concentration."

"It's the latest thing, right up my alley. No two colors ever the same."

"Color affects the keel I've heard."

"Yes, that probably is true. On a ship the keel is part of the hull that rests above the water line. Color is where the ship docks."

Lewis remarked, "In a movie the keel records talking. I wonder what makes that job so desirable?"

"Keel measures ground up to maximum thirty feet."

"The catch on the ship elevator rests over a low floor called a low trim. On a movie set a trim is used to eliminate sounds."

Jones asked, "Are you thinking a trim and keel operator may have bought these murders?"

"Well, here's an option. You have to inquire, How often does keel for movie stage work ship plaster? I think it's at one-quarter total work experience, about ten years. Then they are acclimated to height."

"Such as at Fifth Street High Bridge?"

"No, it's an outside job. That's why a film shoot cannot occur outside. Let's assume the drug dealer had a problem getting his stash onto a reliable vessel. Where could that person have gone to? A movie stage might be an ideal place."

"Or the individual is already on the island residing there. Where did you want to take this?"

The Intersystem ship computer placed all parties on two ships, each which docked inside a month. The first ship, the Turkish vessel, originally headed to sea to join a cruiseship master making its passage to Grenadines when the body of a radio man was discovered and put to dock. Intersystem officers boarded, removed the body, and returned an hour later to collect passports and take statements from the staff. Later, nearly a week after the passports were processed and matched to Steigmund tests, short order form of polygraph based upon obtaining first two fingerprints, matches were released. After a day all hands were sent to Saba to a work farm and staff to Nevis to await orders. Neither Bauterrie nor Coffey were on board. The second ship, a medical supplies ship making its twenty-first voyage from Australia brought Bauterrie to After island and took Coffey across the strait to Nevis Gale Wind Prediction Center. Once Bauterrie encountered the five male hands she proceeded to take vitals, draw bloods, and record eye exams, check for written proficiency, and otherwise provide day cooking and light housekeeping.

The primary subject prints on Bauterrie proved that she was originally an employee on the set of South Pacific filmed in the north island of Tahiti prior to the Bay of Pigs fiasco when the U.S.S. Nordstorm allegedly sank off the coast of North Carolina. Having made her maiden voyage across the gulf stream she deplanked for three days in Charleston then departed south stopping in Miami for sightseeing and instamatic photographs. The island pirate theme would become a popular notion once housing was built in the Bahamas and around the interior Gulf of Mexico. Gale storm warnings became the precedent as to when small boats could set sail for the Grand Isle or when groups could proceed to a new housing town for work communities and housing.

The two match book prints belonged to one Laurence Amundsen of upper tonk Norway who shelved ships for arctic expedition and to one Norwegian unnamed whose record log came in as having been ordered off a barge ship Titanic was stranded on the ice at 0, 20. Their files were attached by nuisance court pledge signifying that authorities knew a man or men were out there but because they had bomb packs on their persons no life saving procedure was allowed.

SABA 5

It is not manhood to rape a son. The sins of the fathers were presumed to be held forever in absentia as when the huge ice flows poured over the Norwegian twin arms in masses of gorged, coagulated, snow crushed rivers. A courageous government would don capes and like furious footed madmen in swirling capes would march out on horses to torch the ice flows for hundreds of miles all the way to the Atlantic. At night during the coldest clime these rivers of fire could be seen pouring down the hundred feet deep glaciers burning the icepack off from the northerly islands to holy hell. Rivers of burning ice, a stunningly horrific sight to behold, would descend, a carnivorous fire, a half mile across its width, branching into forks, pushing the floes westerly against the bitterest chill of snow, turning a smothering density of ice into gushing water which hung in the sheerest of window panes against a further retreat of the harshest of weather conditions.

In Norway the country shuts down in the winter. An entire nation stays indoors for seven months waiting out the storms and pinnacles of ice to wash off the land and leave it exposed for spring yuletide days. The ocean above her is cracked with shifting ice, her fisher vessels slow thorough the intricacies of cracking ice, covered the ocean speaks to no one, she is at once a grave and a fortress. In the difficulties of such a world, the civilized world far off in the tidal coastal regions under no concept of the descending ocean of ice, in a small village below the crevice lay just such a man Manheimm on his death bed, his small son tending to the ardors of play. The heat burned strong in an interior chamber, in the summer it would go low, the home about five hundred square feet, the only castigating element the comprehension of what could be occurring far north if the ocean had receded off the thousand islands allowing the snow to bloom in over a vast tundra. The burning rivers had tracked a plateau of ice down to their hollow depths, some lit like an incandescence of shining empiricism seen at a distance, and everyone knew it would be a long winter. The old man knew his brother would return by spring, less aged, greater in capable strength, of alert mind and promising recalcitrance; only his small son, contented by wanderings throughout the house, might someday wonder by what door his aged father left, and a young man, his uncle, entered.

He called his son Bram to his bed and told him to fetch the porridge in the master bowl and mix in some dried bacon, sea bass, cube vegetables, carrots and tomatoes, and a bowl for himself. His son, today age nine, dutifully obeyed, returned with his father's supper and feeding it to him gradually gave him the entire meal of some six bites. The old man would never tire of the same dinner over a winter, every Norwegian stayed indoors five months some seventy winters since youth, went summers to work the causeway, sometimes to Fin or Cope, and returned healthy, tanned, fit. Until he ended his seventies he would feel a complacent solitude and a recognizable remembrance of times past of wading into the swirling encapsulation of a quarter mile deep snow before he laid his first torch and watched fire pour out to feed the massive floes as they spilled above terrain and rock on their way to the north ocean.

The ice descended to the rocky bairn spending its corporal insinuations far beneath a gigantically surging ocean, corking underwater in stupendous formations of ice rock in below zero depths, spreading out under the water in sheets of pale yarn until it floated on top of coastal drift, solidifying. Without the burn-off the menacing forty-mile-an-hour snow cozened high in blizzards that grew on the land as they flowed in all directions; three months of rivers of fire receded the floes into glacial caverns. They sailed north by wind stern with swells lashing at them routing through speckled islands to locate the spills into the ocean, roped up rock blairn through a density of icy snow seeking footholds into crags, their spiked boots striking at a solid ground, hauling themselves onto the plain into trenches long ago prepared for such a purpose. They walked swiftly, hanging lanterns attached to the rock, observing the amount of snow, seeking a hundred rock ice packed above the chairn before they inserted into hollow ice a specially made chairn waster, never a chemical was considered, having about an hour to leave, jumping through space into the ocean, the first year the work took roughly ten months, thereafter a month for every ten years. Only in Norway was blairn permitted where it was a severe problem, outside Norway it did not exist to even a minor extent, no where else in the world could wasting be forgiven.

There was not so much as a house beneath blairn even if there were a rising sea wall of dirt with caves littered about the tairn. No habitations so far north were built along the plateau, not like the caves of Denmark which were a perpetual problem because boats were able to pull into them, an antithesis of human life were so many clouds billowing up, miles of ice and snow pouring over cliffs into the sea, all parables squelched in the affront of the Almighty force of nature, no surrender over the lives of a population grouped together in often cramped village cellar to avoid this one corner of uncontrollable destiny. Manheimm had trained as a boy of an earnest era with his family to serve in the bitterest realm in the face of wreaking devastation. Dressed in dark garb he learned every secure hold of the coast during summer and fall, by winter when snow descending fast, piled quickly over the land to its swirling consequence of rapturous ice, he and his uncle with thirty others climbed the twelve hundred high dairn, fetching the narrows to some sturdy point in the heavens, clawed their way along the gravenstein valleys to the ice meeks, their bodies already fiercely grim, chill depositing in essential gnome, crawling their way along the stone piled gheen to light the lanterns. They knew a raw inescapable truth, that they two men of youth might release one gaol light too many before they turned and ran from a freezing damp cellar to descend the ravines of soil.

A scrutiny of indomitable insolvency, other than awakening in a body of chill water, the ice could shift and freezing able bodied men drifted from the coast washing upon sand embankments who would be hauled in upon frame catamarans onto soggy turf. Far from siberdclairn the wholesome winter lathered on a downwind sweep claveling over the mean shelf over cliffs and like amassing lather poured down, tangling with mist and bramble to the coldest blue straits of the honestad. Manheimm would describe to the blondest male of couvairn that the ice itself rocked upon an ebb toward a straightaway, upright an impossibility, gavenhurst a proximity, always a brook of warm water emerging oddly up to surface from the sudenfeld. This was yet a governing velmenad which by Spring sequestered in lace over nesting broods and wild brushken dairn. Who can see the ocean through all that reaming mist, he would say, a sly smile to ward off any remaining doubt that he too was shaken in his rigors to an utmost declaration of what is valued as an absolute. Norwegian salt, a beveled revelment arising from frost and misting marsh when taken by the filtration of bogs heavy with remissions of effluent from factories poured over the rock in summer when the land was dry in the bitter north fifteen hundred miles above Shetland Isles to form what was called negative blue ocean. Norway's problem was she required additional water in her rivers because so much of it froze and drifted to a northernmost sea.

At sixteen having completed two lantern marsh evvils, Manheimm, staunchly strong and confident, married into a bistern, together with someone, lashtivastiv, brought about by ephisttivad, coming upon a new realism of living. His spouse was Irina, a lass of eighteen who had completed her second year in physician sailing, was modestly tall with a sash of silver blond hair to her waist, thin shouldered and long legged, a small breasted girl with narrow high cheekbones, who loved to hike hill country. Together in the fashion of farming roots they journeyed inland up rivers to their origins. A few times having slept on a bedroll beneath the stars, they encountered abandoned villages the homes which were crushed under the oppressive weight of advancing snow. Into the third year of marriage in a house situated above the clanmarn Irina had a son, a tithing of a lash-driven sailor who at twenty would chart a course for any island which in winter could stay land warm so as to settle new villages directly beneath the blairn.

It was in dark winter when Manheimm was away from the

house, his son in attendance with him, walking through the coven to the electric circuit, the tairn alit with lamps, the swirling snow piling high over the blairn that Irina, wreaked by a second pregnancy in her thirty-second year passed in her sleep, a long object box prepared for the new child silvereen. It was all Manheimm could do to see a visitation of her ghostly cairen as he steadfastly set the waster into the ice, pasted the shield with dismal gupish and fringed the torch, each shield a fathom from the subsequent door within a partial tunnel, the exterior tairn just beyond humanly grasp. By the time they returned Irina had lain dead for the better of two months, her body deceptively tan and cool. Manheimm took to his bed in grief closing the door on his beloved, the cradle empty in a hallway, the bout of his fulfillments abandoned. He wept for the tairn, for seaward minstrels, numbly listening for some far-off clavicle twanging in an imposture of ocean pounding insensibility. Davash mirables poydanken, all my treasured graces have separated.

Who may look into that cistern of joyous memory without regret? Few, who could within a reasonable discernible time escape the long habit of isolation. With utter remorse his son completed the tasks of housekeeping seeing to meal preparation, washing clothes and general tending, on occasion bringing home a girlfriend Clara, a silvery blonde like his Irina from the Ebanisbaads, her contender for their navy being that sewage salts would degenerate tough silver mines, that green aurora borealis lights when longer than a week of nights a year could sink the land below an inferior atmosphere. Manheimm took this in half heartedly for what is a man without the stills of life, his one misfortune but the desultory sweeping betrayal of life lived, that very meaning of the consummate lost permanently, toiled, troubled, ascended. When the twinkling silvery lights of the nord dimmed, there was a transcendent blue crystalline sparkling afar above any horizon, the tinkling chime of snow-white ice descended into the freezing waters above the coastal plough. Over the years Manheimm sat by the hearth, his inescapable sorrow borrowing on the freezing tairn outliving any realm of endurance until quite by chance he drew his son and his son's fiancée to his bed to explain he would be leaving soon and a younger brother soon thereafter to arrive. He took their hands, told them he had willed the house to them, and asked only they look after their uncle when he came.

Young Amundsen, Manheimm's brother, arrived that spring to the house one afternoon while Bram and Clara were out attending to the marketplace. When they returned they found Amundsen, a tall vigorous male of stalwart disposition, dark black straight locks, in the sitting room reading through a sailor book of shipping terminology having scrubbed the basins and towel room, cleaned the cupboard's, stored dried folded clothing into the cradle, and set up a lightweight bed inside the hall at the rear of the house, a chest moved beneath a window that overlooked the yall. He was in his late adolescence and required in the new winter to fetch for the newbeggin in the north oceans to train for falling yarn to dispatch the coastal hills into climbable footpaths up to the tairn.

SABA 6

Above the inveterate snow packed density and myriad of icicles hanging off every edifice, there was a sonorous frost inevitable to vast regions of clawing landscapes of ice. I had long clung to the idea of walking the Siberian frost fields above the bobbing boulders of cracking ice that landmarks a continuous coastline stretching above Russia, Finland and Norway, the compelling need having arisen out of a fear of the unknowable, the concern that people could become stranded in unlivable tundra or icy pinnacles blasting with cold. In those days I was a youngster, a marsh bunny whose adolescent preoccupation gave me no solace other than to travel with my uncle annually to monitor the potash forming from muddy eddies beneath strata of glaciated ice and discernible rock. I was fifteen to be precise, a nature loving boy born of a sturdy mother of a similar disposition, caught in an attentive measure with high places to which one might hike or track, schooled in a wooden room by a stern reproachful aged termite whose only goal was to prepare a class of twenty youths for college professions in the arctic. Without his constant marshalling roost, a finite bearing of trapper or industrialist, I could scarcely have beveled myself to endurance. When at nineteen I took my first assignment to fly a prisoner south to a blazon destruction of sobering cold on Sail Island I fixedly remanded myself that prison must hold its warrants elsewhere and left that world before I entered it. If life is a practicality for formal bench work, it would leave my senses invaded and flattened because life imprisonment no matter its essential cannot sustain a spirit destined for wanderings. The engraver would no further question his ink than the gatekeeper his locks or loaf of bread passed through a door window to the prisoner in the shovel.

Blue is the color of the unknowable, forever intrinsic, surging, iconoclastic ocean, the nameless creator of catastrophe, of all endings, all majestic governances of trade. Blue, abstract, immense sky, infinite ocean, a tarnish on which to affix other color, a streak of immortal red, clandestine stippled yellow, the narrowest path of glinting winter, sharp curling waves, indelible thunderous calamity wreaking havoc against a shoreline, indigo, tortuous abbreviated aggradations of rising diurnal, crashing, pounding, unfurling sea, hostile habitat, unrecognizable latent landscapes, churning froth escaping into sand leaving an imperceptible glide, how brief the encounter, unknowable the blue, all time – morose, signified a diaphanous inlet on an instant translation of monochrome shining water, invisible, immediately vanishing, until a succession of gradually rolling waves magnificent as a curling wall, all glistening deep blue, a curvature of the watery world, a surfer riding the distance, a swift fleeting movement of unending precision, sight and adroit control, the wind demanding an exhilarating brevity of definition and form. Time elapsed, retracted from reality, a marine training for the forces of nature.

He lay on his back allowing the saturated sand to release him from the arduous task of focused concentration, the glaring sun to obscure the jumble of rocks cropping fifty feet out of the ocean, the whirling columns of sand shifting to the water. The relational objectivity of enchantment to the perfection of methodology, first the racing waves, then the momentum of the crescendo, far from any conceptual cross accompanied only of the pleasure of endurance, deciphered the tiniest entities of ocean sailing onto a collaborative whole, a spellbound destination without demarcation – felt, perceived but unknowable, the solace of waves rushing up described the endless time of the sometimes dangerous occurrence of undertow, an ironic unsuitability of massive changeability meeting chronicles of human experience, a recurrent incessant adaptation for which the finality of days became synonymous with regret. As he slept the stilling sensation of the infinite left, in its place he was a swimmer on a beach, a man among thousands historically whose sense of himself could become persuaded by the routine of duty. When he awakened he was possessed of a sight of the calm ocean, so blue the color was indefinable, as unlike his canvas at his bungalow on which blue appeared almost black, smears of dark ultramarine dried with a palate knife soaking it in turpentine and allowed fluid to pool to distill to a softer blue until the shape of the center looked like the floes of the ocean underwater, dark, dark blue and surface azure as when a submersible rose to the surface from a hundred feet. The color of blue both knowable and unfamiliar held the work captive, standing across the room the room the almost black slabs were what snagged the focus, the 64" by 40" was a mired descent of drippings controlled by a sheen, blue of all hues actually derived from one color subsiding to lapis flecked with small grains of indigo, cobalt, sapphire, madder, cyanic, cold smalt; in one florid enactment at the bottom of a canyon a diaphanous scintillating pneumatic blue. Blue adhered to the canvas impossible to be reduced, altered or in any way negated by tests, it always consisted of often darkness, infinite and undying as deep dark satin, mythical, mystical, a plumed serpent. In the manner of fashionable art, the thousand canvases he had painted with oils were of intrinsic blue, flat one dimension without detection of motion, obscure. In essence blue was gracelike, an associated state of truth, for to gaze upon it there was a perception of inner tranquility, a response of peace or beauty. Blue represented a constancy of the world of mysticism that he had ever known, the most true of living, always he returned to either the sea or the color blue to reform his weariness in a resplendent soothing calm of Self to imbue himself with mystery, non complication, of the phenomenon of the divine.

He had begun his youth living in a land where the land was not yet formed. In his adolescence and early adult years he trained as a diver on missions to recover sunken harbor piers that detached in the turbulence of a storm, drifted and sunk with seaweed to the underworld where they became enmeshed. In several years he was admitted to training to sail a wind sail on a board before he operated a rescue on the rivers of Copenhagen extending a line to wind capsized deck mates crouping them to a plank in a jacket all the way to the knees. After a year he returned to the southern Norway coast to ride the reverse curls lunging into massive rolls straddling the board until he mastered a proficiency for staying afloat. The first years catapulted him into horror, without a sail he lacked control except for the utter hold, his arms and feet steering direction, shoulders aligned to the curl. If the wave didn't curl, it slammed into a side wind, he had to sit at the rear, a long board proved best – the sea humbled a man to his astute ability to sense wind. By the years he rode for the harbor fence he had sailed schooners, flying jibs, topsails, rolled in fish nets, taken fish barrels to the Arctic, commanded a strait, creosoted soft ice drifts, when he dove for his first harbor he found it had been hurled miles off shore, it rested in a trove of weed growing from a sunken ship, hauling it back to the coastline was a simple task, a matter of starting the ship engine with a duplicate haul, no towline needed nor plank bed rail.

My associations with blue are of perception. Blue is the color of the sky, of the ocean. To the patient The Blue of prisons of danke dashad, or immortal dangerous life-threatening horizon, is a sky for which sky and ocean seem as one. I began seeing the patient after he was admitted for wandering lose on an iceberg. His crew could not get him in. They reported he heard his name being called. He walked off the ship, lit a cigarette, took a walk and could not be coaxed to return to the ship. The patient's psychology is of mother and son where the dyad is thwarted, a subject of consternation for the public for the thinking seems to reflect an interior repression of a presumed fundamentally necessary proof of maturation. It is of course incumbent in the role of mother to bridge the pseudo-aggression of the adolescent as he celebrates mastery over powerfully intoxicating changes to manhood by providing a foundation of healthy day to day functioning. His eventual accommodation of relational coupling is based upon his observation in kind of his parental bond of both positioning and affection. The duality of relationship is suggested when that fundamental give and take becomes ethically compromised, translating for the stability of ego a coercive, if not dominating, fashion from which the dyad is weakened or strengthened but nevertheless fixated. Thus when the symbiotic duality of the parental bond is severely conflicted, this maturing adolescent embodies an incomplete gathering of essential tasks, giving himself an exterior of uncompromising and belittling qualities. In the mother/son relationship that we see here the father while stormy is ineffectual, found to be frequently slumbering off drunkenness and so in time the mother in a misdirected need of a consulting opinion has coveted the lack of common sense in a son who like his father must to some degree capture something of the ineffectual; indeed the son masters denial while also shoring up his own ambivalence toward hostility at his ineffectual father. This mother clearly has not adequately dealt with any of the severities that have been thrust upon her, she does not know why she lacks evidence to emotionality, with conviction to restore her son, or her dead husband for that matter for incompetent custodial supervision, but her internal unwillingness to find grievous fault with her husband catapults her past any real sanity and there she remains, caught hold in suggestion.

The transference is a psychological term that speaks of conflict with exposure between two people. To speak of a transference of object ambivalence or object compassion is to enjoin two people of like or unlike minds who as they proceed come upon a sense of uncanny similarity such that one is drawn to use the reflective element of the other to pursue self insight. In the therapeutic encounter of awakening a sleeping dragon, long dormant in unobservable consciousness, the transference begins as a wholly captivating admiration of the physician. Sometimes there is a twinge of anger, sometimes it is a clarity that is aroused mentally. Its purpose is to stir memory such that it engenders aid in coming to terms with often painful wearisome experiences not previously permitted to the surface. Thus, when he speaks of the Blue, as the more altruistic minds of Norwegian-stammer Copenhagen describe their ocean-bearing landscape, gains a stark, cautious regard as light bounces off its waters to pronounce a barely perceived crystal-like sound that can be charted to a source by use of a radio much the way a captain steers a vessel to harbor or across the ocean frozen ice. This suggestion, a tinkling of ice as air freezes, mystifies, mesmerizes, shimmers as it were on a close by horizon with a metallic resonance that raises an alert, increased sensitivity of mirage that surely someone else must also be on the ice. The further north one goes, as one approaches the Arctic, that crystal tinkling beckons like a teasing mother.

Of course the ocean is unknowable, a mysterious mystery, a clandestine wilderness of torquing icebergs and sliding slabs, both simultaneously a brevity of breathless laborious breath and a bitter wind blowing driven mass of cold, a confrontation of white non dimension wherein one might imagine they hear wailing chanters lost on slippery ice or with misty blizzard evaporating suddenly an ushering universe that holds back the impossible strain of snow blind accompanied by panic, hopelessness and utter skin numbing chill. Out there even God does not know if a traveler will live or die, the life of the arctic ocean freezing beyond remotest survival, any glazed film of ice unreliable and potentially treacherous. We are a seeking people motivated by far out-of-reach reality where the attraction to save life is great, sometimes motivation as strong as instinct, a primordial calling, a tinnitus of doubt ever-present, ever-glistening, radiant, clairvoyant. Psychic awareness jettisons all of a certain flinging of ourselves to answer the calling of open space. In seeking that tinkling crystal sound we glide on the unknowable ocean course toward it, in awe of the platitudes of glacial caverns, reticent endangerments, to harbor on a fantastic voyage with a crash course with fate.

SABA 7

Rare police video footage showed four jumpers diving off the Fifth Street Bridge. Coffey was sent for to examine the video and had come by train from Reno, Nevada where the movie Spartacus hiring two thousand extras for battle scenes had completed and film had been sent to the cutting room in South San Francisco at a studio warehouse at the end of the train line for what was then an illegal use of train film movies. Primary transportation were trains, each train station had a post office, baggage claim, bathroom cleaned hourly by a porter, a small coffee shop with food, and benches to sit on, and only one station in the country had a Western Telegraph that approved funds based upon photo transactions. The post office was an essential part of the government and was not private. Telegraph services for money orders fingerprinted for the warrant and a series of cameras took photos of all entering and requesting cash transactions. Someone had photographed the end of the Reno train yards of silver backed compartments of 1953 train yards for the motel lot and north Cypress Memorial cemetery where the high desert train stopped to let passengers stretch their legs before it crossed the aqueduct that supplied irrigation on the opposite side to rice farms, rice grew in flooded fields, their long green stems finally produced a small thin grain as water was absorbed down to its nitrogen base. In those days there were three companies which made goods to ship by train throughout the west, Bauterrie developed radiation for mapping, Randolph burned refined sugar for the production of molasses and with rice made Turkish baklava and Filo dough, and Mitchell produced movies. It was in 1953 that a Korean transpacific ship carrying aircraft bound for San Francisco plundered off the coast of Hawaii as a result of six men swimming out to sea bringing charges with them. The bounties for ship bombing were severe, for illegal use of post office at train stations even worse. For one ship bomb twenty-seven businesses of any type were erected in any state and a bomb to any aircraft necessitated eight highways of which two were built in Los Angels, three in San Francisco and three in Oakland. A bomb to a train netted four interconnecting freeways. The public view of outdoor movies was that these were methods for undesirable activities such as abductions, legitimacy, arson and bombs, none of which the Federal Bureau of Investigations agents could be acting in nor on set. In 1957 a shooting death at a train station resulted in a cemetery being moved over state lines from Searchlight to Sparks, Nevada. In 1959 a thunderstorm burnt much of the Sequoia-King National Park eliminating timber and industrial suburbs comprised of about a hundred two-story insured homes each. In 1960 San Francisco train yards were shut down because they were referenced as movie studios. Also in that year the extensive Kaiser Aluminum ran out of aluminum. The lower deck for trains discontinued trains while the upper deck of the San Francisco-Oakland Bay Bridge for buses intended for two-way traffic became one direction to the peninsula and the low deck for vehicles traveling to the East Bay. In 1962 in Orange County a refinery bomb took out all refrigeration lockers along the wharf and put these in Oakland beneath the Nimitz Freeway from Fortieth Street to the Jack London Square. Further inquiry determined that the five men found dead had each served prison convictions, one at Freedom, Pennsylvania Institute; one at Charlottes, North Carolina; two in the Birmingham, Alabama located on the Midnight Line; and one in the Rockies of Wyoming. The women had completed hard-weather internships through Department of Bureau and Justice to become document appraisal sub-contract agents working primarily on shipping wharfs. Coffey went to Nolte Ranch's Huntsville and Bauterrie went to Petaluma in San Rafael, both located in the non-prison state of California.

Lewis gave all this information a mere glance. This was going to prove an exhaustive find to track the auspicious data that led to the murders in the Atlantic rather than in the mist forests of Norway or eastern Austria. He nevertheless pulled a section on polygraphs and narratives. Immediately he received a rather oddly mysterious photo of a train petrol explosion in front of the long-time hotel building and ground floor ball-room and casino dubbed affectionately as an MGM for the reels the establishment showed there. Buildings tended to resemble one another, there was a Grand in downtown Oakland off the lake, another in San Francisco, yet another in a town slated to become a city once population increased to two thousand residents; this one in Buelton Isles also a Grand. Anyone with a name or reputation clamored to live in their spacious one bedroom studios for sixty-five a week. Only the Grand in Iowa City took reservations for pencil boys freed out of the Gates Way Penitentiary, a studio with coffee in the lobby looked unrestrained at a surprising thirty-five a week, nights only. More than one out of the clink thirsted after a little action, reel to reel was for a mature man who was headed for ship duty working the rotating light or the mast poles. In the annals of registries for the Grand Hotel the name Amundsen Bjorney, Ship Captain, stood out in bold script like wrought iron ink distinct on the page for four nights docked into Oakland London Wharf.

He happened to glance to the water in time to see Rhonda dressed in tan pegs and a black sleeveless showing off an even sun exposure climb off a single kayak. She looked fresh, awakened. She was in good shape – glowing, healthier than he had seen her in years, blond and silvery hair twisted and drawn back tightly from her face. She was all of four minutes coming up the elevator to his top penthouse striding in with the breeze.

"Hi, babe," he said to her from the balcony. "Pour yourself a drink."

She helped herself to the champagne on the blue tiled counter pouring the 10 into a gold edged glass and dropping in a white sugar cube. Out on the water was a solo windsurfer, three stripes to his sail, white, green, yellow. She wandered outside. "How's your drink?"

He held up an amply filled green edged fluted stem glass to indicate his was fine. "How've you been?"

"Can't complain." She picked up a tiny spoon of black caviar with creamy cream cheese and ate it. "You? How's Abby?"

"I packed her onto a yacht and sent her to parts unknown."

"She was young, Lewis; it would've taken years to adjust. It was a second youth for you."

"She came with the job on Grenadines."

"Right. I forgot that bloodshed. That case went on forever."

"Don't I know it. I'm still tracking where the money for the movies came from. Now I'm winding my way through that Saba Island massacre."

"I know. Jones told me. I brought some first shots, all top row. Are there pertinent files?"

"One is of the ship captain who is killed. Others include ex-cons and Janice Coffey. The female was targeted by five shipmates. Bauterrie was assigned to follow reel hands where bridge ship film near train stations shot scenes of movies. Coffey only met Bauterrie through the polygraph agency after 1970 blast to the wharf."

"Do we know what brought Bauterrie to Florida?"

"Appalachachola tornado apparently, she was already on the train from Goodwin, North Carolina; a public bystander in the Norwegian marathon races turned up in northern Florida. Here's the issue," he said, and took a sip. "These men are in photos with border crossing felons working on a film crew."

"Abby should've been helpful."

"She wasn't quite to the degree I'd hoped."

"Who found her?"

"A dog."

"How come? Was she in a field or something? Actually I thought she was at home."

"No, she had to stop off at the lab; it occurred on her dinner break on the lake. Only way to find a body is to drag through water is with a dog, terriers lick hands to preserve prints, Scots find the head under the soil, patrol dogs only find the gravesite."

"And what has that told the forensics?"

"No lab on the movie. Way too much publicity."

"Someone was bound to recognize her after all those races."

"What, are you kidding? That's Europe."

"That's the movies," she said gently to point out a fact.

"Movies bring people in from around the world and this guy used two thousand extras; has to be a legitimate reason."

"It's an idea, I won't say I'm sold on it."

"Who does battles that way, you may as well take over a town."

"Could explain the amount of money raised for the production, a dollar each."

"Who knows. Do you want to eyeball these?"

"Sure. What've you got for me?"

She handed him the envelope, explaining, "There are a dozen black and white of Baja hotel men, as you'll see Coffey isn't there, she's still working the last shift on the office at Petaluma Prison Fort. The men are considerably younger. Bauterrie is a wife of one ex-chief on the wharf side port entry and that is a difficulty."

"The files are relatively straightforward. Stiles were places below road that led to stone stairs with mason stone rooms where one could hide. Bauterrie was a film notary. She had to review every film, magazine, newspaper to perform comparative analyses. Findings would have been slim anyways."

Lewis studied each photo cautiously impressed with the photo detail. A fine eye had honed in on culprit suggestibility. As in the littered rooms in central Baja and Mexico's Capistrano beaches, there were the evidence of drugs, of counterfeit and as usual through a slightly opened window of a far-off port, the height of ships distinctly visible. The surfeit of cargo alongside individual docks lent an air of movement, ships coming and going, products departing for other islands, some destined as far as Florida. The drug tarnish that slaved a kitchen only indicated illegal trade, whereas in remote shots of compartments standing empty in an inhospitable host of border train yards fronting the Texas El Paso drive-in there were numerous rooms, most of them bathrooms through which passed obvious men in drag, young prostitutes seeking their fortune, and a bevy of young mustached clandestine drug operatives, all intent on just getting a glimpse of the promised land. The government's latest policy was to bring every family over the boundary into Harvest, Southern California at the Tijuana border to interview for potential hire. From time to time bajo lingos showed up on filmed excursions in and around Nevada's deserts as far south as Nogales all the way past James Hooper windmill in the desolate, dust-driven windy, hundred and thirty degree furnace heat, car motors destroyed, dependent upon the cheap motel rents of thirty a month awaiting border patrol or patron-sainthood labor of a dollar a day.

"Who runs this sort of operation?" he asked her, shaking free a French cigarette and lighting it.

"He's a film editor runner out of German-dutch-Seigfert out on the islands. He's known to exchange film of studios with their historic landmark sites."

"Do you have a file on this man?"

"Nothing docu-proof-able. Occasionally he has a piece in a mainland magazine."

"Has he ever shown up in movie excerpts?"

Rhonda gave a guess. "I suppose they all do eventually if they are anybody, not the ads themselves, travel sidelines, usually it's Tijuana, sometimes Corpus Christi, rarely of a boat dock in the lower Keys, almost usually of bays."

"So these are border transients who frequent boats along the beach coasts of the peninsula and the islands."

"Yes, could be. Their disposables show up at market supply marinas, it's where they tend to make their reputations, at outboard and canoe rentals, fishing sport for the day. Do you have Jan Coffey on board the cruisers?"

He said, somewhat complacently, "The big ships, yes. It's doubtful that any polygraph service in the gulf kept her. I think she worked that line a few days a year wherever a reel-expert turned up, could be a ship jumper, someone practiced with realistic ship heights. We know she hauled medical supplies to island clinics, my suspicion is she may have been sent to verify actual scenes of movies."

"Outgoing communications of a Western Telegraph are always photo docu-proofed with voice recorder. The producer of Spartacus was a grip known for his touch, his talent made him sought after, he could match the camera to line up with the focus. It's for the distant shots the entire cast of extras went to Salt Lake to film battles below the beige hard sand mountains. Those producers were each clapper loader who ran the film and steadi-cam which shot the picture. The foley artist mixes up the sound for dialogue of the actors with other sounds."

"Diminishing sound is weeks spent in a sound room. What do your consultants say about enhanced color?"

"That's a Scratch system that relies on an image loader such as Pandora for True Grit with John Wayne. Then there's Pluto Launch that takes a projected display to visualize images as they are in reality removing the need to make film take-outs."

"But how does it work?"

"Doubles two fields of a video frame to capture a picture taken at two different times to reduce flickering. Dogs of War, made originally in 1955, shows a plane taking off amidst bombs exploding in fields near a runway and has a segment of vehicles on the low deck of the east bay-south bay bridge in two-way direction traffic including the overhead train in early Los Angeles near the aqueduct and the brick Kreiss building."

"Maybe original video shots were used as actual footage to enhance viewer interest."

"Oh, sure," she agreed.

"Is Spartacus the movie with the shafts of silvery sun in a blue forested terrain raising mist with a falling tree and balls of fire emerging downhill from on high? It's vivid in my mind."

"Genghis Khan. It's another memorable study. It's predecessor Leviticus by Kubrick in 1960 was remade, I think, as the girl with the dragon tattoo released several years ago."

"I thought it was Inherit the Wind."

"You may have that right."

"About the teacher who is expelled for teaching descent of man."

"I remember now. That was actually quite good."

"Expert," he said. "Why did they take their battle scene for Spartacus to Salt Lake, do you suppose?"

"They ran into a problem, the studio burned down."

"Maybe it's worse than that. Their check for production was held at Western Union Telegraph and sent to the nearest postal station."

She digested his answer with a sip of champagne. "Entirely possible the money wanted to film the battle scenes themselves, or someone just got talked into it and wanted to develop land for houses near a railroad."

"Or some smart ass sent the money by telegraph."

"Do we have any of the island dead found in the crack house who may have performed for that movie?"

He said, "Both Foley artists, they would've known what to listen for."

"They could do anything except be dead. There has to be a direct reductionist connection."

"Yes, there is, they were stoned on exceptional stuff."

She laughed. "Could I stay the night?"

The fact of love was once learned never released even in the throes of resentment, boredom or distraction. All matters estimable and candor, the description of apathy eventually was replaced by familiar seeking, by often small subtractions of breathless heaven, the knowledge that herein lay soft surrender mingled with destination, a still slightly open aperture, a sudden cresting of passion, considerate in thought, the last of which came with the surprise of relaxation. Below him she lay trans-hypnotic in enjoyment fixed on a permanent image of him he was certain, neither wayward nor craving, subdued to tenderness, no longer cloying, attempting to control or possess. He grew aware then of the moment, an awareness he must have abandoned years ago, either having lost his own boundary or having found hers wanted her willingness to forfeit whether or not she agreed. He supposed love was a recalcitrant resistance to indulgence, perhaps of emotional effort of being dependent, a house-hold structure meant to regroup one's interior dignity, integrity or continual craving for eliminating the tyranny of need. How much was too much, how many sunsets looked to be helplessly cavorted – he had long ago lost count and had assumed rightly or wrongly she could no more not choose him than she might burrow to independence of the spirit. Yet here they were, sinking in passion, the threshold met and reconfirmed, subjective in every sense, she holding him easily, for the first time showing none of her disclosure, and for whatever else he assumed he knew of her, she gave no exposure. She seemed to come to for a brief pulse and looked into his soul and he knew he wasn't lost. Only for the mortality of the surrender he took that revealing treasure to some dark place evident to him in his knowing and whispered to her that he had had no one for what seemed eternity. She didn't cry as she once had, causing him to shudder momentarily, she maintained a momentum, and he had to go with it. If she controlled him now, if she gave not enough indication of if she could break, if he wanted a symbolic gesture, he warned himself against the idea of it. He could bear the notion of an intimate barrier, a non-concealing, risk was barely present, he closed his eyes and felt himself give in.

When the telephone rang, they had been sleeping for hours. Lewis felt the late afternoon sun warmth on him like a damp humidity, a light ocean breeze wafting through the open window. He lifted the receiver and settled against the headboard, Rhonda's back curled away from him. Jones had hunted down the peculiar happenstance of the dead girl's itinerary finding she had fled on foot to the train station and taken a night special cross country and transferred in Chicago to the mid Atlantic New York to Florida line coming down the eastern seaboard in a defeatingly hurry to escape time and threat of injury. She was already with a book of notaries established for physician-approved films promised to be paid out of the Union Pacific drawer, nothing without full districted authority, the mail key around her neck stripped off her body sometime after death. Jones was assured of a bevy of information, the majority of it hosted by the Grand's Jerome Offam who had curtailed an occasional movie when the stress of hysteria beset upon a cast and crew as it apparently had in the final takes of Warren Gregson's last show. The sheriff bureau had combed every inch of the yard, the three apartment dwellings of elite flats, as well as the studio and turned up a body and compromised ethics. He was certain if he had the liberty he could track the corporate holding signature to determine how the battle scenes were advised and who underwrote the final picture. Lewis gave him four days.

"That was Jones," he said, when he rang off.

"What did Jones have to say?" she stretched, turned onto her side, and slipped her hand over his tight muscular frame.

"Not much. The deceased female, Jan Coffey, stipped as physician-notary on the set for two remakes of battle scenes made simultaneously by Craig Morely – Spartacus and El Cid. Why she died is not yet clear."

"What does Jones think, Honey?"

He lay against her. "He thinks it's a money item. The alternate producer raised four dollars apiece per actor and brought in over two thousand extras funding both movies and setting up an account on which to base loans. He has a claim that says the one grouping of scenes for the first remake ran five hundred bucks with distribution to go to four projection houses – Grand, Universal, a show studio owned by Laurentis and the other owned by Pandora, all backed by watch making corporations Renoit, Silversmith, and Forny, predominantly Swiss, starring show girls like Charlotte Wesler, Vivian Leigh, Delores Bratton, and film agitators Mihael Stemley and Stan Bamy, essentially anyone who can sing and waltz. Jones said Grand wants to move away from 'hospital' movies to gambling-raised funds. Apparently Wafer Hospital in Daytona financed Leviticus."

"Remind me, where was her body found?"

"Past a walking lane that led to gardens with statues near a mill and pond."

She was awake now. "Maybe we should be looking for a disgruntled husband."

"We'll wait to see what Jones returns with."

"My guess is he'll bring in a previous hospitalization with injuries."

"It reads the same to me also, man beat his wife in a 273.5, payout by federal victims of train wrecks. Poor woman."

"Senseless," Rhonda agreed.

Not always were the reel images as improving upon life as stalwart honest juris for balance of authority. From time to time life hung like a train fallen off a bridge or suggested itself the same inspiration as in Skeptics moral instruction of Deuteronomy, do not copulate your son's wife for in the end you will discover if you live to earn wage from him, you won't be yet loyal. It was impossible to miss that Coffey had worked the medical clinic less than several months before she was called out to California to approve studio funds for the remake, less impossible it would've been she to sign off on rail yard passenger cars to bring in the casting crew. Coffey had just that day purchased a townhouse condo in Miami South Gardens that was nicely put above market value because it was close to the train post office, shops, retail and restaurant patios and had coastal access. Jones substantiated with photos, one of a studio bedroom on set taken from the light rack. A similar train yard photo taken from a high turn gate showed a young man seen asking her for money jumping rail tracks crossing a yard of about ten separate tracks. It was a mystery why anyone wanted Coffey after they had already murdered a ship captain, five from the relief bin and a frantically shrieking Bauterrie. A snippet of a studio surrendered in cash deposits showed on the dateline. If the one threat that tied Coffey to the battle scenes was that she could only approve for inside scenes, the problem least understood was who had approved outside film.

SABA 8

Jones kept his hunches under his hat. He worked task-driven until he had answers, foregoing lunch with Lewis, golf on the green, mint julep drinks at the Avalon. The answers were elusive, the situations long forgotten or denied. The delving instigation at intangible shadows kept him under the desk light into the damp night, pages of a report surrendered to the pen, tired of making telephone calls, looking up deeds and disposition orders, checking against construction templates and government contracts and against photo permissions and circuit number assignments.

No matter the instances of studio laws that were not adhered to, there was still the fact that post office money wires made the world go round and these were derived on ship availability along the coasts and on number of families of teens not yet nineteen. Gemma Stone herself was the second wife of a Norwegian ice-gate keeper by the name of Bram who worked the avalanche trench, entirely staked hiking up by spike. As a teen he had lost footing and plunged falling down the lengthy damp trench into deep water, a turbulent sapphire blue ocean estimated by fierce blustery wind that hung about one like a tethered heavy sheet flapping wildly in a frozen cold capable of cutting breath in the lungs causing the body to become cleft with tension in the shoulder. At four hundred and fifty kilometers from the steep gravelly torwinds cliffline the ships rested placidly on the ice, periodically buoyant amidst floes, the cold factor consistently minus two degrees. Here morning light tumbled down from on high like a waterfall, splashes filled with the multitudinous spectrum glints of blues, purple, mauve, lilac, and muted teals, the air all around crackling with a mysterious crystallizing calving of chill and ice – the only thing one hears – even rain twinkled. Up that steep glade of iron oxidized hard strata, it was a fourteen hour climb with kites adhered to the back and shoulders to any cave deep enough to house seven men, a rigorous death-defying leap of faith as steep as Mount Everest, all snow and hanging ice, pinnacles of torque-twisted frozen ice emerging from cracked sternums of jutting rock, the air teeming with light rain, one could hear nothing but the bitter raging wind; from inside one could see sunlight coming through the cracks, moss and wood beams of the house on the outside. It was said these were people who survived the continent because the average age of life was a mere forty years; winters were long, despite heat all year long from November 20 to May 4, snow packed in a minimum of eighteen feet high, buried houses and shut in doors, as insane-stirring madness cackled amidst hearth fires until as soon as one ventured outside, the first venture through the hills of ice engraved snow burned with frostbite and took life. The summer was meant to offset this harrowing madness – tri-athalons every summer began with age six to age nineteen for the hundred meter, four thousand meter and the steeplechase run with jumps, until after twelve years training one was ready to climb the trenches, captain's ropes hanging from the misted on-highs for mis-steps. It was straight up starting at age nineteen, one's pack strapped to ones shoulders, kites lifting into the wind from the belt, preparation by snow sport for ski, cross country, mush, and gravel riding down a narrow escalante in a rocket sled up to speeds of a hundred and sixty miles per hour feet first, hands at sides on the bars of the sled, wind whistling over the face.

There was a week of intense madness when all hands of twenty-one barrel kleg slid rope burn all the way to the soil into churning waters and swam for the ships. The water rose with spitting mist, barely evaporating indiscriminate fog, shadows and shapes and the likes of which parted over blistering surface water only to gather anew and obscure the ground. Ocean ramparts flooded and froze and splintered and cracked and drifted and bobbed a giant massive soldiering entity, for days one could stay there, the all-around whiteness causing pulsing headaches and snow blind, but freed of the densely aquamarine ice, the ocean in a floating ship was a promise of awe to be held. The blocks of ice were thunderous, the air its own spinnaker, snapping and oozing ocean as though the breath of ages might part from its very husband nature, lapping bays an infrequency, the stillness décor of arches, windows and caverns contained the rarest and bluest purity of nature, sights unparalleled, rivaling mountains and ravines shadowed by low moving cloud cover far off on the ice, life not yet discovered, or realized. The sting of chilled cold as it swept like driven sand over the snow continued for days once the ship pulled its anchor and moved several yards past its previously moored century-post. Carnivorous entreaties grouped the men although once sleep took hold they were as ghosts, slender flannel-attired, hunched-over wanderers aboard a ship they could have commandeered had they been three times their age. Their ship shook along portals of coastal snow crunching against mighty tables of bluish ice destined for nowhere, perhaps another far-north town or the distant emptiness of ocean, sinister dark blue, waves so high that ship and soul could be flung to the insurmountable indefatigue-able grave of ocean depths. Given up for dead – the belief was the ship flooded in the engine and sank a slow death and her men lay scattered across a vast landscape of ice. Search and Rescue airplanes sent up fleet-water-overland-balloons day and night until a full month gone the coast guard cutter mid-Florida honed in on all hundred and eighty-nine ligfiturists and the ship was ordered into the port of Miami. When the bodies were finally transferred from Nevis to No polo, the postmortem inquiry summarized the incident as follows: five sail-mates took over the steerage of Norwegian Star, repainted her renaming her Morphin, and landed in Florida where upon the ship was seized and all five sent inland to prison dockets. Illegal manufacture of lithium killed the five deck hands after an unknown person or persons eliminated life from the ship captain for his docking key and it is believed subsequently killed the two female physicians, one Janice Coffey in Nevis and her co-associate Gemma Bauterrie553 in central Delando for refusing to grant pay for the production of outside movie battle scenes.

DEFINITION MURDER
IN THE FIRST DEGREE

Causes

Aggravated arson
Aggravated assault
Aggravated rape
Amphetamine, methamphetamine
Anger killing
Armed robbery
Pyromania, firebug
Gangs, street terrorism
Auto theft
Extortion scheme
Bait and switch
Bite wounds
Blind date bombings
Infections
Bludgeons/clubs
Bullets, firearms
Burglary
Carjacking
Child abuse
Psychological maltreatment
Cocaine abuse
Carnival bunco
Cookers, drug manufacture
Mafia activity
Counterfeit

Crack cocaine
Crank, speed
Crime lab, handling evidence
Transporting
Snitching
Homicide
Cults
Dangerous drugs
Date rape
Dirt
Drive-by shooting
Drug selling, stash
Entrapment
Search warrant
Ephedrine
False evidence
Handling procedures
Hanging by ankle
Trace elements
Weapons
Explosives
Fabric
Feces
Lasers
Food, poisons in
Force
Glass
Hallucinogens
Hate crimes
Hells angels
Heroin
Homeless
Hit and run
Hostage-taking
Hypnosis
Threats
Jailhouse incarceration

Jealousy killing
Joyriding
Kidnapping
Killing for hire
Knives
Involuntary manslaughter
Marijuana overdose
Serial killing
Moving surveillance, tail, shadow
Narcotics
Payoff swindle
Pigeon drop
Pills
Poisons
Outrageous conduct by a police officer
Undercover agents, sting
Kiting
Package, postal
Patrol handguns
Premeditation
Pseudoephedrine
Random killing
Ransom
Revenge killing
Ruby ridge incident
Runaway teens
Sedatives
Sex crimes
Shopping marketplaces
Stalkers
Stimulants
Suicide, murder-suicide
Surgical procedures
Target blue ambush slayings
Triangle killing
Unknown identity
Vehicles, manslaughter

Videotaping
Vomit
World Trade Center bombing
Wounds

CASINO

1.

There was a healthy amount of snow on the ground. The Thursday was sunny, a hint of warmth. The Christmas crowd had arrived early to the grill restaurant which was busy all morning. By eleven-thirty there was a line into the lobby. The flooring was a snazzy light blue carpet with darker blue lines through it like a 21-pick-up game. The walls consisted of solid wood paneling alternated by brick. For $1.99 breakfast of three stack pancakes, a side of sausage, hash browns and two eggs any style were served with beverage.

In the lobby the desk manager was checking in a large group of twenty-one students, verifying visas, assigning rooms, ticketing luggage, providing menu passes, and selecting tours for a five night overstay. They would be grouped on the only two couches for an hour before the bus arrived to transport them to their wing. The two girls stood close to their luggage talking about their proposed itinerary. That evening they would travel by van to the Italian Palacio to see colorful golden, orange and green waterfalls, take a floating glass boat on a serene lake passing Venetian buildings and domed columns, and finish with an opera sung by actors on marble stairs. This was a first trip to the wonderland of Vegas casinos that fronted the Green River along its cartwheel extravaganza strip in western Nevada at Bullfrog City where yearly twenty thousand tourists poured into enjoy the massive marble gargantuan sites. The girls were each in their late teens, stunning redhead beauties, paneled hair to their shoulders, a duo of sculpted modeled faces, thin upturned noses, brown yellow eyes, small bosomed, straight waists, small hips, dressed in white shimmering silk shirtwaist dresses and matching high heels that showed off their legs. The blond male who had come with them was a lab coat, physician credentialed, forensic analyst. He wore white trousers, white long sleeved top shirt, green jacket and beige suede shoes. At some point in the evening they would find themselves sandwiched onto a small deck, he making light of his profession as a pellet frame expert in the same town where they resided and worked; in this tense waiting for papers to be processed they barely took notice of one another. One girl Veronica had removed a lipstick case and applied dark red lipstick as she looked in the compact mirror. Her cousin Darien was brushing her hair in an under curl and arranging it on her back. They seemed to flourish in the awareness they had drawn lots of looks. A tour guide finally arrived, a rather tallish reddish blond man in his mid thirties attired in tight black jeans and a sweatshirt that said Casino in bright gold letters. He grouped them outside on the top of five stairs, made sure they had their registrations, passports or driver's licenses, and luggage, before he directed them to board a van.

"Isn't this utterly exciting," Veronica said to the blond male whose seat she had slipped in next to.

"Oh, wonderful. Have you been here before?" He leaned forward to include Darien. "Bit of confusion back there, isn't it?" he said to her, as the van became filled.

"Yes," Darien said, eager to appear pleasing. "That wait. It took over an hour."

"Every tour is that way," he said.

"We're from Richmond, California," Veronica said. "Where are you from?"

"Crescent City. It's a small place, not much to recommend it, but then I don't suppose Richmond is much either with all those smoke stacks."

Darien leaned forward as the van backed out into the street, saying, "Our house sits on the bay, we see the water from our living room."

"That sounds very pretty," he said. "My name is John Mattel."

"Veronica."

"Darien."

"Nice to meet you both. Are you planning on taking the tour to Carlsbad mine?"

"We didn't sign up for it," Veronica said. "Will you be going?"

"Yes, it's three days, overnights in the desert. It's truly wild West."

The van swung to the left causing Darien to grasp the handle in front of her.

"We're signed up for tonight's cruise on the river, tomorrow is the museum and a rodeo, the next day is the Roseville tour ---"

"That's the one. Great, we'll be traveling down together."

"Oh, that's splendid," Veronica said. She turned to her companion. "He means the Roseville tour."

"Yes, we are scheduled," she said. "Are you in any line of work?"

"I'm not the famous Mattel, if that's what you are thinking. I'm a physician laboratory. I study death scenes of people who are disposed of by gun powder cartridges."

"That sounds very interesting," Veronica said.

"How'd you get into your field?" Darien asked.

"Every man in my family is a pellet expert."

"That's amazing," Darien said. "We are both court stenotypists. I work for Richmond City, Ronnie works for the county."

"Do you girls handle any criminal?"

Veronica nodded. "I do. She does mainly probate."

"See any estates of homicide?"

"One. It's almost unheard of. The usual comes from natural deaths."

"I'm surprised. Which county do you serve?"

"Alameda. There are a few county courthouses, but we are the furthest east along the Suisun."

"We ought to compare notes. Crescent sends most of its analyst documents to Alameda for final notation."

"Might I have taken stenography on a file of yours?" Veronica asked.

"I was thinking you might. We sent several this year. One was a group of murders in Nevada City."

"It's possible that file was referred for venue to San Mateo. I would have remembered a mass grave case."

He said, including both girls, "It was a ghastly item. Ten men were found dead in their blood, shot by pellet. Recovery thought they had lain dead almost a half year. I had to send a report to your county for second opinion on pathology."

"Sounds awfully gruesome," Veronica said.

"Oh, it was much worse."

The van pulled alongside a covered entrance bordered on both sides by snow and opened front and back doors. Everyone inside the van stood at once and fetched their luggage. The tour group filed into the warm sunlight into single file to be escorted inside, each led to suites one set at a time.

"You girls enjoy yourselves. I'll see you tonight on the river tour."

"Yes, we'll see you," Veronica said. "Bring a camera."

"I will. See you."

"He was cute," Darien said, once Veronica and she were alone in their hotel room.

It was a large room that contained two double beds and lamp tables, a separate sitting alcove of a hundred square feet with two dark blue sofas and two vinyl chairs, a nice sized round table, kitchenette complete with range, sink, counters, refrigerator, bar, and overhead cupboards, and drawers for silver, utensils and napkins, and a long bathroom with full amenities.

Veronica made fresh coffee and poured two cups.

"Yes he was. He makes the world seem awfully small," she said.

"It's unusual we wouldn't have heard anything about it," Darien answered.

"Very. I'm trying to imagine the file names. Possibly they were heard under different headings."

"What about that Berkeley hanging on Campus Hill off Scenic Drive?"

"That was opened as a suicide because of the chair. It was straight forward, open and shut. A James case. The man was a local resident studying religion." Veronica stripped down to lacy white underwear. "He was in his thirties, a handsome dark brunette. His wife worked in downtown Berkeley as a wait-ress."

Darien removed a clip from a small luggage case, wrapped her long red hair into a twist and clipped it. "Did you bring a pack of cigarettes, Ronnie, Love?"

Veronica looked through her black leather purse and finding an unopened pack tossed it to her. "What do you think about his job?"

Darien unwrapped the pack of Cool's, drew out a cigarette and lit it. Even in the pale sunlight Veronica thought her friend looked stellar, a subdued red, tapered long legs without so much as a muscular lean, thin throughout, firm breasts that rose off her ribcage with an after-thought of seduction, they had enjoyed good times with several handsome males, who themselves were steno-typists seeking entry into law practices.

"He's a physician," Darien said. "Pellet is rather unusual. He'd have to apply to causality. No idea if he thinks the stub nosed refractory lens is capable of relying upon lethal adminis-tered fire target."

Veronica lay on her side, the sharp side of hip bones pro-truding with visual compliment. "I think we ought to seduce our Dr. Pellet, take him dancing, loosen his tie."

"You do that, Ronnie. He won't want me, he likes you."

"I thought he gave us equal time."

"He was being polite."

"Well, he is cute, I agree."

Darien finished her coffee and took a long drag. "How many homicides have you really had?"

"It's not many and they aren't all that gory. I've told you.

Toss me a cigarette?"

Darien got up and handed Veronica the pack and matches, to which Veronica took her by the wrist and brought her to her and kissed her on the mouth. Darien fell beside her, allowing herself to be discovered, Veronica somewhat feverish, and slowly placed her hand on Veronica's hip and drew her against her.

"You can always have me if the men disappear," Darien said. "I'll never say no."

Veronica lit her own cigarette. "We are wicked, Sweetheart."

"I know, but it's fun."

"I always ache a bit."

Darien smiled. "You are more beautiful every day, Ron. You take even my breath away."

Veronica gave her a peek below her brassiere to where the swell of breast strained to be free. "Will he want me?"

"I'm sure it won't prove impossible."

They wore tight, tight fitting backless black lace dresses to their ankles without an article of undergarment. Veronica had parted her hair to one side. Her lips were moistened with wet gloss. Darien wore her hair in a tight French braid, her nape creamy bare. She had painted her eyelids dark pink mauve and on her lips, a very obscure dark blood lipstick stain. Both females wore the same lilac cachet and carried small sequined gold purses. They joined John on the deck, each taking a side.

He wore dark tweed casual men's slacks, a light tan thin sweater, heavy knotty tweed jacket, Mock Beans with dark stretch socks.

"You both look absolutely gorgeous."

They laughed teasingly.

"I mean it. You two take my breath away. You must be the two most stunningly attractive women I've ever laid a glance on. How will I choose between you?"

"We will help you," Darien said.

"Ah," he exclaimed, and put his arms through each girl

beside him. "Aren't you chilly?"

"Not me," said Veronica.

"Nor me. Do you like her dress?"

He held her slightly apart to appreciate it, gaze taking in the barest suggestion of skin. "Did you make it?"

"Oh, no, we bought them."

Darien lit a marijuana cigarette. "We should relax," she said, handing it to him.

He accepted it from her fingers, whereupon she kissed him lightly. He allowed her to do so and took a long inhalation, passed it to Veronica who also inhaled deeply and passed it in the other direction.

"This is fast acting," he said.

Darien removed the cigarette and smoked the last of it.

Veronica said, "We were trying to figure out your case this afternoon. Were all the crimes in California?"

"Only the one crime in Nevada City," he said to reassure her. "It was apparently committed after hours, many of the men were at a nearby bar; the thought is they were followed home to a flop house."

"Did your report give any reason?"

"No, that's not my department. I had to state causes of death for those murders involving pellet."

Veronica leaned against him as she said to Darien, "I told you so." To him, she added, "It's possible the cases that come to our court don't involve pellet."

"That's what you stated. One pellet isn't really all that consequential, but I looked up your county on my computer. You heard a hanging suicide and a drowning case in the bay off Pt. Richmond."

"So we did. A man was knocked semi unconscious and his body dragged into the bay."

"There are lots of those. This river here probably sees a few in winter. Some are established to be accidental deaths."

"We don't tend to hear investigations."

"No, we don't either."

"I'm getting hungry," Darien said.

They walked down the deck to the entrance to the dining hall, joined the already long line, waited a mere several minutes, and selected platefuls of food. Alaskan crab, sole percale, bass, squid, blue clams, stews, roast beef, turkey, roast ham, Jell-O salads, fruit salad, garden salads, carrot raisin, tarts, cakes, pies, and custards were piled on six plates. Over dinner John discussed his laboratory describing the complex intricate index graven stains that isolated tissue lacerated by pellet spray from numerous causes.

The blood on the surface of the skin became consistency of jam, there was almost no bleeding; thus it was odd blood had pooled suggesting a worse crime, stings of sharp introjections appeared, after weeks skin would become emasculated as opposed to some victims having white soft doughy tissue listed as death attributed to fire torture using soluble garden chemical.

"In pellet there is the immediate question as to type of pellet resin. Is it mercury, coal or platinum, known as bullet strength? Coal comes up all the time. It's most usually what causes the skin to become blackened. Coal pellet is manufactured at a paraffin plant that produces those. The difficulty with my case was the skin was definitely corroded by pell but contained shrapnel-looking markings."

Veronica had sampled each of four servings and was on a vegetable stew. "What did you write in your report?"

"I described the found state of the victims, how thoroughly they could be rinsed, head microscope examination of limbs and facial composure, movement, as well as capable artery maintenance. I started with full tests including recovery of skin, nail clippings, hair follicles, groin recapitulation, sturdy cultures, and a handful of additional sensitivities. The entire evaluation takes four to seven hours per vic. For at least six I had to cut, suture the incision, compare interior to any laceration."

"Full physician competency," Darien remarked, having touched nearly none of the meal. "It must be questionable for knife wounds or for wire cork semi explosives."

"Very," he said, eying her carefully, hearing the legal use

of terminology referred to for exclusion contests of restoring physician license. "Have you heard many court proceedings as to restorative measures post evaluation?"

"Hundreds. A fraction of the intakes for immediate disposition."

"Ever handled any on inmates?"

"Thirty."

"How about on legal proof residency complications?"

"Ten, if that."

He fixed on Veronica to be conversational. "You?"

"Almost none. County hears on gun permit, reckless discharge, wild out of control frenzy, death by asphyxiation, morbid causes."

"You certainly have me impressed."

"We aren't physicians," Veronica said.

They all laughed.

"Do you ever receive a copy of the other opinions of other pell experts?"

"Yes, I have completed files. On these Nevada City boys, San Mateo read in all findings and sent me the final slip."

"Who read second?"

"I would have to guess because I don't determine. Possibly Los Angeles. I only obtain the court order as final copy."

"Were there any knife wounds among your grouping?" asked Darien.

"Several. Knife wounds don't usually kill. They leave clear passes, easy to see lacerated tissue all the way through. These particular wounds were described by poison tips suggesting that the knife, it was one knife evidenced by tissue of previous vic's, was placed for a long time in chemical, in this instance paint sealant, that did the men in instantly."

"I've seen reports of that description," Darien said. "Parking lot stabbing crimes."

"That would about do it."

He invited them to his hotel room for a nightcap once the yacht docked. John poured sufficient drinks in crystal high glasses and they retreated to the alcove. The two girls sat on a black sofa and he on an upholstered black and grey striped high backed chair. From his position they seemed receded by their net dresses, thinly slender remarkably long legged females although also inaccessible in an elusive manner.

"Would you like to stay to watch a movie?" he offered.

Veronica replied. "We thought you might like some entertainment. We've done this for other men we have dated. It's quite harmless. We'd like to have you watch us make love."

"I've never seen that except in porn."

Veronica stood and walked over to him and sat on his lap. "It's wicked. You are just asked to enjoy what you see." She kissed him longingly as she ran her hand across his chest. "Say you want to see. I'd like it if you would."

He was aware that Darien was lighting a marijuana cigarette. "You are so beautiful," he told Veronica. "You would be hard to resist. You two decide."

Darien approached him, placed the cigarette between his lips. She bent over his arm letting him feel her length and kissed Veronica who took the cigarette and took a few drags, then gave it to Darien.

Veronica said to him, "You are hard to resist yourself. I knew straight away in the lobby I wanted you."

He put his arms around her waist, pressing her to him. She acknowledged him running her hand down his chest and down his abdomen. He kissed her again feeling heady, consumed. When she placed her hand beneath his pullover he felt surges of attraction.

Darien kissed Veronica on the neck, shoulder and breast and he soon found himself watching, she slipped a hand beneath Veronica's gown up her bare leg, still planting kisses down her ribs and stomach, until she had exposed Veronica's thigh. Veronica arched while she stroked his chest.

"We love getting dirty," Veronica said to him.

"She's so smooth," he said about Darien.

Veronica reached behind his belt and whispered to him, "Hurt me."

He felt an absolute rush. He curled his free hand beneath

her right breast, surprised she wore nothing beneath, aware of an unusual hardness, and squeezed her roughly.

"Harder," Veronica said.

He squeezed her full nipples.

"Oh, good, do it again, both."

Darien separated her legs, pressed the gown to her hips showing dark blond hair, gazing at John, catching his glance downward, and kissed Veronica's inner thighs to which Veronica withdrew her hands and crushed Darien's head to her body, clutching her braid with force, beginning to breathe faster.

He pulled her nipples in turn, seized them tightly in succession, bit her ear. She had her hands on either side of Darien's face and moved her head, parting her legs, thrusting her hips at her face. He realized Darien was kissing and biting her and he raised her face toward him and suggested they lie on the bed. Veronica stood and he rose with her, taking her feverishly in his arms, running his hand down her body to bare skin, Darien stood and led Veronica out of his grasp to the bed where she sat and drew her to her.

John lay on the bed. The two lay beside him, Darien closest to him. Veronica ran her hand over Darien's body, kissed her neck all the way to her thighs.

Veronica said, "Now you have to make love to each of us."

The maid had called in the report of a dead man inside his room. It took the Sheriff four hours to respond. He arrived with five men attired in black suits – two police, a photographer, a fingerprint man, and a laboratory inspection analyst. The Sheriff directed tasks. The police cordoned off the entry and walked through the scene. The other four sat on the furniture drinking cups of coffee smoking cigarettes while the police detectives searched the scene and made notes. They were long at their jobs, used to the commonplace, as attentive to details as strip handling nurse detectives to the human body. Their search of the entire contents took an hour; by the time they finished note-taking, they had the crime well-disposed. The photographer shot ten rolls of the scene and left, leaving the blood man to take seven vials and swab the mouth and drinks and food. The fingerprint technician had the remainder of the day to laser and dust off windows for technical expertise.

"What do you make of the crime?" the fingerprint man named Cantrell asked his boss. Cantrell was in his late seventies, a red haired slender stocky man with freckles.

Sheriff Dyadf ran fingers through his silver brown crew cut and sighed, "Sex and drugs. Only problem is Mattel will be our fourth pell to get nabbed. The two females chimed and dimed him. My guess is they came looking for him, tuned him up a bit; killed him. No marks on the body, death could be damn near anything. It could be we are dealing with an active group going about, they wanted to learn some particular information, once they understood the status, they knew what their endangerment was."

"This must be your tip that came in a few hours ago."

"Sure. 'Another crime is set to go down.' I sent it to Voice analysis. The person making that call is male, man by name of Starn, lives in west Bullfrog. I don't know who he is to this crime wave. Apparently he's the same person who called in Oakland for the Fruitvale murders, house of six dead grave yard employees at West train station."

"Any idea whether he knows the female duo?"

"Until this moment I didn't know any females were suspected."

"Did any victims survive in that melee?"

"Several, but they don't know anything."

Cantrell said, "I'll send you names along with objective surveys by tomorrow afternoon."

"Fine. That will be right about fine."

Mathew Dyadf had worked the train towns since the beginning of time as far as he was concerned. By and large they began as average sized mining towns, each approximately a hundred and fifty houses, a county hall built of sandstone mill slate, a handful of warehouses to accept cut lumber feet, and a half dozen restaurants, shops, and furniture stores. Nevada City lay toward the top of the line, houses had tin roofs, snowfall every year was five feet; public parks saw as many as eighty families for fairs and frog jumping shows, not to mention a few surrounding national parks and lumber mills. Life had retained a moderate pace for well over fifty years, generations had moved up the line; and crime had pretty much left these small towns alone.

The ten murders in Nevada City had all but befuddled investigators. Oddly the victims were unknowns. Their data sheets said they were linemen who worked towns as extras, living off the land primarily picking up summer jobs for under-staffed mine corporations, obtaining rooms as renters as they moved across the country. Those ten had frequented a talkie bar parlor a few miles outside of town. It was the same with the murdered groupings in Oakland. The grueling realities were still a mystery. No one knew a goddamn thing. He had his suspicions. For starters all lab physicians associated to the Permanente, Kaiser Aluminum Plant had been killed. Second were chief accountants to the plant. The category of work for others dead in groups were industrial lights in towns with high cement walls keeping homes and stores separate from a main thoroughfare.

2.

Mathew's case began with two Genoca brothers burning
the mint in western Nevada, his photograph stills removed
showed the shadows in the ceiling of rotating oars of a fan, an
upside down multi-reflection shower of prism crystals of glinting pink Romanesque light specks, a febrile stirring of spatter
at the height of the wall, instantaneous motion of trembling,
directly overhead slats of alternate light and shade running over
dark shadows of beams, a lone whistle in the distance moving across the silken plateau, rain patter on tin sounding like
a washboard, barely visible downpour in bright sunlight, tin
staccato – all day, all night, fading incoming trains, a sigh of
disputed lust reaching far above the clear windows, remorse
driven afternoons like studies of desolate hunger etched by
tragic demurs to be surrendered, Veronica Estis awakened to
the sickly pungent scent of death, in the film she was the more
adventuresome, a cunning diver losing breath as the man came
deep in her throat, the other girl inserting a long metal penis
into his rectum at full charge all the way in, he trying to remove it and being unable to, he bent over trying to reach it and
was still unable to, he insisted it be removed, but the girls kept
kissing him, teasing, Darien shuddered in orgasm, he collapsed
begging them, saying the pleasure was just too intense, he was
in pain, both girls pressed to him and he went unconscious, it
was a tantric last meal, an act of disposal, the females eventually bathed, kissed each other's breasts, they dressed in their
gowns and removed the dildo and left, prints matched, he was

dead face down, shit-faced; this was a crime of domestic do-
micile, no suspects, if all witnesses said two gorgeous females,
then somewhere there was at least a forensic report that said
that, after two identical crimes what told them who had such
a report, what act called it to their attention, in the mint profiles, all redacted, a long legged brunette modeled in a room in
front of a wire fenced window in black lace bra and leggings
with mask while in the basement below seat men were getting
shot over wine crates, an elevator was detonated, in the receipt
room where a hundred chief accountants approved checks it
was peaceful, not a disturbance perceived, although in the dye
engine wing bill staff, chef, and cooks who combined the dyes
were sprayed with charcoal split assault weapon fire, all but
their faces painted streaks of coal tar, esoteric duck webbing
and grain rinsing techno-experts who poured gallons of ink
through slush ponds, drip clerks who watched the dark green
ink pour through floors like liquid hemp, who among them
was to be trusted, none but work they did, long hours, three
shifts, term sentences for the march of dimes, there were a
hundred ways to die, and only the shotgun analysts, maybe a
dozen men, who tested by special chemicals to make certain
the dye was the right color on the paper, escaped unscathed,
without knowledge, nor sense any massacre had occurred. The
Genoca's had turned up dead, drowned in the port estuary canal, feet tied, not to be discovered for at least a week, the other
sixty bodies in houses identified as lab and accountants who
worked the aluminum tin factories situated throughout Emeryville and west Oakland, none known to be guilty of any
crime, a dozen factory electricians soiled by their own blood,
left dead in the already paid-off houses of miners who in final
months of November and December had boarded trains to new
plants in the blue mountains of Tennessee and Virginia to dent
coal and Galveston, Texas to work sand, over four hundred industrial factory miners whose early fifteen years were lived in
the tenement flats off San Pablo and Telegraph Avenues; the
causes for the plethora of deaths were unknown, brutally sadistic, prints long obtained with no known referents, bodies were

spongy adhering to the carpets they lay dead on, the morgues refused them without correct tags, it was safer to leave them where they lay. Mathew often warned himself the killing was not over, that this ongoing mission of malice was nowhere near ceased, glass stains continued to arrive monthly which proved another spree and despite prints or in spite of them, killers were not sufficiently apprehended, either evidence gleaned unlikely suspects, plant yard managers or train stock clerks or they were hiding somewhere watching the streets waiting for another cadre of mint detectives to arrive. His first series of photos, all rows removed, gave the fetching long legged, semi clad brunette staging inside the dime store while a few men toting Winchester rifles shot all bill dye manufacture agents in a basement immediately below the dime certification office. A good thirty workers saw her. None said anything. The other girl Darien showed up on stills as a minter, short hair, coveralls, tight bodice, no clear indication she was not male. Neither securities nor bonds were ever paid to any mint operative whose contracts would not be due payable until 2019 and then only payable in Oakland, California; all others would be sufficed if they continued to reside in original houses purchased on or before 1950. So that had to be the predominant motivation for these crimes, although change of names could not be affixed. He considered himself smarter than most of his immortal counterparts, a species of known commonality, he had denied all files that listed brethren who hadn't formerly existed, he squandered any still involving procedural findings to all jurisdiction prudent eyes, he tossed in the merry widows to completion of any crime, forgave no omissions, the duty of crimes were piling up as fast as crime could be planned and implemented, previous co-miners who attested to family sponsorships would someday be sent to the gallows and gas chambers. As of December 30th, 1971 there were hundreds of fake domiciles alleged to, each one without pardon, the aging elderly were kept at home probably anticipated for youth by the subscribed to year, who knew what treasures of murder rested in wait, until then food was a shortage, houses were listed incorrectly, deeds were sought by seedy lease lend carnivores, the pistol, chain and whip Mac-Nulty forbearance bond lenders on the trot, every institution to come along since the advent of substitute recorders bargaining for parcels and damnation. Whereas this rationale explained every crime nationwide, it did not appear to proscribe to any congruence for mass murder off the California rail lines.

Veronica lay on the divan sunning in front of the wide sitting room window. She wore an extravagant all black strapless swimsuit gathered at the bosom. On the floor Darien slept in an angle of bright sunshine. Their sole roomer Aaron with whom Darien had been in love with since their days at the mint was in his separate entry apartment that led to the garden and three hundred yards out to the sandy shoreline of the San Pablo Bay. Veronica eyed the transcript on the bureau, as far as she could infer, the analyst's signature matched the handwriting of the Mattel they had met, in his report he described a virtually unknown incident in which she had plunged a metal bard through a competency mackerel bonds analyst before robbing his drawer of stiletto weapon causality findings which probably did condemn half a dozen guards to prison and the chair, but the whereabouts of these analysts worried her if in fact they were deputized witnesses to one crime committed on Adam's apple farm church yard, an adjunct across from Ellis Island where European land holdings were photographed, itemized and indexed and prints compared. John had proven a good chump like many physicians whom they had wandered to, usually it was Darien whose spent emotion gave her a clinging dependency on Veronica who soothed her, hushing her as she entwined her legs about Darien's waist, sucked Darien's ears until Darien was burning, then had her insert her fingers into her and rose on her as on a phallus. That was joining, they were always fresh, often unburdened, hard in one another's enthralled seductions, Darien varied the release, it was like their first time when Darien came upon her after a dive and found her releasing herself with another diver and then knifed her, turning in dim twilight to discover Darien who all but raped her, charging at her, grabbing her by the shoulders, trembling with the arousal of taking a girl she talked to every day at lunch.

"I like you," Darien had said in early summer that year, twenty-one years ago.

"You'll have to take a number," Veronica said. "I have a man I'm sweet on and every weekend I take my passion with a senior analyst here, a she."

"I have a man too. Maybe you'd like to meet him."

"Maybe. Are you wicked?"

"Every time I look at you I'm in uncontrollable love. It's getting harder all the time."

"Don't take me home, save me for yourself. I'll be over my analyst in another week."

"Then come find me, destroy me."

That was their first time. Darien had consumed her, positioned herself on her slightly bent leg, felt her until Veronica couldn't resist, inserted into her backside, held her and finally almost a half hour later forced her to submit. There were men on line who liked a hard thrust in the mix corridor, it wasn't enough for her but she set a schedule for the older ones at a dollar a gush. One afternoon Veronica paid her a two-bill.

"I want to reserve you every Friday at nine in the post bail office and we'll entertain the crab master."

"You don't have to pay me," Darien said, as she drew Veronica's string on her blouse.

"I want to. I have to get inside his desk and I can't think what else to do for it."

"I'll talk to him. He'll show me." She pressed the bill into her hand.

Veronica placed it inside her bra. "We'll keep it here in case you need it."

Darien kissed her breast, withdrawing the bill in her lips, rolled it and jammed it inside her, telling her, "You'll have to pay that way," and then partly withdrawing the rolled bill said, "I saw you kissing a young man yesterday, do you give him what you give me?"

She had left her desk that Friday and walked to their

secluded spot when she came upon Darien and her Aaron making frantic love.

"Just do it as hard as you do her," she overheard a jealous friend say. "I won't be good until I have all of you."

"Darien, you are so perfect, you're an angel, take me, take me, do it, kill me."

She had her arms wrapped around his head, having demanded as he entered her that he bite her nipple, she gave him as much tightness as she dared and as he rushed into her, he bit her harder than anyone had and she came, desiring him as though she had never been in love.

Veronica went home with Darien that Friday for the weekend to meet Tom. While Darien lay sleeping she entered their bed, awoke him with oral sex and rode him without awakening Darien. She told her the next morning.

"I did it to get back at you; you can't have everyone I need."

Darien was a bit astounded. "I have to possess you."

"You possess Aaron; that should be plenty."

"Then I'll break it off with him."

"What should I do with Port? Throw him out?"

"Sure, throw him out."

She acquiesced to Darien, let her make most final decisions. They were each tramps out to settle a score, each score was taken without Aaron, he was a place to go home to and after so much time had passed, she gave up the notion she had had him first. Darien used him as a wedge between them, if Veronica went out and brought someone home, Darien descended to Aaron's flat and spent days and nights with him. Occasionally it was good with Darien, they kept to a flirtatious stemming, Darien was at her best when Veronica became ravenous, and then the dynamic began again, Darien didn't let her out of her sight and she felt hemmed in.

Veronica padded into the kitchen, poured herself a glass of chilled white wine and retreated to the living room. Darien had awakened from her nap.

"Is Aaron about?" Darien asked.

"I suppose. Are you still depressed?"

"I'm alright. I rather liked John."

"He was nice, I thought it ended fine."

"He identified you."

"I really wanted him to give us his wording. That would have been much preferable."

"Yes, I kept after him about it, but he wouldn't budge."

"None of them have. It's sort of pointless."

Darien went into the kitchen for a glass of wine and stood in the doorway sipping her glass. "What do you want to do for dinner?"

"Pizza might be nice. Why don't you send Aaron out to pick up some?"

"I could. Maybe he should get a few movies?"

"That would be decent. I'd like that."

"Shall I call him?"

"Sure, tell him seven new movies, we'll stay up all night."

Darien made the call. "And, honey, be sure not to get horror, only stuff we can stay up all night with." To Veronica, she said, "He'll be back in an hour."

"Let's take a walk to visit Mr. Detri," Veronica suggested.

"Great idea," Darien agreed, feeling more cheery.

They donned jeans and tight long sleeved light blue shirts, Darien twisted her hair and clipped it, Veronica brushed her hair tying it with a dark red scarf. The air was windy with a hint of rain. The beach beneath their sneakers crunched.

"It could've been worse," Veronica said to Darien, touching her breast lightly in a slight gesture meant to impart affection. "He could've asked us to go. I expected that when he couldn't make up his mind who he wanted."

Darien briefly slid a hand between Veronica's legs. "He was annihilated by you."

"I'm not altogether certain he wasn't just being generous of spirit. When he made love to you, he was in dark need; he didn't anticipate your surrender."

"He was tender, sweet almost. It's odd, but I hoped you might change your mind."

"Well, what had to happen when he had me? He was beside himself all night to be touched by me, when I finally took him, you didn't wait long."

"It's never quite enough. I wanted him to have me several times, I wanted you to make love to me for hours; then I wanted him again. With you it gets down to business. It's over too soon."

Veronica paused standing in front of Darien, the wind blowing their hair, smoothed her palms across Darien's breasts, pressed them, looked deeply into her liquid eyes. "You only want it when you think I won't."

They broke free and continued their walk. The ocean rolled in up the incline dragging in oil rich muddy water, strands of sea weed, frothy waves. On the horizon the golden sky was striated by white lines giving off a surreal appearance.

Veronica said, "It's apparent to me with all the news on Iraq that we may see some real changes on the American continent. Oil may start diminishing, for starters. The society may chart a course away from resorts to staying at home more, rationing industrial incentives, spending more of its dollar in France."

Darien thought about it. "I can temp again. I still maintain two hundred words a minute."

"Well, there is that. I was thinking more along the lines of an orchard rental."

"We might. What will it tell you?"

"Who is buying stocks, how is money getting utilized."

"Did you have something specific for an entry?"

"I'd like some experience staying where money stays, on the Russian coast above Mendocino, a bed and breakfast could do, early spring."

"I'll check the Earnest Poor as well as the Dow Seven at work, maybe you'd consider a smaller house in southern San Mateo to beef up our live-ability."

"A small stipend from a renter is what I'm thinking of."

"I can check easily."

They climbed the white peeling wooden stairs to the rambling ranch style wooden house that sat high on the bluff.

"Mr. Detri," Veronica called out as they entered through the narrow kitchen into the living room.

A very handsome widower, strikingly tall with jet black wavy hair, dressed in dark olive khakis and a mustard color, short sleeved shirt with open collar and sandals appeared. "Girls, girls, you took me up on my invitation, so good to see you;" he grasped a hand each, drew them to him, pecked their faces.

"Wine?"

"We can only stay for a glass," Veronica explained, slipping her arm about his thin compact waist. "We sent Aaron on an errand for pizza."

He pulled Darien into his embrasure. "Can I show you my home?"

"We'd love it," Veronica replied.

"Yes, yes, show us," Darien said, shedding shyness.

He held them fast, standing in the room that faced the ocean momentarily to permit the influence of the view of ocean to affect them. The room was large, almost empty, soft walnut flooring, an abundance of cabinets and counter tops, two refrigerators. "I am so glad you walked over. You must come by every day."

"We've been meaning to since you asked, but we both work, you know," Darien explained.

"Have you?" he asked, as he looked down at her.

She held him firm. His shoulder muscles rippled with taut fitness. "You don't object, do you?"

"No, dear, I don't," he remarked, and squeezed her again. "Do you?"

"No, it's rather nice."

"What does Ronnie say?" Without waiting for an answer, he wheeled them into a second living room made of walnut flooring, terra cotta soft rose walls, a dark stone hearth, book shelves crammed with books.

"This is stunning," Veronica said.

"It is my palace. Maybe you would like to spend several days here."

Veronica looked to Darien who said, "She'd love to. Our place is actually very small."

He laughed. "I suppose you should both stay over, make yourselves at home. Nothing would suit me better. Should you phone your roommate, let him know you're here?"

Darien said she would.

While she called, he gave Veronica a walk through. The hall gave way to a spacious sunroom with reddish tile; through it he showed her a large bedroom and a bathroom with sunken tub, when Darien returned. He held Darien's neck as he explained the deleterious condition in which he bought the home. She slipped her arm around him again, while he resumed the tour to another bedroom with two modest size beds, a reading chair, and a wall of walnut shuttered doors containing closets. The carpet was thick white pile. He had them pause before a gilded mirror in the tiled hall, smiling at each.

"Here we are. I am seventy-four years old, and you are beautifully youthful. I could stand to offer my graces to you both, may I one day?"

Veronica ran a hand up his back. "Would you care to join us for dinner this evening?"

He turned to Darien. "You must invite your friend, we will eat in the garden; then I will keep you all night."

Veronica and he locked gazes as Darien went to ask Aaron to bring the pizza and movies. He kissed the top of her head.

"Do you like my house?"

"It's stunning. I'm in awe."

He beamed at her. "Are you often available?"

She kissed him. He circled his arms about her, kissed her eyes. "I've been alone for over thirty years."

"Do you think I'm as pretty as Darien is?"

"You misread my intent. She is saddened, I imagine."

"She's been depressed. I didn't realize it was that obvious. Do you like me?"

"Yes, beautiful Aphrodite, I do." He kissed her cheek. "You are an enigma." He grabbed her hands and kissed them reverently. "Let's go find your friend."

They returned through the house holding hands. Aaron had arrived with the pizzas, h'ordeurves and VCR movies. Aaron was handsome, grayish bronze haired, blue eyes, six foot, slender, tanned. He planted a kiss on Darien's lips and pat her backside. They helped set out four glass light green plates on the deck, Detri poured burgundy wine into goblets, and Aaron served the French pepperoni and bell pepper; tomato, clam and linguini; and teriyaki chicken, purple onion, tuna and chives large pizzas.

Once they were seated beneath the grey umbrella, all servings accommodated, Aaron asked Detri what he did for a living.

"I verify designed reproductions of color tweed. I've worked what is known as tweed for sixteen years. Prior to that I ran a small mill operation rebutting errors prior to final runs. You?"

Aaron swilled his wine. "All match, stick and dye. I was hired as a kid off the mule dock. That's where I met these two."

"Appreciative," Detri said. "I graduated up to first run."

"From third?" Aaron inquired.

"Correct. I've done solely offset which means there is no plating of currency."

"Ronnie worked off for years. Darien had the wine spillage."

Veronica gave a nod of agreement. "I tracked wire thread."

Detri smiled to her. "Did you complete justification?"

"No, I only did piece. Much of what I looked for was either mule, dark color, and faded blemish."

"That's considerable for any female."

"Yes, it probably is. I could have worked cut, but the bosses sought aged male photographic plate stringers. I also attended college at Dartmouth for a year to learn batch."

"Money is a trickery to produce correctly. The prejudice opposing females is that the continued contact with inks becomes prohibitive. One finds that unusual criminal intent, preplanned disposition relates to fine chalks, even more seductive webbing, and lace pillory are laid on spread which makes an appraiser capable worthy of redesign of paper, and that's where

I start with my procedures."

Aaron remarked casually, "My guess is they enter seat work; it seems to me that the reduction of image is what attracts counterfeit."

Detri agreed. "Superb analysis. Have you always owned on the beach?"

"Yes," Aaron replied. "We've resided at our home for almost twenty years."

"Did you transfer to the west coast?"

"Yes," Aaron said. "We saddled money for the western unions when packaged bills were chained to the train under flooring."

Darien spoke, "He went into resin for a brief three years turning cloth for parchment. It was fairly decent pay, nothing like what I imagine yours would have to be."

Aaron said, "Twenty-two a half season."

"That is excellent. I wasn't aware belt paid so well. Mine is estimably high. I've often entertained the idea of a beach cottage at San Diego."

Veronica drank a good portion of wine, for that her glass was refilled. The breeze had wafted, the air temperature was moderate. With no hint of rain, they might sit here all night, long past dark.

She said, "We've had the toe of the industry. The pay for various sites has always attracted top-notch belt, not to mention other industrial standard chemists, arrangement, as well as bread for soaking the offset color, blemish, and transfer, all of them."

She saluted with her full glass and the others joined her.

Detri said, "Oddly enough to lay text for newspapers requires stint which is similar to crate composition. I spent a season during a layoff working the husband newspapers. I think that's how I wound up inviting Ronnie. I was struck by a similarity in our work, you had to examine under sedition law a bound set of bills for your court, and over the years I have been asked to define goof, that peculiar webbed background that appears on any greenback."

Veronica remarked, "I recall being surprised to encounter you, if you remember I told you it was quite unexpected."

He continued with, "The nature of our field brings a sort of denouncement of money. I wonder how many people are aware of the intricacy of duck or makeshift, the timing of having set the plates over the first paper bin wrap, then applications of subsequent layering."

"Too involved to know about, much less comprehend by actuary."

Aaron left three crusts. "The matching takes almost a month ---"

Detri interrupted, "Oh, good God, no, it takes minimum a year."

Darien put her arm around Aaron's shoulders. "Sturdy was eliminated just shortly after I began work. All that cotton, some bright green, laying about, one could scarcely make it out of the operation box."

Detri smiled. "That is Nevada, nothing but goof, endless barrels."

"They brought in newer equipment, some with photo determinants."

"Very steep expenses, but that's the issue; money is always up against a field of diminishing returns as it remains longer in circulation, changing hands, the felt becoming too soft, eventually it tears."

The sky darkened, and Detri hastened them inside. They took their wine with them into the living room, Detri put the first movie into the VCR, Darien and Aaron sat on a couch, and Veronica and Detri on the other. Veronica removed her sneakers. The movie began, an internationally acclaimed drama about an older woman who seduces a teenage male while her husband traveled to India. They watched through most sipping wine, cautious of talking, Darien permitted Aaron to put his hand on her leg, Veronica tucked in her legs.

Detri asked Aaron, "Were you assigned Kaiser tin?"

"No, none of us. The plant hired strictly non corporate accountants, not one from U.S. Steel, Batchelor Commodities,

Proof Western, or any of the Nebraska Trumpet Court."

"I wondered. There must have been a hundred who arrived with the tin mill change croft crew."

"Strictly payroll. Tin doesn't require chemists and therefore no change turn screws who are the analysts who itemize use per material."

"Very clear thinking. My recent task was to compare thread weave on siding of small indented coin. Normally dimes contain an opposition of crank, a mixed blend of dollar silver and nickel copper, but overproduction has determined the interior should only have nickel band." To Veronica, he asked, "Were you ever required to tinker coin?"

"No."

"So you plied bills?"

"Yes, only the minimal thread on first actual paper."

"That's slightly different."

The drama concluded, and Darien and Aaron said they had to be going. Detri encouraged Aaron to take the uneaten pizza but he refused. At the door Darien hugged Detri in lingering affection. Detri held her face in his hands, kissed her, and whispered a remark in her ear to which she hugged him again, before departing.

"I told her I had as much desire for her as for you," Detri said, as he closed the door.

Veronica caught him in an embrace. After a minute of silence, she pressed to him, took his hand and placed it on her waist, kissing him as she removed his shirt. He undid the buttons to her shirt glancing with swelling pride at the tops of her breasts, setting them free, motivating her through the hall to the bedroom pushing her onto the bed lying on her.

"It's turned into a wonderful evening," he said.

"For me too."

He spread her hair across a pillow. "Of course I like you better. I have dreamed of you since that day we met."

She clasped him around the back. She was all fever, burning, a goddess in his loins, a knot of rising tension, her kisses were searching, her eyes closed, she took his leg with hers and told him, anything, anything.

He stripped nude but kept her clothes on around her thighs, aggressed toward her, dipped, his instrument hard, withdrew, dipped again, withdrew, over and over, letting her want him, until she was beyond satisfying, until he came in a sensational stupendous climax, brimming to the fullest, hot with torrential desire, made manly, made whole.

They lay tangled in one another.

"You are a lifetime of fulfillment," he said.

"I am all yours. There is no one but you."

He kissed her longingly, drew her hand to his chest, raked her hair with his fingers. "I have given you my entity. You alone know me as no one does. Will you stay the night?"

"Of course I will. I require you."

"You are my will."

She kissed him holding him until he was breathless. By degrees she toyed with him, stroked his face, brushed back his hair, giving him new passion, pressed his face against her neck, pushed his head down to her breasts, asked that he talk to her, he told her she was perfect, a vision, and he made love to her breasts, all the while lifting her leg to his thigh, he continued to kiss her, moaning, she was every bit a wet dream, a goddess, he had to consume her, had to know her, when she ravished him surrendering in small breaths until weakened. He would go on talking to her, they were so close, not a mile, he could see her every night, review her documents if she liked, be her flame, drive her to work, keep her; he continued talking until he could see she was asleep. She slept with relaxed peace, breathing quietly. He felt her cheekbones, her long neck, her collar, cupped each breast and rubbed her nipples, taking his time to enjoy her feminine form, caressed her ribs, her stomach, each hip and thigh; hardened, he mounted and thrust into her, exploring her, waiting for evidence of arousal, finding he was wild with abandon, a stallion, a carnivore, he thrust, her sole movement of her hand touching his side caused him to race against time, tear primitively at her, beseechingly, he felt his impassioned soul perceive a flail of agony but he ignored it and his emotion spilled, his body flying, he was intoxicated, in a pronouncement of rapture, fighting her, the pleasure of such harnessed thrilling ecstasy he could not imagine where it would take him, he no longer possessed control, he was an assignment of euphoria.

It was dark. Veronica walked the beach mildly aware dew had fallen. The night had been provocative but she realized as she gathered her clothes and dressed that in truth there was no way she could ever allow herself to become known to him. The moon was a silver sliver; dampness caused her to run toward the house. She entered by the gate, opened the door to her flat. She slipped into bed beside Darien. She had long ago resolved that Darien's jealousy bore a vindictive rant. Darien was possessive, always wearing a solicitous armor. She often kept to a perception that Darien really wanted to control or contain her.

Officially, the hotel stiff Mattel died of arrhythmia, nothing could anyone say about his heart giving out because he got over-stimulated during a consensual act. It must have occurred to him that once he ejaculated there could be no further stimulation. But that wasn't Dyadf's problem. Mattel had worked wood crates in Chicago at the time of the disaster at the mint when five floors lowered crushing the chief lab analysts who had not yet completed their assignments. The crisis crushed sternums, fractured pelvis, eliminated limbs, feet, arms, hands; such a disgusting act he could not comprehend the intention. No money was produced there; none was stored there. The drawer trowels had not been raised in an hour when the fire broke out on the third floor and zoomed through the facility. Mathew thought most likely Veronica reset the schedule of rinses. He also thought Darien had just left the suds room, but still wasn't convinced she was involved; Darien's boyfriend Aaron had worked stock barrel and would have known who the finger men were; and Aaron was the first on the ground. Dyadf retraced his assumptions to the motivating interest; in addition to land copper available on site for the manufacture of pennies and disposable tract of platinum for dimes and coin, there was the ready theft of ink which was associated to the laying of presses for the bill. The bill seemed to be the desired objective, if only because it was easier to carry. It was bill design operators who were getting killed in small groups. Whether they were identified and later stalked remained unknown.

3.

The wayward hills of Wisconsin while attending to neither a primacy of green sloping foothills nor to a tracked phenomenon of green flaked natural copper, as impure in recidivisms of hilly hill hocks of sparse pasture astride mountains invested with boron, granite and zinc, nevertheless renumbered flanks of redundant authentic rheumatisms of nature borne of colonized rivulets of oxidized salt. By late season all finalities of surveyed land tracts measured suggestive columbines of wheat grasses interspersed with lilies, blue wild iris, crimson ferry, and an abundance of Romanian thistle smartly cavaliered over suds stone up to primitive canyon deep marble strata indoctrinated with wild asparagus lung. The more relevant anchored trees like blizzard driven wandering cassocks over an interminable plateau bleached clean by scoring winds retained the clandestine desert in its chalky cracked moon swept surface glinting in the furthest voids of chill nights, seemingly recalcitrant beggarly demise. A rare howl of ground sniffing coyote terminated the reconnoitered sense that time was sufficiently lengthy in its twelve hours; it surfeited the lonesome terrain in an unreasonable strained terror, a prickling of the spine, a sudden sweat of sensibility, a forlorn mitigating austere scrutiny for distance on the horizon. Night, then, was an enemy. A precarious distress to guard against. Except for very distant garish lights of an installation at the far reaches of the hardened paper Mache sand gulches, the night released a dismal prostrate awareness that the traveler could find safety, let alone an assurance of security. Until one encountered the ends of prairie and discovered the nearly frozen bailiff waters of Superior Lake between Bayfield and Duluth to the northeast, there was no appointment of barrier; life accommodated no repression, scarcity stood sentinel, constraint was both aboriginal and brutal. Washouts like any prosaic parallel gave way to a paralysis of diaphanous tenancy; nomenclature, a stillborn accord, described a paucity of panorama of grain and nap. Occasionally a pungent acrid breeze deported the rustic unrefined landscape divorcing it from its recalcitrant coarse rube. Prickly pears and worsted kiwi brooded over the quadrants of irrigated farm like recursive overgrown runts, shadowy bona robe grew in savant braiding raked acrimonious in prophylactic offense. In winter the lake changed from deep blue to opalescent grey, ice clouded over in fallible fissures. Slack marsh fed a rapid extortion of briny sweep; along the inlet gull cries scorched the air with multitudinous flapping, boisterous crank; defiant purchase. By late summer the land had shrunk, its captive shoreline held firm by paroles of uniform scatter, a priceless conceit of unguent occupant deposits.

The analysts at Bayfield Corporation, Inc. studied the latest photographic half sheets to determine where the three assailants may have been employed during their ten year stay working for the laboratory that rinsed dye for currency. Litigators spent weeks in Decipher sorting through valued bands of imagery in an attempt to best determine which cast of dye had been applied to a bill, and to do this evaluation the department hired in another ten lab coats to assess chemical additives, phenol acid tone, pilfers, barley as well as a number of groupings by element in their determination of same content offsets. Once each host combined to a natural linen and grave indexed according to pro rata document sheet, the sector was sent to the computer crayon offices for contrasting comparison. Dye, white water, permeable resin, double sided stamp demarcations were installed into a series of tumbling rag and then compared to known circulation. Often too purple had mixed with dull black and light yellow with bluish gold. Enhancers often subtracted exactitude of necessary font. This quiet December morning a reference had been submitted on blood type for the light ray chamber known by its employee nurse stations as the death chamber because any enhanced offset meant a deceased run. The other excitement was generated by hustling staff to discern an answer to Dock once the files were identified which might take thirty to a few hundred hours. Two combat reconciliation technicians gathered photo receiving data from plant operations opening and work station assignments searching for day to day object administered barrier closures and found the twenty year old Aaron inside an interior weave frame cloth graphics detriment office on the fifth floor of the baseball pitcher mount building which to anyone standing in the plaza square resembled a gigantic score board. Such assignments worked at night to first dawn when unfiltered morning light prepared the web for distilled color refinement. Aaron was one of nine pitchers whose job included task setting accomplished on separate pages per fold. Hours just prior to the hold being fired upon he removed a plait sheet discriminated against for too much grey in the web cutter conduit. Aaron placed it inside his interior jacket, signed out, registered it at Plates, received a ticket, and walked pipe stairs down five flights into the cellar. There he handed the receipt to an Underwater sewage pipe cleaning diver, an apt looking thin female dressed entirely in skin. Upon his return he dropped off the web cutter sheet to Dead Office.

The tank was controlled by a rotunda of bathe scopes for which any of fifty computers restored pressure readings as the video movie camera swung horizontally allowing periodic pipes to be color stocked. Two divers submerged while uncorking canisters of opaque dye scavenging for plate breakage; once seen, they took Casio photos with long filters which flared and dimmed almost immediately. Up in the underwater containment cylinder they pulled off their gear, logged in by time and station referred to on video and commenced defibrillation protocol. In those photo Lorries, Veronica was a long legged blonde, her youth, agility and capability assessed. She scanned a handprint and nearly a half hour later the door opened to a flight of stairs that led to the treatment plant. Darien worked the crate room, she entered at half past eight, lathered the all cement floor and scatter-proofed it with a beam pellet duster, re-entered after four to iron cork well the space before the first row of crates was lowered. Hunt profile analysts noted that their encounters were accidental, nominal non-injuries except for the month subsequent the crates all dropped at once onto ninety heads of dye analysts.

The kiss was registered in the park. Shoes were calibrated from point of origin in a pantomime of activity under grey scope. Darien had found Aaron rinsing suds at the moment Veronica appeared on the movie screen emerging to the first hold where an underwater joiner joint blew. The suds room primarily released valve activity easing the plug-like device to enter. Dead Office retraced their presumption that Darien understood the attachment device significance the moment she saw who went down.

The salt mine flats on north shoreline Chicago required a school of dark water divers whose head gear were their physician head lights, a pro-A team of trauma worthy line spool wire fray schedule keepers, who illegally dragged coil from building to building until they could predictably trip wire a building's electricity shorting it for days, finally necessitating a dam to rewire to depth. Every so often the summer weather receded surface water of lakes to its baser algae components leaving a dank emerald saturated pool on the great lake, a physical endurance for any diver no matter how expertise to succumb to, infiltrating to any realizable depth a disgrace of plummet. Surely as natural copper became lake resistant and imbued itself into surrounding rock co-established of salt wafers and lactate, the lake suffered tragic bleeds causing the wells to become obstructed and pipes to crust over, their platitude for recovery brought by a denizen of confectionery Brackens known to the world as severe Dutch birthed anywhere in Poland, Dutch West Harbor, northern Germany, down to Lisbon and some as high as the Toe of low peninsula Finn. Because copper was relatively easy to manufacture, combined to Bracken wrought iron, it was made for sheet metal, copper coiling, doors and roof tops, each watershed of laid waste was in time turned over to barrel sheeting. Each Veronica and Aaron grew out of this milieu; Darien herself was solely wine crate for dye, not yet graduated to rinse, suds or grain tail.

Matthew Dyadf took the four sheets of single frame shots by occurrence along with the written narrative to compare to. Each suspect damned by one thread of content – a short wire circumference plug which shut off the suds, governing the amount of release from the dye rooms – its significance picked up by apparently only two people, Darien and the Release Chief upstairs inside the lit office. Chief Engineering confirmed there was a breakage. Matthew looked up where Darien worked now, found her in Richmond working for the county of Alameda in torts and complaints, no longer in accounting, now a treasury print volume analyst whose responsibility was to verify print column documents to the federal government in any form. He assigned his weekly calendar secretary to arrange an interview with her.

It took him four and a half hours to drive to the West Richmond County Courthouse and parked on the grass square of 37th Street and Bissell. He walked up the broad pebble-studded cement stairs into the cool exterior of the glass building, spoke to the African American elderly female dispatch clerk in blue at the window and was escorted to an interview booth with recording equipment. Darien entered wearing an all tan business suit, white bib blouse, and dark tan high heels. He introduced himself and showed her his badge and sheriff number.

"Is this dye section representative of work you once performed?" he asked, handing her a plastic file from a binder showing a dark purple bill.

Darien put on her glasses and gave the ten dollar note a circumspect review. "I have worked with gray color that has deceased, but this lacks a box of yellow, so I would have to say not this particular bill," she replied, and gave it to him.

"Are you aware of how gold ends up on a pan bill?"

"Yes, I am. The rinse room bypasses suds."

"Approximately, what gross aggregate have you deceased?"

"It might be a ream of three-quarter sheets. That would make seven hundred bills of ten dollars apiece."

"Have you had any occasion to study smelter breakdowns?"

"A few times. The suds shut off, for an hour the run was produced without incident, but then outside pipes began to burn."

"Is it customary to then send down divers?"

"Yes, absolutely necessary. They have to pipe weld the obstacle."

"Where were you in 1968 on May 19th?"

"Is that the date of the death chamber fire?"

"Yes."

"I had just left my final shift and was on my way to collect my sweater when the charthouse room iced in causing a fire inside the closest stairway."

"Did you ever determine who caused it?"

"Not completely. I thought my traveling companion Veronica started it."

"Was she an experienced diver in those days?"

"Yes, at nearly everything, sewer can, dye calliope, margin excess."

"Do you know who may have gone down with her?"

"Possibly Jerome or George Capone."

"When did you leave that job?"

"October, 1968."

"What was your next job?"

"I went to work in Nevada City below Truckee, I worked for a group of web cutters, four of them. I was there about two years when their uncle started an ink factory in Old Sacramento and transported ink to the six counties including Alameda."

"Why did you leave?"

"Richmond city hall asked for me because I knew the plate formats for plate making. False money had been introduced into circulation; the city wanted someone with hammer dye web expertise. I was given numerous bills, most hundred dollar notes, to verify as to same such original dyes."

"How many have you come across?"

"Probably as many as a thousand."

"Do you keep legal document of what you send?"

"Yes, we photo knife it on maps for backgrounds."

"Are they vaulted?"

"Some are. Many are in tin, coarse glass or felt."

"Who do you send your results to?"

"He's a warden on Father Island offshore of the Richmond State Bridge and the oil refineries."

"Do you know his name?"

"Laurence D'Antigone."

Matt Dyadf was permitted to use an office in the Alameda County lab. There he reviewed Darien's answers. Certainly it was possible her interest in her job was entirely to verify correctly made bills. The ten men sent by the Treasury to distribute money were dead inside their houses, and the money was in circulation. It was a reluctant observation that all dead were killed for the latest release of currency who constituted a handful of agents at labs who made every effort to bring in stolen bills. The shift warehouse storage agents had to know which bills looked fraudulent under the appraiser lens, which dyes turned color after terms, type of paper became discolored. Even D'Antigone had no real answers; most threads he received lacked correct backgrounds, the fault lay in the use of black color which eventually bled on the surface turning the note a rancid fuchsia. If an expert could see the black, the notes couldn't be released; chartreuse was more problematic, because it gave the bill a wet yellowish light green sickly look. Matt decided the fraud had to have been perpetrated by an insider with access to plate during a time when work was seasonal. His possible candidate might be Darien's boyfriend who worked the containment grid light house outside Detroit. If any politic was readily divined, it was that along the Sunset train line through Oakland there was a lack of industrial jobs, the easy availability of work had shrunk, without the Kaiser Aluminum yards nearly six hundred mining jobs trans-located to Appalachia with coal for heat and industry and to the Great Salt Lakes for household salt and boron for bathing salts. The demise of mining was to be expected every twenty years replaced in kind by the post office, taxation, paper making and accounting of every kind at city, county and state proving to require a burgeoning industry of magnitude for many thousands of jobs per major region. Dyadf had to rely upon his sense of this transition that brought the three-some west, that an instantaneous need to possess trade tools of a modern mechanized society now was open to subsidiary industries of many determinations. If not for the basic economy that garnished small banks, teachers of elementary, secondary and college, librarians, hospitals and medical staff, markets, entertainment and restaurants, and cloth mills and shops, then these several hundred jobs were viewed as too few to also provide remaining tasks of new roads and county services. Hundreds of shop photos delineated a historical transition, a depredatory urban blight given discretionary factories and nearby hotel looking apartments. By the end of the day after procuring the top six files, reviewing rows of photographs along with bleach out-takes, and sorting through legends of industrial grids, gin reproductions of non absorbent curd, hours of punch and yet more of quit, he gave a shrewd guess as to the nature of the raid. Perhaps the proof was right there on the mat board; the dead were in respective tasks that put them secondary to the approval that verified the final note process, few times a year Veronica worked with the fans who pulled the stiff dollar to the mat in preparation for the mill run, and selectively were noticeably speeded up creating goofs, tears, misplacements, and downside dollars. The furled covenant that automatically discarded a trader's mixture of bad print would in time become a dementia praecox of drab declassed living who were always on the run. Matt decided it was inside the light house that the final sop run was suppressed; if Veronica was primarily a diver in the treatment tank to open hatches and Darien had guessed the elaborate scheme between her and Aaron, it stood to reason he controlled the measurement of released dye for pre-print soakers from the font gutter of the light room. Had he to assure the schedule to package money, then he had to be able reasonably to assure its arrival date to destination.

He stood far from the computer panorama screen and reviewed the display line-up. He had what he thought he had, each suspect's last action prior to leaving the plant on the night of the destroying fire, Darien leaving the dye room, Veronica opening an underwater hatch, Aaron batch code file recording; his one-time utterly shocking act utilizing the wrong background of the Superior lake skyline for easement for document proof. He examined the file again, stopped the stiller, magnified it, snapped the side operator's fingerprint, ran a cross match through Birmingham, Alabama; sure enough he was the suspect. Dyadf matched the prints and name aliases for any known location for employment. Within minutes VIACOM listed the sources, Treasury Office; Montana Draft File; and Oakland Pell. None meant any damn collusion; Matt would have to take a tedious scrutiny to under files to look for further redacting. Without him Darien might not have been hired; he was, after all, the master print card.

Matt went for dinner across the street on Broadway at the deli, purchasing a cup of coffee, a burger, and powdered donut. The traffic at five conspired with congestion all the way to Harrison; inside three years they had lost sixty agents including the Capone group of Chicago, two web cutter analysts had been killed in the parade of painstaking commerce of proofing bills, delivery men along the train line, pellet and lab chemists, and commensurate analysts as well as morgue document proof transcribers. It was still anyone's guess what aspect of crime connected them.

He eventually returned to the lab. He went through a second examination of close-up photographs of the dead homeowners, searched street traffic for them, pry marks on doors inside the eight ransacked buildings – the Twentieth Street

Grosvenor Studios, Blenchley's Grand Storage and privately owned morgue, the lab on Nineteenth, the Garnier floor, the Pickle yard where photos of the dead were examined, the Pell Building, and the dozen or more accounting and individual lab offices between Fifteenth and Eleventh on both sides of the street including Mooreland, Skylar and Lawson offices – all handprints in blood, paint or foreign substances; latents, food and shoe prints with case number, date and time, and location, officer's name, and evidence item number. Matt cross matched to the DNA lab in Berkeley and to federal crime labs for the FBI, ATF, DEA and military services. As it became evident, each piece of evidence was traced from its discovery to courtroom trial, prints were photo lifted from cross lighting and special high contrast film and fogging and placed on a white card, and latents were compared with registrars of inked prints. Due to the sensitivity of the cases, there were over a hundred motions to suppress narrowly limiting the State's ability to grant access about most evidence.

4.

Proposition 115 gave courts the ability to hear hearsay evidence when considering weak or circumstantial evidence. This was done by an expert whose opinion could suffice as evidence.

Inside the Pell Building on the second floor two halls were lit; at night they resembled the grid building near Chicago where bill designs were approved. A special task force from UCLA was assigned to go out in unmarked vehicles to get an idea of what had occurred there. The team of five sheriff found a partial floor with vaulted shelving on which were compartmentalized stacks of bills ranging from one dollar value to a thousand, estimated to be a half million dollars. Photographs were taken. Technical services were called for scene sketches. The money was not confiscated. There were no bodies or signs of entry or tampering. A search warrant was issued by the State District Attorney to interview the fifteen people who were believed to have delivered money to the site. Between the hours of 10 pm and 6 am suspects were ordered interrogated. Each suspect was found dead, all sixteen in Oakland appeared dead due to violent methods, cause of death listed as fractured distal lumbar, after it was ascertained that the head in each case exhibited a wound to the skull, completely healed, which caused fractured skull involving the frontal and both parietal bones, occipital and sphenoid bones with subdural hemorrhage present; upper spine not involved. Underlying skulls were found intact. Wounds exhibited some pellet tattoo. Damaged pug nose retrievable metal was photographed on carpet. There were signs of recent semen ejaculation. No samples of blood or urine taken. Despite these findings, an order not to remove victims from premises was issued and photographs of each body including close-up photos to match fingerprints were made. An investigation was initiated as to extenuating circumstances to determine truth of facts in order to identify when and where the victim was seen in the company of another person likely to have wounded them. This investigation took approximately one hundred hours. The suspects were two females, one aged twenty-seven, red long hair, and one aged twenty-two, dark long hair, and one male, aged thirty, red curly hair, all Caucasian. The case never went to court.

Matt contacted the UCLA Forensics Department for any investigative consultant able to discuss the bills found inside Pell. The file when pulled had been expunged; there was no mention of bills, nor description of physical premises. He thanked the assistant coroner and asked to be transferred to medical. The physician was a typically reticent individual with a deep sonorous voice who possessed a belief in an absolute order of forensic medicine. He stated he had testified in court. Matt spoke to a soft spoken secretary at the county clerk office of the courthouse and was able to get her to send a facsimile of the transcript. Dr. Barringer was sworn in at approximately 1003 hours on August 4, 1971 and was on the witness stand three full days. He said he examined a dozen rolls of Cool Pix camera film under several microscopic lens. He examined both glossy black and white as well as brilliant color photos taken of the same physical scene. All photographs were thought to be digitalized hubris, a term meant to describe flaws of webbing suggesting the bills were produced by a counterfeit artist, not a mercurial duck webber, someone who may have worked density. None of the bills had been handled yet. When he attempted to locate any scratch for a similar batch production, he read to the clay backed photo the man Aaron had used for the first three backgrounds. It was his reverent opinion that the bills were consistent to old scratch and that no bill could be utilized in the marketplace.

Q: Do your records in any way show these or similarly made bills have been used for transactions?

A: Yes.

Q: What does this fact suggest to you?

A: The hubris is very similar to original bills.

Q: How similar?

A: At least a tenth resonance for accurate blue visor combined by high pinpoint recognition.

Q: Do they meet requirements for counterfeit?

A: No, counterfeit passes at a twenty-fifth resonance.

Q: Is it difficult to trace counterfeit bills?

A: It's fairly easy. People usually make transactions with certain vendors. The vendors combined might be a rather large crime ring.

Q: Were the bills packaged?

A: Yes, they were packaged in white wrapping.

Q: What does white wrapping signify?

A: The bills were scheduled for burn.

Q: Do you know whether white contains a toxic chemical?

A: Yes, it does. The wrapping is treated to strychnine which when exposed to air produces a vapor.

Q: Did you ascertain why the packaged bills were separated from the crates they were shipped in?

A: No, I did not.

Q: Do you know whether the bills were burned?

A: They were not burned. The burn factory did not receive them.

Q: Generally how long does it take to burn once bills are received to storage?

A: It is about a month.

Q: Is it your opinion these bills were set into circulation?

A: Yes. I believe the unsecured bills were brought to markets and drugstores in Oakland.

Q: Upon what factual data is your opinion founded?

A: The photo lab at UCLA has photographs of transactions for wrapped bills.

Q: Where have these transactions occurred?

A: A market at the corner of Broadway and Twenty-seventh, the old wharf, seventeen private estates in Oakland and Montclair, Joseph Magnin, and a pundit of small hotels throughout the state.

Q: Has your lab contacted these companies?

A: All, we closed most. The Broadway market was bombed last month displacing the pavement in an explosive arson.

Q: Is there any wording for white that brings you to a conclusion arson was a choice predicator?

A: The law is ambiguous. It states that scratch must be burned on a mattress inside a factory or warehouse designated as such, but it allows for housing in an industrial division. Target spray fire may be administered by aircraft and may be conducted on ice or aboard an industrial carrier.

Q: Has your lab conducted a historical analysis?

A: Not yet. Not all information provides a clearly defined database.

Q: Does the information give you any indication of a future crime?

A: I couldn't say.

The transcript proved little on an indictment of a treasury patch except by inference. Scratch had been assigned to burn in Reno. Due to a murder the train transporting scratch had been sent onto Oakland arsenal for disposal. There, the crates were planked off the train and held inside the Pell. In the interim the treasury transportation crew were murdered and left for dead. Over the next several months as many as ten lab analysts in Oakland were killed. Matt referred to a plethora of photos. His belief that many white packages were socked into hideouts in the ground was scarcely confirmed by a few hundred photos of mostly men shoveling earth out of their yards and placing locked tool kits inside dug out areas and potting plants on top soil. Some were inventive burying a lonesome package in park grounds; some merely shoved their packages inside bus depot lockers or hung them by boat anchors in shallow lake harbors. A few exchanged the sum of money for diamonds and emeralds. The fact that mausoleums with furnaces were built across the state was a hopeful but impractical idea. Raids on Brinks armored vans later were found ditched with white wrapped burn money, apparently real money exchanged for scratch. A thousand agents flooded into the state to manage the crisis. At the bottom of the evidence cache lay the all-too-inescapable reality, no longer just a perception, that scratch was traded for real estate and assignments against impoverished circumstances, a panoply of transactions, among them nation-wide thousands of restaurants, copier stores, film instamatic shops, bed and breakfast nooks, jewelry outlets, movie theatres giving the new FBI an indentured servitude of reams worth of receipts to chronicle for owners who had previously never held down jobs or inherited money. In every California juris-diction, sea coasts sprung to life, museums and landmarks lit squares at night, festive weddings flowed into the streets and limousines parked at the curb offered wine and tourism prom-ising a life of envied passage. A new moon had risen over many Times Squares, stage at fifty dollars a ticket captured the neon light, lazy trombones bleated out tunes of discontent while at newborn resorts waiters carried circular trays of champagne and lovers kissed, finally blessed in a coming of age of mineral spas, mud tubs, and suites overlooking violet and dark green orchards bearing promise of seedless grapes and expensive dry and fruity wines. Matthew felt a tryst of angry debauchment, a faint denouncement at a mildly agreeable society not far out of infancy gone berserk. Chocolate crème glace filled cake had symbolically come to replace an evening with the family at a ballet, the crystal orb was turning casting off flakes of shim-mering golden incandescent light, a debauchery of greed was summoned to substitute for a solid college education, temper-ate mores constituted by organic salads and oven baked raga toile stymied intimate inducements for a whirlwind tour of ex-perience; to Matt's way of thinking, this distilled living made life seem too brief. It raised the question of temporal climates incongruent to the world of politics.

It provoked a hostility borne of easy spending without a

sensibility of keeping one's wits about them. Life ought not to become too complacent, although by any similarity of understanding an attainment of life well lived should be imbued with having worked hard to achieve one's dignified respectability. Youth should be happy to wait for recognition. Likewise the professional adult had to tolerate milestones of adulthood including middle age, sending children off to graduate school, maintaining pace with unanticipated divorce, staying independent in older years, staving off the infrequency of meal taking or the stagnant loss of remorse driven libido and alienation.

Frankie took the call matter-of-factly. He checked with Dispatch at Homicide Division to determine that their office received a confirming call. An old silver and gray Plymouth which had arrived in the hen compartment car of the train; with a body of a primary mint stale producer lay in the back seat, required fingerprint dusting of all vehicle glass and upholstery and stain or glue procedure at an Alameda County laboratory. Frankie contacted his best security and asked they ground the car onto the street and bring it to the Seventeenth Street dock yard before he had an opportunity to check his E-fax for incoming submissions and found Dyadf's analysis.

The dead were mint control analysts, they scheduled bar and code design sheets, they were trained to find sheet layout determinations for inadequate dye, dye was scheduled in rinse using natural color for what was called box curds which hit any computer on print wells by six reference releases, the starting series of dye flooded into the death chamber and took approximately thirty hours, the next series of dye took another twenty hours. Both flowed through tiny intricate cells in iron plates giving the background a look of lacy webbed distillery, analysts inside the light room timed the aperture to seconds once a lather of gray was applied; upstairs in a long room like a narrow hall nine detriment color analysts viewed the product for measurement, here the clerks who batched coded bills logged in the hundreds of bills by numerical use notifying a segment identifier supervisor whether each side was placed correctly, in this twilight task it was Darien's boyfriend Aaron who batched, the bills that were hung on a wire section lay propped indicating that any number of bills might be discarded later; Darien worked dye; her friend Veronica was one of five divers who secured tanks off the bin premises, all divers were filmed for location in the event there was a mill shut down.

Simultaneously in the junket house where the U.S. minted two dollar coin was a russet half penny size the copper wheel was slowed and copper pennies emptied into a standard carrying case, eliminating copper stripping and alternating to metallic bronze used to coin silver dollars. The lone computer that regulated this alternate silver smith manufacture was handled in pellet staging; as the coins became minted a stream of pellet sparks were released and the host enmeshment paper recorded each firing.

Two senior mint analysts, never found, walked off the line that afternoon after a shotgun pistol was administered to one of the pellet analysts killing him. Although photographs went off at four second intervals, and every last employee on site was filmed, by the time it became necessary to place his body in a morgue vehicle, the gates were shut and the controlling gate mechanism was broken. From that moment on it was each man to himself, the analysts who made it to flood line were stabbed or bound, tossed into vehicle trunks and fired upon repeatedly.

It went without saying that a pellet analyst and numerous bill detectives were murdered and that three individuals working the Wisconsin-Michigan nights were looking for anyone who might be able to place them on the crime scene. The matching rows of photographs showed direction and exact distances of the plants, they showed exterior and interior, activity and disposition; each photograph contained a number, date and time, case number, crime, location, subject and photo ID number. A small number of assailants had been detained, identified in a court and sent to prison; they had booking photos, ink fingerprints, and photo lineups. Reports came with names, addresses, motive, weapons, injuries, and suspect vehicles.

From Frankie's viewpoint Chicago had descended the Staircase into high chaparral desert, through whirling dervishes of beige sand, beneath limestone formations of escarped rock formation, cautious of the old gunslinger west, in clear advance of a team of wardens equipped with little else than booking procedure and gummy vans to cart off alive or dead prisoners.

The body was sent to the Oakland morgue and the Plymouth was re-crated inside a transportation van belonging to Van Storage Lines, Inc. and shuttled to an empty warehouse in El Cerrito off Highway 17 on the other side of landfill accessing the bay. There, the car was driven off a ramp into the larger of three windowless rooms. Frankie himself and his men gave the car a thorough study: this make of manufacture was a Nakimura manufactured in Peoria, Illinois; all other Plymouths being released in either Nevada or California. The exterior was a minted beauty, paint was fresh, not a dent on her; windows had been rolled half way as though the dead required the air; the bluish gray upholstery had been shot up several times along the ceiling on the right side as if the pistol had intended to miss its victim; the square trunk was large enough for a couple to sleep inside. They set up their testing equipment spraying the window glass with smear resistant chemical which produced a series of smudged prints which lifted easily onto Bandex tape. At least one individual appeared to have attempted to deter the vehicle from departure evidenced by six prints evacuated from the top of the driver's side of the windshield; another set of clearer prints was lifted onto tape from the rear window above the trunk that indicated a person had clung to the car briefly or for a distance. The underside of the engine casing and interior grill of the radiator contained flung blood as if the car mowed down its victim.

They worked detail taking most of the morning, eyeing the resultant trace under appraiser lens, circling smudges with a brown grease pencil, photographing and removing prints before they fed the tapes into a computer that produced names. Oddly the names came in as obvious aliases. They were Shovel Franklin, age 26, and John Pell, age 37, both names of buildings in downtown Oakland between Seventeenth and Eleventh Streets, probably bearing no relation to building owners.

The blood taken from the underside of the car matched the blood taken at the morgue of the victim identifying him as Type AO negative. With contusions all over his body he was the probable victim; his fingerprints declared him as the son of Frank Capelli, vehicle maintenance of the Chicago Trumpet Court building of the mint declaration building.

When Frankie tried to pull photographs of acts of violence committed at the mint shore plaza, he was locked out. The file read, Denied, Classified. He requested that the walls of the garage where Vince Capelli had died be partitioned and shipped to a warehouse on the far East Bay Strait near Port Costa for evaluation by the State.

As the final order of business of the week he sent his team of retired officers who had worked warden routine in upstate New York into every building occupied by any Aluminum analyst who remained since the closing in 1970 of the aluminum factories of west Oakland. The team found four dead males inside the Hawthorne building on San Pablo and Twentieth Street, an older beige stone building with column tile entry taking up two blocks by one half block, each apartment approximately five hundred square feet consisting of kitchen, sitting room, two bedrooms and large bath, sixty in all. The dead lost their lives to an unknown explosive that severely damaged their lungs deflating them and rendering their torsos fractured. All four were of French descent similar in appearance to the dead who delivered scratch discovered inside Victorian houses, red skin, dark brown hair shaved short, each male about five foot ten inches, slim, wearing night garments, who worked downtown corner pharmacies as guards. By the time the first analyses were submitted to the Bureau of Demographic Data, it was commonly held by public opinion that the killers had entered the city sometime during the mid 1960s seeking whereabouts of detectives who staffed the Treasury halls monitoring computers. Thus the subsequent field investigations attempted to isolate any photograph that showed any dead officer who had talked with any individual who worked in any treasury office or who showed on a camera monitor.

The wind was a flying ninety degrees, sultry and mysterious. By all accounts the city had settled on its single largest contract to keep non essential services including on site labs open twenty-four hours a day. The immediate boon was to local cemeteries for burials and for flower casket services. Frankie dressed for no occasion planting himself at a tiny closet of a bar called Kings Row off the drugstores and theatre parlors on a lone alley a mile from the memorial gates fronting the city of the damned Rumanian Turkish post war memorial cemetery. He had ordered a bloody Vodka with celery, and sat at the counter attending to a football game on the television. The joint was crowded for a Thursday evening, even the arch celibacy were present to keep an eye on their clerics satiating themselves on fresh brewed house coffee. Students from a nearby monastery filed inside while with roving gazes took in the scene all the way to the dimly lit anterior where a jukebox bleated out Sinatra and Holiday. Niceties to each and every gent, the brusque British bartender nevertheless shot out a few opinions of his own to the handful of regulars whose drinks gave him his bar tab; roil their duffs in governor's sod, dab a grave with none but silver crude, bound the lads whose whips steer a horse to bay, and so on, all hours into darkness, a shine to intolerance his stiff whimsy.

"Are there many stones at the yarn?" Frankie asked, the moment Riley returned for a refill.

"I'm told you bury the taciturn," a mild Riley, plum Brighton in his late seventies remarked, his meager expression denying any unjust sentimentality.

"I'm only the Cad man. I don't as a rule whistle in the wind."

"Fry up my scour dough if you want despair, it's the ale will send you to hunger." Riley rinsed his shot glass and placed it on the mat for the next Yankee martini.

"We've been laid to rest in our tarp houses."

"Life says first a man lines up his green, then he spikes his bourbon."

Frankie smiled, always a bit wry. "There's a mercenary war afoot."

"Aye, Mon, that I'm convinced. Eight steeds harness the box to sleep upon the stone."

"Seen many in the last month?"

"Two to the pickle, one to a fair lady." He moved to a two-some who ordered tap, let drinks with twists of freeze dried lemon and rang the tab.

Returning, he leaned on the bar and said, in a tone laced with sarcasm, "Depends who wanted the step door unlatched. Now, the way I heard it was the house asked to move its property deeds."

"Who would have inherited on Charney?"

Riley shrugged. "As I understand it, the trumpets sounded for divine guidance. It's one thing to ask for a booty of apartments off the lake, quite another to arrange markets in city office blocks."

"That's city planning, you see that everywhere."

"Well, consider the calling. At every throng to hell stands a bishop."

Frankie coddled his drink in bewilderment. "I found their bodies, Monica died nearly a month ago."

"It bothers anyone to know they are so young, barely out of the cradle."

"I agree. I'm given to understand the wind caught her skirt on the fender and she was unable to extricate herself."

"That's an accident, my friend. Why look past it?"

"Too many murders. Everyone at the morgue is dying."

U.S. Treasury tarp agents fanned out over six miles posting an occasional man at the Paramount and a nearby Kelly girl, testing silent alarms, flaming all suspects by Intel, sending in a walk-by into the Hawthorne lobby and 21st Street lounge, and running security on money changing hands. Tarp was the easiest method by which to assess scratch. Agents ran daily tabs, placed secure markers on each trans-disposed bill, targeted all bills to origin, matched voice to fingerprints, and devised a hood specter for each thief. At the end of the month, they had on file composite profiles for each crime along with vehicles, addresses and contacts. Their information was instantly sent to each city for location identification of actual address whereabouts of contacts.

Frankie himself holed up with market purchases from a 711 inside his apartment on Harrison overlooking the lake intending to run a few spools on street walk-ins and travel by cabs to determine what activity Monica may have encountered late in the day. He placed her on her routine coming to the yard and leaving for lunch five days a week, several days at her desk working through lunch, bringing ex parte summaries to the courthouse to obtain a judge's signature prior to filing with the county clerk, shopping evenings at I. Magnin on Broadway, attending showings at the Fox. He collected filter photos of a trip to Copenhagan through metro tunnels of concentric well lit arches from Vestamager to Forum to grey hazy skies to dutch brick and modern five story semi industrial museums, office sites and outdoor festivities with a close female friend; another trip to Czech Prague Castle, of the stunning green narrow canal waters of the Mala Strana, Lesser Town plazas, lost in the crowds, an evening in the plaza of spire stone cathedrals, a tourist boat downwind, a young female on the go; paralleled by a ten day river cruise the following summer in attendance with childhood friends and a few courtroom lawyers from San Francisco down the Rhine past sumptuous irrigated rows of cabbage, squash and spinach; crystalline waters, frothy splash off the stern deck; a smooth ride home to SFO and their rack of luggage delayed a day, obviously a bother necessitating a return. Work photos inside the Grand yard collecting bills of lading from arriving transportation vans and admitting evidence. Aside from the Capone van car, there wasn't anything much to suggest there was anything out of the ordinary to see. Twice she had taken a cab to the Catholic cemetery to stand witness to two funerals in City of the Damned line-up of alabaster sepulchers and soap-blue copper mounted doors, a few having a glass pyramid roof light and then to pick up signed burial papers for silk casket, placement and expenses. Frankie examined the archived templates and origination approvals and found himself looking through a lens rather abruptly onto a death certificate of Veronica, her described last name given falsely as Mangini. He copied the image of certificate onto a sorting computer in order to determine whose fingerprints had handled it. Three prints showed one thumb belonged to a county coroner technician, one to the cemetery document file examiner, and the last registered for a dye analyst at the lit building next door to the Tillery building down on Seventh.

The glass door interconnecting the dining room to the living room opened slightly in the breeze that came from the window stirring in his imagination, somewhere evident in these photo files lay the forensics of predatory acts, an enslavement of freedoms by people who injured others for their own predispositions, the syllabus of evil crept about the city as a dark lantern, a sort of blister plaster over breakwater; he hoped it was far off, unknown to life and the living, but a perceived expediency was evident in medical offices, tenement apartments, prowling about as if all who encountered it were blindfolded by fate, unable to identify it for what it was, a henchman waiting to strike; a mean trickery, possessions taken by force, a knife in the water. He waited for the breeze to subdue, for his sub-conscience not to be aroused, where was this Veronica seen first? The question lingered over a barely digested meal. How was she declared dead, was it a substitution for a form?

He sent a picture fax to Chicago.

It was his conjecture that Monica's document for putative damages for the dead Capone subsequently delivered to Garnier for his lab finding as to cause of death killed them both, but what was the substance of the finding, but that Capone, lead tarp, had succumbed to air pressure when in June 1971 an outside valve released air suffocating the agents inside the clock room during a print run; indicated by his fingers had turned grey, despite his sternum had compressed he had no dislocation of vertebrae, and he had bit his tongue stopping life. Who was there in Oakland who worried that anyone would discover cause of death? They were two thousand miles away from Chicago and her tarp presses. Even for medical personnel, the query seemed far removed to have motivated death; so it had to be these individuals had stolen a great deal of money, too much to forgive, and there had to be some sort of association that proved their crime; a smart lead at the mint had discontinued the copper half penny and produced solely a one cent copper penny thus derailing potential mint thefts. Since a crime of felonious assault combined with felony theft was in progress, the murders seemed retaliatory.

Matt Dyadf arrived to his office in Nevada City by six in the morning. The first findings on the garage wall for the last body in a van car had come in. Scrapings revealed smudges of green ink used for the greenback indicating at least one male who worked clock or batch had wet hands or a wet belter's apron. This secured motive. The fact that the garage mechanic responsible for transport of packaged web had been struck and carried beneath the moving van car made the death an act of treason. The fingerprints showed the assailant, a Mathew Borrows, age fifty, residing in Chicago, deeply red hair cut modish. On at least one occasion he was photographed helping Aaron load a van for transport to a Michigan yard for disposal which was properly seen to. Matt wrote his narrative and referred the file to the State Attorney General Office.

Aside from green ink, and package-able scratch which by now could be anywhere, the problem of verifying money was still afield. In addition someone wanted any capable person familiar with the look of real money dead.

The arson on the Nebraska train line of 1972 returning out of Omaha burned a train cargo of red bean crop in order to ignite a train moving in the opposite direction of two dozen safes carrying each two hundred dollars money.

The suspects were delinquent young adults whose underage truancy, suspension from school, arrests, drug use and drunkenness, and vandalisms gave way in subsequent years to failures to abide by the law, inability to maintain long term intimate relationships, usually relationships were unstable and demanding with periods of serious depression; not uncommon acts of severe impulsivity in which feelings shifted within moments to emptiness or hostility culminated in untoward aggression of physical assaults or intentional injury, who defaulted on debts, usually traveling as a drifter without job or residence, and a disregard for truth and use of aliases, and violating the rights of others without interruption for five or more years.

The sentencing was to a living laboratory in the Nevada foothills of four story concrete, seven such buildings forming a square surrounded by high prison walls and two guard towers with a sentry entrance made a deprecatory existence to repudiate any visceral vicious acts verified by fingerprints.

Once the lot of these criminals was co-associated to actual known complicities, they could be arrested and charged. Until then, their crimes could not be proven; a dildo was inconclusive to establish intent to murder; the sad fact was the guy's heart gave out after the two females left him. Likewise, there was no proof that Veronica had in any way killed agents in the clock or that Darien removed bills, only Aaron who worked the light in Michigan knew which scratch was ever removed and sent to a warehouse. A covert identifier had to exist somewhere which tied these people to their deeds. Darien was the last one out because she brought that month's plates into the death chamber where dye would be administered by the assembly trained to run dye; Aaron was suspected of removing a laundry bag of scratch; Veronica was thought to have placed an interconnecting tubular between stacks; garage staff was suspected of loading plates that had provided actual tarp runs; light staff was believed to have removed protective wax from used plates; warehouses were identified by van pool transportation drivers; and closets found to be identified by bill denominator and date scheduled for taping. In Oakland and Richmond there were eighteen stores owned by members of the ring. The group might stay put for awhile as they came off the streets or retired;

as their businesses were replaced by legitimate owners and the pool of flowing money diminished, their options would eventually peter out.

Reluctantly Dyadf checked the status of his seventy files, matching for actual addresses, finding stores at which his suspects shopped, verifying fingerprints to every transaction, posting to street sectors for vehicle driven, workplace, parking meter utilized, he noted apparent inability to be alone, drug use which struck him as excessive, hourly in quantity, easily a half bag a day, possibly to subdue overt anger or other intense unpredictable outbursts. At the moment, their lifestyle was complacent, they each worked full-time, owned cars, owned a home, went out on dates. He took no chances. They had selected another target, an elder man with two houses paid off; Matt posted a security detective to him for round the clock detail with photos. The two girls were hungry; they wouldn't readily pass up an opportunity for survival even if this period of elopement extended a handful of years. The news of Borrows' captivity would circulate quickly. Were he their last and final bag man, they might begin turning tricks as soon as their resources dried up.

He hadn't forgotten the evidence of the Oakland morgue screens nor of the established facts of the identities of two dead men. He had a few other bodies to contend with; not just Garnier or the pellet chemist. There was the man placed in the canal at London Square tied by his feet to rope, presumably witnessed by the living Monica herself and called into the police; there was the dead postmaster whose body was deposited in tar and concrete, twelve dead analysts in five buildings, and the men who transported scratch found dead with healed wounds inside their homes. He had each of their pertinent data on the parallel computer and was still seeking cross-matches to crimes. The relevance on the admissibility of evidence was debatable, that Monica had administered the tabula test on substance found inside the van car inside which was a dead man, and she had to obtain the court order to allow the test required by law to take the document to Garnier seemed the greater of convincing proof than her call in the middle of the night of an alleged crime which she did not see with any real clarity. It was Garnier who concluded that the person who murdered the man in the car worked in the light room in Chicago with the victim. No one else knew the murderer's identity. The judge who wrote the order was Charney; Garnier was murdered, as was Monica.

Garnier's proof showed on the computer. The prints he established as to chain of custody cross matched to sets of other previously unknown prints. The hallway leading from the light room to the vaults was covered by infrared prints, otherwise invisible, of seemingly non-intrusive individuals. Dyadf color referenced each set of prints, positioned them by identified person, and then reversed the tape, running it to determine what illegal activity occurred. Five employees had waited until dark at their tables when the station was nearly empty before they locked wooden windows over glass panes; they poured dilute over the boxes of sheet paper, locked the print timers, stabbed the wax which protected the dye on any number of loose plates, tossed accountant ledgers into the hall, and released giant spools of thin wire thread using it to force open doors. Aaron took a cart, picked up the plates from the wool and tossed them into a briefcase and latched it; Veronica removed design and retardant from a wheel and placed them into a cardboard box; three men unlocked safes, removed fifty wrapped packages, and set fire to the furnace. With the vaults open, when they pushed open a door to the outside, the fire drafted through the hall decimating the cribbage rooms in minutes.

The guilty were Aaron, Veronica, Barrows, Mattel brother, and Pro Tem John Charney.

It was a very satisfying feeling to know that at last he had them. Now he could initiate findings on other crimes. He contacted the Office of Forensic Findings for composite suspects by their fingerprints, fraudulent documents, any hit and run transfers for oil, paint and blood; fibers, use of firearms, cloth, quick tests for drug analyses, photo files, liquid chemicals and powders. The computerized services which were national comprised of half a dozen databases based upon collection and determinations of physical evidence might take seventy-two hours to list. Matt grabbed his jacket, said goodnight to the guard stationed at the desk in the lobby, and walked to the parking lot in front of the building to his black sedan.

Life was stultifying, rarely gratifying. No women, no one to greet him at home, a mildly agreeable lifestyle. After the cases he had had – men killing their women for another female, or for a property deed, or the best exit plan a wife chilling a lover while she flew to another country on a joint bank account and a string of aliases – he didn't believe in romantic love. He was a realist. There were no martyrs and there were no saints. His associates were divorced, some paying handsome alimony, at least half like him had never remarried, had adopted careers as partners. They lived in the here and now, no less available than he to any demand their hours foisted upon them.

As he entered his studio, flicked on the light system, a glance at the alcove with grey black tweed sofa, matching recliner and ottoman, and built into the wall TV, small kitchen, long black Formica counter, refrigerator with ice water which he poured over green tea and sipped as was his nightly custom, maid polished gleaming stainless steel island stoves, two computer desks facing French doors and patio with several dozen flowering lilac, white and yellow tropicals tended to weekly by a gardener for a small fortune, and separate bedroom and gigantic bath, all opaque glass, he considered the reality that Life had finally graced him for hard earned recognition. This fucking case with three perverts had at long last shot winded into a closed alley. He turned on the TV Channel 7 news, sat in his big grey tweed easy chair, removed his tie and prepared to relax. He felt justified as a public servant, his time spent in a worthwhile endeavor, all rewards to he who waits. The hands of time moved into position and the chimes sounded at six. In an hour he would eat leftovers of turkey and sautéed mushrooms and spinach remaining from his Monday night out with his boss and detective unit. Then he'd settle into bed with a good book reading until he fell asleep.

Dyadf had been married in his youth while in the service but the Army had better uses for him and shipped him overseas to the far reaches of Germany into the mountains. There, he tested car motors for a Nissan industrial pact with France. He found he was a bitter replacement for stalwart lads whose careers took them into engineering. Just as he was learning to make up for sprint driving, they sent him to Stockholm for a month to report on a food crisis where he cruised on the port to Gamla Stan and walked cobblestone alleys past hundreds of shops between orange, pink, yellow and white buildings; to the glass United Nations Plaza flying flags of every country at Kungsgatan, to Chinatown for something of everything and watches which kept the country well guarded, and to Ostermalmstorg for cuisine arts and expensive semi outdoor cafes for wine and broiled sausage roll. Then home – he spent four long years on a hospital ward patching up the near dead. Had he returned to his girl he was certain middle years would be comfortable, but she had left for another male nurse and was saddled with two small children. He never looked over his shoulder. He told himself life had other plans for him. When he left the service, he was admitted to Forensic Services where he sat at a desk and tied report inquiries to crime specific information. He was adjusted to long hours of tedious work with almost little results, spoon fed on an indoctrination that evil people eventually received their days in hell.

Yet, as he dressed for bed in blue and red plaid flannel pajamas, the window ajar to the fresh air breeze conjured by the babbling creek in the gully, his mind wandered to the alert on his computer. For all anyone knew, Aaron and Veronica were long term married, definitely never apart, looking out for the other, Darien as good an alibi as any, what was she besides the female who had to possess Aaron? A girl who watched a heist go down and got out safely?

Early morning brought the usual anxiety, a postponement of answers, as he awaited his computer to call forth the day's priorities. Who inherited off Aaron and Veronica? Matt steadfastly searched through a database. A bail bondsman listed as Weymouth located in Emeryville had declared Veronica dead after she called him from jail as a result of a possession charge. He ordered a search of City of the Damned to tear the two roads of sarcophagi apart, each threshold dismantled by funeral service photos of all repairs, replacements and grave sites. He hoped he might strike it lucky and turn up the bunch of stupid hens who in waiting Charney's orders to send them home had instead died in houses in Piedmont and west Oakland of dummy wad.

Someone had already done the dirty work, evidenced by rolls worth of film taken at night under bright lights; cemetery personnel had awakened the dead, moved tile floors stone by stone, removed sand bags worth of lazy makeshift money, somewhat printed; had brought in heavy scorpion bulldozers to unearth dirt in the middle of meadows along the freeway near the coliseum and laid down shredded mill deep into cement shafts, ready for any war that might ensue. Almost instantly a modern all pink tile and green glass Chinatown was erected, the opera house got a makeover, previous gardens of flowers and tile were exchanged for an extended on-ramp to the Alameda tunnel, no stone for seven blocks left unturned. If small groceries and soy product fresh eggplant and chili markets lost their aged shoppers to a new Mecca of commodities and packaged foodstuff, no one really paid much attention except perhaps the betting merchants who dined at the oyster bar or at Le Cheval's spacious restaurant. All but West Street profited by the erection of new buildings, stunning blue glass commensurate with extravagant mezzanines and galactic skyway walkways. Per each construction site, under bright lights, the city rose by lavish glass, the Internal Revenue Service twin towers, the arch angels on top the white stone church clock tower, black glass county buildings, bronze metal, broad pebbled plaza and stairs, Sauvignon sanctuaries to throng in a bloodstone metropolis dwarfing the once elegant three blocks containing the Hawthorne, Fox, Pell and Pillar. Always grateful to Sweden's museums of medieval art, slabs of Aged Street, part cobble, nothing but male teen pharaohs and broken pottery, he took rare comfort in the valences that some historian analyst had recognized a rather disconcerting problem and take matters into his own efforts. He had to assume the heist money had vanished into thin air, the engraver plates also, leaving only taped tarp, possibly only undesignated scratch. The original Oakland of the late Fifties gave no sign of having expulsed a crisis, the Greyhound Bus Company, the morgue, Western Union flower services, libraries, post offices, and lanes of apartment buildings stood non-oppressed by the passing of years. Supposition had it that at least a cemetery priest took vows and subsequently returned to commit the tarp crime.

His file arrived, a terse, all too thin document with photos. He lined them up by description. The Chicago take-over began two days after killings to purge pellet analysts in New York State's bombings of two banks. A bomber had driven in a Manhattan county morgue van painted black from blue, arrived to the Chicago Trumpet Court all glass front western clock building, entered at midnight while state computers were counting the cribbage rooms and sewage dye plant, set charges against the glass for half past three, and blew the trip entrance to complete oblivion. Within minutes a silent alarm went off and iron gates descended locking the place in. Exactly a day later the tarp was fire bombed leaving forty accountants crushed in the death chamber and two tarp executives dead upstairs in the cooling plant. No warden responded; the order from their chief was to not work shift and not to call. Eleven city watch tower officers who disobeyed the command were later found dead on canal streets.

This was the file. Not a shred more. Dyadf had to assume all dead died by one hand due to the similarities of puncture scars to the neck and arms. Deaths in underground parking yards were gruesome. He had to assume also crimes followed the path of real money. Why Oakland and not Los Angeles with train lines to anywhere – perhaps it was expediency.

Every last person seen in a photograph had a clear set of prints attached along with aliases, addresses, friends, and stay-over's. Anyone attempting to leave the boundaries on ship sank. Anyone in exceptional circumstances was locked up in a federal pen. In thirty-one years forty-three of sixty adults had been rounded up. He sent the Michigan state bureau the prints on Aaron and Veronica and a two page description with whereabouts.

OAKLAND

ONE

The day was a salty air breeze circulating at a winsome sixty degrees. Morning had begun at 7:05 am with scarcely any indication of pardon. Car drivers had scraped their windows free of ice and turned on their defoggers permitting a gradual thaw. At the far end of Seventeenth Street just dead set ahead of the Caldecott Freeway sat the Coroner Cadillac, a grey limo with white walls Calabash struts venturing three inches past the rim. Spin the wheel would call the hour when it pulled slowly into traffic. The Grand Lake Drive docked in palm prints as surely as the courthouse calendar had its priorities. If the cad was called to the bus yard it could arrive solely by an advance notice ring to the staff office which necessitated the hat check-in to the drive-in. A message request for a cad transport if received before noon might be left in the car display room at the Paramount movie hall. Preceded by its desolate wail, the train from Reno arrived at one before it made its way toward the valley and peninsula. As it stopped in Oakland station four blocks from the city hall the statistician disembarked with his short case chain cuffed to his wrist. He had first to enter the rail building office on Seventh; then had to proceed by arranged taxi to the permanent dew declarations office on Twelfth, pick up the stamp at the post office in the Memorial Building on the lake and proceed to the Fox stage for a billing. The extravagant frontals of these stone edifices screamed money falling in gold bronze trinkets of information, anyone having contact with the deceased and knowledge as to last activity was posted at all halls. It was scarcely opportune that there were any accidental defining acts but the police placed their pretty girls wearing striptease in the public eye and the notices poured in, reams of paper worth slotted into tiny boxes for a dozen police investigators. The celebrities created play billings to frazzle dazzle with innuendo and stalking peddler mincing dialogue. All the distance from tumbleweed to Chicago fountains and wishing wheels life gamboled at the hard edges. Glint and glitz formed a wall of sparkling barely recognizable deceit. The spiral staircase of the dance glittered beneath angelic lights, stunning women whose bare frames made their audiences wince with envious awe paraded under burdened headdress of plumage. When the desert finally blew away, the train's whistle was all that any town could recollect.

The girl who checked the vans in at the dock was a Laney business college graduate of eighteen whose 180 words per minute typing and 90 shorthand gave her a job working dispatch for six-county transportation. A sensible junior accountant, Monica was in her tender years a mild blond with looks. In her first month of clerking the van transport dock she already had received a body in a ford and another toe tag inside a trunk of a Chicago Chevrolet. Procedure called for the cad man to roll prints and view the body head to toe for marks. Her written explanation gave her a sentence identifying shipper and next of kin authorized release. She added the costs for photographing the body, new clothing, assigning a motel address, the cad man's routine exam and signed report as well as notifying a process server to visit next kin for legal recorded interview. The Ford brought in an elderly stiff lacy blond from Reno whose shock of white hair suggested straight brandy poured over an iced cooler who managed a fur wrap and sequined purse shop, and the Chevrolet held a dark black haired male in his seventies with a metal hook for a hand, whereabouts unknown with a billet train stub in his pocket deemed a chronic severe alcoholic due to his dark actual purple skin tone. Otherwise the fifty vans returned at half days billed at thirty dollars or from outside Emeryville having clocked one or more overnights having distributed newspaper crates, furniture, cut flowers, and billable product goods as far as the border.

On an October afternoon 1971 shortly before five Monica Neville-Herald, daughter of a newspaper broderick, was sent in a van to the train station to collect four hundred bags of clothing. As she pulled open the Rocky Mountain insignia glass doors to the small station lobby, she saw at once the daunting number of brown bags lined up in four long rows. It took her a second to realize she alone had to load them up. The train porter was busy processing tickets for the last train to Wyoming where the standing line looked to be a good fifty people. She returned to the van for the crate handyman, left the side door open all the way and went to retrieve the itemization list among the stockyard items. She took a clipboard, put on sequined eyewear and jotted down the count. After a cursory gaze she wrote in "400 brown bags filled clothing and paper goods; lading document in top of 392." On an attached sheet was typed by dot matrix printer with heading "pleadings and proceedings before trial, Cincinnati Ohio," followed by an extensive itemized listing beginning with "Parole board code 1000" of the Welfare & Institutions Code of the Ohio Penal Code under Section 602 and remitting "12 woolen scarves, bag 7; 50 small purses, bags 9, 11, 16; 41 lip roller and eye shadow compacts with mirror, bag 10; and went on for three pages." On the third last page was the summation which read "1000.9, restitution of criminal proceedings, grounds, hearing; and 1000.11 Statement to probation officer or community program worker, inadmissibility – overturned." She remained until 5:30 pm finally approached by a whistle man once the people had gone out to the platform. He checked her remarks and at 7:09 pm signed his initials.

By the time Monica entered the speedway headed north she planned the section of warehouse where she intended to stock the bags once the contents were reviewed and photographed. It meant two all night work schedules which would require indefinite status verification by time card along with thumb print at top left hand corner inside the square. She turned down Fourteenth Street entering through a third wrought iron gate which closed behind her automatically and circling to the unloading dock parked alongside it. The ramp was laid out, the roll-top raised. Inside the lights infused the cement walls with a cool complexity. The hopper had been turned on for the scarabs of corn which were covered in phencyclidine, a substance that would test clothing for residues of crystalline containing cocaine base, cocaine, heroin, methamphetamine and marijuana. One half gram or less declared grounds for special proceedings in the handling of narcotic intoxication criminals. The corn test was considered more reliable than lab procedure by swab or refrigerated sampling. Based upon coloring, red and white proving stone cold dead, basis for continuity of prosecution leading to final determination was established. Blue and yellow confirmed ocean death below freezing for genetic changes to the skin, important in establishing presumed murder. The evidence index on materials consisting of clothes and bedding gave two murders with six ocean deaths. The docket was prepared and sent by special courier to the city district attorney for last known whereabouts and prosecution. When the task was finally completed and the two vehicles passed into the prints room of the gigantic warehouse for dusting, the ambulance having retrieved the bodies for post mortem, the storage supervisor sent Monica home for seven hours sleep.

Monica lived with a Foothill Security Patrol officer in a small flat off Adeline on Thirty-Fourth Street upstairs overlooking a backyard garden of gladioli bulbs, wisteria and grass and a brick patio with table, benches and parasol. Inside the entry with maple blond hardwood floors throughout was a large sitting room, dining room with mirror over an adequate hearth, average sized kitchen, hall bath and two large bedrooms, furniture of three green, yellow and purple velvet bench sofas, walnut dining table and six matching chairs, dark blue and green Turkish-oriental rugs, and each bedroom with large bed with bronze deco headboard and lamp-table with moon in a crescent lamp. She worked days; her man friend worked graveyard. Rarely they talked weekdays, but they left written notes on the dining room table. Their friendship was platonic – soon he would marry and then Monica would inherit the flat. Because late afternoon formality became a routine of brewed coffee taken black, a dim sum shrimp and green onion and potato smallish dumpling purchased across the street from the police yard chased down by a shot of cognac and finger bite cinnamon roll while reviewing monthly billings, she sat to her meal as she perused the worksheet of the past night. The entries were correct, lab testing properly signified, columns added up, explanations at far right noted for remarks. The testing strips had been cut off at the end and attached below with references. At the end of the week, she would have receipt from the district attorney and the bulk of material transported to a lab location. Her meal took her forty minutes. Once done, she ran the water for a shower. She had graduated at the top of her business college class for a law-medico to work in lab, clinic office, or dispatch, as this job was considered. She had attended city lab for four weeks, coroner for seven weeks, medical charting in downtown Redwood City an entire semester, and pre-trials in three county courthouses assigned to more than one attorney. Someday she wanted to run her own lab.

The shower relieved her of anxiety. She drew a towel and shut off the water and slipped into a terry cloth robe, tying into a ribbon band around her shoulder length blond hair. Sleep was always an adjustment filled with tense rethinking of each case and the bothersome notion she was forgetting a detail of her college training. While she rethought judgment, serious felony for cost of incarceration and order for payment and cost of parole, as sleep overcame her, she remembered there were other known properties involving a house on Eighth Street and several legitimate businesses for the dead male in the driver's seat of the 1957 Ford, and for the other deceased, also owning a house in south Oakland, substance abuse related felony, use of minors as agents.

It was a pleasant day. An alleviation of rain succeeded by a nightly downpour had left the streets clean and fresh. City hall was filling up for its morning calendar on which were three fatalities. The morgue had tried its sole contender at an 8:30 am hearing with a finding for death by deadly weapon. Lawyers in business suits gathered in small groups, the few experts waited in the main hall for their names to get called. There were to be heard the first hearing on 289s for acts against victims by force, violence, menace and unlawful bodily injury. The presiding judge, Honorable Sault, who sat on such matters had never failed to convict.

The first case called announced on loudspeaker. "Paste, calling on the matter of Paste to Department 1."

A bevy of lawyers and their assistants stood and walked to the tall wooden doors situated immediately in the center of the hall. A police deputy checked their names off a list and permitted each to enter.

Inside the courtroom was a semi-circular assembly of upholstered seats, at the stage was the judge's podium with court secretary stenographer directly below, the legal setting fronted by two long tables where counsel and defense attorneys would sit, the jury panel to the right against the far wall. Dark brown drapes secured against sunlight over tall sash levered windows. The dark copper and tan carpet gave a distinct impression of conservative appropriate proceedings.

The clerk's thunderous voice boomed. "Here ye, here ye, the Honorable Judge Sault presiding. The Paste matter, 71-00034 to be heard."

Judge Sault stared intently over the podium at county counsel. The judge wore a brown crewcut toupee that surrendered a benign fatherly expression. "What is the county's position?"

District Deputy Jan Feare began in an equally sonorous voice that belied no hesitation to a very thin trustworthy demeanor constitution of six feet, silvery hair, fair complexioned. "We intend to demonstrate, Your Honor, that James Paste did willfully and with premeditation commit murder to one Monica Neville-Herald, daughter of San Francisco Herald Newspaper owner, Marin Lakerity. If it please his honor, we intend to establish a series of communications between Mr. Paste and a hotelier in Oakland that prove beyond any doubt intent to cause great bodily damage."

Judge Sault turned his considerable attention to the defense. "Do you have a statement, Ms. Defense attorney?"

"We shall prove that the named was not in Oakland the week of the death, Your Honor. He was traveling from Chicago in a black sedan owned by his sister."

The light filtered down from on high onto the yard and patio of the warehouse alighting the entire parking section which past the monitored gate ran from Fourteenth and Fifteenth clear through to Seventeenth Streets. The hearse stopped at the dock and pressed a handle allowing the rear door to open. The driver, a small time operative Franklin Rely, slid out to have a cigarette while the staff made ready the body for transporting. The driver was an all-time academy quickie who had seen his nifty share of vehicle theft, vandalism, and child abduction and had saved more than one employer with parking lot enforcement and material safety. As a result he ran his own detective agency supplying a few thirty nighttime retirement guards to vehicle patrol, patrols outside, gate access and traffic for county hospital and the three hospitals on the hill, Peralta, Summit and Samuel Merritt. The October wind addled through allies causing a bit of breeze to kick about.

"Where's Nicky?" Frankie asked the dock man about Monica.

"I thought you heard. She wound up dead on arrival to the emergency."

"That's insane! What do they think happened?"

"Drug overdose. I hear she was loaded."

"Jesus, poor kid. I really thought she was going places."

"We all did. She was a very perky kid."

"Who's the old man going to bring in to replace her?"

"No idea. No one's said a word."

"Where'd you park her car, the crimson and white T-bird?"

"Downtown Eleventh before the tunnel to Alameda island."

At lunch break Frankie sent his chaser in search of the kid's car. It wasn't on Eleventh Street or anywhere in Chinatown for that matter. It had gone straight to the has-been shop in one of two display rooms where it sat spiffed up on the eastern corner of the first block as traffic emerged from the tunnel onto the short section and onto Main Street. Medical offices dotted the streets with hotels. Orchards replaced trains except for twenty-one townhouses on a central plaza of five blocks. Tennis courts, a bowling green, a small yacht harbor and outboard wind sailing imitated the enjoyed life of retired physicians, many relocated from ivy league campuses on the eastern seaboard. The Costa Brava had eloped with ex-wives in the middle of the winter from champion skating iced over ponds in Delgrada outside Boston blowing a wad purchasing everything in sight to convert to studio and one bedroom apartments. At the top of their lists their scar face thugs were hunting coifed blondes with hourglass figures and expensive fur wraps and glittering hair clips for midday thefts in clothier storefronts and working the odds at the racetracks. Whatever the rationale for chewing up the wife's white wheels, marriage was at an all time premium that included a parcel acre. Not a single girl from Alameda Island would jet set as an EMT through the tunnel or over a train bridge, each one would be skirting clandestine hours working up a tan on a second story balcony or clerking for a husband's medical office; only girls from the Broadway Terrace or along the Telegraph thoroughfare would be training for speed in a typing pool classroom of fifty law, business secretary or medical clerk females, hair in sequined nets, white blouse, grey box skirt and pale pink sweater vest.

It wouldn't surprise him if Nicky turned out to be a kick-in-the-pants by some grade A. Her drug screen toxicology said sniffer, positive for cocaine 45 mg. and meth 90 mg. She was tooting. The zero gravity index said stone dead as a result of a vehicle taking too fast a turn which should have been impossible. Traffic drove fast every day and no one died. She may as well have been blood shot drunk. As if that wasn't enough the muted sun in the traffic lane photograph revealed a dark sail on the lake three miles across town suggesting the tangerine light of day may have been a factor in death obscuring a lineup of vehicles approaching the corner of Seventeenth and San Pablo early that morning on her way to work. Blue light from shadows cast by buildings may have been another. By all indicators she was a happy young adult, nice, friendly, no problems, newly employed, having departed breakfast with a close friend from high school at Crest's lounge, and started down the street in the direction of work.

She went down in a second flat. An icy blonde female in a short navy culotte skirt and white seersucker ran out to help and called 911 on her cell phone. The Oakland Police arrived in twenty minutes with an ambulance. Two attendants placed Nicky on a stretcher and sped off admitting her to Merritt on hospital hill at Thirty-Forth and Hawthorne where the supervising physician tried to revive and failing pronounced her dead. No scars, marks, tattoos, or fractures were evident. A patch test was administered to look for suspicious causes. The time of the death certificate read in at 3:05 pm.

Death was a world unto itself. The traveler's journey, abruptly cut short, became the lament of which ballads were conjured. The grind and holler of the final hour departed in absolute shock without anyone the wiser to understand what had taken place. Deadly motivations occurred behind locked palisades where life was pronged by the sweet scent of inhospitable age and unsightly illness. There was no funeral service nor acknowledgment as the body was prepared for its next existence and at the day of notification to family of origin no one requested viewing. The family knew nothing; even less was there any trepidation on the part of the friend who was last to see Monica alive. She had talked freely about her new case; the dead man slumped behind the wheel whose clothing tested for chromo somatic DNA factor for a bleeder with Rh-positive blood. Her task that day was to send the imprint to the Dolphin Corp. for a sea water saline match. In and of itself that objective was routine; who would attempt to negate a court order on the basis of felony causality, but there it rested for anyone with a suspicious reasoning to extrapolate.

Frankie telephoned and left a message with his street contact, a black man in his thirties who operated afternoon movies at the Paramount and Grand Lake theatres. By the time the contact returned the call with a message that Monica was observed on Telegraph Avenue passing below the windows of the 45 rpm train sound studios, approximately at 8:35 am that day, Frankie was on his way to Grand Avenue to talk to his first witness, a gal whose husband he had investigated a previous year on an old flame case involving stalking.

TWO

"Can you tell me what time Ms. Herald was admitted?"

The female in front of him was a frosted blonde in her seventies who was still trim with every bit the humorist. Stella Ester wore an all white nurse's uniform and white leather shoes. She had uncapped her nurse cap and was sipping a fresh brewed cup of coffee.

"The ambulance pulled into the emergency at about 9:25 am and the attendants wheeled her to the O.R. where she was hooked up to a stat screen, an IV was inserted, and a heparin solution administered."

"Was she breathing?"

"Yes, she had a faint pulse. Her skin was damp. We treated her for a cardiac although she had eaten recently and her saliva contained a bit of liquid food. She was prepped for an abortion. It was lights out during the aspiration, we did all medicine gives us for to restore her to no avail."

"Did the scope deadline?"

"Not for at least a half hour, but pulse rate lessened

considerably. As it turned out, it was too weak to sustain."

"Was she reported to have said anything?"

"She came to at one point and said, 'get Ron, tell him what's happened.' It was noted on the intake. The physician did not feel the call should be made."

"Did you place the call?"

"No, I did not. Why? Was a call made?"

"We have reason to believe someone tried. Were you given his last name?"

"The victim had an address book. The name may have been in it."

"Were any words uttered while she was in the O.R.?"

"Yes. She came to for about a minute when she said the test read gray. Gray indicates gravened for dusting a body and causing palpitations."

"Is that statement produced on the treatment report?"

"It should be. You should be able to get a copy with a subpoena for the information."

Lakerty resided on the southern side of the lake off Harrison in a glass and tile highrise with large comfortable balconies, once the foundation had been a neatly mowed vista and grass plaza with benches and several posh French restaurants, the apartment was in the middle on the fifth floor overlooking the lake and sand beach and walking path, it was a large sitting room and kitchen and terrace. Lakerty was a partner, offices in the new mecca behind the church across from the twin IRS and FBI glass towers, an extravaganza of portfolio destiny at the Jack London waterfront, he was tall, face etched with lines, shock of vivid silver straight hair, penny for your thoughts mien, able bodied, a man who minced no words, who meant his business, at the moment he was enjoying a stiff latte while writing a travel piece combined off desks of foreign offices, of course he had heard about his daughter, who the hell hadn't, he had a search out on this guy Paste, as far as he was concerned she had been knocked off by the syndicate, no, he himself wasn't mob or gob, the KKK. He was a single-minded man with straight forward business interests, he suspected his daughter of seeing someone, knew of no man named Ron, didn't give a hoot who disliked his politics, they didn't have to buy his newspaper, last time he spoke to her was a few nights ago, she was tied up at work and couldn't make dinner, she gave him a rundown on the hundred bags, clothing, makeup, scores of fingerprints she had to proceed on, the codes and penalty provisions, he had agreed to handle some research for her. Sure, everyone in lab work knew how dipstick worked, the PCP test was salt proof, like any test it required minimal paraffin, it was like auto mechanic grease, he had made a few calls, to her mother Frenchy Neville up in the tower on 12th, a slick debonair sophisticate, all catch words spiked with a few jabs, for instance – who had promoted to chief county lab, who was the new white coat at coroner staff, which Cayman executive had just enlisted to obit circulars to enhance his pilot-flyer lists. Well, you know how that goes, we step on tippy toes to weep on garden plates, the convention of the era was to purchase by objective, he was all in favor of landmark aristocracy, had he known who was a player he could have bid on corner lots to pay off the cost of newspaper.

How were the fees these days? Herald inquired.

Can't complain, the work just piles up. So how did Nicky land such a prized job to begin with?

Her mother insisted, to make a pro out of her; imagine, over talk of stocks they argued about her, she was unusually bright, had instantaneous recall, he actually wanted her to waitress at the dock, her mother was the ingénue, made party favors that had Nicky guessing chemicals in perfume, paint doctors to remove sleazy spills, barf tickers, residue counters, all in a good day's work. It had worked, she thought like a junior morgue classifier, sure was plenty of garbage on the streets.

The dead were held by joint tenancy. This meant a search revealing the names of parents and legal guardians were included under writs even after post mortem, on the issue of gray section on the beetle cob, the accurate description read for who was guilty as well, all relevancies taken into consideration. It's whoever dusted, take that Ely mine disaster, once inside the criminals dust sprayed resulting in any investigator who entered getting subdural latent prints on their own hands; snippets like these become an entirely suggested treatise. The newspaper syndicates are a homemade family of many dozens of distributors who over years wind up in different capacities, this winds up in amoral terms once a magazine man encounters beat-up chickie-do's and toe tagged vagrants. Had Nicky to have been slightly older she might have regarded the nature of these assignments in very divorced relationships. By now, the second day of forensic review, it should be known which paths of any essential previous crime her body became disposed to, could be morgue franchise, which should have indicated how she became involved besides primary scene abduction, including littoral subjugation, this would be that she was on film crossing any area proven by the facts to be linked to each part of the origination, as indicated by mental deduction, what Nicky herself deduced. Could I obtain any persuasive medical indication, I might know who to track.

Frankie was not permitted discussion with a grieving parent no matter how rated and compelling the matter seemed to warrant. Sudden grief often took on its own harbinger, it knocked at any door without proper search and seizure designated by the outcome of a forensic principal.

"We are examining your daughter's death with every scrutiny available. In the meantime I have to ask you not to leave town without notifying me first with a four day advance."

He had to assume Nicky was appreciated as lively remorse with such a high toxicology screen evident, her early pregnancy made it all the more questionable, but she didn't reside on the fringe which was defined by any living area northeast of Lakeshore going through the avenues as far as the start of Hayward, Monica Herald enjoyed the life of an upgraded secretary stenographer belonging to a morgue site, if she had lived anyone could have seen her rise to investigator in charge of all packages delivered off both train and postal service; the problems for fringe involved shakedowns usually of small retail businesses, some delineation of therapeutic relief by encroachment of one's family or extended relatives, borrowed goods off clothier racks, and straight approach wire buzzer shutdowns of storage and warehouse. Frankie had co-habited with many a street walker, a few who were the nicest a man could ever hope to know, they lived a worthy fringe life frequenting bars, both gay and straight, seeking johns who were regular habits and eventual husbands. Their dead bodies turned up in attics or on the wharf storage or lying in a street near the Seventh Street Post Office, skin torn, arms twisted, this was an indelible worst life, not yet a hospital admit, these females had once been some retailer's nightmare, hey honey you want a quick score while a pimple or send-off ran out a back-door with stolen money, school teachers the same looking for years for an underage minor who had left home to marry some brainless man who stole more than their youth and beauty, how had Nicky found her way to hell unless it was with a man. Well, who the hell ever got lucky enough to find out, but Frankie decided the answer had to be somewhere on the cold Oakland pavement perhaps running a loot shop operating under a half dozen aliases.

The train brought in a new wind. It pulled into the brick and light blue glass station in time for the cocktail hour, all sparks flying free of the cog wheels. The Pullman coach porter dragged the two crates onto the broad platform and left them for the man who drove the luggage cart who would be along after the train headed south toward San Jose. The apple man drove his van up to the tracks and loaded up the crates. It would be his expertise to test by injection any glass proof for evidence sent by the Chicago lab for substances found on the ground. He slammed the van doors shut and headed for the main thoroughfare. He was a sensible man in his forties whose test expertise had taken him on a bloodhound's search for money stolen from the upstate New York mint on the Washington Street Parkway, a job that had culminated with seven dead federal agents and ten million in missing notes. The Ford cars that had been sent were waiting in a drive to the underground that was detonated. The bail bond man had turned up dead some twenty-five years later, ankles tied by heavy twine, his body loaded down underwater secured to the deep channel dock in Alameda across the water from Jack London Square. The situation caused quite a flap, with a sensational flood of investigators, ambulances and tray cars between ten at night and three in the morning working a dredge under bright lights. When it was over and the victim posted to an adobe in Ranch Meadows in west coastal wetlands of Hayward, the dead man's mug shot photographed, the identity was hush-hushed due to his transfer of billing bonds out of the zoo to Nebraska state yard. The pressure was on, the necessity to learn who had killed mint agents a longtime authorized priority.

THREE

Frankie obtained the medical summary with a subpoena.

The victim was admitted unconscious, wheeled in on a folding stretcher under bright ceiling lights, through double doors into Room 2, transferred to a fully arranged bed. The attending head nurse, a forty year old male nurse residing on the premises, dark striated cut hair, moderately distal lumbar, prepared a saline 60 mg consisting of ammonium chloride 2.75 mEq/kg nasogastric injection until the urine Ph was less than 5.0 intended to restore vitals, which it never did. Normally urine acidification took diuresis using Lasix furosemide 30 mg. intravenously to introduce adequate excretion, and then afterwards a week of treatment under close supervision adding potassium supplements by prescription to reduce the large amount of PCP in the body, his instinct was to act swiftly, the patient could have entered cerebral coma, requiring minute by minute life-saving methods, he expertly rolled the left arm at the elbow, inserted the cuff, let blood squirt through and fill six vials, near death offering no resistance, his gaze never left identifying status of the subject's raised vein, watching for flattening which was too big a problem, specifically that the blood was pooling, and that was a disaster. Tests were standard with electrolyte and serum glucose levels, complete blood cell count, hepatic and renal profiles, these were taken while the initial treatment was evaluated for medical complications.

The operation team exhausted all efforts to save her, but as pulse went thin line, pupils became pinpoint, skin faded bluish, disparate respiration resulted in pulmonary edema, electrocardiogram, utilized a chart monitor to determine artery blood sufficiency for internal injury for massive hematoma, drug and alcohol screen, and a brain wave tomography read to determine brain death that consists primarily of rapid eye movement in conjunction with auditory stimulation. If the patient feared restoration and mentally withdrew, it was nevertheless impossible for that person to fall short of full capacity if they could be brought to consciousness.

The presence of a fading hematoma the color of deep red along the left side of the lateral body confirmed the certainty of purposeful murder, open and shut, because there were visual lacerations that the driver stepped on the brakes hard and slowly released allowing the wheels to reach as far as the body. Normally an hour post injury the tissue would become discolored to red and visible blue, light green in splotches, due only to the front grid having forcible contact with the body.

PCP gave a confusing picture by itself. An individual covered with it daily could at the point of immediate handling of a hundred items become intellectually impaired and have serious medical problems, PCP was a frequent impurity found in marijuana and cocaine, producing initial calmness, little early irritability, loss of orientation to place or self, unpredictable elevated mood and compromised rational thinking. Could a chemist or a handling operative become contaminated through contact with the formula? The district attorney would have a field day with these findings.

The DA and Special Handling Office would send out for a chromatogram to establish length of stopping distance and shoot their info upstairs to the pro's who assessed for criminal evidence in drawing a legend of the scene.

He went to see Frenchy whom he knew well. A little shy of fifty she nevertheless knew every ballroom dancer and sports coach who worked parking. It came to her once that a child who entered adult life prematurely should face at least a setback; unfortunately she herself was forever retracted having witnessed a bad stabbing. She came to the door in black tight stretch pants, a casual, white swaying rug top, backless heels, all the fashion with bronze hair tied in a black glittering clip. The flat overlooked Broadway's medical terraces, there was a thin view of a park green, the sitting room gave her a clear glimpse of roof tops and cars on the 880 freeway. She believed her child had been told to talk to Ducky at the law college at Laney about a clerk steno job, she had her suspicions that a close friend to her daughter wanted a parade listing, what sort of education was the city specializing in these days, if her child knew a Sally, then to whose benefit was an introduction if there were a Sally at the moving van and transportation, if the Sally's were tracking the lawless Caps maybe they were crooks too. Her own father, the John Neville, God of gods, had tracked the three mint Capone tycoons. Even her husband who grouped all inserts and page ads had an item or two on them, from bouncing chairs to stripping refrigerated shelving and sticking the dead bills in basement closets for months. She herself had ranged newspaper photos, had tracked mean wicked hoods, had looked up coroner reports and wrote obits, she had stripped down dummy pages and managed classified advertising; she knew the crime traffic, nothing was beyond her surmise. In addition she got the goods on every last crime planned.

The city's troubles began in 1960 with the building of four freeways. Milky Way Marvin wanted to be state controller to manage funds on old buildings, many which he owned having purchased when real estate was cheap. Despite that Lake Berryessa was submerged after an old aqueduct dam was eliminated sending his five mansions packed with silver drayage under lake water, the silver mines could not produce. A good deal of favor was being sought from the state for silver shorelines and inland reservoirs that could feed lakes for a steady supply of manganese. After a horrifying arson of manganese at Sequoia Park that left not a living forest, the state pushed to the north. While the State Recorder tracked these menacing youths and placed liens on small houses and buildings across the state, Alameda County created newer systems for greater local authority from its San Francisco controlling law, hiring in a hundred new physicians to staff hospitals in addition to running private practice and five hundred civil suit attorneys to research law and torts. Included in the new system was the formation of the Public Defender which could now be assigned to any case outside felonies. The old system of trial attorneys for the claimant was put into the appeals on writs, torts and injunctions requiring over three months of court.

What did that give Oakland, except the opportunity for its own public violence: shootings in hospital lots, stabbings in restaurants, knifings in alleys, gasoline fires to furniture stores; gay disco drive-by gunshots, movie theatre nude flashers, broken windows on rooftops, bombed out cars, a distilled disintegrative society periodically trading newer homes for seedy clandestine factories; inside old resorts a stale damp air pervaded by closeted shitload bags of empty food cans, buildings to let, carpeted floors inside musty offices used by the homeless whenever a sympathizer left a back door ajar, a track record of forget-me-not's, lost minds functioning on empty registrars, once someones' children destined for good jobs with good pay.

There was no one to explain the hit and run to her daughter, not a possibility Monica used drugs, out of the realm of probability she sniffed after being covered in PCP up to her elbows every day; the coroner summary concluded nothing that made sense, so it had to be the work itself, a letter in the mail or a dead Capone on the street.

He pulled the traffic shot, first three pic's in the front row. Sleeping on the bus bench was a young man beneath a zebra

striped sleeping bag, a bus pulled up too far to the corner going north and a morning newspaper male distributor, blond,
aged 41, stepped off almost colliding with her. Down the cross
street on 17th Street a hearse and motorcycle entered a parking
lot behind the fire department, a mail van came down toward
Telegraph and the driver waved to her, a large station wagon
driven by a short haired brunette pony-do pulled to the opposite street blocking Monica's passage while she walked through
the crosswalk; inside a car sat the impatient look-alike to the
Cad man, who sped down the street and slowed to a stop barely
grazing her causing her to fall, then inched upon her, got out,
went to look, saw her there, as a female rushed into the street to
feel for a pulse. Frankie was certain the prints wouldn't match
on the Cadillac driver, didn't know where he was at the time of
the accident, if he was in a medical office watching the scene.

"Who is the driver by proof?" Frankie asked.

"One John Charney. He is five foot nine, dark red black
hair, American. He does the assault and battery."

"Where does he first come across her?"

"San Francisco, Battery Street."

"Does he want her for the glue stain?"

"Well, my thinking," said the district attorney assigned to
research the girl's case, "is that the bugs proved money, not just
blood, and the Ford was anticipated to bring the money."

"It's your conjecture that the getaway car would arrive with
the money. Maybe the Capone's converted it."

"I've considered a double cross."

Frankie responded, "The money was arraigned in Chicago
before it was sent to Ely; there wasn't a dime on the frigging
car so I think, if it existed at all by then, it was driven to and
placed in the Ely mint."

"The rooms which were subsequently blown up. It was the
older Capone who went into the Oakland estuary presumably
for a bomb to a bank vault in New York tied by his feet who
was fished out."

"I knew the identity was denied publication. The younger
Capone arrived in the Chevrolet that the Chicago Herald girl

had to test, but it was the consulting chemist who got murdered by the punch. Are you intending to prove a connection?"

"Her death may not rest with the fact that she could be sworn in as to the younger man's identity. We can only testify as to actual fact."

"Which leaves us with how her blood coagulated."

"Under exposure to handling PCP to wash the corn bugs for test preparedness, obtaining uncut cocaine bug proof as to a victim's blood, testing apple for substance on the killer which gives you the meth content, and then going home and sipping one or more glasses of white wine which leaves her still under the influence when she is grazed by the slowly moving Cadillac."

"Will you introduce the emergency room attending physician as expert?"

"Yes, and the State will ask for term sentence."

It wasn't sufficient to his logic that Oakland terminated the lives of ruthless criminals who had murdered twelve federal agents under the most brutal of behaviors and staged their bodies in underground compartments meant to be obscured semi-permanently. As these perpetrators were identified, they were turned over, booked, fingerprinted, and prosecuted and convicted, sent to prison to serve out sentences, and those who had murdered were robbed of life. Frankie saw they would get their conviction without any real answers. They wouldn't really learn which piece of life had cut her the no-win bad luck, which car she could not test, which test she could not write a description for, if she witnessed a murder, if she knew the decedent. A month prior to her death, she spent a dinner on board a yacht on SF bay hosted by Scoma's during which she was escorted by the trial attorney on gaming, a black man who was putting the screws on illegal gambling run by Harvey's casino in Reno. Somewhere in all the morass of death and autopsy, there had to be a reason why Oakland's Cad man ran her down. Frankie would have to turn the place over to get to any reason and he didn't think he had enough information.

Four

Oakland's downtown below her hospital zone was defined by two thoroughfares, Broadway and Telegraph, the YMCA to as far west as the train station and wharf with fishing trawlers and a half dozen restaurants, and her commercial shipping offices and apartment flats between Eighteenth and Twelfth Streets including Chinatown and the lake, pharmacies and newspaper storefronts on the street corners, several shops open that sold watches, cookware and household appliances, a travel agency, liquor shops, small customer banks; independent retail shops that cleared out after a few seasons, medical staffing came and went year after year, buses ran every half hour and were crowded enough for standing room only. The long existing buildings were high schools and park recreation, nearby eateries, a bookstore, a section of department store malls, a few furniture stores, hospitals and clinics, medical uniforms, car lots, and college campuses with their student housing, theatres, museums, and churches; no police or security patrols or accountants, enough jobs for a hundred people. U.S. Steel and Kaiser Aluminum hiring thirty-eight hundred people had shut down, removal of the train off the Bay Bridge ended ships and ferries between Oakland and San Francisco and ten dockyards, five hundred telephone switchboard operators were replaced by automation, and housing construction which put in forty-four hundred homes in twenty years was over.

This was the year that underwater wharf excavationists who had to secure the wharf against a loose ship pulled a body, tied up, bound and gagged, out of the bay. The man was older, possibly in his seventies, mottled tan-grey skin, chalk white hair, clear as day a Steglione out of industrial Chicago, a Brewster man who worked for the replacement of worn dollar notes, a big bag man as this set was affectionately known by marble-punch die and square alike. The disappearance of the senior funk man who ran new bills out to the western unions in Reno, Oakland and Kite's Land, Los Angeles by shop van carrying also a key shop created an all-out search involving a hundred bonies, skeleton key deputies for the postal green union supported by accountant Argonaut lazies situated at each downtown minter's office building. The body brought in two trains, a few Cad men, several lazies, and a dead shift bony, all to evaluate on-the-spot physical circumstances that may have contributed to finality. A specialist in reading blue light arrived on the 4:05 pm the next day out of Flagstaff. The body was transported across town to a Richmond shoe cutting factory where his hands were soaked in wool dye and read under chromium match stick. Obviously at some point in the past four days he had handled a code bill for a vault that he presumably found a paper match key for somewhere in personal possession. Other than that, the butcher found only the usual striations for marking batch by square, no big deal since no one could touch these without getting covered in plait dye. On the man's forehead rested the blessing by blunt pick, he had been struck by a whaler once and despite the relatively tiny thrombosis, it speedily took his life in less than five seconds.

The long shore man job title was born that week. Fifty meat packer accountants combed every last office in downtown. The findings were atrocious, two accountants, both middle aged white, were found bag punched onto window grills, another found pressed into fresh cement at West and Broad, one was locked inside the rail storage house with his face hacked open, another in the brick facing Pinkerton building stabbed in the shoulder scapula, palms of hands having turned blood green. The word on the street was the lamp light was left on, which signified someone on the lakes was tearing the place apart tracking the whereabouts of the vault timer Capones, the belief is they were dead, all nine. It was a year of merciless bloodshed, a year of shucking the jarn, as was politely referred to the Chicago steal-y worth mint glove men. Who knew into what lame alley any of these men were lured or by whom. In another ten weeks new jobs were posted for accountants to work wharfs and three hundred males with junior law degrees applied.

Monica was sent by her boss to pick up the interview list on the day John Charney's new blue Bel Air was released by the manufacturer and was seen parked in West Hollywood on La Cienega Avenue and a man inside a hotel leapt to his death to escape a 4-star alarm fire in the hallway outside his hotel suite door. He opened the window and tried to make the opposite hotel roof narrowly missing secure footing and falling five floors. The news release hit the bulletins the same hour that the acceptance of all applicants went public at the charcoal broiler duffy-flop house for retired wolfers, longtime assistants in law numbers for ship products whose stops were on any marine and bay on the California coast. She consulted her father and not getting him at home called her mother who was putting out the evening paper. The sensation of a man losing his life in such an error was on all the news slumber margins, a parade of untimely death and worse, her mother told her, a fried west-all case in which the deviants were certain to be listed as pay-out brats for the Chicago-Seven, yet another strong-arm box case running the circuits.

Frankie stopped by to interview the glue stain man whom he took downtown to the hof-brau on Broadway for coffee.

"I need to know what else was received in, if anything."

"A crate cardboard container of portrait glass with snipping tool, the bill of lading read for one window windshield, possibly mint restoration. We have two, Nebraska and Ely. Request was to read by laser plate only, no specimens, projection to ground only."

"Did she open it?"

"Yes, she placed the shield on a frame easel, she did administer powder with which to test and verify substances. It had to weather dry air temperature at cool temperature 48 hours without lights. The shield was treated on the sides with chromium solution to allow restoration of wastes and liquefiers, this for liquid that hit the window, the solution fixes prints, hair, vomit. She would have gotten to it that afternoon."

"And that arrived by train also?"

"No, that was sent express by bus."

"From Chicago?"

"I think from Maine."

"From lab storage?"

"Yes, the lab name was Winthorp. The label read Farner, Garden Land, Greenland."

"Was there any other reference enclosed?"

"No, none. That was it."

The city's hearings convened in the state building amidst a bevy of reporters and halls filled with attorney representatives and their key case witnesses. The calendar was packed with two trials, one at 9:00 am anticipated to take an hour and a half on death review, and twelve minor hearings on new construction costs, a traffic accident involving the mayor's son, and several probation progress reports for wards of the state. Inside a private courtroom a trial had been going on since 8:30 am to consider county disposition on material evidence. Frankie sat beside his prosecutor, a thin elegant statuesque elderly black man dressed in white business threads who as far as anyone was concerned ran the county.

"From whom do you rent your space?"

"We rent the basement of the Grand Storage building from a lease corporation owned by the Grand Casino in Reno. The parties are Klompfer and Broom."

"What were the tests for the second Ford General Motors car?"

"We conducted three tests for stain, apple and tray. On every vehicle we are required to test residue, submit a report to the state recorder office here in this building and get it stamped."

"Would you describe the tests?"

"Certainly. The first test is a screen on glass the size of a windshield for substance on the upholstery. In this situation the stain was green. There are two other test colors, red means money and black is for a dead body. We then looked for where drugs were carried. To do this we had to pull the car apart. The paper tray test is a curbside lab in which a laptop computer is hooked to a cup containing a blood specimen, and the apple test conducted by an approved state examiner injects any substance on the ground which goes with table, chairs and loose clothing but nothing found on the victim."

"What did you determine?"

"There was evidence of a tiny amount of crystalline on the seat, the floor and oddly on the vic's suit."

"Why do you say it is odd?"

"Well, it seemed that when he was killed he was providing a test in the vehicle. It is crystalline that turned the stain green with minute blue. However there was no presence of formula anywhere."

"How would you interpret the results?"

"Green places victim in a mine, blue confirms for presence of drugs."

"What was state of death due to?"

"We suspect it was removed before he was shot."

"What was he shot with?"

"Hard to say. There was no evidence of bullet. We got a read for extreme sudden and violent death to a federal agent whose blood shot onto the steering column, all windows, upholstered ceiling of car, as well as on his person."

"Did you have the wounds examined?"

"We photographed three wounds and sent them to radiotelemetry. Of course, you are aware of what happened."

"Move to strike last sentence," Opposing counsel declared, a medium height dark tan lawyer with blond curly hair who wooed his opposition with conservative dark navy suits and black tie.

Judge Paste instructed the court reporter to remove the statement and asked county prosecutor to inquire for clarification.

"Did you receive written report?"

"No. We were sent a copy of a photo showing the forensic specialist was murdered."

"Is this that photograph?"

"Yes, it is. It has my initials with the date on it."

"Witness is excused."

Judge Paste asked, "Does the defense wish to cross?"

Counsel for the Defense stood. "Yes, Your Honor."

"Very well, the witness is asked to remain seated. You may proceed."

"Were you at any time brought to the morgue to view the telemeter examiner?"

"Yes, I was."

"What was his state?"

"He was dead. There was a ram of upholstery punctured to his shoulders."

"What were you told killed him?"

"A cow punch."

"Were you told there was consistency in the wounds between the dead man in the Ford and your medical study chemist?"

"Yes."

"Who told you?"

"Chief Medical Examiner, Michael Onerow."

"Does he have a professional relationship to your service?"

"Yes, he signs off on all our trial transcripts."

"Calling Michael Onerow," the bailiff shouted into the hall above the din of chatter.

A silver haired man in his seventies dressed in a blue suit came forward. He showed a subpoena and was admitted inside. The judge invited him to the witness stand where he was sworn in placing one hand on the bible and raising the other to take an oath.

The defender approached the witness. "Please tell the Court about your examination of George Garnier."

"George Garnier was brought by morgue van to the Alameda County morgue on the fourth Thursday in October. He was placed on the operating table for examination. He had attached to his backside a rather lengthy plat of upholstery typically found on walls of vehicles but in this instance it was assumed the cloth was intended for apartment use. The plat had been administered crudely by bolts which penetrated his shoulder blades and hip joints. It was evident after thorough examination of the body that this was cause of death. Based upon clotting of blood and eventual edema, I put time of death at around 2:00 pm with rate of heart failure taking approximately three hours or longer."

"How was his body discovered?"

"A janitor arriving for work came across him. The victim was lying on the floor but conscious. The janitor called 911."

"Did you learn if anyone working in the building contacted the janitor service?"

"Yes, a secretary for a physician staffing agency overhead the victim's cries for help and responded."

"I have no further questions, Your Honor."

"Counsel?"

"Did you learn anything else about the decedent?"

"He had just completed two reports submitted for analysis by the requesting agency that held the two transported documents."

"What does your evidence say about the two reports?"

"Examiner Garnier concluded there was blood evidence that proved both cars were owned by Capones."

"Did he indicate to you who the Capones were?"

"Onerow produced a report he had signed. The Ford owner was John Capone and the Chevrolet owner was Pers Capone. Both men are in their late eighties."

"Have you attempted to ascertain local addresses for either man?"

"Yes. John Capone has an address on Fifth Avenue and Pers has a flat on the Oakland estuary waterfront. They purchased homes as a result of the death of their oldest cousin Laurence who they lived with on Lake Superior."

Jason Klompfer was a surly looking, blond and gray curly headed beefeater faced businessman attired in an attractive blue and brown striped suit wearing expensive tan Mocktoe shoes. On the stand he looked tired, haggled by life's many disadvantages, the more noted a fidgety restlessness owing probably to continual stress.

The prosecution walked right up to him.

"Are you the legal owner of the Grand Storage building located on San Pablo Avenue?"

"Yes. I co-own with my business associate Ash Broom."

"Do you have a lease agreement with Dr. Kiddo for a forensic service?"

"Yes. It's a good contract. Kiddo pays a thousand a month."

"Have you had any management difficulties with him?"

"No."

"Do you own other properties in the state?"

"Yes, a small casino at Tahoe, a large warehouse complex in El Cerrito and ten medical office buildings on Grand Avenue in Oakland near the lake."

"Does your partner Broom supply the janitorial services to these buildings?"

"Yes, to all."

"Was Examiner Garnier discovered by one of your staff?"

"Yes."

"Who sent your janitor?"

"I did. I keep a very close guard on any of my buildings."

The judge took the lawyers into chambers.

"Will we be ready to go on Monday?"

Frankie said he would need another week.

"You have three judicial days. We'll begin Wednesday. How will the county plead?"

"We intend to show murder. Charney was at the wheel, Monica Herald was a duck. She had witnessed Charney in the hard bed and he killed her over an insinuation."

"What does the defense intend to show?"

"Charney was out of town. He sent his brother, but his brother had no motivation."

"Are the traffic photos available?"

"Yes," Counsel replied. "They show a van pulling up to the corner causing the girl to step into the path of an oncoming coupe which hit her."

"Did it stop first?"

"Yes, the driver got out."

"What does the medical evidence support?"

"Murder."

"Make sure you distribute exhibits. I don't want a post-ponement."

FIVE

"Please state your name for the record."

"John Charney."

"Are you legally married?"

"Yes, I have been married since 1959."

"To whom are you wed?"

"Her name is Martha Struant. She is an actress."

"Does she reside in this state?"

"No, she lives in Denver."

"Where were you born?"

"I was born in the State of Minnesota."

"In what year were you born?"

"1947."

"Have you ever been employed as a state warden?"

"Yes, at the hole in Ely, Nevada."

"What were your duties?"

"To review and sign off on all death review cases."

"Is that your job for the County of Alameda?"

"Yes. Here I also have to coordinate morgue availability by dispatch after 3:30 pm."

"Do you have a vehicle for this purpose?"

"Yes, I drive a white Cadillac, year 1967."

"Do you own and drive an off-duty vehicle?"

"Yes, it is a blue Bel Air 1970 with four wooden doors."

"Were you making a turn off Nineteenth Street onto Telegraph Avenue the morning of December 10, 1971 at about 8:47 am?"

"Yes. "

"Which car were you driving?"

"The Bel Air."

"Will you tell the Court what occurred?"

"My car accidentally struck one of my lab employees. I saw Monica Herald pause to let my car pass, and next thing I knew I heard a thud. I stopped immediately, got out, found her lying there, and called both police and ambulance."

"What was her condition?"

"She was breathing but woozy. I reassured her that the ambulance was on its way."

"Did she say anything to you?"

"She asked me to call her boyfriend, James, and I said I would."

"Did she say anything else?"

"Yes, she said the green stain turned black after eight minutes. I told her she was one of my best stenographers."

"Was she alive when the ambulance arrived?"

"Yes, she was still holding my hand in a firm grip."

"Did you ride with her?"

"No, the attendants said there wasn't room. I followed in my car. I told them Merritt because Permanente had a nurses' strike."

"Was she alive when you arrived to the hospital?"

"Yes, but she reported sleepiness."

"Was your relationship with Ms. Herald ever friendly?"

"Yes, I took her to dinner about four months after she began working. We went back to her place — "

"Objection," the defense was on his feet. "No ground has been set for this line of inquiry. The information was not made available in discovery."

"Overruled. I think the weight of this may be crucial. Please continue, Judge."

"I spent the night. I dated her for about three months. I continued to see her on occasion."

"What was your most recent visit?"

"I went the night prior to her death."

"Did she inform you as to her morning schedule?"

"Yes, she had given word to my secretary."

"Did you have sexual relations with her?"

"No, but we kissed."

"What time would this have been?"

"It was around seven."

"What did you discuss?"

"I asked whether she had been inside the Fielding building. She said she was there a few weeks earlier in the month to give him the findings on tests that proved blood spatter. A name did not accompany the body. She was under an order by State Recorder to submit the folio to that particular historical consultant."

"Why did you want to learn if she had been to the Fielding Building?"

"I received a written note that she was seen entering around the time of the consultant's established untimely demise."

"What did you suspect?"

"Well, nothing. I didn't think she discovered him."

"Did Ms. Herald ever lead you to believe she took matters up herself without discretion?"

"She asked me if she could consult her father as to a rendering of evidence."

"What was the nature of her request?"

"Our office received a threat."

"What did the threat say?"

"Something like, 'The Cad man was seen drizzling someone on October 20th at 9:08 pm.'"

"What was your answer?"

"I said the law was very clear. She could only discuss a law issue."

"Do you have reason to believe the victim disclosed to her father as to a law issue?"

"Yes," John Charney stated. "She wanted to know how many Capones were in Chicago."

"Wouldn't that be on public record?"

"Yes, I guess so."

"Did you receive a copy of a call she made to the police?"

"Yes, that would be the telephone call on October 20th."

"Do you think that was how the message to your office came to be asserted?"

"Yes. "

"Did you at anytime attempt to have a body of October 20th sent to an outside morgue?"

"No."

"Did you arrange stock room renovations for the next day?"

"No. I didn't. It just worked out to begin the morning of the 21st. The van transported Drizler by mid-afternoon from the island because the body wasn't military."

The judgment against John Charney read involuntary manslaughter due to the accused not watching where he was driving. Three days after the pronouncement of the death of Monica Herald a full investigation into extenuating circumstances was ordered.

SIX

Despite the best of intentions, the funeral was late in getting off to a start. The organist arrived a half hour into the choir and the pallbearers had to pick up their suits. The family stood in the church entrance to greet their friends, shaking hands and exchanging kisses. A hundred and forty people showed up in traditional black, silver and blue. Frankie kept a keen gaze from the last pew. The coffin was enthroned by lilacs and pink and red gladioli on stands, up and down the aisles were stands pillaring with flowers. People wept, the Methodist minister read from the Old Testament, the solace of life taken too short was a felt sentiment. Seven pallbearers lifted the coffin and carried it up the center aisle to a hearse waiting outside.

Beckoning waited at every gated crypt, stone angels rising on high of rooftops, a city of the dead for its twelve gravel paths for the hearses, corner stone houses within walls and lawns, rolling hills of shrines made of carved alabaster and windows with hanging lights inside, lawns here and there. About a third gathered around the grave to throw long stem roses as the coffin was lowered. It had begun raining by the time the welcome wishers started to leave.

By the late hour in the afternoon when he made it on return to his tiny cramped office on the estuary, Frankie had received the latest series of obits which made Oakland of 1971 seem like a chronicler of doom and foreboding. Each description left him with a salutary finding of chaos, an extreme chillingly decreed barometer of malice.

Caucasian adult male, presumably Barrister Capone, feet tied by twine, body immersed up to legs in the strait of water of the Oakland channel;

Boat house − body of Caucasian adult male presumably a Courtere found scrunched up in kayak and boat turned over on its side;

Portuguese adult man found bolted to window of chief accountant office in Fielding building;

Chancelory Building, north side − adult Negroid male, law accountant, found in dumbwaiter on far side of hall, third floor;

Fire department building − Portuguese adult man who had headed payroll for Kaiser Aluminum grants found dead inside trunk of Chevrolet; and lastly

Beneath street at Sixth and Broadway − Caucasian adult man, steel foreman, found on inner shelf of walking tunnel leading to frontage wharf.

This was some pretty picture. Nowhere did such a line-up make sense for who was discovered dead. It was as though the mining treasury vault pay system had been disclosed and its chief officers forced to kneel at their own graves. Within hours the remaining two hundred steel yard employees had been deployed to parts unknown in deference to their lives. The State was at war and no one had the slightest idea what the hell it was all about.

Of course, once the steel yard was gated and shut down it

became readily apparent that something of severity was gone awry. Instantly television monitors were installed in every street front store including in bars, pharmacies and beverage halls, and these televisions blared all day and all night causing streets to seem vacuous and oddly absent of ample foot traffic. Circuits were relayed to major surveillance sites, not the least which were police precincts. Seeing eye curtain rods were positioned in every ditch throughout downtown and in hours police had a body count estimate of sixteen, all accountants, most law hired to conduct to weekly payroll for previously fifteen hundred steel yard miners. Additional findings were gruesome. Bodies had been cruelly assaulted and some bloodied and gored had been stuffed into basements, laboratories and stairwells. The police force quadrupled in a month. No one knew how the killings had gone down so fast nor whether this was the work of one or ten. No one knew how many eye witnesses there might be either.

By J. Lea Koretsky

WALL OF DARKNESS
ISBN-10: 1-58790-020-3 / ISBN-13: 978-1-58790-020-4 / 126 pages / paperback / $14.95
This novel takes a hard look at cults that kill. Based upon real accounts of runaway teens, the story about a group of pedophiles is set in a garden paradise in Hawaii and depicts an investigation of the etiology of sex on the Internet to exploit vulnerable children.

> *A psychological profiler of extensive expertise, the author writes from her work in the trenches of cyber crime.*
> —William B. Sloan, Attorney

> *Teenage Violence — a whole new planet.*
> — James Delessandro, script doctor, author *Bohemian Heart*

THE ETERNITY LOOK
ISBN-10: 1-58790-052-1 / ISBN-13: 978-1-58790-052-5 / 231 pages / paperback / $14.95
A whodunit introducing U.S. Marshal Dalton Keys who staffs high security prison wards and tracks down clandestine drug manufacturers. Keys goes after a bonemaster paper manufacturer whose vendetta begins with the deaths of a captain who provided tactics and deployment and his disabled son in a pool of kaolin and cyanide.

> *A convincing plot, attractive protagonist and winning prose.*
> — Publishers Weekly

> *Reliably mystifying. A pro book from a pro tracker who goes with the detectives on beat patrol and into the field with the sheriff coroner.* — Sisters in Crime, San Rafael

DOMINO
ISBN-10: 1-58790-068-8 / ISBN-13: 978-1-58790-068-6 / 238 pages / paperback / $14.95
In this second Dalton Keys thriller, U.S. Marshal Keys sets out to avenge a fellow officer who is killed in the line of duty. Isaiah Du Bois is the first African American gay cop to be reassigned to highway 395 after an inner city corruption case in a police department blows sky high.

> *Exhaustive descriptions of locale and detailed analysis.*
> — Mystery Column, Rex E. Klett

THE SWEAT BOX
ISBN-10: 1-58790-106-4 / ISBN-13: 978-1-58790-106-5 / 216 pages / paperback / $16.95
A series of unsavory acts ties a rancher in Texas to old farming money in California. In this third Dalton Keys mystery, U.S. Marshal Keys wends his way through an entanglement of relationships to corner a barn burner and killer.

> *A fast-paced whodunit — you never know what to expect next.*
> — SACRAMENTO MYSTERY READERS

UNDER DRAGON HOUSE
ISBN-10: 1-58790-090-4 / ISBN-13: 978-1-58790-090-7 / 238 pages / paperback / $14.95
This fourth Dalton Keys mystery finds the illegal sale of firearms to insurgents leading to a statewide manhunt for the son of a priest turned tracker. Addie Marjoe has all the makings of a maverick cop except he's his own dungeon keeper in this novel on customs and abortion rights.

> *Full of complex, twisty suspense.*
> — David Doerrer, MYSTERY SCENE

BLUEPRINT
ISBN-10: 1-58790-157-9 / ISBN-13: 978-1-58790-157-7 / 170 pages / paperback / $22
Fifth and last Dalton Keys based on the actual 1951 New York subway bombing, leads to a suspected reunion of terrorists who commit a mine bombing in the California desert.

> *An excellent, well-portrayed loot book, fast paced, gripping action.*
> — MYSTERIES IN BRIEF

SNAPSHOT, COLLECTED STORIES
ISBN-10: 1-58790-158-4 / ISBN-13: 978-1-58790-158-4 / 170 pages / paperback / $20
A collection of compassionately told stories that include eight short works previously published in Ellery Queen Mystery Magazine under the author's pen name Lea Cash-Domingo.

> *Superb, substantive well-crafted puzzlers.*
> — Library Journal

> *One of the most notable features of Judy Koretsky's stories is the vivid depiction of setting. Judy brings her background so thoroughly to life that she seems to create a painting with words.*
> —ELLERY QUEEN MYSTERY MAGAZINE

CHERISHED MEMORY, POEMS & A PLAY

ISBN-10: 1-58790-152-8 / ISBN-13: 978-1-58790-152-2 / 92 pages / paperback / $18

Written in the style of Shakespearean sonnets, there are over two hundred poems in this book. This is Ms. Koretsky's first work of poetry. "How many days will it take to know you?/ When sweet designs their answers echo clear?/ Once agreed will you tumble fast and true/ And hold me close and always keep me near?/ Or will you fickle for sweet restraint/ Fall for some other woman's arduous complaint?"

ROPE

ISBN-10: 1-58790-171-4 / ISBN-13: 978-1-58790-171-3 / 344 pages / paperback / $27

Three novels-in-one book also featuring ROOM and DEATHMASK each about Criminal Intelligence Division investigations in Scotland and England. In ROPE three physicians-in-training and five nurse shipmates are murdered by rope hanging at their college of medicine in Edinburgh, Scotland after a day outing consisting of military exercises. In ROOM the controversial "no egg" case focuses on a team of divers whose bodies were found in opaque morgue bags after a locked room shooting death of a county planning commissioner. In DEATHMASK the famous Brughel murder of a young Backwalk girl who is brutally stabbed haunts forensic detectives in the Clough in Ireland.

Barnes & Noble gives ROPE a five star rating.

Tower Books ranks ROPE #1 in Fantasy-Historical

TROJAN PARK

ISBN-13: 978-1-58790-211-6 / 212 pages / paperback / $18.00

TROJAN PARK *A California Mystery* is a glimpse at the narcissist prone culture of the society noir which upper elite artists careers ascend as quickly as they recede. From ritzy Terra Linda to glitzy Montclair the social climb to wealth seduces a young socialite, whose flirtation with thrill-seeking and reckless danger leaves dead two husbands on the Fourth of July. A fast paced page turner, this novel sizzles with intrigue and tawdry motivation and a questionable cast of characters. Who stands to earn a killing on the senior Roark's life? Alameda County Deputy District Attorney Lenny Cliford tracks the desperate dealings of a family at war with its adolescent heir-son. Through tantalizing art and state-of-the-day security systems to protect a museum, a fail-safe chase takes this investigator-attorney to Paris to the Musee du Louvre, to the Los Osos coast and then Seattle to dragnet a diamond heist of staggering proportions.

BORDER

ISBN-13: 978-1-58790-225-3 / 445 pages / paperback / $24.00

These stories tell of shipping and trade in the Puerto Rico islands, commerce with the United States, and border custom's patrol in the South and Florida. They attempt to explain causes for numerous shipwrecks, predominantly over the mid-Atlantic, and causes of three airplane crashes worldwide during the nineteenth and twentieth centuries.